P9-ECN-843

Killens, John Oliver, 1916-
Great Black Russian.
1989

SANTA BARBARA PUBLIC LIBRARY
CENTRAL LIBRARY

GREAT BLACK RUSSIAN

AFRICAN AMERICAN LIFE

General Editors

Toni Cade Bambara
Author and Filmmaker

Wilbur C. Rich
Wayne State University

Geneva Smitherman-Donaldson
Wayne State University

Ronald W. Walters
Howard University

BOOKS BY JOHN OLIVER KILLENS

A Man Ain't Nothin' but a Man: The Adventures of John Henry
Great Gittin' Up Morning: A Biography of Denmark Vesey
The Cotillion: or, One Good Bull is Half the Herd
Slaves
'Sippi
Black Man's Burden
And Then We Heard the Thunder
Youngblood

GREAT BLACK RUSSIAN

A Novel on the Life and Times of
ALEXANDER PUSHKIN

JOHN OLIVER KILLENS
Introduction by ADDISON GAYLE

WAYNE STATE UNIVERSITY PRESS   DETROIT   1989

Copyright © 1989 by Grace W. Killens. Published by Wayne State University Press, Detroit, Michigan 48202. All rights are reserved. No part of this book may be reproduced without formal permission.

93 92 91 90 89   5 4 3 2 1

Library of Congress Cataloging-in-Publication Data

Killens, John Oliver, 1916–
  Great Black Russian.

  (African American life)
  1. Pushkin, Aleksandr Sergeevich, 1799–1837, in fiction, drama, poetry, etc. I. Title. II. Series.
  PS3561.I37G74   1989   813'.54   89–16717
  ISBN 0–8143–2046–5
  ISBN 0–8143–2047–3 (pbk.)

To Harry Belafonte
who was the initial catalyst
And to
The Creative Writers Workshops
of
Howard University, Bronx Community College and
Medgar Evers College
whose members believed in this work

A Note of Appreciation

For more than twelve years, my husband, John Oliver Killens, researched the life of the Russian poet, Alexander Sergeievich Pushkin. He visited the Soviet Union during the Pushkin festivals, talked with Pushkin scholars, went to the Pushkin home and museum, and throughout the years became totally immersed in the life and times of Pushkin, the "Bard of the Decembrists" and the literary hero of the Russian people.

It was also during these years that John traveled throughout the United States lecturing to students and literary groups on Alexander Pushkin. The manuscript went through many stages of writing and rewriting in my husband's efforts to capture the essence of this legendary figure and his time. The book truly had become to John a labor of love and admiration for this great Russian poet.

To Wayne State University Press, our thanks. To Lawrence Jordan, who brought the good news of the book's acceptance to John a few weeks before he passed, our thanks. And to my son-in-law, Louis Reyes Rivera, who meticulously worked on the final editing, love and much gratitude.

We do hope that the readers will enjoy and savor this beautiful biographical novel about a romantic revolutionary poet, written by a romantic revolutionary writer who was also a realist.

Grace Killens
Brooklyn, New York
June, 1989

INTRODUCTION

Addison Gayle

Alexander Sergeievich Pushkin was born in Moscow on May 26, 1799. He was descended, on his mother's side, from Hannibal, an Abyssinian Prince, who became a ward of Peter The Great. Hannibal served his Czar so well that he became a confidant and favorite, was revered at the court, and began the aristocratic Pushkin lineage. In an unfinished work, THE NEGRO OF PETER THE GREAT, Alexander Pushkin pays homage to his illustrious ancestor. Though his father did not possess as distinguished a lineage as his mother, he was also descended from the Russian nobility. Perhaps more important for Pushkin's development as a poet was his father's literary ambitions. As a result the household was often filled with various writers, including Pushkin's uncle, who had a reputation as a minor poet. Among those who also visited the Pushkin household were such leading Russian writers as Karamazin, Zukovsky, and Dmitriev. Though by the time of his birth the family had lost much of its wealth and Aristocratic pretensions, he and his brother and sister were educated in the tradition of the nobility. Pushkin had a private tutor and access to his father's personal library, where he early became acquainted with the masters of French and German literature. His voluminous readings, in addition to attendance at the literary soirées given by his father and presided over by his uncle, began his interest in writing poetry. By the time he entered the Lyceum—a school established for educating the children of the nobility for important state positions—he had begun to compose his own verse. His early efforts were patterned after the compositions of classic writers, Russian and French, and centered around such youthful themes as lost love, the pursuit of pleasure, alienation, and occasionally such political pieces as "On the Return of the Emperor-Czar From Paris" (1815) and "Liberty: An Ode" (1817). Such offerings won him respect and acclaim. Derzhavin, Russia's "greatest eighteenth-century poet," praised his accomplishments

7

and he was invited to join Arzamus, a respected literary society. When he graduated from the Lyceum and took up his post as a foreign affairs officer in Petersburg, he had already acquired a sizable reputation as a writer.

He was also renowned as a rebel. The pursuit of wine, women, and song was characteristic of the young men of the nobility and Pushkin found comrades as enamored of each as he was. Yet his own appetite for sensational and atavistic behavior seemed obsessive. His actions not only appeared fatalistic, as John Killens intimates, but the many duels fought and the many more contemplated suggest an excessive challenge to authority. The source of this need to engage in combat with those in power may be traced, on one level, to his lifelong feelings of alienation from his parents. Later in life he became convinced of his father's hostility towards him, and he was never really certain of his mother's love. Thus he grew into manhood, harboring intense feelings of alienation, uncertainty, and despair. Such feelings led to participation in radical causes and membership in radical groups. He supported the emancipation of serfs in Russia and of slaves in America; and he opposed the absolute power of the Czar. His activities led to involvement with a radical group, The Green Lantern, and to friendship with many members of the Decembrists, a revolutionary group so named because of the aborted attempt to overthrow the Czar in December of 1825. He lent his powerful voice as a poet to such groups and their efforts. Among the poems he produced in the interest of liberal causes were "The Country Side," which denounced serfdom, and "Christmas Fairy Stories" and the "Ode To Freedom," which attacked tyranny and despotism everywhere. He writes in "Ode To Freedom": "Tremble you tyrants of the world? And you degraded slaves, give ear / Be strong, take courage and arise."

His activities with radical groups and his political poetry soon brought him into conflict with the authorities and precipitated his first exile from Petersburg. He was sent first to Southern Russia, where, after three years of riotous living, he was allowed to move to Odessa, a cosmopolitan city near the Black Sea. Here he wrote some of his most important works. He began THE GYPSY, wrote the first chapter of EUGENY ONEGIN, and finished THE FOUNTAIN OF BAKSHISARAI, THE PRISONER OF THE CAUCASUS, and GABRILIAD, an "irreligious" poem depicting a sexual liaison between God, Gabriel, and Mary. Later, he would deny authorship of the poem. He soon came into conflict with the Governor General of Odessa, Count M.S. Vorontsov. His continual pursuit of the Count's wife intensified hostilities between the two and Pushkin was dismissed from the foreign service. He was exiled to his mother's estate, at Mikhailovskoye, near the village of Pskov. Here he was placed under the supervision of his father, with whom he was frequently, sometimes violently at odds. When he discovered that his father reported upon his activities to the Czar's secret police, he broke all contact with the older man. His relationship with his sister and brother, who also lived at the estate, was good and their friendship helped him to confront the loneliness and alienation of his exile. In 1825, two events occurred that helped to release him from the boredom of Mikhailovskoye.

In November of 1825, Czar Alexander I died and on December 14, the Decembrists attempted to take advantage of the confusion brought about by the question of succession. They began a short-lived revolt in Petersburg, which was soon crushed. In what was seemingly an unusually harsh act, the new Czar, Nicholas I, sentenced many of the conspirators to death and exiled over a hundred to Siberia. Most were either friends of the poet or avid readers of his poetry. Yet, because of his exile, he was safe from accusations of actual complicity, though suspicion about his involvement persisted. When he wrote a letter to the new Czar, asking permission for health reasons ("a kind of aneurysm"), he lied to end his exile and go "to Moscow, to Petersburg, or to foreign lands," and surprisingly his request was granted. Nicholas' motivations were twofold. He wanted to demonstrate that his extreme action against the Decembrists was not motivated by cruelty and vengeance, that he was a merciful and compassionate Czar. To end the exile of the man quickly becoming Russia's best known poet and, perhaps, secure his services for his regime might enhance his image in the eyes of his subjects. At the least, he would be better able to keep watch on the poet's activities were he near the court. Pushkin was summoned to Moscow, where, in a meeting with Nicholas on September 8, 1886, he impressed the Czar with his intelligence and honesty. He admitted his friendship with many of the radicals of the Decembrist movement and acknowledged that were he in Petersburg at the time, he would undoubtedly have been among "the rebels." However, he would not now, he agreed, provide any form of opposition to the new regime. After calling him the "most intelligent man in Russia," Nicholas ended the poet's six-year exile and he was allowed to resume his social and literary life in Moscow.

The Czar's largesse was not given without conditions. The poet's works were to be carefully scrutinized before publication and travel restrictions were imposed. From time to time he was called upon to defend certain poems—the atheistic GABRILIAD for example—and he had to account for his actions time and again to the Czar's secret police, who were charged with monitoring his movements. Yet, he was back in Moscow, back in the social setting of which he was so enamored. Once again, he became a popular figure at the court and the opera houses and he continued to enhance his reputation by publication of such works as BORIS GODUNOV, COUNT NULIN, and POLTAVA. After awhile, however, he began to tire of the constraints upon his life, the harassment by the Czar and his emissaries, and even the social life of Moscow. He appealed to the Czar to allow him to become part of the foreign mission, with duties in Paris or even China, but was rejected. On his own, without permission, he journeyed to the Caucasus, where he spent time with his brother's troops on the front line in a war against the Turks. Upon his return he was severely chastised by the chief of the secret police. During this period he became increasingly morose and despondent, and his constant bouts with depression may have led to his surprise marriage to Natalia Nikolaevna. Though she was purportedly one of the most beautiful women in Russia, friends and critics of the poet were bemused by such a seemingly incompatible marriage. Natalia had little cognizance of his literary achievements and ambitions, was not interested in the arts, and was obsessed with the social activities at the court of Nicholas—activities with which Pushkin had become bored. Her family had neither money nor titles and she consented to marry only after the poet had engaged in persistent, sometimes embarrassing pursuit. After marriage, though she eventually bore him four children, she continued to cause him embarrassment. At numerous balls and parties— many of which she cajoled him into attending, some which she attended accompanied only by her sister—she was the stellar attraction. Flirtatious and naive, she encouraged the attentions of many men at the court, including the Czar. Over the years, Pushkin increasingly found himself compromised by her actions, but was powerless to restrain her from pursuing her social aspirations. Gossip, which had begun early in the marriage, concerning her purported liaisons, intensified. She was said to be romantically involved with not a few suitors, but when she encouraged the attention of d'Anthes-Heckeren, a handsome young French foreign missionary and the adopted son of the Dutch Ambassador, the poet was forced to act. After receiving anonymous notices informing him that he had been chosen "coadjutor of the Order of Cuckolds and historiographer of the Order," he challenged d'Anthes to a duel. The duel was twice postponed, but on January 27, 1837, the two men faced each other. D'Anthes, a good shot, fired first, wounding the poet, who managed to fire his round, inflicting only a slight wound in his opponent. Pushkin was rushed back to his home, where he struggled to regain his strength, only to succumb two days later. News of the poet's death produced an upsurge of fever and passion, and crowds thronged the streets of Petersburg, surrounding the Pushkin apartment and showing signs of possible political action. Fearing the possibility of a riotous demonstration, the civil authorities held a secret funeral service, moving the ceremony from the large church for which it was slated to a much smaller one and allowing attendance by invitation only. On February 6, 1837, Pushkin was buried in Svyatogorsk Monastery, near Mikhailovskoye, near his mother and great-grandfather, "The Negro of Peter The Great."

Pushkin's reputation as the founder of Russian literature is secure both in his homeland and on the continent. Praise for his works and his rebellious spirit have come from Gogol, Turgenev, Wordsworth and Matthew Arnold. Gorky wrote of his countryman: "Pushkin is the greatest master in the world. Pushkin, in our country, is the beginning of all beginnings. He most beautifully expressed the spirit of our people." Though his works are little known in America, his reputation is also secure among one very prominent group of Americans—black intellectuals— who have long looked upon his literary successes with admiration and respect. Dubois cited accomplishment in Russian literature as proof that black men, free of racial bias, could develop their genius to its fullest, and Richard Wright cited the achievement of the Russian poet as proof of his theory that blacks who lived in a congenial racial climate could produce literature, void of a "racial content." Pushkin, wrote Wright, "was at one with his culture."

In GREAT BLACK RUSSIAN: A NOVEL ON THE LIFE AND TIMES OF ALEXANDER PUSHKIN, John Oliver Killens moves beyond the summary praise of both European and black American intellectuals. He refuses to reduce such an important poet to simply "the beginning of all beginnings" or a vehicle to counter racist claims to moral and intellectual superiority. Instead, Killens has adopted as a starting point for his own exploration of the life and times of this Russian writer Dostoevsky's tribute to Pushkin, over twenty years after his death, that without him "we should have lost, not literature alone, but much of our irresistible force, our faith in our rational individuality, our belief in the people's power, and most of all our belief in our destiny."

The Pushkin of John Killens's imagination is a multidimensional character. Anguish, pain, torment, hope, the search for love are all aspects of his character. The young boy who was despaired of his mother's love because he hungered for it so much is the mature man who wishes to transform fantasy into reality. "My mother loves me. Poor woman, she doesn't know how to express herself to someone like me. And who can blame her? I'm not easy to get along with." These conflicting emotions concerning his mother remain ever present and contribute to his varied feelings of compassion and concern for others, to his constant bouts with depression, and to his feelings of alienation and despair. And a contributing factor also, indeed, a most important one in the development of this poet as man and writer, is the overwhelming impact made upon him of his African ancestor. This fact is often overlooked in the works of academicians who write about Pushkin or downplayed in discussions of his life and works. In a compilation of Pushkin's poetry, one such academic never mentions the fact at all; and a "respected scholarly" work, published in 1970, also ignores the fact of Pushkin's ancestry. But the poet himself was fascinated by his great-grandfather, as his unfinished story "The Negro of Peter The Great" demonstrates. Realizing this concern, after careful and meticulous research, Killens, the novelist, depicts Hannibal as a central figure in the development of his great grandson. Writes Killens: "He [Pushkin] had lain there in his terrible loneliness and thought about his great-grandfather, the friend of the great Czar Peter . . . and the tall black man with dark eyes . . . came to his bedside and talked with him about the times gone, when he himself was a boy in faraway Africa, a young Ethiopian prince."

The prodigious gifts of the poet are part of the heritage bequeathed by his ancestor, "the African blood" impacting upon his emotional and moral character twofold. The poet who loved human freedom and who despised chains and shackles everywhere, "Alas, where'er my eye may light / It falls on ankle chains and scourges / Perverted law's pernicious blight / And tearful serfdom's fruitless surges," is the poet of rebellion and revolution. But the poet who hungered for his mother's love, who, perhaps, saw reflections of his mother in every woman he intimately knew—and there were many—is the poet of extreme passion and sensitivity who often recoils at his own behavior, and who seldom hesitates to take responsibility for his actions. When he exercises a "master's perogative," seduces and then

11

impregnates a young servant girl, "He still felt guilty toward her. . . . He was no better than the very bastards [the nobility] he despised and wrote against. He said, 'I'm a devil. Stay away from me.'"

The young girl realizes what Killens enables the reader to realize, that Pushkin is not a devil, but man, one driven, as are all men, often by forces beyond their comprehension or control. He suggests in the case of Pushkin that among these forces were his ancestry and his need for love, and that because of the strong influence of each, the poet is neither the complete revolutionary, as, perhaps, is Kyo in Malraux's *Man's Fate*, nor the writer at one with a society in which his ancestry is of little consequence to his countrymen. Killens, the poet, realizes that the mythical life is never lived, that somewhere between the myth and legend of the man and the fact and reality of the man is the man of worth and substance. Thus Pushkin is able at one and the same time to censure the relatives and friends of the Decembrists for their vacillations after the aborted uprising against the Czar, while himself courting the very Czar who sentenced some of them, his friends, to death and exile. He is capable of denouncing those who lie in order to achieve favor at the court, while in denying authorship of several of his own poems, he rationalized his own fabrications: "I do not owe the imperial court the . . . truth. The only things I owe it are damnation and exposure." Pushkin's explanation of and attempt to understand his complex character however are no rationalizations. "A writer," he muses, must suffer many contradictions, among them loneliness, the need for quiet and space, and "THE ABSOLUTE NEED FOR PEOPLE, PEOPLE TO LOVE, TO KNOW, TO LOVE WITH, TO BE HAPPY WITH, TO SUFFER WITH." Every time a writer begins a new work, it is "like falling in love again."

Not surprisingly, outside of heredity and the quest for parental affection, Killens discovers that the animus for Pushkin's complex personality, as well as his prodigious talent, lay in his continual belief in the energizing power of love. I have written of Killens elsewhere as the poet of love, for the key to the complexity of his own characters, from the novels from *Youngblood* to *Sippi*, is the love they possess for themselves, for black people, and for humankind. It is progressive this love, beginning first with the self and moving on to embrace one's culture and race. Afterwards one is capable of love of the oppressed everywhere. Such love, which moves beyond the Platonic, must be carved out of the tumultuous, turbulent world in which men and women must live. But the achievement can be made and the effort is not, as the existentialists suggest, a lonely and solitary one, but instead, a quest in which the very sensitive are aided by their ancestry, history, and sense of commitment to the elevation of humankind. Such men and women, Killens has argued, include Frederick Douglass, Sojourner Truth, Fannie Lou Hamer, Malcolm X, and Martin Luther King Jr., among many thousands gone, who through love of freedom and hatred of oppression sought to redirect the course of human history. Pushkin is the newest star among Killens's constellation of such lover/warriors and is different from the Pushkin conceived in the minds of either academic scholars or black intellectuals. To ignore the impact of Pushkin's ancestry, Killens realizes, is to ignore an important source of his artistic and moral strength. But to suggest that the absence of racial conflict produced the climate necessary to write literature about the cares and concerns of all humankind is false. Killens has argued that black literature of necessity addresses such concerns, for blacks remain, as Wright once depicted them, as the metaphors of the twentieth century, and to write about the concerns and struggles of blacks is to write about those of Everyman.

Killens has carefully integrated fact and fiction and produced a portrait of one of the paramount figures in world literature. He has depicted a man of power and intellect, of sensitivity and concern. He has etched out the contours of the life of a writer and universalized his experiences so that they bear resemblance to those of writers everywhere. He has draped over the shoulders of this nineteenth-century Russian writer the cloak of his own concerns and fears about our ability to love and to hope and to create a better world. He has shown us a Pushkin who, for most of his life, believed in justice, compassion, and freedom, and who, like Byron and Goethe, two literary models, was enamored of revolution as a means of liberating men and women from serfdom and slavery as well. He has shown us a Pushkin imbued with a sense of romanticism, and it may well be that the strongest link between the nineteenth-century Russian poet of African descent and his twentieth-century counterpart is the romanticism shared by both men.

For Killens is among the last of our romantic poets. He believes fervently in the promise of humankind; he believes that black men and women can vaunt the barricades erected out of the experiences of many holocausts and point the way for the oppressed of the twentieth century, for the men and women in Angola, Mozambique, South Africa, and Nicaragua as well as for Blacks in America. Despite the rhetoric of current prophets of despair, he believes that love is possible between black people and black people and that this love has enabled millions to survive the American racial Armageddon. In all of these concerns, he is, like Pushkin, "the people's poet," one for whom concern with people is more important than wealth or fame. It is this concern which enables both him and the subject whose life he so carefully researched and ably presented in fiction to remain vibrant forces in the daily lives of revolutionaries/romantics everywhere. When he visited Moscow and was taken on a tour which included the shrine to Pushkin, he stood looking down at the crypt of this black Russian poet. At that moment, two centuries of history merged and one poet reached across the vast expanse of time and distance to embrace another. GREAT BLACK RUSSIAN: A NOVEL ON THE LIFE AND TIMES OF ALEXANDER PUSHKIN is the result of this encounter. The novel is a great effort and a tremendous achievement.

No Russian writer was ever so intimately at one with the Russian people as Pushkin. Those multitudinous writers who have taken the people as their theme, compared with Pushkin, are, with one or at most two exceptions, only 'gentlemen' writing about the masses. Even in the two gifted exceptions (Tolstoy and Turgenev) there is apt to appear on occasion a flash of haughtiness, which seems like an effort to bring happiness to the people by raising them to the writer's level . . . Without him (Pushkin) we should have lost, not literature alone, but much of our irresistible force, our faith in our national individuality, our belief in the people's power, and most of all our belief in our destiny.

Feodor Dostoevsky, Moscow, June 8, 1880

Pushkin is the greatest master in the world. Pushkin, in our country, is the beginning of all beginnings. He most beautifully expressed the spirit of our people.

Maxim Gorky

ON THE EVE

ON THE EVE OF ARMAGEDDON

By evening, it will all be over. This old earth will be no more for one of us, me or the Frenchman, d'Anthes.

It is eight o'clock in the morning, January 27 in the Year of Our Lord Eighteen Hundred and Thirty-Seven. It is still dark outside on the streets of Saint Petersburg. Notwithstanding, the street lights are slowly being snuffed out. Death to the night. Die slowly, slowly, Russian night.

My Russia of the snow and steppes.

I wipe the mucous from my eyes. My wife, reputedly, objectively, realistically, the most beautiful woman in all the Russias, is still sleeping the innocent sleep of babes and angels. I go over to the bed and stare down at her. Her mouth is slightly parted. Her shapely rosebud lips are like an infant pouting because it cannot have its way. A pale angelic face haloed by curly ringlets, black-as-midnight-on-the-Russian steppes. My lovely wife is softly snoring. More like a happy kitten purring, really. Her bosom climbing and descending. I feel a sweet warmth in my loins. My lips have known those sweet bare breasts in their natural state, honey-combed and unencumbered. Natasha is so beautiful and guiltless, my eyes begin to fill, almost. The parted lips are two red rose petals perched in the middle of her pallid face. The most beautiful poem I've ever written. My great achievement in the arts. A great sadness descends upon me now. I feel old before my time. And I am not quite thirty-eight years old.

Whatever happens on this day, I pray that she will not be blamed. The duel —the duel—the goddamn duel! My entire life, it seems, has been a succession of stupid duels, one after the other. One continuous never-ending struggle with my relentless and implacable fate. My parents—my loneliness—the aristocracy—my loneliness—my mother-in-law—the Emperor—my terrible unutterable loneliness.

16

Duels—struggle—duels—struggle—my head throbs like a beating heart underneath a stethoscope.

Will it never cease? Senseless, you say. Perhaps.

On the other hand, perhaps life is one great endless duel . . . I smile grimly in the darkness. Last night we made love together. It was good, warm, soft, sweet, tender, salty, achingly desperate. The earth quaked and then stopped hurtling into space, she enjoying, I enjoying, together, maybe better than it's ever been. As if it were the very last moment on this earth. For us. The Holy Virgin knows I love this woman!

I bend over and brush my full lips softly on the sweet mouth of this woman-child who is the mother of our children. Her gentle breathing titillates my nostrils. My breath blows softly onto her face. The very special sweet-and-musty smell of her sleeping body excites my senses, sends a heat throughout my face and shoulders and a great warmth in my loins. I tiptoe around the chilly room. My nostrils wrinkle at the familiar pungent smell of her urine in the chamber pot beneath the big brass bed. Natasha's urine. I don a red striped robe and proceed to do my toilet.

Staring now, quizzically, at myself in the looking glass above the dresser, a practice I began when I was seven or eight years old and did not love my reflection. Myself sees a high wide forehead. A fuzzy beard surrounds my face, a crown of wooly hair atop. My sallow jaundiced skin is much, much darker than most men of this Northern province. I have my mother's pinched and pointed nose, my great-grandfather's African lips. My eyes bluish-black, black on blue, as if the gods could not make up their minds.

GOD.

Where is God, who looks indifferently down on us and allows this thing to come to pass? This stupid duel. I have so much work as yet undone. No time. No goddamn time! There's never been enough time. For me. And yet, this is all the time there is, or will be; all the time there ever was. I feel a silent screaming in my head.

I have fought so many duels, hundreds of them. I was always expert enough not to have to kill my adversaries, excepting two. Usually, it was a bullet in the shoulder, in the leg, in the chest barely missing the heart. An expert on how to win the duel without killing the opponent. The two exceptions were accidents. I have this strangely deep regard for life. But somehow I know that this one will be fatal, for me or d'Anthes. By the end of this day one of us will be mortally wounded. And then oblivion. Escape?

I can hear the servants stirring, waking up to greet the day, to make things easier for the rest of us. But nothing is ever easy. Not even for the Emperor. Everything is relative. It is a sound I've heard so many times before. The symphony of pots and pans, the steamy smell of sibilant samovars. Bells resound outside for early mass. In the eyes of my sleepy mind I see priests in long black cassocks with black cowls hiding their frozen faces, gliding shadow-like along the empty frozen streets, past the bonfires at the intersections where the homeless street people gather, swap yarns and jokes and, hopefully, keep from freezing to death.

As usual, I sit down at my desk to do my mail, to answer correspondence, before getting to the work for which I was placed here on this Russian earth. I smile confidently. This day, it will end one way or the other. One of us will live to tell the tale. Me or the Frenchman. And I am the story-teller. I am the writer. So—it stands to reason—if there is such a thing as reason.

Nikita, my faithful valet, brings me a cup of steaming tea. There are so many years between the two of us. I think, "So many joys, so many tears. Banishment. Alienation. Loneliness. I recall the riotous living of my young life raising hell with the Hussar Horse Guards. There were some good times. Some triumphs. Some achievements. To paraphrase my favorite "Othello," *I have rendered the Russian people some service, and they know it.*

Nikita sees me smiling. "Master is feeling good today."

"Why the hell not, Nikita, old friend? It's good to be alive!"

"It is for sure, Master." Why is he calling me *Master* today? He does not usually call me *Master.*

"I'm not your master, Nikita. You're more like a father to me." My voice chokes off. Why have I not spoken with him like this before? My surrogate father all these years.

Nikita smiles patronizingly. "But of course, Master."

I rise from my desk and embrace Nikita warmly, and kiss him on his grizzly-bearded cheeks. The old man stares at me with a fatherly affection and a great wondering in his bleary eyes. I notice for the first time the lines and wrinkles that age has etched relentlessly in his wizened face. I turn from him and sit down again to conceal the tears that have begun to fill my eyes. He stands there for a moment, then turns and shuffles out of the door, almost noiselessly.

I can hear the snow now softly lapping its wet, sloppy kisses against the frost-bitten windows. Hear the sleigh bells jingling through the early morning darkness, the ennobled young mam'selles and roues heading homeward from one of their all-night parties. I used to be a part of all that. Oh, the great waste of my precious youth!

If only I could have made my mother understand me!

It is a day like any other day of winter in the Northern heavens. It is snowing with a terrible vengeance in Sweden, Norway, Denmark, Finland, and across the Finnish marshes to Great Peter's city on the frozen Neva, Saint Petersburg. The wind comes roaring off the Baltic. Sighing now, I close my eyes and I see everything through the mist along the Neva River.

St. Petersburg! O mythical city of fantasy and dreams and vast boulevards constructed by Great Peter on the banks of the River Neva. O Renaissance city of Grand palaces and baroque mansions. "Window on Europe!" . . . "Venice of the North!" City of the "white nights" and the Winter Palace and Senate Square. City of martyrdom

and "Decembrists." City of Ibrahim Petrovich Hannibal, my illustrious great-grand-
father, City of great wealth, city of abject poverty. Magnificent vision of Peter the
Great, Emperor of all the Russias.

I breathe deeply and I open my eyes again. The city fades into the misty myth.

First, a letter to Madame Ishimov, translator of literature from English into Russian for my magazine.

> Dear Madame:
> May I compliment you on the crispness and simplicity of your translation. This is surely the way to write! I'm sorry I will not be able to fulfill our luncheon engagement. etc., etc.

My correspondence completed, I read the latter pages of an unfinished novel I am writing about my great-grandfather, a novel I have already titled, THE NEGRO OF PETER THE GREAT.

I stare at the unfinished manuscript. I am talking to myself again. "I promise you, Grandfather Hannibal. I will finish this novel soon. I shall put all other work aside and get it done."

I remember my great-grandfather's grave at Svyatogorsk Monastery on Holy Mountain near Mikhailovskoye. I can see myself and hear the promise I made to him and me that day, so long ago it seems, as I stood there midst the falling leaves of autumn and felt the nearness and the oneness with my great-grandfather. This morning, I put the novel aside, temporarily. I wish I had known Grandfather Hannibal. I mean, outside of all the dreams I've dreamed so many times. I am, incorrigibly, a dreamer.

Now I work briefly on a slender poem I read aloud.

> "I have ripened for eternity.
> And the torrent of my days
> Has slowed . . ."

I try hard now to concentrate, but the duel is heavy on my mind, my senses are as sharp as the biting wind outside my window. Stories, faces, incidents crowd themselves into my aching consciousness. Amelia—Zizi—Tanya—Arina Rodionovna—Marya Ravsky—Grandma Hannibal—my pitiful mother—Eliza—Oh, the women in my life! Were they real? Or were they poems that I have written? Dreams I dreamt? The thousands of words that came from me, the hundreds of titles—EUGENE ONEGIN—BORIS GODUNOV—ODE TO FREEDOM—THE DAGGER—GYPSIES—THE BRONZE HORSEMAN—GABRILIAD, I smile. Gabriliad was a naughty poem. Folly of my jaded youth.

"No!" I argue heatedly with myself. "It isn't true!" Gabriliad was a serious poem. One of my better and more truthful moments. Satire is the profoundest expression of a poet, irony is the blood of life. Especially of Russian life. Humor is a very serious venture. It is not a thing to laugh about.

I remember my prose. THE TALES OF BELKIN—THE SHOT—THE QUEEN OF SPADES—DUBROVSKY, THE CAPTAIN'S DAUGHTER. My mind's eyes see the moody, brooding, endless steppes of Russia. I shall never solve their mystery. I know that now. I think of my children sleeping innocently in a room nearby. I see the faces of the children in the hilly Cossack country, the land of Pugachov, the magnificent pretender. I see Nina's face. Little undernourished large-eyed, pock-faced Nina. Dead these many years. Nina—beyond the Jewish pale at Kichinev. The wondrous steppes, shapers of the Russian psyche all down through the centuries. I remember the old Gypsy woman who warned me years ago, "Beware of a white man in your life."

I think to myself, the snow is snowing and day is breaking, and it will never break again for one of the two of us, me or the Frenchmen, d'Anthes.

And the world will go along its jocular way.

Hour after hour. Day after day. Time after time after time after time . . . Mais, c'est la vie.

PART ONE

CHILDHOOD DAYS IN MOSCOW

CHAPTER ONE

Except for the eternally optimistic and perceptive prescience of his Uncle Basil, there was no sign at all, at birth, that he was very, very extra special and divinely blessed with genius. *Au contraire*, he seemed a terrible throwback to his African ancestry, as far as his parents, Sergei and Nadezda Pushkin, were concerned.

Alexander Sergeievich Pushkin was born in Moscow on May 26 (June 6 by the Gregorian calendar), 1799, on Holy Thursday, as church bells rang out all over that city of a thousand churches, and all over Holy Russia. His favorite uncle would always swear (exaggeratedly?) by a host of Holy Virgins that it was high noon and the time of the day when the Angelus rang out all across the land, across the vast and endless undulating steppes, across the majestic mountain ranges, in the thronging metropolis, in the little nameless villages along the Volga and the River Don, all across the frozen stretches of the North, they held devotion for the memory of the Holy Babe's Annunciation. Indeed, the bells rang so loudly Nadezda Pushkin could hardly hear her baby crying, according to Russian myth and legend, and his boasting Uncle Basil Pushkin.

Admittedly, Alexander Sergeievich was not a thing of beauty, according to Russian standards. When his father's mother first saw him in his mother's arms in the large four-poster bed, she exclaimed, "How on earth did you give birth to such an ugly creature? You must have been frightened by a monkey!"

His mother was a handsome "mulatto" woman, raven-haired and swarthy with a pointed nose which gave her face a haughty countenance befitting her aristocratic class, as she imagined it. In Russian society, she was known as "The African beauty," the "Lovely Creole," the "Beautiful Arab," and so on. Aside from the olive-skinned and glowing darkness of her beauty, the only trace of African strain was her plentiful curvacious lips which were forever between her teeth, as if she sought to bite them down to proper Russian beauty standards. She seemed descended from the Moors, unwillingly.

"I don't know how this thing came from me," Nadezda told her mother-in-law. "He must be a reversion to my savage grandfather." The "African beauty" turned her face to the wall and cried. She turned away from Sasha during most of his lonesome childhood.

His nickname was Sasha, and his parents should have seen it as a joyful omen, when, at two months of age, he sprouted three large teeth, and that he was born with a full head of hair. Instead, they were upset, because his hair was downy, not unlike the wool of sheep. He was the black sheep of the family. At least, with those three teeth they should have expected he'd have a ravenous appetite for life and living.

He was raised by a contingent of nurses, governesses, tutors and various other servants, most of them French. It was a time when the Russian aristocracy possessed a severe inferiority complex vis-à-vis the rest of Europe, especially the French. Most of the Russian nobility worshiped the French as if it were a kind of fetish that would secure them the keys to the Kingdom and bring all happy things to pass. A man might have been a garbage collector or a street hoodlum back in Paris, but in this turbulent country, most likely, he was a tutor in one of the great households of Russia.

On a summer afternoon in dusty Moscow, Nadezda Pushkina took her children out for a walk in the park accompanied by a French nurse; people walked up to them admiring the children. There were three of them. Olga, the pale-faced blonde-hair, gray-eyed sister; Leo, the white, blonde blue-eyed brother; and Sasha, the darkly visaged child with the black-on-blue, deep and penetrating eyes.

An over-fed woman dressed in the very latest French style, complete with parasol and lorgnette, came over to admire the children.

She oohed and aahed over Olga and Leo. "Oh, how cute! How divinely beautiful! *Ils sont très charmant!*" But when she came to Sasha, she stared down at the boy whose lips were already thickening and widening, his skin developing a deep, deep olive-like complexion, she adjusted her lorgnette for a closer, surer inspection of this rare phenomenon. She frowned and the child made a face at her in self defense. She turned to the mother: "How did this swarthy one get in here?" she asked Nadezda, accusingly.

"They all have the same mother and father," Nadezda said defensively. "And he is a very alert child. Smart as a knout." She turned to Sasha. "Count to ten for Madame, Sasha darling, *s'il vous plait,*" she added to show off her proficiency in French. But Sasha heard the annoyance underneath his mother's cooing. He stared at the lady and stuck out his tongue.

"Well!" Madame said, "Wherever he came from you should send him back *toute de suite!*"

These kinds of things happened with too much frequency for Nadezda Pushkina. The "lovely Creole" rarely took her older son out when she could avoid it. Possibly she thought the Russian sun would make him even swarthier. And whenever he came to her for affection, which he always starved for as a child, she would pass him on to an elderly nurse, his *nyanya*, Arina Rodionovna, a peasant woman who gave him the affection his mother denied him. She also gave him a love and deep regard for the Russian idiom and folklore with her countless stories of Russian heroes and heroines of olden times.

His nyanya told him stories of how Moscow had evolved from a small 12th-century village surrounded by a wooden stockade to become the Holy City of Russia, revered by all Russians. Her voice would assume a mystic tone, sending shivers all along his spine. "It is where Ivan the Terrible was crowned the first Emperor of all the Russias in 1547 and ruled till 1584." He would sit on the floor near her, his dark eyes ever widening at the wonder of it all.

Every time he went toward his mother she was ill with a headache. So as a little boy, he came to realize he was a headache to his vainglorious mother. Most of his childhood Alexander Sergeievich spent alone with his books. He was an avid reader by the age of six.

His mother was a moody woman. In certain moods Nadezda Pushkina went through periods of extreme devoutness, during which she kept her Bible with her everywhere she went, as if to ward off evil spirits. The Pushkins were deeply religious people, believed devoutly in the Bible and the Holy Virgin and Her Immaculate Conception. Indeed, there were sacred icons all over the Pushkin household, hallowed images of the Virgin and her baby, Jesus. Candles were forever burning. In the evening, Nadezda would gather her three children about her before the nurse put them to bed, and read to them from her Good Book. Sometimes she would dismiss the nurse and see to them herself.

One evening she read, "In the beginning God created the Heavens and the earth." Her voice dripped with piety like molasses on a winter morning. The children's sleepy eyes were wide awake with the mystery of it all.

"Who created God, Ma-ma?" Sasha asked. His innocent eyes stretched even wider now, as he tried to imagine the vast, deep void of great white nothingness that must have been here before the Good Lord had created. A chill moved swiftly across his boyish shoulders.

"Nobody created God, you little idiot!" his mother whined, exasperated. "How could anybody create someone as great as God?"

His brother, Leo, laughed at him for asking such a foolish question.

He grasped the enormity of his stupidity. If nothing was as great as God, how could anything less than God create him?

"Holy Mother of God!" Nadezda exclaimed, holding her forehead, as if to contain the headache he was giving her. "You are enough to make a saintly angel curse and lose his piety."

Holy Mother of God! he thought. But how could God have a mother or father when there was nothing here before he was? He figured it was a reasonable question to ask his mother. So he asked it.

But she stared at him as if he was something inconceivable. She left the room with her Holy Book, shouting to herself, "Holy Mother of God! Sinless boychild of the Blessed Virgin!"

It gave the bad boy cause to ponder.

The Pushkins lived in a large rambling wooden house in the back of a court on German Street in Moscow, which was now the second seat of national government, and had been ever since Great Peter moved the capital to his brand new city on the Neva River.

Alexander Pushkin was educated early on by a steady stream of *uchitols* (house tutors)—nearly always of French vintage. Eventually each of them was sent packing, due to repeated instances of debauchery, sleeping through the day after a rough exhausting night of chasing after the governess or the pantry maids, or overindulgence in excessive drinking of alcoholic beverages stolen from the Pushkin cellars.

Sometimes Alexander Sergeievich's nyanya would take him for walks into the heart of the city and you could almost hear its throbbing, wild and frenzied. There were all kinds of exciting occurrences forever taking place. Little Sasha thought his Moscow was the largest city in the world. Actually, Moscow was less a city than it was a bunch of villages huddled together for its own protection. A few cobble-stoned streets that ran reptilian routes through the center of the city. A cluster near the heart of town of large handsome palatial mansions where the aristocratic boyars lived uproariously like a bacchanal that went on and on and never ended. And further in, there was the busiest of marketplaces, rows upon rows of seemingly endless stalls as deep and as mysterious as caverns, selling all manner of strange and exciting merchandise.

Sasha smacked his lips as he savored the assorted smells; his narrow eyes all encompassing and alive with seeing, learning; his ears alert with the amazement of it all, tasting, smelling, experiencing. The meats in the stalls, the smell of new wood and leather titillating his senses as did the sounds and unusual accents of the vendors huckstering their wares. He was stimulated into dizziness.

The awe-inspiring walls of the Kremlin with their crenelated battlements atop reminded Sasha of pictures he had seen of the famous "Great Wall of China." His nyanya told him the mighty Kremlin had been constructed almost a thousand years before, at the bend of the Moskva River which bestowed its name upon the city. The mysterious Kremlin. Even outside the walls, he could see the tops of the countless churches and cathedrals with their golden gleaming cupolas shaped like giant onions and sharply pointed heavenward. He'd heard of numerous harems inside those sainted walls. When the bells of the numerous Kremlin monasteries began to ring, they seemed to drown out the endless noise around the city's center and its marketplaces.

25

One afternoon while walking through town with his nurse, Alexander stole away from her in the milling multitude around the marketplace. The old nurse looked for him frantically, frightened witless. She went feverishly along the Moskva River banks where she knew he loved to go and watch the boats go up and down the river, and dream of far-off places where he imagined these great "ships" had been, the wonderful things the men and ships had witnessed. She asked for him along the waterfront among the sea merchants, men who had brought their fabulous wares from as far away as Kiev on the Dnieper River, Norway on the Baltic Sea, and even distant Constantinople. Men who dressed strangely in tunics and caftans and long brilliantly-colored robes and wore skull caps and fezzes and some with beards that reached beneath their knees, who laughed boisterously and spoke many foreign tongues and accents.

Arina Rodionovna looked for her Sasha in the blacksmith shops where she knew he loved to go and watch the smithies with their bulging muscles and watch the sparks and embers fly. She looked in several of the churches, sought her little boy among the Arabers, the produce farmers, who brought their fruits and vegetables from outlying farms into the city by horse and wagon to sell them on the streets directly from their wagons. Among the thronging crowds of thieves and beggars and cutthroats on the streets of throbbing Moscow she sought her little Sasha.

A growing fear began to seize Arina Rodionovna's old heart as the day began to cloak itself in shadows. How could she go back home without her Sasha? And he was *her* Sasha and she loved him with a motherly passion as if he were her very own. Sometimes she imagined that she had actually birthed him. She'd known and loved him ever since the day he was born, and she had midwifed his mother. Her old legs were wobbly now and her body bathed in sweat, as her weary mind conjured up stories of children in this ancient city of Muscovy being lost and never found again. Of notorious children snatchers who roamed the city day and night, carried them to far-off lands and sold them into slavery, kidnapped children and held them for enormous ransoms. She'd heard that there were men who roasted children on spits on open fires like shaslyk and ate them for their suppers. All day long she looked for him, and now the sun was going down, sinking like a golden ball of fire into the river across the way. And she knew not where to look or turn. She felt faint, as she wandered, without hope, within the walls of an ancient monastery. And suddenly there he sat on the dusty red clay earth watching open-mouthed the monks in their long, shaggy mysterious beards and grayish cowls and long black cassocks, as they rang the great bells of the monastery. He stared at them in amazement as they worked on those giant bells above them, pulling on the long ropes in a kind of rhythmic unison that lifted them off the ground.

Arina Rodionovna was immobile at first. Then a rage began to build within her, filling up her face and shoulders. She was furious with her Sasha for the fear and anguish and anxiety he had put her through. She wanted to box his ears, cuff him around, beat the beautiful innocent expression from his face. She went toward him and scooped him up, and she overflowed with love for him. Her great love washed away her anger. She smothered him with hugs and kisses, even as she scolded him for giving her such a terrible scare. He told her, "When I grow up I'm going to be a monk in a monastery so I can ring those bells so loud it will wake up the Lord from napping like my mother."

That night Sasha questioned his mother about the larger than life-sized, copper-colored icons he had seen on the walls of the monastery, larger than he'd ever seen before, images, he imagined, of the Blessed Virgin and her babe.

Sometimes, Nadezda didn't gather them together before the nurse put them to bed. Some nights she went from room to room. Alexander was usually the last one she attended to. He thought it meant she loved him less. She would listen to him say his prayers and was impatient to be away from him. Some nights he asked her questions to prolong her stay. He loved to have her to himself.

"Why are they black, Ma-ma?" he asked. "The mother and the child?"

"Black?" she said excitedly, as if Christ Himself had been blasphemed. "Are you going crazy, stupid child?"

"Was Christ an African, mother?" His Grandmother Hannibal had always taught him to love the land of his great-grandfather. Grandmother Hannibal's father-in-law, Ibrahim Hannibal, had been an Ethiopian prince.

"African?" his mother shouted. "The Good Lord never heard of Africa."

Sasha insisted, "But God knows about everything, Ma-ma. And he must have told his son about such a wonderful place."

He used to drive his mother crazy with questions about the Bible, especially the Annunciation and the Immaculate Conception.

Before he was eight years of age, Sasha had read so many French romances, he knew where little babies came from. One night he asked his mother, "Did Joseph really believe the story Mary and the angels told him? Didn't he know he was a cuckold?"

"Oh!" his mother squealed. "Oh! You little atheistic pagan! The devil must have stolen into my bed and made me pregnant when I birthed you!" She boxed his ears and slapped his face.

The tears streamed down his face, as he came back with: "Somebody must have stolen into Mary's bed."

"Oh!" Nadezda sighed, as if it were her last breath on earth. "Oh!" She went to a corner of the room where a large icon hung above a table where a candle was forever burning. She fell upon her knees. In the poetry of his mind, Sasha imagined a smile on the face of this image of a walnut-colored woman with her dark brown babe in a mother-of-pearl encasement. "Holy Mother of God," Nadezda beseeched the calm-faced woman in the icon. "Forgive me for my daily sins. Blessed Virgin, punish me not for giving birth to this monstrosity, this demon in the disguise of a human being. Forgive me, Holy Mother, and I will go and sin no more!"

Sometimes even as she pushed her darkest child away from her, something deep inside of her wanted to reach out to him and pull him to her bosom. It was almost as if something in the depths of her remembered those nine months when he lingered, waited, in her womb. Remembered the ecstasy her erected nipples knew when she suckled him as a baby. She could never have explained it to her husband. There were no words for it. She would have been too ashamed. It was a love affair that a mother knows with her infant that a father never even dreams about.

Sometimes at a party in the Pushkin household, the children would run in among the grown-ups as they stood there in idle conversation with their cocktails in their delicate hands. Capriciously, Sasha would dash out to his mother and lose himself amongst her hooped skirt and clasp his arms around her legs and intoxicate himself with the smells of perfume and powder and other feminine fragrances.

Embarrassed, Nadezda Pushkina would push him away. "Get away from me you naughty child!" But he never remembered seeing her push Leo or Olga from her. Each time the evening would be spoiled for him, and her. Sometimes, later, she would look for him and find him sulking in a corner somewhere, and she would take him to her breast and kiss him. Sometimes her heart would ache and her eyes would fill, and she would wish fervently that he had been more like her other children. No matter, he was the way he was, and there had been too much between them; there was a memory of love for him there deep deep in the womb of her in that eternal place where the people of this earth are born.

Sometimes, he himself wished secretly he were more like his brother and sister: blonde of hair, fair of skin, light-blue-eyed. When he grew tall enough and no one was looking, he would stand for long extended intervals and stare at himself in the mirror above the washstand in his bedroom, biting his lips as if he thought to make them thinner. Sometimes he bit them till the blood spilled from them and stood there crying in his loneliness.

Alexander was shy around most people. Every time he expressed an opinion his parents ridiculed him. At seven years of age he began to stammer terribly. They thought that he was surely stupid and inept. And sometimes he believed them. He stopped speaking for many months. He escaped into his books. He began to write. If he could not articulate or verbalize, he would have his say with the written word. Sometimes he practiced talking to himself. He was not the kind of boy who gave up easily.

If he was shy, then he would overcome his shyness. If he stammered, then he would exercise his mouth with words until he did not stammer anymore.

On summer days his nyanya took him for walks in the Imperial Garden, where the fresh intoxicating smells of flowers in full bloom and green trees and grass assaulted his senses pleasantly. He wanted to know the name of every tree and flower. The smells of Moscow were not always pleasant. The air was usually filled with sharp odors of horse dung and dead garbage, the foul stink of human excrement in a badly working, almost nonexistent sewage system. Imperial Garden was a haven to those with dainty nostrils.

It was Alexander Sergeievich's first encounter with the House of Romanov. Czar Paul-The-First was a brutal tyrant. His madness was a rampant rumor. He required, by Imperial ukase, that every subject doff his hat when he passed by. When the Emperor passed them in the park on his great high horse, officially attired in his red Imperial cap and his Cossack uniform with the black gleaming boots, protected front and back by the not-so-secret Secret Police, Arina Rodionovna was so terrified she forgot to take off Sasha's cap. Mad Paul knocked the lad's cap off with his riding crop, scolded the old woman and threatened to have them both jailed for treason and sedition.

Life to the Moscow aristocracy was one continuous round of parties. Ennobled boyars slept straight through the mornings and went partying all through the night. The Russian serf did all the work and had no rights his lord or master was bound to respect. It was Heavenly ordained, they continually explained to Sasha, who was forever asking questions, some of which were embarrassing to his patriotic parents. A serf was chattel, owned every limb, tooth and genital by his ennobled master. Like slavery in the "New World," he could be sold at any moment to satisfy the slightest whim, away from his wife, mother, father, son or daughter. By the time Sasha was eight years old, he knew that a dissident serf could be hung by his fingers, get his ears chopped off, could be flogged to death with knout and cudgel tipped in heated melted glue. Imperial law provided him no protection. His only protection was that he was property and to kill a serf was to destroy one's property, to decrease one's wealth. It is probably where the expression derived: "To flog one within an inch of his life." Sometimes the measurement of life's endurance was miscalculated. In which case the master would weep bitter tears over the loss of his valuable estate.

As a lad, Alexander Sergeievich saw a serf receiving the "pipe" treatment at a garden party at one of the boyar residences. The amiable pleasant-faced master of the household entertained his drunken and ennobled guests by having one of his serfs stripped naked and flogged with knout as he slowly puffed away on his long oriental pipe. Sasha was seated next to his mother, and he reached out and grasped her hand. The male serf was dark of skin, almost black, of medium height, slimly constructed, with dark narrow brooding eyes, heavily eyelashed. His eyes seemed entirely black, shaped diagonally from his wide forehead toward his long slender nostrils. His left ear was missing, had been chopped off for listening too closely, Sasha surmised. He stood there straight like a ramrod, as the huge clean-headed Tartar, likewise a serf, administered the knout. When the first blow landed, the smaller serf did not move, his eyes were absolutely quiet. It was as if the whole thing were on stage, a theatrical performance, and he had a role to play, and he was determined to play it according to the script. Sasha winced as each blow landed.

The giant Tartar grunted at each downward descent of the knout. Alexander Sergeievich thought there was a kind of nobility about this little black man, who stood there silent and undaunted, even as the cruel knout bit into his back like an angry cobra, leaving long red streaks across his back and shoulders. Perhaps it was the contempt that Sasha thought he saw in the man's eyes that shone now like rare diamonds.

"Whack!" It was a lovely summer afternoon. A blue translucent cloudless sky hung over the city of churches, over the yard, redolent with the fragrances of roses and of lilacs.

The flogging continued as the overfed master with the pleasant face and double chin and hooked nose finished smoking his first pipeful. This would be the "two pipe" treatment, and possibly the "three."

Nadezda Pushkina tried to pull away from her son, but he dug his fingers into the flesh of her hand and held onto her as if his life depended on it. The amiable master was halfway through his second pipeful, and the proud serf began to groan quietly as each blow landed, and the sweat began to pour from him, from his hairy armpits, the summer sunlight glistening on his ebon shoulders, draining from the black and angry hair around his male organ hanging limply from between his legs.

It was a lovely sunlit afternoon. Flowers were in full bloom everywhere. The noblemen were wild-eyed now, even some of the noble women, saliva dripped from their slackened lips.

"Whack!" They sometimes called this rich man's backyard the "Garden of Eden." The trees that ringed the yard were heavy now with the smells of early-blossomed apples and peaches and pears and cherries, and why couldn't he enjoy himself like the rest of them? It was a beautiful afternoon, and they were all aristocrats.

Nadezda felt the body of her son begin to quake as each blow landed now and the blood began to splatter, and he dug his nails deeper into his mother's hand.

"Marvelous!" the aristocratic gentlemen shouted.

"Magnifique!" Countess Dubinskaya squealed in orgiastic ecstasy. The male serf winced slightly now as the flogging continued and the master began his third pipeful, puffing furiously now. The male serf never lost his composure, even though he lost control of his body functions, and urine flowed freely from the middle of him.

"Beautiful!" the ladies shouted.

As far away to the west a flash of lightning streaked across the summer skies.

"By the Holy Virgin! He's like a horse!" Count Stroganov shouted.

Sasha had somehow understood long before that to these ennobled ones the man before them was not of their species. He was an exotic artifact. He was no more than an animal.

"Bravo!" "Bravissimo!" they shouted. "Magnifique!"

Suddenly Sasha felt a growing fullness in his neck and shoulders filling up his face. He pulled away from his mother and ran toward the giant serf who was administering the knout, screaming. "Stop it! Stop it! You'll kill him! You'll kill him!"

There was a rumbling of thunder to the west of the city.

The ennobled people laughed uproariously at the tender-hearted boy. His mother was embarrassed. At the same time she understood and loved him for it. She had also sat there horrified. His father ran to Sasha and dragged him away, kicking and screaming as the bald-headed Tartar continued the flogging. He ran away and threw up his dinner in the sunlit yard by the side of the great stone mansion, heavily cloaked all over now in bright green ivy clinging from the bottom all the way to the tower. The vomit seemed to come back through his eyes and ears and nostrils. He could not understand himself. Why was he so different from the rest of them? Was he less noble than they? Amongst all these ennobled people he felt his great aloneness wrap around him like a winter cloak. Why couldn't he enjoy himself as they did? He felt an arm around his shoulders. He looked around and up into his mother's understanding face. She wiped his mouth with her silken handkerchief and kissed him on his cheeks and forehead. Tears spilled from his darkening eyes. He loved his mother deeply. But she was so inconstant with her love for him.

"You're no nobleman!" his father told him later that evening. "You're not even a man, let alone a nobleman."

"You're right," the boy agreed.

Later that night, Bible in hand, Nadezda gathered her children about her in Sasha's bedroom to hear their prayers.

Sasha asked her, "Why are some men masters over other men, Ma-ma?"

"Because the Good Lord ordained it," his mother answered wearily.

"How do you know that God ordained it?" Sasha insisted.

"Everybody knows it, excepting you," his brother Leo said disdainfully.

"Excuse me, my little brother who knows everything," Sasha said sarcastically, "but I *was* speaking to my mother. I did not know you were called, 'Ma-ma'. Shall we call you 'Ma-ma' from now on?"

Leo made a face at his older brother. "Come on, Ma-ma," he whined. "Put me to bed and kiss me goodnight."

The mother started out of the room with Leo. Olga lingered behind with Sasha. He seized his mother's other hand. "How does everybody know, Ma-ma? Where do they get the information from?"

Now she was torn between her two sons. There was a kind of desperation in Sasha's eyes, a need to know that his mother loved him as much as she loved his light-blue-eyed, blonde-haired younger brother. He stammered. "I—I—I want to talk with you, Ma-ma. Don't leave me, Ma-ma. Kiss him goodnight and let him go to his room by himself. He knows the way. He's not quite *that* stupid!"

31

She looked from Leo to Sasha to Olga. Olga said, "He can find his way to his room, Ma-ma."

Leo was absolutely certain that his mother would leave Sasha and go with him. She had done it so many times before. But this night she seemed to understand how much her older son needed her affection. She said, "Wait a moment, Leo."

A smile broke across Sasha's face, as triumphantly he led his mother to a chair near a table where an oil lamp sat, dimly lit. An icon candle burned brightly in another corner of the room. "How does everybody know, Ma-ma?"

He sat on the side of his bed and watched his dark-haired olive-skinned mother leafing through her Bible. He knew she was the most beautiful woman in all the world with her large dark eyes and her curvacious full-lipped mouth, her tiny feet. He watched her as she lip-read through the pages of her Holy Book. "Here it is," she told him, finally. "The Epistle of Paul the Apostle to the Collossians, the Third Chapter, Twenty-Second to the Twenty-Fourth verse. 'Servants, obey in all things your masters according to the flesh; not with eye service, as men pleasers; but in singleness of heart, fearing God: And whatsoever ye do, do it heartily, as to the Lord, and not unto men; knowing that of the Lord ye shall receive the reward of the inheritance: for ye serve the Lord Christ.' There," she said, "You see it's all right here in the Holy Book." She read further. " 'But he that doeth wrong shall receive for the wrong he hath done'. There," she repeated. "It's all here. It covers everything. That serf had done some wrong, and he received his punishment."

She rose from her chair to go with Leo, but Sasha was not through with her. "But it does not answer the question—why was this man a serf? Why was this man not the master and the Baron the serf?"

She was tired now. He always exhausted her with his interminable questions. Why couldn't he be like the other children and accept things just the way they were? "It's Fate," she whispered to her older son, "and nothing can be done about it."

Fate! God's Will! The Holy Virgin! And God preserve the Emperor! were words he'd heard ever since he could remember hearing words. They all meant the same thing to him. "I hate Fate!" he told his mother in a shouted whisper.

"Yes," she said wistfully, "I know you do." And she kissed him lightly on his forehead. And Olga kissed him. Nadezda left his room along with Leo and Olga.

CHAPTER TWO

Left to himself and his books, Alexander Sergeievich spent some of his lonelier moments observing, with an interest far beyond his age and capacity to comprehend, the amorous playfulness that went on between the tutors and the chambermaids.

There was one chambermaid in particular who made his head spin and evoke many childhood fantasies. By the time he was almost twelve, he daydreamed his fantasies and always with his golden-haired Tatyana. He wrote poems to his enchantment. Every morning she would bounce into his room to make up the bed and straighten up after the young master whose room always looked like it had just survived an Uzbekistan earthquake, with books and scribblings strewn all over the place. He had already begun his life's commitment as a writer. And worked at it in deadly earnest.

Some mornings Tatyana would pinch his cheeks; sometimes she would slap him on his nervous buttocks. Some mornings she would kiss him awake. Always the taste and smell of her would linger in his mouth and nostrils long after she had gone about her business to other parts of the house. He loved her sensuous lips. Therefore, sometimes he only pretended to be sleeping so she could "awake" him with a kiss. He would lie there in his bed in a sweet and sweaty expectation of her fullsome mouth, her smell, her femaleness, and he would feel strange sweet things happening to him that he did not fully understand.

Long after she'd left him, he would lie there wondering about the way she obviously felt compared to how he always felt. For she was always gay and joyful after she had kissed him and stroked him, singing her happy songs, whereas he was always left gladsome, but at the same time he was somehow terribly ashamed of his gladness. But why shouldn't he feel glad about being loved by his secret Tatyana?

And why did she love him and why did she love to kiss him? And somehow he knew she was not ashamed. And why did he know that he must keep it a secret that she was the only one in the whole wide world who loved to kiss him fully on his full-lipped mouth? Whenever his mother kissed him she usually kissed him on his forehead, a brief swift kiss as if it were a gift of some tasty confection she sought to take back before she gave it, before he could savor the deliciousness of it, as if she thought his forehead was contaminated. And even his nyanya only kissed him on his cheeks. But his secret love, his Tatyana, always kissed him lingeringly and fully on his generous mouth with her plenteous lips, and it made him feel good. And how could it be sinful, and why did he feel so guilty about his secret love? Sometimes, he wanted to go to his mother and tell her all about his secret love, but then it would no longer be his secret. For his mother would tell his father and his father would—who knew what his father would do? No, no, no, he'd better keep his secret Tatyana all to himself. She was his. She did not belong to his brother Leo, she did not belong to his sister Olga. She was his Tatyana. And in all those French romances he had read, you did not go around telling everyone about your secret love. But why did he somehow know it was sinful to love his Tatyana, when actually it was good and she was good and love was good, so how could it be evil? How on earth could it be sinful?

Some nights Sasha would sleep fitfully and think disturbingly of his Tatyana and when he slept he would dream that he lay in a large mysterious, luxurious bed in which he had never lain before, and it was cold in his big bed and he shivered and his teeth chattered, and he was freezing, and Tatyana came to him, to bed with him, and she took him in her arms, and he nestled closer to her and the great warmth of her body as if he slept near to a fireplace, and his head lay in that dear spot between her chin and her soft shoulders. And he felt peaceful, oh so sweetly peaceful he felt, and he slept the whole night through. But all the same he still felt guilty about something even though it had not really happened, but was merely a dream. The knowledge that it was only a dream did not mitigate the guilty feeling. If anything, it intensified the terrible feeling. Because only a boy who had the devil in him would ever dream such sinful dreams.

All the day long, sometimes, he would walk around with a look about him, like a humble borzoi dog not sure if he is going to be kicked or petted. And when his mother or father would look at him, or even if his brother or sister stared at him intently, he would be certain that they knew his deep dark sinful secret. No matter, he looked forward, shamelessly, to her coming to his room each morning. She was his secret Tatyana, and she belonged to no one else on earth.

Sometimes he thought the devil's hell was burning in him and that was why his limbs were all aflame when she came into his presence, or sometimes even when he only thought about her. Perhaps Tatyana was the devil in the disguise of a lovely chambermaid. Everybody knew the Good Lord and the Emperor performed their wonders together and mysteriously. But of course God and the Czar had nothing to do with the devil's business. The devil was not in God's dominion, nor was he in the Emperor's. And Tanya was much too beautiful to be a devil or one of the devil's imps.

Tatyana was not of the *Underworld*. She must be an angel sent especially to him from Heaven, a balm to soothe him in his loneliness. Why then did he feel guilty? Was love bad, was love sinful? What was wrong with loving Tatyana? The feeling, the wanting, the warmth, the taste in his mouth, the fullness in his face and shoulders. How could it be bad? How on earth could it be sinful?

Sometimes, after she had "awakened" him and after she had tidied up his room, in her own fashion (she was not the tidiest chambermaid in all of Holy Russia), she would lie sprawled back in one of his easy chairs, her petticoats and long peasant dress pulled up above her gleaming knees, and blow and breathe aloud her tiredness with her legs agape.

"Your Excellency, you sure can disarrange a room! You'll work poor Tatyana to death trying to keep this room in order." There was poetry in the way her fine legs opened and closed and opened and closed like scissors to a rhythm only he could hear.

One morning, Tatyana came in and Sasha pretended to be asleep, and she kissed him and did funny things with the thrusting of her busy tongue which got him all excited everywhere. She nibbled at his ear as her peasant hands wandered like an experienced explorer and found their way down to his crotch and felt the hardness in the middle of him, which was a new and fearfully strange delight to him. He laughed loudly like a whopping crane. Tatyana said, "Not so loud, Your Excellency. Everybody in the house will hear you."

Then she whispered in a strange and sensuous voice, "You are the sauciest devil in the world, Your Excellency. I swear by Holy Friday, you ought to be ashamed of yourself at such a tender age. Tanya ought to take the baby across her lap and give His Excellency a terrible spanking."

And when she left, singing some merry tune to herself, she left him in a terrible upset, and the smell of her lived for hours in his nostrils and all amongst him. He knew then she was his first and only love, and he read the French romances in desperate search of explanations of the way he always felt. He loved her and he would die for her, if it came to that, and he almost died each time she left him, very high and dry, and strangely damp.

Moscow literati gathered frequently at the Pushkin household to talk and drink and versify. Uncle Basil was a famous Moscow versifier. Usually in French, of course. Alexander's father, Sergei, like his brother, Basil, served briefly in the Czarist Guards, retired at an early age and lived precariously on a pension and, as an absentee landlord, on the meager earnings of inherited estates. Sergei had no stomach for business and landlordship. He rarely went to the country to manage his estates. Therefore, the stewards whom he'd placed in charge reported to him infrequently and added up the income from the crops and livestock always in a manner that put more rubles in their pockets than in the pockets of the landlord. Sergei Pushkin was a descendant from a long line of aristocratic ennobled boyars in the court of Peter the Great and long before, maybe even of Boris Godunov. But it profited them very little in these days of Emperor Alexander.

At these literary soirées, where the most prominent men in Russian letters would gather of an evening, oftentimes little Sasha would sit in a corner unnoticed with his narrow eyes opened wide, his plenteous lips agape, and drink in all that Russian erudition. They were some of the great influential minds of Imperial Russia. So how can you blame his parents when men like Nikolai Karamzin, His Imperial Majesty's own famed Imperial Historiographer and founder of the Sentimental Movement; Ivan Dmitrev, one of the great Karamzin's gifted disciples and the Minister of Justice; Alexander Turgenev, Director of the Department of Non-Orthodox Denominations; and Basil Zukovsky, founder of the Russian Romantic Movement and Imperial Tutor to the heir-apparent Czarevich, showed no awareness of Sasha's genius? These great and powerful men paid little attention to the sleepy-headed, swarthy-skinned, crinkly-haired boy who would one day be known as the father of their literature.

Even before he dared go into the Pushkin salon when he was six and seven years of age, he would steal out of his bed and down the stairway and sit outside the drawing room and eavesdrop, and he would wonder why these great men almost always read their poems in French when all of them were Russians. One evening his Uncle Basil found him asleep outside the door and picked him up and brought him inside. He had been attending these soirées ever since.

One night Zukovsky was reading a poem he'd written, in French. All was quiet except the resonant sound of Zukovsky's voice. The candle-lighted chandelier burned brightly overhead. Zukovsky paused to clear his Adams-appled throat. He was a tall, stately nobleman with a thin face and the long nose of a mountain hawk. The room seemed heavy with the ambience of their erudition.

Sasha Pushkin swallowed hard. He breathed deeply through his mouth and nostrils. His small voice invaded the momentary silence. "Why do all of you write your poems in French?" He broke into a damp cool sweat. All of their eyes turned toward Sasha, and he felt himself growing smaller and smaller. He felt that he might vanish altogether. And he wished fervently that he could.

Zukovsky sputtered, "I say, my dear boy, I mean—you see—"

"But I do not see, Your Excellency. Are you ashamed to be a Russian?"

His father Sergei stared at him furiously. "What are you doing in here? It's past your bedtime. And whoever heard of writing in Russian? It isn't *comme il faut*. A writer must be universal. Now off to bed with you, you impertinent scamp."

Sasha had begun to stammer, "Are—you—are—are—are the French universal then?"

"Of course, of course. Everybody knows they are," his father replied.

"But they write in French. Why—why—why don't they write in Russian?" Sasha insisted.

"Certainly not! It's unthinkable. It's absurd!" Sergei told his son.

"And—and—and it's equally absurd for us to write in French. Russians are as universal as anybody else."

"The lad is right, of course," his Uncle Basil interjected. Basil was taller than his brother, Sergei. He seemed to be smiling most of the time with a mischievous twinkle always in his grayish-blue eyes. "The only reason we write in French is because we feel inferior to the French." Uncle Basil was more cosmopolitan than Sasha's father. He was articulate in several languages, including French, German and English. He'd read the classics in each language. He'd even read the English and American Nursery Rhymes.

"Preposterous!" the chubby Dmitrev snorted excitedly.

The nine-year-old boy announced heatedly, "When I become a writer, I'm going to write in Russian for every literate Russian to read, and the devil take the universal French!"

Zukovsky and Uncle Basil applauded. "Bravo, Sasha! Bravo!"

Zukovsky's face flushed red as he came over and picked the boy up and embraced him. He turned to the others and proclaimed, "Out of the mouths of babes and angels." He laughed and kissed the boy on his flushed cheeks. "And a little child shall lead them."

Each time afterwards, when Sasha would attend one of the Pushkin soirées, he would promise himself beforehand that this was the night when he would share his own verse with these Russian giants of literature. This night he sat there with his heart beating as if it would, at any moment, leap from his boyish chest. He thought certainly they could hear the thumping thunder of his crazy heartbeat. No matter, this was the night he was going to read; it did not matter if they laughed at him. Alexander Turgenev had just finished reading, and there was an agonizing moment of silence in the candle-lighted drawing room with the handsome bearded portrait of Alexander Romanov, Czar of all the Russias, smiling at him from the wall above. He cleared his throat to speak, but the words stuck in his throat like glue. How did he dare to read his puerile verse to gentlemen of such literary preeminence? The atmosphere was so dense and so utterly overwhelming, he felt as if he was suffocating. He would read at the next one. This was not the proper moment. His father had been in ill temper all day long. If his reading went badly his father would surely scold him and embarrass him in front of these literary legends, most of whom had the ears of the Great One Himself who smiled at them from up above.

Sasha took the paper from his pocket slyly. He glanced around him, furtively, to see if anyone had noticed him. Perspiration dripped into his eyes and he could not see the wording clearly. Again he cleared his nervous throat. But just as he opened his mouth to speak, the venerable Nikolai Karamzin began to read in his incomparable prose. He sighed deeply. He felt an overpowering relief and at the same time a keen disappointment. The old man had a young man's voice. His diction, in French, was elegant as was his exquisite prose. After he finished, they applauded excitedly, Sasha sat there quietly, transfixed and transported.

They began to discuss Karamzin's offerings animatedly. When they had exhausted conversation and the room got quiet again, the boy broke out with a fine perspiration again on his face and neck and shoulders. He took the paper from his pocket again. His hands shook terribly. He closed his eyes; it was as if one dove into the icy Moskva River and had not yet learned how to swim. He found that he could not read his poetry with his eyes closed. He opened them and began to read softly.

Zukovsky said, "*Pajalsta* (Please), a little louder."

Sasha tried to read more loudly but his voice would not cooperate. It was something he had done in French. He didn't dare to read his Russian poetry to these noblemen of Russian letters.

When he finished, they shouted, "Bravo! Bravo!" His uncle kissed him on both cheeks.

"We have a genius in our midst," his uncle said excitedly. His father stared at him, unsmiling.

Sasha stood there in all his boyish modesty, smiling ecstatically inside himself. He was almost trembling with the excitement of the moment. It was a poem he had written effortlessly the night before. He thought, "Perhaps I am a genius." But he wouldn't take his uncle seriously. He knew for certain that his father wouldn't; couldn't.

Sasha wrote a comedy, THE PICKPOCKET, in French when he was not quite twelve and acted all the parts with his sister, Olga as the audience. The audience hissed the performance. Sasha bowed as if on stage. "Merci beaucoup, Mademoiselle. You are a perceptive critic." But then she saw his eyes begin to fill. "What do you know about theatre?" he demanded.

Olga knew she had hurt him even though she loved him; she adored her brother. She told him she was sorry and kissed him on his pouting lips.

The next day he thought better of it, and he wrote a poem and gave it to her.

The house at the pickpocket's opening kicked
Up a terrible row. And it's clear
that the author deserved it, his play being picked
from the pocket of one Moliere!

When Sasha wasn't scribbling frantically, his eyes were searching the printed page. His brother Leo once boasted that by the age of eleven Sasha knew all of French literature by heart. He was already familiar with giants like Racine, Voltaire, Moliere—

38

Sergei Pushkin took little interest in his children. It was a jurisdiction he had long ago assigned to his wife. As far as he was concerned, children were things to pat on the head, give advice to with handy proverbs, to boast about to colleagues of their cunning and precocity. Never to be picked up or attended to. He never changed a breech-cloth or took the children for a walk, not even to the bathhouse. A show of affection on his part was as rare as a heat wave in Siberian winter. And when this rare occasion did occur, it was hardly ever wasted on the older son, Alexander Sergeievich.

One spring morning Sergei Pushkin got up feeling good and took an interest in his elder son. He went to Sasha's room in his absence, sat down and began to read the poet's manuscripts. Sasha had just begun to write his poems in Russian rather than in French. It was his first attempt at Russian idiom, heavily influenced by his nyanya. It was like discovering a new invention, giving birth and voice to a new way of speaking, singing. He went around in a kind of creative ecstasy, his face and shoulders all aglow. He lived in a heavenly ambience. He was absent-minded, talked to himself, went without eating.

This morning, his father went through one manuscript after another, changing Russian idioms into French expression, scratching out this, erasing that, tearing up entire manuscripts. Whoever heard of anyone writing a poem in Russian idiom? Sergei Pushkin was as busy as a kitten covering up his excrement when Sasha walked into the room. Tattered papers littered the floor.

"What are you doing?" Young Pushkin's voice was trembling.

"Helping you with your writing, son. Why are you writing all of this Russian garbage? Any idiot can do that."

Tears blurred the poet's eyes. He was so angry he was speechless. When he could speak, he said, "Get out of my room! You have no right to tamper with my work!"

"This is my house, you ungrateful wretch!" his father shouted. "This is the thanks I get for trying to help, you little pagan bastard!"

Enraged and livid, Sasha looked around the room, screaming, "Get out! Get out! Get out!"

"You little African bastard! I was trying to help you!" Sasha seized a lighted candelabrum from beneath its glowing icon and went toward his father. He waved the heavy brass candelabrum at his paunchy father. "Get out before I kill you! Never touch my work again! Never again!" Tears were streaming from his eyes. The hot wax from the lighted candles spilled upon his hand. He didn't even feel it.

"You dare raise your hand to hit your father! You dare threaten me in my own house!" Sergei went toward his son and slapped the triple-candled candelabrum from his hand. He hit the boy with his fist and knocked him to the other side of the room. But the angry boy came back for more. "Give me my manuscript! Give me my manuscript!" His nose was bleeding.

They wrestled all over the place, even as the lighted candles in the candela-brum set fire to the rug and began to smoke up the room. Sergei Pushkin was puffing and blowing when Sasha's nyanya hurried into the room. The strong sturdy old woman pulled them apart. She scolded the father. "You ought to be ashamed of yourself, imposing on a poor little innocent child like that! What are you trying to do, burn down the house?"

"Mind your tongue around your betters, old woman. You're a servant in my house. You're nothing but a serf," Sergei Pushkin shouted.

Arina Rodionovna paid Sergei Lvovich no attention as she took the blanket from the bed and smothered the smoking rug. Sasha, his nose bleeding, his eyes overflowing, told his father, "You're the one who had better watch your tongue. You'd better watch how you speak to my nyanya. She surely is your better!"

They stood there now, Sasha and his nyanya, side by side facing his father, the man of the so-called mansion. Sergei Pushkin felt himself at a disadvantage. He couldn't continue beating on his husky son forever. He was already out of breath. And he certainly couldn't beat on this old woman who was a fixture in the Pushkin household. Like the old dutch stove that cooked the food, and the timber used to construct the house. It would never have occurred to him that as the master he might have her whipped with knout or cudgel dipped in hot molasses or have her impertinent tongue cut out. His fat stomach was too squeamish for such practices, which were every-day occurrences between masters and serfs.

He backed out of the bedroom, mumbling, "I'm not afraid of either of you. And you haven't heard the last of this, neither of you, I promise both of you!"

That night Sasha dreamed his mother came to him and kissed him on his warm forehead. Had he been dreaming? Had it really happened, actually? He was oftentimes confused between his dreams and his reality.

Tatyana came to him late one morning. Sasha was just barely past twelve years old and wide awake, dressed and waiting for her, impatiently. Usually, he could never begin his writing until she had come and gone. He broke into a sweat and his heart began to thump inside his boyish chest as he heard her coming down the hall singing a Russian folk song.

Igor, Igor courted Mary
punched her bowl to make her merry . . .

Sweat broke out all over his body. He felt a jumping thumping as if his heart beat in between his legs. His mouth knew an unfamiliar taste. What was happen-ing to him? What kind of spell had this woman cast upon him? Was Tatyana a witch in beautiful disguise? Sometimes he told himself she was a poem he had imagined. With her long flaxen hair and her double-breasted bosom. Long-waisted was his poem and constructed solid in the shanks. He smelled his poem before she came into the room. She had grown up on a farm on the steppes of the River Don.

40

At fifteen she was forced by her family into a marriage to an older man, a Don Cossack, who used to beat her each night when he came in from the steppes for what he suspected her of doing, or "for what she was going to do," as he jokingly explained it. She ran away and made her way to Moscow three years ago to seek her fortune, as it were.

"What's the matter with you, Your Excellency?" his poem said teasingly. "Do you have a fever?" She came to him and put her hand on Sasha's perspiring forehead. He felt the sweat pour from all over him. From his head down to his crotch. There was this queer taste in his mouth, and he could smell his own dear shamelessness.

His mouth worked but no words came forth, at first. Then—"You are —you're—you're very late this morning, Tatyana." His full curving lips were pouting.

"Oh yes, Your Excellency, Tatyana is very very tired. What untidiness they made last night at their party!"

This morning there was a new and special smell on her sweetish breath mixed with all the other smells that drove him crazy. He knew it was the smell of wine, cognac or vodka which she had scavenged by sipping from half-empty glasses left over from last night's party. His poem was slightly intoxicated and it gave to her a new excitement. Things often got out of hand in the Pushkin household. Servants all over the large rambling disorderly house. Launderers, footmen, cooks, housekeepers, chambermaids, tutors, getting in each other's way. Sometimes drunk and stumbling over one another.

Tatyana threw herself backwards on his bed, her legs spread wide apart. "Come, little naughty one. Let me see how hot you are."

He came hesitantly and stood above her. She said, "Come, darling boy, Tanya isn't going to bite you." Then suddenly she pulled her dress and petticoats up to her navel, and he beheld a world of ivory thighs and a blessed triangle in the middle of her flaxen-haired profusion. She pulled him atop her, pulled down his pants, and began to work her hips, slowly at first, then gaining tempo, furious and frenzied like she was going wild in her excitement. And he felt his boyish manhood growing hard against the middle of her. His head began to swim. He knew a heat wave in his shoulders, his thighs inflamed. What was he supposed to do? What did his poem expect of him? It wasn't long before his poem took matters into her own hand, and with an upward thrust she guided him to the proper target. And began to work and sweat and moan and groan as if she were going out of her mind. She locked her strong legs around the middle of his back and he thought that it would break in two. He tried desperately to free himself from the clutches of his lovely poem. All those books of French romances he'd read had not prepared him for this moment.

He was badly overmatched by this buxomy, powerfully-constructed peasant woman. Tanya was an earthy woman, whose hair was like the hay she'd gathered all those years along the River Don and the flax that grew wild on the steppes. She smelled of hay and earth and fresh coffee cooking, the sun and sky and the river in its overflow. She was a woman and she knew she was constructed differently from men, and she imagined the Good Lord in his infinite wisdom must have had some purpose in mind, and she meant to make the most of what the Lord had given her, Heaven bless the Emperor. It did not take her long to overflow.

When she arrived, she lay there whimpering like a tortured kitten, for the briefest moment. The poor lad thought that he had wounded her. It was not long before she disabused his fears. She pushed astonished Sasha up and backwards and jumped sprightly from the bed with an expression on her face, as if she had just partaken of a sumptuous feast, with sparkling eyes and swollen lips. With a rustle of cotton fabrics and a twist of her wide hips, she straightened her dress and underclothing. And quickly made the sign of the cross. She moved flowingly over to Sasha's icon and mumbled thank you to the Blessed Virgin. She was a devout and pious woman. Before he'd had time to cover his astonished nakedness, she kissed him quickly on the thing that had given her so very much happiness and pleasure. And now she went about her business straightening up his room and bouncing about and singing a Russian folk song.

See the wench run to her love
Hear them giggling in the clover.

That night, as he sat at the table eating supper, his mother stared at him in irritation.

"Sasha, why aren't you eating your supper like a good boy? Look at Leo and Olga. They're almost through eating already."

Sasha sat there staring silently at his plate, perspiration pouring from him as if his body had sprung leaks. There was a pounding in his head and a crazy dizziness.

"Why can't you be like your brother and sister?"

Why can't you love me, Ma-ma, as I am?

His father asked, irritatingly, "Why are you so different from your sister and your brother?"

His Uncle Basil was the only one in the family who saw worth in him, besides his grandmother. "You're damned right, he's different. He has the making of a genius if he isn't one already." His father stared at Basil as if he had suddenly lost his senses.

His versifying uncle, his only true friend in the household, came to his rescue. "Can't you see the boy isn't feeling well?"

His mother said, "There's nothing wrong with him. He just has the devil in him. It's his African blood rising up in him."

Ma-ma is so beautiful even when she scolds me.

His uncle rose from the table and went toward him and felt his forehead. "This boy is burning up with fever. He's got the grippe! It's raging all over Moscow! People are dying off like midges!"

42

Uncle Basil rang for the coachman and went out into the freezing winter, where the snow was falling steadily, for the doctor.

The long Russian winter night had already begun. The little coachman, bundled up in his bright red suit, woolen cossack jacket and high boots, waited near the shabby carriage outside the Pushkin residence, jumping up and down and flailing his body with his arms and hands to keep from freezing to death. The horses shivered, pranced and snorted. The saliva from the horses' whiskers changed immediately into icicles that glistened in the winter darkness. The clatter of horse hooves filled the night, trotting to and fro along the icy streets, and the merry sound of laughter and the jingle of the sleigh bells. The round of winter parties had begun.

Uncle Basil had to go to the other side of town and drag the grumbling man-of-medicine away from a riotous drunken celebration.

The doctor examined Sasha from head to feet. He could find nothing wrong. "The boy does not have influenza." But he bled the boy with Spanish flies and leeches just to be on the safe side.

Sleep did not come easily that night, as Sasha lay there in his terrible loneliness, listening to the nighttime sounds of the old house creaking and of the ghosts and spirits tiptoeing around the old place that was surely haunted. He heard the rasping sound of the great rats scratching inside the walls of his bedroom. Perhaps they were devils in disguise. He stared out at the darkness and he could see the evil spirits dancing around the icon with the lighted candelabrum burning brightly in the corner. His nyanya told him he need not fear the ghosts. There were good and there were evil spirits, and only the good spirits visited good boys, and since he was undoubtedly the very best of good boys, he had nothing at all to worry about. The rats inside the walls made a terrifying racket. If spirits came, and they surely would, he would welcome them and have a talk with them and learn some good things from them about the other world of elves and spirits. But his nyanya did not know about his sinful carryings on with his secret Tatyana. And surely there were evil spirits dancing all around his room even at this very moment. As he stared at the icon staring back at him from across the room, he imagined the image of the Holy Mother frowning disapprovingly at him, even as his own dear mother often did. In any event, the terrible noise they made unnerved him. He thought they might one night scratch their way into his room, and there'd be thousands of them. The Blessed Virgin seemed to open Her mouth and speak to him from Her Icon corner and scold him for his sinful ways. He could hear Her saintly voice, though the words she spoke were unintelligible. He began to sweat a frightful kind of perspiration. And now he heard distinctly the other spirits in the room reproaching him for his terrible depravity. He closed his eyes, but somehow with his eyes closed he could still stare at the darkness and the darkness stared back at the wicked boy, rebukingly. His eyes were shut as tightly as he could shut them, but he could still see a great redness from the brightly lighted icon and the candelabrum as if he were gazing at the setting sun. It was strange the colors he could see even though his eyes were shuttered tightly, especially the redness. A bright orange kind of redness. Perhaps it was the devil's own fire burning for him deep in hell. Perhaps he had died in his sleep and was down there with the devil and his fire and brimstone.

The next morning Tatyana came. She was surprised to see Sasha in bed and especially to find his mother at his bedside. "Alexander Sergeievich! What happened to you? Your Excellency," she added for the mother's benefit.

His face flushed as she came toward the bed. "What's wrong with him, Madame?" Tatyana asked the mother.

"How should I know if the stupid doctor doesn't?" She was irritated with the boy for inconveniencing her with his illness. She suspected him of feigning illness just to cause another headache for her.

Tatyana said, "I will watch over him, if Madame has something more important to do."

The mother fussed around a moment longer, then left without saying thank you to Tatyana. Tatyana came and sat on the bed beside her confused young lover. "Tatyana knows what troubles the bad baby."

"I am not a baby and you know it!" Sasha sweated more than ever as he flustered in his terrible agony. He hated her for poking fun at him. To put her in her place, he said, "And you're the chambermaid!" And hated himself for saying it.

"You're Tatyana's baby and you know it! Your Excellency!" She lunged at him and she began to tickle him in the ribs and under his arms—"Your Excellency!"—and the bottom of his feet, and he jumped about the bed giggling like he was crazy and begging for her to stop. "Your Excellency!" He forgot about his illness, as he howled with laughter, pleading all the while.

"Shhh," she cautioned him. "Not so loud, Your Nobleness. You'll wake your mother from her precious headache." And she continued tickling Sasha until she was tired and she threw her body on the bed beside him with her dress and underskirts up to her rosy hips. She lay beside His Excellency red-cheeked, flushed with perspiration and breathing hard, with the pungent smell of her all over everything. Now he felt a sweet and terrible disturbance, for she was the fever that caused the seizure, with the agonizing smell of her femaleness with which she effortlessly assaulted all of his senses. She sent his temperature soaring.

She leapt from the bed when she heard Sasha's mother coming wearily down the hall, awakened from her headache, and calling out to him in that irritating whining voice of hers. "Alexander Sergeievich . . . Alexander Sergeievich. . . ."

Tatyana flitted around the room straightening it up, as she quickly swept the dust and clutter underneath the rug, and by the time the mother reached the room, she held an open book before her (upside down) and was patting Sasha on the forehead with a damp towel.

"What are you keeping up such a racket about? You woke me from my morning nap."

"His Excellency's doing all right, Madame, I was reading a book to him, and he was laughing at a very funny part."

"Well," Nadezda Pushkina said, "I'll sit with him for awhile. You have other rooms to clean." His mother drank vinegar each morning to give herself a paler complexion, but it never worked.

"Yes, Madame."

"Go on now and fetch me something for this headache." And now she sat by her older son's bedside, sighing and blowing as if she had done a full day's work. Earlier, she had argued with the housekeeper about the house expenses. These daily arguments always left her exhausted. The steward and the housekeeper were the greatest swindlers in all of Holy Russia. It was traditional! Expected. Their cheating was an open secret.

She picked up the book that Tatyana had left near Sasha's bed. She stared sleepily at its pages. She turned it right-side up and soon was fast asleep and snoring. The frost that lingered on his window made him think of icing on a cake. The presence of his mother in the room did not help abate his fever.

When Arina Rodionovna heard of her Sasha's illness, she hurried to his bedroom, and his mother left him with the peasant nurse who truly loved him. A tall, gangling woman with wide roguish eyes, strong and sturdily constructed. She was the balm that exorcised his loneliness.

His nyanya sat with him, nodding and napping all night long. The old woman told him stories of olden times and knights of honor who swept through the night on great steeds to rescue pretty Tanyas and Natashas in distress and all in Russian idiom and nuances. He lay there, his heartbeat quickening, his great dark dancing eyes aglow with wonderment, as she took him into another world of ghosts and elves and great awesome spirits, always spoken in a mystic mood. And the world she brought to him was much more real than the world of parties and the French-styled soirées performed regularly in the Pushkin drawing room. She administered to him old-fashioned herbs and poultices, wrapped his head in a kerchief soaked in vinegar, and he was loved and he was happy and the fever left him. By morning, both of them slept peacefully.

CHAPTER THREE

The only other person who gave him love unstintingly beside Tatyana and her erotic love, and his nyanya, was his maternal grandmother, who told him stories of the grandeur and heroic exploits of his great-grandfather, Ibrahim Petrovich Hannibal. The same one who came as a boy from a strange and wonderful land far far away, a land called Africa, and served with great distinction in the court of Peter the Great. His deep dark blue eyes would gleam, his plentiful mouth would motion wordlessly and his boyish chest would swell and almost burst with a burning self-esteem. He loved his maternal grandmother for the great self-pride she instilled in him, which he needed desperately. And many nights he dreamed he lived in those far-off days and shared in his great-grandfather's feats, as they strode the country side by side. It was a dream that came to him with a welcomed frequency.

Even as Sasha grew toward manhood, he always cherished the days he spent with his grandmother. He loved to remember, dimly, even as a baby, when she would put him in her knitting basket, and puff on her old Oriental pipe, and spin yarns to him about Ibrahim Hannibal, as he sat there in the basket with his eyes stretched wide and his mouth hanging open. His grandmother was a beautiful wondrous poem he knew by heart. She would tell her favorite grandchild of a time during the early part of the eighteenth century when Holy Russia was already vast and much of it unexplored, stretching from the eastern edge of Europe over great mountain ranges and broad steppes and desert land thousands of miles across frozen Siberia all the way to the wide Pacific. He tried with all his young imagination to envision the poetic vastness of this land called Mother Russia. She spoke of Peter the Great, the little White Father, Czar of all the Russias, Creator of Saint Petersburg! "Oh, what a mighty man he was! There's never been one like him before or after and most likely there will never be. Truly, he was God's emissary down here on this sinful earth."

"Tell me about my great-grandfather, Grandma-ma," he asked excitedly.

"He was a great one," she stated proudly. "And Czar Peter really loved that man. Those two were inseparable. All the courtiers were jealous of him. He was so tall and Black and comely."

"How did he come to Russia?" She smiled at the boy and ran her bony hand through his wooly head. She had told him the story many times, but he never tired of it.

It is my favorite poem, Grandma-ma.

She puffed on her pipe. "The Turks and Ethiopians were at war with one another. Your great-grandfather was a nine year old African prince. He was captured and brought to Turkey as a hostage. And they put him in a harem. It was fate that saved him. Thank God for our Great Peter. They would have castrated your great-grandfather. They would have made a eunuch of him. But Peter had sent the word out to all the embassies in Europe. 'Find me a Negro!' or Ethiope or Arab or Black-amoor."

"Grandfather was an Ethiope," Sasha stated proudly to his grandmother. "Yes," she answered. "The Ethiopes were a grand proud people. That's why Peter thought so much of him. Your court was not considered to be a proper one without at least one Negro. Every court in Europe had one. It was the fashion in those days."

"What did they do at the court, Grandma-ma?"

His mouth would work, soundlessly repeating as she went along. "Some were footmen." *Some were footmen.* "Some were court jesters," *Some were court jesters,* "clowns and pets and lackeys. But your great grandfather was nobody's lackey." *Grandfather was no lackey.* "Right away Peter saw the worth of Ibrahim Petrovich. And it wasn't long before he became the private secretary to His Most Imperial Majesty."

Sasha knew he was his Grandma-ma Hannibal's favorite among the children. She seemed to know he needed more affection than Leo or Olga. She was always secretly giving him sweets. She told him he was special, "because you resemble your great grandfather much more than the rest of them." She baked cakes especially for him. Ibrahim Hannibal was a great man, the handsomest in Peter's Court, and I suspect he was the most intelligent. And you take after him in every way; in looks and in intelligence. And I'm as proud of you as I can be." She kissed him on his mouth and slapped him gently on his backside.

Whenever Sasha visited his grandmother she would let him play with the peasant children, much to his mother's deep chagrin. His mother said the *muzhik* devils had fleas on them and he would be contaminated. But every chance he got he played with them. He ran and romped and wrestled, got in many friendly fights. Danced, played ball. Learned to swear and use his head and butt them like a mountain goat. He would come home sweaty, sometimes with a bloody nose and darkened eye. His mother would box his ears and scold him. But he was happy with his new-found comrades. He felt loved and very much at peace. He did not mind his mother's beatings. The fun he had was worth the price.

Some evenings he would steal away and go out on the darkened steppes with Anton Ivanovich Aniskushk, the shepherd, and his brothers, with his flock of sheep. He would sit by the open fire with them and other peasant children and listen to the thin-lipped older shepherd boy tell his tall tales in a lusty Russian idiom about the mysteries of the eerie steppes. Anton Ivanovich would sit there with his pipe in his skimpy mouth, sometimes his mouth would be filled with snuff, and he would spit the dark brown stuff out into the night so that it landed near the sleeping sheepdog. The old dog would move around and look up at his master, stare up at the moon and howl. He'd scratch the fleas on his lousy mangy underside; sometimes it would feel so good, he would start to gnaw at where the fleas were biting him. Then he would fall asleep again.

One night, Anton Ivanovich told them about a man who had put a curse upon the entire village. "All the crops were failing, the sheep were dying by the dozens. The enemies of Igor Igorovich Berinsky, a one-armed Uzbek from Bukhara in Uzbekistan, in the far-off eastern desert, spread the rumor that the old one-armed hermit was a witch causing these disasters to their crops and sheep. A holy man led a group of righteous, outraged subjects of His Imperial Majesty, peasants all, to the Uzbek's *isba* (hut) with torches flaming. 'Come out and get your just deserts, you devil's nephew,' they shouted to him. They beat the side of the house, they screamed, they whooped and hollered. Finally he came to the door.

"Tall and firm of jaw and as wide as he was tall. 'Come on out you black devil!' they shouted, ropes in hand. 'We just want to hang you so our crops and cattle will stop dying.' He told them they must be crazy. He was no devil or witch. He was just a humble peasant, a hard-working muzhik like the rest of them. They began to scream and curse at him. He slammed the door in their faces. They banged against the house again. The next time he came to the door they told him if he did not give himself up, they would set fire to his isba. They assured him that they meant him no harm. They only wanted to hang him to a tree to save their crops and sheep. His was the only isba with a windowpane of glass in the entire village, which proved absolutely his connections with the devil, the window blinking at the sun and moonlight, like he was sending signals to the devil or receiving them. He told them if they set fire to his house, if they burned him to death, he would surely come back from the dead to haunt them forever and the very next day following forever. His image would always be there in the window of his isba, which proved, of course, that he was in contact with the devil's underworld. All the more reason why they should destroy the black devil. He stood there in his little door looking at them mean and evil. And they looked around at one another, and one by one, two by two by three by four, they slunk away like cowardly dogs with their tails between their legs. After midnight, a few of the courageous ones came back and set fire to Igor Igorovich's isba. They burned the isba to the ground, and Igor Igorovich was never seen alive again.

"But the next morning they went to see what they had wrought, and there was the isba just like it had always been, windowpane and all, blinking in the morning sunlight. There was just one difference. The white pasty image of old Black Igor Igorovich was grinning at them from the blinking windowpane. They fled like thieves to the Emperor's Secret *Politseyskii*. They went back the next day and broke out the window. The image still grinned at them. Old Igor is right there till this very day."

They had all been very quiet during the entire telling of the story. Sasha stated flatly, "I don't believe it."

Piotra Ivanovich said, "You aren't supposed to believe it. You're supposed to listen to it. You weren't born with a veil over your eyes like all us muzhiks."

The other children laughed at Sasha. Anton Ivanovich said, "It's still over there in that isba near the old church." He pointed through the darkness across the eerie steppe. "Old Igor's still grinning his fool head off. Nobody lives there because they're scared of the ghost of Igor Igorovich." He looked around at their young faces gathered around him near the fire, as it crackled and spit sparks all over the place. "Anybody want to go and see it for themselves?"

There was at first a roaring silence. Then Sasha said quietly, "I'm not afraid." His voice was trembling.

To show everybody he was not afraid Sasha went up front alongside Anton Ivanovich. The rest of them dragged along behind. It was late in autumn and the grass had been cut, and neat piles of hay had been stacked here and there on the steppe. In the darkness of the steppe, the stacks of hay looked like gatherings of ghost people from the dreaded underworld come up to conspire against the righteous and patriotic people who loved God and served the Emperor. Sasha's eyes were widening every fraction of a second, as his face broke out into a cool damp sweat, and he could hear and feel his heart beating all the way up in his mouth, and he was glad that it was black-dark so no one could see how scared he was.

Finally they reached the little isba sitting there on the edge of the steppe all by itself as if it were infected by an incurable disease. It was a neat little log cabin with a roof of hay and straw and shaped like a Chinese pagoda. There was just a single window without a windowpane. All of them stood there staring at the little pagoda-shaped isba. It looked so lonesome, Sasha began to feel sorry for it. He knew the feeling of loneliness.

"You see him, don't you?" Anton Ivanovich asked them in a scary voice. The other children answered, "Yes! Yes! There he is! There he is!" Sasha swallowed the cool night air deep into his nervous belly. He stared at the window hard and long. "I don't see anything." He didn't even see a windowpane.

"Look good and strong. There it is plain as day." Alexander Sergeievich thought, "It's plain as day, but this is night."

All the other children sang out, "I can see him! I can see him!" Sasha narrowed his eyes and strained them. Suddenly there was an eerie sound like the bleating of a poor sheep lost forever on a frozen steppe. Old Igor began to howl and then he ran around in circles, a chill danced across Alexander Sergeievich's shoulders, and his flesh crawled as if centipedes were on the march across his back. And then right before Alexander Sergeievich's eyes there appeared an apparition in the window, a white hideous smiling face. "There he is!" the children shouted, and then they beat a swift retreat back across the darkened steppe. Sasha was not very far behind them, except that while running back across the steppe he ran into several haystacks and he was sure that he was in the clutches of the people of the underworld who had risen from the dead and meant to take him back with them to make a true believer of him. When they got back to the Aniskushk isba, he was too scared to go home by himself. Anton and Piotra walked with him.

Some nights he would spend with Anton Ivanovich and his family. His mother would punish him the next day but it didn't matter. She was afraid he would acquire bad habits of speech like muzhiks; she wanted him always to speak like a proper nobleman, with all the French nuances and intonations. Anton's youngest brother, Piotra Ivanovich, was Sasha's best comrade. He would sleep in the drafty isba with them atop a stove and shiver all night long underneath a flimsy blanket. When his teeth began to chatter Piotra Ivanovich and his brothers would laugh at him and put him in the middle of them to keep him warm. He loved the Aniskushks and felt loved by them. In many ways they *were* his family.

One night he went with Piotra Ivanovich and his family to one of the other isbas nearby. The hut was overcrowded with people sitting on the floor and standing along the wall. Three of them sat on top of the oven. An old man sat in the middle of the floor, his head thrown back, his eyes closed. He opened them and looked around him at all of the expectant faces, peasants all, except Alexander Sergeievich, who, with Piotra Ivanovich and his family, had sidled into the crowded hut and found spaces on the floor to sit. Many stood outside the isba and listened.

Finally, the old man began to sing a *bylina* (epic poem), a narrative of heroics of the great Prince Vladimir and Ilya and Igor and Olga and Ivan and Boris and even of Dmitri, the great impersonator. He closed his eyes again. At first, his singing was possessed with a sorrowful and haunting quality, and the tears spilled down the old man's cheeks. Some of the people gathered were also weeping openly. It was as if he were endowed with magic and hypnotic powers.

He was a *skazital* (storyteller), and he made them laugh and made them cry, as he taught them their own history.

Now he sang a rousing bylina, a song of triumph, and the people clapped their hands and felt triumphant. Sasha smiled and felt a great warmth as the tears spilled down his own eyes, and he felt he was in the presence of a truly great man, this skazital, and he felt close to the muzhik, the lowly Russian peasant, and he wondered about the land of his great-grandfather. Were there also skazitali in Africa, men who traveled from place to place and sang their history to the people?

Natalya Ivanovna was Piotra Ivanovich's fourteen-year-old sister. She worked in the fields each day and the sun had put a warm and burnished tan on her body. Her face always glowed and glistened. She was a girl who laughed and smiled most of the time, though Sasha always thought her dark eyes were full of all the sadness in the world. He loved to watch her supple body as she moved about, her sloping shoulders, one held higher than the other. She walked as if she took great pleasure in the feeling that the walking gave her. Every limb exuded pleasure. He thought she was surely one of the most beautiful girls on this entire Russian earth. Her full-lipped mouth that loved to talk with him and him to listen. He thought her dark wide-set eyes held all the mystery in the world and he wanted to know their secrets. She loved to tease Sasha, called him "Old Man" and said he must have lived before in another life. He had too much sense for one so young, she told him. He loved for her to call him "the Old Man" although he pretended to dislike it. In the evening they would walk together along the countryside and sometimes venture out on the darkening steppe.

One day he went to see the Aniskushks and found the household in a great disturbance. The bearded old man was walking around the isba cursing to himself, and the mother was trying to console the smiling laughing girl with the tears streaming from her sorrowful eyes. The two-room isba was pulling apart with tension, from the little kitchen where the boys slept to the front room where Natalya and her parents slept with a heavy curtain of sack cloth dividing the room in half and providing them with pride and privacy. Piotra Ivanovich walked outside of the isba with Sasha.

"What's the matter?" Sasha asked his best comrade. Piotra Ivanovich's voice was choking with emotion.

"Natalya Ivanovna is going to be one of His Excellency's handmaidens!"

"That's good," Sasha commented. "Isn't it?"

"It's terrible!" Piotra Ivanovich exclaimed. "She will not be living with us anymore. She'll be living with His Excellency," he blurted out. "My father says she'll be sleeping with His Excellency and before long she'll be having a baby for him!"

Piotra Ivanovich's father had always known it would happen, had known it was just a matter of time. He had watched the Master with his covetous eyes on his little girl ever since she was nine or ten years old. Count Melenkov would come into the field on his great roan horse and watch her work.

One day he commented to Piotra Ivanovich's father, "Natalya Ivanovna is going to be a beautiful woman one of these days. She's too beautiful to be working in the field like a drayhorse. She should be in the manor house."

Natalya's father had responded anxiously, "She's a good field worker, Your Excellency. She works harder than anybody else. She loves field work. She has the skill for it. She could entice wheat to grow out of rock in the middle of the desert. She would be no good at all in the manor house."

"We shall see," His Excellency mumbled. "We shall certainly see."

Sasha thought his heart had stopped beating. He stammered. "But-but-but-but why doesn't she tell him she'd rather work in the field? I mean he can't make her work in the manor house against her will—." Even as he said it, he realized it was a foolish statement.

Piotra said, matter-of-factly, "She has no say in the matter. He is the master and there is nothing for it."

"But he's too old for her," Sasha protested. "She is too young to be his wife."

"She will not be his wife," Piotra said bitterly. "She'll just be one of his concubines!" He uttered the hated word like an oath.

Sasha stared at his comrade and looked up at the clear diaphanous sky. He felt a deep all-encompassing sadness. He reached around desperately in his mind for words with which to console Piotra Ivanovich, but there were no such words for him. And he realized that it was like he was losing his own sister to the evil master. He would no longer watch her move about. She would no longer call him the "Old Man." They would no longer go for walks together. He had not realized how much he loved Natalya Ivanovna with the sloping shoulders and the laughing face and the most sorrowful eyes in all the world. But more than anything else he felt the futility of his anguish, his deep frustration, his overwhelming impotence. As Piotra Ivanovich had said, there was nothing for it. There was nothing anybody could do about it. He remembered the serf at the garden party in Moscow. His mother said it was Fate, God's will. How could he love a God like this? He hated the Russian phrase, "There's nothing for it." He had heard it all his life. "Fate, God, the Emperor, there's nothing for it!"

That next summer Sasha went to visit his grandmother in the country, and looked for Piotra Ivanovich and his family. He went to the isba where they had lived and found other muzhiks living there.

Grandma-ma Hannibal took him in her arms and told him, "They're gone, little darling. They belonged to the Melenkovs. And they sold them to the Kaparins. Last week they moved off to Novgorod."

He was surprised at the question that first came from him. "And did Natalya Ivanovna go with them?"

"She's in the manor house," his grandma-ma told him. "She's pregnant with the master's baby."

Sasha felt a heat collecting in his face. He saw the laughing face of Piotra Ivanovich before him and the sad dark eyes of Natalya Ivanovna and it was too much for his young mind and heart to encompass and contain. He fought back the fullness in his face and shoulders. He wouldn't cry. He was too big a boy for that. His father told him only babies and women cried. The more he fought against his tears the more the tears pushed themselves forward spilling down his anguished cheeks. He buried his face in his grandmother's lap and he cried and he cried as if the world were coming to an end.

PART TWO

LYCÉE DAYS AT TSARSKOYE SELO

CHAPTER ONE

Alexander Sergeievich was twelve years old, and his family still had not the vaguest notion of the coming greatness of the boy who dwelt among them. He lived outside their understanding, in the real world of his poetry and his heightened consciousness.

His Uncle Basil assured them they had birthed a genius. "I don't know how you did it. But I swear by Holy Friday, he's a natural genius. Neither of you deserve him. The Lord works in mysterious ways."

His mother said, "Sasha? A genius? Don't be ridiculous!"

His father said, "That insolent, impudent pagan! He'll never amount to anything."

His mother agreed. "He's too much like his African great-grandfather."

When he was just past twelve, he left his turbulent beloved Moscow. Uchitols were fine, but when a lad was reaching toward his teens, house tutors no longer sufficed. It was time to think of higher education, even for worthless Ivan Ivanoviches, good-for-nothings, like Sasha. It was traditional and expected of the children of aristocrats, of the male species, that is.

It had been decided that Sasha would attend the Russian Jesuit School, which was far beyond the means of the Pushkins' economics. It was a school where the wealthiest of the nobility sent their boys. Sergei Pushkin was rescued from financial embarrassment only when his brother, Basil, brought home the good news of the free-tuitioned elitist school being set up by Czar Alexander on the grounds of the Summer Palace at Tsarskoye Selo to educate the future "pillars of the Empire."

Uncle Basil busied himself and pulled all kinds of Imperial strings to get his favorite nephew into the new Lycée. Then came the Imperial communication inviting Alexander Sergeievich Pushkin to come for entrance examinations at Tsarskoye Selo, a small city situated near the outskirts of the fabulous Saint Petersburg.

As much as the boy loved his noisy unplanned Moscow, he felt no sincere regrets at leaving it behind him. There were no family ties to keep him. No nostalgia for the good old days with Mama and Papa. He was fond of his grey-eyed sister, Olga, but his younger very blondish brother, Leo, was his mother's favorite, and Sasha would not be heartbroken by departing from him. He would miss his nyanya, Arina Rodionovna, and his maternal grandmother. He would also miss Tatyana, who, in a few month's time had taught him all of the mysteries of love and the giving and the making of it. He was hardly the innocent lad he'd been when she used to give him fever every time she came into his presence.

And she came to him that last night, and they made love, and she cried herself to sleep beside him, because "I truly love my baby! His Excellency!" And it was a shame His Excellency could not take her with him to Saint Petersburg. Sasha could not sleep that night as he lay there immersed in the smell of this generous tender-hearted woman and in the sweet salty smell of the love they had made together. Near the dawn he finally dropped off with visions of Saint Petersburg and a new day borning for him. He would be alone, really alone, for the first time in his lonely life, and his imagination ran wild, made his heart thump in his manly chest, as he listened to the soft snoring of Tatyana and drifted slowly into dreams.

The family accompanied him to the gates of Moscow, which was the custom, and they cried as if by Imperial decree, which was also the tradition, wept like professional mourners at some great man's funeral. Even his hypocritical mother wept bitter tears for her "darling angel Sasha!" Hungrily, she held him tightly to her bosom, and it all conjured up long forgotten memories of when he was a new born babe and sucked from her his nourishment.

Even his Uncle Basil summoned up some tears from somewhere, although he was making the trip with Sasha to see after him until he hopefully gained entrance into the Lycée.

Uncle Basil was actually glad to be going to Saint Petersburg where the really artistic and intellectual occurrences were, where the latest style in French coiffure and French apparel came into the city once a week, and the latest word on liberal thinking. It was a time of George Gordon Byron and *Childe Harolde*, when fashionable Europeans wore their hair cut short in sturdily ragged locks. Uncle Basil could travel, intellectually, with the truly elite of the Russian versifiers. And there was this beautiful serf girl, Annette Vorozheykin, seated meekly opposite Sasha in the stagecoach. Uncle Basil's wife had left him recently, and he had been so terribly upset he had taken this dear child to soothe his broken heart and save himself from suicide.

Sasha wanted to be away from all the hypocritical moaning and groaning and gnashing of teeth, as he sat there impatiently nibbling away on his fingernails down to the actual bone. Finally, the steps to the carriage were taken up, and the coachman lashed his horses and Sasha could not keep the smile from spreading over his eager face. He was on his way! Going north to that notoriously fabulous city of Peter the Great.

Uncle Basil, Sasha and Basil's amie, Annette Vorozheykin, stopped at one of the fashionable hotels in Saint Petersburg while waiting for the school to start. The people in this fantastic city were different from the folk of Moscow. Sasha felt like a country bumpkin come to the city from the provinces. They seemed a different breed of Russian altogether. And the city intersecting at right angles instead of like in Moscow where an unplanned conglomeration of villages went off in all directions and sometimes with no direction at all. Moscow was like a wayward orphan that just grew up without rhyme or reason or parental guidance. But here was a city planned by man. A city of stone and granite and gleaming marble and concrete and man-made canals. The people seemed likewise to be made of stone. A cold city without a heart or deep emotion. Even the Neva River seemed to have been constructed. Everywhere he heard proud Russians describe their city as "a window on Europe!"—"The Venice of the North—" as Europeans poured into the city and the hotel by the hour. He heard all kinds of foreign tongues and accents.

His uncle took him to several literary soirées and he stood around, his narrow eyes dancing wide with wonder as Uncle Basil introduced him, casually, to men who were household words in the literate homes of Russia. Then the day came to travel to Tsarskoye Selo (the Tsar's Village), to the Summer Palace of Czar Alexander.

His uncle took Sasha around the Palace grounds, breathtaking in their flamboyant splendor and pomposity. He was open mouthed and his head was in a whirl as his uncle told him, "This palace is the ostentatious alter ego of Empress Katerina the Great. During the reign of Peter the Great, Empress Elizabeth was a playmate of your great-grandfather on your mother's side." Peter the Great! His heart leapt about. Empress Elizabeth! Katerina! Ibrahim Petrovich Hannibal! His great-grandfather! He was catapulted back through time and space through Russian history. He was dizzy with excitement. He felt a part of it all, as if he had lived it all another time. A déjà vu! His uncle laughed his booming laughter.

"Elizabeth was the one who invited Catherine to Moscow. She was the German Empress after Elizabeth. Like they say in the American nursery rhyme, Great Catherine was like the old woman who loved in a shoe. She had so many lovers she didn't know what to do. Your great-grandfather used to sleep with her," his uncle boasted.

To Sasha, the Summer Palace was a vast grotesque monstrosity of harsh yellow colors. Beginning from one end to the other, it seemed to go on and on forever. A four-story colossus of stone and marble and concrete with more than a thousand arched windows gilded in gold, the edges trimmed in gleaming white. He blinked his eyes, unknowingly. It was an awesome sight. Long wide marble steps flowing endlessly down from the Palace into a man-constructed fairyland of shaded lanes and artificial lakes and ancient obelisks and gigantic monuments of bronze and marble, the lingering after-summer redolence of jasmine and hyacinth. Tall majestic ageless trees. It all put an aura of romance around the Palace, especially for a romantic one like Sasha, especially in September when the grounds around the Palace seemed aflame with early autumn. Fall seasons always summoned up his muse and made our poet lovesick.

The vast green-carpeted Palace grounds hung heavily with peaches and ripening apples, the fragrances intoxicating, and he imagined the grounds were a lover's paradise, and then remembered, forlornly, that the Lycée provided no place for girls in the Imperial scheme of things. But it was a romantic time in Russia, Sasha thought, in real life and in literature, and love would find a way, inevitably. He felt a fullness in his face at the beauty of it. His uncle and he stood alongside a broad flat sleepy lake without a single ripple in it. Sail boats went quietly up and down the man-made lake. Lotus leaves and water lilies sat upon the glassy surface and seemed to grow up out of the tranquil water. Majestic swans sailed out from under the bushes along its banks like an exquisitely choreographed ballet.

That first evening just before the day was falling along with the golden leaves, Sasha watched, open-mouthed, as Czar Alexander-the-Pious-One, Emperor of all the Russias, strolled along a lane with several sparsely disguised policemen at a discreet distance in front of and behind him, with his great Siberian husky just up ahead of him.

Sasha pointed excitedly, "That's him! That's him! His Imperial Majesty!"

"Of course, that's him," Uncle Basil responded. "My darling nephew, you're at the Emperor's Summer Palace. But you must never point. It's gauche. It isn't *comme il faut* to point, especially at His Majesty." Uncle Basil always professed to know all of the gossip at the Court. He laughed at his favorite nephew. "Everybody knows, dear innocent boy, His Most Imperial Majesty is on his way to bestow His Imperial blessings upon a sixteen-year-old serf girl with an enormous bosom and great frightened eyes. His nightly assignations are an open secret. What's more, they have the Czarina's benevolent approval." He smiled at the look on his nephew's face. "You see, my dear innocent child, the Emperor and the Empress are terribly sophisticated."

Sasha was among the thirty boys out of hundreds who passed the examinations. "Why should it surprise you?" his uncle asked him. "How many times do I have to tell you you're a natural genius?" They were eating breakfast downstairs in the restaurant of the only hotel in the village.

He stared at his uncle, as Uncle Basil shoved the food into his mouth and made slurping sounds as he gulped down the steaming coffee. "What is a genius, Uncle Basil?"

"You have a natural creative ability, an exceptional capacity for imaginative and original conceptions." His uncle answered. An extraordinary sensitivity and perception. That's why you are a genius. You are one of the most original human beings on this entire earth."

The young lad's face flushed violently.

Uncle Basil smacked his greasy lips and wiped his mouth and smiled at his embarrassed nephew. "God has blessed you with the rarest gift of all, and he hasn't made you arrogant. That is the beauty of it. Stay as you are, my boy. It is not necessary to flaunt one's genius."

Sasha smiled nervously. Genius? Should he take his uncle seriously? "Genius is a blessing then?"

"Of course it is," his uncle told him. "Though it does not guarantee happiness or wealth. Wolfgang Mozart was buried in a pauper's grave. As often as not, men of genius come to grief. Ignorance and envy and avarice. The world is hardly ever ready for the geniuses of this earth."

"What's the good of it then?" the nephew asked.

"Some men hide themselves from their destiny. But I have watched you ever since the day you were born, almost. You've always moved boldly toward your destiny. And that is as it always should be. You made a commitment to your genius when you were six or seven years of age," Uncle Basil said.

He felt the tears standing just out of sight on the other side of his eyes. His face filled up to overflowing. He thought his uncle was being tremendously extravagant. Yet deep deep inside of him somehow he knew at least a small part of the truth of his uncle's great extravagance. He had long ago, in Moscow, in that rambling old house on German Street, made a lonely commitment to himself and to his muse.

His Uncle Basil rose from the table, wiping his mouth with his napkin. "You've hardly touched a bite of your food."

"I'm not hungry, Uncle Basil."

"You're going to be a genius for a long time, so you might as well get used to it and not let it spoil your appetite. You'll starve to death if you do." He smiled down at his flustered nephew. "Hurry now, dear boy, and finish your breakfast. This is your first day at the Lycée."

His uncle left him with Herr Director Englehardt.

The first Lycée days were full of pomp and ceremony. The school, located in the left wing of the Summer Palace, was divinely blessed with the presence of His Imperial Majesty and his entourage of courtiers and sychophants on that first day of the installation ceremonies.

They were gathered in the vast Lycée dining room. The air was pregnant with lofty expectations and excitement. They were the chosen few from all the rest. What did it mean to be so extra special, he asked himself. Were all thirty of them geniuses? The bands played the National Anthem. Standing proudly with his head bowed, patriotic, Sasha knew warm unfamiliar feelings for the Motherland. He was Russian and a part of this. He no longer felt alone. It wasn't long, though, before Sasha turned and twisted in his chair, fighting desperately against falling asleep through a long endless litany of boring speeches exhorting the new students to loyalty and dedication to the Motherland and to His Imperial Majesty, which were, of course, synonymous. Finally, it was time to eat, the most important moment for the young and future pillars of the Empire.

By now Sasha was starved. The hefty dowager Empress of German stock with the great nose and the heavy mustache, came over to a table of hungry students and asked one of the flustered boys, "And is the soup goot?"

Alexander Sergeievich answered, "Oui, Monsieur!" His soup went down the wrong passage and came back through his eyes and nostrils. The dowager Empress smiled and moved along.

Lycée days for Alexander Sergeievich were spending very little time with the school books that bored him to distraction, like mathematics and engineering and Latin. Getting into all kinds of mischief. Falling in love with anyone who wore skirts, had lovely eyes, fulsome lips and tiny feet. And getting into trouble with the very strict instructors. He was assigned to a seat in the back of the classroom because, they said, he could not learn.

"Alexander Sergeievich, would you kindly give us your opinion on the period of the Inquisition?"

His name had to be called several times to capture his attention. He got slowly to his feet. "I beg your pardon, Monsieur."

"Please answer the question, *s'il vous plait*."

"What was the question, Monsieur?"

"About the Inquisition."

He sweated. "Well, Monsieur, it was a time of great inquiry."

Laughter from his fellow classmates.

"Very well, Monsieur Pushkin. Go back to the poem you were writing. You may take it from under your desk."

After a few weeks came the announcement at Assembly that the boys at the Lycée would be confined to the Academy until they graduated. By Imperial Decree, against which there was no appeal. They would not be allowed to go home on holidays to visit their families. Six years at the Lycée with no vacations!

Lonely Lycée days were spent watching the Russian world pass Tsarskoye Selo dressed in army boots and uniforms, sometimes barefoot landless muzhiks marching sloppily along to face the Napoleonic Plague that had swept over most of Europe. His beloved Moscow was in flames. He worried for his family. It was knowing an ephemeral feeling of great patriotism for the Motherland. It was Emperor Alexander marching into Paris. Czar Alexander, the Messiah, Savior of Holy Russia, Little White Father and protector of the universe from the anti-Christ, Napoleon. Hero of all heroes. Glory to his name. It was truly a patriotic time when Alexander Sergeievich sat in his room at his desk, sometimes all through the night with the candle burning low and dim till his eyes began to burn. One night, at thirteen years of age, he wrote:

"Where are you, lovely Moscow of the thousand cupolas,
Wonder of our land?
There where the solemn city reigned,
Nothing but the ruins remain.
Moscow! All Russians quake at the sight of your grieving face.
Gone, the palaces of noblemen and Czars!
The flame has consumed them all, the crowns of towers
And homes of great fortunes.
Along the boulevards of wealth,
In gardens and in fields.

His inflamed eyes began to tear, and he fought against the patriotism he felt, but his remembered Moscow of the thousand churches, the grandiose mysterious Kremlin, the marketplace, the waterfront, the cobblestoned boulevards with grass growing wildly up between the cobblestones, all of it put a queer taste in his mouth and fullness in his face and shoulders. He missed all of it. He longed for his beloved Moscow. And he wrote:

Where the scent of myrtles hung and lindens shook,
Now there are embers, ash and dust.
Everything is dead, silence everywhere.
Take comfort, mother of all Russian cities.
See how your invaders shrink,
They have felt upon their boastful company
The avenging night hand of the Lord.
See: they are running away, they do not turn to fight.
And their blood is flowing in long streams through our snow.
And in the night hunger and cold cut them down.
And at their backs the Russian sword pursues.

And Lycée days for Alexander Sergeievich were going over the wall with his new friend, Ivan Pushchin, and making it to the quarters of the Hussar of the Czarist Guards who drank and reveled outrageously and talked revolution and wined and womanized and sang risque songs as well as ballads of rebellion. The Emperor's Horse Guards exuded anti-Monarchist sentiments. Some of them had been to France with Alexander Romanov as conquerors and heard all of the talk of *Egalité, Liberté* and *Fraternité*. They yearned for the same in their native Russia. At least they talked of nothing else. It was the kind of group that went perfectly with the mood of Alexander Sergeievich and his inflammatory poetry, for which he was already becoming famous, or infamous, depending on one's point of view.

The years at the Lycée passed swiftly, and at sixteen Alexander Sergeievich could curse and swear and wench and drink with the wildest of the Hussars. Under the guise of hell-raising revelry, the Emperor's Hussar Horse Guards carried on frenzied subversive activities, mostly consisting of polemicizing pyrotechnic rhetoric. With numerous pictures of Czar Alexander hanging like Holy icons all along

60

the wall, they exorcised each other, harangued at one another. It was at this time that Alexander Sergeievich met Nikolai Raevsky and the renowned "moral revolutionary," Peter Chaadaev, a colonel in the Horse Guards.

At the center of the Hussar group, along with Chaadaev, was a handsome, blue-eyed, tow-headed, hard-drinking, philosophizing womanizer by the name of Kaverin, who had also been with Alexander the-Savior-and-Conqueror in France. A hell-raising, antimonarchist Constitutionalist. Both men were hero images to young Pushkin, and six and seven years older, and had traveled outside Imperial Russia. The younger poet was always wide-eyed in their presence. Captain Kaverin, for his raging all-consuming lust for life, drinking and fornicating as if tomorrow were the very last day on this Russian earth; Chaadaev, for the calm and beauty of his countenance and soul, the brilliance of his mind and his absolute commitment to the moral urgencies and imperatives of his times.

It was also at this time that Alexander Sergeievich formed the habit of leaping on tables, a dark blue flame burning in his animated eyes, arms outflung and declaiming his electrifying verse. These activities escaped the all-seeing eyes and ears of the Czarist police because of the sound and fury of their raucous revelry which was a tradition with the Hussars.

Beautiful women were always within arms' reach at these endless bacchanalia, and Hussar arms were always reaching. There was, particularly, a very articulate, dark-eyed, sloe-eyed, freckled, red-haired, curvy-mouthed beauty named Svetlina who was of very facile virtue, and who had special eyes for Alexander Sergeievich. Her rich avid lips exuded sensuality. Her dear dark black eyes overflowed with fun and frolic. She was one of Kaverin's wenches, but she made it very clear to the young sapling poet that she could be his for the asking. But he was in such awe of this romantic revolutionary, he fought against temptation. She was an agonizing enticement, with the tiniest feet of any woman he'd ever known.

Sometimes they would be seated around the long rectangular table, overflowing with all kinds of drinks and delicacies. Shaslyk, pheasant, mutton, caviar, cabbage soup, plover, wines, cognac, vodka. Spouting revolutionary rhetoric. And he would feel Svetlina's warm hand underneath the table caressing first his trembling legs, then stealthily creeping along his young thighs, and his face would glow with a terrible embarrassment, and a warmth would gather in the collar of his tunic. Svetlina always managed to sit next to the poet. If he moved from his customary seat, she would always, just accidentally, find herself seated next to him. And her hand always began to rove and roam, till she ultimately took hold of his very youthful hardening manhood. And each time she reached the goal he would be staring across the table into the smiling face of Captain Kaverin.

One night Alexander Sergeievich sat amongst them, listening fervently as they discussed the evils of the monarchy and serfdom. His heart leapt in his boyish chest. He had never heard such dangerous talk before in all his life.

61

"The rest of Europe moves progressively into the nineteenth century, while our Motherland drags her hobbled feet, mired down inexorably in the quagmire of the Dark Ages. We are the bastion of medieval times. A horrendous anachronism."

Alexander Sergeievich shivered as he stared into the craggy-bearded face of Boris Gregorovich Shokilov, as a terrible bitterness spewed from his thin angry lips and his square-jawed chin that seemed to have been sculptured out of Michelangelo's marble.

He heard Chaadaev's velvet voice, bitterly sarcastic now. "Our Imperial Russia is not a European country, my love. We are barbaric Asiatics." The boy had never heard such bitter anger in men's voices.

Igor Bolinsky's great bush of hair was so red it seemed aflame. Sometimes it seemed a ring of fire burned violently around his leonine head. "Talk. Talk-talk," he mimicked himself sarcastically. "Let us talk about how we can kill the son of a swine, the pious bastard, Alexander Romanov. His most Imperial Majesty! He deserves to be assassinated!"

They talked and schemed in fearfully whispered tones of how the assassination would be carried out. By gun or dagger or by poison? And when? And where? And ultimately by whom? There was a roar of silence in the room. Sasha knew that they would laugh at him if he volunteered to be the assassin.

Oftentimes Alexander Sergeievich did not know where the words came from. His own temerity frightened him among these mature men of the world, these intellectual giants, who had been so far and seen so much. Yet he heard himself say in a trembly voice that was going through changes from high to low, sometimes from word to word, "But-but-but what good would it do to kill the Czar? Nothing would have been changed. Constantine or Nicholas would take his place. The monarchy would remain intact. The serf would still toil underneath the knout." He felt that he'd been bathed in perspiration. When would he learn to keep his mouth shut among his sophisticated elders?

It seemed a century before Chaadaev said, "By the Holy Virgin, the boy is absolutely right. What good would it do to kill one Emperor and have another take his place?"

Kaverin looked as if the burdens of the world had been lifted from his shoulders. He gazed fondly at Alexander Sergeievich, as the boy's face flushed hotly and he stared down at the table. "What has our precocious one got for us tonight? Let us hear from the little genius."

"I am no genius," he protested as they lifted him up on to the table. "A poem from the little genius!" Kaverin shouted. And the others joined him. "A poem from the genius! . . . A poem from the genius!"

Alexander Sergeievich stammered at first as he began to recite a poem he had been working on, calling on the serfs to rise up and throw off their shackles. It was always like this when he began. He was terrified before the older more experienced men. The words seemed to stick in his throat, his tongue seemed lazy and inept and absentminded. But as he went along his face lit up and a crazy flame burned in his eyes. He felt himself grow taller and taller and he was no longer a babe just out of swaddling clothes. He was a man among other men. He was the one they called "the genius."

When he finished they stood up and applauded him wildly. "Bravo, Pushkin! . . . Bravo! Bravo!" When he got down from the table, they embraced him and kissed him on his burning cheeks. Svetlina took him in her arms and kissed him fully on his mouth. Lingeringly.

A few nights later, as she sat beside him as they supped, he felt her gentle hand move sweetly along his throbbing thigh, and he felt her hand go inside his breeches and take hold of his member as it stood stiffly and attentive. "My! My!" she whispered out of the side of her mouth. "His Majesty is certainly bold and dignified tonight. Upright and majestic, like a nobleman of the highest rank." He stared into the smiling countenance of Captain Kaverin.

One night early in the before-day morning, when he was about to take his leave, Captain Kaverin put his arm around the lad in an older-brotherly gesture. "A certain lassie here wants to bed down with you, Alexander Sergeievich, my little genius. *Voulez vous couchez avec ce belle femme ce soir?*"

Alexander Sergeievich stared at him all innocent and speechless. Kaverin laughed uproariously. "You sly young dog! You think I don't know what's going on between you two?"

"But she's yours. I mean—." His young face warm with shame and guilt.

"Nonsense! She adores young yearlings like yourself. She'd go to bed with a six-year-old if he could rise to the occasion!" The tall handsome Hussar Captain turned from the poet and called Svetlina over to him. He had his arms around both of them. "Take your baby home with you and suckle him. Induct him into all the rites and mysteries of revolutionary passion."

Alexander Sergeievich feebly protested. "But—but—but—."

"You don't like this lovely wench?"

"Yes, but—"

"Well then what are you afraid of? That you cannot rise to the occasion? She has assured me that everything is ready and all is very well proportioned." Kaverin broke into a raucous laughter.

That night Alexander Sergeievich went home with Baroness Svetlina and she initiated him into all the secrets of "revolutionary baccahanalia." She knew artifices and legerdemain his chambermaid in Moscow never dreamed of, dear innocent cornfed Tatyana from the blessed steppes along the Don.

Svetlina's bedroom was arranged to put the coldest ascetic in the mood for the wildest orgy, aphrodisiac from wall to wall. Soft candlelights in golden candelabra dimmed almost down to utter darkness. Three-quarters of the walls hung in soft brocaded Chinese silk. Svetlina's bedroom was heavily drenched with the smell of Eastern incense and fragrances from Bombay and Calcutta. She was Aphrodite reincarnated. Across from her silken quilted bed there was a mirror that covered the length of the wall, top to bottom. They shared a round of hashish in the semidarkness.

As Alexander Sergeievich inhaled the expensive hemp into his naive unaccustomed throat and deep into his unsophisticated belly, he lay back in the luxurious plush of the chaise longue and stared down at her seated on the thickly carpeted floor in front of him. He looked around him, and he wondered how she could commit herself so totally to change and revolution and yet spend so much of her time and energies with the sensual comforts and indulgences of this life. He thought Svetlina was an outrageously lovely contradiction.

As if she were clairvoyant and could secretly police his thoughts, Svetlina said, "The contradiction is more apparent than actual, my precious young falcon. Love, itself, is revolutionary, the most revolutionary of emotions. Undying love of the Russian people!"

"What has revolution got to do with all this?" He waved his arm around the room. "Drenched in all this opulence. The time and energy and rubles it takes to put all this together. It's utterly obscene."

As if she had not heard a word he said, she continued. "Love and peace and happiness. These are the aims of the revolution. This is what we want for the Russian people, for every worker, every muzhik, every lowly, hapless peasant."

There was something recklessly specious about this lovely lady's rationalization, and our precious young falcon was well aware of it. "But-but-but how do your erotic overindulgences, your drunken brawls, help the muzhik to achieve your love, your peace, your happiness? I mean, he's still deep in the potato furrows all around Tsarskoye Selo. I mean, what we consume certainly doesn't make your hapless peasant corpulent. Your self-indulgence does not give him peace or love or happiness, not even bread upon his table."

Svetlina inhaled deeply of her hashish. Her large dark shining eyes were half closed now. She took off his boot and caressed his foot and kissed it. She giggled. "At this very moment, in this house, here and now, you and I are creating the new audacious world in miniature, the new earth we are striving to bring about. An earth of love and peace and happiness; a world that's never ever been before!"

She passed her long pipe to her young precocious falcon. "And revolutionary love, my dearest, must begin with you and me, the actual revolutionaries!" He pulled it deep into his lungs. His head knew a delightful giddiness. They began to giggle. He felt as if they might actually float away on a silvery cloud to that revolutionary paradise she had just described to him.

"You and I and love and revolution." She sang a crazy song to him. Now she took off the other boot and kissed the foot, and she began to undress her dear young lover, all the time murmuring to him and to herself. "Baby! Baby! My sweet little precious revolutionary genius of a baby!" As if he had protested, she said, "But you are my baby because the Captain gave you to me!"

64

Svetlina could hardly talk for giggling now. She had removed his tunic and undershirt now and was nibbling on one of his ears. "His majesty! My little baby with the big thing in his breeches!" She kissed him in his sweating armpits. "I'm a baroness. You're His Majesty! We were fated to be lovers! For the revolution!" she added as an afterthought. The peachy fur above her curving lips was bubbling now with perspiration. She kissed the sparse grass growing early on his downy chest, her mouth pulled on the nipples of his manly breasts. His nipples hardened, even as he pretended nonchalance, and was going crazy with desire. All this opulence is obscene and decadent, Alexander Sergeievich thought, and he wanted to argue with her further, to disagree violently with the lovely "revolutionary" baroness, but he was light-headed and they both were much too giggly. He surrendered to the moment, to the erotic fragrances, the incense, the wine, the hashish, the total sensuality, the loveliness of this lovely woman, his own needs, his wants, to the terrible terrible throbbing in the middle of him.

Now she was pulling down his breeches. She pulled him to his feet and stepped away from him and stared admiringly at his ever-stiffening shameless member. "My! My! What have we here? His Majesty!" She did a rhapsody. "His Most Imperial Majesty! Firm! Regal, bold, proud! Majestic! Prodigious! Astonishing for one so young!" She kissed his sunken belly button. "Please excuse me if I eat you up!" By now she had worked herself into a frenzy. "So dark! So prodigious, so handsome and so beautiful! Majestic! Magnifique!"

She stopped, momentarily, as frantically she shed herself of her remaining petticoats and other underthings. She was Venus come up suddenly out of the ocean. And now she stood before him, just as he was. Her golden skin possessed the texture of the softest velvet. She was so beautiful she took his breath away. His Majesty grew even nobler and more stiffly dignified.

Abundantly equipped she was with female pulchritude. Almost had too much of everything. The Baroness was not overly breasted, just bosomy enough, and highly freckled in those ample parts. Rounded out like honeycombs. Her hips were neither fat nor thin, but slimly rounded. And now he saw that she was freckled all around her fiery-haired pubescence, this woman who volunteered to kill the Czar.

She said, "Oh!" And she took him by the mannishness protruding boldly from the middle of him and led him to the wall-lengthed mirror. "Look," she shouted softly to him. "Look! Do we not look lovely? We look beautiful together! Yes?" And she lay down upon the deeply-piled carpet imported from the Orient, and they made love before the mirror, she shouting all manner of obscenities unheard of by this experienced Lycée poet, this comrade of the Hussar Guards. She heaved this way and the other, fast and furious, then suddenly she slowed down the tempo, shouting, "Baby! His Majesty! His Most Imperial baby Majesty! My sweet majestic baby! Look at us! Aren't we pretty? Aren't we beautiful together? Look in the mirror! Look in the mirror!"

He took a quick look and saw himself and her in a frenzied kind of mortal combat, saw himself atop this wild voluptuous revolutionary heaving to and fro as if they rode an ocean wave. How ludicrous we are, he thought. And he was almost moved to laughter. How ridiculous we look! But he only got a hasty glimpse, and he had no time for laughter. For the business at hand was much too serious and getting more so by the second. He had to work so hard just to stay there atop the tidal waves and ride them home to culmination. He heard her, as if from far away in a wild and frenzied poem he'd written, dream he'd dreamed. "*Yebat* (Fuck) me! *Yebat* me good!" she shouted, she commanded, "*Yebat* me beautiful!"

And now he felt himself hard, so hard inside of her, the hardest he had ever been, as he began to fill up with the overflowing, and she began to throw her head from side to side, and her entire body began to shake like the limbs of a palm tree at the ocean's edge in the time of hurricane, as she went all the way for the greatest treasure of them all, and he felt a shiver move across his slender shoulders, and he knew a giddy feeling tantamount to vertigo.

And as he reached toward the crest of the highest wave, she made her desperate move to go there with him. Higher, higher! They rode out the storm together as the waves of love washed over them. And he felt the great love they had made flow sweetly from the middle of him. Her darling body quaking now in a fit of spasms. Little spasms, quick spasms, continuous unabated spasms. She let herself go, and he could hear her cursing now and thanking God and Emperor for him and her, and heard her blowing hard with the joy and pleasure of it all and snorting now and breaking wind. She said excuse me, and *pajalsta*, but it didn't matter, as they fell asleep in each other's arms on the thick red rug from Samarkand.

He was in her great canopied bed when he awoke, amongst softly padded quilts and silken counterpane. Subtly sunken on a mattress made from the down of geese. And at first he knew not where he was or what he was or why or when or otherwise. He had been awakened by a ticklish kind of sensation that sent rivulets of sensuousness along his spine and back and forth. At first she nibbled at his toes, then she moved upwards towards the top of him. By the time she reached the middle of him, he was leapingly alive. When she saw that everything was right and ready, she mounted him astride and impaled herself and rode him like a Cossack on a wild Arabian steed. Now she was pumping away atop and swearing to the heavens again and losing all control again and moaning and groaning and breaking wind and shouting for the joy of living, loving, she wished glad tidings for the Holy Virgin.

Afterwards, she stared at His fallen Majesty who looked so forlorn and dejected, now that he had been dethroned. And she remembered how bold and regal and noble and darkly dignified he had been just a short time past. Tears spilled from her eyes, as she took his limp and limber member in the cradle of her hands, caressing it affectionately. "Poor, dear, sweet darling, so despondent and crestfallen!" Murmuring and cooing, a tear fell on the Him of him, and she kissed the tear

66

away, endearingly. She fondled his testicles and held his member close to her cheek as she felt it coming awake again. She smacked it tenderly, like a mother spanking reluctantly a naughty child, and it began to move about in little jerky motions as if it had a life of its own, an existence separate and apart from him and over which he had no control. She watched it as it began to make little leaps about, and she began to laugh, almost hysterically.

"Oh my! Look at that! By the Holy Virgin, His Majesty has come alive again! He thinks he is a toady frog!"

Three more times Svetlina took Alexander Sergeievich through the streets of passion, each time it was a different journey. Then as she drifted sweetly off to sleep the last time, she whispered dreamily, "That's all right, Your Majesty, my dearest fondest falcon. We'll finish it in a little while—in a little whi—" as softly she began to snore.

He thought. "This woman is insatiable!" When he heard her snoring soundly, he got shakily out of bed. He felt a great exhaustion, a dizziness, his head whirling. He thought his legs were changed to iron. He moved, stumbling around the room as quietly he got into his clothes by a softly glowing candlelight, with the smell of love all over him. And he left this lovely sleeping revolutionary who seemed to live for love and love alone, and walked, giddily and heavy-legged, all the way back to Tsarskoye Selo. He bribed the sentry at the palace gate with his very last kopeks.

CHAPTER TWO

The next time Alexander Sergeievich was at a Hussar celebration Svetlina was there. This time she sat across from him and smiled at him as if nothing at all had happened between them, as if the entire episode was a fantasy he had dreamed. A crazy lovely sonnet he had written. Sometimes he thought that possibly it was, especially when he heard Svetlina spout her revolutionary rhetoric. She was the most articulate woman he had ever known. He sometimes listened to her open-mouthed.

He had long discussions with Colonel Peter Chaadaev about the function of art vis-à-vis society. The Colonel would discuss a poem with the poet and dissect it in its minutest detail. What did every single word mean, what did every comma? What did it all mean put together? Alexander Sergeievich's head ached and whirled with the excitement of it.

"Revolution!" . . . Constitution! . . . Destruction to all emperors!" It was still a wonder to Alexander Sergeievich that the Secret Police did not pay them more attention.

If a gendarme stumbled accidentally upon the Hussar quarters, he would be overwhelmed by the sound and smell of wine, rum, vodka, cognac, drunken men and women and bawdy ballads. They always kept someone on guard. The gendarme with his Cossack coat and his nifty waxed mustache would be slapped on the back, given a drink in a golden tankard and pushed into one of the drape-hidden booths with one of the available women "eager to serve the cause of revolution."

"And how's that for good old Hussar hospitality, *tovarische?* (comrade) Eh? She's a good and lively wench, yes?" By now, the wild-eyed voluptuous women, Tatyana, Natasha, Olga, Alexandra, Katrina, Larisa, would be stripped down for immediate action, eager to do their bit for the cause of revolution. The Hussar reveler would shout, "Long live the Third Section!" which was the popular nomenclature for the hated Emperor's own Secret Police. And—"Heaven bless the Emperor!"

Early in the before-day morning, Alexander Sergeievich, sometimes with his Lycée comrade Ivan Puschin, would leave the Hussar gathering place, where whiskey bottles and uneaten food littered the floor, as did men and women in various stages of dishabille amid the laughing sounds and acrid smells of lively copulation, and make their way back to the Summer Palace and over the wall to that hallowed seat of learning known as the "Capstone of Russian Education."

But above everything else, Lycée days for young Pushkin were writing poetry about anything and everything. Always it was leaping upon the tables at the slightest provocation and versifying, vehemently. He had made very few friends at the Lycée, but he was respected by all, students and teachers alike. For it was a romantic time in Russia when everyone was poetizing, good, bad and damned indifferent. And already he was recognized as the major poet at the Lycée.

It was a new experience for Alexander Sergeievich being articulate, people listening to his every word, as if he were a sage. It had never been like that at home in Moscow. From his mother and father almost always it had been: "Shut up, stupid child! You don't know what you're talking about."

Perhaps, he thought, this was what had driven him to writing. A way of expressing himself without being disputed at every other word. Here at the Lycée, when he leaped onto tables and declaimed his poetry, people shouted and applauded.

"Bravo, Pushkin! Bravo!"

The battle with his shyness was a fight that never ceased. Nobody at the Lycée could believe he'd ever been a bashful boy. Quiet, sullen, introverted.

He was not entirely alone at the Lycée. He roomed next door to plump, round-faced Ivan Pushchin, and they had become warm fast friends from the very beginning. And there was the mild-mannered, chubby Anton Delvig who loved Pushkin like a brother and recognized in him the genius that was inevitably to be fulfilled, if he lived long enough. Pushkin and Pushchin were politically of the same persuasion. There were a few others, "Crazy" Kuchelbecker, Vasili Needleman, a serious and studious student, and the hell-raising, hard-drinking, woman-chasing Constantine Danzas. But Alexander Sergeievich was basically a lone Russian wolf, known by some of his fellow schoolmates as the African, because of his wooly hair, swarthy features and plentiful mouth, his open generosity and his sometimes "savage temper." He was also known as "the monkey," possibly because of his propensity for leaping upon the nearest table when he did impromptu versifying.

Sometimes his friend Pushchin and he would sit alone in one of their rooms sipping vodka smuggled into the Lycée and talk far into the night about war and peace and freedom and revolution and the meaning of man and art and literature and last, but not least, about women.

One night the African was in low spirits. "Why don't they like me in this place? You're the only comrade I have here. You and Delvig. And Crazy Kuchelbecker and Needleman." The candlelight flickered near the open window. "And perhaps Danzas and Nicholai Raevsky with the Horse Guards."

He took a swallow from the bottle of vodka and passed the bottle to his comrade. Ivan Pushchin gulped a swallow down his thick throat. His blue eyes darkened in a heavy frown.

"They like you all right," Pushchin told him. "Even those who don't like you have to respect you. You're the finest poet in this place. I can assure you."

The African got up and walked the floor. He stopped and stared at a moth encircling the candlelight. "I don't mean for my poetry. I mean for me, myself. Is it because of my African great-grandfather?" The moth cast a giant bat-like shadow up against the wall.

Pushchin said, "Of course not. I mean—"

"Well all the pompous haughty swinish sons of syphilitic pigs can drown in the fornicating Neva for all I care. I'm proud of my great-grandfather. You hear that? He was a great man, a general in the Russian Army and he owned a thousand serfs. His name was Ibrahim Petrovich Hannibal—Hannibal! Do you recognize the name? Hannibal! His ancient ancestor was a military genius. He made the Roman Empire tremble! And my forebear on my father's side fought with Alexander Nevsky against the Swedes at Novrogrod in 1240." Alexander Sergeievich stood before his friend, grabbed him by the shoulders and shook him. "I'll show these condescending bastards one of these days what it means to be the grandson of an African prince!" Would he always be an outsider? At home? At school? What in Heaven's name was wrong with him?

Pushchin told him, heatedly, "It has nothing to do with your African ancestry, Alexander Sergeievich, I can assure you."

"What is it then? Is it the way I look? My mouth? My hair? The color of my skin?"

Pushchin shook his head as if he'd have it leave his body. "No no, No, I can assure you!" Then he added, "Perhaps they are jealous because you're such a damn good poet, the best in Tsarskoye Selo!"

Pushkin said, "The devil take them! I don't give a damn!" But Pushchin knew he gave a damn.

In his spare time, Ivan Pushchin would always seek out the African. Go for walks in the Summer Garden with him, oftentimes along with Delvig and Lomonsov, sometimes with Crazy Kuchelbecker. It wasn't long before all of them realized that Pushkin was far ahead of them in knowing what the world was all about; he had read books they had never even heard of. He knew of the colonizing of Africa and the slave trade in America. They stood in awe and admiration of his erudition.

At the age of fourteen the African had already published his TO A FELLOW VERSI-FIER in a very prestigeous Petersburg magazine, the *Vestnik Europi* (The European Herald).

In a frivolous mood he'd written:

Oh God I am at fault, Before thee I repent:
the small clerics dear,
Thy servants, I do fear;
I fear their conversation
And shun the obligation
Of sharing wedding feasts
I hate and find no deep regard
For all thy village priests."

To Colonel Chaadaev, who spoke four languages and philosophized in three, more seriously, he had written in his FOR THE PORTRAIT OF CHAADAEV:

Heaven sent him into life, chained
To the orders of the Czar. In Rome
He had been Brutus, Pericles in Greece;
Here: an office of the Hussars.

A few months later, he wrote in TO CHAADAEV:

Listen, comrade, it will come,
The adorable dawn of blissfulness.
Russia will awaken.
On the ruins of despotism,
It is our names they will inscribe.

As a young boy growing toward manhood Alexander Sergeievich was never tall in height. At nine, ten and eleven he had been tall for his age, growing like a wild weed on the steppes, but when he reached the age of twelve he seemed to stop growing altogether. Pushkin was possessed of a short wiry body leapingly filled with nervous agitation. When he wasn't getting off his nervous tautness through his writing, or leaping on tables versifying, he was engaging in such activities as fencing, target practice and other aspects of the art of self defense. Running for miles around the Palace Grounds. He felt gladsome when he exercised. Every limb of him seemed to feel the pleasure of it. Grappling with boys much larger than himself. Using the skills he learned from childhood peasant friends who lived in Grandma-ma Hannibal's village. He was the champion butter at the Lycée. When a boy was much larger than he, our poet used his head to bring him down to size.

Some days in the too-brief autumn season, when he wasn't writing, he would go out to the countryside and watch the muzhiks harvesting their master's crops. He watched them bow almost to the ground beneath the terror of the omnipresent knout. He watched their muscles ripple underneath the muzhik sackcloth that

71

thinly clothed them. Sometimes they pulled off their tunics and the sweat from their naked bodies glistened in the midday sun. Old men and women, young and middle-aged women in varied and various stages of pregnancy, little children dragging the heavy bags along. The overseer, himself a muzhik, on his great horse riding hard down the furrows with his knout or cudgel that he would lay on the backs of men, women and children alike. It seemed to make no difference to him.

It was as if he watched a scene that he would some day paint a picture of: he etched it deeply into his consciouness, and he would paint it some day with words on paper instead of oils on canvas.

Then one day as he watched, he knew he would never really get close enough to the feelings of the muzhiks unless he joined them in the field and worked as they did like illiterate beasts. He had to know their tiredness in his own bones, smell the stench of sweat on *his* body, and even feel the sharp sting of the knout, if indeed it came to that.

Another day Alexander Sergeievich found himself suddenly pulling off his tunic as he joined a group of potato pickers. He worked all day taking the hard tuberous vegetables out of the earth and putting them into a sack he dragged beside him. He worked till he was drenched with sweat, as the perspiration drained from every pore of him. Pouring from his armpits, his head wringing wet, dripping down into his eyes, onto his lips, the sweat and sweet dark earth got all amongst him, his face, his nostrils, ears and mouth, his neck, earth and sweat, salty tears stinging, pouring from between his legs, angered bugs of dirt and perspiration moving across his back like an army on the march. And still he picked. He had to know the feeling of it, had to grasp its deepest meaning.

He remembered Piotra Ivanovich and Anton Ivanovich. Their whole family sold away like insensible cattle. And he remembered their laughing sweet-faced sister, Natalya Ivanovna, with the dark and sorrow-laden eyes. He worked beside the muzhiks, heard them groaning, grumbling, saw them fall like midges in the early autumn heat. He pulled the hard round bumpy vegetable out of the dark earth till his fingers blistered and he was blinded by a salty perspiration, his back aching like a mouth of rotten teeth; he didn't know where he was, or why or when. Still he picked. He began to see white liquid spots before his eyes that were not there for him to see. He picked blindly. Stabs of pain shot through his legs. He pulled potatoes from the black soil until his head began to swim around and around and the earth began to whirl. And still he picked, stumbling. Blinking his stinging eyes, tasting his salty grimy sweat. He picked. Smelling his own angered perspiration. His aching legs became unwieldly. He walked around in a daze. The ground began to dance beneath him. Still he picked until the earth came up and smacked him hard.

When he awoke he lay there shivering in the cool of an autumn evening beneath a grove of apple trees. The earth had chilled and night had begun to fall all over the Northern Russian countryside.

He heard the voice of the tall muzhik overseer with the wide shoulders and wild blonde growth of beard and mustache and a long nose that extended from his broad forehead like a foothill near the highest mountain. He growled, "Another malingerer, eh? I'll show you tiredness." Alexander Sergeievich watched detachedly, the blonde-haired, blue-eyed overseer with the rotten teeth as he raised the knout above his head. Then he heard another voice.

"Don't you dare strike him, you vicious son of a pig!" He recognized the voice of his good friend, Ivan Pushchin.

"What's he to you, Your Excellency!" the overseer asked respectfully. "Does he belong to you?"

"He belongs to no one. He's a student at the Lycée. He's an aristocrat!" The overseer removed his cap. "Excuse me, your Nobleness. But how was I to know?" He looked around him. "All right, you lazy swine. Help the gentleman to his feet."

The overseer went toward the poet, but Ivan Pushchin pushed the burly man away and with the aid of an old peasant he got Alexander Sergeievich to his feet. He took his cloak from his own back and placed it around the shivering poet and they went to a carriage that waited at the side of the road. All the way back to the Lycée he scolded Alexander Sergeievich as if he were a misbehaving child.

"What in the hell were you trying to do, kill yourself?" Darkness had begun to fall and the countryside had come alive with the sounds of giggling crickets and croaking frogs. Fireflies blinking in among the trees.

"I have to know what it feels like being a serf, a hapless muzhik. How can I write about it unless I experience it?" Pushkin said.

Ivan Pushchin stared at his comrade with exasperated admiration. He took him in his arms and squeezed him warmly. "You are one crazy African! And I love the excrement out of you!" He kissed the crazy African.

Alexander Sergeievich said heatedly, "You spoiled everything. You shouldn't've interfered. I wanted to know everything, even the feel of the goddamn knout!"

Ivan Pushchin shook his head from side to side. "I repeat, you are the craziest African I have ever known in all my life, and I love every bone in your body!" He kissed Alexander Sergeievich on both cheeks, animatedly.

Alexander Sergeievich asked him, "How many Africans have you known?" Ivan Pushchin broke out into peals of laughter.

When they reached the Lycée, Alexander Sergeievich fell on his bed too exhausted to undress himself. His comrade helped him out of his clothes and into a night shirt, sweat, dirt, grime, stench and all. As soon as his body hit the bed, he fell into a deep sleep, snoring loudly. He slept through the night and stayed in bed the following day, missing all of his classes.

A few weeks later, Alexander Sergeievich went with his comrade to the Hussar quarters. Later that evening dear Svetlina took him home with her, and they bathed together in the vast Louis Quatorze bathtub in sweet and heavenly scented waters.

After the bath, they lay in the luxurious bed, laughing spasmodically on expensive hashish, she reading aloud some of the rough draft of his work in progress. He was working day and night on a lengthy poem that would one day be known as his ODE TO FREEDOM. She shook her head wonderingly. "When I watch you up there on that table declaiming your poetry something takes hold of me. I feel strangely good all over me. I feel a quivering all down into the quick of me and my toes begin to tingle."

Svetlina read parts of one of his unfinished poems. "This one is truly revolutionary!" She looked at him, her dark eyes all aglow with adoration. "The way you write is unbelievably beautiful! Why haven't others written a poem like this?" She kissed him fully on his mouth. "This one will surely get you in trouble with the Emperor. How do you dare to write like this?" She kissed the nipples of his breasts. "But of course you must! But how do you know so much about the lowly muzhik? Where do these magnificent words come from, these revolutionary sentiments, your understanding of the serfs?"

He was always amazed at the power of his poetry to arouse her sensually. He knew all of the signs by now, the fuzzy dew above her mouth, the unconscious movements of her lovely backside, her roving hands tenderly exploring, even as she read his poems aloud, as if she sought some new and sudden revelations. They had become familiar with each other. Perhaps too familiar, he thought. From "His Majesty" she had begun by now to call him, "My African." He wasn't sure how he felt about her calling him *her* African.

In the dimly candlelighted room immersed in sensuous fragrances, they went through all the rituals of erotic foreplay which had almost become routine with them. The reading of his poetry, the kisses, the fond caressing, the fine exotic hemp. Nothing helped her African this night. He was tired; simply exhausted. She fondled the *him* of him, teased him lovingly, teased his testicles, his buttocks. Nothing aroused him.

She began to cry, sobbing angrily. "What tricks are you playing now, My African?" she demanded heatedly.

Even though Alexander Sergeievich thought he understood the sobbing woman he heard himself say, "I am not *your* African. Neither am I your stud nor your Arabian stallion!"

Svetlina wept now without restraint, sobbing and talking interchangeably. "You think I'm a courtesan, a hapless bitch always in heat. Well, I have desires the same as any man. And who whores around any more than the men of the Russian nobility? Catherine the Great had a hundred male concubines. They say she went once with a horse! And who wenches more than those so-called revolutionary Hussars? Answer me. Every one of them have laid their hands on me without so much as a by-your-leave, and they never even say *spaciba*. I'm neither your whore nor—"

"Who said you were my whore?" Alexander Sergeievich asked uneasily.

"I'm neither your whore nor your mistress," she continued, as if she had not heard him. "You do not keep me, neither do you pay me for my favors."

"Neither am I your pander nor your Monsieur, since you do not keep me nor do you pay me for my favors," the mannish boy responded angrily.

"I was born in Tashkent in the province of Uzbekistan, and my father was one of the richest men in Tashkent, and he was a great White Russian—" Svetlina went on, sobbing, talking—"And he adopted Allah and the heathen religion of Islam, so he could have as many wives and concubines as he could afford. And he had hundreds of them, I can tell you. My own White Russian mother was the unhappiest woman on this earth. My father died and left it all to me. I was his favorite, and I got as far away from Tashkent as I could." She went on. "He used to sit me on his lap until I was past fifteen. I think he wanted me for one of his concubines. My own mother—poor woman, may she rest in peace—accused me of sleeping with him. My father lusted after me. He was a monster, and there was nothing for it. He was so rich and powerful and ennobled. And why can't I lust after you, or any man that catches my fancy? Answer me. Why can't I seduce you instead of you seducing me? Answer me!"

Alexander Sergeievich said, unconvincingly, "But you do, my princess. You seduce me every time. I'm just simply exhausted tonight." The boy sought wearily to turn the whole thing into a joke, to make his lusty lover laugh. "I'm just very very tired and cannot rise to the occasion." If he had not been tired before, her continuous talking had certainly exhausted him by now.

She tried to laugh at him as she took hold of him. "I want your young dark handsome African penis hard and firm inside of me." She put her flaming head between his legs and she kissed, she kissed, she kissed, she kissed. Laughing, sobbing, kissing. But there was nothing for it. And it saddened him profoundly, for he knew it was the end of something terribly important to his growing into manhood. He was not sure why or where or when, or even what, but he knew with a definite certitude he was not the boy that he had been before he met his lusty revolutionary baroness.

He left the bed and he got into his clothing, methodically, deliberately.

"What do you think you're doing? What is the matter with you?" she exclaimed.

Alexander Sergeievich pulled on his boot.

"Come over here," Svetlina commanded with a growing terror in her voice. "Where do you think you're going?"

He slipped his arms into his hareskin jacket.

She sat up on the side of the bed and stomped her tiny feet. "Come over here, my naughty African."

He walked over to her and kissed her matter-of-factly full on her mouth. "I am not *your* African! I am not your Arabian stallion!"

He left her and went out into the night.

CHAPTER THREE

In his loneliest of moments Alexander Sergeievich remembered and cherished the love and warmth of his maternal grandmother. And he visualized his great-grandfather, as if he'd actually known and lived with him. He liked to remember sitting in a corner of the room and listening to the old woman's stories of other and nobler days, when grandfather Hannibal walked the Russian earth with his special and prodigious steps. Sometimes in his lonely room, he imagined he could hear Grandma-ma Hannibal's silken voice.

"Peter the Great adopted him. Peter became his godfather. The Queen of Poland became his godmother. But your grandfather was proud of his African ancestry, indeed he was. And he refused to adopt his Imperial godfather's Christian name. That's why he called himself Ibrahim Petrovich Hannibal after an ancient ancestor, that magnificent Carthaginian."

Grandmother Hannibal, smooth skinned for someone her age, would be sitting there with her knitting, as she wove her tales of olden days. "After Great Peter died, the jealous bastards at the Court sent Ibrahim Hannibal to the salt mines of Siberia. They kept him there till Elizabeth and Katerina came to power. They said Catherine the Great truly loved your great-grandfather."

Alexander Sergeievich's mother would come upon the two of them as if they were co-conspirators. "Mother, you simply must stop filling Sasha's silly head with a lot of fanciful nonsense about his savage great-grandfather!" Almost against her will, his mother found herself running her hands longingly through Sasha's wooly locks.

"If he was a savage," his grandmother retorted, "Emperor Peter must have been one too. And there never was a greater Czar in all of Holy Russia. He was God's representative here on earth for truth." She turned back to the smiling

Sasha. "And he did admire your great grandfather, my dearest darling. Peter the Great surely did admire that man. And for good reason. He was so handsome and intelligent and so manful."

After each of these sessions with his grandmother, Alexander would go to his room and stand before his looking glass and stare at what he saw, and he would grow more handsome in his own eyes. Ultimately he did not bite his lips, nor did he wish them scantier. Anyone in the whole of Russia could look like his brother or his sister, but how many could you find who looked like Alexander Sergeievich? He stood out in a crowd. He licked his thick curvacious lips and smiled at his reflection.

It was after one of his treasured soirees with Grandma-ma Hannibal that he came to realize the awesome power of concentration with which he was possessed. He had just left her one evening and he lay there in his terrible loneliness and thought about his great-grandfather till his head began to throb, and he had wished him into existence. The tall Black man with dark eyes that seemed to pierce the darkness with their intensity came to his bedside and talked with him about times gone by, when he himself was a boy in far away Africa, a young Ethiopian prince. He had accompanied his kingly father from the River Nile, in which he bathed each morning, on an Imperial caravan across the mighty Guna Mountains, across the broad plateau of fertile plain, all the way to the Red Sea, the same Red Sea across which the legendary Moses had led the Hebrews out of Egypt. There was a soft deep lilting quality to Grandpa-pa Hannibal's voice. Sasha's lips quivered as he stared up at his great-grandfather. Was he awake or was he asleep and dreaming? His body was covered with a cold and frightful perspiration. He was in that dawn-of-dusk zone between sleep and wakefulness. He knew he was not entirely asleep, because even now he heard himself gently snoring. How could he be asleep? His great-grandfather leaned over, kissed him on his damp forehead and said goodnight to him and left.

The night before he left for Tsarskoye Selo and the Lycée, Sasha's grandmother had been visiting them in Moscow and he had had a long talk with her in her bedroom. She was growing old and she seemed to live in softened shadow lately. Her skin still pulled tightly over her elevated cheek bones. And yet he realized she was aging because her voice had weakened. It no longer reminded him of the sound of violins playing. Her voice had always made him think of water falling gently through the summer morning sunlight. He thought that now she smelled like old and ancient lived-in houses, she who used to smell like Eastern spices, eggnog, cinnamon and dried apples.

Grandma-ma Hannibal spoke in a strange and unfamiliar voice, as she lay there in her canopied bed with the candles flickering in the candelabrum underneath the golden icon, "Stay strong, my courageous falcon, and study hard. Show them what a boy with African blood can do. Learn everything you can about the land of your great-grandfather." Her old eyes were flashing now as if they were ablaze.

He stared at Grandma-ma Hannibal. His heart beat quickly in his manful chest. He knew she had not long to live, no more than a year or two he thought. He heard the old clock on the wall tick-tocking away the final moments of her life, this one who surely loved him. She had always loved him. There was so much he wanted to say to her. The Russian language was so terribly inadequate, especially in times like this. And he was a boy who had a mastery of words. His stammering came back to him. He said, "Grandma-ma!" He repeated, "Grandma-ma—Gran-Gran-Grandm-ma—" He did not recognize his own voice. He wanted to tell her that he thanked her for the deep love of himself she had inspired in him. He no longer dreamed of thin lips and a light complexion. He no longer envied Olga Sergeievna and Leo Sergeievich. Because of her, he looked with favor on his darker image. The words gathered in his mouth and seemed to get in one another's way.

Then he simply said, "I love you, Grandma-ma."

She said, "I know that, my grandson. And you know that I love you."

Even as she said it, he felt the moments slipping from them. He wanted desperately to capture them, to hold them close to him forever. His eyes began to fill as he took her in his arms, sobbing, "Grandma-ma! Grandma-ma!"

She responded, "My baby! My baby! Sasha darling!" Her shoulders shook. And he knew that she was crying too.

Alexander Sergeievich haunted the Imperial libraries and searched them avidly for literature on Africa. He read agitatedly of the colonizing of Africans by Europeans, the African Slave Trade and of slavery in America. His grandmother had often spoken to him about it. He empathized with African slaves away off in the *New World*. He sympathized. He agonized. Sometimes he was moved to tears.

He told his comrade, Ivan Pushchin, "Slavery in America and serfdom in this Holy Russia. What is the goddamn difference?"

He also immersed himself in research of the Russian oral tradition of the bylina, the heroic poem and the original writings of the monks and Saints of ancient Kiev where the flowers of Russian culture first began to bloom and blossom. Sometimes Ivan Pushchin would look for him all over the countryside among the muzhiks in the orchards, deep in the potato furrows, and for miles around Tsarskoye Selo. One night his comrade found him deep among the dusty books in a corner of the dimly-lighted room in the Lycée Archives. A flying cockroach leaped about him. He heard the scurrying of rats. A moth flew around a flickering candle nearby. Fireflies blinked about his head. He was oblivious to everything, in a state of total concentration.

"What in the devil?" Pushchin began. "I—"

There was a bright glow on our poet's grimy face, as Alexander Sergeievich turned toward his puzzled comrade. "This is it! The vitae and the paterics! It's all here! Even the bylina!" he shouted softly. His dusty dusky face suffused. "This is where it all began! Look! Look! Here it all is!"

"What in the devil are you talking about?" Ivan Pushchin asked his wild-eyed comrade.

Alexander Sergeievich acted as if he'd had too much to drink. "The *vitaes* and the *paterics*! The *bylina*! The epic poems, the songs of the minstrels!" His mind conjured up an isba in his grandmother's village and the people gathered there, inside and outside, the old minstrel man singing, his eyes closed. He could hear the poem the old man sang. The mournful chanting. Vibrations moved across his shoulders. "It's all here! The Kievan monks, they left it all here for us. To know ourselves! Now we can understand what it is to be Russian. We're not Frenchmen. We're not Germans. We're not even Europeans! We're Russians, my dear comrade!"

Ivan Pushchin stared at his darkly-visaged friend. What was he so excited about? What was so important about not being French or German, not even being European? Why was it so important to know you are a Russian?

"Don't you see?" Pushkin said excitedly. "Before we can have a revolution, we have to come to know who we are—our culture, our literature. We need a *national* literature. That is what we have in common with the muzhik. A history, a culture, a folklore. A *narodnost*, a national pride we can share with every Russian, every Tartar, every Cossack, every Uzbek, every Kalmuk, every Tadjik, every Jew and every Turkman!" He stared at the quizzical expression on Pushchin's face. "Can't you see? All of us are Russians. Every single one of us who labor under His Imperial Majesty's yoke are Russians. And that is one of the keys to bringing us all together and making a revolution."

Pushchin argued, "But we have very little in common with the muzhik, you and I. And we don't labor under the Imperial yoke. We're the elite. We're white Russians. We're—" His fair face reddened.

Alexander Sergeievich said, "Precisely. Obviously, *I* am not a White Russian. Yet my forebears rode with Alexander Nevsky. But all of us are Russians with a common destiny and that destiny is revolution."

Pushchin reminded him. "But you always say you are an African."

Alexander Sergeievich was nonplussed, momentarily. He swallowed the dusty air. Then: "I'm an African-Russian," he said emphatically. "A Russian with an African descendancy."

It was long past midnight. The old palatial mansion of Svetlina Oshnikovna was deathly silent. Less than a half an hour before it had rung from the rafter with laughter and drinking and hemp smoking and animated dialogue. Dancing to the music of an Uzbek band. Alexander Sergeievich had argued heatedly and drunkenly with Chaadaev and Kaverin and Nicholai Raevsky about literature and war and peace and love and culture. Kaverin professed to believe that fornicating and drinking and other forms of debauchery would hasten the day of the Russian revolution. It was the annual "brawl" of the Imperial Hussar Guards.

"*A bas le roi!*" Raising their glasses and shouting drunkenly, "Down with the monarchy!"

They sang *La Marseillaise.*

"Up with Constitutional government! Up the revolution!" As if by drinking to it, everything would come to pass.

Secret police were all over the place, eyes popping, eavesdropping; they were hardly secretive. The way they dressed, attired in Uzbek, Tartar and Tadjik costumes and speaking in Northern Moscovite and Saint Petersburg accents; they stood out in the crowd of hell-raising Hussars with their intense faces. They were much too interested in the varied conversations all around them to be authentic Hussar Guardsmen or their comrades. Everybody knew that they were Czarist spies, members of the Third Section of His Majesty's personal Chancery.

At precisely fifteen minutes after the great ancient clock had sounded throughout the old baronial palace, the band played a rousing "good night" song, then departed from the baroness's medieval mansion. Some of the revolutionary party people had exchanged their drunken *dosvadanyas*, kissing one another lips to cheek and taking leave in their well appointed troikas and their mink fur-lined barouches that waited outside replete with coachmen and footmen.

Alexander Sergeievich thought, they are the wealthiest and most prestigious revolutionaries anywhere on the face of this earth.

Not all of them had left the Oshnikov Palace. Some of them had drifted off, men and women, to one of the twenty-five or more bedrooms Svetlina's baronial mansion afforded. Kaverin had escorted *le petit genie* and Svetlina to her bedroom and departed to another bedroom with one of his lovely wenches.

They were alone now, and Alexander Sergeievich sat there on the chaise longue with a glass of champagne in his hand sipping it slowly and watching the lovely baroness Svetlina silently disrobe. Now she stood before him in all her gleaming and intoxicated nakedness. He worked hard to maintain the nonchalant expression on his face. Her scarlet tongue passed over her upper lip and then the bottom lip, her dark eyes narrowing. He put the champagne to his own lips and slowly drank it. "It's time to go to bed, my dearest. Why is it taking you so long to undress?" Svetlina said.

He stood up. "I have to go back to the Lycée, my pet. We have examinations tomorrow and I have to prepare for them. I'll probably be up the rest of the night."

"Nonsense," Svetlina said. "Everybody knows you're a genius. You don't have to study. Come now. Let us go to bed."

He said, "I think not—"

She said, "I know you want to make love to me, my young African stallion," she said teasingly, as if the whole thing that happened that night more than two months ago was not to be taken seriously. "You're too young to be so serious."

"How old does one have to be before it's time for one to be serious?" he asked her.

"You are much too serious, my beautiful young genius." She came up to him and put her arms around his neck.

He said, "No!" and took her arms away. But the hardness in the middle of him told her a different story, as she leaned herself against him.

Svetlina smiled knowingly, arrogantly. "My young genius of an African stallion."

"Have I ever called you a bitch or a whore?" he asked her, heatedly.

"Of course not, my dear child." she replied. "You're much too chivalrous, and after all, I am a baroness."

"You are a baroness, my dear Svetlina," Alexander Sergeievich said sarcastically. "And you are the most beautiful, the loveliest, the most desirable trollop in all of His Majesty's empire. And I bid you *dosvadanya*," as he moved out of the bedroom, with the baroness screaming after him.

"Come back! Come back! Come back, you African stallion! How dare you!"

Alexander Sergeievich had begun to write a diary. That night he wrote, drunkenly and sleepy-eyed:

> The end of an experience for you, Alexander Sergeievich, with no regrets, and what did you learn from it?"

His head throbbed, felt like it was twice its usual size. His whiskeyed mouth tasted like the smell of bedbugs, dead and bloody. He swallowed hard the foul feeling in his mouth, as he wrote:

> That there are women in this world who can be beautiful and at the same time be articulate, and intellectual, who, at the same time, are sensual and diabolically lascivious. Thank you, Svetline Alexandrovna. Spaceba, my dear Baroness.

The next time Alexander Sergeievich went to the Hussar Quarters, Svetlina sat next to him and teased him underneath the table, causing him to get excited and upset, and he sat there hating her and despising himself because he could not resist this beautiful baroness. In his mind he rejected her completely, but his body contradicted him, had to deal with different memories and responses, played malevolent tricks with his determination. She squeezed his warm rigidity. He determinedly took hold of her hand and moved it away from him. She smiled and immediately placed it back again. They had been drinking and eating for more than an hour.

Kaverin raised his tankard and shouted. "All right! All right! Let us hear from the little genius!"

Alexander Sergeievich did not feel like declaiming his poetry. He didn't feel like performing for them this wintry night. He told them he had nothing for them, but they would not hear of it. They insisted. He thought, "That's what I am, their

81

entertainment. The court jester!" They stomped their feet and they banged their tankards against the table, and they lifted him onto their shoulders, shouting drunkenly, "*Vive le petit génie! . . . Le petit génie!* Our own little genius!" He struggled and kicked, vainly, as they thrust him up on to the table.

He turned to them, panting angrily. He was not their *petit génie*. He felt the perspiration pouring from him. Somehow he felt this night he did not belong to them at all. He belonged to himself. He belonged to his soul, whatever his soul was. He belonged to his heart, his mind. Though he was only seventeen, he belonged to no one save himself. He was his own man, and he was answerable only to this man with whom he lived and with whom he had always lived even when he was a boy.

"I am not your little genius," he told them in a trembly voice, as the bedlam slowly subsided. "I am a man, a rather young one, to be sure, but a man nevertheless, belonging only to myself. One day I hope to belong to the Russian people. One day I hope I will deserve to be called the people's poet."

"Bravo!" they shouted. "Bravissimo!"

"There is, though, something weighing heavily on my mind and I would speak to you about it." He was nervous and the perspiration rained from him.

"Speak to us about it!" Igor Igorovich shouted.

"Tell us! Tell us! Speak! Speak!" they shouted and began to bang the table with their tankards and crash their glasses up against the oak-paneled wainscoting, sometimes up against the pictures of the Czar of all the Russias.

"Speak! Speak!"

Pushkin stared down into the unsmiling face of Colonal Peter Chaadaev. "Most of you are not listening to me. You're too drunk to pay attention." Suddenly the wide and long rectangular room got quiet. The candelabra along the walls stopped flickering.

"If drinking and smoking hemp and brawling and carousing and fornicating could overthrow the monarchy, His Imperial Majesty would be in very serious trouble. Because that's about all we ever do." He stared down into their faces now. Even Svetlina was unsmiling. "Drink and smoke and yebat. We spend so much time and rubles and energy fornicating and drinking and debauching, we have little time for anything else, except rhetoric. We are the great rhetoricians, tovaraschi." It was as if he had turned on a spigot and could not turn it off again, as the words poured from him. "What do we know about the muzhiks, the peasants or the serfs? Do we know what their souls are like? Do we know what they suffer? Do we know what their hopes and aspirations are? What do we know about the working men and women of Saint Petersburg? Do you comrades have in mind a revolution or a coup d'état?"

Igor Igorovich Belinsky stared at him in disbelief. He growled at Alexander Sergeievich. "Where in the devil do you come off lecturing us? What do you know about revolution? All of us have been to France!"

Peter Chaadaev said, "Let him speak. Allow him to continue!"

Alexander Sergeievich continued heatedly, feeling painfully his youthfulness and inexperience, in comparison with these men who had been so far, seen so much. "A revolution is a serious undertaking, comrades. It requires the participation of all the people, the serfs, the peasants and the working people. It requires all the thought and energies we can muster. *Tovarischi*, it seems to me we're *devant-derrière*. We're putting the *droshky* before the donkey. We seem to be always celebrating the revolution before it has taken place. We are premature revolutionaries." He had their undivided attention now. They had even ceased their drinking. He felt good now about what he was saying. He felt bolder. He felt older than he was, and much wiser. His voice was stronger.

"Go among the people, comrades," he continued. "The peasants and the serfs and the impoverished working people of the city. Work with them. Live with them. Learn from them, learn their ways, their language, their thought processes. Talk with them. Eat the food they *have* to eat. Know everything about them. Their fondest hopes and aspirations, their foibles and their prejudices!" He swallowed hard. "All their superstitions. Know intimately their hurts, their ills, their pain. And most important of all, know their bountiful humanity, their indomitable instinct for survival. They are not illiterate beasts, comrades, even though they are treated as such. They are your brothers and your sisters, flesh of your flesh, blood of your blood. Know all this, tovaraschi, then speak to me of revolution! Otherwise, everything is bombast, hypocrisy and empty rhetoric."

There was a deafening silence at first, as he got down from the table, bathed in sweat. He'd made a fool of himself, he thought. Then Peter Chaadaev stood up and began to applaud. "Bravo! Bravo! *Vive le petit génie! Vive le petit génie!*"

Suddenly he was afraid of his own temerity. He fought back the tears. It was like running the gauntlet, as he stumbled through the claps on his back, the embraces, the handshakes and the kisses, and made his way out of the hall.

He walked alone underneath an opaque winter sky entirely black, past the bonfires where the homeless beggars gathered along with the other Ivan Ivanoviches. He stumbled over the gaps and ditches and made his way back to the Lycée. Had he been utterly ridiculous? Had he made a complete fool of himself?

Alexander Sergeievich swore off women for a time, especially the baroness. Wenching was too time consuming. There were worlds that needed changing. Months passed before he went back to the Hussar quarters. He'd had his fill of riotous revolutionary escapades and the empty rhetoric that went on interminably. He was learning nothing from these older men now who had been to all those foreign countries, and had all those experiences unimagined by him. He was no longer awestruck in their presence. He was young, impatient, he wanted change, to learn everything and all at once. He wanted to know what the world was all about. What was Imperial Russia? What was revolution? Empty rhetoric no longer sufficed for him.

He was drawn toward the fields, to the bonafide Russian who knew not one exotic word of French, had never traveled more than fifteen *versts* from the earth that spawned them, muzhiks, serfs, men and women who seemed to have grown straight up out of the dark sweet earth of Russia. He worked and sweated with them, went with them to their homes, their miserable huts, their isbas, and broke bread with them, and even went to church with them. He began to talk like them, with their idioms and accents. He danced with them in the village square.

Each night when Sasha came in from the fields, he would work on his ODE TO FREEDOM far far into the night until the goose quill fell from his trembling fingers. As he wrote by the feeble candlelight, with the moths circling the flickering flame and sometimes getting into his matted hair, sometimes on his face, his ears, his plenteous lips, he would stare through his exhausted eyes and beat out a rhythm on his desk with his goose quill pen, his head cocked to one side, waving at the pesky moths. And his weary mind would summon up the images of the men he had worked with in the fields, the strong invincible Russian and ennobled faces of the women and the men. His mind would conjure up a revolution.

And he wrote:

But lend an ear, ye fallen slaves,
Gain courage and arise!

He remembered Piotra Ivanovich and Anton Ivanovich. He remembered the day the landed squire took Piotra's fourteen-year-old sister into his manor to be one of his handmaidens.

The anguished sweat dripped from his eyes, and he wrote:

It was law, not nature, tyrants,
Put the crown upon your heads.

Sometimes Ivan Pushchin went to the fields with him and worked and sweated with him, never really understanding the whys and wherefores of it. He just went along with his beloved comrade for the sake of comradeship. Possibly he thought that understanding would rise out of the potato furrows and rub off on him. Sometimes even Delvig went with them, sometimes Crazy Kuchelbecker went along. The muzhiks thought them Czarist spies.

One evening, underneath a lowered opaque sky, Alexander Sergeievich was coming back from the fields alone. He was exhausted, the perspiration streaming from him, liquid spots dancing dizzily before his eyes. His head knew a sudden giddiness, his steps unsure, as he dragged along through the blossom-covered lanes around the Summer Palace, placing one foot carefully before the other like a blind man. He could smell the stench of his own perspiration, feel the sweaty dirt crawling like bugs across his neck and shoulders and down his paining back. Now the fragrances of the orange and cherry blossoms filled his nostrils and went down deep into his stomach and mixed there with the smell of human perspiration. His mouth and belly knew a queasiness and feeling of great nausea. He felt faint. He stumbled along. I must not faint! I must not faint! Must not—! And he dimly saw a vision there before him. A vision of unadulterated loveliness. Had he already fainted? Was she an optical illusion?

She was a comely dark-haired wisp-of-a-lass with large dark-black eyes, a plentiful scarlet mouth that seemed to have just had its fill of wild strawberries. She watched him stumbling toward her, and she rose from where she sat and came toward him just as he fell forward into her arms. Even as he fell, he fought against her catching him. He was aware of the stench of his grimy and perspiring body, as compared to hers, all scrubbed clean and dressed in white and smelling of rosebuds and jasmine. "*Pajalsta!*" Alexander Sergeievich protested weakly. "I'm all right! I'm all right. I really am!" As he lost contact with his consciousness.

CHAPTER FOUR

Hours later, he lay between white and scented sheets. He felt clean, he knew he had been bathed from head to feet. He seemed to remember the bathing, the gentle soothing hands that were like a balm to him, as he had lain there in his semi-consciousness. As he came slowly out of it, he remembered the vision of the lovely girl seated on the bench and coming toward him and the smell of jasmine exuding from her slender body, the full, ripened, strawberried lips.

He heard a voice say, "Well, we are back among the living. Good!"

He turned toward the voice, and the vision was still with him, seated there beside the bed. "What happened?" he asked feebly. "And who are you?" The room was simply, neatly furnished with curtains of white muslim at the window. A dressing table in a corner with a looking glass above it, and on top of it, a bowl and pitcher of white gleaming crockery. A trunk sat lonely in another corner.

The vision answered, "You fainted and I had you brought to my room. And I took care of you. You've been here several hours. It is nearing morning and my name is Natasha Ashnikovna. I am the maid-in-waiting to Princess Volkonski, and I have to get you back to your own room before the morning or the wrath of God and His Majesty will be on both of our heads."

Alexander Sergeievich wrote poems to his comely vision, and ultimately he climbed into her window and kept her warm on wintry nights. Sometimes he thought her sensuous swollen lips were bleeding, so red were they. And he longed to bite into them further. Natasha was a playful lass. He called her his pussy cat. And sometimes he wrestled with her all night long. When she got to know him better she would whisper to him heatedly, "If you want it, take it!" in a voice that filled him with excitement. And finally she'd give in to him, as if it were the first and only time. She loved it that way. And after it was over they sometimes laughed themselves to sleep. He'd leap out of the window early mornings at the sound of chambermaids approaching.

He sat in his lonely room and wondered about his leaping from one bed to the other. What was this sickness with him? What was the meaning of it? What was this terrible agonizing need? Was it the African in his blood, the savage lust? Or was it because he'd always felt he was not loved by his parents as much as his brother and sister? Was he trying to prove to himself that he was lovable and worthy of being loved? He knew he needed desperately to be sustained by somebody's unequivocal devotion. He needed love, he needed adoration. It frightened him. He was so vulnerable to anyone who offered him affection.

One evening he was going along the corridor of the Summer Palace, and he heard a door open and the rustle of gowns and petticoats and got a whiff of the tantalizing fragrance of jasmine. He knew it was the heavenly smell of his sweet red-lipped Natasha. It was near the room where she worked as maid-in-waiting to Princess Volkonski. He went toward her and took her in his arms and kissed her long and passionately. He felt her hot breath on his neck. "My little pussy cat!" Breathing heavily on her cheek. His hand became a rover with its own consciousness and he seized her precious buttocks, thinking, what's happened to my darling pussy cat? She's lost so much weight just since the other night. Her backside is so scrawny. No matter, he would not be dismayed. Her lips were not as he remembered them, soft as overripe peaches. His heart knew a sinking feeling, maybe this was not Natasha. When she tried to pull away from him like she always had a way of doing, he chuckled with delight, and his busy hand went up her dress. "That's right! Wrestle with me, my pussy cat!" At which point his darling sweetheart pussy cat screamed as if she were being ravished. He thought to himself, She's carrying things a bit too far. After all, we *are* in the Summer Palace. We *are* just outside the old Princess's apartments.

Alexander Sergeievich leaped backwards and stared as a door opened near them and cast a light upon the corridor, into the wrinkled seventy-year-old face of the Czarina's aunt, Princess Volkonski. His heart leaped in his crazy chest. His perspiration turned to icicles. He mumbled unintelligible apologies and turned and ran as if his life depended on his swiftness.

Nothing could possibly save him this time. Alexander Sergeievich's elitist education would cease abruptly and unceremoniously. He would be lashed with the knout and sent home in disgrace. Though the Emperor took no real interest in the Lycée for which he took full credit, he had been kept abreast of the student career of one Alexander Sergeievich Pushkin and of his many escapades.

One morning the Emperor sent for Englehardt, the new director of the Lycée. Standing in his Imperial study near the giant-sized windows draped in silken burgundy, Czar Alexander was cut of the fine and stately cloth of the House of Romanov. Straight nose, broad forehead, firm mouth ringed by a handsome black beard and mustache, sprinkled here and there with gray. Tall, heavily handsome, regal in his every movement, intelligent looking, firm of jaw. Each kingly movement seemed deliberate and carefully considered, yet entirely without conscious effort on his part. A gift of birthright from that King of Kings and Lord of Lords, of the heavenly Kingdom up above. He prided himself with the ability to put other men at ease. But it was unease that Herr Englehardt felt before this noble personage. The Czar stood regally in front of the gargantuan mantlepiece. He waved the nervous director to a chair, then sat behind his glazed desk.

Alexander Romanov offered Herr Englehardt a snifter of the finest Imperial cognac which the director politely asked to be excused from taking. It was a bit early in the day for a man with such serious responsibilities to partake of alcoholic beverages. He watched Czar Alexander sniff dreamily at his tiny pear-shaped glass, sip from it, uttering an Imperial sigh, then gulp the rest of it down his handsome throat.

"Not that your Imperial Majesty does not have a million more important responsibilities than I, but some men have far greater capacity for this life than others."

The Emperor smiled benignly. He stood up again and gestured to Herr Englehardt to remain seated. Despite his regal appearance, he was developing a little bulge around the middle of him which seemed to make his bearing even more imposing and majestic.

Englehardt continued. "I just feel that Your Imperial Majesty has conferred upon me the honor and tremendous responsibility of training and shaping the moral character of the future pillars of the Empire."

"Yes," the Emperor said impatiently. His Imperial Majesty had not changed the expression on His handsome face, but Herr Director knew that His interest had strayed. His concentration span was very brief, especially when in conference with mere earthlings. Englehardt knew all this because he himself had begun to perspire. The Emperor liked to test a man's mettle by staring him coldly in the eyes. If the man gave the Emperor stare for stare, it either meant he was honest and manful with nothing to hide, or that he was impertinent and fool-hardy, and didn't know where the center of gravity was. Or he was concealing something utterly mendacious. Such a man could not be trusted. Or could he?

Across his broad chest from left to right the Emperor's cossack jacket hung heavily with military awards and decorations.

The Emperor said, "Well, it certainly seems that the future pillars of the Empire are on a very shaky foundation. And if things continue as they are the future of the whole world is in jeopardy." His Majesty always equated Russia with the entire universe, the moon, the stars and all the things below the Heavens and above. And if He were the benign ruler of Holy Russia, He must be the greatest man throughout the earth.

Englehardt stared at His Imperial Majesty hoping for a smile on that majestic face to tell him that the Emperor was having a little joke. His reputation as a liberal thinker, a benevolent monarch—but the Emperor was not smiling.

"The discipline for the future pillars of the Empire must be much stricter. The moral codes must be adhered to, to the letter. And. . . ." the Emperor continued.

"But surely, Your Majesty, you understand that boys will from time to time get into mischief. It is inevitable."

The Emperor did not take kindly to interruptions. "And when it reaches the point when my wife's ladies-in-waiting are not safe in the corridors of the Imperial Palace, then things are surely out of hand."

"Your Majesty undoubtedly refers to the recent Pushkin escapade?"

"Princess Volkonski has complained to the Czarina who is furious about the incident. She wants the boy thrashed soundly with the knout and expelled from the Lycée."

Herr Englehardt did not approve of Pushkin the student and his debauchery, as he deemed it, and he knew that Pushkin did not like him. But he had a deep appreciation for Pushkin's potential as Russia's most important future writer. And he wanted nothing to stunt the lad's development. Also he felt a responsibility to his students, even the delinquent ones.

"It was a perfectly understandable mistake, Your Majesty. I can explain everything. The corridors in that part of the palace are dark, as you know, Your Majesty, and the boys were coming along there on their way to the weekly concert. When Pushkin heard a door open and smelled a familiar perfume, he assumed it was worn by Natasha, Princess Volkonski's maid, with whom he is madly in love at the moment. Poets are naturally romantic and impulsive, so he flew to take her in his arms. Unfortunately, it turned out to be the Princess. Apparently they wear the same perfume." Herr Englehardt smiled weakly.

The Emperor sighed. "Your Pushkin is a reckless blackguard. He's gone from one escapade to another ever since he came to the Lycée. I know all about his drinking orgies. So now he not only is a bad influence on his fellow students, leading them to drink and various other debaucheries; the feminine personnel at the palace are no longer safe with him at large. Word has reached me he is sleeping in Imperial beds."

"If I may be perfectly frank with you, Your Majesty, Pushkin as a student leaves much to be desired. He is wild and is hot-blooded, but we can attribute that to his African ancestry over which the poor lad had no control. But no one denies his genius as a writer. Turgenev and Vyazemski and Zukovsky regard him as the hope of Russian literature. Monsieur Karamzin, himself, Your Majesty's own venerable Imperial Historiographer, even at his age, came all the way to Tsarskoye Selo solely for the purpose of seeing and talking with this young rapscallion. They all believe he has the making of true genius."

"And what do you advise as punishment?" the Emperor asked. "Twenty-five lashes with the knout and probation instead of expulsion?"

"It would break his noble spirit, Your Majesty. He is a proud boy and an aristocrat. May I plead for Your Majesty's gracious clemency?" Herr Englehardt was drenched with perspiration.

The Emperor stared at the director sternly, then in a change of mood, he said, "On second thought, perhaps the Princess was not as upset as she pretended. Perhaps the old cow was delighted at the rascal's blunder." And He broke into a loud and raucous laughter, which of course Englehardt joined in with, though not so boisterously. How heartily did one dare to laugh at a member of the royal family, even with the Emperor? It was like skating on the thinnest ice out in the middle of the Neva River.

Meanwhile Alexander Sergeievich wrote his poems and leaped on tables to recite them. He ate and slept and drank his verses. He thought in verse, sometimes talked in verse. He even dreamed his dreams in verse. And he dreamed all night long every night.

At eighteen and a month Alexander Sergeievich graduated. The official evaluation was that he was "Good" in Religion, Logic, Fencing, Philosophy, Athletics, French and Law; "Excellent" in Russian; "Poor" in Conduct and in Mathematics. His Imperial Majesty assigned him the rank of one of the "Assistant Secretaries" in the Ministry of Foreign Affairs in Saint Petersburg at a salary of seven hundred rubles per annum. It was a token appointment, Alexander Sergeievich thought, reward for doing six years of penance at the Lycée. In his new position he had very little to do and a lot of time on his hands, which he spent on philandering and using up the seven hundred rubles on a regular seat at the theatre and buying gifts for his latest passion, Olga, the actress with no talent save her bountiful bosom and her tiny feet and her flamboyancy.

But after six years behind the wall at the Summer Palace, he was more than ready for the madness that was Saint Petersburg's social merry-go-round.

PART THREE

SAINT PETERSBURG

CHAPTER ONE

By now, his parents surely must have realized that their own son was somehow different, even if his Uncle Basil were mistaken as to his capacity for genius. Basil Lvovich Pushkin had always been one for exaggeration. After all, he was a poet. Yes? Surely Nadezda and Sergei Pushkin should have concluded, by now, that Sasha Pushkin, flesh of their undeniable flesh, blood of their own red ennobled Russian blood, was no ordinary specimen of the homo sapien species. And let it go at that. Sasha's brother Leo would certainly have grudgingly agreed, as would his sister Olga, who always had worshipfully adored him. Not that the wayward son and brother really cared one way or the other. He was much too busy getting into mischief with the Imperial government. And if Nadezda and Sergei ever thought of their older son as a genius, it was certainly as an evil genius. They should have been alerted way back at the time when he neglected to remove his cap in the presence of Czar Paul the First who had sired the present Emperor Alexander. They might have seen it as a bad omen.

Meanwhile, Alexander Sergeievich dove headlong into the dizziness of Saint Petersburg society. His fame as a poet had preceded him. He was invited to all of the artistic and intellectual soirées. He was inducted into the *Society of the Green Lamp*, founded by young I.N. Tolstoy and millionaire Vsevolshsky. The millionaire's home became the meeting place for these radical literary roués. There were about twenty of them, most of them young, idle, brilliant and studiously cynical. Meetings were held in a large expensively furnished drawing room with curtains of brocaded silk under a great green glittering chandeliered lamp, symbolizing hope eternal. Each member wore a green ring with a lamp engraved on its emerald stone. Each was given a nickname. They called Alexander Sergeievich the Cricket. Sometimes, they called him the African. They gathered fortnightly to discuss literature, art and all the burning questions of the day. A young, liberal, irreverent, fun-loving bunch with having-a-good-time too much at the center of their activities for them to be involved in any dangerous conspiracy against the monarchy, as the Secret Police had at first surmised. Now and then Pushkin met his comrade Chaadaev of the Horse Guards at these sessions. Nicholas Raevsky and Captain Kaverin were sometimes present.

After heatedly debating the most important issues of the world and Russia, they would have supper in the great baronial oak-paneled dining room at a long mahogany table covered with a silken tablecloth, underneath the candled chandeliers, always in the company of beautiful young women, very agreeable and of questionable virtue, with the male Tartar serfs in their bright red suits coming and going darkly, with the never ending trays of shashlyk, caviar, plover, pheasant— rekindling the candles of the flickering chandeliers—cognac, rum, champagne, vodka. Sometimes, in the midst of all the orgiastic merriment and drunken brawls, the slapping and pinching of plumpish feminine backsides, the crash of champagne glasses thrown against the wainscoted walls, he would look around him and wonder what it was all about. What was he about? Captain Kaverin, drunk and handsome and lying where he had fallen underneath the table, snoring, spittle dripping from the corners of his mouth. Flush-faced flaxen-haired Larissa lying full length on the table with her petticoats above her lovely head. Raucous laughter everywhere. What was he doing in this place? He longed for the cloistered surroundings of the Summer Palace at the Lycée and the fields nearby where "his kind of people" toiled and sweated.

The strong smell of the peasantry, the feel of his fingers digging into the sweet black soil, to feel weary in every marrow of his bones, to know the stench of tiring labor. What was he doing in this place?

One night he went home and wrote:

Veuve Cliquot, Chateau-Lafitte,
Couplets, amicable disputes.
They were but games played in boredom,
Laziness of our young heads
Playthings of overgrown boys.

One evening Alexander Sergeievich bet his hell-raising colleagues that he could drink an entire quart of rum at one standing without losing consciousness. The moment he proposed the bet he knew it was a foolish thing to do and wondered why he'd done it. What was he trying to prove? Why did he feel he had to prove anything at all? What was wrong with him? A bearded serf was playing wildly on the balalaika. Over in a corner Captain Kaverin was doing a furious mazurka with a beautiful young woman who reminded Pushkin of Svetlina. The ambience was pregnant with the smell of alcohol and hashish and the sound of clicking dancing heels.

"No, Cricket! No!" Ivan Pushchin, his chubby comrade of Lycée days, ran up to him shouting in sincere alarm. "It's too dangerous, Alexander Sergeievich. It has killed better men than you!"

Pushkin turned drunkenly to his Lycée buddy. "I'm surprised at you, Pushchin, you old bastard. There are no better men than I. Or you," he added.

"Bravo!" his other comrades shouted. They took him on their shoulders and thrust him up on the table amid the delicacies. He stumbled over the table stepping in the caviar and cabbage soup and pies and cakes, knocking over whiskey bottles. Someone handed up the bottle of rum. "Bravo, African! Bravissimo!" The bets were placed. "No, Alexander Sergeievich! Don't do it! Don't do it!" Ivan Pushchin reluctantly placed his bets on Alexander Sergeievich.

Our poet bowed to his drunken comrades as they urged him on. It was an asinine thing to do, but there was no way he could get out of it. There was nothing for it. He looked down and around at his crazy comrades. He put the bottle to his lips and felt the burning liquid searing down his throat as if it sought to set his insides on fire. He tilted his head back slowly till he drained from the bottle every drop. His head felt as if it had been stretched, enlarged to twice its normal size. Veins in his forehead seemed about to burst. His slim body swayed as he turned the bottle upside down to show that all had vanished down his throat. He threw the bottle up against the fine wainscoting with a loud crash, spraying the carpet with splinters of glass.

"Bravo, Cricket!"

His head knew a growing giddiness, a sense of teetering on the edge of a precipice. Nausea filled his throat. His eyes lit up like lanterns, then the lights went out and he sank slowly down upon the table amongst the Kievan chicken and potato pancakes. Ivan Pushchin ran towards his stricken comrade. By the time he reached the fallen poet, Pushkin had begun to snore.

His comrades began to laugh and chuckle. "That's one time we put one over on the Cricket!"

"He put one over on himself!" another shouted.

But his friend, Pushchin, noticed that the little finger on Pushkin's left hand was wriggling. When the Cricket came to, he argued that the wriggling finger proved he had not lost consciousness. He argued persuasively and won the bet.

The palatial home of old Karamzin, the venerable historian for His Imperial Majesty, and his youngish wife was another gathering place of the young intellectuals. Among these young gems of the Russian literati, Alexander Sergeievich was the star that gleamed and glittered more brilliantly than all the rest. He was clever, an expert with the *bon mot*. He who used to stammer as a child. Amongst all these attractive people, he was the center of attraction.

Madame Karamzina was a handsome, clear-eyed, soft-faced woman, thirty-fivish, exuding sensuality from every pore effortlessly. There was an undeniable charm about this lovely lady that was difficult to resist, and Alexander Sergeievich

Pushkin did not try very hard. Each time he came into her drawing room she would greet him with a kiss, full on his mouth. Always a very warm embrace. "Oh my darling boy! My one and only love—*Mon ami, mon chèrie!* My secret passion! How sweet of you to take time out of your busy schedule to visit with an old, decrepit woman like me. How utterly chivalrous of you!" And always the merry sparkle in her blue translucent eyes, overflowing now with mischief.

So naturally he imagined himself hopelessly and helplessly in love with this sophisticated noblewoman. And accordingly, he wrote a letter to her declaring his undying devotion, his commitment to adore her for the remainder of his days.

Katerina Andrevna Karamzina laughingly brought the letter to Karamzin as he worked in his study. His majesty's grizzle-bearded aging Historiographer, long past sixty, looked up from his mahogany desk and told her, "A young man of Pushkin's undisputed genius must be forgiven certain excesses and extravagances. It is expected of people of genius. But you are too mature a woman to encourage him like this."

Even though she knew her husband to be deadly serious, and could hear the irritation in his voice, she said, "You're having a little joke with me. You cannot possibly be jealous of him. He is a mere child. You cannot take this letter seriously."

"That is precisely the point, my dear," Karamzin replied. "He is a child and you are a mature noblewoman. Please put an end to your flirtations with mere children, especially when they are of the likes of Alexander Pushkin."

Katerina Karamzina smiled. "By the Holy Virgin, I do believe you are jealous. Well, I suppose I might regard your jealousy as flattery of a sort."

Karamzin said, "The problem with you, my dear Katya. You flatter much too easily." He turned from her and went back to his work. He had angered her, then dismissed her as if she were a chambermaid. He knew he could not leave it like this. He turned back to her. "Any indiscretion must be forgiven a man who writes like Alexander Pushkin. Artistic genius is its own justification. But if you are not careful, my poor foolish dear, you will become the laughing stock of society."

Alexander Sergeievich went on drinking sprees with Hussar Guards that lasted several nights and days. Debated poetry with the great Chaadaev. Every word and comma, every colon must be analyzed in the minutest detail. What was the obvious meaning? What was the implicit meaning? How did it advance the coming revolution? He made the rounds of all the parties, sometimes three and four in a single night. Dueling was the fashion, and he had a reputation as an expert duelist, sword or pistol, you could choose your weapons. He was known to have an African temperament and would challenge anyone at the slightest insult, actual or imagined, intentional or otherwise. Why was he forever dueling? What was he trying to prove? To himself? To whom? He did not understand.

In some sophisticated circles he was the talk of the Capital City. He was the topic of their conversation. The talk was that he attended the theatre three nights a week, drew attention to himself by talking loudly and yawning when the drama bored him. Coming late to a performance and walking on people's feet to get to his own seat, then turning with his opera glasses, looking from box to box to see how many pretty faces he could flirt with and make faces at.

He was almost as notorious for his antics as his epigrams. Thus was the talk that went the rounds of Saint Petersburg, having very little to do with the real Alexander Pushkin. He was truly fond of opera, especially did he love the music of Wolfgang Mozart.

But poetry was the mistress that claimed this master poet. Just as some men ate to live while others lived to eat, Alexander Sergeievich lived to write, to create with the goose quilled pen. And it was his writing that sustained him. All else was mere pretension.

Games played in boredom—Playthings of overgrown boys. By now, his epigrams were being read all over Holy Russia. Bored with the continued round of parties, some days he would get up and his faithful valet, Nikita Koslov, would prepare his bath and help him get dressed in his walking clothes. And he would spend the day walking about Saint Petersburg, seeing, smelling, staring, feeling, tasting, hearing anything and everything. Drinking in the sounds and smells of this cold and heartless city made of stone and granite, so unlike his beloved Moscow.

In the summer days which never ended, when twilight lingered after midnight and the sun came up three hours later, he walked the streets of Peter's City and oftentimes it held no beauty for him. The city with its white nights and its vast wide streets and boulevards. He walked all alone, sometimes with Nikita Koslov, and stared and wondered at the yellow-jaundiced purplish houses with inverted windows like sunken eyes of decadence and dissipation, where the little merchants and the civil servants and the petty clerks lived out their lonely desperate lives. He felt that the windows stared back at him in all their utter decadence.

In the midst of all this decay was the Cathedral of St. Isaac with its gleaming golden dome; then came the nearby garish Stock Exchange. He did not feel he belonged in this city with its endless markets and their ragged marquees, the wolfish competition of the marketeers; across the way and over the Neva River the walls of granite of the Peter and Paul Bastille fortress stood, a fearsome relic of the Middle Ages, the contemptuous splendor of baroque palaces of gleaming marble of the fashionable people of nobility, the wooden roadways, the man-made canals, Peter's City! On the Neva River with its granite embankments. Poverty in the midst of arrogant abundance.

Counts, beggars, barons, lepers. There was so much for him to love and hate in Great Peter's famous city on the Neva.

When Czar Alexander came to power he promised the people a liberal and progressive government in which the arts would flourish and freedom would flow

96

like the waters of the Neva. In former and less liberal times, when a child had the misfortune to be born in winter, it was baptized by being plunged into the icy waters of a nearby river. If the river were frozen over, a hole was broken in the ice. But Alexander Romanov was an avid reader of Rousseau, Racine, Voltaire and all those other radical fellows of revolutionary France. And "Bravo to the liberalism" as far as Alexander Sergeievich was concerned.

Under Emperor Alexander, those ice-cold baptism practices were relaxed, for the aristocracy, that is. In the wealthy and ennobled homes of Russia, two tables were laid out in a drawing room by the priests; one was covered with holy images, the other with an enormous silver basin filled with warm water and surrounded by small wax tapers. Alexander Sergeievich attended a baptism for the child of one of his Lycée comrades. The ceremony took place in the rich man's private chapel with icons glowing all along the walls and incense burning heavily. Fire burning in the giant fireplace.

The head priest began by consecrating the font and dipping a silver cross into the water. He took the red-cheeked child and, after reciting certain pious prayers, undressed it completely. He totally immersed it in the water twice and vigorously. The child began to kick and scream. Then the howling infant was given to the nurse and the sacrament was administered.

But the Czar's revolutionary benevolence did not reach the common people who still had to adhere strictly to the ancient practices in all seasons. There were no expeditious pathways to those Pearly Gates for their children.

One day in a cold December, in his wanderings with his valet around the frigid city, Pushkin came upon one of these baptisms. The Neva River was frozen over as hard as the marble used by Peter to construct the baroque palaces. Workmen worked all night long in the freezing cold to break holes in the ice. As usual, two or three hundred infants with their mothers stood in line to be baptized. Also, as usual, many babies were doomed to die of cold, pneumonia and exposure.

Because of the severe cold, the bearded priest hurried through these ceremonies with very little waste of words or motion. As the holy man in his long black robe intoned his pious mumblings, white steam jetted from his thin mouth in cloudy streams like tea boiling in a samovar and settled on his beard and eyebrows like the first frost of the winter. His long red beaky nose was frost-bitten, his holy face was frozen. He could hardly talk.

The man in the long cassock and black cowl hurried also because the days were very short in Northern Russian winters. And because he hurried, several times that day, as the poet watched appalled, a child slipped through those holy hands and disappeared forever beneath the icy depths.

The mothers' wailings were like the bleats of poor sheep lost forever in a snowstorm. Pushkin's stomach did somersaults at the sound of every wail.

It was the third child lost that day to the ice-bound river that sent Alexander Sergeievich into a helpless rage. As the bawling babe disappeared beneath the ice, he heard the tall saintly man in his long black robe unexcitedly intone: "The Heavenly Father has been pleased to take this infant to Himself. Please pass me another."

The stentorian chant of the holy man could be heard distinctly above the bawling infants and the wailing distraught mothers. Alexander Sergeievich could not believe what his eyes beheld as the priest impatiently waved the weeping woman away and reached for the next child. He watched the next woman hand up her infant without protest. His Majesty and God's will must not be questioned. Everything was foreordained. Fate, God and His Imperial Majesty. There was simply nothing for it.

Alexander Sergeievich felt his own tears turn quickly to icicles. He closed his eyes, breaking the thin trickles of ice, his body shaking violently with chill and anger. In the eyes of his optimistic and triumphant mind he saw the line of mothers with their heads wrapped in rags and ragged babushkas break the line now and move inexorably toward the priest with their babies raised above their heads as weapons. He heard them chanting now, victoriously, as the babies changed to cudgels, and they rained blow after blow upon the head of the Godly priest. It was one of his most vivid daydreams. It was happening! It was happening! But when he opened his eyes and saw that things were as they always were, and perhaps as they always would be, the tall bulky man in the long black robe still intoning, the babies bawling, the women wailing, the great wind howling, he somehow heard his own voice shouting to the helpless women:

"Why in the devil don't you good women baptize that holy son of his mother fornicating with a pig? Put his pious head under water and hold it there till hell freezes over!" He felt as helpless and as impotent as the hapless mothers. With the wailing and the bawling and the wind howling, they did not even hear him. He moved toward them now over the slippery frozen river. Nikita Koslov pulled him back.

"Now, now, dear boy, you mustn't upset yourself like that. You mustn't be so headstrong."

He turned angrily to the older man. "I suppose it doesn't upset you then?"

"When you have lived as long as I have, dear heart, you learn that if you must upset yourself, you upset yourself quietly. After all, in Saint Petersburg, even the Neva River has ears and it babbles to the Little Father."

"Ah, Nikita, my dear friend, you are much too cautious."

Nikita told his young master, "Render unto Caesar the things that belong to Caesar, dear innocent child. When one is alone in a forest with a bear, one does not scream and call attention to oneself unless one has a gun to dispose of the big fellow or wishes to become his supper."

Pushkin chuckled angrily, frustrated. "That is too profound a point for one as dense as I." He turned to watch the continuing baptism, infuriated, mostly with himself and his deep sense of futility. Perhaps he did take life too seriously. Perhaps in this life, especially this Russian life, one must be fatalistic, philosophical. He no longer felt the sharp piercing cold as he watched the endless line of stocky peasant women in their long dresses dragging along the ice, with their heads and feet tied up in rags as they handed their babes to this holy man, like sacrificial offering. A scene out of Biblical days.

"Your parents charged me with a sacred trust, dear boy, to keep you out of mischief in this wicked city. But it isn't easy."

"It isn't easy," Alexander Sergeievich agreed as he turned and headed away from the baptismal scene, striking his cane against the frozen and unfeeling river. At three o'clock, night was already falling in the Northern and Western skies. How he loved and hated Russia!

That same night he stole away from Nikita Koslov and went on one of his drinking sprees for which he was becoming infamous. Dressed in his tight breeches and great worn-at-the-heel boots with frock coat and high hat, he went from tavern to restaurant to tavern carousing, running into old cronies of his Lycée days and Hussar Guardsmen. Singing anti-clerical songs and leaping onto tables and declaiming anti-monarchist verses that frightened even his revolutionary comrades.

For after all, everybody knew by now that reading Rousseau and Voltaire was one thing, but putting them into practice in Imperial Russia was a horse of another color. And the horses of the Horse Guards were regimented and mostly of the same color, as were the Emperor's Secret Gendarmerie. Czarist police were everywhere, had even infiltrated the "secret" societies that were springing up like birch trees all over Holy Russia. The Emperor was omnipresent. The Eyes and Ears of Europe, the personification of the *Holy Alliance*. And it was colder in Siberia than it ever thought of being in petrified Saint Petersburg.

Five o'clock that morning found Alexander Sergeievich with a comrade of his Lycée days in a notorious after-hours cabaret that engaged in illegal traffic of drugs and women and everything else that was against the moral code of the sainted Emperor Alexander. His comrade, Needleman, had gone to medical school after leaving Tsarskoye Selo. One of the first persons Pushkin saw at one of the tables was Benkendorf, a man high up in the echelon of the Czarist Secret Police. Seated with him at his table was Count Stroganov who also had the ear of Czar Alexander.

Young peasant women danced out on the floor and kicked their legs high while the drunken nobility, men, women and young mistresses, applauded boisterously and pinched their plump backsides and made lascivious remarks. Most of the dancing girls were fifteen and sixteen years of age and Alexander Sergeievich could see the terror in their eyes as they danced with smiles of tragedy etched onto their faces, or perhaps it was only his imagination. He knew no matter what indignities they suffered at the hands of these ennobled persons of the great metropolis, it was better than life back on the farm where slavery was a natural fact, especially for womenfolk. Certainly he knew that the landed squires were no different from the lordly counts and barons of Saint Petersburg. And the living in the city had more glamour and afforded more amenities.

A few of the girls were women, twenty-five and twenty-six years old, but no less fearful for their longer sojourn on this Holy Russian earth. Alexander Sergeievich was nodding drunkenly at his table when he noticed the girl at the end of the line as they danced across the floor. His stomach knew a funny feeling as he stared through the haze of smoke and the smell of opium. His eyes were burning. There was something strangely familiar about this woman of the flaxen hair and the diaphanous blue eyes of burning ice, the way she moved and was constructed.

Where had he seen her before? Known her? He tried painfully to put the woman in the time and space of his experiences. At the Lycée? Hardly. With the Hussar Guards? Her frightened face was on the tip of his memory, playing games with his remembrances. He had known so many women in the brief span of his stay on this Russian earth. Natasha? No! Alexandra? No! Marya, Olga, Larisa? Was it Tanya? Of course! Of course Tanya! Tatyana, his first love, the chambermaid in Moscow. Now he was completely awake and leapingly alive. He sobered instantly. What was she doing in this Godforsaken hole? He'd known that she'd long ago escaped the poverty-stricken aristocratic Pushkin household. But Saint Petersburg! And this decadent cabaret which had the worst reputation in all the city. He could hardly contain himself.

Now the drunken ennobled men were slapping ten and fifteen ruble bills upon the table, and girls were dancing through the opium fog up to the tables and lifting up their dresses and squatting over the bills, and when they moved away the rubles had disappeared as if their vaginas were constructed with built-in suctions. These miracles of dexterity were accomplished to the frenzied applause and squeals of the ennobled gentlemen and ladies.

Count Stroganov took a ruble out of his pocket and called a waiter to his table, who lit his cigar and then set the ruble aflame. The Count took a ruble gold piece from another pocket and held the flame beneath it in his gloved hand till it glowed as red as fire. He was a hulk of a red-faced man, massive and fat-faced from overindulgence, over-eating, over-drinking, excessive debauchery. He lit another paper ruble and held it to the coin till it was flaming red. He belched loudly. He placed the glowing coin upon the table and motioned to the last girl in the line. The coin had been so hot it burned his glove. She danced toward the table and squatted over the coin. She screamed, pitifully, as she leaped away from the table. The Stroganov table erupted now with laughter and applause. But the girl lay on the floor groaning. Alexander Sergeievich sprang from his chair and ran toward Tatyana followed by his friend, the medical student. Tatyana had passed out, but when they lifted her dress they saw the hot coin still in place. Her pubic hair was scorched and darkly crisp. Alexander Sergeievich took the coin from Tatyana. It burned hotly in his hand. The medical student attended her as Alexander Sergeievich turned to the Stroganov table where the laughter was finally subsiding.

"Which one of you bloody bastards is responsible?" he asked.

Benkendorf said, "Careful, boy. Watch your tongue around the aristocracy." The Secret Policeman was a slimly-constructed distinguished looking gentleman with receding forehead, thinly mustached, with small intelligent eyes.

"You have the privilege to be speaking to an aristocrat," Pushkin told him. "And now I repeat: Which one of you sons or daughters of a bloody pig is responsible? For I am a gentleman, Sires. And I will have satisfaction."

Count Stroganov spoke up, jovially, "Oh well, if you are a gentleman of the aristocracy, what are you so upset about? She's a mere serf girl of no particular account." He was a highly educated man, one of the most literate gentlemen at His Majesty's Imperial Court. And he was thoroughly decadent.

"She is a woman and a human being, Sire, who once worked in the household of the Pushkins." He stared from Stroganov to Benkendorf and back again. "Since you cowardly bastards will not speak up, I will have satisfaction from either or both of you, separately or simultaneously." He deliberately took off the glove from his right hand and resoundingly slapped Stroganov and then Benkendorf. "You have the honor of being addressed by Alexander Sergeievich Pushkin, at your service."

Stroganov's face turned the color of a carrot, as he sprang from his seat. But Pushkin turned his back and went to see after Tatyana, who was slowly gaining consciousness. "Is it very bad?" he anxiously asked Vasili Needleman.

"It is not good," Needleman replied. "She should be in a hospital."

Tatyana was fully conscious now. "Oh no!" she cried. "I don't have rubles for a hospital, Your Excellencies. And besides, I have to work tomorrow night and they might keep me in that place!" Her blue eyes filled with terror.

He covered her nakedness with her dress. Alexander Sergeievich wanted to tell her that if she couldn't work at this hell-hole-of-a-cabaret, she would not be losing anything of value, but what alternative could he offer her? He could hardly maintain himself on the rubles graciously bestowed upon him by the generous Emperor. And his family was among the most impecunious aristocrats in all of Holy Russia.

Nevertheless he said to the medical student, "Take her to the hospital in my name. I will take care of the expenses."

Tatyana said, staring bleary-eyed at her benefactor, "But who are you, Your Excellency?" Her eyes were heavy with suspicion.

"And is your memory so short, Tatyana? Alexander Sergeievich Pushkin! At your service, Madame."

Her whole face smiled. The eyes, the lips, the cheeks, the teeth, "Sasha! My own darling baby, Sasha! His Excellency!" She took him in her arms and the tears spilled down her cheeks. "Such a gentleman he has become!"

The wheels at the Czarist court turned swiftly. Dueling was against the law and it was enforced ruthlessly by Alexander Romanov and Benkendorf, except in special cases where it would be advantageous to the court to be rid of some notorious Ivan Ivanovich or anti-monarchist. No matter. Duels were fought weekly, sometimes by the day. This time the Emperor took no chances. Alexander Pushkin was too dangerous a duelist; Stroganov and Benkendorf too valuable to the Court. There would be other ways of dealing with this irreverent rascal. The Emperor would bide his time.

CHAPTER TWO

Alexander Sergeievich Pushkin seemed determined that the Emperor would not have much time to bide. Even so, the Emperor used his omnipresence to make sure no duel took place. Alexander Sergeievich raged in his terrible frustration. Bored with the corrupt life he was leading, which was not much different from those around him whom he disdained, he was filled up to the brimming overflow with self-loathing and contempt. The Cricket and his comrades of the Green Lamp knew all the institutions of ill repute in Saint Petersburg and were on speaking terms with every madam in the numerous houses of prostitution. Harlots knew them on a first-name basis.

Then one day, suddenly it was spring. And the sap was in more flow than ebb in the poplar and the linden trees, the evergreens of fir and pine and cedar. The thaw of winter's frigid blast was ebbing; there was a brand new smell in the air above and all around in old Saint Pete. Some thought of it as new Saint Pete in relationship to Moscow, which was still the ebb and flow of Russian life. Pushkin longed for his remembered Moscow. Moscow of the palaces of Emperors and barons and counts. Moscow of the hundreds of bazaars, of the thousand churches and cathedrals and sharply-pointed cupolas, Moscow of the mighty Kremlin, citadel of *Muscovy* and the Russian spirit!

Released from their winter prison, people thronged the streets again. The very proper nobility rode in finely appointed troikas and carriages that splashed the snow-changed-to-slush-and-mud upon the common everyday pedestrians, as if the mud and slush were kopeks thrown graciously to the unwashed undeserving multitude. The sky above Saint Pete was cast in mauve, as Alexander Sergeievich rode with his wealthier Green Lamp comrades in an open-air barouche owned by young Boris Rabinovsky. Inside, the carriage was garmented in the luxury of Russian mink. The poetry in Pushkin's mind stared behind the mud-splattered faces of the street people, the beggars, panders, hard-laboring honest-to-goodness working people, hustlers, whores, petty tradesmen, as they bowed and scraped and spoke pleasantries above their sycophantic breaths.

"The best of the morning to Your Excellencies. . . . Your Noblenesses . . . Your Highnesses. . . ."

"May the Holy Virgin always bless you."

His poet's ears happily heard obscenities underneath those sullen smiling breaths. More than likely it was his imagination forever taking poetic license. For how could smiling people be unhappy? Everyone, especially the wealthy, knew that most of the blessed poor were happy and contented with their lot. The tender-hearted son of the Holy Virgin Himself had said, "Blessed are the meek."

On a sudden impulse Alexander Sergeievich leaped from the open carriage as it meandered slowly through the throng of the people-of-the-street. He melted into the crowd, blended into the landscape of the people like a chameleon. He left his hat in the carriage as it clattered along the cobblestoned boulevard.

"Where is Alexander Sergeievich?" his comrade Ivan Pushchin asked excitedly.

"Where did the Cricket disappear to?" from Prince Vyazemsky, uneasily.

Basil Zukovsky said, "It is not safe out there among the rabble."

Alexander Sergeievich suddenly loomed up out of the multitude and came up to the carriage. He bowed obsequiously to his astonished comrades.

"May you live forever, Your Noblenesses," he said softly to them. Then he muttered audibly, "YOU MISERABLE SONS OF YOUR GONORRHEA-INFECTED MOTHER'S MISBEHAVIOR!"

He bowed slowly and respectfully to the carriage containing his startled laughing comrades. They shook their heads at his audacity.

"Go ahead, laugh, Your Eminences, YOU LAZY, PARASITIC, GOOD-FOR-NOTHING SYPHILITIC SWINE!" he mumbled *sotto voce*, loud enough to be clearly heard.

The street people of the Nevsky Prospekt were taken aback at first, then snickered hesitantly. Who was this cheeky bastard that looked like them, even sounded like them? Was this one of the Secret Police's tricks? The hated Third Section? This one wasn't dressed much better than they were. He spoke their language and voiced the sentiments they would not dare to utter publicly.

"The best of health to Your Excellencies, *you miserable offsprings of filthy dung-eating pigs! May you choke to death in your mother's excrement!*"

The street people of the Prospekt began to cheer Alexander Sergeievich now as a larger crowd began to gather. He had maneuvered himself directly in front of the expensively fur-lined carriage with its handsome well-groomed horses. He fell in front of the horses and pretended they had knocked him down. He leaped to his feet.

"See how they treat us!" he shouted to the gathering crowd of ragged people. Professional beggars, one-armed lepers, straggly-haired foot-sore ladies of the evening and the boulevard, procurers, hustlers, working people. "They think more of their goddamn horses than they do of us. We should break their horses' dainty legs!"

"Break their horses' dainty legs!" somebody shouted from the crowd. "Break their legs too!" another shouted, as they gathered around the carriage, preventing it from moving now. Some of them had seized the reins. The ennobled comrades were no longer laughing. Mounted *gendarmes* moved toward the noisy gathering mob, dispersing them with knouts and cudgels.

"Is everything all right, Your Excellencies?" one of the mounted gendarmes inquired. They were no more than two versts from the Winter Palace.

"Everything's fine. Thank you very much," Alexander Sergeievich answered. He was back in the well-appointed carriage now, underneath his top hat. "They, the people, were just expressing in their own inimitable way their great love for the Nobility and His Imperial Majesty."

The police horses pranced and snorted. The mounted gendarmes in their handsome Cossack uniforms looked about them dubiously.

"You're sure Your Excellencies are all right? You're safe?"

"But of course. What could be safer than the love of His Majesty's subjects? Are you implying that the people do not love His Imperial Majesty?"

The confused policemen saluted the carriage people and rode off again. Alexander Sergeievich shouted after them. "Long live the Russian people! Long live the Russian *politseyskii!* Long live His Imperial Majesty!"

The crowd had dispersed by now, and as they went cloppidy-clop down the mud-spattered cobblestoned boulevard, his comrades bombarded him with questions and recriminations. The rattling sound of the carriage wheels grinding and creaking into the slush-covered cobblestones made his flesh crawl.

"What in the devil did you think you were doing?"

"You carry a joke too goddamn far!"

"We almost had a rebellion on our hands!"

"Just a little demonstration," Alexander Sergeievich told them calmly. "To show you how really little you know about the true mood of the masses. And you fraudulent bastards call yourselves liberals and revolutionaries." He laughed at the quizzical looks on their faces. His comrade, Ivan Pushchin, began to laugh hysterically.

One night that spring, Alexander Sergeievich found himself with some of his revolutionary comrades in a house of ill repute with one of the better reputations in Saint Pete among the upper classes. "The Home for Wayward Girls" was chaperoned by a certain Madame Marya Dubinskaya, who regarded the young ladies in her charge as her adopted daughters. She was a handsome matron somewhere in her middle forties, sturdily constructed and well preserved for one who had labored so long and earnestly in such an ancient and honorable profession. The two-storied brothel was located on Bourgeois Street just off Nevsky Prospekt. Of wooden-framed construction, it consisted of six large rooms on each floor, with oaken front and back stairways, a darkened hallway running down the center of each floor, with a secret back door entrance for the extra special clientele. Gaudy, gold embroidered draperies adorned the shuttered windows. Each room had its icon corner where the candles burned eternally.

The first time Alexander Sergeievich had gone there, Madame Dubinskaya had taken the already-famous poet on a grand tour of the premises. Into the back and front parlors with their overstuffed chairs, where the demi-virgins languished, hastily washed, gaudily dressed and heavily perfumed. Alexander Sergeievich's head swam from the pungent fragrances.

"These are my wards," Madame Dubinskaya told him proudly. "I regard them as a sacred trust. Poor darlings, some of them never had a mother or father."

Alexander Sergeievich looked around at the poor little half-naked, motherless and fatherless darlings, wiggling their plumpish backsides and licking their painted lips at him. He said, "It must have been very difficult for them, coming into the world without a mother or father."

Madame D smiled graciously. She wiped a lone tear from a darkened eye. "Yes," she said, "but they're human beings like all the rest of God and His Majesty's subjects, aren't they? Aren't they?" she repeated. "And by the Holy Virgin and His Imperial Majesty, I have dedicated my life to see that they are always treated humanely. I'm a Christian and a humanitarian, don't you know. Some people say I'm just too tender-hearted."

She took the poet to the back room on the right just off the rear staircase into a chapel complete with altar and confession box and icons of various sizes and de-scriptions, the candles beneath them burning brightly. Alexander Sergeievich gazed, transfixed, now at a life-sized portrait of Our Savior hanging behind the al-tar and staring down from his cross and crown of thorns with ever saddening eyes. A chapel in a whorehouse? But Madame Marya Dubinskaya was a very devout lady, as she explained to the flabbergasted poet. He learned later that her young mischievous daughters called her "Ave Marya." Not to Madame's face, of course.

To emphasize her piety, she introduced Alexander Sergeievich to the chaplain of this famous and nightly brothel, one Abbe Igor Podolinsky. "Father Igor is a very modest gentleman," Madame explained. "But you should know that he is the esteemed assistant to the head of the Orthodox Church, who is Metropolitan of all Saint Petersburg, who is second only to His Holiness the Patriarch Himself in the whole hierarchy of Russian Orthodoxy!" Madame Dubinskaya had a way of speak-ing as if she had just completed some arduous chore and the very next breath would be her last. Listening to her, Alexander Sergeievich felt himself almost out of breath.

"We always insist on the very best for our poor darlings," she assured him, breathlessly.

Abbe Igor was a soft-spoken man, nearing fifty years of sojourn on this Russian earth, quite obviously a glutton at the dinner table, obese and puffy-eyed and paunchy. It was said of him that when the young daughters came to him for sacred counsel, this pious gentleman would place his divine hand on their heads and sometimes other places and stare down their loosely bodiced bosoms, and usually with a few well-chosen phrases in Greek or Latin, would bless them by patting them fondly on their playful buttocks. It was further rumored by the fun-loving daughters that this Orthodox Abbe gave his blessings to "Ave Marya" in a very unorthodox fashion. It was even rumored that Abbe Igor was so solicitous of Madame Marya's soul that he hardly ever left her side, except when he was bestowing grace upon the girls or receiving their confessions. And that he even went to bed with her to protect her sainted soul from the devil while she slept.

This particular evening, Crazy Kuchelbecker had taken a buxomy lively redhaired lassie to a room upstairs. Plump-faced Ivan Pushchin had also disappeared with another double-breasted maiden.

Alexander Sergeievich sat in the front parlor with a dark-eyed full-lipped girl, no more than seventeen, pure and angelic in every aspect of her countenance. The sincerity was all there in the utter blackness of her eyes, the innocence in her generous mouth, the way her girlish pointed breasts lifted high up toward her shoulders, the way she primly sat before him, her tiny voice, her earnestness. All this spread around the girl an aura of saintliness that sharply contradicted her presence in this house of prostitution. She should be in a cathedral or a convent, he thought. Belongs in Heaven, up there with the other angels. His idealistic heart imagined a halo around her lovely head. How could this pure one be a prostitute? He was certain she was here by some quirk of an implacable fate. He would bring her to Abbe Igor's fatherly attention.

He surprised himself when he asked her, "What's an innocent one like you doing in this God-forsaken place?" The question was a cliche he had read in many French romances. His face flushed with his own embarrassment.

His angel answered him demurely. "This place is not God-forsaken, Alexander Sergeievich. We have an Abbe and a place of worship here. We have prayer each night after work."

He felt foolish even as he spoke. "I'm going to speak to Brother Igor about you. We must rescue you from this place. An innocent one like you—"

He got no further when a terrible scream went through the house. Then another, and another one after that, as if one of the poor darlings were being raped or murdered. Doors opened and slammed and many feet ran down the stairs, all converging on the back room across from the chapel, all in various and varied states and stages of dishabille. Alexander Sergeievich almost collided with Kuchelbecker at the entrance to the back room where the uproar was continuing. Fun-loving, red-haired Louisa lay there naked on the bed screaming with laughter and pointing at the man bent over the bed before her, tears streaming down her appled cheeks. The man's breeches were down around his ankles, his round, fat-cheeked backside glowing in the candlelight.

"Your Grace," she began and then went off into gales and gales of raucous laughter.

"Now—now—daughter—just play with it a little. It will pucker up and the Lord above will surely bless you."

"But your Grace! He's so tiny I can't find *him*. Your fat belly's in the way of everything—." She began to laugh again, uncontrollably.

"Now, now, dear daughter, the Holy Virgin will not smile on you—making fun of Her apostle—."

"When was the last time you had a glimpse of *him*, your Grace? How do you find *him* when you urinate?" She laughed so hard she had to hold her stomach, falling out of the bed, kicking her fine legs all about as she continued to whoop and holler.

By this time the room was filled with naked gentlemen and daughters. The air was pregnant with the overwhelming aroma of cheap exotic perfumes all mixed up with the smell of body stench and very recent copulation. The room across from the chapel shook with laughter. The chubby bare-assed man turned, and it was true what Louisa said. His stomach was so fat and round it was impossible to glimpse his male protrusion. His round face reddened by the second. Our poet was thunderstruck and speechless when he recognized the identity of this noble personage. He heard, "Your Grace! Your Holiness!" He was no less a holy one than the Metropolitan of all Saint Petersberg. Next to the Patriarch himself, second in command of God's holy work and mission on this entire Russian earth. He was His Imperial Majesty's personal connection with the Great One up on High.

Naked men and women went immediately down upon their knees and made the sign of the cross. Let it be said for the Metropolitan that, though his cheeks were roseate as new-bloomed roses, he did not lose his dignity as he, with difficulty, pulled up his silken breeches. He made the sign of the cross and with a proper gesture, blessed those kneeling, cleared his throat and spoke in a deep and saintly voice. "I was bestowing upon this young daughter my divine blessings, but she did not appreciate the precious gift I offered her. And for her unseemly behavior, may this ungrateful, wanton bitch rot in hell's fire till eternity!"

By that time Abbe Igor came to The Holy one's rescue and led him away from the band of infidels who had erupted now again with howling laughter. But the Holy man never lost his dignity.

The next day he went to see Count Miloradovich, the Governor-General of Saint Petersburg, demanding that Madame Dubinskaya's "den of iniquity" be closed down at once. "It is an outrageous affront to this Holy Russian Empire!"

"But, your Grace, we have no evidence—how do you know that the one who brought this tale to you does not have some evil axe to grind against the dear woman?" The Metropolitan did not appreciate the twinkle he saw in the Governor-General's eyes. "Isn't Abbe Podolinsky her counselor? Madame runs a school for wayward girls—I mean—"

The Metropolitan was clearly agitated. "It is a danger to the morals of the youth of Saint Petersburg, and it has come to my attention—and if steps are not taken against this woman immediately, I shall have both of them, her and that lecherous bastard Podolinsky, ex-communicated."

Count Miloradovich promised, "I shall look into this very grave matter immediately. You may rest assured, your Grace."

But His Grace refused to rest assured. He got into his carriage and went immediately to Benkendorf, Chief of Saint Petersburg's Secret Police, where he received assurances of immediate action.

A few nights later the disillusioned Pushkin was again at Madame Marya's Home for Wayward Girls, making himself at home in bed with his innocent Larissa. The innocence was still in her face, her lovely young-girl's breasts still pointed heavenward, the imagined halo still encircled her angelic head, even as her lovely darkly cloven spot received his energetic truncheon. Even as her limbs went up to meet the challenge and she murmured softly sweet obscenities, she still had that angelic look about her. He thought, guiltily, I'm fornicating with a saintly creature, an angel recently come down here from Heaven, and against his conscious will, he got an extra perverse pleasure from the idea of it. Just as they were about to reach those Pearly Gates together, hearts pounding like claps of thunder all the way up in their foreheads, there came a loud pounding on the doors and windows front and back.

"Open up in the name of His Imperial Majesty!"

Sounds of quiet giggling turned instantly to shouts of alarm and screams and scrambling. Gentlemen leaping out of windows. More pounding now on doors inside the house. Fortunately for Alexander Sergeievich, he was in a room on the first floor and did not have too far to jump. A few legs were broken that fateful night. Fortunately, also for our poet, it was not the cold of winter, due to the fact that Alexander Sergeievich left hurriedly and without his breeches. He had to walk through the cool spring night in his meager undergarments.

It was during these times of his profound debauchery when he wrote, and pretended to believe:

Love and wine
We need together.
Without them men
Would yawn forever.

But his poetry was the thing that kept him going, made him think his life worth living. As spring moved toward summer and the white nights of Saint Pete began, he immersed himself in his poetry. Night and day, the anti-monarchist, anti-cleric verses poured from his angry pen. Satirizing his pro-Czarist, long-time friend and patron, the Emperor's national historian, Karamzin, he sat in his lonely dim-lit room and wrote:

In his elegant simply told history
He explains to us most objectively
How autocracy necessarily came about
And all the good effects of the knout.

He licked the tip of his goose quilled pen and relished the taste of his bitterness. He was a man possessed.

Attacking Father Lev Gregorovich Photius, a famous mystic of Saint Petersburg society, he wrote:

Part fanatic, part pickpocket
The only spiritual weapons he waves
Are opprobrium and cross, sword and knout.

And of a wealthy countess who contributed great sums to this holy mystic, he wrote:

This so pious woman
Has sold her soul to God,
And her sinner's skin
To archimandrite Photius.

Alexander Sergeievich made enemies by the hundreds amongst those in powerful places.

He went to visit Tatyana at the hospital but she was no longer there. He raised hell at the cabaret where she worked, but to no avail. He looked all over the city for her, but it was as if she had been kidnapped from the planet.

Every time he thought about the baptism scene on the frozen Neva and the incident with his Tatyana at the cabaret, he flew into a trembling rage. At home he worked far into the dim-lit night. He thought that if he could not take it out on a field of honor, then he would have his satisfaction with his pen and paper. He would do combat with the cruel monarchy through his writings. He would burn the pages up with the inflammation of his verses, even as his own eyes burned with sweat and anger. But to write against the throne was to curse the Good Lord up above, to dare the thunder and the lightning. He had this strange trembling fascination with personal disaster, as if he somehow knew it could not come to him. Death seemed to have no terror for this enraged poet, not even far away Siberia.

One evening he went to a party and met Countess Oshnikovna, a low slung, darkly-mustached, flat-chested woman of middle age, a self-proclaimed apostle of Father Lev Gregorovich Photius, both of whom Pushkin had written about in several of his recent poems. All evening long the fanatical, wild-eyed woman followed Alexander Sergeievich around the brightly-lighted drawing room.

"I have read all of your poems, Monsieur Pushkin. I am a great admirer of your work. But you are grievously mistaken about Father Lev Gregorovich."

The little mousy woman had Alexander Sergeievich cornered now. Her high-pitched voice verging on hysteria. Alexander Sergeievich tried to modulate the woman's voice by speaking softly to her, but the softer he spoke the louder she became.

"I love your work," she shrieked. "But Lev Gregorovich is an angel sent to earth by the Holy Virgin Herself. Ask him. He will tell you. He—"

He could vaguely hear the music of a serf band playing at the other end of the vast drawing room. What was he doing in this place? He should have been home working.

"Madame," he said, "Madame Oshnikovna, I have no doubt that Father Photius is on speaking terms with the Blessed Virgin. However—"

She had not come to listen to him. She went on and on. "Father Lev has also read your work. He's anxious to meet you. He adores you. We are having a soiree at my home next Tuesday evening. Please say you will come and meet this great Messenger of God. He loves your work. He's an angel and he even forgives you those mischievous poems about him. And I forgive you too."

Alexander Sergeievich looked around into the ennobled faces, looking desperately for a way to escape this mad woman whose eyes were flashing fire, her thin wet lips quivering. She had worked herself up into a wild excitement.

"Say you will come, dear boy, and I will send my coach for you." She simmered down. She was all soft and sugary now, cooing gently, though the crazy gleam still lingered in her eyes that were forever changing colors. She took his hand and began to caress it tenderly. "It's only fair, my darling. After that sacrilegious poem you wrote about the dear man and the one about me, and both of us forgive you, because we love you." She patted his hand. "There now, there—it's settled then. My coach will call for you at seven o'clock on Tuesday evening.

When Alexander Sergeievich arrived that Tuesday evening at the Countess's palace, night was falling. You could almost hear it coming down, with frogs and crickets croaking and giggling. It was early autumn and had rained all through the morning. Then the rain ceased and the leaves began to fall, turning golden brown all over Saint Petersburg, turning orange, turning scarlet as if all Russia were aflame. It was Pushkin's season of the year.

A long rectangular table overladen with all manner of Russian delicacies was in the middle of the vast baronial dining room underneath a glittering chandelier, with candles flickering under golden icons all along the wall. There were hundreds of them. One might have been in a cathedral. His boots sank deep into the thick red carpeting from Persia. Alexander Sergeievich heard a loud chattering of excited voices before he entered.

"Monsieur Alexander Sergeievich Pushkin," the huge male servant announced him in a mystic tone.

A sudden hush fell over the noisy gathering. And he heard, "Alexander Sergeievich Pushkin!"

A female voice said, "Is it really Alexander Pooshkin?" The Countess trotted toward him. "Monsieur Pushkin!" the Countess gasped, "What a pleasant surprise!" As if she had not sent her own carriage for him.

She extended her hand to him. He took her slender bony fingers and kissed them. She led him to the table and sat him at the foot of it. The band began to play a mournful hymn. The air was alive with the smell of burning incense. The room was foggy with the smoke and smell of opium. The walls were ignited by the softly glowing candles under icons, burning blue and red and yellow. Alexander Sergeievich watched a big lumbering giant of a man enter the room and move toward the head of the table. As the man approached the table everyone rose from the table excepting Alexander Sergeievich. It was only then that he realized that most of those present were women, with a sprinkling here and there of eminent noblemen, a distinguished count, a baron, several ministers of state. Men close to the Emperor and their spouses. As the priest stood now at the head of the table there began a slow chant of mostly female voice.

"Father Lev Gregorovich—"

"Father Lev Gregorovich—"

"May the Holy Virgin bless him."

"May the Holy Virgin bless him—"

The figure standing at the head of the table was a hulking monster of a man, who lumbered like a bear with a head like a lion. His eyes were fierce black pools of moonlit midnight. His head was framed by a blonde and ragged beard and a head of bushy hair that seemed not to have made acquaintance with a comb in months. He was bulky and appeared to be as wide as he was tall, all six to seven feet of him. In his bright red tunic and his black baggy trousers, he looked as rumpled as an unmade bed that had been slept in for many months without a single change of bed clothes.

Glaring down the table at Alexander Sergeievich, Lev Gregorovich's eyes were hypnotic, like lanterns gleaming forth from two black coals. Alexander felt himself about to rise as the eyes of Father Photius were demanding, but he held on to his seat with both hands, even as he felt a fine perspiration breaking out upon his brow. He grabbed the arms of his chair till his fingers ached. The mystical chanting continued. Finally the hoary archimandrite held out his hands for the chanting to cease and for the faithful to be seated.

Now Lev Gregorovich Photius sat there eating and drinking with a leg of lamb in one hand, a glass of wine in the other. He wiped his greasy mouth with the back of his hands and wiped his hands on his crimson tunic. And every time he belched or broke wind, the faithful said, "God Bless you!"

Lev Gregorovich bit savagely into a leg of lamb and passed it on to the lady seated next to him, who took a bite and passed it on. He kept reaching for legs of lamb, taking bites like a ravenous bear and passing them along. Now the stench of this holy man mixing with the smell of incense and opium reached Pushkin down at the other end of the table, and the whole impact was overwhelming. Eating, drinking, belching, breaking wind—"God Bless you!" Eating, drinking, belching, breaking wind—"The Holy Virgin Bless Your Holiness!" Alexander Sergeievich felt an awful nausea building up inside of him, his stomach in an uproar now.

A slow mournful chant began again gaining tempo as the men and women rose and moved rhythmically toward the holy hulk and kissed his hand and kissed him on his mouth. He was standing now and so drunk he could hardly keep his feet. And Pushkin thought, these were some of the favorites at His Majesty's Court. Consultants to the Emperor of all the Russias!

Father Photius looked down the length of the table with his mesmerizing eyes and roared.

"What's the matter with our famous poet? Does he deem himself above the grace of God?" He stumbled down the length of the table to Alexander Sergeievich and reached down with his hairy, ham-like hands and picked him up as if he were a baby, held him close and kissed him fully on the mouth, thrusting with his big fat tongue, as Alexander Sergeievich tried vainly to extricate himself. This holy hulk exuded an odor from his body that was overwhelming, like an over-used overflowing water closet in continual disrepair. His hot breath a cesspool of assorted stenches. His breath reminded Alexander Sergeievich of the smell of dead rats in the springtime who had starved or frozen to death during winter inside the walls of the ancient Pushkin house on German Street in Moscow, and of rotting food and age-old semen. His body was enveloped with the stench of death and decadence. Father Photius roared with laughter as Alexander Sergeievich kicked and pummeled, until Pushkin kicked him in the crotch.

The Holy one grunted. "Oh my, you are a naughty child." And threw Alexander Sergeievich back into the chair. "The Holy Virgin even loves Her infidels."

Father Photius went back to the head of the table. The music had reached a frenzied tempo now. He raised both hairy hands again. "Purify yourselves before the Holy Virgin. I am Her representative here on this sinful earth! I am man and woman, boy and girl and even little infants!"

The men and women began to disrobe as did Father Lev Gregorovich.

"I am the devil and the saint! I am the holy contradiction! No one reaches the Blessed Lady except through me!" His eyes were black coals ablaze.

They were fully naked now and dancing around as if they were possessed by demons.

"Come to me and be blessed! I have slept with the Virgin many nights!" he shouted. "Come to me and I will bless you!" Father Photius was naked now and as hairy as a blonde baboon. They gathered around him now, and he would grab one of them, man or woman, it did not seem to matter to the holy man. They danced till they were exhausted and fell onto the carpet where they lay amongst one another, and wriggled like a mass of snakes.

Alexander Sergeievich thought he must be asleep and had stumbled upon a nightmare, as he sat there with the smell of the holy monster all over him. In his nostrils, in his eyes, he could taste the terrible stench of garbage in his mouth and throat. And he felt the nausea building up again, filling his shoulders his throat, his mouth, his nose, his face, his eyes, and he vomited and vomited till he thought his dear guts were erupting. He wiped himself with a silken napkin and the embroidered tablecloth, then struggled to his feet and went unnoticed from the palace.

He awoke the following morning with Tatyana on his weary mind. With the evil smell of Father Photius still with him. He went into one of his habitual rages. In one of these rages, he completed his famous ODE TO FREEDOM. He had worked on it ever since his Tsarskoye Selo days. He remembered his days with the muzhiks, potato picking in the fields at the time of autumnal equinox. He looked at his hands to see if the dirt was still beneath his fingernails. He could smell the salty perspiration. His limbs remembered the great exhaustion.

I will sing of freedom
And scourge the evil that sits on the throne . . .
Shudder, pupils of blind fortune
Tyrants of the world;
But lend an ear, ye fallen slaves,
Gain courage and arise!
It was law, not nature, tyrants,
Put the crown upon your heads.

Perhaps Pushkin was so sick of Saint Petersburg, he wished to be banished from the scene, but nobody in their right mind wanted the salt mines of Siberia, or the bastille across the Neva River. It was not possible to get that disenchanted. Sometimes he would walk the floors of his two-room apartment all night long, the candles burning low. He went around like a mad man hell bent for his own extinction. Indeed, he acted as if he would challenge the Emperor Himself to a bloody duel, with the Heavenly Father as his divine second who would make all of the arrangements. His anger even frightened him. Deep inside of him he wished a confrontation with the one on High, His Most Imperial Majesty, the Emperor of all the Russias.

114

How else to explain his poem, even to himself, HURRAH! HE'S BACK IN RUSSIA AGAIN, in which our celebrated poet mocks the Emperor upon his triumphant return from Paris and satirizes the speech the Emperor had made in Poland promising liberty and justice to Poland and to Holy Russia! While everybody still sang the Czar's praises for his defeat of Napoleon—He was known throughout Europe as the Inspiration and Grand Architect of the Holy Alliance, Blessed Savior of the Civilized World—the incensed poet wrote of the child Jesus weeping bitterly for the nations of the earth. Marya tries to stop Jesus's wailing by threatening him with a visit from the Czar. He put words into the Emperor's mouth;

Know, O peoples of Russia,
What no one does not know;
I have ordered new uniforms
From Prussia and from Austria.
I am fat, well fed, in very good health . . .

Then standing lovingly and majestically over the cradle of the peasant woman Marya's baby, the Emperor promises that he will bestow upon his beloved Russia liberty, fraternity, equality and justice. Pushkin relished this taste of bitterness in his mouth, as he licked the tip of his quill and laughed angrily as he wrote:

At these words the baby wriggles
Vigorously in his cradle;
Can it be possible? Should I believe it?
Could it perhaps be true?
His mother tells him,
"Close your sweet eyes, little one.
For our good Czar
Has finished his fairy tale."

What decided things for the Czar was other than the mere motive of revenge. Alexander Sergeievich was the first "People's Poet" that Russia had ever produced. And he wrote in Russian! Not in French, as so many Russian writers had before him. The people read his verses! Students knew his poems by heart. Recited them with wild enthusiasm wherever they went. Workers who could read, read Pushkin. Czarist informers sent word to the Emperor of workers walking off the job after students read to them from Pushkin in Bukhara and Samarkand three thousand versts from Saint Petersburg, out there on the eastern desert amongst the brown Uzbeks.

His poem, THE VILLAGE, was the ultimate. Like his ODE TO FREEDOM, it was a poem he started while at the Lycée in Tsarskoye Selo. He finished it in his crowded two-room flat in Saint Petersburg, which he shared with Nikita Koslov. It was passed around from hand to hand and mouth to mouth. A romanticizing of country life. He waxed nostalgic for his great-grandfather's estate at Mikhailovskoye.

I love this meadowland with its fragrant haystacks
And bushes enlaced by singing rivulets.
Far off, two lakes spread out their blue expanses
Where the fisher's sail blinks white from time to time. . .

Suddenly, in that incommodious dimly-lighted two-room flat, he found he could not get his family out of his mind. He had seen them only once since he'd left home for Tsarskoye Selo. During his third year at the Lycée they had come up for a visit at Christmas time. They had genuinely enjoyed each other for the first few days, imbued as they all were with the Christmas spirit—eating, drinking, dancing, laughing. But then the violent argument with his father over serfdom and the monarchy. Of course, even afterwards there were the letters from his father exhorting him to patriotism and loyalty to His Imperial Majesty, reminding him always that, "You are an aristocrat! Never forget it!"

No matter, they were his family; so one day he took off by *telega* for his beloved Moscow. They were genuinely happy to see him. They put out the welcome mat, gave a party in his honor. The party was a huge success except that toward the end of it he got into an argument with one of his father's ennobled friends. He spent three days in Moscow with his family, then went back to Saint Petersburg. He realized that the less he saw of his mother and father, the better. As soon as he returned to Saint Petersburg, he went to work again on THE VILLAGE.

Remembering the days of youthful yore spent in the little village in the Pskov Province. Running, romping with the muzhik children, playing, carefree. Mikhailovskoye! The resurrected smell of pine sap and apple blossoms put a funny taste in his mouth, a crazy quiver in the pit of his stomach. And he wrote:

Chains of hills and patchwork fields,
A few flocks grazing at the sodden banks;
Farther off, smoking ovens and winged millet.
It all breathes labor and felicity.

As romantic as he was, his realism usually conquered his idealism and often got our poet into deep trouble. This wintry night he watched, dim-eyed and amazed, as if some unknown presence had come into his room and taken control of his poem, as his VILLAGE evolved itself into an attack against the *boyar* landlords and the institution of serfdom, the very foundation of the monarchy. It was a poem he had begun working on when he loved his lusty revolutionary baroness. He thought of the potato pickers around Tsarskoye Selo, and somehow it brought back memories of the serf friend of his young days, Piotra Ivanovich, and his brother, who'd lived near Grandma-ma Hannibal. He remembered Anton Ivanovich, the shepherd boy, and the mysteriously romantic steppe—Piotra Ivanovich's dark-eyed sister, Natalya Ivanovna, impregnated by the gentleman of the manor house. He also remembered Grandma-ma Hannibal and the day he had found that the entire family of Piotra Ivanovich and Anton Ivanovich had been sold away like drayhorses or any other beasts of burden. He remembered the terrible helpless expression on the face of the father, Ivan Ivanovich, the day he learned his Natalya would be taken to the manor house. He remembered, vividly, the potato pickers around Tsarskoye Selo. He fought against the softness in him that caused his eyes to begin to fill and the tears to spill upon his manuscript. And angrily he wrote:

Head down, docile under the pursuing lash,
The gaunt old serf struggles down the furrows
Of some implacable master,

And again and again remembering, anguishedly, happy faced, sorrow-eyed Natalya Ivanovna, he wrote:

Not daring to dream anymore, or hope for them:
His little girls growing up
To feed the lust of some vice-sodden old monster . . .

In Kharkov, more than a thousand versts away from Petersburg, ten men were arrested for subversive activities against the state. Pushkin's poems were found on every one of them. Shopkeepers, hustlers, whores, working men, working women. Alexander Pushkin was their poet.

Alexander Sergeievich himself was genuinely astonished at the impact the words of his brain had wrought on the Russian people. Sometimes it actually frightened him. Why couldn't he just write and have others just enjoy his writing?

Common soldiers in the garrisons knew his works. This young upstart, this ingrate who would bite the hand that fed him, must be stifled, squashed like a Russian cockroach.

The benevolent Czar felt especially offended. For he gave himself credit for giving the African vagabond an education, giving him a second chance at the Lycée, giving him a position as Secretary in the Ministry of Foreign Affairs. Siberia would cool the thankless African bastard off, or freeze him to his natural death. He sent for Count Miloradovich, the governor-general of Saint Petersburg. After a heated discussion with Czar Nicholas, the governor sent for Alexander Pushkin.

While the Imperial storm was gathering like a whirlwind around Pushkin's head, a member of the Secret Police approached Pushkin's valet on the street near their apartment and offered him fifty rubles to steal all of the poet's manuscripts and bring them to him for his scrutiny. He would be rendering a service to the Emperor, God and Motherland, in that order of importance. Nikita refused the bribes and threats and hurried to his master to alert him. Alexander Sergeievich hastily burned all of his revolutionary writings, some of which he had been working on since his days at the Lycée.

And now he stood leaning on the mantlepiece with tears in his eyes, as he stared at his own soul turned to thinnest ashes in the fireplace. At twenty years of age, he felt something deep deep inside of him dying at that dreadful moment. He thought, a flame had died within him that would never be rekindled.

Count Miloradovich lay sprawled on his green divan in his drawing room attired in a gold-embroidered Chinese dressing gown. He had sent for young Pushkin. He wanted the interview with this *enfant terrible*, this incorrigible sower-of-wild-oats, as he saw him, to be relaxed and informal. He was disposed this morning to be generous and paternal. He recalled the days of his youth when he had sown his own wild oats of revolutionary liberalism. Also, he disliked being rude with those on his own aristocratic level, men whom he had met at balls and parties and with whom he would be associated on a class and social basis. After all, they were both aristocrats.

When Alexander Sergeievich was shown in by a manservant, he made an immediate positive impression on the Count, who had expected a wild-eyed irascible young Ivan Ivanovich.

"Your Highness, I can't tell you how flattered I am that a gentleman of your eminence and busy schedule would take the time out to grant such an unworthy one as me an interview," Alexander Sergeievich said, as if *he himself* had requested an interview and had been granted one by the Count. "Your generosity, Sire, is incomparable." Our poet continued as if he was rendering a poetic rhapsody.

Count Miloradovich offered the young man some of his best cognac and a pipe to smoke and they drank to the Emperor's health. Alexander Sergeievich was effusive. "Your reputation as a humanist, Sire, is legend. You're one of the few men close to His Majesty who has never lost touch with the little people. Every single one of us adore you."

The good-natured Count knew he was being intentionally and expertly flattered, but he liked the musical sound of it. He smiled expansively. "We're all human beings, you know. Some more human than others, perhaps." His voice trailed off as if he had lost the train of his thoughts. He was an elegant gentleman, handsome and stately, dark intelligent eyes. Perhaps, not unknowingly, Pushkin had touched a sensitive spot, a spot where the good-hearted nobleman lived. For the Count fancied himself a humanitarian of first magnitude. He was an avid reader of the French humanists. He believed in a benevolent monarchy. He believed in social tolerance, within reason, that is, to be sure, of course. Everything in moderation.

After a few moments of chatting and laughing together like long lost comrades, suddenly Count Miloradovich turned to the question at hand. "I started to order your quarters searched for your inflammatory manuscripts, but we are the same, you and I, just different ages, different generations. We're both of us aristocrats and that must mean something in Holy Russia, or what is the use of anything?"

Alexander Sergeievich turned the comment over in his agile mind. Was the generous Count asking a question? Rhetorical? He answered, "What is the use of anything indeed, Sire?"

The good-natured Count stared at the young poet who had the entire Russian nobility in an uproar, even those who did not read. He could not understand it. Where did the aristocratic youth of today pick up all that revolutionary liberal rubbish? Though he knew that the Emperor was irritated by this Alexander Sergeievich Pushkin who was flooding Holy Russia with subversive unholy literature that many students knew by heart, he could not help feeling kindly disposed to this easy-going fellow. How could a good-natured, well-mannered chap like Alexander Pushkin actually be dangerous?

He said, "I decided instead of having your place searched, to ask you on your own honor to bring your papers in for my inspection. What do you say to that then?"

"It would be a waste of time, Your Excellency. I have already burned all of my manuscripts, but it's all written here," Pushkin replied, tapping the side of his forehead with his index finger. "And if Your Excellency wishes, and gives me pen and paper, I will write down everything I have composed, excepting that which is already published."

"Fair enough," the Count answered, and rang for his manservant to bring him pen and paper. The Count puffed on his long Oriental pipe, sending out aromas like the smell of burning apples, and smiled at the young vivacious poet with the generous lips and the dark blue animated eyes. "This is really chivalrous of you to go to all this trouble."

With Alexander Sergeievich's photographic memory it was really no trouble at all. He sat down and for several hours wrote furiously all of the poems, all of the prose and essays, parts of manuscripts he had not completed, some he'd never written before, as the Count looked on in pure amazement. Alexander Sergeievich forgot, conveniently, his most revolutionary material, but the Count didn't know the difference. When he stared at what Pushkin gave him, he knew he had much more before him than all the material the secret police had been able to steal and confiscate. The Count was pleased and told the poet, "You have behaved like a gentleman of your class, and we will forgive you the folly of your youth. We have all gone through these foolish stages."

Pushkin could not restrain a deep sigh. He thanked the Count, "Merci beaucoup!" pecked him briefly on his graying whiskers, "Dosvidanya," and took his leave without delay.

It had been a pleasant interview to all concerned, but the good Count wondered about his next interview as he dressed in his formal uniform with sword swinging at his side and decorations on his breast, and rang for his man to have his horse harnessed for his ride to the Imperial Palace. He was going to meet the God-like Emperor of all the Russias, and was worried already about his promise of forgiveness to young Pushkin. He knew Alexander Romanov to be a moody and vindictive man. Like Almighty God, the Emperor believed that vengeance belonged to him alone.

Meanwhile, the word had gone around that the Czar would reprimand Pushkin. Would it be Siberia this time? Would it be the terrible bastille known as the Peter and Paul Fortress? Was this the end of Alexander Pushkin's brief career? Old Karamzin, the Emperor's own historiographer, donned his uniform and decorations and went to the palace to plead the poet's cause, as did Zukovsky and Vyazemsky, all of whom claimed the impertinent poet as their wayward protege who was the hope of Russian literature and would one day come into his own and render service to the Crown and become the great pride of the Motherland. Would His Majesty please have patience? *Pajalsta!* It was a stage young people must go through, especially one of Pushkin's artistry and temperament and genius.

Now His Majesty listened agitatedly to Miloradovich, at one point rising from His Imperial seat and pacing back and forth before the flustered Count, who had given Pushkin assurances of Imperial clemency without consulting His Most Imperial Majesty. Everyone spoke on behalf of this irreverent Ivan Ivanovich. Even Herr Englehardt, the Lycée director, had come all the way from Tsarskoye Selo to speak for him a second time. What did all these impressive influential gentlemen see in this young African trouble-maker?

Then the moody Czar remembered General Insov, Inspector General of the Southern Colonies, who had sent him recent letters begging him to send some young officials to assist him. The Emperor said to Miloradovich, "I would love to send him to Siberia, as far away from here as possible. God knows he deserves it. But you have made him a promise, and I suppose I should support my Imperial officials. Though it displeases me that you would give him such assurances without my previous approval. See that it never happens again."

The Count wiped the perspiration from his forehead. "Never again, Your Majesty. You can rest assured."

The Emperor sighed. "Let us send him south to Insov in Ekaterinoslav. Cool his African temperament. Travel broadens the perspective of young people. Perhaps he will appreciate more fully the responsibilities of Empire."

When Pushkin heard the news, he was overjoyed. As far as he was concerned, he had been rewarded not punished. Instead of banishment, he had been liberated from the prison of decadent Saint Petersburg with its hypocritical society, its interminable orgiastic parties, its stupid chatter and idle gossip, its pretensions at intellectualism and liberalism. He was sick of it all and now he could do what he was born to do. He could write! He could be true to his talent and his muse!

He sat now in a tavern with his friend, Ivan Pushchin, telling him of his future plans away from sick Saint Petersburg. "I never felt I really belonged at these interminable balls and parties."

"But you do belong, Alexander Sergeievich. You *are* an aristocrat."

"You're damn right, I am!" Pushkin exploded. "My family's ennoblement goes back centuries before the Romanovs came to power. One of my ancestors rode with Alexander Nevsky, not to mention that my great-grandfather was an Ethiopian prince! Six Pushkins signed the charter declaring the elections of the Romanov to the Imperial throne. Two more affixed their marks, because they could neither read nor write." Would this ambivalence never cease? His great pride in the nobility of his ancestry, his contempt for the present crop of aristocrats?

Pushchin said, "Well, there you are—"

"But I despise this current breed of ennobled gentlemen, a bunch of pompous illiterate asses!" Alexander Sergeievich exclaimed, "I had already made up my mind to stay away from these parasites and their Imperial orgies. This move by Alexander Romanov helps me to carry out my resolution. I shall pray to the Holy Virgin to give Her blessing to the Imperial bastard."

Ivan Pushchin looked around to see if anyone was listening. He wished his friend would lower his voice.

Alexander Sergeievich stared at Pushchin now. He would miss his Lycée friend more than anybody or anything else in Saint Petersburg. He was relaxed with Pushchin now and drunk with wine and vodka and tremendous expectations. He effervesced. He felt unconquerable, invincible, excitedly creative. He related to Pushchin how he had outwitted Count Miloradovich.

Pushchin was astonished. "You mean you didn't write down all that you had burned? You deceived the kind-hearted Count?"

Pushkin stared at his friend, put a glass of vodka to his lips and took it away only after the glass had emptied.

"Do I look like an idiot to you?" He laughed harshly at his Lycée comrade.

"But you were dishonest. You—Pushkin—of all people! The Apostle of Truth! Lying to the authorities!"

"Don't get so excited, my beloved comrade. There are truths and there are truths. There are Imperial truths and there are gospel truths, and they are just about the same, mostly lies. But then there are the truths that liberate the people, which are different altogether." His deep dark blue eyes leaped with animation. He had never put it together in his own mind before. He articulated it now for his own clarification as much as for his admiring comrade. His voice hardened. "I do not owe the Imperial Court the people's truth. The only things I owe the court are damnation and exposure."

Ivan Pushchin stared at the heavily-mustached man seated in the booth across from them. He seemed too interested in their conversation. Ivan Pushchin shook his head in wonder at his great friend of Tsarskoye Selo days. It was a good thing Sasha Pushkin was going far far away from Saint Petersburg, away from the eyes and ears of the secret police. He was too impulsive and outspoken.

Ivan Pushchin marveled at his comrade, who at twenty years of age was riding the wave of an unheard-of popularity as a Russian writer. "You are absolutely incredible," he told the flamboyant poet, "admired by serfs and working men alike, literate and illiterate. Those who cannot read have your verses read to them. Can you imagine? There are men among the Imperial elite who love you, and even among the Emperor's own Horse Guards." He paused to catch his breath. "But of course, my dearest comrade, you have powerful enemies at the Imperial Court."

Pushkin's friends wished the three weeks would pass quickly. Not that they wanted to be rid of him, but they feared for him, for he seemed determined to dig his own grave before departing. He wrote like a demon anti-monarchist and anti-cleric epigrams and had them distributed gratis at the theatre under pseudonyms that fooled nobody as to the identity of the author. His style, the Russian idiom, the stark beauty of its simplicity, were Pushkin's signature.

His enemies circulated the rumor that he had been called to the Imperial Palace and thrashed naked like a common serf and criminal. That he pleaded like a miserable mouse, without pride or dignity. That finally he had kissed His Imperial Majesty's feet each in their turn. Crawled on all fours like a snake.

When the rumors reached Alexander Sergeievich he was livid. Gentle mannered Anton Delvig, had been visiting him at the time at his apartment. He told Ivan Pushchin that Alexander Sergeievich literally foamed at the mouth in his helpless rage. It was that feeling of utter impotence that frustrated and outraged the poet. He spoke to Delvig of actually challenging his Imperial Majesty Himself to a duel, which was like slapping God Almighty's face. In Delvig's presence he sat down and wrote the Emperor as obscene and insulting a letter as he could imagine. He was talked out of sending it to the palace by Delvig. Poor Delvig got on his knees and begged him.

From thought of actual suicide, Alexander Sergeievich went around for days plotting in his anguished impotence the assassination of highly placed officials in the Czarist Court, even thought of taking Emperor Alexander's life. He discussed his schemes with Pushchin.

His Lycée comrade pleaded with him. "No, Alexander Sergeievich, no! Put such ideas out of your mind, dear friend."

"Why not?" Pushkin demanded, staring at his best comrade as if he had been betrayed. Everybody was against him. Nobody loved him, not even Ivan Pushchin. He stared at his comrade and felt his aloneness more than ever. Why did he feel the need for change so deeply while others seemed content to wait forever for the revolution?

Pushchin told him, "Your schemes are scatter-brained and doomed to failure. It is your life that will be taken. Besides, what good would it do—to kill one tyrant just for another to take his place? Your own words, don't you remember? And Russia needs you. There's no one to take your place. Give me your word, old friend, you will not attempt these foolish ventures. I beg of you."

Pushkin gave his word to Pushchin.

Nevertheless, Pushkin openly displayed at the theatre a placard with a picture of a man who had assassinated the King of France, upon which he had written in bold letters: LET THIS BE A WARNING TO ALL MONARCHS.

Finally on May 6, the Day of the Ascension, in 1820, Alexander Sergeievich Pushkin took leave of Saint Petersburg.

PART FOUR

BANISHMENT

CHAPTER ONE

Technically and officially, Alexander Sergeievich was not imperially exiled or banished from His Majesty's Capital. He was still a governmental employee at the same seven hundred rubles per annum; his duties had simply been transferred to another part of the Foreign Service so that he might perform them in an environment more suitable to his temperament. The kindly Emperor at all times had Alexander Sergeievich's interest at heart, first and foremost. So the saying went at the Imperial Court and throughout the capital city.

All day long that first day out he traveled by clumsy awkward telega, seated behind the driver atop his luggage, a flat-topped, rectangular pasteboard trunk, and lying on a bed of vermined straw at night, his heart overflowing with the joy of leaving decadent Saint Petersburg. Nothing could dampen his spirit as he marveled at the vastness and the beauty of the Russian landscape. The endless blue translucent skies, the rage of changing colors of the mountain range, the savannah land, the wondrous Russian steppes. The vast expanse of time and space, of earth and land and sky. The smell of wood smoke in the early evenings, clean intoxicating fragrances of wide and open spaces so different from the city stench. This was Holy Russia, vast, endless and eternal.

The air out here is freer, purer. My muse will surely love me now! In contradiction to his euphoria, the travel by bumpy telega was arduous and exhausting. The telega afforded no seats for passengers. The roads, interchangeably, were bumpy, rocky, flooding, muddy and or dusty, depending on the moody heavens. Always the roads were hazardous, abounding as they were with brigands and ruthless highwaymen. The food was horrible in the cockroach-ridden roadside inns and posting stations. Most of the time Alexander Sergeievich preferred going hungry to risking death by food poisoning. Practically starved, he ultimately took his supper one night in a dimly-lighted roadside inn with flying cockroaches leaping about the table. He was kept busy knocking them off his bread and out of his plate. They were fonder of the cabbage soup than he was. The fourth day out he came down with the bloody flux.

What is happening to my joyous feelings?

Even before he had left Saint Petersburg, a storm kicked up over one of his lengthy poems, RUSLAN AND LUDMILA. It was a sophisticated fairy tale of Russian folklore, to be savored and enjoyed and laughed at and not to be taken seriously. In this poem, Alexander Sergeievich had tried his hand for the first time at the epic, or, more truthfully, the comic epic or the non-epic epic. It was a satire on Romanticism and specifically the ultra patriotic Russian epic that was the fashion of the times in Russian literature. It was a whimsical tale of ancient Kiev where the cultural history of Russia had its beginnings.

It came naturally with Alexander Sergeievich, disdainful as he was of Imperial pomp and circumstance. Sometimes it was a naughty poem fraught with sexual undertones. The moment the comic epic was published, the public took sides violently, pro and con.

Cries of "Atheism!" "Sedition!" Shouts of, "Patriotic genius!"

Sometimes he thought that surely the critics had read somebody else's poetry and had mistaken it for his.

As he had worked with RUSLAN AND LUDMILA, it had conjured up the memory of Piotra and Anton Ivanovich and the night with them in the isba with the old man, the shazitel and his bylina. He could hear the old man's haunting song. The tears began to fill his eyes.

His poem was probably the first of its genre in all of Holy Russia. It was a joke that Pushkin was sharing with his public, but almost no one appreciated it. Why didn't they have a good laugh and then leave it alone? Where is the Russian sense of humor? If the Russian psyche lacked a sense of humor, damn it, he would give it one.

The pompous critic of Saint Petersburg's *Neva Observer* decried the lack of taste of this talented poet who misused his talent in an open display of vulgarity, whereas, "the purpose of poetry is to magnify with praise the beautiful aspects of Russian life, extolling the heroic aspects of religion and virtue, for the glorification of His Majesty's government and empire. In this pretense of an epic poem, so-called talent is wasted on trivialities. Possibly we have misjudged and overrated this young upstart, Alexander Sergeievich Pushkin."

Goddamn! Pushkin thought. *Can't the Russian even laugh at himself!*

From other quarters he was attacked for having one of his characters engage in such an ordinary pastime as sneezing. "Who needs it?" the indignant journalist asserted. "What is so extraordinary about sneezing? Leave such obscenity out of poetry!"

Where did all the beauty go? I grow older like the saints and monks of olden times.

The critic of the magazine, *Vestnik Europi*, threw up his arms in disgust over a scene in RUSLAN AND LUDMILA. "Spare me such detailed descriptions and permit me to ask: Imagine a bewhiskered fellow dressed in a drab peasant greatcoat and bast sandals intruding into the club of Moscow nobility and shrieking at the top of his voice: 'Howdy, fellows!' Is it possible that they would look with admiration upon such a wag?" Pushkin threw the journal from the telega, shouting, "*Gavno!* (Shit!)"

Much of the literate public was not ready for the commonplace in their literature. They wanted to escape into the imagined lives of kings and queens and emperors and empresses and others of the upper classes. On the other hand, critic Merimee praised Pushkin's RUSLAN AND LUDMILA precisely on this point. "Enough has been written about kings and queens and emperors. Pushkin wants to give the commoner and the peasant his day in the literature, and hurray for him! Bravo!"

To hell with all critics!

The journey to his banishment was endless. It seemed long and hard and everlasting.

One of his friends and former mentors, Basil Zukovsky, recognized the poem as a highly successful burlesque of an epic poem Zukovsky himself had attempted. Upon the poem's publication, he sent Pushkin an autographed picture of himself upon which he inscribed: "To the victorious pupil from the vanquished master on that most important day when he completed RUSLAN AND LUDMILA, Good Friday, March 26, 1820."

Pushkin pretended to himself that he didn't care a kopek what the journals said about him. Nevertheless, he was more than grateful to his friend, Zukovsky.

Many many days later—it seemed centuries of time to the harassed bedraggled poet—he arrived at Ekaterinoslav.

Ekaterinoslav was just about as far away, southwardly, from Saint Petersburg as the Emperor could send this literary pain-in-the-arse without shipping him out of the tremendous reaches of the Empire. Pushkin's fortunes did not extend that far, nor did the Emperor's benevolence.

Ekaterinoslav was the rear end of the very last outpost of Russian civilization. It was a pretentious mudhole making a pitiful impersonation of a city. When Pushkin arrived he observed a single unpaved main street bordered by one-story wooden shacks. Bearded unbathed muzhiks, adorned in baggy trousers like outsized bloomers and wearing balloon-like blouses, led their straggly goats and horses down the muddy street stepping gingerly over steaming piles of horse manure. Some muzhiks were not so careful or fastidious. On an arid day, peasant women gathered the dried up dung for use as fuel to keep their houses warm in winter.

A two-story house, almost non-existent, was looked upon in awe as a thing of palatial elegance. There were three in the village, and there was, of course, the

Potemkin Palace, constructed by the famous foreign advisor to, and favorite male concubine of Great Catherine the Second.

Actually, as any citizen of Ekaterinoslav would tell you proudly, it was a town brought into existence by the great Potemkin and named for his great Imperial and Majestic mistress. There was this cathedral constructed by him, the founding ceremonies of which were attended by Great Catherine Herself, at which time Potemkin boasted that this "humble edifice will, in time, be larger and more bountiful than the Vatican and Rome." The citizenry awaited patiently the time Potemkin had predicted. They boasted that the day would come!

One quick look around this mud puddle of a city and Alexander Sergeievich imagined he finally understood the meaning of the word godforsaken, that is, if the Holy Virgin's boy child ever knew Ekaterinoslav existed.

He dutifully reported to General Insov, Inspector General of the Southern Colonies. The General was an elegant middle-aged man, vague and absent-minded looking. An oversized head and pleasant face were set in a frame of black heavy hair sprinkled with gray. He wore a neatly trimmed mustache and a handsome vandyke beard. They took an immediate liking to each other. Pushkin's lonely heart lay half awake, catnapping on his frayed lapel, and he was vulnerable, susceptible, ready to love anyone who offered warmth and love to him. General Insov was instantly attracted to this brash young man with a parental affection, a thing Pushkin had always vainly ached for from his own father and mother. An inveterate bachelor, Insov looked upon Pushkin as the son he never had. General Insov was the father Pushkin always longed for. A sensitive and intelligent man. Insov, seeing that the poet was troubled in mind and not enjoying the best of health, gave him practically no work at all to do. He imagined the lad needed rest and relaxation and time to think things over and get together with himself.

And there was nothing for Alexander Sergeievich to do in Ekaterinoslav. No theatre, no opera, no soirees, not anything. There was one down-in-the-mouth pathetic alibi for a hotel crawling with cockroaches, fleas and thirsty bedbugs. Each day as the sun went down, the sleepy-headed town pulled in its non-existent sidewalks and bedded down for the night along with the chickens and goats who walked the street like human beings.

Alexander Sergeievich Pushkin was the greatest excitement to hit the town since it had been colonized and established several decades back. He strolled through the village with his heavy stick and high hat, tight trousers, frock coat, and everybody turned and stared at him like he was something escaped from the circus. Alexander Pushkin! The infamous poet! With the swarthy complexion and the African countenance. Was this the way people looked and walked and dressed in fabulous Saint Petersburg?

The thing that Alexander Sergeievich thought he would never miss was the false sophistication of the capital city, the eternal orgies, the corruption, the fraudulent values, the literary movements that were hardly literary; the theatre where the upper classes went, not because they appreciated drama, or ballet, or opera, but to be seen and to show off the new style of dress and coiffeur, to hear the latest gossip. He had thought he wanted a place like this in which he now found himself, far removed from so-called civilization. But the change had been too sudden and too drastic. Probably had it been more gradual, it might have been different for him. But after the frantic noisy pace of Saint Petersburg, the hushed pace of this frontier village became a deafening roar inside his head. In a couple of weeks he was bored into a nervous wreck. Each morning he went to the wide Dnieper River, recently unfrozen, and went naked for an icy swim. Some days he went boating, always alone.

The peasants of the town made up stories about him. They said he wore voile trousers you could see through, prancing back and forth in His Excellency, the Inspector General's drawing room. You could see everything there was to see! The ladies were deliciously horrified. He was overnight a scandal. He began to long for city life and all of its vast corruption. He had rented a horrible vermin-infested shack to live in. He lived with rats and roaches who refused to share the rent.

Completely demoralized, Alexander Sergeievich kept to himself. Tried desperately to escape into his poetry, create a world for himself to live in, but his muse forsook him. He sat for hours in a quiet maddening meditation. He thought about the tales his grandmother used to tell him about his great-grandfather. He conjured up the dreams he'd dreamed of the land called Africa. Sometimes he sang, sometimes he talked loudly to himself.

When nothing at all worked to arouse his sleeping muse, he would sit half naked in a corner of his room and shoot grapeshot pellets at targets on the wall. Sometimes the pellets were of bread or wax. He was an expert marksman, could hit a rose dead center from forty feet away. His walls and ceilings were pock-marked from target practice. Sometimes he used real bullets and picked off rats as they came boldly from their lodging places.

One day as he sat half naked in his shack drinking cheap wine and trying to conjure up his cantankerous muse, someone knocked upon his door. He went to the door and standing there before him were two young men from the nearby university, looking scared to death. One with large thick glasses perched on his long thin nose, precariously.

"Well?" Pushkin said, with obvious irritation.

The bespectacled member of the delegation said nervously, "We have come to see Alexander Pushkin—"

What did they think he was—something on display for their amusement, a circus performer, perhaps? Alexander Sergeievich said, "Well, now that you have seen him, good-bye!" He closed the door in their startled faces, and felt badly for his rudeness afterwards.

After they left, he went for his daily swim in the icy thawing Dnieper. The next day he came down with fever. There was one doctor in the town and he was more expert at trimming hair and bleeding cows and horses than he was with curing human beings. He was a barber and a veterinarian, and in this town, cows and goats and horses were more important than people. Animals meant kopeks and rubles, a meager commodity in these parts.

Two carriages came to town the next day. The occupants were obviously of the wealthy aristocracy, and they were very well appointed. It was the family of General Raevsky, a legendary hero of the Napoleonic War. His son, Nicholai a member of the Hussar Horse Guards, had lived in Tsarskoye Selo, when Alexander Sergeievich was at the Lycée. They had been good hell-raising comrades. The Raevskys had heard of the famous poet's transfer to the South and had inquired of his whereabouts when they reached the city. They found him in his miserable lodgings delirious with fever. They searched the town over and dragged the aging veterinarian out of his bed at midnight in his nightgown and nightcap, grumbling to himself, but to the Raevskys it was, "Yes, Your Excellencies . . . No trouble at all, your Magnificences." To himself he mumbled as he stumbled into his clothes, the goddamn haughty bastards think the world begins and ends with them!

The old bewhiskered horse doctor with the thick eyeglasses went with them to this horrible rat-infested hovel where the crazy infamous poet was raving out of his head. Dutifully he examined him as the Raevskys stood around and anxiously urged him on. Conscientiously he did bleed the ragged-arse aristocrat with Spanish flies and leeches, as was the custom in those days.

Custom was custom, but Alexander Sergeievich got no better. His delirium continued, worsened by the hour. Nicholai Raevsky went to see Inspector General Insov and asked permission to take the poet with them when he was able to be moved. They were on their way to the mineral health springs in the Caucasus Mountains. Insov saw no reason to refuse the request, and when his fever finally abated, they took Alexander Sergeievich along with them.

The Raevskys traveled in the style they could afford in two well-appointed fur-lined *barouches*, one open and one closed; the legendary father, General Raevsky, with nineteen-year-old Nicholai and two lovely daughters, fourteen and fifteen. They had taken Pushkin up in their arms and put him in the open carriage with Nicholai, the rest of them crowding in the other carriage with the father. But in the evening when the wind began to blow across the wide and open steppes, and the poet began to shiver as if he was having a convulsion, they packed him into the closed and ermine-lined barouche.

All day long and through the night they moved across the broad grassy plains, with the tall stalks of barley and maize and flax dancing a wild mazurka as the soft winds blew their hot breaths on them, yellow, brown, green and gleaming in the sunlight, dark and eerie in the golden moonlight, the great wide legendary steppes, verst after endless verst of rippling grain undulating from the river all the way to the hills and back. But now, as day broke dripping blood, streaking across the eastern skies, they were in among the foothills of the magnificent Caucasus which lorded over everything and everybody. Nothing could escape its awe-inspiring beauty and majesty. Further and further in among the lesser ranges, Alexander Sergeievich knew a feeling he had never experienced before. He forgot about his illness. He had a feeling he was being drawn by a magnetic power from which he would never escape or ever want to escape. Off into the distance stood the highest mountain range in Europe. His excited mind began to write. Every round went higher and higher into the enveloping golden mist of the morning. You could wash your face in the wetness of it. Away off to the right lay a wide expanse of purplish plateau—the whole damned world is one bad poem, he thought to himself, but you can make it beautiful, even in its ugliness. These mountains possessed a beauty that was grandiose and everlasting. He could see the road like a skinny serpentine trail outlined up against the bright and blazing beige of the mountain, a magnificent piece of natural sculpture. In his mind he wrote a poem to all this feral and spontaneous majesty. A few hours later he would be over there looking down at the place where they were at this moment. The excitement of it all made his heart beat up against his chest as if it would break out of its prison. Danger would always affect him like this. Danger was possessed of a terrible beauty. It fiercely fascinated him. And the danger was beginning. It was real. It was not a poem he had imagined. There were men and women who lived in caves among these ranges whom the Russians had not yet pacified. Wild men, yet uncivilized, who without warning, would come howling out of the hills and caves like savage Indians of the far far farthest West, armed with bows and arrows and machetes, to raid and kill and pillage, seize arms and ammunition and noblemen for ransom.

The Raevsky entourage was escorted front and back by sixty mounted Cossacks armed for action, dragging a huge cannon to the rear of them. The possibilities of an attack made Alexander Sergeievich's imagination run amuck. He hoped secretly for the Circassians to attack the Raevsky party. He worshiped danger and excitement. The Circassians were reputed to be the most beautiful white men in the world, the prototype of the Caucasian race. There were other dangers too. The narrow roadway snaked along the mountainside between a great wall and a precipice with no parapets or railguards at its edges. He felt that one false move by the horses and the carriages would plummet off into a great white void and drop forever off the side of the world. He would fly around the earth for an eternity. There was the deep and awesome feeling of infinity amongst these mighty ranges of the Caucasus.

Alexander Sergeievich said to pretty Marya Raevsky, "In the distance there is Mount Ararat where Noah and his ark were stranded thousands of years ago and the world had its rebirth. And over there is where Zeus chained the great freedom-loving Prometheus." Nicholai Raevsky's young sister laughed with him, adoringly.

They reached a point where Asia merged back into Europe, and Pushkin imagined the two continents engaged in mortal combat all amongst these mountains for world imperial supremacy, and neither of them victorious. The mountains gurgled gleefully with underground streams of boiling water. It was like champagne bubbling over. The ranges trembled constantly with half asleep volcanoes. It was an experience he would never forget. Especially would he remember the lovely fifteen-year-old Marya Raevsky. And being a romantic poet he naturally fell immediately in love with her. At least, that is what he told himself. And why not? Marya reasoned. Were not poets supposed to fall in love with lovely young things like herself? Darkly beautiful Marya with the sparkling eyes large and wide and filled up with the greatest expectations from this life, her own dear life. Mischievous Marya. Bubbling joyously over on the brimming brink of womanhood. Her breasts and body were not yet fully formed, but there was plenty of evidence that they were on their way. And they would be ample and womanly.

The coaches made a turn around the mountains, and suddenly there was the open sea before them lapping its frothy salty tongue at the edge of Russia. Marya cried out in pure ecstasy at the beauty of it, and she called upon the driver to stop, and leaped gaily from the carriage and ran toward the edge of the sea pulling off her shoes as she ran, uttering little whoops of joy. Alexander Sergeievich watched as she waded out into the water's edge, her dress lifted almost above her knees; he glimpsed a gleaming flash of ivory legs and calves, as the waves came in and kissed her tiny feet, and went out again and then came back for other kisses.

Alexander Sergeievich was moved to poetic ecstasy. That night he conjured up the spectacle again, and he wrote:

> . . . and I envied the lucky waves
> And longed like them
> To lap your feet with eager lips.

Late one evening, as blackness hovered in the mountains like heavy funeral drapes, and as the Raevskys slept the sleep of death, drowsed by the sleepyheaded rareness of the mountain air, Alexander Sergeievich left his sleeping bag and sneaked away into the hills with a burning torch to light his way. Afterwards, when he looked back at his escapade, he wondered if he had dreamed the whole thing. And if not, then surely he must have been out of his mind, still in a state of delirium. Sometimes dreams and so-called reality were all the same to him. Perhaps it was a crazy poem he'd written. After several hours of fumbling around the rugged, ragged cliffs, slipping and sliding, almost falling off the side of the earth, he stumbled into a ravine and emerged into a Circassian camp. When he recapitulated the experience, dreamed or real, he remembered scantily-clothed men and women seated around an open fire. These men and women spoke in strange un-Russian tongues. He walked toward them, his face aglow, his arms outstretched as if he would embrace them all. "Tovarischi!" he shouted to them, joyously. These wild folk chained our hero to a tree. They disrobed our enraptured poet and examined him from head to feet, his mouth, his tonsils and his teeth and tongue, his chest, his loins, his genitals. Alexander Sergeievich wondered why he wasn't frightened. Why did he stand there grinning like a mindless idiot?

Morning came rosy-pink and apple-cheeked into the mountains, and they tried vainly to make conversation with him. The beautiful, nearly-naked women came and stared and snickered at him in all his shameful nakedness, their breasts bare and gleamingly tanned by the very nearness of the sun. They wore nothing save a cloth no larger than a small fig leaf. It was like an infant's breechcloth, and it never covered entirely the blonde silken curls of their innocent pubescence. They tried to talk with him and he answered them as best he could. The tall handsome men with eyes as blue as the Tauric sky above them came again and again and talked to him, and he knew somehow they were asking questions of him.

He should have feared for his life, but he was too excited to be frightened. "No! No! No!" he shouted. "I am not a spy! I come as a friend. I'm ashamed of the way my people have treated you!" Then he told them, desperately, "But they're not my people anyway. I'm an African!"

Despite their golden skins, they marveled at his olive darkness. They tried to rub it off. One of the women rubbed him till his skin was raw. She could not keep her gentle hands away from his wooly head. She was flaxen-blonde and smiling with strong white teeth and wide, wild blue eyes that always seemed astonished. Her newly nubile breasts were golden-toned and pointed toward him in invitation.

They fed him wild delicious grapes and goat meat, hand-fed him till he felt filled up to above his eyes. The hetman of the tribe came and examined Pushkin's clothing time and again. Alexander Sergeievich finally imagined that the hetman was trying to evaluate his worth in terms of ransom.

They bathed every morning in a warm waterfall that flowed upwards through the mountain, defying the laws of gravity. The girl whom he decided to call "Marya" could not keep her eyes or hands away from him. On the second morning she took him with her to the falls and they bathed together, took him back to camp and they chained him to the tree again.

This time they chained him so he could sit himself down on the sun-cooked earth. She came and squatted nearby as she filled the almost weightless air with questions. Despite the language difficulty between them, with muffled words and signs of hands and sighs and grunts, they somehow made communication.

"You not Russian?"

His memory of the conversation was, at best vague.

"Not exactly . . . "

"Exactly?" She was rocking back and forth.

"I'm a Russian with an African ancestor. Ancestor," he repeated. Her breasts were golden-brown and burnished as if they had been polished.

"What is African?" Her lips were full, her teeth gleamingly white and even. Her thighs were smooth and satiny, and the fringes of the curly tufts of her pubescence shone like silken threads around the edges of her breechcloth.

"My great-grandfather came from a land far away called Africa. The people in his land are black."

134

"*Black?*" *she questioned. She touched him and smiled and talked with her hands and mouth and eyes. "You my friend?" she asked him. "How you my friend? Russians do not like Circassians. Circassians do not care for Russians. I love you but I cannot like you. You too much Russian even though grandfather come from far off land called Africa.*"

He told her that he understood, and he spoke to her of revolution.

"*What is revolution?*" *she asked.*

He answered, "Revolution means to change everything, overthrow the rulers, make all men and women free, Russians and Circassians. Make all men and women everywhere sisters and brothers."

"*I like revolution!*" *she said excitedly, rocking back and forth, her gleaming thighs the color of the bright beige of the earth they sat on.*

The next morning, as the sun exploded, splashing its warmth and light all over the mountains, she came to him and kissed his body . And when they went to the falls for a warm bath, he took her in his arms and kissed her, lingeringly. They held each other warmly and trembled in each other's arms. When they returned to camp, she took him by the hand to the hetman and she spoke to him excitedly of love and change and revolution, and Alexander Sergeievich understood then that his Marya was the hetman's daughter. The hetman turned to him and took him in his muscled arms and embraced him, almost crushing him in two. He kissed the astonished Pushkin animatedly. And the poet finally understood that he had either gotten married or was about to be. They did not chain him to the tree that day. He was free, in a manner of speaking. They celebrated with him his good fortune. They sang, they danced, they ate the sharp tangy meat of the mountain goat, drank the strongest whiskey he had ever swallowed. It set a fire in his throat and belly. Everybody hugged and kissed him. Everybody danced with him. Everybody marveled at the texture of his skin, pounded him on his back. Drinking, eating, reveling till he felt filled up to the top of his head. His neck, his face, his eyes, his ears were entirely sated. It was only then that he regretfully remembered his tried and trusted friends, the Raevskys. They would be looking all over the mountains for him. The hetman broke into his thoughts, pounding him on the back and embracing him again—he was sure he had a fractured backbone. It took him all day long that day to persuade the chief that he must leave them and Marya whom he truly loved. The hetman raged with anger, seized Pushkin by the neck and lifted him off the ground threatening to hack his head off with a mean machete. But Alexander Sergeievich pleaded and gestured and talked his way out of it. And that night a couple of men led him back to the Raevsky camp.

The Raevskys found him the next morning asleep in his sleeping bag and darker than he'd ever been. They ranted and raved at him.

"Where in the devil have you been?" young Nicholai demanded.

"I was captured by the Circassians," Alexander Sergeievich answered.

"Captured by the Circassians?" the general repeated skeptically. "Why you?"

135

"I could never find the answer to that one," Alexander Sergeievich stated. "We had a slight language difficulty. They chained me to a tree, but last night I escaped and made my way back to camp. Several times I almost fell off the side of the mountain."

Marya gasped at the horror of the thought of Pushkin falling off a stupid mountain. Encouraged, he began to make fanciful stories about his capture and escape. The Raevskys were so taken in by his fancies they forgot their anger toward him. He came out of the escape a legendary hero.

They continued on their journey through the mighty Caucasus. When they reached the mineral spa, they joined up with the older brother, Alexander Raevsky. He was handsome and demonic of nature, a self-styled philosopher, nihilistic in the extreme, with yellowish skin and eyes like a venomous snake. He, like many of the literate youth of Europe, was under the heavy influence of Lord George Gordon Byron, a jaded poetic renegade from the British upper classes. Nothing at all was worth the effort. There was no cause worth fighting for. Alexander Raevsky imagined himself the *Childe Harold* of Imperial Russia. *Sophistication* was the ship. All else was the open sea.

After his own jaded experiences in Saint Petersburg, Alexander Sergeievich was ready for Alexander Raevsky's "analytical" mind and his studied cynicism. The two would sit for hours, Pushkin seemingly mesmerized and all ears as he listened to Alexander Raevsky analyze society into oblivion and worthlessness, including love, marriage, nobility, women, family, motherhood, morality, convention, evolution, revolution. Nothing from nothing left positively nothing. Civilization stank to Heavens, except that there was no such place as Heaven. And bravo! as far as Alexander Sergeievich was concerned. And then came Pushkin's introduction to the actual writings of Lord George Gordon Byron. The impressionable poet dove in head first and splashed about. *Childe Harold, Bepoe, Don Juan.* He digested everything.

But Lord Byron and Alexander Raevsky were not the only things that held the poet's raptured attention. He was aware of the two lovely Raevsky damsels, especially Marya of the raven hair and the gypsy eyes, the mischievous mouth and the darkly beautiful countenance and the tiny feet that the sea had kissed.

They lived in tents situated beside the springs that were all over the place like wild mushrooms. Hot springs, warm springs, ice-cold springs. Good for every ailment man and woman could get themselves afflicted with. Rheumatism, consumption, madness, flat feet, stomach trouble, bad breath, flux, dysentery, aneurysm, floating tumors, and so on. Pushkin spent most of his time in one or the other of the many springs. He took a new lease on his life.

Leaving the springs they journeyed to Gurzuf where Alexander Sergeievich lived with the Raevsky family in a palatial mansion, a two-story villa overlooking the sea. He spent many hours in the Raevsky library with books by André Chenier and Lord Byron. One of the older sisters, Katerina, who was already there, helped him to decipher much of Byron. They were all happy to have this famous poet in their midst and the feeling was certainly mutual. He had never known the warmth of family life, and he luxuriated in the midst of it. And fell in love with all the girls. Reading, discussing, eating all the luscious grapes in sight, wallowing in feminine aromas and affections, the sounds and rustle of skirts and petticoats. It was a time in his young life he would always cherish and remember. He loved all of the sisters, but it was little Marya of the dark eyes and tiny feet and lapping sea waves who won his susceptible heart of hearts. In all her youthful wisdom and precocity, she found it difficult to take our poet seriously.

She said of Alexander Sergeievich later: "As a poet, he felt obligated to fall in love with every pretty girl he met. But he was really in love with the idea of being in love. His only mistress was his muse."

During his stay in the Caucasus, he was also soaking up experiences for his poetic muse. He did very little actual writing. He was too busy drinking in everything around him—wine, books, women, mountains, wild grape orchards, shrieking mountain eagles in their great flights toward the heavens. And one day he would take his goose quilled pen in hand and resurrect it for posterity.

Katerina spoke perfect Italian. Pushkin came to her one day and asked her to teach him. She was a tall slim majestic young woman, and she was self-assured, with light blue eyes and a sense of humor lurking in the corners of her skimpy mouth.

"I'd love to, Alexander Sergeievich, but you will not be here long enough."

He hung around her day and night, talking, reading, asking questions. He concentrated totally. Inside of three weeks he spoke the language fluently. He made jokes in Italian. She was awesomely amazed at the power of his concentration.

Every other day or so, Alexander Sergeievich would come up to Marya and ask her, "Did I dream that Circassian experience? Did it really happen?"

One day she stared at him, as they stood together on a steep cliff overlooking the sea. They could hear the monotonous sound of the sea waves washing against the mountainside. "And do I sleep with you and share your dreams then? How do I know where you were those days we lost you in the mountains. Maybe you were out of your mind. Perhaps you still are." He could hear the shrill cry of the mountain eagle. Marya stared at him again and saw his dear face flushing with embarrassment. His darkening dark eyes were so dear to her. She turned and ran away from him.

He watched her fading in the distance. He turned and stood there for a seemingly endless moment staring far across the sea at the rugged cliffs across the great gorge. He knew his aloneness more sharply than ever now, dwarfed as he felt by the vastness of the earth and sea and sky around, below and up above him. He looked down into the deep and endless gorge and his head knew a sudden dizziness. All the world was a blinding beige. He backed away from the edge of the cliff and stared across the way again, and watched a tiny speck of a bird take to its wings. Absently he watched it as it soared higher and higher. He wondered at what he imagined to be its unutterable loneliness up there in an infinite sky. The bird turned in the sky-blue heavens and began to loom larger and larger as it winged its way toward his side of the gorge and sea. Pushkin stood there mesmerized, as the bird came closer and closer and grew even larger. He could hear the flapping of its great wings now. A quivering sensation moved swiftly across his back from shoulder to shoulder. He wanted to move out of the path of this giant mountain eagle's flight, but he was transfixed by a tremendous fear and great amazement. The fear was momentary. The amazement lingered. He thought surely the great bird would alight on the cliff where he himself stood. Perhaps he was the great one's target. But the magnificent bird winged its way swiftly past him, leaving a gust of wind in his path that almost blew our poet out into the great beige gorge, and came to earth on a cliff close by. It turned its golden-brown head toward Alexander Sergeievich and fixed its beady eyes upon him. Alexander Sergeievich shivered. The great king of fowls stared at the little man disdainfully. They gave each other stare after stare. Then it turned and flew away again. Pushkin watched it enviously. If he could only fly like mountain eagles!

Alexander Sergeievich stood there for an eternity of time, it seemed, entranced by the flight of the regal bird soaring majestically through immeasurable space, and he thought about himself, tied down as it were, to time and space on this uncommodious earth. He remembered Tsarskoye Selo and the potato pickers, muzhik serfs shackled forever, tied irretrievably to the soil and sweat and tears and dirt and unrewarding toil. He could see them even as he watched the great bird swooping earthward one moment and soaring toward the heavens moments later, see them knee-deep in the potato furrows, driven like insensible beasts of burden. If they could only fly like this majestic bird. If Piotra Ivanovich, his childhood comrade, and his sister Natalya Ivanovna could fly. The tears began to fill his eyes at the beauty of so much plumaged elegance in full flight.

But now things were coming to an end, his holiday was over, and the next morning he would have to set out along with Nicholai for Kishinev in Bessarabia where General Insov and the headquarters for a branch of the Southern Colonies had been transferred from Ekaterinoslav.

The night before he was to go he opened up his heart to Marya. He loved her and her alone. He could not live without her, he fervently declared. A smile trembled on her ripening lips. She was genuinely moved by these professions of undying love, but she remembered he was Alexander Pushkin, the incorrigibly romantic poet. "You love all the pretty women in the world, Alexander Sergeievich." She wished she could believe that he loved her and her alone.

"No, Marya, you! You! Only you and always and forever you!"

She laughed. "Why then were you cooing like a sickly dove last night beneath my sister's window?"

"You had been acting so cool toward me, sweet lady. So in my crazy desperation I thought to make you jealous. Please tell me that I succeeded."

Her dark eyes, usually full of mischief, now overflowed with tears. She kissed him on the cheek. "Poor dear Alexander Sergeievich," she said. "I do love you darling, Sasha, like I love my own brothers. Perhaps I love you even more deeply. I love you for yourself, I love you for the beauty of your soul and spirit, I love you, I love you, I love you for your poetry, for your revolutionary genius. There is no person on this earth whom I regard more deeply. I shall always love and revere you. But, as for the other kind of love, there is another fate for me."

Fate! Fate! he thought. Fate! Fate! God-and-the-Emperor's will. Damn fate! Damn the Emperor! There was simply nothing for it!

This time she kissed him warmly on his sensuous lips. And she turned and left him as she ran sobbing toward the mansion.

Later, and far into the night, they sat alone underneath a tree and they talked seriously of love and change and revolution. They swore to one another that whatever happened, whatever fate held in store for them, conjugal and otherwise, they would always use their minds, their skills and energies for change and revolution.

CHAPTER TWO

From Gurzuf it was back through a part of the Caucasus with Nicholai Raevsky, most of the time beneath the deep blue sky along the Tauric coast. There was the terrifying experience of crossing a deep and gaping gorge along a narrow shelf of earth with a five-thousand foot drop on each side and no parapets on either. After that, it was going straight up-mountain at an angle of ninety degrees holding onto their Tartar horses by the tail, a thing that brought them vast amusement only after the ordeal had ended. Way up in the Caucasus they visited the Saint George Monastery with its long steep steps reaching down to the sea. They stared in wonder at the legendary Temple of Diana as it lay in solitary ruins. They went to the fabled Fountain of Bakshisarai, a rusty leaky reminder of its prior days of splendor. They walked around the empty sunbaked palaces. Tall, vast, blindingly beige, deserted, awe-inspiring. They gazed in solemn reverence at the eerie monument of the mythical lovelorn Khan. Alexander Sergeievich had taken ill again but dragged himself along with Nicholai to see the great Khan's harem and his cemetery. They wandered through hundreds of rooms in the palatial harem, vacant now, except for startled lizards who scampered underfoot.

It was in September of 1820 when Pushkin arrived at Kishinev in Moldavia, a Bessarabian province. It was even closer to the border than Ekaterinoslav. A dumpy frontier city. Pushkin observed from atop his Tartar horse that it was an unlikely concoction, a dab of Greek, one part Rumanian, one part Jew and a large general dash of Tartar sauce thrown in for good measure. Greeks were streaming into the muddy down-at-the-heel Bessarabian metropolis in escape from Turkish persecution. Kishinev was larger than Ekaterinoslav. Added to the horses and goats impolitely using the narrow streets for an outhouse were the ungainly camels defecating all over everything and grunting and belching and polluting the air with the sound and smell of camel farts. Most of the streets were so narrow, if you stood in the middle and yawned and stretched, you would touch the one-story building on both sides and more than likely break your knuckles. Homeless urchins sat in the streets picking lice off their scabby bodies.

Alexander Sergeievich was kopekless most of the time. He was still on the government payroll to the miserable tune of seven hundred rubles per year, a pittance which he usually spent at the gambling tables before it arrived. Sometimes he felt the government, like the rest of his friends, had forgotten he existed. His father wrote him pious letters extolling His Majesty the Divine Emperor for his generosity and understanding, and telling Sasha how grateful he should be, wishing upon him the blessings of the Heavenly Father Up Above.

"Ponder over your childish sinful ways and ask Almighty God His forgiveness as the Emperor himself has forgiven you." But he never included a single copper kopek in the envelope. If only once he'd said, "We love you." But his father never did.

With camels groaning, belching and breaking wind outside his window, along with the Emperor's spies, Alexander Sergeievich drove himself into his work. Letters from his father made him feel his aloneness more acutely than ever, brought him to the verge of tears. He told himself he must not go mad. He was totally submerged in a melancholy mood. No matter, he must not go mad. He looked around desperately for something to laugh about, to raise his sunken spirits. His mother never wrote to him. She was a woman who never wrote letters to anyone. He tried vainly to seduce his fickle muse. He moved frantically toward humor as a saving grace, an act of simple desperation, pure and unadulterated.

He started a poem about the Annunciation and the Immaculate Conception, in which he depicted the Archangel, Gabriel, as God's procurer sent by Him to earth to speak with Mary on behalf of the Almighty. It was an act of recklessness fraught with unimaginable danger. Now, when Gabriel comes down and sees how lovely Mary is, he conveniently forgets his Heavenly mission. After fighting off Satan who has already seduced the Holy Virgin, he makes love to Mary, as does finally God Himself in the form of a dove. Thus the Blessed Virgin has carnal knowledge with all three of them, one after the other. And then she tells her husband the fanciful story about the Annunciation and the Immaculate Conception, which Joseph is gullible enough to believe. Thus Joseph becomes the most infamous cuckold the world has ever known. When he wrote the poem THE GABRILIAD, it became so real to him, he actually believed that this was how it really happened.

Alexander Sergeievich broke into a terrifying perspiration when he thought about the consequences should the poem fall into Imperial hands. Chills danced across his shoulders. He enjoyed the writing all the more, spiked as it was with danger for him. For to mock the Immaculate Conception, to poke fun at the Blessed Virgin was tantamount to advocating the overthrow of the Monarchy, like casting aspersions on the chastity of a member of the Imperial family.

141

He walked the floor and wrote his poem aloud, listened to its rhythm, changing a "the" or an "a" or an adjective or verb or noun when he heard the tempo violated. Clarity and rhythms were virtues to this poet, and he listened carefully to himself read aloud, his mind on sharp alert for fraud in any idiom or nuance. Our poet worshiped at the altar of Truth and Authenticity. He despised all that was fraudulent. In his poem, God appears to Mary in a dream.

He is surrounded by His Heavenly entourage. The Great Lord speaks to her:

"Most beautiful of our dear earthly daughters,
Of Israel the youthful hope and joy!
I summon thee, aflame with burning love,
To share my glory. Harken to the call.
Make ready for a fate not yet revealed,
The bridegroom comes, draws near unto His slave."

As Mary's dream fades, one of God's couriers, Archangel Gabriel remains, tall and handsome.

She wished indeed to love the king of heaven
The words he spoke were pleasing to her ear,
And filled her with humility and awe—
But somehow Gabriel took her fancy more.
Thus the slim figure of some adjutant
Finds favor, maybe, with the general's wife . . .

Meanwhile up in Heaven, the Creator, frustrated, agitated—

And loudly sang: Mary I love, I love,
My immortality means nothing now.
Where are my wings? To Mary I will fly
And on her beauteous breast I will repose!
He summoned his favorite Gabriel
And explained to him his love in prose.

Gabriel listened to his Master, and

Reluctantly became the faithful
Of heaven's king—on earthly terms a pimp.

But Satan gets there before the handsome angel, Gabriel. He appears first as a serpent and comes upon dear lonely Mary in her garden. Then before her eyes he transforms into a handsome young man.

Prone at her feet, not uttering a word,
Fixing on her his wondrous shining gaze,
With eloquence he supplicates, entreats
And with one hand he proffers her a flower,
The other hand rumples her simple blouse

And hastily beneath her vestments steals
And the light fingers playfully caress
Her hidden charms . . . The marvel of it all
For Mary this is, oh, so subtly new.
But Lo, her virgin cheeks light with a flush,
A crimson that is not the blush of shame.
A languid warmth and an impatient sob
Cause her young breasts to rise and fall—and rise.
No words she speaks; but she can stand no more;
Scarce breathing now, her languid eyes half-closed
She bows her head toward the expectant Satan,
Screams: "Ah! . . ." and falls full length on the grass.

Our hero, Gabriel, God's pimp, walks in upon this ghastly Satanic seduction scene, drives Satan away in a hard fought battle, then turns to the innocent and violated virgin and kisses her hand, fondles her breasts. The innocent girl succumbs again and is made love to by the angel, Gabriel.

What shall she do? What of her jealous God?
Be troubled not, my beauteous maiden fair.
O women, you know love's ins and outs,
You know full well the wiles that can deceive,
That cover up a pleasant little lapse
With all the trappings of sweet innocence.

The errant daughter from her mother learns
The lesson of submissive modesty
And on the first and all decisive night
She feigns false fears and pains that do not pain!
And on the morrow feeling better slowly,
Gets up, can hardly walk, is languid, pale.
Elated the proud spouse, relieved her mother,
And once more the old flame's back again.

Meanwhile, Gabriel flies back to God and reports with an honest countenance that everything is in readiness for His Heavenly Majesty's Visitation. God prepares Himself for the trip.

Pushkin laughed aloud at the satire of his own creation. The poem took him out of himself, rescued him from his loneliness, the depths of his depression. He was right there in the garden when it happened. Of course he was! Perhaps he was Gabriel, Satan, was the Almighty. Perhaps he was even Mary. In any event that's how it was, undoubtedly. This was the way it had to have been! He bit the nib of his goose quilled pen, got up and walked the floor. He sat, and, as he read aloud, he beat his pen to the rhythm of his poem, nodding his proud wooly head in cadence to the beat. Sometimes he'd cock his ears and think he heard African drums his grandfather had once listened to, and that the rhythm of his poetry was African-influenced. He liked the idea of African influence in his work. He heard African violins playing in his poetry. The servants tiptoed softly around the house thinking that the houseguest of their master, General Insov, had lost track of his senses, laughing and talking to himself like a madman.

It was a moment in the poet's life when he overflowed with anger at the church and its hypocrisy, as he saw it, and its collusion with the monarchy in oppressing the Russian people. The mass baptisms of the infants in the frozen Neva. The pious Metropolitan at Madame Marya's Home for Wayward Girls. The sanctimonious Abbe Igor. Father Lev Gregorovich Photius, the saintly monster. It angered him to no end that he was forced by Imperial decree, as a civil servant, to attend church every Sunday. Some Sundays he had been out all night and would come stumbling into church roaring drunk. He would be too drunk to keep up with the proper genuflection. Oftentimes he would be kneeling while the devout were standing and vice-versa. His carryings-on in church became a scandal. Sometimes he would write a line so outlandish it would frighten him. He would change it to a more moderate tone. Then he'd say, "To hell with it!" and rewrite it even more outlandishly. It made him feel good to live at the edge of the steepest precipice. He remembered vividly the dangerous lonely freedom of the mountain eagle.

And he wrote dangerously!

A sweet enchanting dove flies in her window
Above her flips and flaps its wings and flutters
And sings its little winsome birdlike songs
Then suddenly between her legs flies in,
Alights upon the rose and trembles there,
Claws, turns around, and claws again, again,
Works with its feet and with its little beak.
Oh this is God! Mary has understood
That this dove is an Almighty guest;
Her knees drawn tight, the Hebrew maid cried out,
Began to sigh, to tremble, and to plead.
To weep, but no, triumphant is the dove,
In love's hot heat he quivers and he chirrups,
Then falls into light sleep, by love undone,
Resting an idle wing across the rose.

The Blessed Virgin falls into a deep though restive slumber. She awakes and ponders over the occurrence.

He's flown away. All weary, Mary thinks:
What furious pranks and happenings are these!
One, two and three—how eager they all seem.
This has been quite a day, I must admit!
In one and the same day I fell prey
to Satan and to Gabriel and to God.

144

He wrote an epilogue to THE GABRILIAD. His epilogues were usually eerie premonitions, as if he were forever looking over his slim shoulders at the future that would come behind him, creep upon him unheralded.

In his epilogue he wrote, wonderingly, ironically:

Days pass. Time, no doubt, unknown to me,
Will whiten my hair with silvery powder.
A sumptuous marriage at the alter rail
Will unite me forever to some gentle girl.
Oh sacred comforter, the ancient Joseph,
Bending my knees, I pray to thee—
Defender, protector of cuckolds—
I pray and I await thy blessing:
Have mercy, grant me peace and tranquility,
Have mercy, and grant me too—hear me out—
And easy sleep, trust in my wife,
Calm in my home and my neighbor's affection.

When Pushkin ran head-on into a problem with GABRILIAD, he fought it for a while, and if it did not submit, he turned to another poem inspired by his visit to the Fountain of Bakshisarai in the Caucasus. Failing there, he turned his capricious muse to another poem which would one day be famous, THE PRISONER OF THE CAUCASUS. The thing to do was to keep writing. Keep writing or go completely out of his mind. He drove himself like a master driving a recalcitrant serf. At night he went out on the town, although there wasn't much of a town to go out on.

He'd been excited at first by the exotic nature of the city. Compared to Ekaterinoslav it was a vast improvement. But it was not Moscow or Saint Petersburg. It was another frontier mudhole, no matter that it was a larger more sophisticated mudhole than Ekaterinoslav. The people turned out in all manner of attire. Alms begging went on all over the pathetic streets. In Russia, begging was a recognized profession, even in Saint Petersburg. Deformed lepers littered the landscape in old Kishinev. There was a constant chatter of alien tongues. The air was permeated with the smell of animal dung and outhouses and smoke pouring into the streets from opium dens. The obese aristocracy sat in their large wooden houses, Buddhalike, and smoked their Oriental pipes and drank thick syrupy Turkish coffee and smacked their greasy lips on halvah and other sweets and fabulous confections.

To this wild and crazy frontier town where anything and everything was proper dress, where people seemed to vie with one another to see who could wear the most outlandish combinations, Alexander Pushkin somehow managed to look eccentric in his velvet trousers and purple cape and scarlet fez. People came into town just to get a glimpse of the revolutionary poet from Saint Petersburg.

It was not that Alexander Sergeievich worshiped at the fetish of sartorial eccentricity. Actually it was an improvisation to cover up his poverty. He couldn't afford the price of a new coat which he badly needed. Sometimes he wore a long Moldavian Cassock. Sometimes he would borrow a coat from a friend and hide the fact that it was too large for him by having one coattail pinned to his shoulder, the other dragging on the ground. Sometimes his spirits dragged the ground.

One day he went to a ball in one of the great houses of Kishinev. In order to enter the palace, he had to step over and round a motley contingent of alms-beggars and crippled lepers, one without legs up to his scabby knees. "Alms to the poor, Master. Alms to the poor, Your Highness! The Heavenly Father will surely bless you."

It was like a chorus of a song in church these mendicants had rehearsed together. "Just a few kopeks, your Nobility. The Blessed Virgin will forgive you all your sins." Pushkin looked down into the man's lifeless eyes. Hope had died aborning in them. Alexander Sergeievich felt the sweat creep over his back and shoulders. There were children whose faces were severely pock-marked by cockroach bites. The hungry predatory roaches would prey upon the children's faces if they forgot to wash them before retiring on their beds of filthy vermined straw. Back in Ekaterinoslav Pushkin himself would always remember to wash his face before retiring, no matter how inebriated he was, and to get the liquor from his breath. One night he had been awakened by an army of cockroaches on a hunger march across his face. This night he thought he might be ill. The beggar began to kiss the nakedness of his sandaled feet. He shook his foot from the cripple man's slobbering lips and gave him his last kopeks and fled into the house.

Alexander Sergeievich was dressed as an Arab in a long white flowing gown and multicolored turban. He made his way up long white marble steps into the hallway hung in heavy damask drapes. A manservant dressed in Turkish attire appeared from behind the drapes. Alexander Sergeievich gave the man his printed card. The tall manservant pulled the drapes aside and announced in fractured French:

". . . the pleasure to present Monsieur Le Baron A. S. Pooshkin." There was a murmur from the crowd as the noted notorious poet entered, thinking to himself, where in the devil did the Baron excrement come from? It was not on his printed card.

The orchestra had taken a brief intermission. All of his senses were assaulted by the thick and sickly aroma of incense and hashish and strong perfumes and body sweat. He breathed deeply and hoped fervently he would survive this night. He made straight for the table where his most recent love, Princess Pulcheria Varfolmei, was seated. He tried hard to make himself believe he was truly in love with this elegant woman, but he demanded of himself that he have some kind of relationship with a woman other than physical. At least they should get along with each other conversationally and intellectually. She spoke in a strange unRussian accent, which seemed a hazy combination of the twain of East and West in a vast head-on collision. She was a plump and lovely doll without a doll's intelligence.

Not overly visible in the breasts, thin of mouth and boyishly constructed, with wide stupid eyes that seemed to stare at him in open-mouthed amazement. The Blessed Virgin knows he tried to get a conversation going, but all he got in return for one of his wittiest thrusts was, "I am laffing too bad, Monsieur Pooshkin! It is too much fonny jokes you is telling me!"

The band of serfs began to play again. Alexander Sergeievich had plied himself with wine and vodka and slivovitz and was ready for some dancing. He loved to dance. Dancing was a poem to him, with cadences and rhythms and idioms and subtleties and nuances. "Monsieur Pooshkin, you ees zee goodest danzieur in ze world!"

The band was playing and Alexander Sergeievich and Princess Pulcheria were doing a frenzied mazurka. Heels were clicking. Hands were clapping. Dancers cleared the floor to watch them. A young Russian officer new to the nearby garrison ordered the band to cease playing the mazurka and to play instead a waltz. When the band complied, Alexander Sergeievich walked over to the band leader. "Why did you stop playing the mazurka?"

The Tartar serf wiped the perspiration from his nervous forehead. "The captain ordered a waltz, your Nobility."

"And I am requesting you to continue with the mazurka."

"To be sure, Your Excellency." And the serf band began to play the mazurka again.

When the mazurka was over, the young captain came over to Pushkin's table. "I demand an apology from you, Monsieur."

"An apology for what?" Alexander Sergeievich inquired. He thought to himself, the fact of his African descendancy had nothing to do with this present infringement upon his dignity. He was just being too damn sensitive. He had to be able to distinguish between mere coincidences and actually intended insults, deliberate affronts to his sense of personal esteem.

"You are an impertinent scamp! Apologize at once, or you'll have me to answer to," the captain demanded.

"It is you who are impertinent. As for apologizing, I am Alexander Sergeievich Pushkin, at your humble service."

When the captain heard the name of his adversary, his face reddened, then lost color. Alexander Pushkin was a famed and feared duelist. But there was no way the young captain could save his officer's face. When he went back to his table one of his comrades commented, "Save your face! You'd better concern yourself with saving your arse! That scribbling African bastard is a cold-blooded killer!"

Alexander Sergeievich's reputation was certainly deserved, though possibly not in such exaggerated terms. He was a deadly shot and preferred always to incapacitate rather than to kill. The idea was to render his adversary momentarily impotent. If the man stood still, he was absolutely safe, but if he moved, too bad! Nevertheless, before the evening was over all the arrangements for the duel were made, the seconds selected. The duel was set for the following morning.

Alexander Sergeievich came to the duel grounds late, as usual. The young captain was pacing up and down a clearing on the edge of town surrounded by slim white ghost-like birch trees, working up a nervous sweat. The field was muddy from a heavy rain the night before. Jackdaws sat silently in the birches as witnesses to the strange occurrence.

Alexander Sergeievich brought a bunch of cherries with him and started to eat them as the duel regulations were outlined to them. He continued to eat them even as the captain raised his shaky gun and fired. The captain missed. Pushkin did not blink an eye. He raised his own gun and fired, striking the captain's cap in the center of its visor. Then he continued to eat his cherries for a moment. After a while he asked, "Are you satisfied, my captain?"

The captain removed his cap and stared at the hole in its visor. He shuddered. Then he broke into a smile, threw down his cap and gun and ran toward Pushkin relieved and beaming. "You are truly a great man, Your Excellency!"

When he reached Alexander Sergeievich he made as if to hug and kiss him. Pushkin disdainfully pushed him away and turned to leave.

It was not the first nor would it be the last duel Alexander Sergeievich would fight in Kishinev, not to mention those that were narrowly averted. His boredom drove him into one dueling incident after the other. The word went around that he would challenge you at the drop of a hat or blink of an eyelash, or if you belched and did not beg his pardon. These rumors were a clear case of exaggeration. But in any event, it was certainly true that you impinged on his dignity at your own dire peril.

Insov was kept busier averting Pushkin's duels than he was taking care of colonial business for the Imperial government. Sometimes, as a last resort, he would lock his impulsive protege in his room and take his clothes and pistols from him.

Alexander Sergeievich was playing cards in a famous gambling house one evening with Russian officers. He did not hold these Russian officers in very high esteem. They were quite different from the revolutionary ones who had been his friends in Petersburg and in the Emperor's Hussar Guards. He described the Kishinev group as "pompous arses constipated with their own importance." He longed for people like Nicholai Raevsky, Kaverin, Chaadaev, Pushchin and his other comrades.

This night he was losing, as usual, and suspected the game was being manipulated. His eyes were smarting and tearing from the foggy haze of hashish and tobacco smoke. His face burned with his anger and his nostrils dilated; his lips quivered as he continued to lose. His anger was aimed more at himself than at these self-important, supercilious officers: angry because he knew he should have been at home at work with his writing. This realization did not help abate his anger at himself or at the officers. At one point he got so angry with himself he swept all of the cards from the table onto the floor and called the lieutenant across from him a "miserable bastard and a swindler!"

The pale-faced lieutenant rose from his chair. "Monsieur Pushkin, you are an infant who should not be out so late at night with real men. Your parents are delinquent in their duties to you. You have not been weaned yet. I can see the milk still on your lips." The other officers laughed derisively.

Alexander Sergeievich stared at the dark-haired, blue-eyed officer with the thinly waxed mustache and calmly replied, "The milk you see, my darling boy, comes from the miserable udders of your whore of a syphilitic mother." He got up, left the table and strode out of the door.

The next morning at the dueling grounds there was a blinding snowstorm. Both of the duelists missed their shots at twenty paces, tried again and missed at fifteen and then ten, gave up and postponed it for another day. Insov got wind of it and put his naughty boy under house arrest until the heat subsided.

Some days, bored and very close to madness, Pushkin would wander neath his high hat with his great stick with the iron crook to the outskirts of town to a village inside the pale where the chosen were allowed to live a precarious existence. Kishinev, itself, was bad enough, but the ghetto went from bad all the way to worse and horror. There was the unspeakable stench that assaulted the nostrils miles away. Inside the pale itself, there were wooden streets with wild weeds growing up between the planks overrun with piled-high heaps of months-old garbage. Cockroaches, rats and other vermin traveled along the streets like citizens. He heard the constant hum of greedy flies who were better fed than people. He saw the holy men, Rabbis, with their long black heavy coats and large fur hats in the midst of summer heat. They were bent over as they trotted along with a strange and off-beat rhythm, as if they came out of their mother's wombs supplied with yokes upon their shoulders. Children adorned with thin and ancient faces, as if they knew another existence some place some time eons ago. Alexander Sergeievich saw faces without hope staring blankly at the world with the empty eyes of the living dead. Professional beggars roamed the streets. Prostitutes of tender ages and opaque eyes and impenetrable faces with younger brothers as procurers.

Life was real and the smell of death was omnipresent. Somehow he knew that this was not a poem he'd written, a dream he'd dreamt. The pale was very very real even in its terrible nightmarish unreality. There were the filthy shops and even filthier merchants hawking their decaying wares. Men and women haggling with filthy merchants over meats completely covered by glutted flies that nobody bothered to disperse. The poet's shoes could feel the slime beneath his feet. From the time he walked into the pale, even before, as he approached, his stomach was in a continuous uproar.

Whenever he left the pale, he wondered if Russia were worth liberating, if the people were really worth redemption. He seriously wondered if Russia itself were not outside the pale of what men called humanity.

Another day back in Kishinev proper, in a more romantic mood, he saw an elderly woman bent long before her bending time, with her head bundled up in rags, her ancient face a wrinkled mass and a yoke on her shoulders, making her way slowly up the dung-heaped streets of old Kishinev. He saw a beauty glowing in her grizzled face, the fire of faith and hope still burning in her tired eyes. Eyes that had seen so much misery and still had courage left to hope. There was a beauty only he could see. His poetic mind imagined a halo gathered softly around her saintly face. And he knew that this was the spirit of Russia. Full of love and hate and openness and prejudice and backwardness, with hearts as large and wide and vast as the Russian earth itself.

Almost unknowingly he walked up to the woman and kissed her on her scruffy cheek. Instantly he felt warmly foolish. She smelled of age and toil and human sweat.

The frightened old woman made the sign of the cross. "I didn't do nothing wrong, Your Excellency!"

This was Russia, he thought, not Alexander-the-Holy-One and his mincy-stepping, lisping, French-speaking sycophants back in Petersburg; he didn't need their love, God's one and only Apostle, Emperor Alexander, who, by imperial decree, set aside a day each year for holy Russians to invade the pale and beat up on Jews at random and with impunity. He didn't write for them. This was the Russia that inspired his poetry. The old woman, the scabby pock-marked children.

One day, as he wandered aimlessly inside the pale, he saw a tiny girl come up out of the ruins of a deserted hovel, with the most beautiful smile on her face, a small pinched face with the largest blackest eyes, shaped like almonds, dark and wide and mysterious as a moonless midnight out on the steppes. He had never seen such eyes as Nina's. The cockroached pockmarks on her face did not, could not take away her beauty, which shone from inside outwardly. She was a miracle of beautitude. His eyes filled with angry tears, as he took her thin-shouldered, almost weightless body up in his arms, and he went from place to place in search of her parents. They were no where to be found. Alexander Sergeievich took her to a filthy restaurant and sat with her and watched her push food into her mouth as if tomorrow were the final day of famine. Children gathered around the table staring at Nina and the curious stranger, some with their hands stretched out suppliantly. He ordered food for all of them. He was kopekless when he left the pale.

The poet went each week to visit with little Nina and brought her food and all manner of confections. One day he tried to take her out with him, but they turned him back at the point of entrance to the pale. Then one day he went to visit Nina and she had gone away to Heaven to lie down in green pastures. The kindly restauranteur shrugged at him in helplessness.

Dueling situations dogged his footsteps. At a ball given by the Moldavian upppercrust, he was dancing with the wife of a Moldavian aristocrat. He had been standing alone and bored, sipping ices and watching the scene, when Madame Jablonskya whispered to him, "My-my, we are honored to have such a distinguished person in our midst." The band had just ceased playing a mazurka, and she had turned from her dancing partner to Alexander Pushkin. "And why aren't we dancing tonight? Are none of the ladies of Kishinev pretty enough or good enough dancers for the famous poet from Saint Petersburg?"

The band had begun to play again, a waltz this time. Couples had begun to dance. She looked into the poet's face, and, behind her busy fan, her eyes said, "May I have this dance."

He said, "May I?" and took her by the hand. He knew immediately he had made a grievous error.

Madame Jablonskya was one of the few women Alexander Sergeievich had met whom he disliked instantly, wholeheartedly and instinctively. His entire being, all of his senses, reacted against this aggressive horse-faced woman of thirty-five or forty. A hank of blondish hair piled atop her head like a hive for busy bumblebees. Her overfed obesity and slovenness, her garishly purple gown, the front of which dipped almost to her navel, putting her flabby sagging breasts on obscene display. He loathed the over-perfumed smell of the lady. Her breath repelled him. She danced with her horsy body heavily up against him.

She suggested in a hoarse and meant-to-be-sensual whisper, "My boudoir at home is as roomy as this place and much more comfortable. And we could really do some fancy dancing there."

Pushkin was indignant. What made her think he was dying to be alone with her?

"Madame, bedroom intrigue does not interest me at the moment. Neither do whores operating under cover of matrimonial respectability."

Perspiration broke all over her face like adolescent pimples, and he could smell the lady's anger. After regaining her composure, she said, "My, my! We are an African tiger when it comes to defenseless ladies. Too bad such ferocity does not carry over to the field of honor. Instead, we are content to nibble away on cherries."

Alexander Sergeievich retorted, "You can be thankful, Madame, that you are apparently a woman." He turned and left her on the dance floor and strode to the game table to her wealthy husband, a prominent member of the Moldavian Supreme Council, and demanded an apology. The prominent boyar sputtered angrily, then went over to his wife. When he returned to Pushkin, he demanded, "How can you ask me for an apology after insulting my wife?"

"Kindly do me a favor, Your Excellency, and keep your whorish wife in tow," Alexander Sergeievich cooly replied.

The two men had to be kept forcibly apart. A duel was averted only by Insov's intervention. He placed the poet under house detention.

One night Alexander Sergeievich sat fuming in his room in Papa Insov's house wearing nothing but his underwear. The General had taken his clothes from him to keep him out of dueling mischief. Papa Insov came into the room and sat near the window. He stared out of the window at the growing darkness. He pulled on his graying Vandyke beard and turned to look at Alexander Sergeievich. He looked around the room, at the iron bed high up from the floor, the chest-of-drawers, the water stand with looking glass atop and a bowl and pitcher, the candlelighted lamp on the center table, the oaken desk, the chamber pot beneath the bed, a trunk over in a corner. There was a picture of His Majesty on the wall above the chest-of-drawers. On another wall there hung a copper-colored picture of the Blessed Virgin and her Child. Pushkin watched the old man as he thought to himself that his room was not exactly commodious, nor was it lavishly furnished, but compared to what his hovel had been in Ekaterinoslav, it was extravagant, palatial even. Papa Insov pulled on his ear where the hair gathered thickly in great tufts. He cleared his throat.

"My dear boy, you just simply must stop this foolish dueling."

"Where are my clothes?" Alexander Sergeievich demanded.

"Son," the older man said softly, "don't you know you can't kill off the entire world all by yourself? And besides, one of these times, someone will outshoot you. Somewhere in this world there is a better shot than you, and he might just be right here in Kishinev."

Alexander Sergeievich repeated, "Where is my clothing?"

"Dear boy, I spend more time keeping you out of trouble than I do taking care of His Majesty's affairs. I love you like my own son, darling boy, but by the Holy Virgin, you cannot carry all the troubles of the world on your shoulders. You're much too young and your shoulders are not broad enough."

"What am I supposed to do when bastards go out of their way to insult me?"

"What can I do to make things easier for you?" the General asked. "What is troubling you, darling boy?"

Alexander Sergeievich stared at the kindly old man who was like a father to him. "It doesn't make me happy, Papa Insov, to sit here in my underwear."

The older man spoke quietly. "Why are you always getting into mischief? Why do you carry this anger seething inside of you all of the time?"

"The question is—why does everybody go out of their way to insult me? Is it because they consider me an African? Well, I'm proud of my African heritage, and if anybody doesn't like it, they'd better stay out of my way, because I'll not stand for any excrement from anybody, not even from the Emperor!"

"My dear Alexander Sergeievich," Papa Insov said, "as I have told you a hundred times, nobody holds your African blood against you. That is entirely a specter of your own imagination."

He wished he could believe this kindly Russian gentleman, his surrogate father. He wished he could believe the things that happened to him had nothing to do with his African birthright, that it was merely coincidental that he was forever running into insults, real or imagined. But how else could he explain it to himself? Was he excessively sensitive and hot-tempered? He knew people spoke (even those who professed to love him) of his "savage African temperament."

The old man walked over to him and put his arms around him, kissed him on his cheek. He felt a tear spill from Papa Insov's eyes. "Dearest of sons, pride of my tired old heart, believe me, the Russian people love you, even as I dearly love you. They have forgotten all about your African blood. It makes no difference to them. They love you because you're beautiful. They love your genius. They love you because your soul is beautiful, because you are divinely gifted, because you make every one of us proud to be a Russian. It is your special gift to Mother Russia and the people!"

Tears were spilling from Pushkin's eyes now as he embraced the older man. "But I don't want them to forget my African blood, Papa Insov, and it does make a difference. It makes all the difference in the world. Whatever I am today, whatever I have given the Russian people, I owe to Africa and to Russia." Would this ambivalence follow him for the remainder of his life, his love for Africa and his love for the country of his birth? Wasn't there enough love in his lonely heart for both of these great land masses and their people?

He sat down and did not realize when the old man left the room. He looked up when he heard him return with his clothing.

He said quietly, "Thank you, Papa Insov." He kissed the old man fully on his trembling lips, then dressed and went out on the town.

Sometimes Alexander Sergeievich would wander out to Gypsy camps on the outskirts of the town. He had long talks with organ grinders with their monkeys, spoke rapturously with the beautiful dark and carefree-eyed, sun-tanned Gypsy girls who held his hand, read his palm and made his kopeks do disappearing acts. He longed for the freedom they seemed to take for granted. He felt a kinship with these almost-brown complexioned people reminding him of his African ancestry, and thought seriously of joining them and losing or finding himself amongst these people whose country had no borders. Citizens of all the earth. Once he followed a camp of Gypsies and wandered with them for a while all over Bessarabia. He tried to go to Rumania with them, but he was stopped at the border.

When Prince Alexander Ypsilanti, following in his illustrious father's footsteps, led an uprising against the Turks in Jassy, of the then Moldavia, Alexander Sergeievich got excited and applauded fervently the great Greek's grand heroics. Ypsilanti called on all of his Moldavian Greeks to rally to his banner. Greeks seemed to stream from Kishinev like the Dneiper River in floodtide.

Alexander Sergeievich wrote poetry applauding the Greeks, he leaped upon tables in public places and versified the glorious rightness of their cause. "Freedom! Freedom! Liberation!" He added verses to his ODE TO FREEDOM. Called upon the Imperial Russian Government to give them its support with arms and troops.

He called, of course, in vain. The Emperor had no intention at all of allowing his religious scruples to dictate his politics. Alexander Sergeievich began to understand that though the Greeks were Orthodox Christians and the Turks were Moslem infidels, His Imperial Majesty lived in terror of people who fought under such revolutionary slogans as "Liberty" and "Freedom!" It just might become contagious. In this case, piety, orthodoxy, infidelity were total irrelevances.

Alexander Sergeievich even disguised himself as a Greek and tried to join the war, but he was turned back at the border by Imperial informers who spied upon this poet every hour of the day. His letters, the few that he received, were always opened and censored before they ever reached him. At the end of every week informers wrote letters to Saint Petersburg informing on his activities.

"Pushkin is doing very little writing as we can see and getting into very little seditious mischief. On the positive side, he spends most of his time in gambling dens and other such debauchery, fornicating with every woman who will raise her dress for him. And there seems to be very few that are not more than willing. It seems they all wish to discover whether it's true what they say about the African penis. It is truly amazing how they go crazy over this so-called famous poet. Without a doubt the women here are spoiling him."

Some days he would wander into the Oriental part of the Bessarabian metropolis. He loved to stroll amongst the canopied bazaars and haggle with the Eastern merchants, the swarthy yellow brown-black people with their high cheekbones and slanted eyes, Turks, Tartars, Russo-Persians, Uzbeks, short and stocky, tall, gangling, swaggering, dressed in high boots, great shaggy dark crescent-shaped mustaches, long robes sweeping the ground, tall fur hats, bright-colored caftans. Listen to the various and varied Eastern tongues. Reeking with smells and incense from the Orient. Men of Muhammad with skull caps and fezzes and swords and pistols dangling from their waists. Oftentimes he felt more at home with these darkly visaged people than he did with Russians of the purest blood.

Men—Alexander Sergeievich thought, poetically, romantically—whose ancestors had swept across the steppes and rain forests and mountain ranges of Eastern Europe all the way to the Dneiper River with Genghis Khan and Tamerlaine. The soft-eyed, slant-eyed, soft-voiced women with the marketplace atop their tilted heads. He loved to watch them walk, like pretty poetry put in motion.

He fell in love with dark-eyed, brown-faced Sofia Petrovna Belinskaya, but his tragic heart was suddenly discouraged by an angry giant Uzbek who chased him with a saber. Dear Sofia Petrovna had neglected to tell our lonely poet she was betrothed to Boris Drasnokov. He had asked her if she were married, and she had answered simply, "No, Your Highness."

It wasn't long before Alexander Sergeievich became disillusioned with the revolutionary Greeks. His heroic poetry was one thing but reality was a different matter altogether. Very few Moldavian Greeks rallied to the noble cause of Ypsilanti. Furthermore, a schism flared up and deepened between the leadership, despite the exalting fervor of Alexander Pushkin's poetry. Valdimiresco, who fought for a democratic government, as against Ypsilanti, who sought to replace Turkish autocracy with his own bourgeois regime.

When the news reached Kishinev of Ypsilanti's inglorious defeat, and when other news filtered through about the atrocities on both sides, the Turks mutilating Greek men, especially their genitals, selling the women, putting the children on spits and roasting them and tying women up in sacks with hungry rats and venomous reptiles. Alexander Sergeievich threw up his hands in deep disgust. As for the noble Greeks, the news was that they had slit the throats of Turks, excepting those who were rich and would bring huge ransoms. The idealistic poet was thoroughly disillusioned and demoralized. He took it out on his poetry. And he wrote bitterly:

Give no freedom to the flock
The miserable flock
Are for slaughtering and shearing.
Their heritage down through the years
Is the club and yoke with a rattle.

He was losing faith in revolution.

In a letter to Prince Vyazemsky he wrote, more calmly: "The Greek issue may be compared to that of my African sisters and brothers in America. It is hoped that they both may be delivered from their condition of intolerable servitude. But they will have to deliver themselves. Masters never free their slaves. It is the nature of the way things are. And it was ever thus."

The Imperial informers were mistaken when they said that Pushkin was not writing. He wrote every day that he lived. He would always do more writing than was apparent to superficial acquaintances and informers, even those who each day sneaked up to his house and peeped into his windows.

Through all his turmoil and confusion, he somehow finished GABRILIAD, THE PRISONER OF THE CAUCASUS and THE FOUNTAIN OF BAKSHISARAI. When THE PRISONER was published, he received a miserable five hundred rubles, although it sold well all over Russia. He went immediately into a deep depression. He'd read the work from start to finish, go over every stanza, every line, every word. He was his own harshest critic. He'd agonize on every page. He'd find fallacies and discrepancies he could never find before the work was put into print. Queasy stomach, diarrhea, crazy headaches, dizzy spells, abdominal spasms.

The poet pretended to himself it did not matter what anybody thought about his work, especially the journalists. But he did care. He wanted people to enjoy the output of his heart and soul, to gain insight and perception from the products of his busy brain. He did not write just for himself alone. His writing was an act of love. He went through all this creative agony out of love for his readers, and he'd settle for nothing short of true love in return. He did not care for unrequited love.

He had finished GABRILIAD long before, but it had not been published. He had done it in his own handwriting and passed it on to others who had copied it and passed it on. He was the most widely read writer in all of Holy Russia, and undoubtedly one of the poorest, financially. Newspapers and magazines happily published his wonderful verses but refused to pay him. Unheard of writers plagiarized him with impunity. He was dying in his poverty and his vaunted popularity.

Embittered and disillusioned, he dove headlong into love affairs. After Princess Pulcheria, who could never understand Pushkin's funny jokes, there was Calypso, the exotic Greek ex-mistress of Lord Byron. Her mother was a fortune-teller, and they lived uproariously in poverty and squalor. Beautiful Calypso was very generous with the gifts of her magnificent body, but she also sold her love for the proper price, a fact Pushkin did not learn of till he came down with gonorrhea. He laughed it off. He told a friend, "It is nothing more than a snotty nose."

During his stay in Kishinev, the General gave him a holiday and he took a trip to Kamenka and fell among a terrible den of rabid revolutionaries.

CHAPTER THREE

Kamenka was in the Kievan Province at the edge of Moldavia, where he visited the Davydovs. They were a powerfully rich family. The matriarch of the household was General Raevsky's mother. The Davydovs lived in a large rambling villa with a man-made grotto and seventy-five or eighty rooms. The family was enormous. Grandma Davydov was Matriarch Supreme, presiding regally and graciously over endless rounds of parties—two, three or four running sometimes simultaneously all over the place. Houseguests came for weekend parties, took up light housekeeping and often stayed for months. Celebrated nobility and prestigious parasites, abundant liquor, exciting and excitable women, music by serf bands, plenty of dancing, flirting, fornicating, revolutionary rhetoric by the bushel. Alexander Sergeievich was in his natural element.

There was Basil Davydov, twenty-eight, dark-haired, heavily mustached, slim, handsome, a revolutionary theoretician of first magnitude, influential member of a famous secret society known throughout the Empire as the Union of the South. He was anti-monarchist to the core.

There was also his older brother, Alexander Davydov, forty-two, as obese as his brother Basil was slender. Feeding his fat good-natured face and developing a rotunda of a belly with excellent cuisine was his declared preoccupation.

Upon his arrival that first afternoon Alexander Sergeievich met Grandma Davydov, a tall handsome white-haired queenly woman, who welcomed him with a kiss and turned him over to a manservant. "Show our celebrated genius, poet laureate of all the Russias, to his room. Prepare his bed for a brief nap." She turned to Alexander Sergeievich, smiling mischievously. "Get a little rest, Your Excellency. There is a dinner party tonight at seven-thirty. We will be honored by your presence. We will be incensed if you do not attend. Leo Adronov will awaken you in plenty of time. Meanwhile, please dream pleasantly."

Alexander Sergeievich took the old noblewoman's hand and kissed it. "It is I who will be honored, your nobleness."

"Ah!" the old woman said, her face wreathing smiles as she sat there, regally, in her elegant throne-like chair of teak wood heavily draped with scarlet silk. "You are indeed the grandson of Ibrahim Petrovich. That man truly had a way with the ladies. He was so handsome and gallant! I remember him at Great Catherine's court when I was a little girl."

He kissed her wrinkled hand again. "Merci beaucoup, Your Highness."

She waved good-bye to him, and he turned and followed Leo Andronov down a long dimly-lit corridor and up the marble winding stairway to his bedroom.

When Pushkin came downstairs to the dinner party it was already in full swing. They were all dressed in the latest fashion as they elegantly lifted their slim-necked glasses of the most expensive champagne and toasted the coming and inevitable revolution. They were the most fashionable revolutionaries Alexander Sergeievich had ever seen. From their attire they were more French than Russian. The women were from another world, a place he'd never been before, not even in his world of dreams. Beautiful, articulate, charming, and all of them *de bonne famille*.

It was Fat Alexi Davydov who introduced Alexander Sergeievich to his wife, the Countess. "This is my beloved spouse, Countess Aglaya." He told Alexander Sergeievich, proudly, "A delectible *pièce de résistance*, compliments of the House of Davydov." Then to her he said, "And this, my dear, is Alexander Sergeievich Pushkin, poet nonpareil in all the Russian Empire."

The lovely French-born Countess stared at Alexander Sergeievich with her dark and knowing eyes. She disrobed him with her dark eyes, as her scarlet tongue passed over her avid sensual lips. He felt warm all over when she said, "Everyone knows Monsieur Pushkin. Certainly every Russian woman knows him in the deepest recess of her heart." She spoke directly to him now. "You have broken my poor susceptible heart so many times, Monsieur. You have moved me like no other."

Alexander Sergeievich was heatedly confused. "I'm so very sorry, Countess. I never meant—"

She licked her generous red lips again.

"Do not apologize, Monsieur, for being the greatest poet in the world. I have read every line you have ever published."

Later that night he lay restless in the vast high-ceiling bedroom. After the stuffy little incommodious room to which he had become accustomed, he felt engulfed by so much spaciousness. It was not the extravagance of the room that caused Alexander Sergeievich to be restless. He was thinking of the way they had received him. Princess Elina Shostagovichna, the prima ballerina of Saint Petersburg; Count Vasilla Rubinsky, conductor of the National Symphony of Moscow; Mademoiselle Frieda Molotovna of the Moscow Theatre; Madame Rubinskaya prima donna coloratura of the Saint Petersburg Opera Company. It was a register of the beautiful and gifted. Singers, famous actors, actresses, dancers, painters, writers, politicians. The crème de la crème of Russian art and politics, all of whom conversed in French. He had not fully recognized till now the importance of his life's work to the Russian people, especially to the kind of people gathered at the Davydovs. They respected him, his work, the delicate thing he had forged out of an alienated life. His work was important to their dreams of a Russian future, of change and revolution. That evening he had drunk deeply of the heady wine of adulation, and he hoped that the sweet taste in his mouth would not turn sour by the morning.

He felt a chill move swiftly now across his slender shoulders, a warm chill of excitement, of self-esteem, accomplishment. Wave after wave after wave of sweet euphoria. His life's work was a commitment to change in this Imperial Russia. When he returned to Kishinev, in the loneliest moments of his endless banishment he hoped he would remember this beautiful interval of self-realization. For the first time in his lonely life he felt he actually belonged. Here in this blessed place he no longer felt outside. He belonged—to them. They belonged—to him. He, Alexander Sergeievich Pushkin, the son of Sergei and Nadezda Pushkin, the grandson of Grandma-ma Hannibal, the great grandson of Ibrahim Petrovich Hannibal, descendant of the magnificent Carthaginian, was one of Russia's most eloquent voices for change. He had the power to move people. *To move people.* To set them into motion. He felt a heaviness upon his shoulders, an awesome responsibility. He tossed and perspired most of the night. Near dawn he heard the crowing of an egotistical cock and another answer from nearby as he drifted off to sleep and to dream of great Grandpa-pa Hannibal.

Running running, swiftly running. They are chasing me, the Russian feldjaggers in their red capes and their cossack caps. I can hear the galloping of their horses gaining on me steadily as I run swiftly into the face of the wind, over the endless midnight steppe. With the national border now in view. Now the sweet winds lift me from the earth, then they let me down again, up down, up down, I am almost bouncing along; this time I stay up with the tender breezes, higher higher higher, I begin to soar above the dimly lighted cities, some of them are bright as daytime. Now I am soaring high above the wide sea waters, soaring, soaring, ever soaring. I have finally left Russia behind me. I feel gladsome, feel transported. I hear voices, "C'est L'Afrique! Welcome to the land of your great-grandfather." Like a large and graceful falcon I circle, then go in and come to earth.

Seated in a vast high-ceilinged room, I have seen this room many times before, it seems I am in the presence of a young Black prince. I have heard this voice before. This is the throne room. Thick and deep crimson carpeting. Brilliant chandeliers. The young boy is dressed regally in a princely garment, a long scarlet robe that sweeps the floor. "You are welcome, my great grandson."

"But how can I be your grandson, since I am obviously older than you?"

The young prince smiles, and in a strange familiar voice he answers, "Think far far far back to a time long before your birth." He pauses. His voice changes, sounds like an older man, his face changes, the prince grows taller into manhood. The same dark brooding face, the same penetrating eyes, almost black, same generous mouth. I recognize him as the man whose picture hangs above my desk in Mikhailovskoye. "It's very complicated," the prince says, "But you'll understand it better as time goes on. No matter, you are destined to do great things. You will give a voice to the Russian people. Your pen will help to liberate the masses."

I recognize him now. "Grandfather Hannibal!" He smiles and moves toward me with arms extended. Just then there is a loud pounding on the door somewhere, upon all the doors throughout this earth, it seems, as a chill moves swiftly across my shoulders. And I hear, "Open up in the name of His Most Imperial Majesty!"

Alexander Sergeievich awoke, lathered in perspiration, an icy coldness in his mouth. His body shaking as if ague-afflicted. Why was he shaking? The high-ceilinged room confused him, as did the silken bedclothes and the sunken goose down mattress. Where was he? Why did he feel threatened? Then he remembered where he was, remembered he'd been dreaming. A feeling of well-being moved through him as he remembered that he was in a place where he belonged.

Belonged! And was appreciated. The people here loved him. For himself. He was no longer the outsider.

Alexander Davydov and his wife had separate bedrooms. "Why wouldn't they have separate bedrooms?" Ivan Mikhailovich said one drunken evening. He was a Colonel in the Engineering Corps. "They have different uses for their bedrooms. He takes food to his room and eats all night. She takes men to hers and fornicates." The revolutionary Colonel laughed hysterically at his own witticism and pounded Alexander Sergeievich on the back and shoved him with an elbow. No matter, Pushkin would not laugh. He walked away from Ivan Mikhailovich.

One night the obese gourmet passed out on the ballroom floor. His manservant, Leo Adronov, came to his assistance as he stretched out on the gleaming parquet floor, sublimely snoring. When Leo Adronov sought to pick the fat one up, Alexi awoke for a brief instant. "Take your black hands off me, you fornicating African bastard!"

It was true about our man, Leo. He was darker than Alexander Sergeievich, and his head was woolier. Pushkin learned much later that Leo was a product of the vast and holiest of empires. His heathen mother was from the faraway land of the magnificent Uzbeks near to India and China. Partially a descendant of the golden hordes of Ghengis Khan. His father, a Russian colonizer for the glory of His Most Imperial Majesty, Paul The One, endowed his mother with the Christian spirit by raping her at the very tender age of twelve. But to give the devil his due, he saved her at an early age from the worship of pagan gods. But Leo Adronov was an ignorant ingrate. He hated the Russians with a cordial passion despite the fact

160

that his fortunate mother died at thirty-one from overwork in an extremely unctuous state of Heavenly salvation. He didn't give a damn that the dear woman was *Up There* feasting on milk and honey instead of roasting in the fire and brimstone of *Down There* on the devil's spit.

So Leo dropped his Master as he lay and left him snoring. Alexander Sergeievich and Aglaya had watched the entire performance. The lovely Countess took the poet's hand and led him over to the manservant who stood near the wall muttering underneath his breath, "Fat white Russian sonofafornicating pig!"

Aglaya took the manservant's hand and squeezed it warmly. "Set the table in the antechamber."

She took Alexander Sergeievich by the hand and they left the ballroom. She led him down a long corridor and up endlessly winding marble stairs till they reached the antechamber of her bedroom. A long oaken table alive with alcoholic spirits, apples, grapes and other fruits, graced the middle of the antechamber, and a bright chandelier lit up the room like the middle of the day. Aglaya led Alexander Sergeievich to the divan and the poet almost sank out of sight in the silky goose down sofa. He had a sudden desperate feeling like going down in deep water for the very last time. Aglaya literally fell upon him and smothered him with kisses and her liquored breath. "I love you, dear Pushkin! I love you, you goddamn infamous poet!"

"I love you too," Alexander Sergeievich mumbled without zest or much conviction, as he tried to readjust himself to the situation. He preferred always to be on top of things. But if somebody "loved" him, who was he to reject any show of human affection?

It was at this very moment that two men came unannounced into the antechamber. The startled poet tried to spring from beneath the frantic woman. Aglaya was not bothered by the interruption. "Put it on the table *toute de suite* and get out of here!" the lady shouted softly at them.

Leo Adronov stared at his mistress with dark and sad contemptuous eyes. "*Mais Oui*, Madame." The dark one and his comrade proceeded to put the delicacies on the table and replaced the melted candles in the chandeliers. They worked swiftly, efficiently and left, Leo muttering disdainfully. Alexander Sergeievich wondered if the contemptuous glance by Leo was meant for him or Leo's mistress.

Aglaya leaned away from Pushkin. "Let's eat first. There's no need to hurry. There's plenty of time. Relax, my sweet. You're overanxious."

Alexander Sergeievich stared at her in wonder. He looked at the table spilling over with delicacies. Caucasian pheasant, chicken in the Kievan style, shaslyk, pickled cabbage, kvas and sturgeon and caviar, black and from the choicest sterlet. Wines of all denominations including his favorite plum wine, slivovitz. They ate and drank till she began to belch and beg his pardon. He wondered where she could put so much food. She was not obese like her husband. Neither was she skinny, but slim and very well constructed. It seemed the food stuck to her ribs in all the proper places. She stood up from the table and stared at him with those warm wide dark and slanted eyes of hers and belched again.

"Shall we retire, my pet?" she asked. "I'm getting sleepy."

"Of course." he replied.

And they went into her bedroom, undressed and went to bed. But sleep was far distant from the Countess's mind and sweet intentions. Aglaya was made for love. With bountiful breasts for one so slender. His hands explored them, even as she explored him with her full lips and very very busy tongue. Now she seized his lips with hers. Her warm wide eyes dilated as he moved into her, and she pulled him even further into her with her long legs wrapped around him. "Make poetry with me, beautiful poet!" she shouted in a desperate whisper to him. "Make poetry with me! Love me! Love me! Love me! Now! Now!"

And he went even deeper into her as they made drunken love together, and they promptly fell asleep.

Alexander Sergeievich awoke perhaps several hours later to the sound of strange inhuman noises coming from the antechamber. He jumped naked from the bed and stumbled around the room looking for his clothes as the terrible sounds continued. He fell over a chair and Aglaya sat suddenly up in bed.

Her bare breasts and lovely shoulders gleamed sweetly in the darkness. "What do you think you're doing?" she demanded of him. Alexander Sergeievich pointed frantically toward the antechamber. "What's that awful noise out there?" It sounded to him like Kishinev camels at a wild uproarious bacchanal.

"Oh that," she answered indifferently. "It's just Fat Alexi eating."

"Your husband! And how in the hell am I going to get out of here?"

"The way you came in, silly." She replied in an exasperated tone. "Through that door. Were you so drunk you don't remember?"

She yawned and belched. "He won't even notice, mon chérie. By now he's drunk from overeating. He's probably passed out again. That's him snoring."

Pushkin stared at her unbelievingly. He looked around the room. With the moonlight spilling into the room he could see the silken golden drapes that matched the moonlight on her breasts. His feet sank deep in the thick rich pile of golden carpeting. How could he go out of the bedroom of another man's wife and face the husband, and he a guest in the husband's house? There were some boundary lines to hospitality. He was not in a dueling mood this drunken before-day-in-the-early-morning. And if he were going to duel, it must be over something slightly less ridiculous. He couldn't kill a man about the man's own wife. He stared at her again and pointed toward the antechamber. "This is no time for making jokes!" he said in a shouted whisper.

Aglaya stared at him uncomprehendingly. Then there was a sudden noise in the next room, a clunk of a sound like the iron doors of a dungeon slamming shut. "What in the devil was that?" our poet whispered seriously.

162

She leaped out of her canopied bed in her transparent chiffon nightgown with the moonlight glowing through the middle of her. He watched the outline of her fine limbs and the dark inverted pyramid of her blessed womanhood as she ran toward him, her youngish bosom bouncing. She looked sensuous and desirable and ten years younger than she really was. She held her busy body up against him, causing things to happen in the middle of him. Forgotten for the moment was his terrible predicament. "That was his face falling onto the table, dear. His false teeth rattling. We can go back to bed now. He'll be that way for hours." She reached down and put her hot hand on his hardness.

But he backed away from her, shaking his head. "I have to get out of here. I would be no good at all for you, or me, with your husband in the next room. I am not that sophisticated. Or decadent." He dressed hurriedly.

Aglaya shrugged. "There will be other times, mon petit." She threw a pink silken negligee around herself.

"Yes," Pushkin agreed distractedly. "Other times." As she led him tiptoeing through the antechamber. And there was fat Alexi with his friendly face upon the table, snoring peacefully, not one care in all this awful world, food scattered everywhere, a giant rat oblivious to everything and everyone excepting the fine morsel of shaslyk he was nibbling near Alexi's mouth. Alexi's snoring did not disturb this greedy monster. Horrified, Alexander Sergeievich forgot where he was and his own predicament, as his flesh crawled crazily across his back and shoulders and dizzily downward from the back of his neck to his spine. He stomped his foot and shouted, "Get !" The big rat turned and stared brazenly with beady, defiant eyes at the unnerved poet. Alexander Sergeievich stomped again and shouted louder than before. The rat, meat still in mouth, scampered across Alexi's face, leaped from the table and disappeared.

Alexi stirred, looked around him drunkenly. By the time his eyes reached Aglaya she had hidden Pushkin behind her. Our poet felt ridiculously foolish hiding behind a lady's scented negligee. "What was that all about?" Alexi mumbled. "Who made that noise?"

"It was nothing, my pet," Aglaya replied sweetly. "You snored so loud you woke yourself up. Did you enjoy your supper, Precious?"

"Very very good," Alexi mumbled. "But who is that crouching behind you? Why doesn't he sit with me and have some supper?" His tongue was thick and heavy now. The words came forth with difficulty.

Alexander Sergeievich stepped from behind Aglaya with enormous nervous dignity, his face flushing with an instant heat.

"Pushkin! You old Don Juan devil you! Have you been sampling my wife's delicacies?"

Aglaya said, "I asked him to come and help get you to your room. I knew you didn't want to be bothered with that African! I mean, Leo."

Alexander Sergeievich said in a shaky voice, "But *I* am an African, Madame."

163

She said, "You are the incomparable Alexander Sergeievich Pushkin, the greatest writer on this earth."

"*Mais Oui*, Madame. At your service. But all the same I *am* an African, a Russian of African descent." He countered.

They took Alexi, drunk and stumbling to the bedroom next door. And they undressed him, Alexi mumbling and laughing interchangeably. "You're the best comrade a man could have. Imagine a famous man like you undressing a big fat nothing like me. You are a m-man of gr-great humility and I shall n-n-never for-for-forget your kindness." They put fat Alexi to bed and left him.

Back in front of her bedroom Aglaya leaned against him again and asked, "Won't you come back now to sleep with me? You know Alexi is never going to wake up now. Maybe by tomorrow afternoon."

Pushkin looked down into the heat of her wide dark slanting eyes and felt her youngish body against him. But the desire for her had left him, had flown in the light of day that was breaking all around them.

She wiggled her body against him. She said, *"Pajalsta!"* He said, "Another time." And kissed her briefly on the mouth and left.

CHAPTER FOUR

And indeed there were other times. A passionate Aglaya made her love with the infamous poet Pushkin. On the balcony at midnight they would stand holding hands, enraptured, and watch the dimly-lighted boats pass along the river like fireflies in the night. Listen to the serf band playing downstairs in the main ballroom and the sounds of drunken riotous revelry of the rabid revolutionaries. And watch the clouds sail softly by a full moon heading in opposite directions. Right there on the balcony they made love beneath the stars.

"Make poetry with me, poet!" she shouted softly.

Downstairs, it was: *"A bas le roi!"* . . . "Down with serfdom!" . . . "Up the Russian Republic!"

One evening Aglaya came to Pushkin's bedroom and spent the night with him. But his visit to Kamenka was not all fun and frolic, wine, feasting, adultery, rhetoric and making love. There were serious creative moments. The poet did some writing. He wrote a poem to his Aglaya. The loneliness in her dear dark eyes reached him, touched him. In a way, he really felt compassion for her. He, of all people, certainly knew the meaning of loneliness. The poetry and the loneliness in him made him know she was not a happy woman. So he wrote:

Other men have known my sweet Aglaya
For their mustache and their braided coat,
Some for money—that I comprehend:
Some because they were French
As was my innocent Aglaya;
Leo was no doubt impressive,
Exotic in his terrible "savage" dignity.
Daphnis sang like all the angels;

But tell me, my Aglaya,
What your husband got you for?

And it was actually in Kamenka and not in Kishinev that Pushkin finished and refined THE FOUNTAIN OF BAKSHISARAI, lying face down all night long in the billiard room on a pool table, biting on the tip of his pen till his lips were blue with ink. He worked without stopping, missed breakfast, dinner, supper. Two days in absolute solitude. Leo brought him food, most of which he left uneaten.

He had thought, at first, that the longer he wrote the more facile it would be for him. But he found out very early in the game of life and poetry that the direct opposite was true. The longer he wrote, the more mature he became, the more excellence and craftsmanship and literary truth he demanded of himself. Alexander Sergeievich was his severest, most apprehensive critic. Deeply suspicious of his own facility and craftsmanship. If it went too easily, there was something seriously wrong, maybe even fraudulent. He wrote, rewrote and then rewrote again. The poet tore up many pages. Agonized over every single word, every comma, every colon. He polished it down until it glowed and burnished, sometimes bled from the abrasion, and its deepest truth could never be denied. He laughed, he cried, he shouted for joy at every triumph of the written word and suffered every tragic incident.

And he had many conversations with Leo Andronov. It interested him that Leo Lvovich Andronov was not the obsequious servant-type so popular in the myths of Russian literature. On his part, Leo Lvovich Andronov took a liking to the famous poet. More than once they talked together in Alexander Sergeievich's bedroom.

"What do you think of our hosts?" Alexander Sergeievich asked Leo one evening.

Leo Lvovich answered, "They are not my hosts. I am a servant in this place." They sat across from one another in the brightly-lit, high-ceilinged fourposter bedroom.

"Sorry," Alexander apologized. "But what do you think of the Davydovs?"

"They are all right, but I'm not depending on their revolution," Leo replied.

Alexander Sergeievich sought to change the subject. He had been so harassed by Imperial spies, he was even suspicious of Leo Lvovich. "You say you're from Tashkent," he said jestingly. "But how did you become so black? Is the sun so hot out there then? I think you have more African blood than I."

"Quite possible," Leo answered indifferently. "In the old days many African caravans came through on their way to China and India. But I'm not from Tashkent. I was born in Samarkand."

Leo Andronov was a handsome specimen. Large head with eyes deep dark brown, cheekbones high up near his slanting eyes. Uzbek. Large mouth, wide nostrils that distended when annoyed or angry. Thick curly hair beginning far back on his high wide forehead. Notwithstanding his status as a servant, he was a man who took his dignity for granted. "They talk revolution, but they don't talk it with me, Your Excellency!"

"I am not Your Excellency," Alexander Sergeievich replied. "You and I are brothers."

"To be sure, Your Nobility," Leo said with amused sarcasm. "But your revolutionaries have no contact with the Russian masses. They are going to have a revolution of the celebrities and elitists and nobility." He laughed heartily at the querulous look on Alexander Sergeievich's face.

Pushkin could not help laughing. Staring into his intelligent face, Pushkin figured Lvovich was a combination of African, Arab, Russian and Chinese. It was a magnificent combination. He'd never seen a more universal face in all his life.

"I talk with you, Alexander Sergeievich, because you're different from them. Your work speaks to the common people."

Alexander Sergeievich was moved. He tried desperately to hide his pride and his embarrassment. It was one thing to be appreciated by the revolutionary elite, but it was qualitatively different to see admiration in the eyes of someone like Leo Adronov. Leo was of the people to whom he actually wrote and hoped fervently to reach, even though he knew, realistically, that most of the Russian masses were hopelessly illiterate. He thrust out his hand to Adronov and embraced him by the shoulders. "Thank you so much, brother!" He kissed Leo on both cheeks.

He poured them both a pony of vodka and they toasted the downfall of the Emperor. "Death to slavery!" Pushkin shouted. "Death to slavery everywhere! In Russia and America!" He leaped up into the middle of his bed and began to recite new verses from his ODE TO FREEDOM.

One evening Ivan Mikhailovich, the self-proclaimed *dangerous* revolutionary of His Majesty's Enqineering Corps, came into Pushkin's room to have a drink with the poet. When he discovered Pushkin fraternizing with Leo Adronov, he demanded, "Why are you socializing with this African serf? It isn't dignified. A man like you, with your genius and prestige—"

Alexander Sergeievich answered heatedly, "We're both of African descent. He might be a long lost relative, for all I know."

Ivan Mikhailovich said, "But you're not an African, Alexander Sergeievich. You're more Russian than the rest of us put together. Your great-grandfather was an African. And this man is a servant, a person of no particular account. I mean— but you, you're—"

Pushkin exploded. "Don't you tell me who I am! I'm an African because I choose to identify with my great-grandfather, and I choose to be an African because it makes me feel more honorable. Anyone can be a Russian. I choose to identify with that part of me that you choose to despise. If that upsets you, what kind of revolutionary are you?"

"But, Alexander Sergeievich, I didn't mean—I only meant—"

"You make me ashamed to be a Russian." He turned to his Uzbek friend. "Please excuse our bad manners, Leo Lvovich. The Great White Russian is as boorish as the Russian bear."

"You misunderstand me, Alexander Sergeievich," Ivan Mikhailovich replied anxiously. "I didn't mean—"

"I know very well what you mean," Pushkin countered disdainfully. "You advocate an exclusive revolution of the privileged nobility, or all the superior Great White Russians. Yet there's more worth to my African brother here than all of you so-called revolutionaries put together. You're as bad as the fornicating Greeks. You'll never overthrow a goddamn thing!" Yet in his heart and soul Alexander Sergeievich wanted fervently to believe in a Russian revolutionary movement, in his time. A movement that would include Russians, Tartars, Armenians, Cossacks, Jews, Uzbeks, Black, brown, white, yellow, every single being who labored under the yoke of His Majesty's Imperialism.

One day the legendary General Raevsky visited Kamenka, with his sons and daughters. Alexander Sergeievich was delighted, though Marya did not come with them. Notwithstanding, they were like family to him. Like the good old times that never really were. That weekend the Davydov's establishment was a hotbed of subversion. They gathered under the pretext of celebrating Grandma Davydov's birthday, but actually they had come to plan a secret conference of the UNION OF THE SOUTH with its counterpart of the NORTH to be held clandestinely in Moscow that next winter. Both Pushkin and General Raevsky were kept on the periphery of the secret society. Both suspected its existence, but were never brought into the fold. The group felt that the General was too elderly and too set in his attitudes to be of any use to the revolution.

As for Alexander Sergeievich, it was his good friend Ivan Pushchin's idea, along with others, to keep the poet out of actual membership in subversive societies. "Don't involve Alexander Sergeievich," Pushchin had argued with them vociferously, "in any of our revolutionary conspiracies. He is too outspoken and impulsive. Also he's too valuable to our cause to risk his life in these adventures which may come to naught but the scaffold or Siberia. Pushkin is our only hope to awaken the sleeping masses."

This attitude toward him had become another source of agitation to our poet. He felt betrayed, rejected, and distrusted. Outside again. Here he was exiled because of his inflammatory writings, and at the same time not taken seriously by the very same men who professed to be inspired and inflamed by his revolutionary output. Here for once he'd thought he was in a place where he was accepted, loved, even revered. To hell with them! He didn't need them. He didn't need anything or anybody. He had his poetry, he told himself. That was where the real world was.

One evening there was a gathering at the Davydov's which General Raevsky and Pushkin attended. The whole meeting was manipulated to prove to the General that no secret organization could possibly exist anywhere in Russia. At one point in the meeting, Ivan Yakushkin, leader of the Southern Union, put it up to the General. "Let's say for the sake of argument that there is such an organization, are you ready at this very moment to join?" They were all gathered in the softly lighted private chapel of the Davydovs.

"Of course," the General answered unhesitatingly, enthusiastically, "I most certainly am!"

"In that case, shake my hand," Yakushkin said, smiling and reaching his hand toward General Raevsky. When the General extended his hand, Yakushkin broke down into laughter. "You see, it's all a joke. There's no such organization." At which point all the co-conspirators burst into laughter.

Alexander Sergeievich leaped to his feet with tears spilling from his dark eyes. "Tovarischi, I have never been so unhappy in all my life. Here I was thinking at long last I would be a part of something truly wonderful, something really ennobling and worth living for, even dying for, and it all turns out to be a terrible farce. I tell you, comrades, I have never been so disappointed in all my life. A revolution is nothing to joke about. It is the most beautiful thing that can happen to a people in a lifetime. It is like the most beautiful poem in all the world."

From conversation with the plotters Alexander Sergeievich came to understand that unlike what he had envisioned, his colleagues were not planning a people's revolution. They planned an elitist military coup like the Spanish, Portuguese and the Neapolitan revolutions of the 1820's.

One evening late at night Pushkin wrote his EPISTLE TO BASIL DAVYDOV, in which he said his "revolutionary" comrades were filling:

The cup of Freedom
With chilled, flat wine,
And tossing it down their gullets
With Toasts to Victory, Theirs and Hers;
But they are playing games in Naples
And Freedom will not yet survive.

One evening he was having drinks with Basil Davydov. Davydov was explaining patiently to young Pushkin that the only way to overthrow the monarchy was through an elitist military coup d'état. "It's the only way, Alexander Sergeievich. Look at what's happening in Naples with Carbonari. It's naive to think of a revolution of the peasants and the working people. They don't have the necessary intelligence. Things would surely get out of hand."

"What's happening in Naples?" Alexander Sergeievich demanded. "Absolutely nothing. As naive as I may be, I know one thing to be as fundamental as the sunrise in the Caucasus. Freedom won by the military elitists will never filter down to the common people."

"Don't get me wrong, Alexander Sergeievich. No revolution is being plotted," Basil Davydov assured the poet, condescendingly.

There was always this lingering suspicion that, even with his avowed comrades, the African in him had something to do with this alienation he felt so deeply.

That night after the fraudulent meeting, he could not inveigle sleep to come. Even though he did not believe in their coup d'état, he resented deeply their rejection of him. Yebat them! he told himself, but his heart knew the terrible lonely feeling of the outsider again. All of his remembered life, since infancy, he had known this agony of not belonging, of being not of this earth. From his vainglorious mother, from his whining innocuous father. And now he found himself outside again, even among his friends and comrades. Outside of everything that mattered. He remembered the exquisite emotion he'd known that first night, of belonging. A welcomed emotion that, heretofore, had been a stranger to him. He had found a home, at last! They loved him, they accepted him, they loved him— loved him! They revered him! Euphoria! He had opened up his lonely heart of hearts to them. He had gone around like a man intoxicated by the rarest wines. And now this. What the hell was wrong with him? "Yebat them!" he shouted softly in his desperate solitude. They were not authentic Russians anyway. Most of them had forgotten how to speak their native language. When he engaged them in conversation he spoke the Russian of the peasantry much to their annoyance. He spoke in broad exaggerated folk idioms and accents. He was a lowly uncouth muzhik when he talked with them. And he made them feel uneasy.

Even passionate Aglaya, who shared his bed that night, could not cure his restlessness. He realized now he'd always sought in the arms of women assurance that he was likable, perhaps even lovable. But it had never been enough for him. He wanted to be loved for himself and not for his poetry or the popularity it had provided him. Sometimes he didn't know what he wanted. Did he really want his comrades to forget that the prideful blood of Africa flowed in his veins?

When sensuous sensitive Aglaya could not arouse this passionate poet as she lay naked up against his nervous body with her voluptuous limbs and her active hands, lustful lips, she held his manhood, soft, relaxed now, in her softer fingers. She asked him, "What's wrong Sasha, Chérie? Am I so unappealing then?"

He held her trembling body close to him, but she knew the feeble gesture from the real thing. "Nothing's wrong, Aglaya, my pet. I'm just very very tired tonight."

"Tired of what, mon petit? And have you grown tired of your Aglaya then?"

He kissed her questioning lips, now eager for his love and passion. Why not just lose himself in the willing arms of this lovely woman who reminded him so much of his Tatyana with her openness, her generosity, her earthiness, her candor, her hungry lips, her almost total lack of artifice? In a world where everything was fraudulent, she was the refreshment that his soul needed, desperately. Tanya! He could see her now. Crossing herself and genuflecting in the icon corner before going into bed with him, like saying "Grace" before the feast.

170

Coming out of his Tatyana daydream he was conscious of Aglaya sobbing quietly, and the wetness on his chest. "So that's it, eh? I'm nothing to you then. Just a thing to go to bed with, to fornicate with. You believe everything they say about me. I'm just an ordinary slattern to you then, to fornicate with and then forget." She went on and on, sobbing and talking interchangeably. "I am not the kind of human being to share your heartache with, or intellect. I'm just a stupid bitch in perpetual heat—"

"Hush!" he shouted softly to her. "Shut up your silly babbling, you sweet stupid sensitive wench!"

"Talk with me then," she pleaded. "Don't treat me like an outsider though I may truly be unworthy of your deepest thoughts."

She had said the magic word unknowingly. Outsider. In his home in Moscow he and Tatyana had always been outside. An outsider because he was too African? "A throwback," his mother said, "to his 'savage' great-grandfather." A pariah in his own home, and now, an outsider among his revolutionary comrades at Kamenka. Aglaya said huskily, "Tell me, dear heart, what is troubling you?" He kept thinking of this peasant woman from the steppes of the River Don. Tanya of the flaxen tresses. Tatyana, the love poem of his agonizing adolescence; haunter of his secret wicked dreams, his sweet and dreadful sensuality. Tanya, who had taught him giving, giving him the gift of love.

"I thought I was among people with a noble purpose in their lives, a group of revolutionaries," Pushkin answered. "And now I find it's all a joke. But perhaps it isn't a joke then. Maybe they were lying to me," he added hopefully.

"They are very dangerous revolutionaries," Aglaya told him. "All of them excepting my beloved Fat Alexi."

"Perhaps they don't trust me then," Alexander Sergeievich said morosely.

"They trust you," Aglaya assured him. "They trust you and they love you, even as I love you. They love you differently, of course. But they don't want you to expose yourself. You're too valuable to their cause, mon chérie."

"They believe I am not trustworthy." Even as he said it, he wanted this lost and lonely woman to tell him that it wasn't true. He needed a faith to live for. Desperately he needed someone to have faith in him.

"You are wrong again, mon petit," Aglaya whispered. "You are trustworthy, sensitive, wise, perceptive, lovable—" She sang a love song in his happy ears even as she nibbled gently at them. She continued her little sing-song love song. "Wonderful, ingenious and ingenuous, desirable, excitable, African, dynamic. You are all these things and so much, much more, but you are also impetuous. And they would save you from your own impetuosity which is an essential part of your irresistible charm. And after all, you are the incomparable Alexander Sergeievich Pushkin. And they must protect you, because there is no one else like you on this entire earth."

He said, "But how can I be one half of all these things, when I have just begun to do the work I have to do?"

"You are absolutely every single one of these things. And even much much more, and that is why I worship you," Aglaya insisted.

He did not know how to contend with a woman who talked as much as he, and was articulate. He said gruffly, "Shut up, you babbling wench. You talk too much."

And he took her into his arms again and felt her tears upon his neck and her heart thump up against his chest, and she took the growing hardness in her hand, and she guided it to the misty place where her love was more than ready for him. And loneliness became a fleeting stranger as they made desperate love together, as the moonlight spilled into the room luxuriantly.

CHAPTER FIVE

Back in Kishinev was like coming from fairyland to a life of harsh reality. His spirits dragged as he rode in the back of a telega atop his trunk through the muddy main street of the town, clogged now with a traffic of ragged muzhiks on foot, horses, goats and belching camels. Camels who seemed, Pushkin thought, to have been put together by a committee that could not come to any agreement as to how these ungainly animals should be constructed. The narrow streets, the smells, the sounds—he felt an overwhelming tedium even before he reached his living quarters with the kindly General Insov.

That night he made entries in his diary.

Where is Russia? What is Russia? What is a Russian? Is it the carefree life of Kamenka by the moonlit waters? Good food, drinking, adultery, lovemaking, the good life with reveling revolutionary rhetoricians? Or is it the illiterate muzhik bent beneath the yoke, standing knee deep in the muck and mire of his poverty, living from hand to mouth and thanking the gracious God and Blessed Virgin for every breath he took, barely living, never traveling more than twenty versts from the place that birthed him? Is it my poem, THE VILLAGE, *head down, docile under the pursuing lash, the gaunt old serf struggling down the furrows of some implacable master?* Not daring to dream anymore, or hope? Is it the Cossack living out his life along the broad endless beautiful life-giving steppes along the River Don, the giant breadbasket of Imperial Russia, the blessed steppes, an infinity of brownish-yellow stalks of flax and grain dancing in autumnal breezes, the broadest plains in all this earth? Is it ancient Kiev in the vast Ukraine? Is it the 'wild' unconquered Circassians of the Caucasus, with their indomitable spirit? Is it the people of the Crimea? Is it the sloe-eyed Tartars, Turks, Tadjiks, the Uzbeks of Tashkent, Bukhara and Samarkand on the far-off Eastern desert? Is it the vast and frozen regions of Siberia? Where is Imperial Russia? Is it Moscow, beloved mother of all Russian cities? Is it in Saint Petersburg? In the Imperial Palace where Alexander the

Great, Czar of all the Russias lives gluttonously in ostentatious splendor? *Venice of the North*, Great Peter's city on the Neva? Is it in God-forsaken Kishinev?

Wherever it was, Pushkin wanted to leave this frontier outhouse behind him for all times.

That same night he wrote to his great influential friend, Prince Vyazemsky in Saint Petersburg.

Autumn is coming to this mudhole of the Southern Colonies, and I am freezing to death in this Southern paradise. Tell 'Alexander the Great' [his ironic nomenclature for the Emperor] I'm a good boy now. I have mended my youthful ways. Tell him any damn thing. How can I rehabilitate myself in this uninspired, godforsaken village where everything and everybody activates against the artistic temperament? Where ignorance and illiteracy run amuck. There is no one to talk to excepting dear Papa Insov, and he keeps too busy with his Imperial Majesty's business and keeping me out of mischief and under house detention. One finally runs out of breath chasing the few interesting and available women. One cannot construct an entire life on fornication, as you call it. I prefer to call it 'Yebat'. The serfs are more poetic than you ennobled Russians at the capital. Perhaps 'making love' is more appropriate for me, since usually I must feel deeply for a woman with whom I make love. I am not a cold-blooded fornicator. I need the fraternal community of fellow artists, my friends and comrades of Saint Petersburg. I was born and brought up in a metropolitan city. Frontier life is not for me. If I don't get out of this place, I shall go quietly out of my mind. No, not quietly, loudly, screaming! If you are my friend, speak to the Great One on my behalf. Ask Zukovsky and Turgenev to put in a good word for me. I am desperate!

Of all the ailments that afflicted Pushkin in his exile, the most debilitating was his terrible sense of alienation. His aloneness was an all-consuming passion, his desperate need for love and comradeship and understanding was ever with him day and night. It was a time when he was constantly taking inventory of himself. Who was he? A Russian with the royal blood of Africa in his veins? An African who was born in Russia? What was he all about? What was he worth to himself? To his family? To his friends who conspired behind his back to keep him out of a revolutionary conspiracy? Sometimes he felt like screaming: "What's the fornicating use!" What was his writing all about? Was poetry its own justification? At the Lycée when he was only fifteen he had written: "Imagination, only thy art my reward!" But it had never been enough for him. Art for art's own precious sake would never be enough for him. It was a time when he found himself deep deep down in the pit of his despondency. He had to know what he was worth, what his life meant. Doubts assailed him. He developed stomach cramps, dysentery. He tried to write himself out of it. In his loneliest of moments in his dim lit room he began to write THE SOWER. There were those who believed that Alexander Sergeievich Pushkin had every right to write of himself, and proudly:

A lonely sower of liberty,
I left my dwelling early
Before the rising of the stars,
And with my clean unsullied hand,
I scattered life-giving seed
Among the enslaved furrows.

Was it utterly arrogant of him to make such claims about his writing? He sometimes wondered. Yet he wrote with lofty self-esteem:

I neither live nor write for praise, but fear
To die unknown in fame and story.
I'd rather win a little place
For my sad name, some share of glory,
One note, one line of poetry
That, like a friend, shall speak of me.

There were days when he dwelt in a roaring living silence, as if he walked on tiptoes through the lonely chambers of his heart. Deep deep in his dreary solitude, he wrote wistfully and confidently, and read loudly to himself:

Perhaps my liens a stranger's heart
May move; perhaps by luck of fate,
At last dark let the will not swallow
The stanzas I today create
Perhaps (what overwhelming hope!)
A simple fellow may some day
Point to my portrait and declare:
"He was a poet, a man of scope!"
A lover of the peaceful Muses,
Receive my thanks and salutations—
O dearest friend whose memory
Will shrine my fugitive creation,
Whose hand of grace may yet caress
An old man's bays with tenderness.

The swift wheels of the capital city turned, albeit slowly, creakily. And it took many days and nights for word to reach him across the steppes more than a thousand versts away from his Saint Petersburg. The talk amongst the capital literati was: "Poor Pushkin! Something must be done to salvage this enormous talent for the glory of the Motherland."

While the wheels turned squeakily in the capital city, autumn came early to Kishinev, putting frost around the windows, and snow began to fall and camels shivered pathetically so far from their desert homeland. Wolves howled throughout the night. Pushkin trembled in his misery and desolation.

As winter swiftly approached, word came across the great white steppes along with the wind and the howling blizzards, that the despairing poet was being transferred to Odessa to work under the wise benevolence of one Count Vorontsov. Pushkin had already heard of the famous Anglophile by the name of Count M. S. Vorontsov, Governor General of Southern Russia in Odessa, not very many versts from Kishinev. The Count had been educated in London and spoke Russian with a British accent. His personal secretary and receptionist was British. He even had a British groom, lackey for his British horses. Vorontsov was a blond, handsome, thin-lipped, pinched nosed, clipped-voiced, through-the-teeth gentleman, who saw himself as Viceroy for His Imperial Majesty, looked down upon the natives of his provinces as his subjects. He had gathered around him a coterie of sycophants and expert arse-kissers, mostly British-born, toadying to his every whim. He set aside an hour each day to receive suppliants at court. He listened to them with a paternalistic smile which thinly disguised his insufferable contempt. Albeit he was a consummate actor and an expert at dissembling.

Odessa! Alexander Sergeievich was overcome with joy. Odessa-by-the-Black-Sea! He had made two brief visits to this seacoast city. It was not Moscow or Saint Petersburg, and no closer to those fabulous places of his wasted youth. Actually, it was a few versts further south. But it was leaving Kishinev, and that was good enough for Pushkin, momentarily. Odessa was a fast growing city with a theatre and Italian opera and ballet! And restaurants and interesting rhetoric and dialogue. It was almost like going home. His most serious regret was to leave "Papa Insov." Somewhere deep inside of him there was this sleeping dread of what a new chief held in store for him.

After Pushkin left Kishinev, Papa Insov went around shaking his head sadly and prophesying to all who would listen. "Oh why did he leave me? He'll see! He will not get along with Vorontsov. And I loved him like a son. Loved him like my very own!" As if Alexander Sergeievich himself had requested his transfer. It was a move by the Foreign Minister, Count Nesselrode, to place our poet under stricter firmer supervision.

In the summer, black dust covered everything in Odessa like desert sand. It drifted along the unpaved streets, crept up to the second floor of buildings, crunchily filled the mouths and blackened the teeth, clogged the nostrils, burned the eyes. Living in Odessa was like working a coal mine. Noblemen and ladies wore shawls and capes to protect their faces and themselves from the inevitable black dust. Alexander Sergeievich came this time in autumn as did the rains, when, instead of dust, everyone was ankle deep in mud. Carriages got stuck in the thick black quagmire. Crossing the street was a perilous venture. One might very well lose a boot or two. Pontoons were constructed for ladies in long evening dresses to step onto out of their expensive carriages.

Odessa was a frontier town fast becoming a thriving metropolis. It was a commercial center where each day ships came in from far away bringing delicacies for the natives, who were more than ready for them. Alexander Sergeievich wrote into his diary: "Wheat, flax, linseed, cloth, dresses, perfumes, china, latest styles, opera, ballet, news from the outside world. Africa, China, Europe. War? Famine? Revolution? What's happening out there in that other world?"

Money changers by the hundreds converged upon Odessa, and fortunes were made almost overnight. A jubilant Pushkin happened joyously along with the happenings that were Odessa-by-the-sea. There was the theatre where troupes come in from all over the world.

Lovely ladies sat in expensive gowns of the very latest styles just off the ships from Europe. Madame sat there in her box surrounded by young gallant admirers, while her rotund wealthy husband snored through most of the performance, his fat smiling face fixed in a smug complacency, while flirtations went apace and long-lasting assignations were consummated.

A rich man's prestige was measured by the number of young stallions and gallants his wife attracted. Cuckoldry was a way of life. Of course, each nobleman had a few mistresses in his repertoire. Each night Alexander Sergeievich went to the theatre, taking in the sights and occurrences. He was truly in his element. Then one night he met voluptuous Carolina at a reception given for a troupe of ballet performers.

Carolina Sohansky was the elegant older sister of Evaline Hansky, who was to marry Honore de Balzac. Carolina was a slim majestic woman. Her overripened mouth seemed lecherous and greedy for life and love and kisses. And particularly for intrigue. Her wide blue eyes seemed always on the alert, expecting or suspecting something. All that, and she was an intellectual, which somehow bothered Pushkin. But why should it bother him, he wondered. Why should he feel threatened by a woman who questioned everything, the Emperor, God, art, literature and politics?

One night as they sat together in her luxuriant salon drinking expensive wine and drinking in each other, she asked, "Did you really mean everything you said in THE GABRILIAD?"

"I mean everything I ever write, especially at the time I write it." He added, "Of course, one's attitude is changing every moment of one's life."

"Do you think there'll ever be a revolution in Imperial Russia?" she asked.

"Ever is a very long time," he answered cagily.

"Do you believe that serfdom should be abolished all over Russia? Do you think the serfs are ready for it?"

This was a question he would never evade. Not even before the Emperor or the King of Heaven. He answered quickly, "Every Russian infant is born ready to be free. Every person on this earth."

Carolina could hold her drinks with the stoutest drinking Hussar. As they got drunker that night, Alexander Sergeievich became more amorous, but the more intoxicated she became, the more she wanted to engage in intellectual conversation.

She wanted to discuss the vicissitudes of Russian serfdom, especially those of women serfs.

"When I think of what a female serf has to look forward to, I awake in the middle of the night and cry," she said. "The first time I read your poem, THE VILLAGE, it brought tears to my eyes. Your poem truly broke my heart."

"Speaking of sleep, my pigeon, don't you think it's time for us to get some?" Alexander Sergeievich stretched his arms and yawned loudly and suggestively.

"And does my conversation bore you then?" She said fretfully. "You never talk to me seriously. You treat me as if I'm nothing but a common serf girl."

"What have we been doing ever since we arrived here, ever since I've been calling on you? Talk-talk-talk-talk!" He stared at her suspiciously. "Don't you believe in making love then?" It was not that he needed to sleep with this voluptuous woman. He was not overcome with an uncontrollable passion for her. It was merely that he had grown weary with the drift of the conversation, felt strangely threatened by Carolina Sohansky's facile intellectualism.

Carolina said, "Yes, but—"

He did not need this woman this night. So why not just drop the question completely? There was no perspiration on his lips, no palpitation of his heart. He felt no throbbing in the middle of him. He was not inflamed with desire. Yet he heard himself continue, "It's been months, and we have not gone near your bedroom." He looked around him drunkenly and began to put on his hareskin greatcoat. It was winter and he could hear the snowstorm howling outside like a pack of wild and hungry wolves. He hated the idea of going out in the cold dark night, when there was a warm bed here to sleep in and a very lusty sleeping partner. He was pretending and the drunken woman did not understand. She was six years older than our poet and he had no illusions regarding her chastity. No woman lived as lavishly in Imperial Russia as she did without being bought and paid for.

"Where are you going, my pet?"

"Home, as if I had a modicum of intelligence," he answered. "As I should have done long before."

"And when will I see you again, mon petit?" She said coyly.

"Since I do not believe in platonic or unrequited love, you will probably never see me in your home again."

"But, my pet, I do love you. Truly I adore you and no other."

"You have a peculiar way of demonstrating your affection." He had his greatcoat on now and moved toward the door, determinedly.

"But, please, don't leave me now, you impetuous darling," she pleaded. "You should see that sensual mouth of yours. You're like a little boy pouting because he cannot have his way. And you can always have your way with me, if you will only persevere."

He had his back to her now, moving toward the door as the swirling blizzard raged outside. He would have to walk all the way to his hotel. There would be no coaches on the street. He hated whatever it was that kept him from leaving. She was undressing as she spoke to him.

"Come now then," she commanded him, "and let us have one more drink before you go if you insist on leaving me in all my terrible frustration."

He turned toward her and there she stood before him in all her stark and gleaming nakedness. Her ample breasts were breathing at him, her long legs so slimly round, inviting and provocative. He wanted to leave, he wanted to stay. He hated her for causing him such indecisiveness. "Come," she said, "my sweetheart. It is freezing cold outside and no coaches on the street this time of night. Come and keep your darling warm."

He stared at her with the heat in his eyes and anger almost blinding him. She'd known all along he was pretending.

She moved toward him with those long lovely naked legs of hers, seductively, smiling, like a regal lioness stalking, certain of her hapless prey. He stood there watching her coming to him, hating the helplessness in him, his utter vulnerability. He wanted to turn from her and be gone away from this voluptuous woman, even as he heard the howling blizzard outside blustering the shuttered windows.

Now she was all amongst him, as she put her arms around his neck and pushed her slim thighs up against him. She felt him growing hard against the middle of her, and she knew she was in complete control. She seized his mouth with her rich licentious lips. She reached down and put her hot hand on his growing hardness.

She smiled arrogantly and said, "Then it's actually true what they say about you Africans. You do possess a handsome and prodigious penis."

Alexander Sergeievich smiled angrily back at Carolina. He took her arms down from around his neck methodically, and stepped back from her. "What a pity you will never know the actual truth from this very particular African."

He turned from her and went out into the howling snowstorm and sloshed his way through the drifting snowbanks all the way to his hotel. He swore off fornicating then and there.

The next day he could not get Carolina off his mind. He tried to escape from her into his poetry, started a poem he called GYPSIES, but there she lay on every sheet of paper, every line, every word and comma, naked with her long legs and slim thighs up against him, her wide eyes blue and asking questions. He told himself without conviction that she was just a poem he had concocted. He had conjured up a nightmare. He had to know all there was to know about this lustful lusty intellectual. How could she afford such a luxurious salon, a palatial villa hanging like a giant beehive on a cliff overlooking the Black Sea, where she entertained her young gallants? Was she independently wealthy? An heiress? Like Svetlina of the Hussar Guards? He had to know. But no one seemed to know anything about this woman.

Then one day there was a knock upon his door, and when he opened it, in walked Alexander Raevsky. The two men embraced and kissed and drank much vodka and sat and talked of old times. Raevsky had not changed noticeably. He was the same tall rangy handsome cynic with the yellowish and arrogant eyes. According to him, "Politics is the game of fools. . . . Serfs deserve their serfdom or they would not be serfs. They would have long since changed their situation. . . . Women were not made to love, but to be made love to or at, whichever, but never to be taken seriously."

Finally, the question came inevitably around to Carolina Sohansky. And of course Carolina was the mistress of the infamous Count DeWitt, who was an acknowledged member of the Czarist Secret Police, the notorious Third Section of His Imperial Majesty's personal Chancery.

Pushkin's heart and spirits sank lower than they already were. He felt his heartbeat quickening.

"Are you quite sure?" he asked.

"Of course, my dear sweet innocent child," Raevsky replied. "Everyone in Odessa knows of it excepting you."

"And Carolina then?"

"They work hand in hand, my poor baby. She invites all the radical young intellectuals to her palatial residence and gets them drunk and opens up those lovely legs of hers and then gets them to tell her all of their subversive ideas, after which they mysteriously disappear and end up in Siberia or some other place God never cast his eyes upon."

Pushkin rose from his chair and began to pace the floor. "God damn that Carolina wench! How could I have been so stupid? I'm undone! Alexander the Great will surely cook my Russian goose this time."

The nattily attired coxcomb said, sardonically, "What are you worried about, my dear innocent child? Sasha Pavlovich Romanov knows all your poems and ideas by heart by now. He is the Emperor of all the Russias. Why do you suppose they won't let you back into Saint Petersburg? Do you imagine it's because he's jealous of your reputation with the ladies at the Czarist court? He's already sampled every one of them."

"Of course," Alexander Sergeievich responded, sighing with relief. "I have no secrets from the Great One. Everything's in what I write."

They sat and talked far into the night, Raevsky doing most of the talking, Pushkin the avid and attentive listener. Alexander Sergeievich still held a fascination for this self-centered genius of a cynical popinjay. Carolina's role was very clear to him now. She was a sweet and lovely trap and a bait for lecherous revolutionaries like himself. And though he agreed with Raevsky that she presented no danger to him, he never sought her company again. He fell out of love with Carolina and fell immediately in love with Madame Amelia Riznicha.

Even while he went about falling in love again, which was a pure and simple act of self-defense against his maddening loneliness, he drove himself into his work to protect himself from madness. The possibility of losing his mind was ever with him. He started working on GYPSIES again. He recalled his days in Kishinev when he sought out those liberated nomads on the edge of town. It had appeared to our romantic poet to be the sanest freest spot on this entire Russian earth. He also wrote a desperate poem: GOD GRANT THAT I MAY NOT GO MAD! He was sick to the heart of words like "civilization," and "progress." In this cold white Russian world, he longed for Africa. He worked in a quiet heat of creative ecstasy. He would not answer the door when visitors knocked. Not even to Alexander Raevsky, who would stand outside and bang on the door and shout his name.

"Alexander Sergeievich! It's me, your comrade Raevsky! I must speak with you on a matter of monumental importance!"

He did not need Raevsky's nihilistic attitudes. He needed to believe in life. The so-called civilized nobility of Petersburg and Moscow was not life as it could be lived. He needed desperately to believe in GYPSIES.

And he spent his restive sleepless nights writing about a man, Aleko, a jaded Russian cosmopolite who escaped from the maddening revelry of Saint Petersburg and had run away and joined a band of gypsies. Aleko falls in love with a young gypsy girl, Zemfira. They live together with her father, the hetman of the gypsy band. Alexander Sergeievich thought a lot these days of writing in prose. He had taught himself to be conversant in English and Italian as well as French. He was reading Shakespeare and was deeply impressed, and he promised himself that he would one day write a Russian tragedy. Imperial Russia was a tragic land. In GYPSIES, he began to move toward these determinations. He still wrote in verse but this time interspersed his verse with dialogue. The gypsy girl, Zemfira, asks Aleko, the sophisticated Russian from the capital city:

Tell me, my friend: don't you regret
All you left behind for good?
Aleko: What did I leave behind?
Zemfira: You know
Your country's people, city life.
Aleko: I have no regrets. Could you but know,
Could you but feel how city life
Imprisons, stifles, warps the Soul!
What did I leave behind? Deceit,
Betrayal, prejudice's voice,
The persecution of the mob—
Or glory, triumph, crowned with shame.

These days Alexander Sergeievich saw his own life as meaningless, shameful, enshrouded as it was with so-called fame. He walked the floor of his lonely room, sat down again and wrote:

Zemfira: But there are mighty mansions there,
And many colored carpets too
And games and merriment and feasts,
And maidens clad in rich attire . . .

The idyllic life between Zemfira and Aleko lasts blissfully for several years, till she falls in love with another man. Aleko comes upon her in his arms and kills them both by stabbing. Zemfira's father banishes him from the gypsy band.

Leave us, proud man. Away, be gone.
We are wild people without laws.
We punish not with pain or death.
Your blood, your groans we do not need;
But we can't brook a killer here . . .
You were not born for freedom's ways
Begone, and peace be with your Soul.

The gypsy band leaves Aleko, the civilized Russian man, alone and desolate on the steppes. With all of Pushkin's romanticism, he was too much of a realist to see the gypsy life as Utopia. The battle always raged in him between romance and reality. On the one hand he saw himself standing firmly committed to change, and on the other was "God's Will and the Emperor's" and his implacable Fate! This life of primitive bliss was at best transitory, ephemeral. In his epilogue he wrote:

But even you, nature's poor sons,
Cannot lay claim to happiness!
And in your tattered tents you dream
Like other men, tormented dreams.
Wandering through the steppes, you feel,
Like other men misfortune's blows.
Everywhere passions wreak their ills
And against the Fates there, there's no defense.

The poet did not, could not finish his GYPSIES all in one sitting. Too many things distracted him. But he was writing. He was writing! And he was saying what he wished to say. He was consciously drifting away from the influence of Lord Byron. Some days he would work all through the night and fall asleep at his desk, the nibbled quill pen dropped beside him on the floor, the papers scattered. And hours later when he awoke, with bloodshot eyes he would reread what he had written and wonder agonizingly how he could have written such tripe, such unadulterated excrement! At other times, he would marvel over the words his weary mind had wrought. And he would laugh aloud and sometimes weep over a beautiful and just-right word, a phrase, a clause, an entire stanza. "That's it! That's it! By the Holy Virgin, there is no other way to do it, say it!" Every time he sat down to his desk, he profoundly felt a sense of mission. He would show them what magic the great-grandson of an African prince could work with the Russian language and its literature. He would excel. He would teach them how to read and write! Grandmama Hannibal was often on his mind these days. She had gone to her eternal rest now, but she had charged him with a great mission and responsibility.

Ivan Riznich, the husband of Pushkin's new love, Amelia Riznichna, was a Dalmatian grain merchant. Her father was an Austrian banker. The only possible problem of a liaison with a married lady was the trifling inconvenience of a pesky duel—that is, if one were indiscreet. In this kind of an affair of the heart and bedroom, no other obligation was expected or intended. A situation accepted amiably by wealthy husbands of the nobility. Amelia Riznichna was a slim elegant woman with dark sparkling eyes—wide, staring and intelligent—and long black hair.

At the theatre one night, Alexander Sergeievich had stared at her distractedly with his opera glasses till her pink cheeks turned as red as apples from the province of the Don Cossacks. Monsieur Riznich was not unaware of Pushkin's eyes upon Amelia, and he felt proud that his wife was beautiful enough to attract the obvious stares of such a famous and notorious roue as A. S. Pushkin, the dashing Don Juan of the written word. They met at the end of the second act as Alexander Sergeievich sat outside the theatre on the marble steps sipping Italian ices underneath a soft spring night that had come unusually early to Odessa-by-the-Black Sea. As he watched her coming down the steps toward him, he sensed an eerie feeling of déjà vu, though he knew in fact he'd never seen her before. Yet somehow he also knew what she would sound like when she spoke. He would know he'd heard her voice before, somewhere sometime perhaps in some distant dreams he'd dreamt. Her voice would be deep and rich and resonant and musical. It would make him think of cellos playing Mozart music.

Pushkin leapt to his feet as she walked toward him. As if by previous arrangement, one of her coterie of young gallants stepped forward and said, "May I have the pleasure to present to you, Madame Amelia Riznichna? And to you, Madame, may I present Monsieur Alexander Sergeievich Pushkin?"

The flustered Pushkin bowed and said, "I assure you it is my pleasure, Monsieur, for which I shall be eternally indebted to you." He kissed Madame's extended hand.

"And how has our esteemed poet enjoyed the play thus far?" Amelia Riznichna asked coquettishly. Her voice was like a symphony composed especially for cellos. Fundamentally, Alexander Sergeievich was bashful, and he covered up his shyness with an air of *savoir faire* and worldliness.

"Madame, there was nothing on the stage as magnetic as was in the Riznich box." He replied. "You are a magnificent distraction. Blame yourself as I know nothing of what was happening on the stage."

Her eyes were dark blazing busy bodies. They stared at him and looked away at the same time. Was she actually staring at him or at other folk in other places? Her wide black eyes were deep and limpid and all angelic innocence, yet seemed to hold in them all the knowing in the world. Every single part of him, intellectually, spiritually, physically, knew an undeniable attraction to this lovely mystery of a woman. At the same time he felt like running for his worthless life. Women will be the death of me! There was a bright dark flame burning in her eyes, and he was afraid it would consume them both if he ever got too close. But he knew he must get close to this woman who would probably change his life forever.

Of an evening Amelia Riznichna was like a queen holding court, and there were many voluntary young slaves-of-love more than willing to pay court to her. She attracted young gallants like the nectar of a lovely flower attracted bees, especially one young wealthy landowner by the name of Yablonovsky. Sometimes Pushkin had to stand in line like a beggar supplicant as she sat on her queenly throne chair in her vast high-ceilinged drawing room. The chair itself was made of the very finest East Indian teakwood, hand-engraved, with a teakwood canopy overhead with intricate carvings adorning each side and extending downward from the canopy in arcs and curves. She sat there regally like a queen, submerged almost in silken goose-down pillows. The walls were hung in Chinese silk. It anguished Alexander Sergeievich to see so many jealous sycophants. He felt the entire role beneath his dignity and hers. And yet against his will, he queued up along with all the other anxious would-be lovers.

One night in her bedroom, he was complaining to her about another handsome young upstart who had come into her drawing room as if he had some undeniable claim on her affections.

"How can we make love the way we do, my sweetheart, while you have another man believing you belong to him? And yet I know somehow you do love me. When we make love I know it has to be the real thing for both of us." He wanted it desperately to be real. "Yet I feel like killing those young upstarts when they act so familiar with you, as if they know you intimately. Tell me, what is Yablonovsky to you, Amelia?"

Her husband, Ivan Riznich, was on a business trip in Vienna. She whispered softly to him. "Be contented that you know I love you, and believe me, I love only you."

"But," Alexander Sergeievich persisted, "that Yablonovsky bastard today acted as if he's slept with you.

"Don't you worry about my sleeping habits. You have more important things to occupy your wonderful mind. After all, you know there is at least one other man I sleep with, and that is Monsieur Ivan Ivanovich Riznich, my most honorable husband."

The truth and sense she spoke did not mitigate the poet's anguish. Indeed the reality of her truth deepened Pushkin's agony.

He lay there visualizing his Amelia in the arms of her husband whom he saw as exercising the rights of property and ownership rather than the nobler rights of love and passion. He'd never loved like this before. If only he had met her before she married Riznich. If only! Fate was like *God's Will* and the Emperor's, the omnipresent malevolent enemy. Fate would always victimize him.

In his desperation he said, "Come away from this place with me, my beloved. Come away with me while he is in Vienna. You are just a piece of property as far as he is concerned, and he will hardly miss you. I cannot live with the thought of you belonging to another man."

"But the Emperor would miss you, my pet. And where would we go? You forget that you belong to Russia, and the Emperor is its ruler. You can't even go to Kishinev without the Czar's permission."

"We could escape to Africa or lose ourselves together up in the Caucasus and live with the Circassian people. The Emperor could never find us." He insisted.

The poet realized that women were much more practical than most men imagined, especially men of the romantic persuasion like himself.

She asked, mundanely, "How will we eat, Alexander Sergeievich?"

"We'll live on wild grapes and game. And on our undying love," he added.

"And what about your writing?"

Even though he knew he lied, he said, "With your love, my dearest, I would not need my writing." And he wondered to himself why it was that true love found it so hard to be truthful. Without his writing he could not love or live. His life would be one interminable unbearable existence. And how well he knew it. Yet—

She kissed him fully on his mouth. "Oh my beloved, if it were only true. But without your writing nobody on this earth could live with you. Without your writing, even I shouldn't wish to live with you.

"My sweet, courageous falcon, you are your writing and your writing is precisely you." Amelia said tenderly. "There is no way on earth to tell where one leaves off and the other begins. You are your ODE TO FREEDOM. You are your VILLAGE, you are your RUSLAN AND LUDMILA, you are your GABRILIAD. You are THE SOWER. Your writing makes love to me. It makes me warm all over. It makes me laugh, it makes me cry, makes me angry and happy. It makes me love, hate, shout for joy. It is as much a part of you as this manful thing, that I'm holding in my hand. I adore every single part of you."

Her lovesome mouth gave way before the passion of his fullsome lips like softest rubber and ripened peaches, as he murmured, "I love you, goddammit! I love you! I'm bewitched! You're a fever, you're a madness, a sickness that I never want to be rid of! I love you so much it frightens me!"

And he lost himself in the special smells of her tumescent breasts and arms and thighs, sighs and moans and groans of this woman who delightfully cast a spell on him as they made love as love was meant to be, but never meant for them.

Sometimes he would sit all night with her among the silks and satins of her lavish boudoir smoking their Chinese pipes together, pipes she kept especially for them alone, sipping their special wines, and he would be intoxicated with feminine aromas of Oriental essences and occidental fragrances. She would be reading some part of his new work in progress and would read aloud a particular line or phrase, and a smile or laughter would light up her face, burst from her lips, or a tear would spill from her wonderously dark eyes, and she would reach toward him and kiss him longingly on his mouth, and ask him, "How on earth do you write so beautifully?"

One night he told her heatedly, "I suppose it has something to do with my love and admiration for the serf, the Russian peasantry. I hate serfdom in Russia and slavery in America and everywhere else on this unhappy earth! The muzhik is the pure and unadulterated Russian. He is the most human of us all. And I love him for it. I love his invincibility. I love his instinct for survival."

They would talk far into the night, of war and peace and freedom and of art and literature, his poetry, his aspirations, his future. She told him she'd be his and his alone some day, and soon. And when he left her he felt as if he'd made the freest, craziest, wildest truest kind of love in all this loveless earth.

But Amelia knew her lover.

Love would never be enough for this sensitive and sensual poet. Sure he needed love, physical, spiritual, intellectual love, but he needed also comradeship of his peers who held him in regard and loved him not just for his verses, but for himself. Someone to appreciate and criticize his creative efforts. Someone who respected him and whom he respected as he respected sweet Amelia. Amelia was becoming to him a grandiose sublime obsession. She was his loftiest, most magnificent of poems, an epic of his own creation. Sometimes he really thought that he could, would steal away to the Caucasus with her, or to Africa, if she would go with him, and let the world take care of its crazy self. She was a sickness in his blood that he cherished and adored, pampered and indulged. He felt aged at twenty-four and sorely pressed for time, especially when he was not with her. Sometimes he really felt he was much older than the actual years he had spent here on this Russian earth. He'd had so very many experiences, there wasn't time for so much living. They'd always called him a genius, but sometimes he thought his genius was in the life he lived and how he lived it. He must have lived before. Was that not why Natalya Ivanovna used to call him the Old Man, even when he was only eight years old? Life was here and now to grasp and live, with his Amelia. And death was breathing on their necks. One lonely night he wrote a poem to her
TIS TIME, MY FRIEND.

> Tis time, my friend, tis time!
> The heart for rest is crying
> The days go by, each hour bears off,
> as if it's flying
> A shred of our existence—
> we two, we plan to live,
> But death may come, how soon?
> And joy is fugitive.

Not happiness, but peace and
Freedom may be granted here
On earth: This is my hope, who by one dream
is haunted—
A weary slave, I plan escape before the night
To that remote repose of toil and pure delight.

Alexander Sergeievich saw nothing in the country changing, not even himself. To the theatre almost every night, flirting with pretty flighty women, restaurant hopping from Kimitraki-the-Greek's where the cuisine was fantastically excellent and renown to Cesar Automne, the Frenchman, a great admirer of Pushkin, who always kept the poet's favorite Saint Peray champagne.

It was a time when he made himself believe that he believed in art for it's own precious sake, that he did not write to create a new vision for himself and humankind, that he was not THE SOWER of his former days when he was young and innocent.

When GYPSIES was published, Vyazemsky wrote him, asking: "What is the purpose? What does it mean?" Pushkin answered, irritatingly, "You ask me what is the purpose of GYPSIES? What should it be? The purpose of poetry is poetry!"

Loneliness. Sometimes he thought that he just might one day lie down and drown himself in the river of his loneliness. He dreamed one night he was back in Ekaterinoslav and was swimming across the wide Dneiper River stroke after stroke after stroke after stroke, and when he'd almost reached that other shore, a great exhaustion suddenly came upon him and he struggled against a raging tide, and asked himself, what is the sense of struggling? If he reached the other shore, he would find nothing but a world of loneliness and alienation. Death would come as a welcomed stranger on a great white steed. No one would miss him. No one cared. Then just before the final gasping breath, he awakened, breathing convulsively short quick breaths. And his happy heart was palpitating, and he was glad that he was still among the living.

Two or three times a year he received letters from his brother and sister. He knew they loved him and revered him. He loved to write them letters in return.

After a few months in Odessa, a familiar feeling of boredom came down on him as it usually did when his muse played frustrating games with him. Except for Amelia, there was no one to talk with, with whom to share his revolutionary fervor. So in desperation he turned to his evil genius of a cynic, Alex Raevsky, who was more than willing to accommodate.

For a time Pushkin's sole male comrade was Alexander Raevsky, who still fascinated him with the sinister doomsday aura that always surrounded him. He almost had our poet mesmerized with his yellow snake-eyed appearance, his nihilistic approach to everything. "The end of the world will be here any moment, and nothing can be done to change anything, so what is the use of trying? What is the use of writing, thinking, working? What indeed is the use of living?"

Sometimes these sessions resembled seances. Alexander Sergeievich would blow out the candles and sit in the dark and listen to his nihilistic prophet. He would break into a sweat. Chills would move across his shoulders. Sometimes he even pretended to be frightened by Raevsky's incantations. But it wasn't long before our poet grew bored with Raevsky's negativism.

For Alexander Sergeievich was at heart an optimist despite his notorious posture as a sophisticated cynic. He wrote to change the world. He was, in fact, THE SOWER. He continually reminded himself that in his ODE TO FREEDOM, he had called on slaves to rise up and throw off their chains. In 1821 he wrote THE DAGGER, in which he extolled the use of violence as a legitimate weapon in the revolutionary struggle against tyranny. He believed in the inevitability of change and the responsibility of men and women to work for change. He gradually began to avoid the sneering Raevsky and sought the comradeship of Tumansky, who worshipped Pushkin as the "Russian nightingale, the Robin Hood of our literature." It was Tumansky, Schwartz, and Varlaam with whom he made the rounds of theatre, restaurant and casino, where hundreds of civil servants, clerks, and such gathered each night to lose their rubles to professional gamblers who roamed all over Russia, sleeping through the day and taking advantage of their unsuspecting victims all night long.

One night, before day in the early morning, Tumansky and Varlaam and Pushkin sat in a booth at Cesar Automn's consuming bottle after bottle of Saint Peray. Tumansky wore a blonde mustache like an elephant tusk. He stared across the table at Pushkin, worshipfully, with his wide blue eyes. "I simply cannot understand you. You write like an angel just descended from the heavens, but your conduct is that of a common ordinary whoremaster. I mean, the way you wench and womanize is a national scandal. Sometimes I think you're undeserving of your heavenly talent, the gifts the gods have given only you!"

Varlaam laughed, "He writes like an angel all right. An avenging angel."

Pushkin stared from one to the other of his drunken comrades. He oftentimes suspected that his so-called legendary sexuality was attributed to his African blood, even by such staunch admiring comrades as dark-haired Varlaam and blonde Tumansky. Even by his own devoted father. He remembered years ago when he was an innocent lad in Moscow. His father had caught him with the chambermaid, Tatyana. He could hear his father as if it had been yesterday.

"You hot-blooded African bastard! No girl is safe with you. Not even your innocent sister!" His father had threatened to send poor Tanya away. The frightened boy had begged his father. "It was all my fault, Pa-pa!" He had pleaded tearfully. He really had believed it was his fault, his hot African blood. In the end his pleading had prevailed, he'd thought. Tatyana was retained.

Then one afternoon, he had been going down the long hall of the rambling house and he had heard a scuffling in one of the many guest bedrooms. He had heard his Tanya's voice.

"Please, your Nobility! Please! Have mercy on me. I'm a good girl!"

"Shut up, you wanton bitch! Don't put on airs with me, you slut! You think I don't know what's going on in my own house?"

He had broken into the room and found his father wrestling with his true love, tearing her dress from her. And he had wrestled his father all over the room.

"Who is the hot-blooded bastard now? Who is the hot-blooded African bastard?"

The memory made his heart beat faster. He looked around at both of his admiring comrades. He said to Tumansky, calmly, "First of all, there are no such animals as angels. I am a man, no more, no less, than any other man. I ruinate, I defecate, I fornicate. Especially do I love to make love with a lovely woman. Some men are carpenters like Joseph, that legendary cuckold of Biblical times. Some men lay bricks, some are cobblers. Some are stone masons. I happen to be a writer. I have the same needs as other men. I get lonesome in this Imperial banishment. I get bored almost to madness. I like the comradeship of lovely interesting women. My interest in women though, goes much much deeper than fornication. Women, to me, are not pieces of meat placed here on earth solely for the surfeiting of my libertine appetites. A woman is physical—yes. But a woman is also spiritual, intellectual. Perhaps, actually I should say I make love with women, because I only make love with women whom I care about, whom I respect, with whom I share something in common, literarily, politically, intellectually, spiritually, and last and perhaps least of all, physically." He laughed aloud at the look on Tumansky's face. "Womanizing is a Russian tradition, especially among the jaded aristocracy. And who chases after more women than both of you, you whoring sons of bitches?" He added, "And you don't have an ounce of African blood in either of your veins."

And then there was the ever present problem of finance. The seven-hundred-rubles dole from the government was a monthly payment that sometimes came across the silent steppes three or four months behind time. In Odessa, unlike Kishinev, it was not so easy for Pushkin to disguise his poverty by adopting different racial and national identities. People in Odessa dressed decorously, and everybody knew who Alexander Pushkin was. He was a proud olive-complexioned, frizzly-haired, sensual-mouthed, dark-eyed man, who went to the theatre in a black frock coat, frayed and buttoned tightly at the neck. Tight fitting trousers that shone so, you could almost see yourself in them. He always carried with him an iron-fisted cudgel, ostensibly "to strengthen my hands and wrists for future duels."

At the theatre, he heard voices.

"Is that really Alexander Pushkin? He's so dark!" Who in the hell did they think he was? An Ethiopian potentate?

"They say he's very, very rich."

"Why does he dress so shabbily then?" *I lend my money to the Emperor.* "I certainly would like to sleep with him. My husband would have something to boast about."

"They say he's a foreigner, an African, not really Russian!"

"Of course, he's not a Russian, he's a genius!"

"But he must be Russian. He was born in Moscow! Moscow is the soul of Russia."

And there was no getting along between his chief, Vorontsov, and our impetuous poet. Pushkin would not—could not—play the role of a sycophant, which was what Count Vorontsov expected of all who worked under him. Pushkin pictured himself an aristocrat on a level with the Count. And even above him, intellectually. Vorontsov was disposed at first, to be kindly tolerant and paternalistic toward the sayward boy, the celebrated African scribbler. He was prepared to be the poet's patron, if Alexander Sergeievich would play the role of court jester or poet to the Court of Count Vorontsov. It would lend prestige to the Court. But there was no way this arrangement could have worked, since each man saw himself in a different light. Vorontsov saw Pushkin as a poverty-stricken African nobody, one of his numerous subalterns, while Pushkin saw himself as an intellectual aristocrat whose lineage went back as far as six and seven hundred years.

Creditors hounded Pushkin as religiously as Czarist spies. There was an especially pesky cabman who had taken him, on credit, out to the Odessa outskirts a few times to visit the camps of Gypsy friends. One day he broke into Pushkin's hotel room while he was shaving, demanding his pay. Pushkin advanced toward the cabman, razor in hand. "Get out of my apartment, you impertinent bastard!" Thinking Pushkin was going to slash him with the razor, the chubby cabman ran for his very life.

It did Pushkin's spirit little good to get a letter from Saint Petersburg, telling him that everybody was reading with excitement his poem THE FOUNTAIN OF BAKSHISARAI, based on his trip to the Caucasus and the legend of the lonely Khan.

He answered his elated friend, Zukovsky:

Thank you very much, and thank all my loyal friends in Saint Pete for me for the pains they take to make me a famous man. It is unfortunate though that one cannot eat fame or popularity, nor can one pay his hounding creditors. I only pray and hope those to whom you have so generously given my manuscript will see fit to buy the printed version which, hopefully, will be published shortly. You probably think it vulgar of me to aspire to make a living from my writing. But it is after all, my life's work. Nothing more. No more no less than to expect a cobbler to make a shoe and give it to one and all free of charge. I am vulgar. I write from inspiration. But like the cobbler, I expect pay for my product.

Then one cold day word came across the hushed white steppes from Saint Petersburg that changed the course of literature, changed the attitude of the Russian writer toward himself and his creativity; Prince Vyazemsky had sold THE FOUNTAIN to a publisher for three thousand rubles, the largest sum ever paid to a writer in the history of Russian literature. People in Odessa looked at the poet differently. Sud-

190

denly overnight he became their topic of polite conversation. He was like their *hors d'oeuvre* before the main course, their cognac snifter after supper.

A few days passed before he did anything with his sudden fortune. He would sit in his simply furnished room with iron bed, a waterstand in a corner with waterbowl and pitcher, a looking glass above the stand, two chairs, bare floor, his flat trunk in another corner, a writing desk, heavy inexpensive drapes at a single window, two inexpensive pictures on the walls. He sat and stared, unbelieving, at the bountiful draft of rubles and the letter from Vyazemsky. It was true he'd made literary history, and he was profoundly proud. He was ecstatic. He had turned a corner in his life. As proud as he felt, he warned himself not to take his sudden celebrity too seriously. He promised himself he would always take his work, his art, more seriously than he'd ever take his fame, which could easily change to infamy. An artist who took his notoriety more seriously than he did his art would always be in trouble with his muse.

CHAPTER SIX

Pushkin's creditors made short work of the munificent three thousand rubles. One morning he went to the window of his hotel room where his creditors had gathered outside in the square, as usual. But this day was special, because the news of his good fortune had spread far and wide. All of his creditors, some he had long ago forgotten, were on hand. He paid them off by throwing rubles from the window to them. The first one to be paid was the insistent cabman.

The people in the street shouted, "Pooshkin! Pooshkin! Pooshkin! Long live Alexander Pooshkin!"

Three nights after he received his monies, he sent 360 rubles to Papa Insov. His letter said, in part: "I am ashamed and humiliated to have been unable to pay you before, and the simple reason is, that I have been kopekless."

He sent a draft of four hundred rubles to his family in Mikhailovskoye.

He indulged himself by purchasing a new outfit of clothing in the latest most expensive style. But no matter that Pushkin became poverty stricken again almost overnight, he had made Russian literary history, and he could not help being proud of it. He felt warm and good about himself, and it lifted his dragging spirits and carried them aloft long after the money from THE FOUNTAIN had run dry like the legendary Fountain itself. His Amelia was also proud of him; she read Vyazemsky's letter over and over, and she wept for joy; they made love as love had never been imagined.

A copy of THE FOUNTAIN lay unopened on his desk in his hotel room since the day it had arrived. He had resisted a compelling impulse to pick it up and open it and read it from cover to cover. He walked around it, warily, as if it were a deadly cobra poised to strike out at him. He wanted to savor this ecstatic feeling of literary omnipotence as long as the taste of it endured.

Then one day he could resist no longer. He began to read THE FOUNTAIN and the depression descended upon him, almost immediately. When he came upon a line he thought might have been done differently, he shouted, "Oh no! How could I? How could I have ever written anything so fraudulent and trite?" And he sank deeper into his indulgent gloom. His head began to ache. When would he ever learn to write expertly?

The poet's spectacularly growing prestige and popularity did not improve the relations between him and Count Vorontsov. If anything they worsened. Each of them kept their hostility to themselves, though each was well aware of their mutual animosity. Vorontsov cordially invited Pushkin to all the formal affairs of the court—the dinners, banquets and receptions. Pushkin attended, bored to distraction, though he accorded Vorontsov a cool politeness and was treated civilly in return. Each man was too sophisticated to display his truest feelings toward the other publicly.

This outward show of civility was not participated in by one of the few non-British sycophants attached to Count Vorontsov's court. A Russian by the name of General Skobelev. Inadvertently, Pushkin had come across a letter written by the General to the Central Authorities in Saint Petersburg which said, in part: "The generous Count Vorontsov treats the young African scalawag too kindly. Pushkin's subversive works should be forbidden to be published. Instead, the author of these perfidious verses should have a few strips of flesh removed from his behind with a knout dipped in heated glue. It would teach him the lesson he sorely needs."

Pushkin thoroughly despised this Russian lackey who was a willing errand boy for the British gentlemen of Court and willing to curry favor even if it came to kissing their English backsides.

The unwritten peace pact between Pushkin and Vorontsov continued for a time. In fact it lasted until Pushkin went to visit Amelia one evening and was met with an empty house and a steward who told him that Madame and Monsieur had left the country for Italy.

Alexander Sergeievich could not believe his hearing. "But when did they leave? How long will they be gone?"

"It doesn't seem they'll ever return, your Highness. They have arranged for the sale of the house, the furniture and everything."

Alexander Sergeievich stood staring incredulously at the steward, not wanting to believe him, but his pounding heart and the hardness in his stomach knew the steward spoke the truth. His beloved had deserted him. He was through with love and women and trust and friendship, for all times. He turned quickly from the steward and made his way back down the marble steps. Odessa was already becoming a terrible lonely experience for him. He felt a stranger in this place. It was spring, but he felt cold like winter, hotter than the burning days of mid-July. The sweet taste in his mouth had swiftly turned to bile. He walked, stumbling, blinded by his tears. As he walked toward town, the ground beneath him was like shifting desert sand. Amelia gone—forever gone! Gone! Here was one whom he loved and who truly loved him and understood him and adored him and valued him. And she had left him without even saying dosvadanya! Gone! Gone! People on the dusty street turned and stared at this famous poet talking to himself.

When he reached his hotel there was a note for him from his Amelia.

This has happened so suddenly my dearest, there was no time to say goodbye and kiss your sweet sensuous mouth and your beautiful expressive eyes, but be sure I shall return to you if you will have me and we will go away together. Nothing can keep me from you except death itself . . . I am yours! Yours!

Forever—

Your Amelia

That night he got raging drunk, loud and boisterously inebriated. When he imbibed, every man was his friend and brother, even Emperor Alexander, maybe. But this night he got evil-drunk. He went looking for a fight. And found one at Vorontsov's palace. He had been drinking since around six or seven o'clock, when he remembered the Vorontsov party. His vodka advised him to attend.

When Monsieur A.S. Pushkin was announced, there was a murmur through the crowd already gathered, as if His Imperial Majesty Alexander Romanov Himself were honoring them with His august presence. All eyes turned toward the entrance. Vorontsov was not pleased by the impact of this egomaniacal poet, which was how he saw the "swaggering African scribbler." The intellectual elite of Odessa immediately gravitated towards him.

Pushkin was standing in a corner of the brilliantly lighted salon in the midst of his admirers, when he overheard a conversation that was probably meant for him to hear.

One of the members of the Count's coterie inquired, "I wonder why Yablonovsky isn't here tonight? I am quite sure that he was invited."

"But, haven't you heard?" another answered. "He left the other day for Italy. He left on the same ship with the Riznichs."

Alexander Sergeievich recognized the slimy voice of Skobolev. A great warmth gathered in his face and a knot doubled up his belly as he turned and stared directly into the sneering cat-grey eyes of Skobolev.

A heavily powdered lady with a thin nose that seemed to have no nostrils gasped. "How thrilling! How terribly romantic! The days of chivalry still live in Imperial Russia!"

"Yes," the General said, deliberately eyeing the famous poet, "but it leaves many broken hearts in its wake, even famous Don Juan poetizers. There is a rumor that a certain scribbler who shall be nameless was madly in love with Madame Riznicha."

194

Pushkin heard the tittering among his heretofore admirers. Alexander Sergeievich said calmly, deliberately, "Better to have kissed the sweet lips of a lovely lady than the buttocks of English gentlemen."

He turned and deliberately stepped on the big feet of the General as he heard the gasps of a few ladies of delicate constitutions. "Excuse me, General, but then you are used to men using you for a footstool, aren't you?"

As upset and inebriated as Pushkin was, he knew exactly what he was doing. "And now," he said to the General, "will you go over there and fetch me a glass of champagne like a good boy, or do you just run errands for those who speak the English language fluently?"

Skobolev's face first turned scarlet, then lost color. "Sir, you will answer for this insult."

"*Pardonez moi*, Your Excellency. I did not realize it was possible to insult lickspittles such as you. I do beg your humble pardon."

Enraged, the General lost his nonchalance completely. Unlike an ennobled gentleman of the Russian Army and the Court of Vorontsov, he charged toward Pushkin like a wild bull on a lonely steppe. Pushkin nimbly stepped aside but left his right foot there long enough for the General to trip over it and fall on his fat face. An even larger crowd of gentlemen and ladies gathered quickly. Pushkin cooly helped the General to his feet, and with the deepest show of sympathy he said, "Come now, comrade. That's no way for a General in his Imperial Majesty's Army to conduct himself. It's not aristocratic, definitely not *comme il faut*. You should never lick boots in public. Even so, my own boots do not need polishing."

The General pulled himself away from the smiling poet. "Monsieur, my seconds will make all the necessary arrangements." He was shaking like he suffered from the mad dance of St. Vitus.

Arrangements for the duel were made, but Vorontsov interceded and promoted Skobolev out of the province. The night of the Skobolev incident was the night that Alexander Sergeievich met Eliza Vorontsova, who took the place of Amelia Riznichna in his broken heart.

Two situations stepped up the tensions between Vorontsov and Pushkin and brought the undeclared war out into the open. One, the insult to his Russian general, his favorite and favored lackey. The second, which really pushed it over the precipice, was our poet's *affaire de coeur* with the beautiful Eliza Vorontsova. This *Ivan Ivanovich* had the nerve to start an illicit affair with the First Lady of Odessa. Damn his savage soul! Vorontsov would show him. Other men of the ennobled gentry would have been flattered by the infamous poet's attentions to their wives. He would get rid of this ungrateful rascal. He began a series of letters to influential gentlemen in Saint Petersburg. "Get this arrogant African bastard out of my jurisdiction!"

Thus brought out in the open, Pushkin's ammunition was his epigrams, his weapon was his goose quilled pen. He went immediately on the attack. The epigrams went the rounds of Odessa. His first shot was a biblical reference.

David was a little man,
But he did vanguish Goliath,
Who was a very big general
And little more than a Count.

His second shot was:

Half milord, half tramp,
Half sage, and half hick,
Half bastard now, but one presumes that
He will make a whole one yet.

Biblical legends and epigrams were one thing, but in an open all-out war like this, Vorontsov had the most powerful guns and ammunition and was in charge of all the rules of warfare. Therefore the cards were heavily and unevenly stacked against the poet. And even God, Fate, His Majesty, and/or circumstances seemed on Vorontsov's side.

A plague of locusts broke out on the southern steppes of Russia. Thousands of locusts descended like a greenish-yellow storm cloud upon the corn and wheat and barley, killing millions of rubles worth in crops. The Russian breadbasket faced starvation and disaster. Vorontsov sent an inspection detail chosen from his underlings on the very lowest rung of his imperial ladder, and in the scheme of things, Pushkin was naturally chosen as a member of the team to go and investigate the damage being wrought by these malicious grasshoppers. Our infuriated poet was given the following orders:

You are to visit the districts of Kherson, Elizavetgrad and Alexandria, and obtain the following information in each town: Where have the insects landed, in what numbers, what action has been advised to exterminate them and how has it been followed up. You are also to inspect the places which have been badly affected by the invasion, evaluate the effectiveness of the methods of clearance being employed, and consider if the measure adopted by the Provincial committees are adequate. Your observations are to be submitted to me personally in a written report.

When Pushkin received the written order, he reread it over and over again as he held it in his trembling hands. Grasshopper investigator! He looked around him at his miserable hotel quarters. He had never considered the seven hundred rubles stipend as a wage for his working for His Imperial Majesty's Government, but as subsistance monies for his survival while in banishment. He went from agency to agency trying to get the grasshopper order rescinded, and though many sympathized with the poet, he soon found that the center of gravity was at the court of milord and that the Count's word was law, against which there was no appeal. In desperation Pushkin even invaded Vorontsov's court, went to Secretary-General Kaznacheev, a sympathetic man who admired Pushkin and delayed the execution of the orders as long as possible, so much so that Vorontsov threatened to send the Secretary General along with the delegation.

Pushkin burst into the room of Prince Veigel, a man recently from Saint Petersburg and in Odessa for a brief visit. Prince Veigel ranked high in the echelon of His Majesty's foreign ministry. "I won't go!" Alexander Sergeievich declared. "Let them shoot me! Hang me! Send me to Siberia! I will not be humiliated by that Anglo-Russian egomaniac!"

Prince Veigel made an appointment with Vorontsov and went to see him to intercede on Pushkin's behalf. "The sensitivities of a poet of Pushkin's genius and temperament must always be considered in cases of this nature."

At Veigel's first words, Vorontsov's face lost color, his cheeks began to twitch, his thin lips trembled. Veigel feared that the Count might begin to froth at the mouth. "My dear friend, if you wish to preserve the friendship between us and our families, do not mention the name of that African scum in my presence." He paused to get himself collected. "And the same goes for his friend Raevsky."

His few trusted friends finally persuaded Pushkin that he must go, and the poet went along with the others and watched the locust fighters standing waist deep in the yellow hissing giggling mass. The locusts clung to his clothes, whispered stupidities into his ears, kissed his thick lips, took up light housekeeping in his matted hair, and literally drove the poet out of his senses, drove him to a decision that he would live with for the remainder of his days. He decided to resign from the employ of His Majesty's government, which was an arrogant and ungrateful act tantamount to inviting great God up Above to kiss his hindquarters.

Upon his return to Odessa from the locust-ridden steppes, Pushkin submitted the following written report to Count Vorontsov:

The locusts were flying, flying, flying,
Then the things came down to earth,
They crawled, they ate up everything,
And then the things flew off again.

He then wrote a letter of resignation from the service, which he addressed to Kaznacheev, the Secretary-General of the Odessa Mission.

For seven years I have had no official dealing with any superior. I have not written a single report till now. These seven years have been wasted as far as promotion and development are concerned. Any complaints on my part would be unseemly. Writing is my profession, and it gives me a living and an independence. I think Count Vorontsov would not wish to deprive me of either. I may be told that I am receiving a salary of seven hundred rubles and must continue to serve. I have accepted those seven hundred rubles not as a salary of a civil servant but as compensation paid to an exiled slave. I am ready to give them up the moment I cease to be master of my time and activities. If I had wanted to serve, I should have asked for no better chief than His Excellency; but feeling my total incapacity, I do hereby renounce all advantages of a diplomatic career that His Most Imperial Majesty, Czar Alexander, has so graciously bestowed upon me.

One more word. Perhaps you do not know that I suffer from aneurysm. I have been carrying my death inside me for eight years. Any doctor will give me a certificate. Is it not possible to leave me in peace for the short time I have still to live?

The aneurysm was fraudulent. He had a not too serious case of varicose veins in one leg, but he was not about to miss a chance to convince the authorities of his dire need for resignation and retirement from the service.

Upon receiving the letter, Kaznacheev hastened to Pushkin's hotel room in a desperate attempt to persuade Pushkin to take the resignation back. He had not yet shown it to Count Vorontsov. "Please! Take this letter back and destroy it. I will not breathe of it to a soul. Think of the consequences. How will His Imperial Majesty react to such a display of impertinence, no matter how innocent the intentions?"

Alexander Sergeievich was adamant. "I appreciate your concern, though I do not understand your fear of the consequences. I aspire only for my independence."

"But what will you do? How will you live?"

"I shall live by my writing," Alexander Sergeievich replied. "I have already overcome my repugnance to sell what I write. As I continue to maintain, I write only by inspiration, but once written, it is merchandise to be sold for a price like a cobbler who sells his shoes, the product of his labor. I am a working man whose trade is the written word."

Kaznacheev was one of the few men in Vorontsov's service who genuinely admired the poet and his work. "But Count Vorontsov will be infuriated. He's sure to take it as a personal insult."

The Count would be no more infuriated than Pushkin was at this point. The poet answered, in a calm voice, "Yebat! Count Vorontsov! I'm sure he'll discredit me in the opinion of the public. But yebat public opinion too! I care as much for the opinion of the public as I do about the adulation of our critics and our journalists."

Meanwhile Pushkin's affair with Eliza Vorontsov went apace, even intensified. He spent many blissful moments with Eliza and Princess Vera Vyazemskaya, his Petersburg friend's wife who was in Odessa for a short vacation. The three went on picnics at a cavern by the sea. As the surf came in and lashed the rocks, he read his poetry to these charmed and charming women. He bared his soul to them. Princess Vera Vyazemskaya wrote many letters to her husband; in each she mentioned the "mad . . . impetuous" poet. "Poor Pushkin, nobody seems to understand him and it's all his own fault. He seems to think the world is against him because of his meager African blood. He insults the most important people and imagines they've insulted him. I do not know what the end will be for him. He is so gentle and charming when he wants to be. At these rare moments he is utterly irresistible. But if he continues on the course he now pursues, he is surely headed for tragedy."

Even as he professed his love for Eliza, he knew that it was Amelia who lay heavy on his heart, in his dreams and remembrances. She was always with him. Eliza reminded him of darkly beautiful Amelia—the dark-to-blackness of her large wide eyes, like smoky topaz, the sensual lips, the sincere interest in his poetry, in literature, in politics.

Meanwhile, the infuriated Vorontsov forwarded Pushkin's resignation to Saint Petersburg, along with a covering letter which requested Foreign Minister Count Nesselrode to come up with a solution that would send the rascal out of Odessa and out of Vorontsov's jurisdiction. "There are too many people here who flatter his enormous vanity and encourage his stupidities. They acclaim him as the world's greatest writer and he believes it. In the summer there will be more of them, and instead of learning and working, he will go even farther astray."

In another rather desperate letter the Count wrote:

I repeat my plea. Deliver me from Alexander Pushkin; he may be a fine young man, an excellent poet, but I do not want him around any longer, either in Odessa or in Kishinev. Pushkin meets too many flatterers here, who praise his works and foster his illusion of literary omnipotence, whereas he is still no better than a feeble copy of an extremely dubious original, Lord Byron. And please do not send him as close by as Kishinev where Insov will surely spoil him and people from here will go there and shower adoration upon this undeserving African scoundrel. He is spoiled enough already.

When the news of Pushkin's resignation reached Saint Petersburg, his friends were furious with their irresponsible genius. They competed with one another in condemning him. "He's impossible!" . . . "It's all his fault!" . . . "God knows what will happen to him now!" . . . "It's that terrible African temperament that always gets him into trouble!

Prince Vyazemsky wrote his wife: "I am really very unhappy for him, even though he is obviously at fault. However, people who do not know how to respect genius such as his, though it be the genius of a madman, are necessarily themselves in grievous error."

Then there was a letter intercepted by the postal service, in which Pushkin went into a lengthy satiric discussion of atheism and took a position unequivocally against the existence of a Superior Being and the immortality of the soul. *When one died that was the end of it. There was no such place as Heaven. Some men were less than cockroaches. Cockroaches did not go to Heaven. When you stepped on one, that ended it.* The letter was brought to the immediate attention of the sanctimonious Czar Alexander the First.

While Vyazemsky, Zukovsky and Turgenev were scurrying around in Saint Petersburg trying to salvage as much of Pushkin's hide as was salvageable, Countess Eliza Vorontsova was spying on her husband's correspondence for some idea of what fate held in store for her beloved poet.

Pushkin tried vainly to borrow rubles from Princess Vera Vyazemskaya and involve her in a plot to board a ship in the harbor and escape the confines of the Empire. He'd go anywhere. Africa, China, Europe—any goddamn-where! Why should he have to live the remainder of his life in this prison that was Imperial Russia?

One week later a letter came across the grassy steppes from Count Nesselrode by the authority of His Imperial Majesty. Pushkin was to be immediately relieved of his official duties, taken off the Imperial payroll, and sent by stage to Mikhailov-skoye in the Pskov Province, there to reside on his great-grandfather's estate and there to remain under Imperial and clerical surveillance until further notice. His route to Mikhailovskoye was outlined in the official letter and rubles were allocated to him for the expenses of the trip. It was a long trip ahead. Mikhailovskoye was more than 1600 versts away to the north.

When the orders arrived, July 29, Count and Countess Vorontsov were on a holiday in the Crimea. Acting Governor Guryez summoned Pushkin, and inside of fifteen minutes he had received his orders, the designated route of journey, 389 rubles and five kopeks for expenses and the hiring of three horses. He had twenty-four hours to depart.

Alexander Sergeievich had thought that when and if his resignation were accepted, he would be free to do his work anywhere he chose to do it. Perhaps he would go to Africa. Or Paris. Or Peking. But he was exchanging one prison for another, even worse, a dungeon. At least in Odessa there were the theatre, the opera, restaurants, interesting and beautiful women. But now he was being sentenced to a Russian village in the middle of a wilderness. He would not even be able to bid his beloved Eliza goodbye and would probably never see her ever again. It was too much! It was devastating.

He went again to Vera Vyazemskaya and again he begged the princess to help him in a plot to board a ship for other parts. But as much as she loved the poet, she was even more fearful of the Emperor's wrath should he find out that she helped him in any way to escape Imperial punishment.

When Prince Vyazemsky heard of the poet's fate, he was filled with righteous indignation. He wrote:

Who is the author of this cruel indignation? It is capital punishment to bury a sharp intense young man in the solitude of a desolate Russian village. . . .Do the people who made this decision realize what it means to be exiled in a Russian village? A man would have to be an angel not to go completely out of his wits. Why is he not allowed to go abroad? His publications would provide for him a livelihood for a few years anyway. Tell me, for the love of God, how the cudgel of Peter the Great could fear the prose and poetry of a mere child? The fine old tree of orthodoxy is full of sap and blossoming abundantly. If Orpheus himself were to appear and intone a subversive chant, none would budge a single inch. All the poets in the world could howl their lungs out, nobody would hear a sound. The Titans did not sing hymns to the Gods when they wanted to drive them out of Heaven.

The shaken poet had to pack hurriedly. He kissed Princess Vyazemskaya a warm passionate goodbye and gave her another kiss for his beloved Eliza in the Crimea. Along with his clothing he packed his manuscripts: THE DEMON, TO THE SEA, TO THE FOREIGN LADY, IMAGINARY CONVERSATION WITH ALEXANDER I, the beginnings of a new poem about Saint Petersburg as he remembered it, and the first two chapters of a new novel in verse with which he had been wrestling during his trials and tribulations in Odessa. His working title for it was EUGENE ONEGIN.

On the thirtieth of July, he left Odessa in a daze and began his long journey toward the isolated Russian village that wasn't even on the Imperial map. All day long the telega moved across the black and sandy rutty roads surrounded by whirls of black dust covering everything within its wake. He lived that first day with the taste of black sand in his mouth, felt its thick grime on his face, in his nostrils and his ears. He felt it creeping up the sleeves of his tunic and into his sweaty armpits. The next day they moved over the inevitable rolling grassy steppes beneath a merciless sun, a blue diaphanous sky, a hot purplish haze that steamed up from the greenish earth. And far away he shook his head at the wonder of the endlessness of the steppes, versts after versts of it. And off to the north where the sky came down to meet the end of the earth, which men called the horizon. It seemed a million versts away. Here and there the steppes seemed afire with pinkish heather.

It was early evening now, and the pungent scorchy smell of wood smoke reached his pointed nostrils from the isolated villages half hidden by the tall grass and the sparsely scattered spruce and poplar trees. He could see the thatch-roof huts, the isbas, sending up wispy smoke signals to indifferent Gods of Holy Russia. The poet thought, these steppes and the people here had seen so much suffering. Foreign conquerors have swept across these plains throughout the centuries. Swedes, Poles and Teutonic hordes from the West; Mongols, Tartars from the East. Time and time again.

He closed his eyes and he could hear the groans and weeping, hear the clash of hammered steel, the swish of arrows, roar of cannons, the clatter of Arabian steeds.

How many times had he been questioned, how could he write so beautifully, with so much verisimilitude? Where did he get his insight, which seemed to have eluded so many writers before him? As he wiped the sooty perspiration from his eyes, he thought perhaps he did have a special insight into the Russian psyche, especially the lowly muzhik, because, like the land of his great-grandfather, his own Mother Russia had been raped by many nations; men from strange lands had come uninvited. Strange men who had scorned the people, considered them barbaric. His dark eyes filled. How long would God and Fate bring damnation down upon this Russian earth and her long-suffering people? How long would there be nothing for it?

This day it was blazing hot. Horseflies clung to the lathered horses. The coachman cursed when the horseflies mistook him for a beast and bit him.

They spent that first night in Nikolayev. He shared his supper with cock-roaches that leaped about like locusts. The next day they changed horses at a post-ing station in Charnigov and stopped again for the night.

The next morning, while walking through the hotel lobby, he met a young man. Pushkin asked him, "Are you from the Tsarskoye Selo Lycée? You seem to be wearing the uniform."

The boy looked down upon this character who had accosted him and whom he mistook for a common hotel porter. Pushkin wore a red Moldavian cape, full blooming trousers with matching color, yellow shoes and a Turkish fez with yellow tassel. He carried a big staff with an iron crook on the end like those used by shep-herds on the steppes. When he traveled he always dressed like someone from the East, a Tartar or an Uzbek.

"Yes," the boy answered curtly, "though I don't see how it could possibly be any concern of yours."

"Well," the unsightly character almost shouted, "so you must know my brother, Leo." Leo should have graduated long before. He had been drummed out of one school years before, had spent three pointless years in the Russian army, then had gone back to study at Tsarskoye Selo.

The boy was taken aback, and spoke more civilly now. "What is your family name, sir?"

"Alexander Sergeievich Pushkin. My brother, Leo, graduates this year."

The boy said, "You're making a jest! You couldn't be—"

Pushkin said, "Yes—, I—"

"You're not the Alexander Pushkin, the poet?"

Alexander Sergeievich's face flushed with embarrassment. "I was one of the first students to attend the Lycée," he told the excited lad quietly.

"Excuse me, Your Excellency, for not recognizing you. You are the most fa-vored, the most famous alumnus of the Lycée! We adore you! We love you! We know your verses all by heart! Ach! I'm talking to Alexander Pushkin himself in person!"

Embarrassed even more, Alexander Sergeievich had begun to walk across the lobby toward the entrance where his telega was waiting. The excited lad ran after him. "Excuse me, Sire. But please do me the honor of signing your name on this piece of paper. No one will ever believe that I actually met you unless I have the living proof."

The boy kissed Pushkin on his cheek as the poet signed the paper hurriedly, turned and left the nervous lad and continued on his journey to the north.

Day after day, landscape after landscape they gained on Mikhailovskoye. One evening just at dusk, six days and many landscapes later, they came into the town of Mogilev. Alexander Sergeievich was looking around the town after having checked in at the only hotel for the night. He was so covered with dust he looked like an apparition come up suddenly off the eerie steppes. He was dressed peculiarly and yet he seemed familiar to a young military cadet who was passing on the road.

"You don't remember me, sir, but I remember you." The cadet said. "You are Alexander Sergeievich Pushkin. I am Alexander Englehardt, the headmaster's nephew. I used to come over to Tsarskoye Selo and you and Delvig and Pushchin used to make me recite poetry."

Pushkin embraced the young man and exclaimed, "I remember—I remember you very well, Sasha. You were a versifying cadet par excellence!"

Young Englehardt was so excited he ran off and told his friends and fellow officers that Pushkin was in town. They hurried back to meet the poet. It was as if they were having drinks with His Imperial Majesty, Alexander Romanov Himself, they were so overjoyed. They had dinner together and drank bottle after bottle of champagne. Englehardt kept repeating, "I can't believe it! I simply can't believe it! Imagine meeting Alexander Pushkin in the flesh like this! People didn't believe I really used to know you!"

They drank to the health of everything they could think of, except the Emperor. They drank to revolution, to an end to serfdom, to constitutional democracy, an end to the monarchy. Alexander Sergeievich leapt up on one of the tables and began to recite his poetry. Their eyes were all alit with joyous adulation. Others in the dingy restaurant looked at them askance. The young officers took him in their arms and carried him kicking on their shoulders to their hotel, and continued downing bottles of champagne.

One of the officers, Prince Obelinsky suggested, "This is one of the most auspicious occasions we will ever experience in our lifetime. Let us celebrate by giving our famous friend a champagne bath as a proper *bon voyage!*"

Alexander Sergeievich was truly moved. The enthusiasm and adoration from the young men took some of the edge off his banishment which seemed everlasting. The youth of Russia loved him. He felt a wetness in his eyes. For after all, the youth were the future of Russia, the only hope that Russia could have a future. And change. His voice choked as he said, "Tovarischi, I appreciate profoundly your sentiments from the bottom of my heart. A brilliant idea. I can think of nothing more exhilarating than to splash about in a champagne bath, but time is against us, and I must get on. But let me leave you young comrades with this admonition." Pushkin himself was only twenty-four, but he felt strangely ancient, so much older than his actual years. "Take the future by the scruff of the neck and change the country. But go all the way! Make a people's revolution. Don't be content with a coup d'état of the elite, which is so fashionable today in Europe. Liberate the Tadjik, the Finn, the Kalmuk, the Tartar, Uzbek, the Don Cossack, the Jew, especially the muzhik, as well as the so-called Great White Russian! Rally every Russian to the cause. Even the Circassians. It is left entirely up to you!" His happy eyes conjured the image of little emaciated Nina inside the Pale near Kishinev. Nina! With the largest darkest knowing eyes in all the world.

It was four o'clock in the morning. Daylight had already broken in the eastern skies when they went with him to his hotel room, helped him get himself collected, put him in the telega and bade the famous poet a rousing farewell.

Sitting there atop his old dilapidated trunk in the rocky dusty telega, Alexander Sergeievich stared across the endless grassy steppe where the heat rose from the earth like waves of steam, and he tried to visualize his future, which he equated with the future of his country. The young folk, the future of the nation, loved him. The older entrenched nobility hated him with an all-consuming passion. He was caught between a crossfire of students, young people, workers, peasants, some middle-class intellectuals, lonely pedestal-placed women, some in far-off unknown unnamed villages. A few ennobled literate gentlemen on the one hand, and on the other hand stood the wealthy businessmen, the entrenched intransigent aristocracy, counts, barons, princes and princesses, landed gentry, boyars, and on top of the pile the Holy One, Czar Alexander Pavolovich Romanov—all of whom hated the very sound of his name. Alexander Sergeievich Pushkin!

He came in sight of the steeple of the Svyatogorsk Monastery high on a hill, and he visualized the nearby cemetery on Holy Mountain where the bones of his famous great-grandfather lay buried with the busy worms. His face began to fill up against his conscious will, and a fullness now was moving through his shoulders. A turn in the road, and he saw in the dimming distance the low-slung, wooden one-story house of his great-grandfather. Now the telega moved irresistibly toward his past, which would be his future. His family would be there to greet him. Greet him, or just meet? Well, they were his family for better or for worse. His brother and his sister loved him. He was their brother and a hero to them, though they lived precariously within the shadow of his name and popularity.

He felt somewhat like the legendary prodigal son as he saw them all standing before the house beyond the little bridge, as it squatted there amongst a grove of pine and linden trees. It looked so lonely there among the trees. He was moved to pity for the proud little house constructed by his great-grandfather. It looked smaller than it really was, and lonelier, dwarfed as it appeared to be by the lordly domineering pines. The telega moved creakily and steadily beneath the giant pines with the storks atop the tallest trees making crazy noises like a howling wind among the shutters. The telega went bumpty-bump over the little bridge and the dried-up creek that ran underneath. He leaped from the telega and ran toward his mother with all her own self-hatred and confusion which caused her to deny him her unlimited affection. Against his stubborn will the tears spilled down his cheeks, and he took her in his arms and found that she was weeping too.

She loved him, yes! She loved him not.
He was confused.
He was upset.
Yet he was somehow happy.
He was home!

PART FIVE

EXILE IN MICHAILOVSKOYE

CHAPTER ONE

While the Pushkin family did not feast upon the fatted calf that first night in celebration of the return of their prodigal son, they did their best to make the prodigal feel at home with a veritable feast of *shaslyked* lamb, stchi (cabbage soup), black caviar, salted cucumbers, sturgeon, kvas, wine, and vodka. He knew they must have sacrificed to prepare such an elaborate banquet. They were not wealthy aristocrats. So they must be genuinely glad to have their wayward son back. They loved him, after all the heartache he had caused them. He knew it was not easy to be related to Alexander Sergeievich Pushkin.

His father was always confronted with: *"You're the man that sired the irreverent revolutionary rascal! It's your fault that you spared the rod and did not beat his arse enough when he was a boy. He must have been an unruly bastard!"*

His mother always feared allusion to her African background. *"It's the African in him. He gets it from his mother's side!"*

Pushkin knew it was easier for his sister and brother because the youth of Russia worshiped him. Yet it was a burden for them also, since Olga and Leo were expected to spout energetic revolutionary verse at a given moment simply because they bore the name of Pushkin. Revolutionary genius was taken for granted. All these thoughts romped through his mind as he looked around at his family, the only one he would ever have until he made one of his own. And there were not many prospects for family-making on his part buried in the sleepy village of Mikhailovskoye, which was not even on the Imperial map.

His old nurse, Arina Rodionovna, came shuffling into the dining room shouting, "Sasha! My little Sasha!" Her little Sasha picked her up and danced around the table with her. He insisted that she and Nikita Koslov, his valet, sit at the table and enjoy the feast with them. She had been his surrogate mother, which had always been a source of superficial envy on his mother's part. Nadezda Pushkina thought Arina Rodionovna did not have to bear the shame or blame of actual motherhood. Neither had she borne the pain.

Even in this ancient house, the impecunious Pushkins were taken by the father through the charade of the wealthy aristocracy. Nobody sat until he arrived and took his seat at the head of the table. The servants always dressed in formal attire, with pomaded skull and powdered wig stood behind the chairs of the now seated family, serving equipment in hands, heads bowed, awaiting the master's pious blessings on the household. Arina Rodionovna and Nikita Koslov eating with the family was a concession to the prodigal son.

The next few days he walked around looking up forgotten places and stirring up memories of his childhood. He sat for hours outside the back of the old ramshackle wooden house staring at the Surot River that ran past. The Surot was more lake than river in its stillness and tranquility. They were drowsy sunlit days with no breeze stirring. Not even the leaves on the pine and linden trees were moving, as they stood still and quiet as if holding their breath for something to happen. Only the crazy sounds of the storks, perched at the very top of the lordly pine trees, broke the stillness with their shrill strange noises that sounded as if they were rattling shutters to awake the sleeping world. The river itself was smooth and motionless, like a long flat piece of glass that you could see yourself in, and the sunlight bounced upon it like a thousand emeralds. He could see the reflections of the trees in the placid river seeming to grow in an upside down direction. He saw the reflection of the old house reaching downward in the river. The entire world seemed topsy turvy. Perhaps this was a true reflection of this old earth's condition.

He walked along the many paths that led from the old decrepit house. Hares scurried through the underbrush. The grass grew tall and unkempt here, and the world abounded with sunflowers. Opalescent butterflies flitting to and fro. Bees buzzing, grasshoppers hopping, darting through the highest weeds. He was intoxicated by nostalgia and the pastoral smells of summer blossoms. He thought about his poem, THE VILLAGE. He remembered Natasha Ivanovna. He came upon an opening and stared at a great big black rock as it sat there in the middle of the clearing. He remembered the legend of the great black rock and his great-grandfather and the serf girl who saw him sitting there one day, as was his habit. She had said, "Look at him sitting there with his black self on that black rock thinking all those black thoughts!"

Alexander Sergeievich was mesmerized as he walked toward the great black rock and sat on it for hours, as if to conjure up the old days when his great-grandfather walked this very Russian earth and thought all of those beautiful black thoughts. How he longed to have known his great-grandfather, the friend of Great Peter the One. He thought of his grandmother who now lay beside him in the quiet cemetery at the Monastery. He remembered all the stories she used to tell him, and the tears began to fill his eyes, and he promised himself he would one day tell the world the story of his great-grandfather.

He spent many hours with his brother and sister, Leo Sergeievich and Olga Sergeivna, in earnest and long extended animated conversations, as if to make up for all the years they had been separated from each other. Their faces glowed with admiration for their famous brother. The love and reverence for him shone in their faces as they spoke with him of love and literature and revolution. They talked of childhood days in the old house on German Street in Moscow, the time he wrote his first play, THE PICKPOCKET. They laughed and cried for the joy of having him with them. They hugged and kissed him, especially Olga Sergeivna. He welcomed it. All this love and adoration were like a balm that exorcised his sense of alienation.

His father came to him one day after supper and put his fatherly arms around his wayward son. "Son, I can't tell you how proud I am of the way you've changed into such a fine upstanding, outstanding and understanding young man. I never really lost my faith in you. They said it was the African strain in you that made you act the way you did. But I knew if you put your trust in the Holy Virgin, she would show you the light. And now that God and the Emperor have forgiven you, you can serve the Crown as your ancestors have before you. Who knows? In the foreign service you can become an ambassador. I can't tell you how proud I am of you. And now you can have a good influence on your brother, Leo. He got drummed out of Tsarskoye Selo again for lack of scholarship and engaging in revolutionary mischief." His drunken father kissed him fully on his mouth. "I'm depending on you, my favorite son. You always were the apple of my eye."

He stared at his father and realized suddenly his father was aging. But he knew that every living thing on earth was aging. Even new-born babes were growing older. But the wrinkles in his father's face, the exaggerated jowls, and the even greater rims and bulges in his neck told him that Sergei Pushkin had crossed that Separating Line from which there was no turning back. The jowls would slacken even more. The wrinkles would increase, not lessen, as the days went swiftly by. He remembered his father slim and young and handsome. What was ahead for him? The stiffening of his joints. Poor circulation, the hardening of his arteries, senility, if his father lived long enough. Tears began to fill the poet's eyes as he thought against his will that his father reminded him of a samovar, especially in winter. Round, short, thick necked, short arms, with the steam issuing from his thin lips and pinched nostrils like tea boiling over.

His father went on and on. "After all, you are my eldest son. They always said that you resembled me and had good sense just like me, the apple of my eye. The very apple of my eye! And God and His Majesty have forgiven you. And so have I!"

He told his father sadly, quietly, "Father, the Emperor is not God."

208

"Not God? Not God?" Sergei Pushkin repeated incredulously. "Of course His Majesty is not God. God does not dwell here on this earth. The Emperor was given to us by God to take His place on earth. He is God's presence here. He is the Voice of God. That is why we call Him the '*Little Father*.'"

Alexander Sergeievich said patiently, "Alexander Romanov is a very ordinary man, who eats gluttonously, swills piggishly, debauches outrageously. He urinates, he defecates, he fornicates just like any other human being. Much much more than most."

His father said, "The Emperor is God incarnate. Like God, He works mysteriously. That is why He and God have forgiven you."

"But why? I don't even believe—"

"We are not meant to understand. Our duty is only to obey God's commandments, which He passes on to us through His Divine One here on earth, the Emperor." His father seemed to lose track of the trend of his conversation with his prodigal son. He came toward him again and embraced him, kissed him animatedly as again he declared, "You always were the apple of my eye."

Pushkin backed away from his babbling father. He had never thought of himself as the apple of anybody's eyes. And while he relished, even treasured, this elaborate show of affection, especially from his father, he knew it had to be on his terms, not based on false pretense and misunderstanding. There simply was nothing else for it.

And so against his will he heard himself say, "But, father, I haven't changed that much. The Emperor has not forgiven me. I don't believe in the Immaculate Conception. And you might as well know it now. I am dismissed from the Foreign Ministry. In fact, I resigned. The Emperor despises me and the feeling is certainly mutual."

Sergei Pushkin stumbled away from his son with a look on his face as if he had embraced a leper and was contaminated. "Why do you always have to spoil everything? Why can't you accept generosity and forgiveness?"

"But you must know the truth, my father. The Emperor has not forgiven me. He has imprisoned me in this godforsaken place. And I love you too much to deceive you."

"Don't you dare love me you, you, you African son of a swine! And stay away from your innocent brother and sister!" Sergei Pushkin was working himself into a lather that reminded Pushkin of the hot foam on the horses that had brought him to this place. "You're trying deliberately to get your own father sent to Siberia! But I'll write a letter to His Majesty! I'll tell the world you are not my son! I disown you, do you hear? I disinherit you!"

Things became unbearable in the low-slung rambling wooden house. The tensions built up by the hour. Each day he heard his father ordering Leo to "stay away from that devil, Sasha, who will try to lead you into the evil ways of atheism and condemn you to hell's fire for all your days before and after death."

Alexander Sergeievich and his father stopped speaking to each other. They even ate at separate times as the tension built. His mother avoided him as if he was unclean.

"Yebat them all!" he told himself. He did not need their love and adulation. His writing would sustain him. But it was not enough. He needed love. He needed love and understanding! There were no substitutes. It was in these miserably lonely moments that he longed for his Amelia.

There were times such as these when Nadezda Pushkina wished for strength to stand up against her husband, Sergei, in defense of her tempestuous offspring, even though she understood her husband's attitudes. She too wished Alexander Sergeievich were different, with fairer skin and light blue eyes, thin-lipped like his sister and his brother, and that he were more reverent, more patriotic and more loyal to the Little Father at the Palace. Yet there was something deep inside her that could not entirely deny him the love that was due him by the rights of childbirth. Sometimes she wished for the time when he was a little ugly baby in the cradle of her arms sucking on her tightening nipples. In times like this her face would flush with shame, her womb would remember those nine months.

One day as Alexander Sergeievich sat working at his desk, Nadezda Pushkin came into his room and ran her hand through his wooly locks. He looked up at his mother and smiled as if he understood. Her husband Sergei passed by and became enraged.

"That's the trouble with that little African bastard! You spoil the pagan too damn much. You still think he's a baby!"

"He's *my* baby," she whined. "He'll always be my baby." But how could she explain it to her husband? He'd never had the morning sickness, had never known the ecstasy of the moment when she knew she was with child and the moment of the first heartbeat. How could she explain it to him when she did not fully understand her own feelings. Sometimes she thought her emotions were perverted. She only knew that they were real.

Two things brought the tension to a head like a boil that had been festering. First, he learned that the government had asked his father to spy on him, and his father had agreed! Every letter he received was first opened and censored by his father who reported to the Pskov authorities. Pskov was the seat of government for the Province in which Mikhailovskoye was situated. His father also eavesdropped on his conversations. This was bad enough, although enraged, the poet kept his peace until one day he overheard his father warning his sister, Olga, against him. His sister had always loved and respected her brother, the only person in the family he'd always felt really close to. "He's surely bewitched by the devil, Olga, darling," his father admonished. "So be on your guard against him. He'll probably try to have sex with you. And failing that, he'll try to rape you. Beware of that black devil!"

Pushkin, enraged, decided it was time to have a civil talk with his confused father. But as soon as he opened his mouth, his father began to scream and shout. "Get out of my sight, you unnatural bastard!"

He turned from his father, went down the hall and out of the house, mounted his horse and rode away. As he left he heard his father shouting to his brother, Leo, threatening him if he did not stop having anything to do *"avec ce monstre, ce fils denaturé!"*

Pushkin rode up the dusty lane across the creaking bridge galloping at full speed along the path beneath the tall pine trees. He thought perhaps he'd write to the Emperor requesting that he be transferred from Mikhailovskoye to an actual prison. Anything would be better than the situation in which he now found himself. He rode miles away from Mikhailovskoye until the great horse foamed. He turned about and made his way back slowly to the Monastery and up the hill to the grave on Holy Mountain where his great-grandfather and grandmother Hannibal slept the sweet sleep of the everlasting. He got off his horse and stood with his head bowed near the pitiable mound of grassy earth that was the only evidence that this man from far-off Africa had once lived and breathed and walked this Russian earth. It was as if the grandson came here for counsel from a man who had seen a land so far away. As he stared down at the patch of dirt, he thought, so this is all it comes to. After all the biting, scratching, screaming, struggling, this is all it comes to. A clump of earth. A feast for worms. He found himself mumbling to himself, and it almost frightened him. It was early autumn and a chill was in the air. It had rained the night before, and leaves were falling, dying all around him. "I promise you, grandfather. I will give your story to the world. Your sojourn on this crazy earth will not be forgotten. Men will know you lived, grandfather, just as they know Great Peter lived."

Tears welled in his eyes as he turned away and mounted his horse, and he thought that he was now able even to forgive his pathetic father, a man he tried to feel compassion for. His father too would one day find his peace in the long and everlasting sleep. He would go back to the house now and ask his father to forgive him. For after all, his father *was* his father. Without him he would not have lived.

When he got back to the house his father was reading in the library. He walked in quietly and put his arm upon his father's shoulder. His father was startled and looked up into Alexander Sergeievich's face and leaped from his chair screaming, as he ran down the hall and out of the house, "My son has struck me! My son is trying to kill me!"

Alexander Sergeievich stood there stunned and speechless. Striking your father was a capital crime in Imperial Russia. You could be hanged or given lifetime in the salt mines of Siberia. His father was hopeless, he thought sadly, beyond redemption.

CHAPTER TWO

The rains came as autumn moved with unseemly haste toward winter, and one day Pushkin's mother and father left him in the old house alone with his nyanya and set out for Saint Petersburg. Leo and Olga had already left a month before. It deeply saddened him, because he could not feel truly sorrowful enough to say goodbye to his parents.

Mai, c'est la vie. Fate, God-and-the-Emperor's-will. There was simply nothing for it.

They took Nikita Koslov with them and left him in the care of his nyanya.

It was not long before winter came. First the cold rain, turning slowly into even colder sleet. Then the sleet changing into driving drifting snow. And then the freezing chill of loneliness, a great white all-encompassing cloak that wrapped around him, giving him no warmth at all.

In these lonely moments his mind often dwelt upon Amelia Riznicha. She had promised to come back to him. But when? Where was she now? What was she doing? Did she ever think of her Pushkin? Did he ever cross her lovely mind?

Lonesome winter days were getting up early in the morning in the semi-darkness, making his way through the snow to the frozen river, breaking a hole in the thinnest ice with his cudgel and taking an icy bath. Remembering Amelia. Having breakfast with his nyanya. Oftentimes, a simple breakfast of kasha and coffee and a piece of black bread. Winter days were also frightened muzhiks crossing themselves, as the woods exploded with pistol shots, as he took his daily target practice for the duels that he would some day fight. Longing for Amelia. Going for a ride on horse back amid the drifting snowbanks. Coming back for hot cups of tea from the steaming samovar. Thinking of Amelia. Working all day on a chapter of his novel in verse which he was now definitely calling EUGENE ONEGIN. Then the night closing in along with the cold chill of the howling blizzards that came through every chink and crevice of the ancient creaking house.

He would sit at work in his leather-worn high back chair alone in his study at the large formidable oaken desk, with a golden four-candled candelabrum alit on the desk to the left of him, his manuscript before him, surrounded by piles and piles of books. There was a worn carpet on the creaky floor. There was an old divan behind him near the fireplace. Shelves overfilled with books adorned two walls. A picture of his great-grandfather stared darkly at him from above the old desk. To his back the fireplace with logs burning brightly, the sound of crackling twigs and fire spitting filled the quiet room, casting dancing shadows all around and on to his thoughtful face.

Sometimes he heard the howl of hungry wolves from far away. Sometimes, desperate, they came and looked in at him through the frosted window, longingly. Sometimes their lonely eyes would meet. In Holy Russia, northern nights came soon and lingered long.

Where are you, Amelia? Come back! Come back! You promised me!

Some cold nights he spent near the fireplace with his old nurse, Arina Rodionovna, and listened to her folksy legends. Of the great Prince Vladimir and Kievan days of yore. Some nights they drank vodka far into the night. He truly loved his nyanya like he loved no one else on earth. He looked at her as she wove her tales and watched her hands as they stabbed the needle into the cloth. He saw how withered her old hands had become, saw also that there were only two teeth left in her mouth. Her dear lips quivered as she spoke. Hands that had held him as a baby, tenderly, firm lips that had kissed him, fully. She had always made him feel that he was somebody worthy of being loved. He watched her nodding now even as she sewed and wove her tales of olden times.

Suddenly something caught in his throat as he realized she was aged and would not be with him much longer. He thought of Grandma-ma Hannibal. Arina Rodionovna would shortly get the long rest she so well deserved. His nyanya was old and tired, had worked hard all her life, and one day she would lie down and never rise again. His eyes filled up unknowingly.

He felt acutely now that all men and women were ensnared by a diabolical and malevolent fate. And his heart knew a consuming anger against an omnipotent Creator who would create an earth in which the destiny of every living creature was death, and the grave. He thought about his great-grandfather out there in his lonely grave on Holy Mountain. He had lived almost a century. But ultimately, death. One day he himself would grow old and toothless, if he lived that long. He felt a fullness building in his face and shoulders. He felt the nearness of his own demise. Thirty years—seventy years—a hundred years—what did it matter? Death. He knew a cold taste in his mouth.

He rose and went toward his nyanya and took her by the shoulders. "Mother, it is time that you should go to sleep." He kissed her on her trembling lips.

She stared up into his face and asked him, "Why do you always call me mother, Sasha?"

He answered, "Because you are my mother, *Matushka*. The only one I ever knew." His voice choked off.

After he had taken her to her quarters, he stayed up late and wrote a poem to her. He read it aloud, this time with tear-filled eyes:

Our decrepit hovel
Is all dark, all sad.
Why do you sit there, old woman,
Mute by the corner of the window?
Is it the long sobs of the wind
That weary you, my friend,
Or have you drowsed off
To the murmur of your wheel?
Let us drink, steadfast companion
Of my poor young years!
No more sorrows! Where's the jug
Come now,
Let our hearts be gay!

In a fight against his loneliness he made up folk to keep him company in his verses, in his novel, EUGENE ONEGIN, Tatyana, Lensky, Olga, in his tragedy, Dmitri, Boris. The people of his novel and poems and plays were real to him. Much more real than his real parents. He often wrote far into the wintry night until he fell asleep at his oaken desk. His nyanya would find him there the next morning and scold him as if he were her child. Sometimes, bored and uninspired, he would wander into the part of the house that was partitioned and constructed as a sewing room where Arina Rodionovna supervised a dozen serf girls at work at their spinning wheels. And he would idly watch the girls bent over their work with the old nurse in charge and listen to the humming sounds of the wheels. His presence made the young girls nervous.

One day a red-faced girl with flaxen hair and supple movements reminded him of another girl another time when he was young and innocent. He found himself going over to Arina Rodionovna and asking her if the young girl's name was "Tanya? Tatyana?"

His nyanya stared at him. "The girl's name is Olga Kalashnikova. Her father is one of the caretakers at your father's estate in Boldino." He could see the girl's face reddening all the way down her long and slender neck to her slim shoulders.

A few days later he glimpsed Olga Kalashnikova coming toward him along a path leading to the old house from the bathhouse, as he came naked from the river. He stood transfixed as he watched her. She walked like she was dancing, slim hips swaying, her lovely queenly head erect, as if she were used to carrying the marketplace atop her shapely bunch of flaxen hair. She did not see him till she was almost upon him, as he reached hastily for his towel on the river bank, to partially hide his shameful nakedness. The blood flowed through her ruddy cheeks, utterly rubescent now. She mumbled something unintelligible, as she picked up the sides of her heavy garments and ran swiftly toward the house and disappeared.

One lonesome evening Alexander Sergeievich sent for Olga Kalashnikova and asked her to have supper with him. She stammered and made excuses, as she stared down at the creaking floor. But he insisted. As a serf girl she could not refuse indefinitely. She sat silently through supper, eating nervously, tasting nothing. And when the dishes were cleared away and the rooms got quiet as the servants went discreetly to their quarters, she stood up to leave, and he held out his hands to her and she came to him, shaking like a slim young birch sapling in a soft breeze of the Russian springtime. She stood before him like a human sacrifice. He knew the irony of the situation. He had written angry poems and essays about the hard relationships between the masters and their hapless serf-maidens. He was the man who wrote THE VILLAGE. He remembered Natalya Ivanovna Aniskushka. The guilty conscience did not, could not stay his lonely hands.

Words from his poem, THE VILLAGE, echoed through his lonesome mind.

The gaunt old serf struggles down the furrows
of some implacable master
Not daring to dream any more for them
His little girls growing up
To feed the lust of some vice-sodden monster.

"What is the matter with you, my child? Why are you trembling?" She was no more than sixteen years of age.

To feed the lust of some vice-sodden monster. Though he was only twenty-four, he felt his age profoundly.

"From the cold, Your Excellency." She replied.

Implacable master—vice-sodden monster.

"Come then, let me warm you, sweet child." He said softly. And she came closer to him, and she stood meekly in his arms as he caressed her with his gentle hands. Olga Kalashnikova was not used to gentle hands. The boys who had fondled her were callous and their peasant hands were rough and toughened. He stroked her buttocks, firm and tender to his gentle touch, as a glow came to her face and perspiration to the little peachy down above her lips that opened slightly now without her knowing. She no longer trembled. She was ready to be taken and Master Alexander Sergeievich Pushkin needed terribly to take her.

The words kept sounding through his brain like a haunting echo. His own words, products of his own intelligence.

Vice-sodden monster!

But they were mere words, he argued weakly with himself. Nothing more. And he was no implacable master—He was no vice-sodden monster. He was a lonely man in need of love, someone to love and be loved by, and she was so upsettingly fresh and pure and beautiful, so utterly desirable. And what were mere words compared to his terrible need, his painful loneliness? He tried to still his trembling hands.

He looked up into her eyes so wide and blue and full of wanting to be loved. Her dear-to-him curvacious lips worked, but no sound came forth. He imagined she said, "Take me, master! Take me! Love me!"

He reached for her but this time Alexander Sergeievich heard his own words again.

Implacable master! Vice-sodden monster!

Then he heard his own voice say, "Goodnight, my child. I'm not a monster. Go to your quarters and take your rest."

Even as he spoke, he wanted to take her in his arms as she hesitated at first, with the portrait of rejection sketched in her puzzled face. Then she turned from him and left.

The poet lived with loneliness, with no word from the outside world. Winter was a cold white shroud that covered everything. He wrote feverishly, but nothing seemed to work for him. Even his muse had forsaken him, did not love him anymore. He, who possessed a heart as large and as vast as Russia, a heart so full of love, it seemed his lonely heart would burst sometimes. Of course, he loved his nyanya, Arina Rodionovna, his matushka, and she loved him, but it was not enough for someone with such a vast and endless reservoir of love. Where were his friends? Had they forgotten he existed? The nights were long and cold and lonely. Sometimes he thought he understood what made some Russians totally lacking of a sense of humor, especially the lowly peasantry, the serfs, the muzhiks, shut up in their isbas by the horrific Russian weather, four or five months at a time, shut off from the outside world. And so much weather there was everywhere, especially in winter; white, oppressive and omnipresent like the Czarist spies. Between the winter weather and the eerie steppes, it was a wonder that they ever laughed. Sometimes at night the old house was so quiet he could hear the flapping of moth wings up against the window panes where the candles flickered. He heard the blind bats as they bumped against the old ramshackle house. He felt like going to the door and flinging it open and screaming to the night.

I'm here! I'm here! I'm still alive!

"Pushchin! Zukovsky! Turgenev! Vyazemsky! By the Holy Virgin, let me hear from you!" Why had they turned their backs on him?

"Amelia, I need you! I need your arms around me! I need to hear your voice! I need your love! You promised to come back to me!" He found himself talking loudly to himself sometimes, and it frightened him. He had to hold on to himself. He must not lose his mind. He'd rather die than lose his mind.

The poet heard the lonely howl of wolves from far away and thought he understood their loneliness. He felt that the next time one came close to the house, he would open the door and let him in and partake of his comradeship. He saw very little of Arina Rodionovna. Time and age had slowed her down, and after spending a day at the loom she was ready for nothing but the bed. If she tried to keep him company, she would sit with him for a moment and immediately fall asleep.

Some lonely nights he would sit alone and the vision of lovely Amelia would appear before him, the physical her, her haunting understanding smile, hear the pure lilt of her laughter, the taste of her fully ripened lips, her special body fragrances, the smell of her Oriental pipe like apple orchards in harvest time, her almost baritone voice that reminded him of cellos playing Mozart's music. And he could not be certain if he were awake or dreaming.

One desperate night he wrote a poem to her, I LOVED YOU ONCE.

I loved you once, nor can this heart be quiet;
For it would seem that love still lingers here;
But do not you be further troubled by it;
I would in no wise hurt you, oh, my dear.

I loved you without hope, a mute offender;
What jealous pangs, what shy despairs I knew!
A love as deep as this, as true, as tender.
God grant another may yet offer you.

Sometimes, Alexander Sergeievich felt sorry for himself, and he was a man who despised self-pity. If only he could take refuge in his writing. He tried in vain to work with EUGENE ONEGIN. From EUGENE he went to his tragedy, BORIS GODUNOV. Nothing worked. Some days he would put on his high boots and go for long walks in the frozen woods and listen to the wind roar wildly through the tall pine trees, watch a frightened hare scurry through the frozen underbrush. It was his way of making sure the world and he were still alive.

One day he had walked for miles and suddenly it began to snow, and before he knew it, the wind had blown up a blinding blizzard. The roads were quickly covered as he started homeward. It wasn't long before the entire earth around him became a great awesome world of whiteness. Everything looked the same, white and desolate. Snow drifts everywhere, ten and fifteen feet in depth. Everything merged into each other—the roads, the paths, from sky to earth, the woods were one and the same and indistinguishable. He was numb with cold. His body felt like a solid chunk of ice. He had a familiar feeling that it had all happened before. The loneliness, the snow, the cold. Did he believe in reincarnation? Had he been this way before? He heard creaking movements in the woods behind him, and he thought some wild beast might be stalking him. Darkness began to fall upon the beautiful terrible awesome whiteness. He felt a weariness coming down on him. His tired legs were like heavy pieces of iron. He could hardly lift them in the snow. He kept telling himself, I must keep going—I must not fall asleep. He could barely keep his eyes open now. When he blew his breath into the cold, icicles formed immediately in front of his face. He felt his jaws were locked with ice. *If I fall asleep, I'll freeze to death. What a stupid way to leave this earth! It would be typical of me to do something so damn stupid! Found in the woods a few months later, a carcass devoured by hungry wolves.* He tried to laugh bitterly at himself. *At least my death would serve some useful purpose. Save some hungry wolf from starving. Keep awake! Keep awake!* his mind screamed out to him in panic. But he felt his eyes slowly closing as he stumbled along through the blinding blizzard. Then as suddenly as it had begun it stopped. And a silent darkness fell all over the earth. The moon threw eerie shadows onto the woods. Silent shadows stalking Pushkin. His eyes completely shut now, he stumbled along fighting a losing battle with his sleepiness. If he fell asleep that would be the end of it. End of Alexander Pushkin.

It was the easiest way in the world to die, he consoled himself. Everybody died sooner or later. What easier way than to cuddle up in one's own sweet everlasting sleep? And never ever ever awaken. And dream. Even in death he'd dream all kinds of crazy dreams. He thought drowsily, this way he could escape Russia and its horrible miserable all-consuming weather. He could not remember a night in his entire life in which he had not dreamed and afterwards remembered vividly his dreams. He dreamed in stanzas, dreamed in chapters. Dreams were as real to him as what most humans called reality. Sometimes he could not tell the difference.

His eyes were almost closed now. Was he already asleep and dreaming? *He was soaring now above the earth; now he hovered above the lights of Paris and went down to visit with his great-grandfather, a young handsome Black man, who at the age of eighteen had gone there with his Imperial godfather, Great Peter, and Peter had left him there to get an education in army engineering.* Alexander Sergeievich had these long extended talks with his great-grandfather in this and many other dreams. *Ibrahim told Pushkin that in Paris he had made a special study in engineering, mathematics, drinking, brawling, fornicating, and usually he came out on top.* Pushkin's great-grandfather made him laugh uproariously. Laughed him awake there in the snow. *For a long time after his graduation from the university, Hannibal resisted Peter's letters and pleas that he return to Russia. Russia needed desperately men of his training and intelligence. Grandpa-pa Hannibal told him he had ignored the pleas of Peter. Paris was where things were happening, and Ibrahim felt no particular loyalty to that vast ice box of the earth named Russia. It was not the country of his birth. So he wrote Great Peter one excuse after another, prolonging his stay. He remained in Paris until all of his money and excuses were exhausted. Back in Russia, it was not long after Great Peter's death that young Ibrahim realized how truly fond he was of his Imperial godfather. His popularity at the Court deescalated rapidly shortly after Peter's death, and he found himself shipped to faraway Siberia, where he remained in exile till Empress Elizabeth came to power and brought him back to the capital at Saint Petersburg. She had been one of Ibrahim's playmates when they were children in the Court of Peter the Great. Now Pushkin heard the voice of Grandma-ma Hannibal in his dream. Under the reigns of Empresses Elizabeth and Catherine, Han-*

nibal thrived and prospered, acquired an estate with a thousand serfs and became a general in the Russian army. It was rumored at the Court that Catherine the Great was enamored of this fine specimen of African masculinity. And that he shared Great Catherine's Most Imperial bed a time or two, or three, maybe even six or seven. Ibrahim Petrovich could never erase from his memory those long dark frozen winters of Siberia. Therefore he served Her Imperial Majesty, amourously, dutifully, patriotically, romantically, and with a rare enthusiasm. For to deny Her Imperial Majesty was to court disfavor and disaster. And disaster meant Siberia. He preferred to court the lascivious empress.

Sleep or awake, Pushkin knew the rest of the story. In his last years, Grandpapa Hannibal retired to his estate at Mikhailovskoye. It was said of him that he was ruthless and tyrannical with his serfs, who feared him for his African features and his non-Christian name. Behind his back, superstitious muzhiks crossed themselves when he strode amongst them with his walking cane and riding crop, which he would use on their backsides at the slightest provocation. These peasants were sure he was the actual fulfillment of the long predicted coming of the anti-Christ. He lived almost a hundred years. And Alexander Pushkin was dying at the age of twenty-four.

Suddenly, a hanging tree limb slapped Pushkin in the face and knocked him deep into a snowdrift, and he went into the snow up above his ears. It woke him up and saved his life, from sleeping, endlessly. Bells for early mass were ringing in his head as he struggled vainly to extricate himself, but the more he exercised himself the deeper he seemed to sink. He had a vision of the frozen Neva River and the infants being baptized, as he flailed about helplessly. At the very last moment he reached for a hanging limb from a spruce tree, and with all the strength left in him, he lifted himself slowly from his frozen grave, straining every muscle in his exhausted body. He heard the frozen tree limb creaking loudly with his weight, and he hoped fervently it would not break. He was out now, but his hands began to slip and he almost fell back into his icy grave.

Wondering now as he wandered aimlessly. Why had he fought so hard to save his life. Ultimately he would end up on Holy Mountain with his great-grandfather and Grandma-ma Hannibal anyhow. He stumbled forward, blinded by the cold and whiteness.

In all this vast cold, he again began to feel a warm cozy sleepy feeling. He wanted to lean against a tree, slide down and cuddle up amongst himself and fall into a deep and endless sleep. At the very last moment he began to beat himself in the face to keep himself awake; he thought his hands would break off, they were so frozen, and yet he beat himself till his arms fell to their sides and refused to be lifted. He was about to give up the ghost. Why not? he thought. Life was not that dear to him. It was as cozy a way to die as any. He leaned against a tree and began to slide downward, and he felt a welcomed peacefulness engulfing him, overflowing now with a sweet tranquility. He wondered, vaguely, why it was that human beings feared death. Was it the mystery of it? He would soon know all of death's secrets. Bravo! Then he realized it was not a tree he leaned against. It was a fence! A fence post! His heart leaped about with hope. He hoped it was the post that defined the boundary of his family's estate. Perhaps it wasn't. In any event it gave him hope. It woke him up again. He straightened up and felt his way along the fence, and when the fence gave out, he turned leftward toward what he hoped was home, the old house of Mikhailovskoye. He stared ahead and saw torches moving about above the frozen earth.

The old house exuded now a ghostly ambience, with the torches glowing in the foreground, as it loomed there congealed in a frozen alabaster in bold relief against the blackness of the night and suspended there in time and space forever, as if it had been eolithically sculptured out of an imagined mammoth floe somewhere out there in the North Sea, eons ago, and no longer now afloat. A phantom conjured up by ancient Vikings.

The torches! They were searching for him, he thought. He was saved! He tried to call out to them, but then he found his jaws were frozen, locked with ice. He screamed but only he could hear. He gathered a scream from the bottom of his stomach and brought it up through his body through his shoulders; it struggled through his neck, his throat, it came screaming from his throat. Once—twice—thrice And he heard them shouting back to him. "Alexander Sergeievich! Alexander Sergeievich!" As he fell forward to the ground and slept.

He had no idea how long it had been since that night they found him in the snow. He only knew that one day he looked up and she was there waiting on him hand and foot. She brought him breakfast, dinner and supper. Fixed his bath, changed his bed clothing, kept him clean, bathed him down, emptied his chamber pot, took care of all his human needs. She was Olga Kalashnikova. His nyanya was in bed with influenza. Then one day when his strength returned, Olga went back to her job at the spinning wheels. He almost wished he had not recovered. He missed Olga Kalashnikova.

One evening she came to inquire of his health, and he invited her to stay and have supper with him. She knew everything there was to know about him, physically. No single part of his body was a stranger to her. She was familiar with every mole and wart. But this night she sat there across the table from him eating silently, saying nothing, staring shyly at her plate.

When they were done with the eating, she came and placed her hand tenderly upon his head. He could feel her body trembling. He looked up into her freckled face, and she blushed a bright vermillion from her forehead downward toward her round slim shoulders.

He mustn't take her in his arms! he told himself even as he reached out to her and she came into his arms. He felt her bosom beating wildly up against his crazy chest.

He wished for strength to send her away from him even as he had done before, but there was no such strength for him on this earth.

And yet he murmured, "I must spare you! I must spare you!" And heard her answer, "Please don't spare me, Master! Please don't spare me!" Perhaps he imagined it.

He said, "I need you, Olga Kalashnikova! I need you! I'm so damn lonesome."

Olga replied, "I need you also, my Master."

His hands seemed to have a consciousness all their own, as they wandered tenderly over her body that was shaking like a sapling pine tree caught up in the winds of winter. He disrobed the trembling child.

In his bed now, he kissed her lips, her tiny ears, her neck, her round nippled breasts, freckled, and in the full bloom of her maidenhood and bursting forth with tension now. He was indeed the master, the experienced maestro playing music on a sensitive and lovely masterpiece of an instrument. She was trembling now but not this time from chill or fear. When he entered her she was ever ready to be entered. And they journeyed together and came out at the other end in a world of joyous transports unimagined by this serf girl. No one had ever been so gentle with her. She had not known such love was possible. She had not known a man could make a woman feel so gladsome. She had thought that "making love" was a term made up to describe an occurrence that had nothing to do with ecstasy for women. A woman was made love to or at. Never ever was she made love with. She was imposed upon. A lot that God had put her on this earth to suffer. Was that not why the Holy Virgin had been spared? She was thankful to her master, and she covered his face with eager grateful kisses.

The poet still felt guilty toward her. He really felt more shame than guilt. He had exercised his master's prerogatives, the exclusive privilege of his degenerate and unfeeling class. He was no better than the very bastards he despised and wrote against.

He said, "I'm a devil! Stay away from me!"

"Oh no, Your Excellency! I swear by Holy Friday you're a blessed angel! There is no doubt!"

"I'm a rotten bastard and I took advantage of you!"

She began to cry. "I was no good then! You did not enjoy the love we made! I'm sorry. It was all my fault!" She pulled away from him and started to take leave of his bed, sobbing now as if her heart would surely break.

But he pulled her toward him. How could he make her understand? "Don't cry, my baby—Please don't cry. Pajalsta! Of course it was good! Of course the love you made, we made, was sweet and soft and blithesome and good and tender and I loved every moment of it. But can't you see it was not on even terms? We must never do this again, you understand?" He was kissing her now and stroking her as she nestled closely in his arms. And he felt himself hardening against this dear child once more. She felt it too and a happiness lit up her face. She felt his weight upon her once again. And they made lovely love again. The dirty rotten gentry bastard!

The colder it became the lonelier he was. He sent letters out to his friends in the city. Though he was much closer now to Saint Petersburg and Moscow, than he was when he was in Kishinev or Odessa, he felt more severely isolated. He wrote Zukovsky, Vyazemsky, Delvig, Pushchin, Turgenev. "Visit me! Or I'll go crazy! I'm not infected! Not a leper! Visit me! Write me! Send me news!"

A week after he first made love with Olga Kalashnikova, he looked up one evening from his supper and there she stood. There was a fright in her eyes, the blue-green of the ocean's edge. Like a bird of lovely plumage poised for flight.

He stared at her and said, "Sit down, sweet child." And she obeyed her master. And later they made love like sweet love was intended, but of which she'd never dreamt.

One night, Pushkin became aware that for the very first time he was watching a woman as they made love, and amazed he was at the changes her dear face went through—from at first a chaste, timid and angelic countenance to shamefulness, the eyelids of her shy blue eyes, long thick lashes lowered, to her avid rich lips now opening greedily all her inhibitions to the winds, shamelessly, her face aglow now losing color, turning pale, breathing deeply, her dear face in sweet agony and covered now with pimples of perspiration, her curvacious mouth agape, as if she were sated from the nectar of the sweetest fruit. There was nothing on this earth so beautiful as a woman caught in the thrilling spasms of the last ecstatic stages of love-making. She was soothing to his loneliness; a balm that he looked forward to. Then one week the young serf girl stopped coming.

When he wasn't writing poems or prose he was writing letters, a desperate voice from the wilderness to his friends who had become afraid to listen. They did not dare to pay this dangerous recluse a visit. They even tried to persuade Pushchin from going down to see the old disreputable hermit of Mikhailovskoye.

"As a friend, I beg you," Prince Vyazemsky pleaded, "don't compromise yourself, dear fellow. The Emperor will know the moment you begin your journey."

"He's my best friend and one of the greatest men in Russia." Ivan Pushchin declared. "What has Russia become then if I cannot visit with him? What's the good of being safe? I have to go. I need to see him as much as he needs to see me. I'll start out anyway. So what can they do to me but stop me on the way and turn me back?"

"They can send you to Siberia," Vyazemsky answered.

Ivan Pushchin said, "It's probably where I'll end up anyhow."

He went to see the "old man of the wilderness" in the winter with the snow packed high and lingering on the ground for months. The icicles glistened in the lordly pines. A stillness lay across the vast white earth, broken now and then by the scamper of a hare through the frozen underbrush. One sleepy chilly morning the Hermit of Mikhailovskoye was awakened by the sound of horse hooves in the snow and the jingling of sleigh bells. He stumbled from his bed and through a small circle on the frosted window he saw the chubby Pushchin alighting from the sleigh. He rushed barefoot out into the snow to greet him. They embraced and kissed each other's cheeks. The poet could hardly see his long time comrade for the tears that bleared his happy eyes.

"Pushchin, old friend! You're here! You're here! You're really here! You came! You came!"

"Alexander Sergeievich! Alexander Sergeievich!"

He stood there for a time barefoot and in nothing but his nightshirt, but the warmth he felt for his comrade protected him. Finally they went inside, and Pushchin took off his bearskin coat and heavy boots.

An old woman came in with steaming coffee for them. Pushchin took one look at her and knew she must be the nyanya Pushkin had spoken of so many times. And he took Arina Rodionovna into his arms and embraced and kissed her as if she were his own nyanya. It was like a family reunion. They had breakfast and then they sat and talked animatedly.

"Tell me everything and all at once!" Pushkin said excitedly. Alexander Sergeievich looked older and more serious to Ivan Pushchin, with his whiskers and his side whiskers that almost reached each other underneath his chin. His dark blue eyes were older, wiser. "How is the Union of the North doing?" Pushkin demanded. "When is it planned? The Uprising? What can I do to help? Tell me. Tell me!"

When he saw his comrade's hesitation, Pushkin said, "I don't blame you for not confiding in me, after all the stupid things I've done. But if there's anything I can do to help—the risk you took in coming here—"

Pushchin told him, "You are the most respected and revered man in all St. Pete. And it's a real debatable question who's in prison."

The exiled poet heartily agreed. "The whole fornicating Russia is a goddamn prison. We are all of us in exile. Our country is the saddest place on earth. Perhaps it is the horrible weather that makes us so damn sorrowful."

He pulled out a book he had brought for Pushkin, one the exiled poet had not heard of, Gribloledov's THE MISFORTUNE OF BEING CLEVER. Pushchin began to read it to him as they drank coffee, when a sleigh pulled up outside the house. Pushkin ran to the window, came back and quickly hid the book and picked up one from close by and opened it. It was the LIVES OF SAINTS.

Alexander Sergeievich introduced the unexpected visitor to Pushchin as Father Jonah, the abbot of the nearby monastery. Pushchin went forward to the priest to be blessed and Pushkin dutifully followed suit. Father Jonah explained that he had heard that a man named Pushchin was visiting Pushkin and he had come over to see if he were the same Ivan Pushchin that he once knew when he lived in Southern Russia.

Pushchin assured the priest that he was not the man. He was merely a friend of Pushkin's who went to school with him at Tsarskoye Selo. "The Pushchin you refer to is a General living in Odessa at the moment. He is not a relative."

Alexander Sergeievich sat silently watching them, listening absently to their makeshift conversation. The priest was making short work of the rum that Pushkin served, and got inebriated very quickly. His tongue thickened even as his voice grew louder. Because the rum had slowed up his fat tongue, he seemed to try to cover up the fact by shouting. Father Jonah was a pleasant-faced man with a young cherubic face and a permanent red nose from excessive imbibition. He was of medium height, thick in the shoulders with a slight pregnancy of the abdomen. He wore a long black cassock that swept the rays of dust up from the old decrepit carpet.

He turned to Alexander Sergeievich, still speaking to Ivan Pushchin. "Your esteemed comrade of Mikhailovskoye never worships with us. He never ever comes to church." He spoke these words in a tone of deep significance.

Ivan Pushchin answered, "Alexander Sergeievich is the greatest writer in Russia. He is very busy. Perhaps—"

Father Jonah was in an argumentative mood, by now, abetted by the alcohol. "How can he get too busy to worship Jesus with the people? He claims to love the muzhiks, but is he too important to praise God with them?" Father Jonah rose and began to walk back and forth across the room agitatedly. The hem of his long black garment made the flecks of dust fly above the surface of the ancient rug like tiny bugs. "We are all very busy in the service of the people and the Blessed Virgin, while some of our renowned poets create unrest among the poor and disloyalty to the Little Father. The poor muzhiks are unhappy enough already. They do not need to be made more unhappy by the driveling of some irresponsible scribbler, who lives off the fat of the land surrounded by little serf maidens growing up to feed the lust of the landed gentry." Father Jonah spoke with Ivan Pushchin as if the poet were not present.

Alexander Sergeievich interjected quietly, "How does Your Worship serve the poor downtrodden muzhiks? How do you help their weary bodies and their starving bellies?"

Father Jonah sat down again and took another gulp of rum. He still addressed his remarks to Ivan Pushchin. "It is the duty of the ordained shepherd to minister to the spiritual needs of his flock. To prepare their lowly spirits to peacefully accept their lot on this earth as foreordained by the Supreme Master—"

"And the Little Father at the Palace," Pushkin interjected, "and the landlords and the counts and barons. The Bible says, 'The Lord is my shepherd, I shall not want.' And the peasant wants more food on his table, a better life. And what kind of shepherd is one who lets his flock be devoured by ravenous wolves who are the landed gentry?"

Father Jonah was screaming at Ivan Pushchin now. "The temporal and wordly concerns do not come within the province of the Shepherds of the Lord! The Lord Jesus, Himself has said, 'Man cannot live by bread alone'!"

Pushkin said, "It is strange that there are so few undernourished holy men, since they do not concern themselves with such secular things as feeding their fat bellies. And so long as the shepherd does not take care of his flock, this poet will not be found in his church."

When the rum had vanished, Father Jonah's religious fervor also diminished. He apologized for interrupting their conversation and left. As the sleigh bells faded in the distance, Ivan Pushchin turned to his exiled friend and said, "I'm sorry if I caused you any trouble by my presence."

"It was nothing," Alexander Sergeievich told him. "He's always spying on me. That is how he serves his God and Emperor who are one and the same to the fornicating hypocrite. What astonished me is how he got the news so quickly."

Pushkin took his friend into the sewing room to watch the girls at work. Pushchin noticed the hermit's eyes lingered on a golden-haired girl with a long slim neck. He smiled and winked an eye at Alexander Sergeievich.

When they returned to Pushkin's workroom where the fire was blazing, the comrade from Saint Petersburg pulled out of his bag three bottles of Saint Peray champagne which he knew to be the poet's favorite. Alexander Sergeievich called in all of the house servants along with his nyanya. They drank to everybody's health, especially to Arina Rodionovna's.

"Long live the muzhiks!" Pushkin shouted, "Long live Arina Rodionovna! May she live forever!"

They drank to the overthrow of feudalism.

"Long live the revolution!"

"Down with the Emperor!"

Some of the servants suddenly lost their enthusiasm. They stared down at the floor and up at the ceiling. It was as if someone had uttered blasphemy against the Grand Divinity and they feared that lightning or an earthquake might strike this sinful and unholy place.

Pushchin noted that the blonde girl he'd seen his friend watching in the sewing room was not among the group. One of the muzhiks brought out a balalaika and began to play upon it. Alexander Sergeievich and his comrade Pushchin danced with the servants till their legs grew heavy.

As he danced with his old nurse, Pushkin asked, "Where is Olga Kalashnikova, Matushka? Is she not feeling well tonight?"

The old woman answered, "Olga Kalashnikova is in good health."

He asked uneasily, "Is there something I can do—for her?"

His nyanya's old eyes scolded him like a mother would a naughty boy whom she loved despite his mischief. "You've done enough for her already. Stay away from the dear girl."

He stared deeply into his nyanya's disapproving eyes, then suddenly he began to dance a wild mazurka all around the room bumping other dancers off the floor until they had it all to themselves. He danced with the old woman till her knees began to buckle, and they fell exhausted in their chairs.

About midnight, the servants gone, Pushchin and Pushkin sat drinking coffee. Alexander Sergeievich was complaining about the people in Saint Petersburg who were censoring his manuscripts. "Most of the bastards are illiterate."

They talked about what the writers in the capital were involved with, intellectually.

"What are they doing?" Pushchin repeated Alexander Sergeievich's question. "Most of the great Russian so-called revolutionary intellectuals spend much of their time in contemplating the esoteric meaning of life." He hiccuped and mimicked. "If there is no God, how can life have any meaningful significance?"

Alexander Sergeievich joined the mimicry. "How many needles can dance on the head of an angel?"

Pushchin continued. "What's the sense of *revolution* and *constitution* if there is no Supreme Being for mankind to be subservient to? When one does not even know the meaning of such erudite concepts as humanity, liberty and democracy. Perhaps we all went this way before, thousands of years ago, and *democracy* and *freedom* and *revolution* proved themselves to be degenerative and put us all back in the cave."

Alexander Sergeievich stared long at his comrade. He sighed heavily. "Sometimes, when I look at the way things are in Russia and in the rest of the world, sometimes I find myself believing that I'm a citizen of future generations. I think perhaps I was born too soon." He mumbled only half aloud, "Fate, God-and-His-Majesty's Will. There is simply nothing for it."

In a change of mood, he said, sardonically, "Perhaps His Most Imperial Majesty, Ivan the Terrible, rescued Russia from the cave belatedly. Thousands of years after the fact."

Pushchin laughed at his angry and bewhiskered comrade. "With an emperor like Our Little Father Alexander to guide us, perhaps we will end up in the cave again, devouring one another." He mimicked, "If there is no God, no Supreme Being, what is the point of anything whatever? Breathing, living, loving, eating?"

Pushkin added, "While the arrogant ennobled swine gorge themselves on black caviar and Caucasian pheasant, muzhiks die daily of starvation." He poured Pushchin another cup of steaming coffee. "Every time Vyazemsky writes to me, which is a very rare occasion, he admonishes me to spend some time in Pskov. He says it's full of history. As if I didn't know that Pskov was where the fire of Russian freedom was extinguished even until this very moment. I've already started a tragedy about Boris Godunov and Dmitri the Pretender."

Alexander Sergeievich was ravenous for conversation. He wanted to discuss everything and all at once. It was as if a grand feast had been set before him after weeks and weeks of imposed fasting. Where to begin? What to eat first? If you piled the plate too high with food, you might lose your appetite, and the famine would go unabated. Ivan Pushchin was equally avid, famished. What role should narodnost, the nationalism of the people, the national psyche, the folklore, play in a country's literature?

"The debate on narodnost is raging among the intellectuals," Pushchin told the lonely exile of Mikhailovskoye. "Is there such a thing as a national literature? Does not the idea of narodnost contradict the whole concept of universality in a nation's literature?"

"Hell no! Nyet!" Alexander Sergeievich answered heatedly. "The human tree is universal, but it has many national branches. And even more, the tree trunk of our art and literature must be rooted in narodnost. The problem with our literature is that it has been *too* imitative. Sometimes it's French, sometimes it's English. Sometimes you can't tell what it is. It has no national personality, no identity." He fussed around his desk until he found what he wanted. "I wrote an essay for one of your St. Pete journals." He began to read from his manuscript.

"Climate, history, geography, language, economy, type of government and religion give each nation a particular physiognomy, which to a greater or lesser extent is reflected in its literature. There is a way of thinking and feeling, there is a multitude of customs, beliefs, and habits which belong exclusively and uniquely to each individual nation. We are speaking about the content of the Russian *soul*. France is a bourgeois democracy, a republic. We are a medieval autocracy, a national anachronism, an agrarian society. Most Russians are peasants. Too many are serfs, slaves, muzhiks! The industrial revolution has not reached this crazy country. We have the steppes. We have the indomitable muzhiks. We have the frozen winters. We are a nation of many nations. Kalmuks, Slavs, Tadjiks, Uzbeks, Tartars, Jews, Ukranians, Cossacks. The vastest stretch of land expanse on all this entire earth!"

"Of course!" his Lycée comrade shouted softly. "And almost every member of the Northern Union read your essay in *Vestnik Europi*. There was a great debate about it. We agree with you wholeheartedly. Most of us know the article by heart." He stared at his lonely comrade in open admiration. He remembered the days of Tsarskoye Selo, when he would look for Alexander Sergeievich and find him working in the fields with muzhiks, find him in the Lycée Archives with the *vitaes* and the *paterics* of ancient times.

Alexander Sergeievich's eyes were getting misty. He had yearned so very long, so desperately for this kind of intellectual comradeship, he couldn't believe it was actually happening. Every now and then he shouted softly, "You're really here! We're talking with each other. This is not a dream!"

Suddenly he felt ashamed of his own outburst. He got up and walked around and slyly wiped his eyes and blew his nostrils. He came back and embraced Pushchin. "I'm so happy to see you, brother! I mean it. I'm so goddamn happy to see you!"

He read parts of EUGENE ONEGIN to his friend, and the beginnings of his tragedy, which he had titled BORIS GODUNOV. By the time they finished the last bottle of champagne it was early in the morning. It was time for his comrade to leave. They embraced again, kissed and said goodbye. And promised to meet each other in the spring in Moscow. Alexander Sergeievich worked hard to keep his feelings muffled under heavy winter blankets, but he had a premonition they would never meet again. This was the goodbye everlasting. He stood in the doorway holding a flickering candle, waving and saying, "Farewell, tovarishi! Beloved friend! Dosvidanya, comrade! Dosvidanya, dosvidanya—" He murmured to himself now, as a sinking feeling settled over him. And he stood there in the quiet cold and watched the sleigh until it jingled out of sound and sight.

Spring came late that year. And in April, his friend, Anton Delvig came, and spent ten happy days with Pushkin. They talked of Lycée days and read their poetry to each other and paid visits to the women in a neighboring estate at Trigorskoye.

One evening in a fit of loneliness, he sent for Olga Kalashnikova. She came and stood before him at the supper table. "Sit down, my child. Why have you been avoiding me?"

"Nothing, Sire. I've just been keeping busy. And I didn't want to make a nuisance of myself."

"Nonsense, sweet child. And did I do something to offend you then?" Pushkin inquired.

Her cheeks began to redden. "How could Your Excellency offend me? You're the master and I'm nothing but a common serf girl."

"Don't say things like that, little one. Sit down and have supper with me."

She sat down across from him, but ate nothing.

He said, "Come here to me, my baby."

She came and stood near him diffident and all atremble. He sighed. He put his hand on her and she shrank back from him, as if she thought he was infected. He thought about what Father Jonah had said, as he took her into his arms and caressed her trembling body. And finally he started to disrobe her. She shrank back from him again.

"Please, Master! Please, Your Highness! Do not take my clothing from me!"

Her pleas only made him more determined, increased the heartbeat in his chest and the thumping in the middle of him. It was as if she pleaded with him to make love to her. He took the blouse down from her shoulder and saw the reason for her reticence. Her young breasts were blue and purplish. She was covered with welts all over her body.

His anger made him see white liquid spots before his eyes. "Who did this to you, sweetheart?" Pushkin demanded.

"I forgot who it was, Your Excellency." She said hesitantly. "Please don't make me tell! He said he'd kill me if I told you!"

He said quietly, "No one is going to kill you, child. No one is going to put their hands on you again and live to tell of it."

He began to kiss each sore spot and she began to whimper like a grateful puppy. "Oh, master! Why can't all men be like you?"

"It's the way things are, my child. Some men have never had the leisure to learn gentleness and sensitivity. Who did this to you? Tell me."

"Igor Ravinowitz, Sire, the son of the peasant in charge of the orchards."

"The sonofabitch!" Pushkin exclaimed. As he kissed her belly, her young heart pounded rapidly, and he noticed a new roundness and a swelling that had not been there before. "Who got you with child, my baby?"

"Sire?"

"I asked you who got you with child?" He repeated.

"Your Excellency, after you, there's been no one else. I refused to let them touch me. That is why he beat me. I deserved it."

"Nonsense!"

"Don't be angry with me, Your Excellency! She pleaded. I love you! But don't you worry. I'll kill myself before I bring any trouble to you. I swear by Holy Friday!"

Alexander Sergeievich felt old and ancient at this moment. He felt terribly degenerate. At the same time he felt full of love and human kindness and passion which he sometimes confused with compassion. She was fully disrobed now. And he began to kiss her tenderly again. He kissed the bruises on her breasts. "You are not going to kill your lovely self." Kissed her slender shoulders. "You are going to be well taken of." Kissed tenderly her roundsome belly just above the nervous breathing pubic hair. Then he put her clothes on gently, piece by piece, as she stared at him with wonder and in adoration.

She told the Poet that she wished that she could remain with him forever, his serf girl at Mikhailovskoye.

"Don't say things like that!" he shouted at her angrily. "You don't want to be anybody's serf girl. You want to be free!"

"But Master—"

"Don't call me Master so damn sweetly. Your mission is to hate all masters. Hate them! Kill them!" Even to himself he sounded hypocritical.

She shook her straw-colored head. "But I can't hate you, Master! I can't hate you! How can I hate you, if I love you?"

"Don't say you love me. Don't ever say you love a master."

She said, "But Your Excellency—"

Alexander Sergeievich felt an overwhelming helpless shame at what his class had done to her, to her body and her mind. He took her by the shoulders and shook her gently. "You must learn to hate your master, sweet woman. You want to be free, don't you?"

Olga Kalashnikova shook her head, her dear confused eyes blind with tears. "I just want to be here with you like we are now, always and forever."

He murmured, dreamily, "Yes. It would be nice. It would be idyllic, but it could never be. Dear sweet child, the world is constructed powerfully against us. Me as well as you. But some day it will be different. I swear to you it will, or all our struggling is for naught. This banishment—this exile—the Russian people will triumph!" His dear-to-her voice drifted into quietness. And she wept bitterly for a love she knew could never be.

The next day the Hermit of Mikhailovskoye went to see the boy, Igor. He was busy wrestling with chopped-down trees for logging. As he watched the blonde-haired Igor he felt his anger rising in his face and in his shoulders. He was consumed with anger. Igor was a giant of a lad, thick in the shoulders and over six feet in height. Pushkin's anger almost blinded him. When Igor came close to our poet, Alexander Sergeievich lashed out with his cudgel and knocked the muscle-bound Igor to the ground. The big lad got up slowly.

"What is it, Your Excellency?"

Pushkin was fuming. "You know damn well what it is, you son of a swine fornicating with a billy goat! You should have choked to death on your mother's vomit!"

Pushkin was aware that the other men had stopped their work and were gathering. Igor turned to them. "The master is upset because I gave his personal whore a well deserved whipping. And now he comes to chastise me, but he doesn't dare to come without his cudgel."

Igor's father came running up and fell on his knees before Pushkin. "Forgive him, Master! Please forgive the boy, Your Excellency! He is head-strong and crazy and don't know what he's saying half the time!"

The red-faced boy said, "I know what I'm saying. I'm saying that all that fart he writes about the rights of serfs is so much horseshit! He's no better than the rest of the gentry swine. He uses his rank to yebat our women. Then hides behind his title and that cudgel. If he was a man I'd beat the living *gavno* out of him!"

Pushkin threw the cudgel aside and charged the giant of a boy with his head lowered like a bull out on the lonely steppes. It was a trick he had learned when he played with the peasants near his grandmother's estate, a thing he perfected in his games at Tsarskoye Selo. With his large head he knocked the wind out of the big bully. Igor got up from the ground fuming. He rushed Pushkin, but the poet stepped nimbly aside and kicked the boot of his right foot into the crotch of the clumsy woodsman. Igor doubled up and fell like one of the trees being chopped down, and screamed with pain. Alexander Sergeievich now was wild with anger.

He stomped the woodsman in his stomach. Igor turned over on his stomach and stretched out on the ground, and Pushkin would have jumped up and down on the middle of Igor's back with his heavy boots, had he not heard the pleading cries of the desperate father. "Don't kill him, Master! Please don't kill him. He's a real good boy, Your Excellency!"

Alexander Sergeievich turned from the groaning prostrate woodsman toward the father. "He is a scoundrel! Tell him to stay away from Olga Kalishnikova if he knows what's good for him."

"Yes, Your Highness. Thank you, Master." The man began to kiss the poet's hand.

Alexander Sergeievich pulled his hand away, disgusted. "You have nothing to thank me for. You just tell that bastard son of yours, he'd better stay away from Olga Kalashnikova." He turned from the man and strode up the pathway toward the house.

He agonized all day long and into the night, and when he went to bed, he found that sleep refused to come to him. He walked the floor. He could not write. His muse took her revenge on him, the vice-sodden monster who wrote THE VILLAGE. He spent three sleepless nights, and the last night he signed manumission papers that set Olga Kalashnikova free.

A few weeks later he sent his flaxen-haired manumitted maiden to Saint Petersburg with a letter to Zukovsky telling him a gentry friend of his had gotten this dear sweet innocent child in a family way. "She is free now. She has manumission papers with her. Do everything you can for her and see that she gets the best of medical attention in her confinement. Whatever the expenses are, my friend will be responsible for them. When the child is born, send them both to my father's estate in Boldino."

Before his lovely manumitted maiden could possibly have reached Saint Petersburg, Pushkin received a letter from his father asking him if he had lost his mind. "You have no authority to free Olga Kalashnikova. I rescind your action out of hand. That girl still belongs to me." Alexander Sergeievich wondered how his father had gotten the news so quickly.

A few days later, his faithful valet, Nikita Koslov, came back to Mikhailovskoye. Alexander Sergeievich looked up from his desk one day and there his valet stood with a tumbler of kvas for his master. Pushkin was overcome with joy.

"Welcome home, old friend. What a wonderful surprise!" He embraced the older man and kissed his graying bearded cheeks.

Nikita's eyes filled up. "Darling boy, I heard about you freezing to death in the snowstorm and came down here to take care of you."

Pushkin laughed. "That was several months ago. But I am glad to see you."

CHAPTER THREE

From his grief at losing Olga Kalashnikova, Alexander Sergeievich went for consolation to the estate at Trigorskoye where women were in great abundance.

The Sorot River, in the spring time, often hovered over by fog and mist, ran placidly behind the Pushkin estate at Mikhailovskoye on its tranquil reptilian course past Trigorskoye almost a dozen versts away. The manor house at Trigorskoye was a large weatherworn structure.

Of a late spring afternoon Alexander Sergeievich would ride the winding twisting paths on his great horse, the flaming color of an Irish setter, the sunlight casting a checkered pattern down through a tunnel of pine and linden trees. The air redolent with the fragrances of spring, the sweet aroma of apple blossoms in full bloom, of pine sap and freshly blooming flowers of myriad denominations.

There was a dazzling green at the top of the pine and linden trees; sometimes, as the early evening sunlight settled in them, the ambience above the trees took on such a sparkling bluish green the emerald sky itself seemed to have descended and to hover just above the trees. The entire world up there was bluish green, aquamarine and blindingly brilliant. Sometimes he would pull his horse to a halting stop and gaze up at it and shake his head in wonder at the beauty of it all. His face would fill and a chill would pass across his shoulders. Beauty always had that kind of impact on him. This poet was a slave to beauty. He loved to ride down the sunlit path to see the women of Trigorskoye. Women—women and more than ready for romance with the famous poet of Mikhailovskoye with the Don Juan reputation. He could not erase Olga Kalashnikova from his memory. Actually, he never tried to erase the memory of her. He indulged himself, remembering her tenderness in caring for him, her gentle hands. The delicate resonance of her voice, her soft and uneasy laughter. The innocence of her large wide eyes. Her walk, her gentle ways. The way she looked when they made their love. The wanting, the trembling, the loving. Olga Kalashnikova.

Sometimes, in a certain mood, he would leap from his great roan horse and climb through a front window at Trigorskoye, much to the delight of the breathless and enchanted ladies. There was Madame Wulf-Osipova, fortyish and twice a widow, a tall plumpish handsome aristocratic woman with a soft face and quiet and reflectful eyes. There were her two lovely daughters of the first marriage, Annettie and Eufrasia Wulf, the latter nicknamed Zizi. The other two girls from her later marriage were just removed from babes in arms.

All of the Trigorskoye women were more or less in love with Pushkin. They knew and loved his poetry, were enchanted by his mischief-making personality, his charm, his wit, his conversation, his tireless nervous energy. He was admittedly the *raconteur non pareil.*

The Wulf-Osipova house was full of ancient furniture, exuded a comfortable unpretentiousness. Femaleness permeated the household, with fragrances of lavender and jasmine, sounds of nervous and spasmodic laughter, sighs of deepest heartfelt passion.

Annettie Wulf, 20 years old, fell madly, passionately and immediately in love with the fabulous poet and went around when he was present breathing as if each breath would be her last. She would sit sometimes all evening long staring at the poet and sighing deep sighs at his every word or glance or movement. Then after he left, she would spend most of the night writing torrid love letters to this dashing Don Juan-of-a-poet. Annettie saw herself as the one and only *femme fatale*, as she understood the term, perhaps mistakenly, destined by a cruel fate to go through this tragic life as an unrequited lover, if alas, Pushkin rejected her.

Alexander Sergeievich was attracted to the dark-eyed beauty, but was not ready to be that serious with any woman at this point in his erratic and uncertain life. All beautiful women brought Olga Kalashnikova to mind. He should have flaunted all convention and taken her as his bride. What kind of a revolutionary was he then? Sixteen-year-old Zizi attracted him, because she was saucy-faced and mischievous, and she ran and laughed in gentle spasms, flirted outrageously, poked out her scarlet tongue at him, winked her dark brown flashing eyes, talked incessantly about absolutely nothing, and eluded him every time he reached for her. She unconsciously reminded him of Marya Raevsky. But after Olga Kalashnikova, he was not ready for a serious affair, unless it was seriously and sincerely serious.

Madame Wulf-Osipova watched the flirtations, enjoyed them all, vicariously, albeit with deep concern and apprehension. She hoped that nothing went beyond the point of what she considered to be propriety. Her girls were of the age when experimenting would come naturally, even dangerously.

Also she was more than a little jealous that her own age and the loftiness of her position prevented her from competing openly for the poet's affection. She told herself that jealousy had nothing to do with it. She had no romantic interest in our poet. She was simply the guardian of these fatherless children, the protector of these innocents' virginity. Her girls were inexperienced, naive country girls, and Alexander Pushkin was the ultimate in urbanity. It was ridiculous for a woman of her maturity and station to think of him amorously. If she were a few years older, she might have been his mother. Her love for him was completely platonic and maternal, she told herself. Nothing romantic at all.

But Annettie watched her mother as she exercised her prerogative as the mother figure. She knew the matronly woman's feelings for the poet went much deeper. Annettie agonized as she watched Madame Osipova discussing literature and politics with him for hours on end and running her hands through the poet's woolen curls, murmuring softly to him: "My darling child! My inspiration and my genius! With the dearest darkest deepest sweetest eyes in all the world!" Pushkin loved it. All of it. He needed it. Wallowed in it.

At night when Pushkin left them, he was inebriated with their love, as if drunk from the headiest of wines. As elevated as the pine trees surrounding his estate on possibilities and creative expectations. Nothing was beyond his capturing artistically, creatively. He could even write a novel. A novel! His heart palpitated. He stayed awake many nights working on EUGENE ONEGIN. In times like these he knew a God-like feeling of omnipotence, he felt close to God even though he wasn't sure he believed there was a God. Sometimes, in these rarified euphoric moods, he felt like he was, in fact, a Creator. And he would create a new world. A really new world. A world of love everlasting, devoid of greed and privilege and misery and poverty and ignorance. A world in which men and women could wage successful war against unfeeling Fate and Destiny. The saints and monks of ancient Kievan times, in their vitae and paterics, had placed much too much stress on submissiveness to God's Will and to Fate and the Emperor, and had firmly implanted these into the Russian psyche, especially the muzhik's pysche. Through his writings he would wage war against Fate and submissiveness. Change! Change! Change the way the Russian looked upon himself, herself, themselves. Change the way they looked upon the Emperor's omnipotence.

If his miserable scribblings reached one individual, only one, and that one changed ever so slightly, he would have begun to change his Russia, he would have begun to change the world. Change! That's what he was about. He was in fact the lonely SOWER!

To change the world was a formidable undertaking, and Alexander Sergeievich needed the novel with its wide sweeping canvas to assume such an awesome task. Was he ready for the novel? Russia had produced no novelists of tremendous stature. Did he possess the wisdom and perception and artistry for so grandiose an undertaking? He wanted to write about the common people of his country. So much had been written about emperors and counts and barons. Did he possess the vision? The artistry? He wanted to give the ordinary Russian his moment in literature. When they read his feeble scribbling a hundred years from now, he wanted them to be able to get some feeling of what Russian life was like other than the occurrences around the Imperial Court. Life at the Emperor's Court had very little in common with the hopes and aspirations of the masses of the Russian people. He would move toward the novel gradually. EUGENE ONEGIN would be a novel-in-verse. He would write this poem in chapters. Just to think of it like this made his heart beat faster. His head knew a sudden giddiness. He trembled at the thought of it.

EUGENE ONEGIN was, moreover, an amazing exercise in creative self-criticism, even to Alexander Sergeievich. For into EUGENE ONEGIN the poet poured much of himself, of those terrible wonderful days of his time's colossal waste in decadent Saint Petersburg, a time of studied cynicism, of arrogance and utter dissipation. Eugene, an idle and sophisticated dandy of the city.

Tatyana, on the other hand, was his idealistic woman, the naive country girl, pure and human and of this earth, a combination of Annettie Wulf and Olga Kalashnikova, and perhaps even his first love, Tanya, the chambermaid of his Muscovy innocence, who taught him of unselfish love, it seemed like centuries ago.

One night the poet looked sleepily upon his manuscript, as the wax from his candle fell hot upon it, and suddenly he realized that Tanya, Tatyana, was the name of EUGENE ONEGIN's heroine. The name had happened weeks before, months perhaps, but this night it came to him like a shock of sudden revelation. He laughed, he shouted, almost cried.

"Tanya!" He couldn't believe it. "Tatyana!" His muse was playing tricks on him. He had not thought of Tanya in such a long long time, so many experiences ago. He didn't even know if she were living or dead! Tanya! Tatyana was the heroine, a pure naive country lass, guileless to a fault. Eugene was the jaded idler, coxcomb, the poet's alter ego, from Saint Petersburg. Through Eugene, the popinjay, Pushkin described his own dissipated existence as a blasé roué of the *Jeunesse dorée* of decadent Saint Petersburg, the youth of wealth and high fashion.

Eugene is on his way to see his rich uncle who is dying in a Russian village. He has seen everything worth seeing, done everything worth doing and too many things that were not worth doing. He is getting away from it all. Through Eugene, Alexander Sergeievich speaks to the reader. Satiric, ironic, sardonic. His uncle is of the wealthy landed gentry.

"Now that he is in a grave condition,
My uncle, decorous old prune,
Has earned himself my recognition;
What could have been more opportune?
May his ideas inspire others;
But what a bore, I ask you brothers,
To tend a patient night and day
And venture not a step away
Is there hypocrisy more glaring
Than to amuse one almost dead,

Shake up the pillow for his head,
Dose him with melancholy bearing,
And think behind a stifled cough,
'When will the devil haul you off?' "

Then Alexander Sergeievich speaks directly to the reader about his alter ego,
Eugene.

Thus a young good-for-nothing muses,
As in the dust his coach wheels spin,
By a decree of sovereign Zeus's
The extant heir to all his kin.
Friends of Ruslan and Ludmila!
Allow me with no cautious feeler
Or foreword, to present at once
The hero of my new romance;
Onegin, a dear friend of mine,
Born where the Neva flows, and where you,
I daresay, gentle reader, too
Were born, or once were wont to shine;
There I myself once used to be;
The North, though, disagrees with me.

One night at Trigorskoye Pushkin caught giggling Zizi in the garden and
kissed her fresh vermillion lips beneath an apple tree in the orchard heavy with the
smell of apple blossoms, and held her softness closely to him, as dear love-sick Annettie watched them from a window. Later, Madame Wulf-Osipova asked her darling son to sit for a moment with her; the girls had gone off to bed. It was well after midnight. She served wine and they sat there sipping silently together, lost in
their own thoughts and profound emotions. Alexander Sergeievich wondered what
the lovely matronly woman had on her mind. There was always an aura of romantic mystery around her. The drawing room was softly lighted by a candled chandelier that hung from the middle of the room. In a corner of the room was a candelabrum with fifteen dimly-lighted candles. He could barely see her face as she sat in
soft shadows across from him in an upholstered easy chair, and he sat nervously on
the long divan, his arm outflung as if someone sat beside him. He felt his all-
aloneness deeply.

He watched Madame Wulf-Osipova take a long sip of her wine. She held the
glass before her, staring at it as if it contained some secret, a solution to the problems of this troubled world. She said, "The problem is, all of us love you too
much."

He was glad she could not see his flushed face clearly. He imagined it looked
silly. Love him too much? How could anybody love him too much?

"Of course," she said, "you understand I love you differently from the way the girls love you, but all the same I love you just as deeply."

The tall handsome woman rose and came over and sat beside the poet on the divan. She moved a little heavily but with such grace, her body seemed to flow without any conscious effort on her part. Now he felt the nearness of her sharply. There was a deafening quiet in the wide vast room. His sense of hearing sharpened so acutely. He heard night sounds he had never heard before. The symphony outside the old house of giggling crickets, honking frogs, hooting owls, the flapping wings of a blind and lonely bat in flight, the love song of the nightingales.

"You know that I love all of you," he said into the dimly-lighted darkness.

"Yes," she said, and placed her hand upon his. "And you have so much love to give the world. You are the poet of love more than any other writer on this earth. It is a crime to imprison someone like you in this isolated provincial village."

The poet said, "If it were not for you and your family, I would not know what to do with myself. I would go completely out of my mind without you." It seemed that once he started, he could not stop talking. "When I miss a night coming to visit with you, I am empty all through the night, all through the next day. The well of my creativity runs completely dry." It was true. Nights when he didn't visit them were nights spent in a vain and desperate pursuit of his elusive muse. Nights spent in quiet frustration. Walking back and forth around the creaky old house, listening to the scampering field mice. Arina Rodionovna sleeping in her quarters, Nikita Koslov fast asleep in his. Nothing worked for him those nights. From his novel-in-verse EUGENE ONEGIN to BORIS GODUNOV to painful thoughts of Olga Kalashnikova and the shame of sending her away from him. The flow of his so-called genius ceased, refused even to trickle. He talked aloud to himself, began to question the worth of his writing. *What was the worth of it.* He was the sower who wrote to change the world, but what was the good of it, if he couldn't change himself.

"I understand," he heard Madame Wulf-Osipova saying. She took her hand away from his and placed it briefly on his knee. He felt a great warmth in his loins, and he fought hard to keep his legs from trembling. "I realize that you need us. And we certainly do need you. You have filled a void in our lives like no other could have done. This house was empty before you came into it, and it is empty when you do not visit us."

He wondered what it was all leading to, this conversation with this queenly woman of Trigorskoye. He said, quietly, "A writer has to reconcile the contradictions of loneliness, the need for solitude to ply his art, and the need for human companionship, the absolute need for people, people to love, to know love with, to be happy with, to suffer with. He can't suck the human experience out of his thumb. He must experience life in order to give it back to the people through his art."

She said softly, excitedly, "Yes . . . of course. That's it!" And kissed him gently on his mouth. "I imagine every time you begin a major piece of writing you have to fall in love again."

The poet started to protest, to deny the truth of what she was saying. "It's not quite—"

Madame Wulf-Osipova continued as if she had not heard him. "You have to have a new romantic involvement to sustain you through your long nights of creative loneliness."

He said simply, "Yes." And he wondered how a provincial matron like her could know so much. Where had she gathered so much insight and perception?

"But meanwhile" she continued, "you must leave a lot of broken hearts behind you. And I do not say this critically, because a person of your genius must be forgiven these terrible extremes. You give so very much of yourself, so much love you give unstintingly to this loveless world."

He stared silently into the darkness.

She said, "I guess what I'm asking you is, to spare me and my daughters. Every one of us is in love with you, and we are very very vulnerable."

He felt a fullness in his face, a welling in his eyes. He reached and took her hand and squeezed it. And he took this majestic woman in his arms and kissed her. He felt her trembling in his arms. And he said goodnight. She said, "Thank you, Alexander Sergeievich."

And she bid him dosvadanya. "Goodbye, my darling son, my sweetest inspiration!"

Alexander Sergeivich went home that night and worked till day broke. Worked on EUGENE's twenty first stanza. In this stanza, Alexander Sergeievich conjured up his own experience and behavior in Saint Petersburg.

> Applause all round Onegin enters,
> Walks over toes along his row.
> His double spyglass sweeps and centers
> On box-seat belles he does not know.
> All tiers his scrutiny embraces,
> He saw it all; the gowns and faces
> Seemed clearly to offend his sight;
> He traded bows on left and right
> With gentlemen, at length conceded
> An absent gaze at the ballet,
> Then with a yawn he turned away.
> And spoke: "In all things change is needed:
> On me ballets have lost their hold;
> Didelot himself now leaves me cold."

Pushkin wrote that night till the pen fell from his hand. It was already morning when he awoke, and he looked outside and saw the fog rolling in from across the Sorot River like something driven by a ghostly presence. It came in tidal waves, came in great swells and surges. It crept into the chinks and crevices and cloaked the house with mist and mystery.

He thought his Grandpa-pa Hannibal must have watched the selfsame fog that seemed to withdraw and always to come back again. He went back to his desk and continued writing till the sun had driven back the mist. He wrote on and on about the jadeness of his Eugene.

By the time Onegin reached his uncle's estate, the old man had gone to sleep forever. The blasé coxcomb decided to remain in the country on his inherited estate. He meets a lovely naive country girl Tanya, who lives nearby, and she immediately falls in love with him. Like Annettie Wulf, she has read all the romantic French novels and believes devotely in them. Onegin is her knight in shining armor. Tatyana writes Onegin a letter telling him of her love for him. A love which Onegin condescendingly rejects with a pompous lecture. Bored to tears by life in the country, he makes friends with a callous young fledgling-of-a-poet, Lensky, who is engaged to Tanya's sister, Olga.

Since Eugene was Pushkin's alter ego, the poet held himself responsible for Eugene's insufferable arrogance and all of his misdoings. The heat collected in the collar of his tunic. He walked the floor. He was Eugene Onegin, and Eugene was Alexander Sergeievich. He went into his bedroom and stared at himself in the looking glass. Wooly-haired, sleepy-eyed, harried looking. He thought he was the portrait of malevolence. He shouted softly at himself. "Oh you bastard, Eugene!" He remembered Olga Kalashnikova. "You miscreant! You miserable wretch!" Tears spilled from his sleepless reddening eyes. He went back to his desk and continued to write.

At a celebration at Tanya's house, Eugene, on a whimsy dances with Olga all night as if he were the one betrothed to her. Olga's fiance, Lensky, challenges him to a duel in the snowy countryside, and Onegin kills the poet in what he realizes is a dastardly act of needless stupidity and cruelty.

Writing of Tanya's distress affected Pushkin deeply, strangely. This was probably why, when he went to Trigorskoye that night and found his elusive Zizi ailing, he took dear long-suffering Annettie, feverish for his love, for a walk among the apple orchard, and held her in his arms. She was his Tanya and he was her Eugene.

Annettie was so in love with her Pushkin. And that night the author of Onegin loved his dark-eyed love-struck country maiden. Trembling in his arms, she kissed his lips, his eyes, his nose, his ears, sobbing wildly in her happiness. "I'm yours! I'm yours!" she softly shouted. "I'm yours, dear Pushkin! Yours forever!"

She was ready to be taken, but Pushkin remembered the unspoken promise he had given to Annettie's mother. He took her, sobbing, back into the house.

In his lonely exile in the rambling house with his EUGENE ONEGIN, he still could not believe his heroine was Tatyana. Dearest Tanya! His face grew hot and flushed. "How came you to be the name of the heroine of ONEGIN?" How had it happened? When had it happened? Of all the names there were to choose, why had he chosen Tanya? Tatyana? It was eerie! Otherwordly! Unbelievable! It was as if he walked this earth with phantoms.

Some days the moody poet grew weary of the world of Annettie's heavy sighs and Zizi's giggling and Mrs. Osipova's maternalistic watchful eyes. And when the mood struck him, he wandered into the little principality of Pskov, the capital of the province, sometimes to a village fair to watch the muzhiks with their peasant songs and dances and listen to their idiom. The muzhiks did not know what to make of this addle-headed aristocrat, oftentimes disguised in the clothing of a peasant. Sometimes he would grab one of the peasant women and out-dance everyone in the village square.

He felt good when he was with them. Felt free, natural, uninhibited, and he was no longer lonely. These were his people. He belonged. He, born of the city, nurtured among the sophisticated cultivated aristocratic European Russians, felt much more at home with these rustic people of the Russian village. There was something beautifully real about them. They laughed, they cried, they cursed, they called a penis what it was, a *khui* (cock). They smelled of human perspiration. They did not fornicate, they did yebat. They were of this earth, and Russian, and he loved them for it. This incorrigible romantic.

One day in the village square, he danced with a peasant woman till he was out of breath, but he continued dancing. She was a buxom full-breasted married woman, flaxen-haired, saucy-faced, built for hard work in the fields, as if the Good Lord had ordained it. She loved to dance. Her husband watched them, as did the other peasants, urging them on with cheers and shouts, and she and Pushkin danced until they fell together from exhaustion.

The village gentry were outraged and scandalized. Pushkin didn't care. He wanted to soak in all the culture of the Russian peasants which he believed to be at the very core of the Russian language and its soul.

He went home late that night elated and exhausted. He entered into his diary that which was later published in a Moscow magazine.

The muzhik is the authentic Russian. The nobleman is a frenchified version of the real thing. Neither fish nor fowl. Counterfeit Russian and counterfeit European. I say to all the young writers: "The study of Russian folklore, the legends and the speech of the common people, the old songs, tales and so forth is indispensible to the acquisition of full knowledge of the resources of the Russian language and its great inherent richness . . ." Young writers, listen to the rhythms and the speech of the people. The most dynamic force in a nation's literature is its folklore. Drink lustily from this life-sustaining fountain that will never cease to flow. You will gain far more from the peasant folk, the muzhiks, than from all the articles in our supercilious journals and reviews!"

And then he learned one day that Anna Petrovna Kern was coming to visit her aunt at Trigorskoye. When Pushkin heard of her expected visit, his heart knew an exultant joy. He felt that somewhere in the depths of his submerged consciousness he had been in love with this raven-haired dark-eyed beauty all the days of his remembered life. Previously, he had met Mrs. Kern in Saint Petersburg when he was nineteen at a party at the Olenin's, and he had followed the dazzling woman all over the place like a great friendly borzoi who wanted to be fondled. But she had ignored the poet's overtures, emphatically. And he had not been able to start any kind of conversation with her. She had ignored him. She was the sophisticated lady, and he was the fresh impulsive lad with his mother's milk still on his lips.

Anna Kern was coming to Trigorskoye, and one of the reasons she was coming was the presence of Alexander Sergeievich as the next door neighbor of Annettie and Zizi who had written many letters to her about this dashing gallant-of-a-poet and of his worshipful adoration for one Anna Petrovna Kern. Anna was also an admirer of his writings and had more or less fallen in love with him via long distance, in a manner of speaking.

She was a devastatingly beautiful young woman who had married a wealthy aristocrat much older than herself due to an arrangement by her parents. Too old and senile to make love with this lovely woman, her husband suggested that she make other arrangements. He even dragged her one night into his nephew's bedroom, who lay naked waiting for her.

After this experience, Anna Kern left her husband and went to live in Poltava and began a serious affair with a man who was a landowner and a writer of pornography. She was an avid reader. She had read everything Pushkin had ever published, and most of that which had not been published, but had been passed from hand to hand. Anna Petrovna was an avid Pushkinist. By the time she came to Trigorskoye she was ready for a new romance, especially with a man of Pushkin's flair and literary eminence. And the poet was more than ready for Anna Petrovna Kern.

Alexander Sergeievich came to Trigorskoye that evening, as usual, after dinner on his great bay horse. This time he did not come through the window as he sometimes did when he was in a playful mood. All of the Trigorskoye women were awaiting the historic meeting of this irresistible force with the great immovable object.

Anna Petrovna Kern versus Alexander Sergeievich Pushkin.

They had talked of nothing else all day long the day before and dreamed of it the whole night through.

They waited eagerly for the great woman-charmer to sweep the magnificent beauty off her feet with an ocean wave of repartee at which they considered him a natural genius. And they were anxious to witness how this Saint Petersburg beauty, this sophisticated woman-of-the-world would handle their debonair poet. Perhaps, Annettie thought, I can get some hints from this lovely and experienced woman.

Pushkin was shy and quiet that first evening. He came in and kissed Anna Kern's hand when introduced, then sat nervously on a divan opposite her and now and then they talked innately about the weather and such trivia as, "How are things in Petersburg?"

Mrs. Kern was equally noncommunicative.

The girls thought this couldn't be Alexander Pushkin. Not their Alexander Pushkin! They stared incredulously at a Pushkin lost for words.

But perhaps, this was a new approach he was attempting. A new tactic for seduction. The truth was, Alexander Sergeievich was simply devastated by the impact of this woman's beauty. He was no fool. He knew Anna Petrovna Kern was experienced. Yet there was about her this aura of purity and chastity he could not dispel. Her dark quiet beauty. Against his will, he thought of his Larissa, the angelic whore of the *Home For Wayward Girls* in Saint Petersburg. The black wide-open staring eyes, large and shaped Orientally like almonds, as if her high cheekbones kept her great eyes slightly slanted and uplifted. Her dear eyes so full of knowing, sorrow, laughter, tears and innocence. Her ripe red mouth, the lower lip slightly larger than the upper one. Her oval face, her ample breathing breasts that pushed her lavender blouse out ever so slightly. Yet, there was nothing flamboyant about Mrs. Kern. No single attribute, like eyes or mouth or breasts or body structure, that pulled you toward her, irresistibly. It was the total impact of her womanness which she exerted seemingly without conscious effort. She was, the poet thought, the personification of what woman was and what woman was supposed to be. She was Eve, he thought, before foolish Adam had corrupted her.

The poet did not remain long at Trigorskoye on that first evening. He sat there quietly staring into space. When he did speak his conversation was so mundane the girls could not believe that it was Pushkin speaking. Mother Osipova understood and envied her courtly niece, who possessed the power to render Alexander Pushkin speechless.

Pushkin did not sleep well that night. No woman had ever cast a speechless spell on him before in all of his young eventful life. She was just a beautiful woman, he told himself, no more, no less. And he'd known many beautiful women in his day. She was certainly not Amelia or even Olga Kalashnikova. She was nothing special or unusual, he argued desperately with himself. Don't let that angelic aura fool you. You know better. She is a woman who exudes sensuality. And she is well aware of it. She's a woman of the world. She has slept with that old bastard husband of hers and with Raminovsky, the infamous pornographer, and only she knows how many more.

Alexander Sergeievich was an artist whose sensitivity and temperament were totally susceptible to beauty. But this time he would not let himself be vulnerable to a lovely face. He was too sophisticated to let that happen.

He went to Trigorskoye every day, eventually emerging from under the spell Anna Petrovna Kern had cast. He was his old charming debonair self again. But his mood would change from day to day, sometimes from moment to moment. He would be light-hearted and irresistibly articulate before her one moment, then suddenly he would be morose and silent.

They discussed the state of the national literature. She had read his essay on narodnost, she told him, and she agreed with him wholeheartedly. "Our literature is too imitative. Especially is it Frenchly imitative. Our writers need to go back to the old ways of our ancient literature." He suggested meekly that they needed to go "not back but move forward with the old ways." She said, "Of course, go forward to the influences of the Church Slavonic which was the original language of our people's literature. That is why I love your writing," she told him excitedly. "It has a Russian personality!" Her bluish-black eyebrows were lavishly endowed. She had a nervous habit of seizing her bright red lower lip with her gleaming-white-and-even teeth and pulling them slowly back across her lip. Her dark eyes were luxuriantly lashed.

Alexander Sergeievich sat before this beautiful woman of the elongated eyelashes that sometimes fluttered nervously and he was like a shy school lad who had never heard himself praised before in all his life. He felt like a commoner being knighted by his Empress.

Anna told him she loved his GABRILIAD. She began to laugh. Every time she thought of it, she could not help laughing. "Such a droll poem," she said, "but so dangerous and truthful. I love it! It's so naughty and so true! I love it! I adore it! I must have read it more than fifty times." She closed her eyes and began to recite the poem. "I can recite it in my sleep," she boasted.

"Most beautiful of my dear earthly daughters,
Of Israel the youthful hope and joy!
I summon thee, aflame with burning love,
To share my glory. Harken to the call. . . ."

And on and on she went until the very end. She even did the epilogue. Now laughing, now reciting, as the other women sat there speechless and awestruck. Then she began immediately to recite his VILLAGE. And now she was reciting the part of the poem that always touched him deeply. But now, the tears were spilling from her lovely eyes.

Head down, docile under the pursuing lash,
The gaunt old serf struggles down the furrows
of some implacable master.
Not daring to dream anymore, or hope for them:
His little girls growing up
To feed the lust of some vice-sodden monster . . .

As he sat there listening to her the tears spilled down his own cheeks as he remembered Olga Kalashnikova, and he wept silently for her and for his own hypocritical and decrepit soul. He wiped his dark eyes shyly, slyly, and kissed her dear hand and departed. They seemed to have forgotten that the other folk were present.

The next evening they sat and talked of change and revolution. Anna Petrovna Kern desired to see it come to pass, the change, in her time. "I want to be a part of it. I want to see our Russia change in every marrow of my body, I want it. I agonize about it!" she said excitedly. Pushkin knew that she was serious. Earnestly and sincerely serious.

One evening the women rode with him in two of the Osipov carriages over to the Mikhailovskoye estate. He rode with Anna Petrovna in a carriage leading the way, caught up in the aura of the romantic moment with the moon full, ripe and mellow. Zizi giggling nervously to cover up how upset she was. Poor dear Annettie suffering exquisitely with her magnificent and unrequited passion. Alexander Sergeievich reached out nervously in the darkness for Anna's hand and grasped it. Anna Petrovna kept up a constant nervous chatter all the way to Mikhailovskoye, about literature and politics and change and revolution. Even as their warm hands engaged in a silent wrestling match. When they crossed over the rickety bridge and reached the old house, Alexander Sergeievich leaped from the carriage and helped his lady to alight. He ushered them all into the drawing room, and Arina Rodionovna served them wine and soft drinks as if everything had been rehearsed or foreordained.

"There's something I must show Mrs. Kern," he told the others. He took her hand and walked out through the garden pregnant with the smell of flowery things and sap from the tall pine trees and apple blossoms, a soft summery moonlit night that was custom-made for Alexander Sergeievich's mood. They walked together, quiet for a moment, with the sound of honking bullfrogs and the giggling noise of crazy locusts, drinking in the fragrances of the night aromas, terribly conscious of their clasping hands locked in desperate combat, the now-and-then contact of the sides of their thighs one against the other as they walked.

Anna Petrovna was the first to break the silence. "What is it you wished to show me?"

Alexander Sergeievich turned toward her, and the want for her was in his face, on the breath of his sensuous lips, all of it was there in the lonely darkness of his eyes which saw a corresponding want in hers and the pimpled perspiration above her scarlet lips.

"I wanted to show you the moon as it came down through the trees. What good is a full moon if you can't share it with a beautiful woman?" His usually resonant voice was froggy with emotion.

He could hear the tremor in her own deep sophisticated voice. "And you have already shown it to the others then? Is that why you left them all inside?"

He swallowed hard. "This moon was only meant for you and me."

And he took her in his arms and kissed her. This sophisticated Russian beauty, this woman-of-the-world, this erudite declaimer of his poetry, this lovely intellectual, this pure virginal Jezebel, trembled in the poet's arms. For she was ready to be kissed and taken. And so the poet took her, they took each other, there beneath the pines and lindens amongst the sweet and flowered fragrances. These two sophisticated people of the city made love there in the country, like common muzhiks on the good sweet earth from whence they came. They heard the primordial call of man and woman and they came in answer to the call.

Anna and Alexander, the lovers, came together.

CHAPTER FOUR

Alexander Sergeievich came to see Anna Petrovna every day, sat there in the Osi-pov living room, discussing literature and politics and narodnost and change and revolution. "I want to see it happen in my time," she told him, repeatedly, "an end to serfdom in my time!" she advocated avidly. But he didn't know whether or not there was a revolutionary movement, he told her. If there was one he was not in-volved. She stared at him incredulously. "How could there be a revolutionary movement without you? You of all people, Alexander Pushkin!" She was angry with him. "Why do you lie to me about it. Are you trying to protect me from the knowledge of it? I'm not a Czarist spy. And I don't want to be left out of it."

He remembered, bitterly, the meeting at the Davydovs in Kamenka. He told her if there were a revolutionary movement, he had also been definitely left out it, emphatically, and he suspected that the muzhiks and all the other lower classes had been left out also.

He talked with her about the novel he was working on, EUGENE ONEGIN. He read chapters of his novel to her, as the other women sat entranced. They shame-lessly made love, the two, with their talk about his manuscript, sharing, loving. He wanted to write a novel, he told her (them), in which the heroine was a realistic Russian woman, not of the city, but of the Russian countryside, a woman who was Russian to the core. EUGENE ONEGIN was the novel, *Tatyana* was the heroine. Alex-ander Sergeievich writing a novel? Anna Petrovna listened avidly, breathlessly excited.

Sometimes they went horseback riding together. They rode all over the coun-tryside, alongside the Sorot River, between the river and a wall of pine and linden trees, which seemed to reach up towards the sky in a prayer to the heavens. The mallards and the wild geese winged their ways across the quiet river, as again she told him she wanted to be a part of something revolutionary.

Revolution or no, Madame Wulf-Osipova figured things were getting out of hand between her lovely niece and her favorite protégé. So she took steps to see that things went no further. Madame Wulf-Osipova firmly insisted that it was time that Anna Petrovna Kern return home to her old husband who was ailing. A week later Anna left with a copy of a freshly written stanza of EUGENE ONEGIN, autographed with passion by its author. From the carriage she held out her hand to the poet, and he kissed it. The coachman whipped his horses, and they lurched away and left the poet standing there amongst the Trigorskoye women.

Alexander Sergeievich Pushkin was alone again.

He plunged into his work again to defend himself from loneliness. But his vindictive muse forsook him. Inflicting vengeance on him for neglecting her for such mundane things as *affaires de coeur*. Struggling with his muse was like fighting with a private Satan, an evil genius. He went from EUGENE ONEGIN to BORIS GODUNOV, thence to a novel in prose about his illustrious great grandfather, which he titled, THE NEGRO OF PETER THE GREAT. He wrote and rewrote, tore up page after painful page. Nothing satisfied him. Some days he mounted his great horse and rode to the monastery and the lonely grave where Ibrahim Petrovich Hannibal lay in deep repose, as if he thought to gain sustenance from this revered ancestor.

One unbearably lonely evening long past midnight, as he sat alone in the old house waging desperate warfare with his capricious and unfaithful muse, he closed his eyes and held his head in his hands, and his elbows leaning on his desk. He wanted his great-grandfather, achingly. Suddenly his entire body stiffened, and he held himself in a rigid and suspended state for endless moments. He no longer heard the familiar night sounds, no longer was he conscious of the moths around the dimly-lighted candelabrum on his desk or those that got into his hair or flicked their feckless wings about his face, as he descended deeper deeper into his private world of total concentration. It was a legerdemain he had practiced fearfully since he was a young lad to save himself from death by an aching heart and loneliness. Now his head began to ache and throb, and he called silently to his great-grandfather. "Grandpa-pa—Grandpa-pa! I need you—need you!"

He felt a sudden surge of intense heat gathering around his desk and a perspiration on his brow. Why then did he also feel an icy chill move across his shoulders? He opened his eyes and stared into the piercing eyes of his great-grandfather, eyes and face as black as the night outside. His grandfather sat opposite him in a rocking chair that had not been there before.

"What is it you want, my son?" His voice was soft of tone and rich and musical, unlike the harsh sound of the Russian tongue.

"I am lonely, Grandpa-pa. I feel so very much alone."

"All men have known loneliness, my son," the older man said patiently.

"Sometimes, I feel that all of the people on earth have died and left me here all by myself." he said.

"But you know this isn't true, Alexander Sergeievich. You know your mother and father are in Saint Petersburg and your sister and brother are in Moscow."

"You don't understand, Grandpa-pa. I—"

"I understand only too well, my son. I lived all alone in this great white Russian world even when I was surrounded by the multitude of sycophants at Great Peter's Court. The great love of my Imperial godfather could not save me from my loneliness. I always felt aloneness deeply here in this place, surrounded by a thousand serfs, even with my wives and families, I always felt alone."

"What is the reason, Grandpa-pa?"

"With me, it was a constant longing I always felt for the land of my ancestors." His great-grandfather replied.

"And with me?" Pushkin asked.

"Aloneness is the price men and women have always paid for dreaming, those whose special and perceptive eyes have seen the suffering of this old earth and dared to dream of changing it. Visionaries have always had to walk alone. It is the price one pays for genius." His soft voice hardened with impatience. "Is it that you'd rather be like your sister and your brother? To sleep restful dreamless nights and walk the earth in a perpetual daze?"

"I have always dreamed, Grandpa-pa, ever since I can remember."

His grandfather's voice softened again. "It means you are alive and having experiences while others waste their lives in restful slumber."

"I think I understand, Grandpa-pa."

"Didn't you ever come into a room or strange place and have the eerie feeling you had been there before?" The old man asked.

"Yes!" our poet said excitedly. "Many times!"

"Be thankful then that you're a dreamer. Think how many more experiences you have known than ordinary men and women. Think how much more living you have experienced. Where do you think your special insights come from? Jesus was a dreamer. Moses was a dreamer. Jeanne d'Arc d'Orleans was a visionary. Geniuses are visionaries."

The air was charged suddenly with a sharp chill, as Alexander Sergeievich raised his sleep-filled head and looked around for his great-grandfather who was no longer there. He stared up at Grandpa-pa Hannibal's picture looking fiercely down upon him from the wall above his desk. His entire body was atremble and a cold sweat lay upon his face.

He went to the cabinet where he kept his rum and vodka. He drank straight from a bottle, then returned to his desk and a peacefulness settled over him.

He worked feverishly till daybreak.

Fall was making way for winter, and Alexander Sergeievich felt like a bear preparing his heart and soul for hibernation. He felt old and ancient though he was only twenty-six. He lived from day to day in a deep pit of despondency. Then one day it all changed.

Without warning, Emperor Alexander died of apoplexy while on vacation in Taganrog in the Crimea, thereby setting a record as one of the few Czars of the House of Romanov who died in bed of natural causes. Pushkin shamelessly rejoiced. Perhaps now there was a chance of pardon by the new Emperor, Constantine, who was younger and, hopefully, of a more liberal and progressive bent.

Meanwhile in Saint Petersburg all was chaos and confusion. Who would be the Czar of all the Russias? The Russian Court was in an uproar. Who to swear allegiance to?" *"Le roi est mort—Vive le roi!"* But who and what and how and when? Bedlam was the order of the day. The nobility, generals, admirals, counts, barons, all fell over each other swearing allegiance to Constantine, Alexander's brother, next in line of ascendancy, the Emperor dying without issue. Even the younger brother, Nicholas, swore allegiance to his older brother, Constantine. There was just one problem. The young Duke Constantine, living the riotous life as Viceroy in Poland was enamoured of the life that he was living, and saw no reason for changing or returning to that Babel that was Imperial Russia, where subversion was a way of life, even among the aristocracy. He wanted to duplicate the record of his saintly older brother, Alexander, and die in bed of natural causes like over-indulgence, dissipation and debauchery. He was married to a lovely Polish princess. A squad of horsemen galloped continually between Saint Petersburg and Warsaw with urgent messages calling Constantine home. Finally Nicholas realized that his brother was not coming. Nicholas, like Julius Caesar, had not wished to appear over anxious or overly ambitious. There were many who despised him at the Imperial Court, a fact that he was well aware of. Nicholas pretended, at first, that he did not seek the throne.

Meanwhile, there were conspiracies and rumors of conspiracies all over the feverish capital city on the Neva River. Members of the subversive Union of the South came surreptitiously into the capital to meet in desperate consultation with the Union of the North.

After many letters to men like Zukovsky, Vyazemsky and others of Imperial influence, asking them to raise the question of his exile to the proper authorities, Alexander Sergeievich decided to take matters into his own hands and steal unheralded into the capital city.

Quietly he got ready against his nyanya's weepings and protestation. He would be putting his head into the lion's den. But the poet had been out of things for so long, he had to go.

Nikita Koslov was set against it. "Dearest boy of my aching heart, listen to one who loves you like his very own and would give his worthless life for you. Stay away from that sinful city. Don't get in trouble with the Little Father, may the Heavens always bless him, whoever he may be."

"I'm already in trouble with the Little Father!" Pushkin said grimly. "I always have been."

The old man countered with: "A horse has four legs and yet it stumbles, but if it stumbles too many times, it will become crippled for life, or else they'll take the damn fool out and shoot him."

There was nothing for it though. He had to go. On his way to say goodbye to the women of Trigorskoye a hare shot out of the bushes and streaked across the path, almost getting trampled underneath his horses. "A bad omen!" Nikita muttered. "Let us change our mind, dear boy. Pajalsta! Pajalsta!"

At Trigorskoye, Annettie wept bitter tears and foresaw all manner of dire results to his going. Even care-free Zizi wept. Mrs. Wulf-Ospiova quietly told him to be careful, because she knew that he must go, and why. On his way back another wild hare dashed across their path. Nikita shook his old head and pleaded, "Now I know we'll change our mind." He began to moan and groan. "By the Holy Virgin, darling boy, listen to a faithful old dog like your Nikita."

When Pushkin returned to his estate he learned that the other servant who was supposed to accompany him had taken suddenly and mysteriously to his bed. Strange happenings indeed. Were the scampering hares really bad omens, as Nikita Koslov continually insisted? Notwithstanding, he would go alone, with his faithful Nikita Koslov protesting every verst of the way. The coach stood outside the old manor house as he kissed his weeping nyanya goodbye.

They were on the way now, and the sleigh bells jingled as the horses took to the drifting snow. The wind was blowing the already fallen snow. Nikita Koslov kept a constant chanting. "It's still not too late, young master." Alexander Sergeievich's nose felt as if it was frostbitten. His eyes burned from the stinging cold. "We can still turn back. Still turn back!" Nikita kept insisting.

Pushkin turned to the old man. "If you can't keep quiet, I will have to take you back and go to St. Pete by myself." It was too cold for him to talk. He thought his mouth and tongue might freeze.

"You can't be serious, dearest boy. You can't really think old Nikita would let you go alone to that wicked city."

"Well then you'll just have to keep your feelings to yourself, because I must go. There is simply nothing for it." But when he passed a priest dressed in black going down the road, it was too much for Pushkin's soul. Some thing out there was trying to say something to him. Nikita began to moan and groan and beat his old face with his hands. "No, no, young master! Now you see the omen, don't you?" The priest in all that blackness was in high relief embossed against the whiteness of the snow. He called to the coachman to turn back. While our poet was not naturally superstitious, Nikita Koslov had gotten to the tenderest section of his nerves, and he was too immersed in the folklore and folk myths of the Russian country people and Anna Rodionovna's great ghost tales to be totally disrespectful of continual bad omens. He would suffer silently in his solitude at Mikhailovskoye till he could learn more of the happenings to the North.

Meanwhile winter closed in on our poet, burying him, so to speak, in his wooden house beneath the constant blizzards. He wished that one day he could escape this cold and heartless Russia.

One night the longing for escape flowed from his pen and joined the verses of EUGENE ONEGIN. Feverishly, by the candlelight he wrote at the old oaken desk, with the fire in the fireplace behind him crackling and spitting and throwing sparks about the hearth. Out of his desperate loneliness, he wrote:

> When strikes my liberation hour?
> It's time, it's time—I bid it hail;
> I pace the shore, the sky I scour
> And beckon to each passing sail.
> Storm-canopied, wave-tossed in motion
> On boundless highways of the ocean,
> When do I win unbounded reach?
> It's time to leave this tedious beach
> That damps my spirit, to be flying
> Where torrid southern blazes char
> My own, my native Africa,
> There of dank Russia to be sighing,
> Where once I loved, where now I weep,
> And where my heart is buried deep.

Pushkin kept a steady flow of letters going to the capital. What is happening? Have you folk forgotten me? He felt buried alive, but he wanted them to give some sign that they knew that he was still among the living. He had to get out of this place. One day he dug himself out of his dungeon and rode his horse through the snow to the women at Trigorskoye. He was having wine and tea with them, when one of their servants came in excitedly with the news of events in Saint Petersburg. Alexander Sergeievich Pushkin was visibly shaken and left shortly afterwards. The bad news reached him piecemeal.

After the nobility had pledged allegiance to Constantine, and the Grand Duke declined to leave Warsaw, the palace courtiers were caught between *Scylla* and *Charybdis* in a maelstrom of disorder. Now Nicholas was forced to call upon the ennobled boyars to change their pledges and transfer them to him instead. Nicholas was known throughout the Russian world as a cruel and ruthless autocrat. Even the entrenched nobility feared and hated Nicholas, which is why at first, he pretended he was not interested in assuming power. No matter, he was the next in line in the ascendency, so that even those who loathed him gathered around him and swore allegiance.

Every day around noon, Alexander Sergeievich would come out of his house and stare longingly and inquiringly toward the north and Peter's City on the Neva, as if he expected the news from the capital to come floating to him on a wave of the Northern wind. A rumor of a plot to assassinate Nicholas and overthrow the government reached Pushkin in Mikhailovskoye. It also reached the Winter Palace.

Good-natured Count Miloradovich, Governor of Saint Petersburg, pooh-poohed the rumor, assuring the Emperor that December 14, the day he would take the oath of office, would pass without undue incident. The Emperor was not so optimistic. He took certain measures just in case his Governor General was mistaken.

CHAPTER FIVE

The world has suddenly lost its way. The Emperor, even more so than an ordinary king, is blessed and divinely ordained. Why then does Czar Alexander, Caesar of all Caesars, Emperor of all the Russias, die suddenly without warning and sans issue? Le Roi est mort, fini! But there is no new Emperor or king to vive to. The world has suddenly lost its mind. Hear the raging blizzard madness come howling across the Finnish marshes to Great Peter's city on the Neva.

More madness yet. About a verst and a half as the snow flies from the Winter Palace, Alexander Sergeievich Pushkin's comrades of the Northern and the Southern unions are plotting feverishly to overthrow that which is divinely blessed. One of these men looks around the room and asks: "Where in the hell is Pushkin?" They are gathered in Rylyev's apartment, where Alexander Sergeievich had intended to stop had he made his way successfully into the capital city.

"Where in the hell would he be?" Alexander Sergeievich's Lycée comrade, Ivan Pushchin, answers indignantly. "He's in exile in Mikhailovskoye."

"I left him there just a few months ago." Anna Petrovna Kern says. Others stare at the lovely matron with suspicion.

"If Alexander Sergeievich were here," Pushchin says, "the first thing he should say is 'where are the muzhiks, the Uzbeks, the Tadjiks, the Cossacks, the Kalmuks, the Jews, the miserable serfs? Where are the representatives of the people we are supposed to be liberating?' "

The dark-haired soft-faced woman agrees again. "That is precisely what we talked about at Mikhailovskoye, the involvement of the Russian masses." There is a tremor of excitement in her usually resonant voice.

Ivan Pushchin watches another woman with a familiar face attired in a long colorful Uzbek peasant dress, enter quietly and sit behind him in a darkened corner of the

253

vast dining room. He hears her whisper in a strangely familiar voice, "Is Pushkin here?" There are several women present among this desperate gathering.

Prince Obelinsky smiles, grimly, remembering a time, a few years ago, when all of them were young and innocent and terribly romantic, idealistic. Remembers meeting Pushkin on his way to deeper exile at Mikhailovskoye. The champagne bath they had suggested for the celebrated poet, his admonition to them to involve all the different people laboring under the yoke of His Majesty's imperialism. Prince Obelinsky looks around the room . His round face is adorned with a great black beard. He is a little older, and hopefully, a little wiser for it.

There is indeed a madness definitely afoot this night throughout this land called Holy Russia. Truly it is a fin de siecle. It has been snowing all day long and well into this Russian night. Outside this house there is a great white Russian world of whirling howling dervishes wreaking havoc at the windows. These mad men and women gathered here would change the world, tilt the entire firmament and point it in a new direction.

Towheaded Yakushkin reminisces dreamily about the meeting at the Davydovs' at Kamenka in the Southern Mountains a few years back. Pushkin's outcry when they assured him that there existed no society plotting the overthrow of the cruel monarchy. "What was it he said to us? 'Tovarischi, I have never been so disappointed in all my life. Here I was thinking that at long last I was a part of something really wonderful and ennobling, something really worth living for, even dying, and it all turns out to be nothing but a terrible farce.'" Yakushkin looks around at his comrades. "You would have to have been there to appreciate the impact on us. At that moment he was the most beautiful person in this universe!" He wipes a silly tear from his eyes. His handsome face hardens. "It's time to get down to business, comrades."

Round-faced, blue-eyed Ivan Pushchin is intoxicated from the excitement let loose by these beautiful men and women and the revolutionary ambience in this room. He remembers the last time he saw the Hermit of Mikhailovskoye in his great-grandfather's ramshackle house. The abbe, his nyanya, the servant girls they danced with. The rum, the Saint Peray champagne, the comradeship, the love, the warmth. Remembering (almost verbatim) the conversation they shared, the excitement in his great friend's voice, the loneliness in his deep dark inflamed eyes.

Kuchelbecker, Bestuchev, Volkonski, Obelinsky, Alexander Raevsky, Ivan Pushchin. Some of the best young minds in Imperial Russia are gathered in this candle-lighted room, from some of the wealthiest and most ennobled families, which proves, of course, that these are mad men sowing their dangerous wildest oats. Certainly Russia has been good to every one of them since birth. What was the matter with these young people?

"Time is fleeting, comrades," says Yakushkin. The dialogue here is as desperate as the howling wind outside that shakes the shuttered windows. "Let us be serious, tovarischi." They stare at each other through a haze of tobacco smoke, the overpowering fragrance of rum and vodka and hashish. Has the Secret Police infiltrated these hallowed

ranks? Can every single one of them be trusted with each other's life? Can each man even trust himself? After much arguing and bickering, they have decided on a plan that cannot fail. Yakushkin, of the blonde handsome head and noble brow, says, "The time is now, comrades. Are we equal to the task before us?"

"Perhaps this is not the time, comrades." Somebody suggests uneasily. "The weather is against us."

"A bad omen," another mumbles .

"It is now or never!" Prince Obelinsky shouts.

Some men are thick-tongued now and glassy-eyed from too much rum and vodka and the hemp. It worries Ivan Pushchin to see some of them so intoxicated. Clear heads are needed here. "These are desperate ventures, comrades," he tells them. "No matter, to change the world is an opportunity that comes to few men in a lifetime. We must make the most of it. No men ever get a second chance." His voice chokes off.

He turns and stares into the face of Baroness Svetlina. She is older now but no less beautiful, and the fire in her dark eyes is, as ever all ablaze.

The time draws nigh. Tempers are extremely brief. The smell of fear is in the room. It is tangible, touchable, tastable. A cold stab in the mouth, a scratching of contracting throats. They are plotting the overthrow of the King of Heaven. Drinking, eating, smoking, laughing, breaking wind, arguing, gesticulating.

Suddenly, the howling snow has ceased outside, as if the Third Section has ordered it so they can eavesdrop on the happenings inside.

As day breaks on the fourteenth of December, the ennobled revolutionaries begin to gather in Senate Square across from the Winter Palace. Some gathering there are not members of the unions, nor are they even participants in the grand rebellion. Some naive ones gather out of sheer curiosity. A silence lies across the land. Some here are suddenly afflicted with weak bladders. Everywhere there is urinating on the quiet ice. These are brave ones, comrades who have conquered fear. There is confusion among the curious. To boost their courage, some of the rebels begin to shout: "Long live Constantine and the Constitution!"

The man in charge of these subversive operations has just appeared. The troops are deployed. Pushchin hears someone among the mass of people ask: "Where is Alexander Pushkin? Show him to me."

Over across the way troops loyal to the new Emperor of all the Russias are also gathering, as if the insurrection were anticipated. What does it mean? Has the Union been infiltrated by the infamous Third Section? Is the element of surprise lost to them completely?

The Czar's troops are ready to fire upon the rebels, but the governor-general of Saint Petersburg pleads to the Emperor that his troops not be precipitous. "Let us speak briefly to the leaders of this unfortunate rebellion. They are young people who have been misguided." The Czar relents.

Good-hearted Count Miloradovich, the very same governor-general who granted clemency to Pushkin in 1820 before he was sent South by Emperor Alexander, starts over to the insurgents to talk them out of their rebellion. He believes in the essential goodness of all men, even crazy evil revolutionaries.

"Now, now. Let us talk this thing over like the Christian gentlemen all of us are. I know most of your mothers and your fathers. Good aristocratic families. We can settle this without resort to violence. His Majesty—"

The dear man gets no further, as one of the crazy nervous rebels steps out of the ranks and shoots the governor-general of Saint Petersburg. He falls mortally wounded.

The ragtag rebels begin to converge across the square toward the Winter Palace, screaming now in exultation. The day belongs to them! Czar Nicholas orders General Orlov to open fire. The Emperor's soldiers greet Yakushkin and his rebels with a hail of grapeshot, killing sixty-five or seventy and causing wholesale panic in the ranks. The disorganized rebels of the revolutionary elite turn and run back across the Square toward the frozen Neva, as the Emperor's Horse Guards surge toward them, slipping and sliding on the ice. The rebels retreat across the frozen river to reach some kind of safety on the other side.

"Regroup! Regroup!" Yakushkin shouts to them. "We can take it, comrades! We can take it!"

But halfway across the frozen river, the sheer weight of numbers causes the ice to give way and hundreds go screaming to an icy grave, where they will remain until the thaw of spring. The still-alive conspirators are rounded up and thrown into jail to await a speedy trial. That night the Emperor of all the Russias slept as soundly as a new-born babe.

Emperor Nicholas Pavlovich Romanov was Czar Supreme of all the Russias.

Even as these unhappy events unfolded in the Nation's capital, "Head down, docile under the pursuing lash, the gaunt old serf (still struggled indifferently) down the furrows of some implacable master," never knowing that the events here had anything to do with him. Slum dwellers on the outskirts of St. Pete shed not a single tear for their would-be liberators.

Months passed with no further news from the capital. Alexander Sergeievich did very little writing. Most of the writing he did accomplish were letters to his influential friends in the capital, men like Vyazemsky and Zukovsky.

Dear Friend, speak to the new Great One on my behalf. Tell him that I was exiled by his brother through a tragic misunderstanding, and that I am prepared to mend my ways. Tell him the exile was due to a silly statement by me about religion in all my immaturity, that even so it was taken out of context. Tell him I am afflicted with aneurysm. I have carried my death around with me quietly lo these many years. But I am growing old. I throw myself upon His soul, that he may let me in my old age find a place for me to die in peace rather than in this dungeon of a village. I will be indebted to him for the remainder of my days.

Then he added, in a separate note:

Show this letter to His Majesty Himself, if you deem it wise.

Zukovsky wrote him back immediately.

Your letter indicates you must be very close to madness. Hold on for dear life to your senses. You're the great hope of our literature. You appear to have contracted a severe case of pre-mature senility. You're only twenty-six. Stay where you are and for heaven's sake keep quiet. Your name is on the lips of every rebel brought to trial. Almost everyone of them has testified that your work inspired them to these desperate ventures. Be glad you're not in Petersburg. The less they hear from you the better. I'll notify you when it's safe to speak.

Prince Vyazemsky wrote him a similar letter as the infamous poet sank deeper in despair and apprehension. "Be calm. Be silent. Let the powers that-be forget you're at Mikhailovskoye."

But the poet, himself, could not forget. He could not get his comrades off his mind, as he lingered in his dungeon, not knowing what their fate would be. He would lie restless and awake at night, as his mind conjured up memories of Pushchin's winter visit, the wine they drank, the great warmth of their friendship, his premonition that it was the last time they would ever see each other.

In these loneliest of times he often thought of Olga Kalashnikova. He had not heard from her in months. In one of the letters from her she had told him that she had left Saint Petersburg and gone to Boldino, so that she could be with her father and stepmother when the baby came. He sent her rubles every month. He should, he often thought, have flouted all conventions and taken her to be his wife.

Then one day that summer the terrible news came to him. Seven of the "Decembrists" including Yakushkin whom he had known at the Davydovs in Kamenka were hanged. The remainder were sent into exile to the salt mines of Siberia, including his best friend, Ivan Pushchin. In the spring when the Neva thawed and gave up its dead, the air of the city was saturated with the smell of the dead amongst the flotsam and the jetsam of the river. Men and women wept as the dead were carted through the city to their communal graves.

Most of the news reached Pushkin in a letter from his Uncle Basil.

The new Emperor has a sense of irony. The hanging was public, in Senate Square where the abortive insurrection was attempted. Seven scaffolds were constructed. Thousands of people turned out to make a witness to this wondrous and majestic spectacle. Russians are a peculiar species. I have no idea why I attended. Perhaps it is the Russian in me. Several times I heard somebody ask: "Where is Alexander Pushkin? Are they hanging him today?" Women came with infants in their arms. Some men brought their sons and daughters. Pickpockets had a pocket-picking picnic.

Basil Pushkin did not trust His Imperial Majesty's postal service, especially when writing to his famous nephew. He sent it by a friend who was coming down to Pskov on business.

257

The seven died with dignity like real aristocrats. I will say that for them, especially Ry-lyev and Yakushkin. They never bowed a single head. It was one of the hottest days of summer. The sun beat down upon the Square as if God were angry about the hangings. Heaven help His Majesty. Men and women put their children on their shoulders so that they could witness everything. The trapdoors were sprung simultaneously. Men and women wept. "God, please don't turn your back on Russia!" Some of them fainted as the bodies hung there helplessly. Then moans and groans were heard from each man on his scaffold.

I heard someone exclaim, "Poor Russia! They can't even stage a proper execution!" I left at this point. I am told though that the ceremonies were performed again shortly afterwards, the second time successfully.

Well, that's all for now. One more word. They're calling the martyrs the "Decembrists." Already you are being called the "Bard of the Decembrists."

Stay well, my favorite famous nephew and be glad you are in exile, or the Holy Virgin only knows.

Your loving Uncle Basil

Meanwhile the Hermit of Mikhailovskoye was steadily going crazy from a guilty conscience. He could neither write nor sleep. When sleep did come, he dreamed he shared the scaffold with them. And he would wake up in a cold sweat with the feel of the rope around his neck, choking the life from him, his breath coming in loud gasps, and he'd be overjoyed that he'd been dreaming. Then he'd spend hours upon hours, days even, ashamed of his gladness, as if he had somehow betrayed his comrades by not being on the scaffold with them or at least being sent to Siberia. And because he couldn't really feel it, he felt even greater shame. If he could only escape into the real world of his writing. But that was not to be.

One evening in the late summer of 1826, Arina Rodionovna looked out of her window and saw a policeman approaching on horseback. She threw up her arms. "Politseyskii! Politseyskii!" She ran frantically to Alexander Sergeievich who was busy struggling with his muse. "They're coming for you, Sasha darling! The Polit-seyskii is coming to get you!"

He ran to his desk and snatched up all of his subversive papers, his manu-scripts and letters, which he always kept at arms reach and thrust them hurriedly into the fireplace where a fire was burning brightly. It was like thrusting his only child into a fiery furnace. They had come for him at last. He sighed. He would be hanged or sent to Siberia. He was frightened but he almost felt a strange relief. At last something was happening. It gave him a curious feeling of serenity and self-respect.

Before the gendarme dismounted and knocked on the door, Arina Rodion-ovna threw her arms up to the heavens. "For the love of the Holy Virgin, look after my poor baby! Save my son, dear Jesus!"

The old woman stood between the poet and the gendarme as he came brusquely through the door, as if she would defend her Sasha with her life. The burly gendarme gently pushed the old woman aside and handed Alexander Sergeievich an official paper ordering him to report at once to the authorities at Pskov for further orders on his journey to Moscow for an audience with the Emperor of all the Russias. Pushkin handed the papers back to the policeman and quietly prepared to go. He left a brief note of goodbye to be delivered to the women at Trigorskoye. When he was ready he took his nyanya in his arms, and she cried now without restraint.

"I'm never going to see my baby again! May the Holy Virgin go with you and stand by you! I'm never going to see my Sasha again." Sobbing, babbling, interchangeably.

Pushkin tried to console the old woman. "There's nothing to worry yourself about, matushka. If they send me to Siberia, the Emperor will see to it that I'm fed well. And if, on the other hand they hang me, I won't need anything to eat." His nyanya began to wail and moan more pitifully than ever. He told her, "The Emperor wants to confer with me on a matter of grave importance."

When Alexander Sergeievich arrived at the dusty town of Pskov, he received further orders to proceed immediately to Moscow where preparations were being made for the Imperial coronation, but "not in the position of a prisoner."

Before he left Pskov, he went, with the gendarme and Nikita Koslov trailing behind him, and stood outside the old wall of the ancient city. He thought, "Pskov —the ancient Kremlin!" He'd come to stand and stare at the walls of this old ancient Russian citadel many times before during his exile at Mikhailovskoye and even as a younger lad. The gendarme followed Pushkin as he went inside the walls and into one of its oldest cathedrals. He listened to the mournful sound of the singing, the sorrowful chants that put a nervous feeling in his stomach, the bearded old men in black skull caps and the old women dressed in long black gowns that swept the earth, kneeling now to the gods of their ancestors, their heads covered with black babushkas, some with their feet bundled up in rags, the genuflecting, the smell of age and human perspiration, the younger women with babes on their backs sitting in the pews alongside the expensively perfumed ladies of the landed gentry in their silk and satin, bedecked in gleaming gems. The Cathedral was the equalizer. This was his inheritance, he thought, the culture he claimed to cherish and believe in and to value. He stared at the walls inside the church adorned with Byzantine frescoes. The sound of the clanging, the looks on their believing faces, the kneeling, the golden icons candle-lighted, hundreds of them along the walls, flickering flames of blue and red and orange and yellow, the bishop in his golden robe, elderly priests with long white pointed beards that reached below their chests, strolling amongst the true believers swinging smoking pots of incense. All around and above him was a feeling of celestial ambience. He gazed up at the lofty ceiling, high high above and brilliantly lit. On the ceiling he beheld a mural of a larger-than-life-sized Christ, that hung there in eternal and grandiose ascendency. The sounds, the smell, the visual effects—he knew it was theatre in its fiercest and profoundest sense, emotionally, dramatically. No matter, the totality of it washed over him like healing waters from a holy and eternal spring. All of it came together and overwhelmed him, made his face fill up with a great love of the Russian people, a new understanding, vaguely realized, of what it meant to be a Russian. And the most important element was FAITH! An indomitable belief that the ultimate triumph would be theirs: FAITH! If this were true, how could he deny the existence of the God whom they worshiped without doubt or question? He looked around him. His eyes began to fill and a fullness moved amongst his face and shoulders. He turned and walked out of the church.

Outside again, he stared up at those ancient walls, one of the oldest Kremlins in all the Russias. It was here in 1240 all around these old white walls, that Russians made their noblest stand against the German hordes, the Teutonic Knights of the Order of Sword Bearers. He wiped his eyes with the back of his hand. A chill passed over the poet's shoulders.

He was proud to be a Russian!

For five apprehensive days and nights he traveled southeastwardly over the rugged Russian countryside. The dust mixed with the midges covered his face, got into his hair and mouth. When he reached the outskirts of the city of his birth, hungry, unwashed, sweaty, bedraggled, unshaved, he was met by another gendarme who had been posted there to look out for him.

"But I'm tired and I'm dirty and I need a shave," Pushkin protested. "I need a bath. Just give me a few minutes to get myself refreshed. I'm sure His Majesty would not mind at all."

"Sorry, Your Excellency," the big-boned stone-faced policeman said. "But our orders are to take you immediately before His Most Imperial Majesty."

Nikita Koslov interjected. "His Imperial Majesty will be displeased with you. After all, it isn't every day, dear boy, that the Czar of all the Russias requests an interview with the greatest writer in all of Russia. Do you know to whom you are addressing with such impertinence? Alexander Sergeievich Pushkin!"

The flustered policeman stared first at Pushkin and then at the wily old Nikita Koslov. He turned back to the exhausted poet. He removed his hat and scratched his head. "Sorry, Your Excellency, but there is nothing for it. The Imperial orders were quite specific."

Pushkin wondered about the wording of the orders he had read at Pskov. But not in the position of a prisoner. Why then did he feel the walls of prison moving in around him? Who was Nicholas Romanov? What was he like? He had already achieved the reputation as a ruthless tyrant. He had hung seven of his comrades. Sent the rest of them into permanent exile, most of whom had mentioned Alexander Pushkin in their testimony.

Bestuzhev Rynumin testified: "My inspiration came from Pushkin and his ODE TO FREEDOM *and his* THE VILLAGE. *Who could read Pushkin without committing himself to the overthrow of serfdom?" He was hung.*

Divov said: "I owe everything, my entire attitude toward life to that greatest of all Russians, Alexander Pushkin!" Sent to Siberia.

One rebel testified, proudly: "Who that is literate has not read Alexander Pushkin? And once you read him, how can you help but work to change this system?" Siberia.

The news of all these testimonies had reached the Hermit in Mikhailovskoye. Alexander Sergeievich did not know what to expect. He felt terribly disadvantaged having to go before such an august and powerful personage in his bedraggled condition. He was within the walls of the historic Kremlin now with its gilded facade of government buildings and palaces and cathedrals and monasteries and numerous seraglios. He felt the same remembered awe he had felt as a boy when he walked the streets outside the Kremlin with his nyanya. He had dreamt that he would one day walk within these walls. The awesome feeling was now multiplied.

"Alexander Sergeievich Pushkin!" He heard himself being announced by uniformed persons as he moved through one door after the other, each time imagining that he could hear the clangor of an iron prison door closing behind him forever, door after door after door, deeper deeper into the dreaded dungeon, down long narrow high-ceilinged corridors, through heavily guarded antichambers, leaving Nikita Koslov at the entrance to the very first door, till now finally he was alone and face to face with His Imperial Majesty, Czar of all the Russias! Caesar of all Caesars! Absolute ruler of the vastest, most endless stretch of empire on this godless earth!

PART SIX

CAPTIVITY

CHAPTER ONE

As he walked into the high-ceilinged room of the Emperor's study, he felt engulfed by its vastness. In width and length and depth, it seemed to go on forever. Like the steppes along the River Don. Alexander Sergeievich stared around meekly at the furnishings which were luxurious and European, especially French. Expense here had been the object. There was the great mahogany desk shining with glazed papers. Deeply-plush carpeting, heavy damask draperies of warmest burgundy at the giant windows. Everything here in exaggerated proportions. Gargantuan. Larger than life. Chairs, sofas, chandeliers. Where was His Imperial Majesty? He finally became aware of a man tall and regal in stature standing before an open fire with his back to Alexander Sergeievich, his body framed by a giant marble mantel.

The mantel was taller than His Majesty, all six feet four of Him. It was at least twelve feet from floor to mantel. The mantel shelf above the fireplace was lavishly decked with miniature replicas of the Muscovy Kremlin, the Cathedral of St. Isaac and the Winter Palace. Further in beneath the mantel the fireplace itself was shaped like a giant horseshoe, a rainbow of gleaming opalescence, with a sculptured profile of Nicholas Romanov embossed in gleaming gold at its apex. On each side of the fireplace stood tall handsome golden candelabras, more than seven feet in height, like giant sentries on guard duty.

His Imperial Majesty turned and looked down at Alexander Sergeievich. The Emperor's handsome ivory face seemed to be hewed out of finest marble, a Grecian statue. His eyes were cold grey immobile steel. He was cut from the very fine cloth of the Romanovs. Heavy handsome face, broad forehead, jutting jaw of granite. He was more handsome than his brother Alexander. His face was sharper, slenderer, clean shaven. This one, Czar Nicholas Romanov, was the beardless tyrant. He was attired in an Imperial Cossack uniform; his chest, that seemed as wide as the Russia over which he ruled absolutely, was covered with military medals and decorations. His stomach bursting from the midsection just above his belt. At first Pushkin had a sudden illusion that the Emperor was in fact a marble statue, an extension of the mantel, until he moved in his high black gleaming boots and a smile spread over his handsome face.

More than ever, Pushkin felt sharply his own shabbiness. He could smell his sweaty need of a bath, and the filth of his five-day-old beard itched him terribly. He knew his nose was red from a cold he had contracted on his way to Moscow. He was brought back to the here and now by the Emperor's voice, at once warm, confidential, imperial and threatening.

"Good morning, Alexander Sergeievich. How does it feel to be back in the city of your birth? Just like old times, eh?"

Alexander Sergeievich forced his head slowly against its will to lift and stare into the Emperor's genial face, as he mumbled, "Like old times." And added almost as an afterthought, "Your Imperial Majesty." He must at all times be acutely alert and observe strict protocol before this all-powerful potentate, he warned himself.

"Well, sit down. Sit down, lad. You must be exhausted after such a journey. I'm afraid my orders were taken too literally. You could have taken a little time to rest and freshen up a bit." The Emperor smiled effusively at Pushkin. He was enjoying the poet's bedraggled state in contrast to his own regal splendor. His orders had been carried out just as he had intended. It pleased the Emperor to have the poet at such a disadvantage.

Alexander Sergeievich stumbled over toward a chair and sank almost out of sight.

"You've been a naughty boy, Alexander Sergeievich," the Emperor said, as he stood over Pushkin with his broad back to the fire. "But you were young and I understand you're prepared to mend your foolish ways."

Pushkin could find nothing in his heart or mind to answer the Emperor with. He wondered at the confidential nature of the Emperor's manner, the almost total lack of formality and protocol.

"I understand that many of the so-called Decembrists were friends of yours." The Emperor continued.

It was like closing his eyes and dashing headlong into a forest fire. The poet didn't want to weigh the consequences or to talk himself out of it. He said quickly, "Your Majesty, almost every single one of them was my comrade."

The Emperor smiled expansively at the poet's temerity and candor.

"Tell me, Alexander Sergeievich, where would you have been on December 14, had you not been in exile in Mikhailovskoye?"

Pushkin felt his heart beat wildly way up in the temples of his forehead. He could smell his fear consuming him. He thought of his friend, Pushchin, somewhere in far away Siberia, and Yakushkin, Rylyev and Bestuzhev Rynumin lying quiet in the cold earth of the Motherland. He, Alexander Sergeievich Pushkin, the "bard of the Decembrists," stared up at the pleasant-faced tyrant who held the poet's life in his hand. He was Nero with the Christians in the Coliseum, he was all-powerful Caesar.

And Czar he was of all the Russias, all powerful, His Most Imperial Majesty, the Emperor of Muscovy, Kazank and Novgorod and Vladimir and Kiev and Siberia, Lord of Pskov, Grand Duke of Smolensk and Lithuania and Finland and Podolia, Emperor of Rostov and Yareslav and Belozero, Sovereign of the Caucasus and Circassia, Grand Duke of Uzbekestan and Turkestan.

A nod of His Majesty's handsome head and the bard would be a feast for the hungry lions. He remembered a conversation he'd had with his friend, Pushchin, years ago in Saint Petersburg in the time of his great youthful innocence.

"You—Pushkin—of all people! The apostle of Truth! Lying to the Authorities!"

He remembered the look on his comrade's face, when he replied: "There are truths, and there are truths. There are Imperial truths and there are gospel truths, and they are just about the same, mostly lies. . . . Then there are truths that liberate the people, which are altogether different. I do not owe the Imperial Court the people's truth. All I owe it is damnation and exposure."

But now, this moment which truth did he owe? He certainly did not owe this cruel Imperial potentate the people's truth. Nyet! nyet! he argued with himself, convincingly. But he could not convince himself as he saw clearly through the speciousness of this argument he was having with himself. It was the truth he owed himself that counted.

Alexander Sergeievich got to his feet, legs apart, and looked up into the tyrant's steel grey eyes and handsome face. Pimples of sweat broke out on his own face. A knot tied up his nervous belly. He cleared his scratchy throat. "Without a doubt, your Majesty, I would have been in the Square along with my comrades." He swallowed hard. "I thank Almighty God I was in Mikhailovskoye."

Nicholas Romanov stared long and hard at this raggedy-arse darkly-visaged poet with the African lips and the frame of frizzly hair atop, and he could not help but admire the courage and audacity of this Alexander Sergeievich Pushkin. He knew of the powerful influence this poverty stricken African nobody-of-a-versifier held with the Russian intellectuals and the Russian people as a whole, the youth, the women, the workers and the peasants. He also knew of the loathing these same artists and intellectuals felt for their Emperor, due especially to the harshness of his dealing with the Decembrists martyrs. Perhaps he thought, it would be safer to keep this mischief-making poet close by where surveillance would be easier. He was a tyrant who longed for love from his subjects whom he tyrannized, like a master wants love and loyalty from his slave, like a father who wants love from his children whom he brutalizes. He *was* the Little Father at the Palace, God incarnate on this Holy Russian earth.

266

Czar Nicholas smiled broadly at the poet. "I admire a man of integrity, one who is loyal to his comrades."

Alexander Sergeievich could not restrain a deep sigh of relief, even as he wondered where all this conversation was leading. He kept remembering that this genial monarch had hung Rylyev and Yakushkin and Rynumin, had banished Ivan Pushchin to a lifetime of hard labor in Siberia. He sank back in the chair again. He knew that Alexander Raevsky was languishing across the way in the Peter and Paul Fortress. What did this all-powerful tyrant have in store for him? Why had he been brought to Moscow where the coronation would be held? He looked up into the face of Nicholas Romanov who stood almost just above him now. Somehow he felt more defenseless than ever with the giant hovering over him. He seemed to be sinking deeper into the cushion of the chair. He struggled vainly now to rise. The Monarch reached out like an older brother and helped the poet to his feet.

He put a fatherly arm around Pushkin's shoulders and began to walk around the room with him. "My brother sent you into exile, and for good reason. I am giving you your freedom. And I hope that you've sown your wild oats sufficiently and are ready to settle down and lend your talents for the good of Russia."

Pushkin was completely flabbergasted. Forgotten was all protocol as he warmed his frozen backside at the fire and faced the Emperor. He had listened carefully to His Majesty. Would he use his talents for the good of Russia? Could he live with such a commitment. Was this a betrayal of his comrades and the cause for which they died and suffered? It was either this or further banishment for life. He had had enough to last a lifetime. Even though he knew the words meant different things to him and the Emperor, he knew within himself what his commitment was.

He heard himself say, "Yes, Your Majesty."

The Czar was in a generous mood. He laughed at the poet's audacity, addressing him in such a familiar manner. For he was a stickler for protocol and ceremony, but he hid his feelings with a smile. "Is there anything else I can do for you, Alexander Sergeievich? Is there anything I can do to make your adjustment back from exile easier?"

"Your Majesty, I'm having terrible trouble with the censors."

"Why would you be writing something they would censor?" The Emperor inquired.

"They censor everything I write, no matter what."

"If you promise you will value our friendship and use your talent for the good of the Motherland and not for evil and subversion, I shall be your only censor." The benevolent Czar declared.

Alexander Sergeievich was speechless. He looked up and saw the clean white hand of the monarch reaching toward him, and he extended his grimy little hand with the long filthy fingernails to be grasped and enveloped by this large white Imperial hand. A wave of irresistible gratitude swept over him. His head knew a giddy feeling. He held on to the Emperor's hand to keep from falling. At the same time he felt deeply ashamed of feeling grateful to this cruel despot.

It was at that moment that Pushkin remembered parts of a poem he had been working on were hidden in his pocket. He had titled it THE PROPHET. He had written it on his way to Moscow.

> Arise, Prophet of Russia,
> Don your shroud of shame,
> Go, the noose around your neck,
> To face the abominable assassin.

He broke into an ice-cold sweat. His thumping thigh felt warm beneath the place where he had put the poem, which would surely remove the smile from the Emperor's face if he knew of its existence. He would join his comrades in Siberia. He felt a swiftly degenerating weakness in the knees. But the Emperor shook him out of it with his arms again around his shoulders as he walked him to the door, opened it and brought Alexander Sergeievich into an antechamber crowded with uniformed courtiers, counts and barons and Imperial sycophants.

With his arm still around the poet, Czar Nicholas announced with Imperial flourish, "Gentlemen, meet my good friend, the new Pushkin! Forget about the old one." He laughed. "I mean of course the younger one."

And they all laughed with the Emperor.

As Pushkin walked down the long wide marble steps of the Imperial Palace with his faithful valet, Nikita Koslov, he thought his feet might just take wings and fly away. He was free. He thought about the majestic eagle high up in the Caucasus. He was free! He felt like dancing down the steps doing a wild mazurka. He was free, he was free! And he had done no damage to his dignity. He had not arse-kissed the Emperor. He put his hand in his pocket for his poem, THE PROPHET, and did not find it. His heart began to leap about, his mouth went cold with fear even as his face broke out with perspiration. Had it dropped from his pocket in the Emperor's study? He would never know good fortune. Fate was playing tricks on him again. Fate had chosen him a victim, and a victim he would always be. Fate and God's and the Emperor's will. There was simply nothing for it! Then he saw a piece of paper a few steps below him. He recognized it as his own. THE PROPHET! He ran down the steps and as he stopped to pick it up, the wind blew it away from him, and it came to rest at the feet of an Imperial guard who stood there like a marble statue. Pushkin hurried down toward it and reached for it just as the statue moved and reached down to retrieve it. The Imperial Sentry stared at it perfunctorily and handed it to the flustered poet.

"Does this belong to you, Your Excellency?"

"*Merci beaucoup,*" Alexander Pushkin answered, "*Merci beaucoup! Spaceeba!*" as he took the poem from the sentry.

He walked shakily with Nikita Koslov amongst a cluster of imposing cathedrals, their steeples reaching heavenward, with their sharply pointed cupolas gleaming like crowned jewels in the midday sunlight. He walked past the monasteries, past the harems and the palaces. He breathed deeply, and relieved, as he walked past the final sentry beyond the walls of that ancient awesome citadel that Holy Russians called the Kremlin.

CHAPTER TWO

Alexander Sergeievich caught a coach cab and went straight way to his Uncle Basil's apartment, and they danced around the room together after he told him the wonderful news. They sat down and drank champagne together. "It is so good to have you back, my famous nephew!"

"It is damn good to be back, Uncle Basil! Tell me, what is happening in this part of the world?"

"Everything is quiet," his uncle told him soberly, though drunk with champagne and with joy at having his favorite nephew home again. His voice was just above a whisper. "Things are very quiet ever since the December incident and all that's happened afterwards. People are afraid to break wind in the bathhouse. So be careful, nephew," he advised with deep concern. "Be very very careful."

"I'll do my best to keep him out of mischief," Nikita Koslov assured Uncle Basil.

From Uncle Basil Pushkin went to see Prince Vyazemsky and visited with him in a Turkish bath. He chatted with the prince as he steamed the dirt and grime out of his weary body. He felt like shouting. It was so good to be back from exile.

"I shouldn't be overelated," Prince Vyazemsky counseled him. "The Third Section is all over the place," he whispered, through a cloud of steamy vapors. "I'll be a monarchist till the day I die. I'll never be a rebel or a revolutionary," he admitted to Alexander Sergeievich, "but I cannot condone the bloodshed that went on and by the Emperor's own hand."

"As you just warned me," Alexander Sergeievich reminded him, half in jest and half in earnest, "the Third Section comes in many disguises. I've just left the Emperor. How do you know I'm not a spy?"

Vyazemsky stared at him through the steamy fog. "How did he happen to pardon you?"

Alexander Sergeievich smiled. "The Czar was playing cat and mouse with me, and I had no desire to be the Emperor's breakfast."

The name of Alexander Pushkin was on everybody's lips. "Pushkin's back!" Wherever he went it was: "There he is, the author of THE FOUNTAIN OF BAKSHISARAI!"

"He is our ODE TO FREEDOM!"

"The Bard of the Decembrists!"

"The living author of the PRISONER OF THE CAUCASUS!"

Czar Nicholas was overheard remarking to another nobleman at a Grand Ball on the night of Pushkin's return: "Today I talked with the most intelligent man in Russia—Alexander Pushkin. We are the best of friends."

One night Pushkin read the rough draft of his tragedy, BORIS GODUNOV, at the home of Venvitenov, one of the most fashionable salons in Moscow. A considerable assortment of writers, artists, actors and other admirers, men and women, some ennobled, were in attendance in this rich man's drawing room. Some of them came just to see the poet and to be able to say they had seen and met the famous writer. Some had no idea what to expect. Pushkin was nervous when he began to read, a fact that no one would have suspected.

A reporter reported the occasion in the newspaper a week later.

At one point in the evening, a swarthy man of African visage and medium stature rose to read. He was dressed in a black tight-fitting coat, a vest of dark maroon that fitted tightly at the neck. The resonance of his voice demanded everyone's attention. Then as the reading progressed, his audience gasped and marveled. Chills raced up and down their spines. Eyes were awe-struck at the star, beauty pouring from those thickened and un-Russian lips.

"African lips with the voice of angels," one lady poet described it afterwards in another newspaper. Pushkin loved the sound of it. African lips. It left a good taste with him. The first reporter continued.

And now as Emperor Boris Godunov made his final speech before dying, men and women were weeping unashamedly. Then it was over, and at first there was an awful quiet, then suddenly the room was detonated with thunderous applause. Then a mad scramble toward the poet to embrace and hug and kiss him. Drinking champagne to his health. Shouts of "Bravo! Bravo! Long live Alexander Pushkin, genius of our Russian souls!"

One night Pushkin went to see the performance of Shakovskoy's comedy, ARISTOPHANES, at the Moscow Grand Theatre. He was late in arriving. The performance had already begun. As he entered, he could hear the whisper—"There he is —Alexander Pushkin!"

People stood as if the Emperor were arriving. All eyes went from the stage to the box where he was entering with his friend, Zukovsky. He heard, "Pushkin!" . . . "Our own Pushkin!" . . . "He's back! He's back!" All opera glasses in the grand theatre, even those from the Imperial box where the Czar himself was in attendance, were trained on his box where he sat with chills racing back and forth across his slender shoulders.

"Pushkin!" the murmur went. "Pushkin! Pushkin!"

The rafter high up in the ceiling of the vastest theatre in all the Russias echoed, "Poosh—kin!" in muffled tones and whispers. The very rafters themselves seemed to reverently call out his name.

"Pushkin! Pushkin! Pushkin!" The murmur of his name grew louder and louder reaching such a mad crescendo no one could hear what was happening on stage. And it didn't seem to matter.

"Pooshkin! Pooshkin! Pooshkin!"

Zukovsky pulled the bleary-eyed Pushkin to his feet, whispering to him. "You must take a bow in recognition of the people's welcome to you, so that the play on stage will be able to continue. This has never happened before in the history of Russian theatre!"

Pushkin bowed to the front, to the right and left as the theatre exploded with applause, as the lights went up throughout the theatre. And the spotlight went to Pushkin's box. Even the actors on stage turned toward him and applauded. He heard cries of "Pushkin! Pushkin! Long live Alexander Pushkin!" He wished his mother were here with him to share this moment of triumph. Even his pathetic father would be proud. He longed for his Amelia.

As he sat down again and the applause slowly subsided, the theatre darkened as the lights went down and the play continued, he blew his nose and hid his face with his handkerchief to hide the tears that were streaming down his face and which he could not control. For he had been in isolation from the city of his birth so long, so very long, he had felt forgotten and uncared for in his desperate loneliness. He had been an outsider all the days of his remembered life. And this sudden adulation and adoration were too much for this lonely poet.

When he left the theatre that night, crowds followed him down the streets. "There he is—Pushkin! Our own, our own, our very own! . . . . The voice of Russia!" Men and women embraced him, kissed him on his bearded cheeks. He was ashamed of how good it made him feel. His banishment was not in vain.

A woman poet described that memorable evening, in the newspaper. Pushkin read it in the Petersburg's *Neva Observer* a few weeks later. She wrote:

The crowd pushed forward;
I hear, "Look, he's coming,
Our poet, our glory,
The people's darling."

Distinguished, though not tall,
Bold, quick and knowing.
He walked past in front of me.
And forever afterward
My dreams were ruled
By his African profile
And lighted by his flaming eyes.

CHAPTER THREE

Parties, parties, parties. Given by the handsome people of the ennobled classes. Attended by the wealthy, the artists and the intellectuals. These days a party without the presence of Alexander Pushkin was considered a social failure. People went to parties just in hopes that the bard of the Decembrists would make an appearance. He luxuriated in his celebrity and fame.

In the midst of all this he would feel a sharp twinge of conscience when he thought of the Decembrists. It sickened him to see the wives, sisters and other relatives of the martyrs living riotously, reveling as if the thing in December never happened and didn't touch them in the least. By now he knew of the abortive insurrection in all its shameful details. He'd learned that immediately after that sad cold day in mid-December, the martyrs had been renounced by most of their families. There'd been a mad scramble to see who could prostrate himself, or herself, most abjectly before the lordly Emperor.

This night he was in the home of the most famous of partygivers in Muscovy. You did not amount to much unless you were invited to Princess Volkonski's grand salon. The princess was the ultimate. Alexander Sergeievich leaned boredly on a long white column in the princess's ballroom watching the women with their bare and powdered shoulders blinking their eyes flittingly behind their pearl-encrusted fans. His thin and pointed nostrils picked up the fragrances of their perfumes; he heard the rustles of their hoop-skirted evening gowns as they whirled and did their elegant quadrilles and mazurkas and their polkas. A footman glided past and Pushkin took another glass of champagne from his tray. The vastly high-ceilinged ballroom gleamed and glittered with chandeliers.

Alexander Sergeievich idly watched the princess moving through the crowd toward him. She had too much for her own good. Too much comeliness, eyes too wide and deep and blue and comely, too much wealth, too much lovely bosom with dress curving at the neck down to the actual cleavage. But he remembered her brother was a Decembrist.

"Alexander Sergeievich!" she greeted him with. "We are so honored by your presence. What have you for us on this most auspicious occasion?"

He stared at the princess, and suddenly he realized she was not actually beautiful. She was terribly pretty, too perfect in her profile to be beautiful. Straight nose, thin mouth. He thought, an unexciting face totally lacking in strength of character. "What makes this occasion so auspicious?" Alexander Sergeievich inquired. He was remembering he'd heard that the day her brother marched away, his head shaven like a convict, in chains, headed for his Siberian frozen hell, his sister and his mother, the old Princess Volkonski of his Tsarskoye Selo days, had opened the ball with the Czar of all the Russias at the Imperial ballroom, and this one, pretty, vacuous Zinaida, the carefree belle of the ball, had gaily danced all evening with His Imperial Majesty.

"Your august presence makes every occasion auspicious, Monsieur Pushkin."

He stared beyond the pretty princess and saw an old familiar face that made his heart stop beating, momentarily. He remembered, agonizingly, the foolish young times of his tremendous waste. She was Madame Marya Raevskya Volkonski, on her way to join her much older husband, Sergei Volkonski, in his exile in Siberia. Marya had always been there just out of sight in a corner of his consciousness, and she had remained fifteen years old, and saucy-faced and mischievous of spirit. He suddenly felt sad and old. Her loyalty and maturity made him proud of the Russian people, even some of the nobility. She was in sharp contrast to her fickle-minded sister-in-law. Where Zinaida was blonde with a flamboyant prettiness, Marya was possessed of a dark and simple beauty.

Pushkin watched Marya move with that special grace born of suffering and inner strength. She was near-sighted and did not recognize him till she was almost upon him.

"Alexander Sergeievich!" Marya greeted him. "What an important man you have become!"

Pushkin stared into her eyes, even deeper darker now than he remembered. "Important? My dear, compared with you and the men you are on your way to join, I feel terribly insignificant. I was so immature and undeserving. He remembered a pretty little girl a long long time ago as she stood outside the villa in Gurzuf among the cliffs above the sea. He could hear the shrieking of the mountain eagles. And he remembered the young girl who said, "As for the other kind of love, there is another fate for me."

He heard her now say in an anxious voice, "Oh no, Alexander Sergeievich. You have paid for your beliefs and you will always be our inspiration. You are the voice of everything in Russia that is decent and makes sense. You are their bard! You are their voice! Never let them still that voice!"

He felt the warmest kind of feeling for this woman. He took her in his arms to hide his deepest felt emotions.

"Give my love to the comrades, Marya, and take care of your wonderful self." The poet said in a trembling voice.

She had been the one so easy with tears, and now he had to fight back his own tears. Surreptitiously, he gave her a poem he had written to the martyrs. It was his MESSAGE TO SIBERIA.

Deep down in the Siberian mines
Your patience keeps with proud disdain!
The lofty dreams of your noble mind,
Your grief and toil are not in vain,
And freedom joyfully will greet you at the door.
Your comrades will restore you to the sword.

He never saw Marya again, and he would never go back to Zinaida Volkonski's salon.

Alexander Sergeievich wasn't writing. He was luxuriating in his ephemeral celebrity. In the midst of it all, the drinking, the flirtations, the gossip, the fraudulent adoration, the music by the serf bands, the frantic mazurkas, he felt lonely and outside of all this. He was a pariah still, even in his renowned celebrity he was their conversation piece, a supernumerary. To some, he was their *pièce de résistance*, to others, he was their after-supper cognac, an amusing anecdote they indulged themselves with after a sumptuous repast.

He visited his mother and father occasionally. They were more than willing to take him to their bosoms and bask in the sunbeams of his sudden fame, now that he had the apparent approval and acceptance of His Imperial Majesty. He tried with all his heart to forget their past rejection of him, to accept them at the value of their glowing faces.

Then one evening at a party, he overheard his father boasting. "I knew he had it in him all the time. I stuck by him through the good times and the bad. I never turned my back on Alexander Sergeievich even when things were roughest and ugliest and the storm was raging about his noble head. Those Decembrists tried to involve him in their damnable conspiracy. But he was loyal to His Imperial Majesty to the end. That is why His Majesty reprieved him."

He left without saying goodnight to them that evening, with the uneasy feeling that perhaps his father spoke the truth about his elder son. Perhaps his father knew him better than he knew himself.

And he was beginning to suspect the best friendship of the Emperor. Had he indeed been liberated, or had he traded a prison that was Mikhailovskoye for a dungeon that was his beloved Moscow?

For he was beginning to understand that Nicholas Romanov the First was not an avid reader. He had delegated his censorship responsibilities to Benkendorf, the chief of the Third Section. The efficient Emperor had simply centralized the surveillance of the pesky poet. One day he received a letter from Benkendorf.

"His Imperial Majesty has directed me to express his dismay at your reading of BORIS GODUNOV without first allowing him to enjoy it. Please to correct this situation immediately and not let it happen again."

Pushkin was infuriated. He felt the rope tightening politely around his neck. He would be gently choked to death. So now he could not even read a rough draft to his peers. He sent his manuscript to the Emperor and within two weeks received a communication from Benkendorf, delivered in person, by the chief of police himself. "The Emperor has read your little 'comedy' with considerable interest. He suggests that you change it to a romantic novel along the lines of Sir Walter Scott."

He felt the heat grow in his face, as the Czar's Chief of Secret Police waited with undisguised impatience for the poet's response to the Emperor's literary counsel. "His Majesty eagerly awaits your response to his suggestions."

Pushkin knew now how the game was being played. The Emperor read nothing, excepting military reports and maneuver dissertations. He remembered his first encounter with the Count years ago in that infamous cabaret. He recalled his first love, Tatyana. Count Benkendorf sat back in a chair and waited. He was sure the Count also remembered. Benkendorf crossed one long leg and then the other. Pushkin walked back and forth in his incommodious room, as he swallowed the heat of anger that was choking him. "Kindly tell His Majesty I am honored at his concern in my literary career, and I shall take his advice about my little 'comedy', which I had unwittingly deemed a tragedy. Meanwhile, I plan to go to Saint Petersburg, and while I'm there I shall go over the little comedy, always keeping in mind His Majesty's kindly and benevolent suggestions." His voice trembled in its anger.

The slender, elegantly-uniformed Benkendorf rose and came back with, "And does His Majesty know of your plans for travel? Has he given you permission to visit in Saint Petersburg?" He massaged his stylish mustache back and forth with a slender index finger.

"Permission?" He could no longer keep the heat out of his voice.

Benkendorf had walked towards the door. He turned and spoke to Pushkin pompously. "You are one of the Emperor's favorites at court, and he'd like to know where you are at all times, in case he needs to consult you on a matter of Imperial import. Kindly always let us know by official letter of any intentions you might have of moving about the country. All reasonable requests will of course be granted. A mere formality."

That evening Alexander Sergeievich wrote a letter to the Emperor requesting permission to travel to Saint Petersburg. A few days later he received an official letter from the office of Chief Benkendorf granting the permission with the cordial admonition, "His Majesty wishes you to enjoy your visit to Saint Petersburg and cautions you to conduct yourself honorably, in a manner worthy of a gentleman of your station."

Pushkin fumed. In other words, "Be a good boy or you will be chastised severely by Your Imperial Father!"

The man who went to Petersburg that autumn was different from the young impressionable and disillusioned lad who had left it more than six years before. It seemed like an eternity. He had crammed a lifetime of experiences into those terrible eventful years. There was a tired lean look about him. Slender shoulders, small in the waist. He had grown very little in physical stature, but he had grown in knowledge of what he was about and what he cared about. He was of medium height with the bold look of the predator about him as he walked with legs apart seeming to move, simultaneously, to the right and left, yet straight ahead steadily and boldly into life, with shoulders hunched forward, and at the same time held them square and back against all adversaries. You impinged upon his dignity at your own peril.

Everywhere Alexander Sergeievich went those first weeks, it was adulation, adoration. Next to the Czar, they told him, he was the most important man in all the Russias. He loved it, at first. He wallowed in it. He took it all in stride, it seemed. He was going around being a celebrity, striking postures, everybody's favorite. After living the role of the forgotten and forsaken man so long, celebrity was heady wine, but it had its morning-after repercussions. He was not doing any writing. Finally he became bored with his celebrity.

He went to the balls and stood around looking jaded, taking glasses of champagne from the trays of footmen as they darted in and out of the mass of pretty people of the nobility and the wealthy and the upper classes. He watched the facile flirtations of the bare-shouldered ladies heavily powdered and perfumed, behind pearl-inlaid fans stomping out a frenzied mazurka with pretty empty-headed look-alike young gentlemen, uniformly attired, and always remembering that so many of them were wives, brothers, sisters, fathers and mothers of the Decembrists who rotted in their graves or in the salt mines of Siberia. Sometimes he tried to drink himself into forgetfulness.

Then one day the entire world collapsed around him. The message reached him from Mikhailovskoye. His nyanya had deserted him. His matushka, Arina Rodionovna, had escaped the confines of Holy medieval Russia over which His Most Imperial Majesty Czar Nicholas I ruled, absolutely. She was no longer a serf, a surrogate person. The message was brief. "She died in her sleep." His nyanya had slipped away from him when no one else was looking, without even saying dosvidanya to him. She was free at last. She was liberated, manumitted. Not even the ubiquitous Third Section could prevent her from escaping.

Alexander Sergeievich sat quietly in his apartment and tried desperately and valiantly to summon up the tears, to feel all at once the totality of his sense of loss. Cry and get it over with. He felt it building in his shoulders, moving up through his throat and filling up his face. But it stopped there stubbornly on the other side of his eyes. Why couldn't he cry for his beloved nyanya, Arina Rodionovna? His matushka! Had he grown so cold? Was his heart so jaded? He rose from his chair and began silently to prepare for his journey to Mikhailovskoye to Arina Rodionovna's last dosvidanya.

He left Saint Petersburg without the Emperor's permission.

CHAPTER FOUR

It was late autumn and already there was the hint of snow coming in from the North. The trees were naked and waiting impatiently for their winter clothing. The Russian earth was ablaze with fallen leaves. The days were brisk, the nights were cold. Pushkin paid little attention to the gold-brown of the landscape. He had no eyes for beautiful Russia in the autumn time. His time. He had only eyes for that which lay ahead of him at the end of his journey. It began to rain the third day out. The rain turned to sleet, then gently to a soft white frothy something, as if the sky were shaking sugar onto this Russian earth. It was snowing steadily when he reached Mikhailovskoye. Darkness was falling as the carriage came down the lane toward his great-grandfather's house. A dread came over him like a shroud. He had traveled there too hurriedly.

They had reached the old house now, and he leapt from the cab. He saw a face in the window. Just as he got to the door it opened and Annettie Wulf ran into his arms.

"Oh, Alexander Sergeievich!" Annettie sobbed.

He looked around him at the empty house. "Where is everyone?"

"Everyone was here. They went back to Moscow this morning."

His heartbeat quickened. He looked around him in bewilderment. "But-but-but-where is my nyanya? I mean when are they going to have the funeral?"

Annettie answered softly, "She is buried. She died two weeks ago."

"But I only knew about it four or five days ago. How did *they* get the news so quickly?" He asked.

"They were here already. They didn't know how to reach you." He took her by the shoulders and began to shake her. "But she was my mother! My nyanya! My matushka! It was me she loved most. It was I who loved her! I, her Sasha!" Tears streamed down his cheeks and his shoulders shook with sobbing. He wiped his eyes.

He stood there now dismally frustrated, and he took her in his arms and kissed her. He said, quietly, "Get your coat and come with me."

Annettie put her coat on and he took her like a man sleep-walking out to where the carriage waited, as the snow still fell, and she went with him to Holy Mountain where he knew they would have buried his nyanya.

By the time they reached the top of the mountain, darkness completely covered the snow-white world of Holy Russia. He was looking for the grave near where his great-grandfather and Grandma-ma Hannibal were buried. The abbe from the dimly lighted monastery came out with a torchlight and called to him. "She's buried over here."

Pushkin stumbled over toward the mound of earth where the abbe stood about twenty-five feet away from where the Hannibals were buried. He stared through blinding tears at the pitiful little clump of earth partially covered with the falling snow. And he thought, this is all that's left of his nyanya. She had not even escaped her slavery in death. The graves where his grandparents were buried were the manor house. Arina Rodionovna was laid to rest forever in the isbas.

He laughed hysterically. "Arina Rodionovna, I hope you get the joke in all this. I hope you're laughing at these mindless sons of bitches!"

And now Alexander Sergeievich stood there remembering the times he'd spent with his nyanya, the love she had always given him when it seemed that love was nowhere else on earth, for him. The songs she sang, the times they got drunk together. He had always been her Sasha and she had been his matushka. And he would never see her again, never hear that dear voice of hers, never kiss those withered lips. Never ever! It was the never ever part that broke through the floodgates of his tears, and he stood there crying shamelessly. The tears were in his mouth, his throat, spilled from his eyes, filled his nostrils. He wept for all the pride she had instilled in him. He wept for the folktales she had shared with him, the love for the Russian people. He cried for the loss of this great heart that had stopped beating, never to beat again, this magnificent soul, this dear voice never to hear again. He wept for this indomitable spirit, for this great love lost to him forever.

He turned to Annettie and she went into his arms. Crying, sobbing. "Annettie! Why did they do this to her? This is blasphemy! This is sacrilege! Burying her away from the family. This is obscene!" He sucked the tears back through his throat. "No, Annettie. I'll never forgive the mindless *mosheniki* (scoundrels) for this. This time they went too goddamn far!"

They rode back to the manor house, and Annettie asked if he wanted her to spend the night with him. He took her in his arms and kissed her warmly on the mouth and thanked her. But he wanted to be alone this night in the old decrepit house. Alone with his magnificent sorrow.

He brought the coachman in out of the cold and they had food and drink together. When they were alone, Annettie and Alexander Sergeievich sipped vodka together silently. The poet talked softly until it grew late, about his nyanya and the great love he had always felt for her, the love they gave each other. Annettie listened attentively, then asked again, "Do you want me to stay here with you tonight, Alexander Sergeievich? Ma-ma will not be worried."

The poet looked at the dark-eyed sad-faced woman and saw the adoration for him in her lovely face. And he said, "Thank you, my beloved princess, but no. I really need to be all by myself."

He helped her with her coat, kissed her warmly on her eager lips again, and took the coachman's carriage and drove her home.

CHAPTER FIVE

Back in Saint Petersburg, Alexander Sergeievich was reprimanded severely by Chief Benkendorf for leaving the capital without His Majesty's permission. He began to drink again. And heavily. He was becoming unstitched at the seams. He tried to inundate the memory of his matushka with rum and vodka. He tried to escape into his writing. But every word, every phrase, every sentiment he put on paper reminded him of his nyanya. Of some experience he had shared with her. She would be a part of everything he'd ever write.

To the people in the capital who mattered to him, to those who looked to him for vision and for wisdom in his writing, he was becoming a dreary disappointment. The word went out that the fountain of his genius had run dry, that he had made a deal with the evil genius at the Palace. The poet's disgusted muse had deserted him. Some days Alexander Sergeievich tended to agree with them. Perhaps he had said too much too soon at too young an age, and had run out of things to say. Maybe what he needed was a change of scenery. He made many trips to Moscow, but Moscow was no better than Saint Petersburg. He was tired of the social life of these two cities. It was as if he had lived this life before at some other time, perhaps in some other place. Sometimes he actually believed that he had been along this way before. He searched desperately in all the likely places for his muse. A couple of futile trips back to Mikhailovskoye and there, alone with his loneliness, he tried vainly to seduce his muse. But he only sat there missing his nyanya, Arina Rodionovna. He made many visits to her lonely grave. One day he had her exhumed and reburied near Grandma-ma Hannibal and his great-grandfather.

Back to Petersburg, back to Moscow, back to Petersburg. To the balls and parties, engaging the delighted women with his repartee. Alexander Sergeievich

Pushkin of the bushy hair, the swarthy visage, the sensual lips and the jaded and disheveled look. He thought sarcastically, Alexander Sergeievich Pushkin the poor muzhik's joy and the noblewoman's toy!

The years passed, and his heart grew colder as he grew older. At twenty-nine, Alexander Sergeievich thought he had written himself out. And there were too many personages who agreed with this estimate of his literary output, or lack of it. He read in important Moscow and Petersburg journals:

> The genius of Alexander Pushkin has run its course.

> Like a blinding comet that shoots across the darkness with a striking brilliance and then is seen no more.

> Monsieur Pushkin's so-called genius must be called into question. We expect lasting power from "genius." But this so-called genius is like a clap of thunder. It makes a loud crash and then is heard no more.

Fall had always been a fertile time of the year for Pushkin. There was something about the early Russian short-lived season after the autumnal equinox that seemed to beckon his genius to awaken. That fall he went to Mikhailovskoye and worked madly on EUGENE ONEGIN. He also ran the women around Trigorskoye wild.

Eufrasia (Zizi) was no longer a child, and, like her older sister Annettie, had fallen madly in love with the cavalier poet in his absence. The women, including Madame Wulf-Osipova, went around making ready for the poet's visit. Redecorating the ancient house, hanging brand new chandeliers, replenishing others with fresh tapers; seamstresses busy all around the place, pins in mouth, fitting dresses, young hearts palpitating, young ladies fussing and exchanging jokes and whispered confidences and anecdotes about the poet, nervous giggling, sighing over fondest remembrances, breathless sighing, working themselves into a state, the old house full of great aromas of pies and cakes and roasted lambs from the kitchen. All in anticipation of the poet's visit. And it was love—love! And our poet truly loved it. It was like old times. Perhaps better than old times. He was not an exile, this time.

He wrote Anton Delvig from Mikhailovskoye.

> I am having the time of my life. Country life is the only kind of life for me. It is just as if I am reliving my youth all over again. I miss nothing at all excepting my dear nyanya, Arina Rodionovna. Sometimes, alone at night with Eugene and Tatyana and the rest of the figment of my artistic imagination, I think I hear the old woman moving around the house like a welcomed ghost. Then when I look for her and she does not appear I am deeply saddened. But enough of maudlin sentiment . . . The rights of passion still reign supreme in this provincial village.

> The Wulf-Osipovas at Trigorskoye gave a big party in my honor, and the gentry came from miles around. Count and Countess So-and-So and Baron and Baroness Such-and-Such, they all came to see the famous addle-head, "the hound of Mikhailovskoye." I'm

told that Countess K., of the large behind and bountiful bosom, wanted to come to the party without her children, so she bribed them with promises of prunes and raisins if they would go to bed like good children. But Count K told them different. That their mother was spoofing them, that she was going to see Alexander Pushkin who was made of sugar, gingerbread and halvah, and his backside made of candied apples, and if they went they could cut me up and divide me between them. They screamed to their mother, "We want to see Pushkin! We want to see Alexander Pushkin!" When they arrived they leapt from their carriage shouting, "Where is Pushkin? Where is Pushkin!" And ran toward me, and when they saw that I was made of flesh and blood, they were keenly disappointed and began to bawl like crazy!

Zizi saw the poet as the great seducer and could not wait to get into his clutches. She called him Mephistopheles and played breathlessly at being terrified of him, and at the same time, a more than willing victim. He laughed at it all, took none of it seriously, even Zizi's tears and Annettie's labored breathing and the mother's jealousy and anxiety. He danced through it all in and out of perfumed and powdered arms. Pretty country girls from all around came to Trigorskoye to be taken by the dashing paramour.

Before winter set in he went back to Saint Petersburg. And back to the parties, the drunken orgies, fornicating with the wives of noblemen, and feeling jaded, old and ancient. There was nothing he had not done in the line of riotous living. While Alexander Raevsky languished in prison and Pushchin in Siberia, not to mention Marya Raevskya Volkonski.

One night on one of his drunken binges, Pushkin found himself at four in the morning in a den of Gypsies. He could scarcely see the Gypsy woman for the haze and smell of hemp and opium smoke and seething incense as she told his fortune in an eerie squeaky voice.

"Beware of a white man in your life. He spells danger."

Pushkin broke into a sweat, felt a chill move across his shoulders.

"Beware of a white man in your life—"

Meanwhile, enemies at the Imperial Court were laying plans to ensnare the "most intelligent man in Russia, the great friend of the Emperor." How could a man be intelligent when he was not wealthy, held no titles, and did not serve in His Majesty's military service? Of what worth was a worthless poet, a raggedy arsed scribbler, who did not even use his scribbling for the good and honor of the Russian Empire?

The Emperor had spoken of Pushkin to one of his beautiful ladies-in-waiting, a Princess Svetlina, whom he knew to be a long-time admirer and intimate friend of the poet. She was having breakfast with him and the Czarina in one of his private chambers in the Winter Palace. "Why doesn't Pushkin serve his country? Why doesn't he enter the service?"

She wittingly replied, "But Your Majesty, he is already serving *dans le génie.*" Which was a play on words, and could have meant "in the engineering corp" or "as a genius." She was Svetlina of his Tsarskoye Selo days and the Hussar Horse Guards. She remembered *le petit génie*. The Emperor never knew she had been one of the conspirators.

Chief spy Benkendorf was a friend of a few of Alexander Pushkin's sworn enemies in high places, men like Count Nesselrode, who was a close friend of the great gourmet, Count Stroganov. They all hated the sound of the scribbler's name. "He's an arrogant African scalawag who gives himself important airs," Benkendorf said. "And the women fawn over him!"

Stroganov said, "He thinks his kopeks are made of silver!"

The first move by his enemies was to bring to the Emperor's attention fragments of a poem Pushkin had written years before the December uprising. He had titled it ANDRE CHENIER. It was about the French Revolution. It was now titled DECEMBER 14, by Alexander S. Pushkin.

Alexander Sergeievich was brought before the Emperor to defend a poem that appeared to applaud the December martyrs.

The walls in the Emperor's high-ceilinged study in Saint Petersburg were covered with awards and honorary degrees and military citations, the giant windows covered with gold-emblazoned draperies.

This time there was no warm greeting from the Czar Nicholas. All pretense was set aside. The Emperor's eyes were as cold as ice. It was summer time now in Saint Petersburg, but in this Imperial study Alexander Sergeievich felt chilled to every marrow of his bones. He could not help himself from shivering. His Majesty handed Pushkin the poem across his glazed desk, rose from his chair and came around the desk and stood over the poet. "What have you got to say for yourself, Alexander Sergeievich, after all those promises you made to me?"

Alexander Sergeievich thought, all of what promises? It infuriated him to be put in a position of seeming to apologize for something he had written. A poem spoke for itself, it was beneath his dignity.

"Nothing, Your Majesty, except that I wrote this poem about the French Revolution. It was written many years ago. It was titled ANDRE CHENIER." He took a moth-eaten manuscript from his own pocket and gave it to the Emperor. "Here it is, Sire, in its original state. I think I wrote it when I was at the Lycée at Tsarskoye Selo."

He despised himself for having to explain something he had written out of inspiration to a non-reading literarily-illiterate like the Emperor of all the Russias.

His Majesty, with his broad shoulders golden-mantled and his chest weighted down with dazzling decorations, stared briefly at the tattered paper and went into one of his celebrated changes of mood. "Well, well, Alexander Sergeievich, it is clear that somebody does not have your interest at heart. Sit down, sit down, my son. I need your counsel for a moment. I know you are a very busy man, but you are a patriot and your country needs your wisdom at the moment."

Alexander Sergeievich could not suppress a deep sigh as he sank deep into one of the plush high chairs in the study. He wondered what was coming next. The gigantic Little Father poured Pushkin a snifter of his Imperial cognac and poured another for himself.

The Emperor of all the Russias sipped his brandy and cleared his throat. "There are rumors of revolt in Kazan and Rostov and Uzbekestan. Unrest everywhere. What is the answer to it all, Alexander Sergeievich?"

Pushkin downed the cognac with one swallow. It relaxed him, dangerously. He almost completely forgot that he was in the presence of the great God incarnate, the most powerful human being in the entire universe. He said, off-handedly and without thinking, "Your Majesty, issue a proclamation liberating all of the serfs throughout the Empire."

The Emperor, seated now, almost strangled on his cognac. He stared at the poverty-stricken notorious scribbler and grudgingly admired him. He had to be the cheekiest bastard in the Empire. The Emperor almost laughed aloud.

"It is not that easy, Alexander Sergeievich." He sighed. "I really wish it were so simple." He was a consummate actor. The theatrics of his Imperial position demanded it. And he had a natural talent for it. "You have some powerful and influential friends at the Imperial Court, Alexander Sergeievich. They talk about you constantly."

Everyone loves me, Pushkin thought sarcastically.

The Emperor was speaking now, as if he were reflecting to himself alone. "Benkendorf," he said, "Count Nesselrode, Prince Vyazemsky, Zukovsky, Count Stroganov." He stared at our poet, his cold grey eyes warming with seduction. He wanted his subjects to love him and to trust him, especially those like Pushkin whom he cordially detested.

Except for Vyazemsky and Zukovsky, the poet knew these men to be his sworn enemies. So what was His Majesty leading up to? Another cat and mouse game?

The Emperor interrupted the poet's reflections. "We are all wondering how a man like you with your popular esteem and touted wisdom, can best serve the interest of the Motherland. How would you like, Alexander Sergeievich, to be an ambassador to one of the courts of Europe?"

Pushkin's heart leaped wildly about in his chest. He remembered the blabbering of his pathetic father in Mikhailovskoye. *"Who knows? The Emperor might appoint you to an ambassadorship—"* And he would be leaving the vast prison that was the Russian Empire. He felt a dizziness come over him. It was too good to be true. There had to be some kind of legerdemain somewhere, some trickery or slight-of-hand not easily discernible. He heard himself say, "But Your Majesty, I am not a diplomat. I know nothing of diplomacy. I'm just a humble poet."

"Hardly humble, Alexander Sergeievich. Overly modest, I suspect. You are one of the most highly regarded men in the entire Russian Empire. And you did render service to my brother in the diplomatic service, so to speak. We could not pay what you'd be worth, of course. A mere seventy-five thousand rubles per annum, exclusive of your living expenses." His Majesty rose from his chair and came and stood above the poet again with his hands behind his back.

Seventy-five thousand rubles! It was more than the poet would make during his entire lifetime even if he lived a hundred years. He tried to stand but sank back in his chair. He heard the powerful monarch say, "You would send your written reports directly to me. Nothing you wrote would be censored, ever."

Alexander Sergeievich said, just above a whisper, "Your Majesty, I'm a poet, a writer, and that is my commitment to myself, to write the truth as I see from an artistic point of view. I'm too outspoken to be a diplomat. Your noble brother Czar Alexander exiled me from the service to a village that isn't even on the Imperial map."

"Well perhaps we can come up with another proposal by which you can render service to the Motherland." Czar Nicholas continued. "Perhaps we can send you to some of the troubled places in the Empire and you can speak to the people and explain to them the problems of the Empire. We would surely make it worth your while. We would not censor your remarks."

Pushkin was sweating now, and he heard, *Will not censor your remarks* and *We would surely make it worth your while*. And he was tired of dodging creditors, he was tired of living hand-to-mouth, pillar to post. He was tired of fighting the might of this Holy Russian Empire. In a word, he was intellectually and emotionally exhausted. And they would not censor his remarks. So he thought, why not? Why should you fight them all alone. He was tired. It seemed that fighting against the Little Father was out of fashion, an exercise in futility. So live expensively, royally, extravagantly. Why not? You only have one life to live. *And they will not censor your remarks!*

He looked up at the Emperor smiling down at him in all his powerful and Imperial contempt, and he thought to himself, but they can send someone behind me and boast of how liberal and republican they are. Were they not the friends of Alexander Sergeievich Pushkin? Did they not pay him well and allow him to roam around at will saying whatever came to his stupid mind? And the people would trust him about as much as they trusted His Imperial Majesty. And in the end he would be the loser. He would lose their love; the people would lose faith in him, Alexander Sergeievich Pushkin, the glorified lackey and court jester, the Imperial pander, the clown, the poetic lickspittle of the Russian Motherland.

This time he got to his feet. "Your Majesty, I am speechless, with gratitude. Your generosity is overwhelming. But I'm a writer, and that is all I will ever be, and that is all I will ever want to be."

It took a strenuous effort for the Emperor to keep the smile on his Imperial face. He put his heavy arm around Pushkin's shoulders and walked him to the door of the Imperial study. "Well, we'll give the matter some serious study, and perhaps we'll come up with something more in your line of endeavor."

Pushkin mumbled, "Let us certainly hope so, Your Majesty." Thinking to himself, will they never let me be?

Many months later Alexander Sergeievich was on his way back to the Emperor's office to explain the sudden appearance of a poem he'd written years ago in Kishinev, a spoof on the Virgin Mary which had never been published but had been passed around under the title of THE GABRILIAD. This one would not be as easy to explain as ANDRE CHENIER. His enemies had placed the looped rope carefully around his neck this time, and they were pulling it tighter. His throat was contracting. In the cab coach all the way over to the winter Palace, as he went past the Yusopov Garden, breath-takingly beautiful now, especially in autumn with the leaves turning golden brown, turning crimson as if the trees had suddenly been set ablaze, past the stately mansions that were like anachronistic castles of another age, past the baroque palaces with their long marble columns of Tuscany standing tall and majestic like sentries of medieval times, deep in amongst the tall majestic oak and pine trees, the boyar residences of Counts and Barons, Romanesque in architecture, an awesome quiet came over him and he could hear his own heart beating. And he wondered how he would explain this current blasphemy to the Emperor of the Holiest and vastest Empire on this earth. He remembered fragments of his poem, THE PROPHET.

Arise, prophet of Russia,
Don your shroud of shame,
Go, the noose around your neck,
To face the abominable Assassin.

He wondered with a strange kind of amused attachment, as if he sat separately in the carriage beside this crazy poet who was getting himself ready for the terrifying ordeal. He thought, perhaps I am beginning to enjoy these intellectual skirmishes. But blasphemy was as culpable as high treason in the eyes of the saintly Emperor. But to poke fun at the Holy Virgin was like advocating the overthrow of the Monarchy. What will you say to His Majesty, you fool? One thing is sure. You have too much pride to crawl before the Emperor and deny your authorship. As he went along the Nevsky Prospekt, he heard people as his carriage went down the wide expanse of boulevard.

"Alexander Pushkin! The Bard of the Decembrists!"

"Our own! Our own! Our very own!"

He felt proud as he saw the strollers pointing at him. He felt good. He was invincible. He left the cab and walked across the wide expanse of Senate Square. He stood now in the great Square on the other side, and stared up at the statue-in-bronze of Peter the Great astride his great horse with the frontlegs rearing upwards, the man who, through the sheer force of his mighty will and genius, constructed this magnificent city on the Finnish marshes. He felt a sense of his Russianness deeply in the place where he lived serenely and excitedly, felt at home with the history of this vast stretch of Holy Empire, its indomitable people, its voracious culture. He was a Russian with the blood of Africa coursing through his veins. He was Alexander Sergeievich Pushkin, great grandson of Ibrahim Petrovich Hannibal whose ancient ancestor made Rome tremble. He was proud.

But now, as he walked up the long endless marble steps to the Winter Palace, he broke into a sweat on this chilly autumn afternoon. He forgot he was amused, forgot also that he was the great grandson of Ibrahim Petrovich. He remembered only the lonely evenings in the room at Papa Insov's in old Kishinev. The anger, the joy he felt as he had written THE GABRILIAD. *"Don your shroud of shame."* His cherished indignation at the Imperial ukase forcing him into church every Sunday morning to be taken through a ritual in which he did not believe. *"Face the abominable assassin!"* The tremendous exhilaration he'd felt from poking fun at the fairy tale legend of the Immaculate Conception. *"The noose around your neck."*

He realized at this last moment that he had not only indulged himself like a little boy sticking out his tongue at His Imperial Majesty, but he had also poked fun at the faith of a people whom he avowed to love and whose instincts he professed to trust. People like the lowly muzhiks, the Russian masses, and above all, his nyanya, Arina Rodionovna, and his valet, Nikita Koslov. But all this was beside the point, he thought, as he went through that final door and heard himself announced.

"Alexander Sergeievich Pushkin, author."

There was no warm handshake. No expansive smiles this time. His Majesty sat behind his desk, stared at Pushkin with his grayish steel-blue eyes, picked up a manuscript from his long, wide mahogany desk with the glazed top and threw it over the desk at Pushkin.

Alexander Sergeievich felt weak in the knees as he stared at the title in bold script. THE GABRILIAD, his one way passage to the salt mines. He swallowed hard the coldness in his mouth. He stared at the manuscript, going through a charade of reading it, his mouth working painfully as he read nothing. He didn't need to read the poem. He could recite it in his sleep. His heart was beating rapidly. Thoughts collided in his exhausted mind. Thoughts of Anna Kern and her visit to Trigorskoye. She also knew the poem by heart. He could see the room at Papa Insov's in which the poem had been written. He remembered the joy he felt while writing it, the fun, the laughter he had known. He suppressed a smile that almost came to his lips. Why should he go to Siberia or to the dreaded Peter and Paul Fortress for a puerile prank he had committed in a fit of childish anger? He thought of the Decembrists. At least they went to prison for a noble purpose.

Then too, his ideas on religion were not that absolute now. He was being put in the ridiculous position of defending a proposition about which he was, at the very least, ambivalent. He had written an article ON RELIGION a few months before, in which, among other things he'd stated:

Finally I came to the conclusion that man found God precisely because He exists. It is impossible, even in the world of plastic forms, to discover anything that does not exist —a truth which was conveyed to me by Art. . . . A form cannot be devised! It has to be derived from something that actually is. Nor is it possible to invent sentiments, thoughts and ideas not planted in us, those having a common root with the mysterious instinct, which distinguishes a creature who at once feels and reasons from that which merely feels. This reality is as real as everything that we can touch, experience or behold. The people possess an innate longing for this kind of reality—The religious sentiment—which they even refuse to analyze. Religion created art and literature, in fact, everything that was great in ancient times. Everything is dependent on the religious feeling . . . and without it there would be no philosophy, no poetry, no ethics and no literature.

He almost knew the statement by heart. He had written it in his diary during one of those lonely nights in Mikhailovskoye, and had it published in a Moscow journal. Had gone to mass the next morning at the village church and worshiped with the muzhiks. And yet he could not deny his own creation.

Don your shroud of shame—His mouth could not form the words to do it. It would be like a father denying his own beloved infant. The Emperor gave him time to read the poem three or four times.

The Emperor cleared his throat. "Well—?"

"What is it you want of me, Your Majesty?" Pushkin asked. It was only at this very moment that he saw at the bottom of the page that it was dated, "June 19, 1829." He made up his mind very swiftly, even as the throbbing in the temples of his forehead quickened.

"This is the most blasphemous, most seditious piece of writing ever written by civilized man. Men have been taken to the block and put on the rack and burned at the stake and stoned to death for far lesser crimes." The Emperor seemed to be deliberately working himself into a rage.

"Surely, Sire, you can't seriously believe me capable of writing this."

"Your name *is* Alexander S. Pushkin?"

"Yes, Your Excellency, however—"

"You didn't expect my generosity to exceed the bounds of human decency and patriotism, did you? After the promises you made when I gave you your freedom. Look at the date."

"Sire, Your Majesty, I did not write this thing at any time. Someone is making trouble for me." Pushkin responded.

"If not you, then who?" The Emperor demanded.

"I have no idea, but I first read this very same poem years ago when I was a student at the Lycée at Tsarskoye Selo. I don't remember who the author was." At this moment Pushkin despised himself more than he'd ever in his entire life. He hated himself passionately. He felt a nausea moving from his stomach to his throat, and he fought hard to keep from vomiting.

Nicholas Romanov placed a Bible on the desk before the poet. "Do you swear that you are not the author of this scurrilous piece of sacrilegious garbage?"

Pushkin looked the Emperor in the eye, unblinkingly. He placed his right hand palm downward on the leather-bound gold-encrusted Holy Book. Perspiration poured from his brow, a coldness in his mouth and throat. "I swear to God I did not write it. I swear it on my mother's grave."

The Czar was silent for a moment. "Very well," he said. "Though I'm fully aware that your mother is alive and has no grave."

"Thank God for that," Alexander Sergeievich said.

The Emperor said as if talking to himself, "I do seem to remember hearing of the poem some years ago long before the date it's dated. It's clear there's someone who does not wish you well."

"Very very clear, Your Majesty." Pushkin quickly replied.

As he left the Palace he wiped the sweat from his face and from around his neck. Tears streamed down his face, unrestrained. He had denied a thing of his own creation. He wiped his eyes. He had escaped the looping rope again. Narrowly this time. The Holy Virgin or Somebody Up There must be watching over him. He smiled grimly as he went down the marble steps. He thought, perhaps His Majesty was beginning to enjoy his game of cat and mouse between himself and the poet.

Perhaps he had begun to enjoy it also.

CHAPTER SIX

The days, the months, the years had passed. At thirty Alexander Sergeievich felt ancient and decrepit. He was weary of the easy love affairs, the ballrooms and the drinking orgies. He was Number Three on the Moscow police gambling list. He had organized a magazine in opposition to Bulgarin's reactionary Anti-Pushkin journal. Bulgarin was an ex-policeman turned magazine editor. Pushkin believed he was still in the employ of the Czarist politseyskii, one of Benkendorf's Moscow spies. Alexander Sergeievich found himself doing most of the writing for the *Literary Gazette*; though Delvig was officially its editor-in-chief, and a few of his other literary comrades made their contributions, he in fact wrote most of the articles under various and varied pseudonyms.

Bulgarin used his magazine *Severnaya* (The Northern Bee) to attack his chosen enemies. It was, politically, a literary hatchet. He went for Alexander Pushkin with a vengeance. Even to the extent of attacking Pushkin's ancestry, with particular emphasis on his maternal great-grandfather.

Pushkin was silently enraged. The memory of his great-grandfather had always been a haven in a time of storm and stress. It was a private sanctuary he guarded with his dignity and shared with no other human since Grandma-ma Hannibal departed.

Pushkin sat down one evening in his study and wrote an answer to Bulgarin and published it in the *Gazette*. This time, he signed his own name to it.

Some literary buffoon said that my great-grandfather was bought by a skipper for a bottle of rum. Fine! And he was the greatest skipper of them all, Peter the First, and they were colleagues who worked side by side constructing this great city of St. Petersburg.

This same buffoon
Now calls me a bourgeois with pretentions
To nobility, But he,
Who heads his family tree?
A nobleman from Bourgeois Street.

Bourgeois Street was the red light district where Bulgarin first met his wife in an infamous brothel, Madame Dubinskya's Home For Wayward Girls.

The attacks came at Pushkin from all sides, inspired mostly by men close to His Imperial Majesty and apparently with Imperial blessings.

The Mercury accused him of having prostituted his talent to win favor at the Imperial Court.

"Pushkin is an imperial sycophant masquerading as a people's poet."

Alexander Sergeievich was infuriated. Not that he ever really gave a damn for the critics' approval. But the personal abuse in literary disguise from men whom he considered practically illiterate was a bit too much for his delicate stomach. It was in this state of mind that he wrote his famous TO THE POET, in which he proclaimed:

O poet, never value popular acclaim!
For thou dost hear fools' judgments and the crowd's reproof;
The present roar of zealous praise turns into blame;
But thou remainest steadfast, quiet and aloof.
For thou art king; live by thyself. In exaltation
Travel the free road, whither thy free mind will lead,
Perfecting the fruits of thy inspired meditations.
And never asking reward for a noble deed.

Pushkin was leading a life that he hated but could not escape. Rounds of endless balls and parties, whoring along with his hell-raising colleagues.

Up to your ears in gambling debts. Hounded again by debt collectors and police agents. Feeling strongly that your life needs stabilizing. Look to marriage as the only answer. When a man reaches your age it is time to be thinking about a wife and family, children. Your posterity. You get no pleasure jumping from one bed to another. Marriage is a stabilizer, and the Holy Virgin knows that you need stabilizing.

He fell in love with one woman after another, hoping to really care enough about someone to spend the remainder of his tortured days with. Late one evening, in a fit of extreme and rare self-pity, he wrote in his diary: "Sometimes my life is like an epigram, but generally it has been an elegy unending."

It was at one of these interminable parties that he inadvertently overheard a conversation. He had assumed his characteristic jaded pose, leaning against a long white column in the ballroom sipping ices.

"But of course, old friend, she died more than a year ago. Died of childbirth all alone in Italy."

Pushkin's heartbeat quickened. He immediately broke into a sweat. He knew a queasy sinking sensation where his stomach should have been. Don't be an alarmist, he told himself. There are millions of women in Italy. Women die every day all over the world.

"Alone, you say?"

"Oh yes, her husband had left her, and that bastard Yablovsky, he deserted her."

"Dreadful! She was such a beautiful and intelligent woman!"

"They do say though that it was Riznich's baby—"

Alexander Sergeievich did not remain to hear the rest of the conversation. How could his Amelia be dead? In the cold ground without him having any notion of it! Amelia dead? Buried underneath some foreign soil?

He should have had some consciousness of it. Some premonition. While he was gallivanting all over the place from Moscow to Saint Petersburg and back again, all the while she'd been all alone in some cold alien earth, a feast for foreign worms. He went home and searched his apartment till he found her note. He sank in a chair and stared bleary-eyed at it.

We have left this day for Italy. This has happened so suddenly there was not time to say goodbye and kiss your sweet sensual mouth. But be sure I shall return if you will have me and we will go away together. Nothing can keep me from you excepting death itself. I am Yours! I am forever yours!

Forever,
Your Amelia

He read it over again and again, as the tears spilled down his cheeks. He closed his eyes and tried to imagine Amelia dead, cold, stiff, rotting, smelling. He could not manage it. He felt he had betrayed his beloved. He looked around his study, as if he sensed her presence in the room. "She'll come back," he told himself. She'll come back. She gave her word she would come back to me. He undressed and went to bed mumbling to himself, "She will come back!" He lay in bed for hours but sleep refused to come to him. Why should he be able to sleep when Amelia was asleep forever?

He got out of bed, lit a candle and went to his desk. Perhaps if he wrote to her and made his message strong enough, perhaps she would come back to him. Perhaps his love could conquer death.

An insensitive mouth announced this death.
I listened indifferent to it all.
Where is love, where its torment? In my heart,
For the poor specter, so light,
For the sweet memory of days that are gone,
There are no more songs, no more tears.

295

He rose from his desk and walked the floor. "Nyet! Nyet! Hell no!" he shouted softly. "It cannot be!" He shouted loudly. "It cannot be that she is dead! I would have known it! Would have felt it!" He sat down again and wrote:

> You said to me: "One day soon,
> Beneath the blue of an unchanging sky,
> Among the olive trees, my friend
> Our lips will meet again."
> Your beauty, your many sufferings,
> Are inside a funerary urn.
> But the kisses you promised me?
> I am waiting. You owe them to me.

He could no longer see what he wrote. His eyes were blinded by the tears that spilled upon his manuscript.

> Come back, adorable phantom,
> As I knew you of old,
> Fair and chill as the dawn,
> Contorted in pain,
> Or like a distant star,
> Or like a sound, a breeze,
> Or a terrifying specter,
> I don't care! Come back! Come back!
> I do not call you here
> To punish those whose spite
> Has struck you down, my friend,
> Or to learn about the other world,
> Or relieve the jealous
> That clutches at me, But I want
> To tell you it hurts, I love you still. It hurts!
> I am yours . . . Come back! Come back! Come back!

He stayed in the house for days, stayed to himself, talked to himself, as if he really thought to conjure his beloved Amelia back to life.

He tried to write himself out of it, but it did not work. Nothing worked to get Amelia off his mind. He had not known she meant that much to him. Weeks went by. Then one day he got up and went outside. Nothing had changed. The world went on its jocular way. The flowers bloomed just as if she were alive. Wars. Rumors of abortive revolutions. Famine. Slavery prospered in the New World of America, serfdom in Imperial Russia. The days lengthened. Spring went blithely into summer and the long white nights. Rumors of wars. Fashion. Rhetoric. Revolution. But he knew that everything had changed. Though the gendarmes still breathed down his neck, he began to be himself again. He had to save himself from madness.

PRAY GOD THAT I MAY NOT GO MAD!

These days his waking hours were usually taken up with thoughts of death and his posterity. What was he doing with his life? If he died he would not even leave a child behind him. He wanted a wife, wanted children, wanted a family to love and be loved by. He had so much love to give.

Then one day Alexander Sergeievich went to a ball at a nobleman's baronial mansion. He stood there half listening to the music and watching the dancing, smelling the scents of the varied perfumes, his ears picking up the idle chatter, the sounds of them stomping a frenzied mazurka, the quadrilles and the polkas. His eyes wandered aimlessly over the gleaming parquet floors, when suddenly those dark-blue animated eyes, eyes that had seen everything, beheld a dark-eyed wasp-waisted girl in a white chiffon evening gown with golden circlets around her black curly head. A ripe red mouth, the plump lips doll-like and curvacious. He knew somehow immediately that his destiny was bound up with this dark-eyed vision of innocence and pulchritude. She was a Florentine Madonna come suddenly to life.

He heard a voice behind him say, "She is very lovely, isn't she?"

He turned and looked into the smiling face of Countess Budensky.

"There must be another word almost equal to describing her, Madame," he replied "but I cannot think of one, and words are the tools of my humble trade."

The Countess fanned her petite oval face and smiled. "Then it is right that the two of you should meet and fall madly in love at first sight. For you are the most romantic man in Russia and she is the most romantic beauty."

She took the poet's arm and led him across the floor to meet his unavoidable fate, he thought. As he neared her the ringlets around her head gave the illusion of a halo. Surely this child was an angel. Her eyes were black as midnight, pure and limpid. Her full scarlet lips perched tentatively in the lower middle of her saintly face. Virginal, chaste. She was the reincarnation of a Tuscan goddess.

"Mademoiselle Natalya Goncharova, may I have the privilege and pleasure to introduce to you our national pride, the greatest writer in all the Russias, Monsieur Alexander Sergeievich Pushkin."

Natalya curtsied almost imperceptibly. At first she stared at him with a shocked expression, as if he were someone come back from the dead. Then she blushed profusely. She looked into his eyes shyly and away again and murmured a polite acknowledgment. It was obvious she'd never heard of the poet.

It was the second time in his life that a woman had rendered this romantic and articulate poet speechless. He did not even take her hand and kiss it. He felt like a shy and callow school boy and at the same time he felt a fatherly attachment toward her.

Whatever the deeper feeling, he was hers forever. She was his ultimate implacable fate. God's irrevocable Will. And there was simply nothing for it.

297

CHAPTER SEVEN

A few mornings later, after several sleepless nights, Alexander Sergeievich went to the home of Count Tolstoy and asked him to attend the home of Madame Goncharova and ask, on his behalf, for the hand of her lovely daughter. Count Tolstoy had told him Natalya's father was a mad man who lived alone in the Goncharov attic.

The next day in the Goncharov drawing room, Count Tolstoy affirmed, "He's the greatest writer in all of Russia!"

Madame Goncharova parried with, "But she is a mere child of sixteen, an innocent!"

"But he's utterly devastated by his love for her."

Madame had come to Moscow from the Provinces precisely for the purpose of auctioning off one, or hopefully, all three of her available girls to the highest bidders. The season was drawing to a close and there had been no outstanding offers. Natalya was the youngest and by far the prettiest.

"Poets are known to be so impetuous," Madame suggested to Count Tolstoy.

It was the third time she had brought the other two girls to Moscow for the marriage season, and living was expensive in the Second Capital. Money was not a thing that the erstwhile wealthy house of Goncharov possessed in great abundance. Madame Goncharova was desperate but at the same time very shrewd. What was a poet, financially speaking? But one must always be dignified and tactful, as dictated by one's class.

"My sweet child is used to a certain standard of living."

"To be sure, Madame. A poet of Monsieur Pushkin's stature, his books are sold all over Russia. He is the highest paid writer in the entire country."

Her dark eyes gleamed like glow worms. Madame had been a beauty in her day, when she had married Monsieur Goncharov who had inherited a legacy of wealth and industry from a great-grandfather in whose blood flowed a combination of landed gentry and crafty Kulaks and who had founded the famous Goncharov Linen Factory. By the time the inheritance reached Madame's husband it had been squandered on grandiose living, stately mansions, fabulous French mistresses and prostitutes. The line infused originally by hard work and Kulak cunning had been bled white with ennobled great White Russian boisterous living.

Count Tolstoy asked respectfully, "Then what shall I tell Monsieur Pushkin? Should he lose all hope then?"

Madame Goncharova smiled. "Patience." Then added slyly, "She is a mere child. Really."

Later that same evening, Count Tolstoy told the impatient lover, "Patience, dear fellow. Patience is the lady's answer. What other answer could a lady of her standing give?"

The next day our poet wrote Madame Goncharova a letter then took off without Imperial permission for the Caucasus where a war was raging with the Turks.

Dear Madame Goncharova: Upon my knees, I express my tears of gratitude at your reply. You have not said yes, neither have you refused me, thereby giving me reason for the faintest hope, because of which I am enthralled with joyous feelings. I understand and agree fully with your cautious prudence and concern. Notwithstanding, it is with a sick and desolate heart that I take departure for the Caucasus intoxicated with happiness and the image of the celestial creature who owes her birth and undoubtedly her beauty to none other than yourself . . . I shall be eternally grateful.

Madame Goncharova sighed and shrugged her shoulders. The utterings of an impulsive and romantic poet were beyond her comprehension.

Madly by stagecoach Alexander Sergeievich rode relentlessly back through the now-nostalgic years of his youth and exile, conjuring up memories long forgotten. Riding day after day across the broad steppes, and now in the foothills, he felt thrills chase another thrill across his slender shoulders. Civilization had come to the Caucasus. Where once there had been caves in the mountains, now there were isbas. Encampments had changed into tiny villages. Many other changes were in evidence, but the Caucasus had not been tamed or fully colonized. Nothing could deny the awesome stateliness and grandeur of these mountain ranges. He went from place to place looking for the war. He wanted foolishly to be in the thick of the fighting. Friends had warned him not to go, argued feverishly with him.

Zukovsky told him, "Your life is enough like Byron's. Don't tempt fate any further."

Uncle Basil urged him, "And by the Holy Virgin, don't dare go to Georgia. Our writer, Griboedov, went there and was recently assassinated. Don't tempt destiny and coincidence."

Naturally he headed straight for Georgia. He arrived in Tiflis, capital of the Georgia province, a country of swarthy earthy people with a raging lust for life, rakish caps and wild mustaches. A crazy mixture of Tartars, Gypsies, Armenians, Uzbeks, Georgians, Russians, Persians, Germans, French, a cosmopolitan center that was both East and West. The twain had met and clashed. It was wine country endlessly abounding in fine grape orchards.

Pushkin was toasted everywhere he went. It seemed that everybody knew the name of Alexander Pushkin. He raised hell all over that part of the Russian world. But where in God's name was the battle front? He sought the regiment in which his brother Leo served, but it eluded him. Finally, by chance, he found his long-life comrade, Nicholai Raevsky, Captain of a battle-weary regiment that had just returned from the front for a brief respite. The two friends embraced and almost wept for joy. It had been a long long time. So much water under the Imperial bridge. His little sister Marya in a far-away Siberia with an elderly husband she did not love. His brother Alexander in the bastille of the infamous Peter and Paul Fortress.

Nicholai could not believe it, Pushkin, looking for a war, attired in tight-fitting trousers and frock coat and high hat. He gathered his tired embattled comrades around him in his tent and announced proudly, "Tovarischi, I have the distinct pleasure and honor to present to you an old friend and distinguished colleague, Monsieur Alexander Sergeievich Pushkin!"

The men stared at Pushkin and back at the captain, absolutely certain that he was playing some kind of joke on them. It could not possibly be true, that this eccentric looking fellow underneath the high hat was actually the famous Alexander Pushkin? Slowly they began to realize that this was really the great man in the flesh. The Bard of the Decembrists!

They drank much wine from the rarest grapes far into the night.

"Long live Pushkin! Long live Alexander Pushkin!"

They gave him a special tent all to himself, despite his protests that he wanted to live like the other men, wanted to be of them, with them. He was their hero and they insisted on treating him as one. A Russian treasure they stood guard over. Even as he accepted their adoration and good intentions, his heart began to know again that dreaded outside feeling.

A few nights later Pushkin was awakened by the sounds of whoops and hollering about a hundred yards from where he slept. Footsteps running down the regimental street. Perhaps he had caught up with the war at last. Mikhail Abramokovich, a lieutenant in Nicholai Raevsky's dragoon regiment, ran into the tent. "Come, Alexander Sergeievich! Come! This is what we've waited for!"

Pushkin's heart beat wildy in his chest, as he sleepily stumbled around the tent getting into his clothes. "Are they here at last!"

"Of course they're here! Come on! Come on!"

He stumbled out of the tent and trotted behind Mikhail Abramokovich down the road between the tents. As he neared the end of the regimental street the revelry got louder. Like a host of frenzied banshees on the loose. What was going on? Had they taken prisoners? As he came closer he realized that the noise came from the very last tent, the vast recreation tent.

"Yeeeeee-Owwww!"

He thought, surely it was one of those crazy dreams of his.

"Come, Alexander Sergeievich! Come on! Hurry!"

He followed the dragoon lieutenant into the recreation tent. Emptied whiskey bottles littered the sawdust-covered floor. Drunken soldiers in various stages of nakedness falling over one another. The carnal smell of fornication and female flesh violently violated. Young Turkish women with their clothes torn from them, some covered with blood. Older women, crying, sobbing, weeping, pleading to the dragoons to have mercy on them. "Please, Your Excellencies! Please, have mercy!" But there was no mercy. Women with crying babes in their arms. Fun-loving dragoons held the pitiful women down while fellow dragoons lined up and orgy-raped them.

The smell of alcohol and opium assaulted Pushkin's nostrils. Shouts of "That's right! Fight back! By the Holy Virgin, I love to yebat a spirited mare like you!"

"Scratch me, will you, you monkey-faced daughter of a swine!" The sound of slapping.

"Spread them legs open, you devil's bitch! You know you live for nothing else! Yebat!"

A dragoon slapped a little girl's face. "Be still, you daughter of a bitch's kitten!"

Alexander Sergeievich was immobile, at first. He could not believe what he was seeing. Surely he was having one of his nightmares. Throbbing forehead, heat in his collar, sweat dripped into his angry eyes. These could not be his comrades, the men with whom he'd gotten drunk several nights before. Hell no! These were not men. They were not Russian soldiers. These were mad dogs.

He felt himself being pulled toward a corner of the tent where a girl lay cringed and weeping.

"This one we saved for you, Alexander Sergeievich! By the Holy Saints, she's probably a virgin. And they are rare among these hot-blooded Turkish bitches."

Pushkin saw that the frightened thin-shouldered child could be no more than fourteen. Her large dark eyes, black as the night, filled now with a terrible fear, her oval face pinched with hunger reminded him of Nina.

"Please, Master! Please! Spare me! Spare me! Do not rape me! I will be your servant for life!"

"Shut up, you devil's puppy!" the dragoon shouted. "You're in the presence of nobility."

He turned to Pushkin. "How does this one suit your fancy, Alexander Sergeievich? I'd swear on my mother's grave this sniveling puppy is a goddamn virgin."

Pushkin went toward the whimpering terrified girl, took her hand and pulled her toward him, and whispered softly "Don't worry, little one. I shan't harm you." He took the freightened girl up in his arms and went with her kicking, out of the tent.

"Oh, I understand, Your Excellency. You want her all to yourself in private. Remember that I saved her for you, Alexander Sergeievich," the dragoon lieutenant called after him.

He took the girl to his tent and left her sobbing on his cot. "Stay here till I return. You'll be safe here." He ran up the path toward Raevsky's tent.

He had to shake the captain awake. "Wake up, Nicholai Ivanovich. How can you sleep through all this bedlam? Your soldiers have gone crazy!"

Nicholai sat up on the side of his cot rubbing his eyes. "What's the matter, Alexander Sergeievich?"

"You ask me 'what's the matter'? Have you lost your hearing then? They're having an orgy down there, raping all those defenseless women." Pushkin shouted.

"Oh that—it happens every time we take a village. It's expected in the ways of war. It's traditional." Nicholai yawned nervously.

Pushkin stared at his friend incredulously. "What in the hell are you talking about?"

"Don't be naive. They do the same thing when they take one of our villages. It's expected. Those women are contraband of war. To the victor belongs the spoils."

"You mean you're not going to do anything about it?" Pushkin asked.

"There's nothing I can do about it. The men would mutiny. The most I can do is not take part in it." He replied.

Pushkin backed out of the tent and ran back toward his own, the din of the recreation room roaring in his ears, his heart beating as if it would leap from his chest. He went quietly into his tent and got his pistol. The girl lay on his cot still sobbing.

Running down the street now toward the great bedlam, his heartbeat thumping in his forehead, sweat pouring from all over his body. He entered the recreation tent. Nothing had changed. The bacchanal continued worse than before. He was almost overcome by the smell of opium, alcohol and lively copulation. He shouted a couple of times for silence. But no one listened. He raised his pistol and shot up through the tent. Everything came to a halt.

"Alright," Pushkin growled in a trembly voice. "All of you soldiers clear out of here and leave these women alone."

"But Your Excellency!" a dragoon grumbled.

"Next time I won't miss, I promise you!" He kicked another on his naked buttocks.

Was this the war he had sought to fight in? These were his comrades. "You goddamn fornicating swine! You ought to be ashamed of yourselves!" They knew he would carry out his threat, and he had the reputation of being the deadliest shot in Russia. They all straggled out in disarray grumbling, cursing and protesting.

The women dragged themselves toward him whimpering; "Thank you, Master. May Allah bless you all of your days."

He turned to leave saying, "Stay in this tent till I return."

He went to his tent and brought the girl back.

Now the women stood around him, some kneeling, kissing his hand, his boots, the legs of his tightly-fitting trousers, mumbling "Thank you," and "Allah's blessing be with you." He spoke gruffly. "Go back to your villages and stay in your isbas till the soldiers leave. Don't leave your isbas for anything."

He went back to his tent breathing freely through his mouth and nostrils, drinking in the fragrance of the clean night air, feeling good about what he'd just accomplished. It had been a long time since he had felt so good about himself.

Alexander Sergeievich slept peacefully that night.

The next day he went into the general's tent and met an old pasha, who, when he heard that he was Alexander Pushkin, bowed low to him and kissed his hand. "Blessed is the man who meets a great poet. The poet is far greater than a rich man or a general or an emperor. For wealth dwindles away, generals are killed in battle, empires fall, but the words and wisdom of the poet abideth forever."

One day the battle front finally caught up with Alexander Sergeievich. Suddenly they heard the whooping cries of a Turkish cavalry as it swooped down on the encampment. Pushkin leapt upon his horse and rode with the regiment of dragoons to meet the charge. One moment he was in the midst of the dragoons, the next moment he was somehow isolated and face to face with a Turkish cavalry man mounted with his sword aloft and charging toward him. A feeling of vertigo raced through his head and chills swept across his shoulders as he spurred his own horse and raised his sword and charged forth, top hat and all, to meet his adversary. At that moment someone shouted, "Pooshkin!"

Nicholai saw the Turk coming down upon his most valuable and crazy comrade. He raised his pistol and fired. The horse fell from under the Turk. Pushkin leapt from his great horse, losing his top hat. He stood over the fallen Turk, his sword upraised. He lowered his sword as he looked down into the fearless dark eyes of the Turk who seemed to be no more than eighteen. He raised his sword again to hack off the defenseless man's head, but something in the boldness of the young Turk's eyes prevented him from striking. Another dragoon rode up, leapt from his horse, and separated the young Turk's head from his body. And Pushkin watched the bloody young head, as it rolled down a sharp incline and disappeared into a ravine.

The next day the general ordered Pushkin out of the area, unqualifiedly. He wrote an official order commanding Pushkin to return to Moscow or Saint Petersburg. Pushkin was more than ready. He had seen enough of what war did to men. Enough to last a lifetime.

CHAPTER EIGHT

Back in Moscow from the Caucasus, his first stop was the household of the Goncharovs.

Madame Goncharova was still the same. Even more so. And Madame had done her research on Alexander Pushkin. Certainly, he was the greatest writer in all the Russias, but what did it mean, financially, status-wise? He also had a reputation for renowned debauchery, and he was considered to be the "bard" of those horrible Decembrists. There was the question of his African blood. She had numerous reservations, and still she would not dismiss our poet entirely. For, as beautiful as her daughter indisputedly was, the eligible young men of Moscow, ennobled, titled, rich or otherwise, were not looking for impecunious young women, no matter how beautiful. So keep this Alexander Pushkin on a leash. Also, they did say, the Emperor had forgiven him. The Czar, Himself, had reputedly called him, "The most intelligent man in Russia."

Meanwhile lovely beautiful Natasha was completely impassive. She ventured to have nothing to say in the matter. She would be there and not be there when Madame and Pushkin haggled back and forth, as if it had nothing to do with her at all. Hers was a cold and marble-like beauty. Pure and chaste, undiluted by thought and the warmth of human feelings. Whatever her mother decided, that was it. They were a sharp contrast in personalities. Pushkin was an unusually verbal person, a genius of the written and the spoken word; Natasha was entirely inarticulate.

It was a battle of wits between Madame Goncharova and Alexander Sergeievich Pushkin. A game of chess, and they were forever checkmating one another. She was like a fishwife haggling in the Moscow marketplace. Pushkin reached back into his repertoire of strategies, and it worked, temporarily at least. He simply stopped visiting the Goncharovs, started chasing other beautiful women, pretended he had given up hope and was looking elsewhere for a bride.

Madame Goncharova sent for the poet. She required a discussion with him. He took his time getting to see her. He might have been having a change of heart. Two weeks after he got her message, he made an appearance.

"Where have you been, dear boy? We thought something terrible had happened to you. Thought maybe you had gone off to that terrible war again and had been wounded, or even worse." Her voice was dripping with concern for him.

"No, Madame. I'm quite all right. I've just been very busy of late and had also given up all hope. It appeared you did not think highly of me and thought me unworthy of your virginal daughter. So I threw myself into my work in an effort to forget it all."

"Whatever could have given you that idea, my dear son?" Madame Goncharova was cooing like a dove.

Pushkin said, "Now where could I have gotten that distressing notion that you disapproved of me? I must have dreamed it. Sometimes I have terrible dreams."

Madame said, "Foolish boy, forget about your silly dreams. Just answer two questions for me, my dear. How do you stand financially? Can you provide for my innocent daughter to live in the manner to which she is accustomed?"

Alexander Sergeievich almost smirked. He had also done his research. Not that it mattered. But he knew that though they were aristocrats, the Goncharovs were not the wealthiest family in Moscow. He knew that darling Natasha was wearing last year's fashions to this year's balls and parties. She was just so beautiful it made no difference. He was too familiar with the situation of his own family not to recognize pretentious aristocrats when he met them.

He assured her. "I make a comfortable living from my writing, Madame. Your daughter will not be deprived. She will live as she is accustomed, and as she certainly deserves. She is undoubtedly a princess and I shall dedicate my life to see that she lives as such."

Madame warmed up the negotiations. "One more thing. There is a question as to your status with the Emperor. If you are in his good graces, then nothing can stand in the way."

Pushkin looked away at his chaste beloved, and she stared shyly down at the floor.

It went against the grain for him to involve swines like Benkendorf and Nicholas Romanov in his personal affairs. He thought to himself, I will not do it! I simply refuse to do it. To go to this avowed reactionary, Benkendorf, for a stamp of approval from the cruel despot Czar Nicholas, to justify himself before the mother of his bride-to-be! He wouldn't do it!

Meanwhile, Natasha sat there, dark haired and dark eyed, the features of her lovely and angelic face immobile and without emotion. He thought, what is she thinking? Why doesn't she say something? We're discussing *her* future as well as my own. The dear one cleared her throat, and he thought surely she would speak this time. He waited, he held his breath, but not a single word came from her. It did not matter though, because he simply would not go to Benkendorf, not even for Natalya Goncharova.

But he did. Because if this was the only impediment in the way of the blissfulness of marriage to this beautiful creature, he would not let his great pride stand in the way.

It took three weeks to get an answer from His Most Imperial Majesty through Chief Benkendorf.

> Your position vis-à-vis the Imperial Court is clear as clear can be, unless you choose it not to be. His Majesty has counseled me, not as Chief of the Secret Police, but as a friend whose counsel he values, to assure you that no gendarme has been instructed to keep you under surveillance. I myself have given you advice from time to time always as a paternal gesture and always in your interest and with good will, never as an officer of the law. Please feel free to show this letter to whomever you wish.

The betrothal was formally announced by Madame Goncharova on May 6, 1830. The war had been won. But the skirmishes were just beginning. Before Alexander Sergeievich could smack his lips over his magnificent victory, Madame began another series of tactics. Attack, retreat and then postponement. Hurry up and wait. Go forward and delay. The sly questions she asked him, the implications, the continual innuendos. Words slipped out like debauchery, atheism, subversion. African blood.

"How do you stand with His Majesty?"

"You have the letter from Count Benkendorf, Madame." Sometimes he felt that the days of the Inquisition had returned.

He stared at Natasha as she sat there demurely beside her mother. He blamed her mother for Natasha's devastating quietude. His romantic heart sensed a storm within her slowly building, imperceptibly, every passing second, every tick-tock of her celestial eternity. Building like the terrible awesome silence before a virulent tempest.

He needed desperately to believe and persist. He thought: I perceive in you, my beloved, a fire slowly burning, stoking itself, unnoticed by those who have eyes to see and yet walk blindly through this life seeing nothing of the needs of such as you. If only I might rescue you from this babbling scheming witch-of-a-woman, then my beloved would bloom and blossom forth and soar high above the majestic Caucasus. There are no heights that you could not attain.

He thought, the fire builds slowly now, stoking itself in the womb of your profound compassion, you who have such a lust for life, a rage to live, a thirst that mere convention cannot hope to quench or sate. And one day, the heat of your passion and compassion will expand and expand and ultimately explode. And then— let the whole world run for its protection.

He had continued staring at Natasha, and now her face was turning crimson as she stared everywhere but into his animated eyes. Then he knew he had been right about her. There was much much more to her than was reflected on the surface. His heart palpitated as rapidly as his mind composed a poem to her:

Quiet one, conjurer of dreams,
I sense the fire burning in you.
I linger near, but fear to come too close,
For fear the fire burning might consume us both,
But I am one like you,
Who loves to play with fire
And to live dangerously.

He was brought rudely from his daydream by the babbling voice of Madame Goncharova.

"They say you have a terrible reputation for debauching women." Her dark eyes blinking rapidly. "My daughter is an inexperienced baby."

"Madame Goncharova, you may rest assured, your daughter's happiness will always be my first and ultimate concern. There will never be another in my life but—"

She approached him from yet another angle. "Natalya simply must have a lovely trousseau that befits her beauty and her station in life. She would be the laughing stock of the young ladies in her class if she were to wed without a trousseau."

Trousseau—trousseau—where would he get money for a trousseau? For a moment, Pushkin could not find the words any easier than he could find the money.

"Surely, my son, you would not have the dear child embarrassed, a writer of your standing and sensibilities would be too gallant to have this happen to your beloved." She babbled on. As articulate as Alexander Sergeievich Pushkin was, he was helpless to cope with this scheming woman. He told her not to worry. The money would be forthcoming for the trousseau. But creditors were already following him around as religiously as the Secret Police. No matter, he would win it all at cards. His luck had to change sometime, somehow. His luck did change. It went from bad to worse. He lost heavily. He played cards against books he had not written yet. He sank deeper and deeper into debt.

Then one day he woke up and realized it was autumn, and as usual he had a seizure of the writing fever. So off he went to his father's estate at Boldino to write.

The manor house was all wood, constructed on high stilts up from the ground. The courtyard was one great mess of black mud and a flock of scrawny cackling chickens who seemed to be suffering from an advanced case of galloping consumption and dysentery. Chicken dung all over everything. Each time he left the manor house he had to pick his way gingerly out of the courtyard. Dirt-poor peasants struggling in the fields looked to the poet like starving ghosts from yesteryears.

The first thing to do was to call the serfs together and advise them of their almost nonexistent rights, then advise them on problems of health and preventive medical treatment. He would have freed them all out of hand, but he remembered the meaninglessness of such a gesture when he had tried it in Mikhailovskoye. There was rumor of a near cholera epidemic. They bowed and scraped to their addle-headed lord and master. He was the most improbable lord of the land these wily muzhiks had ever seen.

After going through these unlikely motions he settled down to the thing for which the Lord above created him. The verses flowed from him like the Neva in floodtide. It was autumn, his most creative season. So he wrote AUTUMN.

I

October comes at last. The grave is shaking
The last reluctant leaves from naked boughs.
The autumn cold has breathed, the road is freezing
The brook still sounds behind the miller's house,
But the pond's hushed; now with his pack my neighbor
Makes for the distant fields—his hounds will rouse
The woods with barking, and his horse's feet
will trample cruelly the winter's wheat.

II

This is my time! What is the Spring to me?
Thaw is a bore: mud running thick and stinking
Spring makes me ill: my mind is never free
From dizzy dreams, my blood's in constant ferment.
Give me instead Winter's austerity,
The snow's under the moon—and what is gayer
Than to glide lightly in a sleigh with her
Whose fingers are like fire beneath the fur?

III

And oh, the fun, the steel-shod to trace a pattern
In crystal on the river's glassy face!
But there's a limit—nobody could face
Six months of snow—even that cave dweller,
The bear would growl enough in such a case.
Sleigh-rides with young Armidas pall, by Jove,
And you turn sour with loafing by the stove.
Oh, darling Summer, I could cherish you,
If heat and dust and gnats and flies were banished.
These dull the mind, the heart grows weary, too.
we, like the meadows, suffer drought; thought withers.
Drink is our only hope, and how we rue
Old woman winter, at whose funeral banquet

Pancakes and wine were served, but now we hold
Memorial feasts of ices, sweet and cold.
They say ill things of the last day of autumn;
But I, friend reader, not a one will hear;
Her quiet beauty touches me as surely
As does a wistful child, to no one dear.
She can rejoice me more, I tell you frankly,
Than all the other seasons of the year.
I am a humble lover, and I could
Find singularly much in her that's good.

Oh, mournful season that delights the eyes,
Your farewell beauty captivates my spirit
I love the pomp of nature's fading dyes,
The forest garmented in gold and purple,
The rush of noisy winds and the pale skies
Half-hidden by the clouds in darkling billows,
And the rare sun-ray and the early frost,
And threats of grizzled Winter, heard and lost.

Each time that Autumn comes I blood afresh;

. . . .
. . . .

My heart beats fast with lightly leaping blood.

. . . .

Our poet truly bloomed afresh in autumn. And then there were the TALES OF
BELKIN! Wonderful stories told in prose. Prose! He was at long last writing prose!
He could not have stopped the flow if he had wanted to. THE SHOT, THE BLIZZARD,
THE UNDERTAKER, THE STATION MASTER, THE QUEEN OF SPADES, THE YOUNG LADY, PEASANT
GIRL. His head grew dizzy with accomplishment. He wrote in clear crisp and un-
cluttered prose with no word or motion wasted. He did very little rewriting, which
was unusual for him. From prose he literally flowed into his "four little tragedies,"
THE COVETOUS KNIGHT, MOZART AND SALIERI, THE FEAST IN THE TIME OF PLAGUE and THE
STONE GUEST, taking Don Juan as the hero of the latter tragedy. It's good! he
thought. It's damn good! All of it's good! I'm happy and I'm free. I could stay here
forever!

Poetry poured from his pen like a fountain that would never cease. He wrote a
humorous narrative poem, THE LITTLE HOUSE IN KOLOMNA. Though he was not sure
he believed in God, he felt Godlike. He felt at the very least that God had touched
him, blessed him. For he knew that everything he wrote was good. He could feel it
in every marrow of his bones, as he sat at the rickety table far into the candle-
lighted night in a constant glow of creative ecstasy and listened to the pouring rain

outside and the rain that came inside through the leaky roof. He reached back and dug deep into the days and nights spent alone with his nyanya, for his inspiration. And he was inspired! Thank you my Matushka! Thank you Grandpa-pa Ibrahim Petrovich! Thank you Grandma-ma Hannibal! He even gave thanks to the Holy Virgin. He had finished EUGENE ONEGIN, and the Emperor had given permission for BORIS GODUNOV to be produced and published in its original state. Morning, noon and through the night he worked. Letters came from Madame Goncharova. "My dear boy, what about the trousseau?"

To hell with the trousseau! Pushkin thought. He didn't want a trousseau. He wanted Natalya, he didn't care about her dresses. He would take her in the raw if it came to that.

Doubts began to assail him. What did he need with marriage? A family? What in the devil for?

He remembered the letter he had received from Madame Kitrova in which she warned him against the prosaic aspects of the institution of matrimony. "It castrates the creative spirit which must be free to go wherever it is moved to go. There must always be the threat of starvation for an artist to be inspired. Marriage for a man of genius like yourself can only lead to obesity, complacency and a complete humdrum existence. For a poet this is suicide. All this distress I felt, when I heard of your betrothal."

From Boldino he had written Anton Delvig: "The only happily married people are imbeciles!"

And now the apprehensions came. He stood up from his desk and walked the floor. Could a man of his debauched experience make a pure girl like Natasha happy? Would it indeed castrate his creativity? Even as the cholera epidemic raged around him, he began to dream of death. The news reached him that Delvig had died suddenly of a heart attack. Death! Death! Delvig dead—Arina Rodionovna dead—it was the finality of death that staggered his imagination. Amelia dead! Death on a great white horse became a ghost that stalked his every dream. Still the fountain of his creativity spurted forth.

Waking from a dream of death one morning he began to write "My Monument." EXEGI MONUMENTUM:

"Unto myself I reared a monument not built
By hands, a track thereto the people's feet will tread;
Not Emperor Alexander's shaft is as lofty as my pillar
That proudly lifts its unsubmissive head.
Not wholly shall I die—but in my lyre my spirit
Shall incorruptible and bodiless, survive—
And I shall now be renown as long as under heaven
One poet yet remains alive.

He stopped and listened to the rain outside. He did not need to finish this one yet. He'd put it aside till later. He had plenty of time. He planned a long creative life.

Dreams had always been a great influence in his life. Sometimes he would wake up in the morning exhausted before he met the day. Sometimes he would awake early in the morning, usually from a dream, and he'd know he had been pursuing some secret of his art, some answer to the problems of this world, the human spirit, and he would know that he had awakened too soon, had not captured all the wisdom that was meant for only him to know. How to create a world of beauty in lieu of poverty and ignorance and ugliness. He would lie there trying desperately to fall asleep again and piece his dream together. Sometimes he'd lie there until his head began to ache and throb. There was no one to discuss his visions with.

He longed for his Amelia. If he shared his vistas with other men or women they would think him weird and brainless. Where was his articulate Svetlina? Where was Anna Kern? He hated Fate and Destiny with a passion. He believed that men and women must fight against an intransigent Fate. Human beings should work at changing their destiny to the ultimate of their abilities. One night he wrote in his diary:

If whimsical Fate destined a man or woman to be born a serf, then he or she, the serf, has a responsibility to wage unrelenting battle against Fate to change his situation. Although Death is the ultimate and inevitable Destiny of all men, all negatives that lie between should be struggled against. Man's mission is to change the world. It is the ultimate *raison d'etre* for humankind.

Then one night he had a dream of Olga Kalashnikova. It was less a dream than nightmare. All day long the next day he could not get her off his mind. What did he need with a family, he thought. He already had one. He had Olga Kalashnikova and a son. But perhaps it was a darling girl. It made no difference. Occasionally he had sent rubles to Olga, accompanied by a letter inquiring as to her health and well being, and she had always answered him. But after awhile the handwriting got shakier and finally was indecipherable, then ultimately the letters stopped coming. He did not know what had become of her or their child who would be more than four years old by now. Then suddenly he realized she must be nearby, he was, after all in Boldino.

With his faithful valet, Nikita Koslov, he went from place to godforsaken place asking for Olga Kalashnikova, all in vain. The muzhiks seemed suspicious of him. Finally after days of searching, he found Olga's father, a tall gangling consumptive-looking man, as scrawny as the chickens that walked around in front of his shack. He was drunk, his eyes were red as he stumbled around in front of his isba stepping in chicken excrement, not bothering to avoid it.

"Where's your daughter?"

"Who are you, Your Excellency?" The man looked at Pushkin with suspicion.
"What business is it of yours?" Nikita Koslov interjected. "Don't you know
how to act before your betters? You're to answer questions, not to ask them. This is
your master. What are you hiding, you sly dog?"

The drunken man swayed from side to side. It had started drizzling. The man
looked from Nikita Koslov to Pushkin. He removed his hat respectfully in a
drunken confusion, as the rain now came down in chilling sheets.

Alexander Sergeievich repeated the question. "Where are Olga Kalashnikova
and the baby?"

"Bell me, your honor," the man answered stupidly. "They was just here a minute ago. Mayhaps they went over there to the commissary. It's down the road a
half a verst." The man hacked and coughed and spat into the chicken droppings
that surrounded him.

Pushkin turned to leave. The old caretaker said, "Ain't you going to leave a
few kopeks for your wife and child, your Nobleness? I'm a poor man and—"

"Watch your tongue, you thievish devil," Nikita Koslov responded sharply.
"The master has no wife." Alexander Sergeievich had turned and put his hand in
his pocket.

Nikita Koslov said to him, "Never you mind, dear boy. I'll take care of this
thieving son of a swine. I'll give him kopeks all right. Before you turn your back
he'd drink it up in vodka."

They started toward the commissary. Behind their backs they could hear the
old man cursing and mumbling to himself, as he stumbled around in the chicken
dung.

They had not gone many steps when they heard footsteps behind them and
heard a woman's voice call out. "Your Excellencies—just a moment, Your Excellencies."

They turned and waited for a big-boned poorly dressed woman. She wore a
heavy long ragged dirty bleached-out-by-time caftan that dragged the ground. It
had once belonged to some noble gentleman years ago. "Your honor, there's no use
of you going to the commissary. You won't find Olga Kalashnikova there."

Alexander Sergeievich asked, "Who are you and what do you mean?"

"I'm Elisa Kalashnikova, your lordship, Olga's stepmother. I will take you to
her, if you'll follow me."

They followed the woman through and around a series of tumbled-down
shacks and came out on a lonely graveyard. Pushkin's heart knew a funny fearsome
feeling, a sickly strange sensation in his stomach and a chill across his shoulders, as
they followed the woman stepping around unkept mounds of grassy graves, until
they came to a mound with the weeds and grass grown over it with a wooden slab
in the ground with a poorly scrawled misspelled inscription on it.

OLGA KALOSHNIKOVA PUSHKINA AND CHILD

DIED 1825

REST IN PACE

312

Pushkin's eyes filled and the tears spilled freely down his cheeks, and he only half heard the woman, babbling. "I done it Your Excellencies. I write the inscription on the tombstone. It ain't nothing but a piece of wood I stuck it in the ground myself."

He turned toward Nikita Koslov and saw that his eyes had also filled with tears. Alexander Sergeievich thought, what was it with him that everything he touched withered and died? Was his the kiss of death? Death struck down everyone who truly loved him. He remembered all the sweet moments he had shared with her at Mikhailovskoye. He could feel her now in his arms, could smell that special smell about her, blue-eyed and flaxen tressed. And trusting. How could it be that she no longer lived and breathed? How could it happen and he not know, not feel the sense of loss till now? Were all he loved destined to an early grave? His shoulders shook with sobs. He turned to the woman. "Why? How did it happen?"

"Died in childbed, Your Nobleness, and the dear baby was born already dead. My poor husband wanted them rubles. Olga was not my daughter, but I loved her as if she was my own. Don't be too harsh with my husband, Your Excellency. He's a poor man, Your Lordship, and he's mighty sick."

Nikita Koslov said, "I'll give him poor and sick, the swine! He's sick from being drunk with vodka."

Pushkin mumbled, "Thank you," to the woman and put several rubles in her hand and embraced her. He turned and went back to the manor house. He tried to drink himself into forgetfulness. How could Olga Kalashnikova be no more? He remembered the day she left him in Mikhailovskoye, the courageous smile on her tremorous lips, as he put her in the telega and sent her on her way. Even as she smiled he knew that brave smile was to hide the tears that were just there on the other side of her eyes. He could not blame Olga's drunken and decrepit father. It was he, Alexander Sergeievich, who had made her pregnant and then sent her to her death! *He, the vice-sodden monster of THE VILLAGE.*

He tried to write himself out of the muck and mire and sorrow of his great guilt and shame, but Olga Kalashnikova was there all around him on every page of manuscript—her smell, the taste of her in his mouth, in his contracting throat, like a lovely phantom. She was omnipresent, an omnipresence in which he suffered and indulged himself.

One morning before daybreak, he was awakened by a presence in his room. It was black dark outside, and the cold autumn rain was descending steadily in freezing sheets. There was a cold sweat on his forehead and a cold taste in his mouth and a great knot in his stomach. He felt a nameless dread, and yet he somehow welcomed it. He knew he was in bed and thought he might be dreaming, as he saw her come into the room and watched her as she came over to his bed. He could smell the special odor of her body, like fresh coffee cooking. She bent over him and he felt her sweet mouth on his lips. "You should not have sent me away," she whispered softly to him. "I would have stayed with you forever." He sat up in bed and she was gone.

Then one day he received a letter from the bride-to-be herself. "Come, we will be married, trousseau or no trousseau." Pushkin read the words over and over again. Natasha Goncharova was not all marble-statued beauty. He had been right about her after all. She *was* alive! She could write letters. She could speak for herself. He prepared feverishly to make haste to his beloved's side.

He left one day in the mud and rain, changing to sleet, changing to snow. The weather could not dampen his spirits. He was going to get married. Then he was stopped at the first epidemic barrier, where he learned that there were five quarantine barriers between him and Moscow. Cholera was raging through the province. The villages were permeated with the smell of the dead and dying. Scores of dead were dumped into common graves. Long endless lines of funeral marchers, wailing and moaning could be heard all over the province. It took him thirty days to finally reach Natasha in his Moscow, where the battle between him and his future mother-in-law erupted once again. The trousseau, of course. The goddamn trousseau!

Natasha's uncle gave Pushkin an old dilapidated bronze statue of Catherine the Great, worth, according to the uncle, forty thousand rubles. All Alexander Sergeievich had to do was to get it restored to its former gleam and glory. It would be more than enough for Natasha's trousseau. He lugged the monstrosity all over Moscow till he found an artisan equal to the task, who told him it was worth at the very most five thousand rubles and would cost Pushkin six thousand rubles to do a good restoring job. When Pushkin took the statue back to the wily uncle, the old man pleaded with him to intercede with the Emperor on his behalf for a pension.

The Goncharovs were driving him very close to madness. Maybe he would end up in the garret with his father-in-law-to-be. He wondered if it was this nerve-wracking before the wedding, what would it be like afterwards?

In desperation, he contracted for a book he was going to write and received money enough to buy a trousseau. Everything was set. All barriers had been overcome. "Let's marry right away. No need to wait a single second," Pushkin urged Natasha.

One day, Natasha Nicholaevna took him to the attic where her father lived. Nicholas Goncharov was having supper when they entered and didn't stop eating to acknowledge their presence. He was eating greedily with both hands. Now and then he would stop and lick his greasy fingers clean. Scraps and crumbs of food lay about the perimeter of his table and on the floor around him. Alexander Sergeievich had seen mice scampering when they entered.

The attic room was wide, deep and spacious. The ceiling was very low. Alexander Sergeievich felt the need to bend over as he moved about, though the ceiling was well above his head. There was a narrow iron bed against the wall away from the single window with iron bars. There was a flat trunk in another corner, a cedar chest of drawers, washstand, bowl and pitcher in still another corner. There was a chamber pot beneath the edge of the bed, a single simple pine table and a chair. And that was all the furniture.

When Nicholas Goncharov finished eating, he licked his fingers again, meticulously, and then licked the plate until it shone like polished china. Natasha said, "Pa-pa, this is my fiance, Alexander Pushkin."

Natasha's father looked up at her for the first time. Then he turned his gaze to Alexander Sergeievich. He stared silently at his future son-in-law. Nicholas Goncharov's lips were curvy, full and sensuous. His eyes were bluish-black, black on blue, opaque and impenetrable. It was as if his eyes had set up a line of defense against the world ever reaching him beneath the surface.

"We are betrothed, Pa-pa," she repeated. He grunted and looked at Pushkin sorrowfully. He was as pale as death. It had been a long time since the sun had shone upon him.

To Alexander Sergeievich, there was something vaguely familiar about Natasha's father's face; the pointed nose, the sensuous lips, the eyes black on blue or blue on black. Then Alexander realized that, save for the pallor of his face, the impenetrable opaqueness of the dark blue eyes, this man of the Goncharov's garret bore a striking resemblance to himself. The father was a paler, older replica of the future son-in-law. He even resembled Pushkin in the structure of his body; medium in height, broad shoulders. Alexander Sergeievich stared at him incredulously.

Natalya Nicholaevna said, "Yes, there is a very strong resemblance. The first time I met you I thought we had met before." She turned to her father. "We're going now, Pa-pa."

Nicholas Goncharov smiled and she leaned toward him and he kissed her gently on the cheek. He turned to Pushkin and took him in his arms and kissed him. Then he turned to a book he had been reading. Pushkin saw that it was his FOUNTAIN OF BAKSHISARAI. "I gave it to him for his birthday," Natalya Nicholaevna explained.

She kissed her father again. And they left him. Madame Goncharova never knew about the visit. . . .

But Madame Goncharova pulled another tactic.

"Of course, there is the question of your ancestry, dear boy. There is a vicious rumor going around that your great-grandfather was an African." A sly smile spread patronizingly over the face of Madame Goncharova. "Not that there is one prejudiced bone in my entire body, my darling. However, one must be concerned with who one's grandchildren will resemble.

"You must realize my dear boy," Madame Goncharova continued, "there is a possibility of the children reverting, I mean, I could find myself with African grandchildren. Please set my mind at rest."

Pushkin stared in shock at his mother-in-law-to-be. Perspiration dripped from his eyebrows down into his angry eyes. He was livid. He was speechless. He had buried his vaunted pride and gone to the hated Benkendorf to clear up the question of his relationship with the despicable Emperor, he had pawned his literary integrity for a trousseau, he had begged and toadied to Madame Goncharova, this witch in the form of a human being. And now he was asked to deny his African ancestry. . . . Why was she doing this? After all the indignities she had already visited upon him, why this?

He spoke to her quietly, trying desperately to keep the heat from his voice. "Madame," he said, "Madame Goncharova, the ancestor of whom I am proudest, I mean, above all others, was born in a land called Africa. I pray that my children will take after my great-grandfather, Ibrahim Petrovich Hannibal, physically, spiritually, intellectually."

It was only then that he realized Madame Goncharova had not been listening to him, as she continued to babble. "Dear Natasha, I'm ashamed to say, she's always been my favorite, of all my daughters. She is my heart. I looked just like her when I was her age. The same beauty, the same purity and innocence."

Pushkin thought, and she'll become like you, and I'll end up a mad man in the garret like your poor bastard of a husband, with the same dead eyes. Maybe he should seize upon this moment, his last clear chance. Perhaps he should, right at this very moment, turn and run for his worthless life. Possibly, fate was finally doing him a favor. His heart beat wildly. His future hung there before him like a guillotine above his head. Then he heard his darling Natasha take a position against her mother for the first time. "Oh Ma-ma, I don't care. I want to marry Pushkin."

Madame Goncharova said, "But your children might be African."

"I don't care," Natasha insisted. "I want to marry Pushkin."

Alexander Sergeievich Pushkin and Natalya Nicholaevna Goncharova were married in the Cathedral of the Ascension on February 18, 1831, with a ceremony of long and tedious litanies, with gold-encrusted icons glowing brightly all along the walls, amidst the weeping of his mother-in-law and his own father and the sickly saccharin smell of flowers and incense. To Alexander Sergeievich it smelled more like a funeral than a wedding. It was all properly done under the aegis and the blessings of the Holy Virgin's Church. Though Alexander Sergeievich thought it a bad omen when Natasha dropped her ring.

Alexander Pushkin, the non conformist, got married in convention with a serious conviction. Which did not keep his friends and enemies from making dire predictions.

"A marriage of Mestopheles to Venus."

"The marriage doesn't have a chance. The first thing he will do is pervert that poor dear girl!"

"Beauty and the beast!"

Some of the gossip and comments reached the ears of Alexander Sergeievich. Our poet could not have been more disinterested. He was disgustingly contented.

And so the Bard of the Decembrists settled blissfully into an idyllic life of domesticity, and a mundane and humdrum existence and ultimate obesity. He looked forward eagerly to years and years of the same.

PART SEVEN

THE BLISS OF MATRIMONY

CHAPTER ONE

It is winter, not autumn, lovely and vivacious auburn-tinted autumn, but winter when Alexander Sergeievich Pushkin finally weds his lovely pristine Natalya Nicholaevna Goncharova. Winter—Ach! Even the Russian bear does not like this season. Winter, the four or five frigid months of shortened days and seemingly endless nights in snow-packed ice-bound Moscow. Crazy blizzards howl like hungry wolves all along the Moskva River. Icicled trees glittering in the winter moonlight. If you are wealthy or ennobled you enjoy the Moscow winter season. Jinglebelled troikas and fur-lined barouches for the elegant party people. A sleigh ride into the country, wrapped forever in the furs of lucky bears and minks and ermines. Winter means romance for them, the ennobled people. Parties, parties, winter parties from the first day of December clear through to the Lenten Season.

On the other hand, some ignoble or plebian people fall asleep in the doorways of the shops and markets on these frozen streets, fall into a long deep sleep from which they never will awaken. A white and sugar-coated death. The white and kindly frost merely bites off your hands and nose and feet, that is if you're among the fortunate. It is not Pushkin's favorite season. He loves autumn, trees ablaze with fall-time colors, leaves golden brown and falling. The woods catch fire with color. September, October, parts of November; the days begin to shorten, the nights begin to lengthen. Preparing for the dreaded season.

Notwithstanding the hated season, the lovers, Alexander and Natasha, settled into a sweet routine of blissful domesticity. Three weeks after the wedding, Pushkin wrote Zukovsky, "I am unbelievably happy. My one fervent hope is that nothing in my life ever changes. Married life! I had no idea what I was missing. In my present state, it is as if I were born again." And he meant every single word of it.

Even Alexander Sergeievich's enemies were impressed by the connubial bliss that was fairly obvious in the relationship. He went around like a man who was completely converted and domesticated. It was a marriage obviously arranged by the angels up in that Heavenly Place. May the Holy Virgin bless them.

As to the marriage couch, Pushkin felt that Patience must be the watchword here. That first night he felt as if he was violating an infant.

Madame Goncharova made all arrangements for the honeymoon. She arranged their first night in one of the most expensive hotels in Moscow, all at Alexander Sergeievich's expense, of course. Spending rubles he did not possess. Pushkin was adamant though, when she wanted to rent a room next to their suite for herself. "Absolutely not! We need no one to hold the candelabrum!"

Natalya Nicholaevna Goncharova Pushkina undressed that first night in the water closet. When she came back in her nightgown, she asked him to turn his head as she got into bed. When he took her in his arms in bed, she shivered as if his arms were made of ice. Each night it was the same. He was an ardent and experienced lover. He knew how to get a woman ready, but a young inexperienced girl was another problem altogether. Natalya insisted that they make love only in the dark. He kissed her lips, as cold as ice and equally unresponsive. He kissed her ears. He teased her belly button with his lips and devilish tongue. She stirred uneasily. It was as if he were making love to the dead. But he never wavered, he was an understanding lover. If she would just murmur something, if she would only show some sign of life! But she never uttered a sound until the poet penetrated. Then she screamed in pain.

"Stop! You're hurting me!"

"I know, my darling. It has to be like this the first time." He thought, at least she is alive and feeling. He must be thankful for the minimal things in life. And he must, above all, have patience. There was simply nothing for it.

But patience has a way of wearing thin and can likewise be wearying. Each night he would prepare her like the expert that he was. Always she was as dry and arid as the steppes in the middle of a summer drought. And each night she would lie there totally unmoved as if he were making love to a marble statue. Her mother had warned her that love-making was something a proper lady simply tolerated. There was no joy to be gotten from it. So expect none.

Their personalities were as far apart in bed as two people could possibly be. He was a sensual, warm and passionate man and she was like a child playing at ma-ma and pa-pa out of a vague curiosity. But he told himself, have patience, please! Pajalsta! He was a man who loved to make love *with* a woman, not *to* her or *at* her. Each time they made love he felt at once like a father, lover, teacher, confidant and rapist. She was the most serious challenge he had ever met. It was left entirely up to him to bring this child alive and warm and humid. He must simply persevere. And he would not let this affect his happiness, his heavenly tranquility.

Then he realized one day that, despite his willingness to understand, to be patient, something was happening that, if it continued, would surely undermine his bid for connubial and domestic bliss. That something was Madame Goncharova.

"Your husband is arrogant. He is unfeeling. He's a savage. It's his African ancestry. I warned you. He is unromantic and debauched, a notorious gambler. Greedy, stingy and unreasonable." After a few weeks in Moscow it became clear that they must put some distance between this undermining influence. So with Imperial permission the newlyweds moved to Saint Petersburg.

The people of Saint Petersburg were astonished at the changed man Alexander Pushkin appeared to have become. Quiet, conservative, very very low octaved, thoroughly domesticated. Stabilized! Marriage was definitely good for him, but what did the dear innocent child, Natalya, gain from the alliance? Some still referred to them as "Vulcan and Venus."

Distance was one thing but the modern postal system was another thing entirely. The post came by telega from Moscow every few days. And Madame Goncharova seemed to have nothing to do with her precious time but to write letters to her poor unfortunate daughter heavy with advice regarding marriage and warning against that "niggardly husband of yours."

That spring Alexander and Natalya moved to an apartment in Tsarskoye Selo. It was quite some time before the mother found out where they were and her letters began to catch up with them. Pushkin was reduced to intercepting letters from Madame Goncharova and to mailing Natasha's letters to her mother in the village garbage receptacles. No matter, it was a time of sweet tranquility. With all the fond memories coming back to him of Lycée days and the Hussar Guards, all the mischief he and his comrades were into, Svetlina, Pushchin, Delvig, Kuchelbecker. A nostalgic time. Some of the happiest moments of his life. A life that had too often been filled with loneliness. And here, Natalya Goncharova loved her Pushkin according to her capabilities and after her own fashion. In bed she ultimately learned the feminine subtleties of showing her emotions, sometimes genuine, oftentimes pretended. There was, of course, another problem. Alexander Sergeievich liked to talk about his work, loved to talk incessantly about the general state of Russian literature. Writing was his life, and he wanted to share every corner of it with this woman named Natalya Nicholaevna Goncharova Pushkina. What did she think of his idea of starting a new national magazine? Did she agree with his estimate on the value of Russian folklore, and the key role of the muzhik in shaping the nation's destiny? What did she think of the impact of narodnost on the literature? What about the national psyche?

"What do you think of Turgenev's work, my pet? What of Gogol? What of Zukovsky?"

Natasha would stare blankly at him. "When are we going back to Saint Petersburg? I want to visit Moscow. I miss Ma-ma and my sisters."

Some evenings after supper they would go for a stroll in the Imperial Gardens of the Summer Palace, and he would be carried away with memories and full of talk about the sweet days of his youth spent in this paradise of Emperors and Empresses. All bad times were forgotten.

"This is the place where I first came alive!"

His senses were intoxicated with the smell of greenness all around them and flowers in the bloom of life. The chirping of a nightingale. Over to the left of them stood a monumental bathhouse of scarlet and gold constructed in the shape of a Chinese pagoda more than a hundred years ago. It shone brightly in the early spring moonlight, an ornate Chinese relic of the Middle Ages.

"Were you dead before you came to school?"

A spring breeze blew a soft sweet scent of peach and apple orchards from the nearby countryside. It was her attempt at humor, he told himself. Irony perhaps?

"In a way of speaking, yes. I mean, this is where I really came alive. I mean, especially with my writing, my vision broadened. My eyes were opened to the world about me."

The garden was exploding now with the red-lipped roses, the sword-shaped gladiolus and the bell-shaped hyacinth. The world was redolent with smells and shapes and sounds and colors. Frogs and crickets keeping up a noisy chatter.

"Perhaps your mother should have gotten glasses for you." She said.

Again he asked himself: Was she attempting to be ironic? Sardonic? Sarcastic?

His mother, his mother. Damn his stupid mother! She didn't love him. Never did love him. And he didn't need her love. And he wouldn't let the mention of his mother kill his spirits at the moment. He'd made his impact on this world in spite of his mother and his fat-faced father who wept at his wedding. It was Grandpapa Ibrahim who had always been his inspiration. And Grandma-ma Hannibal. And Arina Rodionovna.

He continued, "The Hussar Guards! What a hell-raising bunch! Pushchin was here—and Delvig—all my friends, Chaadaev—Kaverin—old crazy-playing Kuchelbecker. The times we used to have!"

As he repeated the names the joy sucked out of him. It was like a roll call of the dead and dying. Delvig was dead. Pushchin and Kuchelbecker were dying a slow death in Siberia as was Alexander Raevsky in the Peter and Paul Fortress. Brilliant Peter Chaadaev had been put away in an insane asylum because he thought too clearly that the monarchy was deathly sick. He tried desperately to capture the looks of their faces, faces he would never see again.

They went inside, as the day was dying, quietly. It never really died completely in that part of Northern Russia. Spring days just petered out. Natasha had tea. He had a sighing snifter of cognac. It was a soft and tender evening. The fragrance of the garden still lingered in the house. His study was a comfortable place of refuge for him which he shared with no one excepting his beloved. It was not a large room, but large enough. Nothing pretentious, but functional and comfortable. A desk of African mahogany, a high-backed chair, a settee *a-la-Louis Quartorze*, golden carpet worn at the edges, two triple-candled candelabra.

He took a manuscript in progress from his desk and began to read his poetry to her. He felt good about himself this night, and even better sharing the meaning of his life with this woman with whom he'd sworn to share the remainder of his life. He read to this woman who was still a stranger to him. And yet he read, feeling a terribly sweet oneness with her. Read for more than a half an hour till he heard her softly snoring and felt a heat collecting in his collar. And he remembered the letter from Madame Kitrova.

"Marriage castrates the creative spirit—can only lead a man of genius to obesity, complacency, mediocrity—a complete humdrum existence—"

Goddammit! If he shared his work with her, the very least she could do was to pay him the courtesy of staying awake. He felt trapped forever in the sweet snare of domestic bliss. He rose from his chair and went over and stared down at her stretched out in her easy chair, her red lips slightly parted, her eyes shut tight as if her conscience was completely clear. No one could bear her any ill. She slept like an angel pure and guiltless. Nobody was that free from sin. Not even Jesus and the Blessed Virgin.

For one brief moment, he could no longer hear her snoring. His mind played desperate tricks on him. His heartbeat quickened, as he thought fleetingly she had left him to join Anton Delvig and Amelia and Olga Kalashnikova. She's dead! Dead! He saw her lying in her coffin. Vivid! Real! She died in her sleep! Like Arina Rodionovna. But she was young! She was still a baby! Then she moved in her chair, her legs sprawled and opened wider like a sensual invitation to him. Her bosom climbing and descending. He thought, you miserable bastard! You wished her dead. Her mother is right. You *are* a selfish niggardly pig! No wonder your own mother never gave you love. How could anyone love you? But he remembered that Arina Rodionovna loved him and Olga Kalashnikova loved him. Amelia loved him. Aglaya Davidoff surely loved him. Pushchin and poor Delvig loved him. Turgenev and Zukovsky loved him. So did Prince Vyamzensky. Anna, Annettie and Zizi loved him. The Russian masses surely loved him. He remembered the spontaneous reception to him that night at the theatre with Zukovsky when he had first come out of banishment. Madame Osipovna loved him. Deep down within his lonely heart he felt his mother dearly loved him.

He stared at Natasha now and the angelic look had left her momentarily, as her mouth hung open all the way giving her face an idiotic expression completely void of human intelligence. He closed his eyes. He couldn't bear to see her look like this. Then the sweet lips closed again, as in her sleep she moved around and worked the gown up to her knees and spread her legs apart. He felt a sweet heat gather in his loins now. And he took her then and there, as she murmured half awake, "I love you, Pushkin!" She'd never told him this before. As he took her stretched out on the floor of his thickly carpeted study. She was aroused this time, sincerely, as he heard her moaning and groaning, striving desperately to reach the crest with him, and she reached it with little spasms. Her palpitating heartbeat told him she was not pretending. Even so, the dear child thought her husband had finally perverted her. Having her on the floor like that. And making her enjoy it. A thing that should be done only in bed. And never ever was it meant for a lady to take pleasure in! After all, her mother warned her, didn't she?

Nevertheless, everything was running smoothly and apparently would have continued so had the Emperor and his entourage not moved to the Summer Palace because the cholera epidemic was approaching Moscow and on its way to Saint Petersburg. Czar Nicholas brought the social season with him. One sunny afternoon as the newlyweds were strolling in the gardens of the Summer Palace, they came face to face with the Emperor and his entourage.

Alexander Sergeievich introduced his wife, and the Emperor began immediately to throw his charm around. He congratulated Pushkin, and staring obviously at Natalya, he said, "Well, my distinguished friend, I'm sure the Empress would enjoy seeing you and your lovely bride at the court."

Pushkin replied, "Thank you, Your Majesty. We are profoundly flattered." He was aware that his lovely young wife was blushing violently.

The Czar said, still staring openly at Natalya like a hunter at his lovely prey, "Alexander Sergeievich, don't be selfish. Share your bride with the Imperial Court. It would brighten the court like nothing else imaginable."

Uniformed gendarmes walked up ahead of and behind His Majesty. The plainclothed gendarmes moved noisily through the trees and bushes on both sides of the flowered pathway.

Pushkin answered proudly, "To be sure, Your Majesty." Even as he wondered at the words of the Emperor—Share your bride. He was well enough acquainted with the ways and customs of the court to know that Nicholas Romanov probably meant the actual sharing of Natalya's body with His Imperial Majesty.

Pushkin stared aside at his fiercely blushing bride. Anything that would bring such a glow to Natalya's cheeks was welcomed by the poet.

Later that evening, she asked him, "When, Pushkin? When are we going to the Summer Palace?" He had been reading his work-in-progress to her.

"Whenever they invite us," Pushkin answered grumpily.

The next time Pushkin met the Emperor in the Gardens he was alone. The Little Father put his heavy arm around the poet's shoulders in a paternal gesture. "Zukovsky was talking to me about you the other day. Now that you have assumed new responsibilities, we must give you something of importance to do. How would you like to be the Imperial historiographer? Karamzin proposed you to succeed him just before he died."

Pushkin's head knew a giddy feeling. "I beg your pardon, Your Majesty. I don't understand—"

Nicholas Romanov had finally devised a plan and found a way of attaching the poet to his court. "It will only pay ten thousand rubles a year."

Alexander Sergeievich was overjoyed thinking not only of the ten thousand rubles, a mere pittance compared to the debts he already owed. He was thinking mainly of the access it would give him to the Imperial archives. His mind was obsessed historically these days. He wanted to write of the days of Peter the Great and especially of his great-grandfather, Ibrahim Hannibal, and about the revolt against Great Catherine, led by the peasant, Pugachev. "How can I ever repay such generosity, Your Majesty?"

"You'll repay me many times over by your writing in the service of your country," Czar Nicholas said. "Zukovsky and I are depending on you to do great things for the Motherland."

Zukovsky had always been Pushkin's loyal friend at the Imperial Court. Twenty-two years Pushkin's senior, he was uchitol to the Czarevich, the future Emperor, Alexander II. He spent most of his waking hours at the Imperial Palaces. He had rescued Pushkin from many a skirmish with the Imperial government. He'd always had great admiration for the younger poet's talent ever since the days of RUSLAN AND LUDMILA, even long before, when he was a lad at the Pushkin literary soirées in the old house on German Street in Moscow. He regarded Alexander Sergeievich as his most outstanding protégé.

Meanwhile Madame Pushkina had suddenly come to life. She was ecstatic over the Emperor's overtures. Two or three times a day she asked him, "When are we going to meet the Empress?"

Pushkin stared at her uneasily.

They were invited to the next ball at the Summer Palace. Madame Natalya Nicholaevna Goncharova Pushkina was an instant overnight success, the topic of conversation among the courtly people. At the very first ball, women stared at her admiringly in envy, men in worshipful adoration. She took her success seriously, which bothered Pushkin painfully. He told himself he did not envy Natalya her smashing impact at the court. It was due her. What irritated him was the seriousness she attached to it. She began to live for nothing else. Her mind was all aglow now and shimmering. Even as she slept she dreamed of brightly lighted ballrooms hung heavily with brocaded silk. She thought, this was the ultimate meaning of her life, what the Good Lord had in mind when He created her. Why else had He made her the most beautiful woman in all the Russias?

Natalya went around for days afterwards with the lingering memory of it all, the music of serf bands playing sweetly in her dainty ears, the intoxicating fragrances of myriads of flowers—hyacinths, roses, camelias—all around in exquisite Chinese vases never left her delicate nostrils. Lilacs and dahlias and jasmines in porcelain pots in alcoves around the vast ballroom.

The Czarina of the Russias approved of Natalya Nicholaevna Goncharova Pushkina unqualifiedly. "She is the most stunning thing that has happened in the court in many years!"

The Czarina invited the couple to an exclusive Imperial dinner. Natalya's inarticulateness was interpreted as naivete and shyness, which was "absolutely charming!"

Every time the Palace held a ball Natalya wanted to be there. Nicholas Romanov was a man who had an avid eye for beautiful women. Believed devoutly in the laying on of hands. He believed it was his prerogative by the Divine Right of His Majesty and Emperorship. It was a prerogative he was known to frequently exercise with the scrawny, aging Empress's approval. Nicholas Romanov longed for the good old days when beautiful brides-to-be were brought to the Palace before marriage to be sampled by His Imperial Majesty, receiving thereby His Most Imperial blessings and His Imperial stamp of approval.

At the Palace balls, Nicholas danced more than his share of rounds with Natalya, whispering into her tiny ears. Most men would have been proud to have a wife coveted by the Emperor. Would have been willing cuckolds to His Most Imperial Majesty. But not Alexander Pushkin.

And Natalya lived for the balls and parties and the vanities of the *haute monde* of the Imperial Court. And wanted a new expensive gown for each occasion. Rubles were no object as far as she was concerned. The party was the ultimate. She never tired. Pushkin tried, but he did not have the heart, nor did he have the words to deny this lovely womanchild.

When the Emperor's Court moved back to the Winter Palace at Saint Petersburg, Natalya wanted to follow. Pushkin refused, emphatically. He had chosen Tsarskoye Selo because he needed solitude to do his writing. He could not write in Petersburg. There were too many distractions.

She wept, she fretted. "You don't love me! You don't want me to be happy. All you care about is your old writing. Ma-ma was right. You're mean, and you don't care about my happiness at all."

"Nyet! Nyet! Hell no! We stay right here where we are!"

But Natalya finally got her way.

Back in Saint Petersburg it was winter, and it was ball after ball after ball. Pushkin despised himself because he hadn't the strength to deny his child bride her every wish, even though he knew it was not good for her, or him, and was in fact defeating their relationship.

Meanwhile he spent many hours every day researching in the Imperial archives. He worked all day and Natalya danced all night and slept throughout most of the day. Ultimately Natalya became pregnant, but her condition did not decrease her social activities until the very last days of her pregnancy. Alexander Sergeievich was very solicitous regarding her health.

"You must slow up, my darling. You must protect your health. You're six months pregnant, but you have not stopped a single moment. It's dangerous. And it's unseemly."

Natalya paid no attention to our poet. Hers was a pregnancy that did not show early. She looked slim through the first five or six months, and as long as it did not show unduly, as long as she looked svelte and beautiful, she saw no reason to change her schedule, especially when the Emperor told her, "Your pregnancy has made you more beautiful and desirable than ever."

As far as she was concerned Alexander was just a crotchety old grouch. She gave birth to a six pound baby girl, went to Moscow to her mother to convalesce. A month later she was back in Saint Petersburg kicking up her heels as high as ever. Listening to flirtations and coquettishly blinking her large dark eyes behind her busy pearl-encrusted fan, while her husband stood around sipping ices and looking bored.

Sometimes he raged at her.

"You are making a fool of yourself, Natasha. Your flirtations are not even aristocratic, not *comme-il-faut*."

"What's wrong with them, Alexander Sergeievich? Everybody does it. It's the fashion at the Court. A little harmless flirtation. Do you think I don't know how far to go? You treat me like a child."

It was an accurate accusation. "Goddammit, Natasha, you're actually vulgar! You're like a bitch in heat!"

"You're the one who is vulgar, Alexander Sergeievich. Just because you've led a life of debauchery, you think everybody else is like you. My mother warned me. You're just a jealous old man, and you don't want me to be happy!"

One day he told her, "You're happy because the male dogs run after you with their tails erect as though you were a bitch, sniffing at your hindparts. It's easy to train the bachelor swine to chase you. All you have to do is to let everyone know you like being pursued. That's the secret of flirtation. Everybody knows it. Where there's a trough the swine will certainly accumulate."

All that ever came of these stormy sessions was Natalya weeping and crying hysterically and threatening to go home to her mother, and muttered oaths by Pushkin, and the losing of tempers and the constant slamming of doors. And always a feeling of deepest guilt on the part of our unhappy poet. It was all his fault. He was a cranky jealous bastard! And in the end she always had her way. Nevertheless, it went abrasively against the grain for this great and famous man to accept the role of *le mari de madame*. To be known in the Imperial circles as the husband of the beautiful Madame Pushkina.

She became pregnant again and, as before, refused to heed her husband's warnings. While in an advanced stage of her pregnancy, she fainted away in the arms of the Emperor at a Palace ball and had to be taken home in the Imperial carriage. She had a miscarriage. She convalesced for a month or so, then back again to the old routine.

Pushkin wasn't doing any writing in his cramped apartment where the tension seemed always about to blow the place apart. He did not understand why he didn't walk away from it all. There were many lovely ladies around the court willing, ready and available to share Alexander Pushkin's bed with him. So why did he fight so hard for this relationship which, at best, was top-heavily one-sided. He sat at his desk far into the night unable to write, wondering why. He didn't understand himself. Everyone, including his best friends, had predicted a short life for this marriage. It was impossible, they openly avowed, for one so footloose as he had always been, to keep his feet to the hearth long enough to make a permanent relationship. Was he going to all this trouble just to prove them wrong? Nyet! Hell no! There were profounder reasons. He loved this woman. He was fighting for his family, the only one he'd ever known that he could call his very own. Fighting against the creeping feeling that he was, in fact, outside again. She would learn. She would grow up and out of this crazy fascination for the frivolous. She was a baby. She was an innocent.

Which infuriated him even more.

For it frustrated him that she was not sophisticated like he remembered Anna Kern. She really didn't mean any harm. She took people as she found them at the value of their smiling faces. And even some of his friends thought him unnecessarily grumpy; he, Alexander Pushkin, a reckless roué if there ever was one, turned overnight into a domesticated grouchy grandpa-pa, suddenly a paragon of piety and virtue. Some said it was due to the fact that he had been spoiled, had always been used to being the center of attraction. And to compound his great frustration, he wasn't doing any writing. If his writing had been going well, he knew, he could have accepted Natalya's fascination with the frivolous with more patience and understanding.

The Emperor called him to the Palace once more. Finally there was something he could do for Russia and the Motherland. His Majesty offered him a commission of fifteen thousand rubles to do the research and write the history of Peter the Great. Pushkin happily accepted. But he would need to get away, he told the Emperor. He requested and received Imperial permission to travel to the land of the Ural Cossacks where in the eighteenth century the pretender-peasant Pugachev had staged his uprising against Great Catherine.

Alexander Sergeievich went far into the Cossack interior to the country villages to Orenburg and Belogorsky and lived among the Baskirs, the Kirghis people and the rugged Ural Cossacks. With his swarthiness and wooly hair, some thought the long-predicted anti-Christ had finally arrived. Others seriously believed Pushkin to be the resurrection of Pugachev come back from his death-by-hanging. They made the sign of the cross every time they met him on the dusty roads. No one would talk to him at first. Perhaps he was a Czarist spy. But after awhile he broke down some of their resistance. No matter, Pushkin was revitalized. Finally he got some of the old timers who had actually ridden with Pugachev, the great brigand, to tell him their story. The story of Pugachev fascinated him so much, he forgot that he had come to do THE HISTORY OF PETER THE GREAT.

He began to feel at home in this godforsaken place. This was Russia to the core. These were the Russian people, he thought. Beatific, illiterate mostly, steeped in ancient superstitions. Mean, generous, narrow-minded, eager for life, humaneness exuding from every pore. The beautiful ragged wide-eyed children. These were the heart and soul of Russia, he thought, untouched by Europeanization. These were the people who would one day make a revolution, though their Pugachev had failed in his rebellion.

He was a new man when he returned to Saint Petersburg, and even the Emperor agreed that the trip had done him good. He was darker, tanner than he'd ever been. He plunged immediately into work on three books almost simultaneously. He was a man possessed with a feverish mission. He worked as if death was knocking at his door and he had a job to do before the bastard broke it down. But he had no desire to leave this world. He would work on THE HISTORY OF PETER THE GREAT, go from there the same day in a great white heat to THE HISTORY OF THE PUGACHEV REBELLION, and from there, in the evening, with his body lathered with sweat, to a novel about Pugachev which he called, THE CAPTAIN'S DAUGHTER. One day he went back to work on a novel about his great-grandfather which he had titled, THE NEGRO OF PETER THE GREAT. This was his great prose writing period, and he felt good about himself. The devil take the critics. He looked up from his dimly-lighted desk at the picture of Grandpa-pa Ibrahim, with the broad forehead, heavy eyebrows and the black intelligent face and the piercing eyes, the sensuous lips. He had brought it with him from Mikhailovskoye. Sometimes he would walk up and down in his incommodious study. The eyes of Grandfather Hannibal seemed always to follow him, and those darkly-bright penetrating eyes never left him no matter where he walked or stood or sat. They kept watch over him, eternally. The Negro of Peter The Great. He smiled inwardly. He knew that he had given to the Russian a poetic tongue. Even his severest critics agreed that Russian poetry was Alexander Pushkin and Alexander Pushkin was Russian poetry. Now he must give to them a vernacular in prose. He felt so very close these days to the Russian soul, its spirit, psyche, zeitgeist, her narodnost. And he would give it to the world in writing, in prose. It would be another Pushkin gift to Russia. Alexander Sergeievich Pushkin, the great grandson of Africa. To hell with imitating Europe! He began to write his Russian folk tales. The *shazka* was the Russian version of the fairy tale told in the Russian folk tradition. His sources were the tales his late nyanya, Arina Rodionovna, used to tell him. They were charming children's stories. He wrote KING SATTAN, THE GOLDEN COCKEREL, THE DEAD PRINCESS AND THE SEVEN CHAMPIONS.

When he came home weary and exhausted at night from digging into the dusty volumes at the Imperial archives, he wanted to discuss his projects with his beloved. But usually Natasha was on her way out to a ball or frantically getting ready to depart.

She had heard how great a man this husband of hers was, a gifted genius, the greatest writer in the Empire, but she did not, could not grasp its deep significance. When he tried to explain himself to her, it was like he spoke in unknown tongues. Her eyes and ears were for the dashing young men at the Palace balls, the Emperor and all his Imperial Court. Her lovely head was filled with visions of the courtly pageantry, stately processions, the music, the pomp, the ceremony, Imperial extravaganza, the sounds of idle chatter, of clicking heels, swirling, dancing the mazurkas, grand marches, or the softly sweetened tunes of madrigals.

Sometimes she would stop dressing and come into his study and try to listen to him. But it never seemed to work. Somewhere along the way he gave up trying to make her understand.

Other times, she manifested jealousy, superficially as it were, of women who could engage her poet-husband with intellectual and literary conversation, especially when they were beautiful women.

Like Baroness Svetlina, auburn-haired, dark-of-eyes, sensuous, mischievous, intellectual, articulate and beautiful, a staunch Pushkin devotee, Imperial lady-in-waiting, unknown to the Czar an ex-Decembrist, who visited the Pushkins almost every morning. One morning she came and, as usual, engaged in a polite conversation with Natasha, then she asked, "Where is Alexander Sergeievich?"

Natasha answered peevishly, "He's upstairs, still in bed. You never come to see me anyway. It's him you're always after."

The Baroness did not bother to deny it. She ran immediately up to Pushkin who sat in bed sipping coffee, surrounded by a clutter of manuscripts. As usual, she pecked him on the mouth and stayed with Alexander Sergeievich for several hours chattering away. Natasha could hear their laughter all the way downstairs. She never learned of their relationship in earlier days.

Sometimes their eyes would meet, and they would remember other times more intimate and more revolutionary, and a hot glow would suffuse their faces. At times, when they kissed, their lips would linger longer than usual. At such moments the Baroness would often whisper heatedly, partially in jest, partially in earnest, "It's all my fault. I should have kept my baby when the Captain gave you to me."

He'd say in equal jest and earnest, "But I could have never been *your* African. Your Arabian stallion."

The relationship was fine, completely harmless, as far as it went, stolen kisses, laughter, teasing, remembering, enjoying one another's company, the Baroness and her African, *le petit genie*. They took a solemn silent oath that they would go no further.

Some days Svetlina would find Alexander Sergeievich in a splenetic mood, morose and sulky, and she would try to tease and laugh him out of it. She would kiss him passionately and pretend that they were merely pretending at being long-lost and ill-fated lovers. And when nothing helped to change his mood, she herself would become morose and sullen.

By this time Natalya Nicholaevna had given birth to four children. Childbirth had no negative effect on Natalya's beauty. She flourished and bloomed forth like a tree in springtime filled with lovely blossoms. She had put on a little weight here and there which gave her a certain matronly and beautiful maturity.

When Alexander Sergeievich came home in the evenings, he would have his children brought to him. He would embrace them warmly and kiss them; sometimes he would play games with them, tell them stories in the Russian idiom. He told them of their great-great-grandfather Hannibal. Sometimes he'd take Alexander Alexandrovich in his arms and he would not want to let him go. They went for walks around Saint Petersburg. Whenever the famous Moscow Circus came to town he would take them. They loved to have their father to themselves.

He marveled sometimes that he could never see them actually growing, see them stretching out before his watchful eyes. But from day to day, month to month, year to year, imperceptibly, they grew. That was the miracle of it all. No matter how closely he watched them, day by day, he could not see them stretching upwards.

Alexander Alexandrovich asked one day, "How does it happen, Pa-pa? Why can't I see myself growing?"

Pushkin told him he did not know the answer. It was a miracle of nature. It was like the old clock on the wall of his study handed down by their great-great-grandfather Hannibal. You could never see the hands of the old clock actually moving, but move they did. "And time does pass, from minute to minute, hour to hour, the days, the months, the years tick away, beyond recall. And before you know it and even before I know it," he told his second-born, "you'll be a grown man just like me."

The smiling boy with the plentiful and sensual lips and the dark eyes looked at the old clock handed down from his great-great-grandfather Hannibal, then looked at his father and back at the clock again in open-mouthed wonderment. "And will I be a great writer like you?"

"If you choose to be, Alexander Alexandrovich. Even greater."

And his oldest daughter asked, "And will I be a great writer like you, Papa?"

"You will be the greatest if that is what you choose to be." He laughed and took his children in his arms and kissed them.

Sometimes he would stare at them and his troubled eyes would fill. He did not want them raised like he was, with governesses and uchitols, always of a French vintage. He wanted them brought up with parental love and care. Wanted them to be unadulterated Russians, not Frenchmen with Russian accents.

Whenever he spoke to Natasha, she saw this as further evidence of his miserliness. "My mother warned me you were niggardly. A gentlewoman does not care for her children. It is a servant's duty." Sometimes he thought he'd like to take them to the land of Pugachev and bring them up with the earthy children of the lowly Baskirs and Ural Cossacks.

Ultimately Pushkin stopped attending the balls and parties at the court and forbade Natasha to attend them unescorted. She wept, she sobbed, she threatened. But this time he was adamant. Then the Emperor made a move that sent Alexander Sergeievich into one of his exaggerated rages for which he was becoming famous. One morning he received an official communication from the Emperor with the Imperial seal thereon appointing him to the office of Kammerjunker at His Majesty's Imperial Court. It was an appointment eagerly sought by noblemen and one you would be justly proud of, that is, if you were only eighteen years of age. But Pushkin was thirty-five and the most renowned of writers in the vast and entire land of Russia. The Kammerjunkers were glorified page boys. And Alexander Pushkin was a man. A man of great import and genius. It was an insult. He would be the laughing stock of all Saint Petersburg.

When the Emperor did not hear from Pushkin on the matter and a week had passed, he sent his Imperial uchitol, Zukovsky, to make an official inquiry. Pushkin was still in violent temper.

"I'm no fool. I know what the Emperor is about. He wants Natasha at all of the court balls. This way I'll be a flunky at the Imperial Court. You can tell him for me what to do with his commission!"

"Surely you can't mean for me to take this message back to His Majesty!"

Pushkin glared at his friend with inflamed eyes. He snatched a piece of paper from his desk and picked up a pen. "Do you want me to put it in writing?"

Zukovsky stammered. "But-but-but His Majesty will consider himself insulted. He. . . ."

Pushkin exploded. "He'll consider himself insulted!? How in the hell do you think I feel about it? For nothing in the world will I present myself alongside these eighteen-year-old arse-wipers!

Zukovsky pleaded with the poet. "His Majesty's intentions were entirely honorable. He meant to be doing you a good turn. He'll consider you ungrateful. You have enough powerful enemies at court. You don't need to add the Emperor to the list. Besides, if you show your ungratefulness like this, you'll no longer have access to the archives. Of that you can be sure."

Pushkin was speechless. He looked around the little room of his study, he felt the airless room getting smaller, closing in on him, finding his breathing difficult now. There was that loop again drawing him more tightly and more securely to the strings of the Imperial Court. He might as well have been hung along with the seven Decembrists. The loop was choking him to death. He picked up the commission with its Imperial seal in his trembling hands and slowly tore it into bits.

Zukovsky pleaded. "Take the advice of an old friend, please! I've known you since you were a baby. Accept this commission in the grace and spirit in which it was intended. I assure you His Majesty wishes you no ill will. But if you turn this kindly gesture down, I can plead your case no longer. And I can't be held responsible for the way your enemies will make capital of your refusal."

In the end Pushkin relented. His decision had more to do with the threat of losing access to the archives than any concern for the feelings of the Emperor. Natalya was ecstatic. But he vowed never to wear the page boy uniform to any of the Kammerjunker ceremonies. He left town for Tsarskoye Selo to avoid the first one.

Before he left Saint Petersburg he met the Emperor's youngest brother, the Grand Duke Mikhail Pavlovich, at the theatre. The Grand Duke congratulated him on his appointment to the Kammerjunkers.

Alexander Sergeievich replied, "My most humble thanks to you, Your Highness. You're the first to congratulate me. Everyone else has been laughing at me."

He wrote a letter to Natalya from Tsarskoye Selo in which he stated: "His Majesty apparently feels annoyed that I'm ungrateful about my appointment as a gentleman of the chamber. I may very well be His Majesty's subject, perhaps even his slave, but serf and clown I will never be, not even for the King of Heaven." In another part of the letter he wrote: "It was the devil's own trick to endow me with a soul and talent and decree that I be born in Russia!"

It was only then that Pushkin realized that his mail was still being spied upon. When he returned from Tsarskoye Selo he was ordered to appear before Benkendorf, at which time he was, by order of the Czar, reprimanded severely for writing such an ungrateful letter. "His Majesty wishes me to express to you his profound displeasure."

Alexander Sergeievich was livid. At first, his lips worked but no words came forth. Finally he said, "So now I'm an enemy of the country. And the Emperor not only opens my personal letters to my wife, but he has the unabashed temerity to call attention to his spying by upbraiding me for the letter he had no business reading in the first damn place!"

Benkendorf smoothed his waxed mustache with his slender fingers and told him with a straight face, "Your mail is not being spied upon, Sire. The letter inadvertently opened. And when the contents were read, an overzealous postal officer brought it to the attention of the Emperor."

Pushkin stared at the supercilious Benkendorf. He broke into maniacal laughter and strode out of the office of the Chief of Secret Police as he sat behind his handsome desk.

Six or seven months passed. Nothing changed at the Pushkin household, for the better that is. One morning, Baroness Svetlina came upstairs to see Alexander Sergeievich, and he was in one of his sullen moods. She demanded of him, "Why do you endure it? That vacant-headed woman downstairs hasn't the vaguest notion of who you are. She has no idea whatever what you mean to Russia and the world." She worked herself into a rage. "I cannot understand how a man of your genius could be so completely vulnerable to a pretty, vapid face. She is vacuous and she's insipid, and she's not even worthy to kiss your boots!"

"You're wrong about Natasha," Alexander Sergeievich argued unconvincingly. "She's very subtle, and there is much more to her than appears upon the surface.

She has more than just a pretty face." Why was he defending her? he wondered. He knew Svetlina spoke the truth, partially, at least.

"Why are you defending her?" the Baroness demanded.

"Because she is my wife," he answered heatedly. "She is the mother of my children."

"She's an insult to your intelligence and your genius. Why don't you come away from here and live with me. I have a palace here in Petersburg. You know the place it's not far from here. You remember the times we had together. You could do your work in complete solitude and read it to me every night." She stared at him wistfully, sentimentally. "Don't you remember how you used to read your work to me? Don't you remember how it was with us?"

He remembered everything, all the sensual signs, the misty fiery down above her red and ripened lips, the busy hands that even now caressed his knees, unknowingly. She was older now, heavier around the middle of her, her dark eyes were older, wiser, but she was no less beautiful and sensual. He felt himself collecting heat.

"I love my wife," he told her fiercely. "I also love my children."

The situation worsened. Natalya had returned from Moscow with her two sisters to live in the Pushkin household. Pushkin, of course, was furious. He raged, he fumed. How in the hell could he afford it? Did she think he owned an orchard in which rubles grew? She wept, she sobbed. Her sisters were there already, *a fait accompli*. They had to move to larger more expensive quarters on Moika Street and the situation became more explosive than ever.

The older sister, Katerina Goncharova, was plain looking, tall, shapeless and ungainly, with the look of a mountain eagle, without the eagle's gracefulness. In comparison with the glittering beauty of Natalya she had to be considered homely. But she was looking for a husband and was enthralled by her youngest sister's access to the Imperial Court. The Czar made her a lady-in-waiting. Alexandra, the middle sister, was the identical image of Natalya, except for a terrible short-sightedness which gave her great dark eyes a squint. She was pretty but not as beautiful as Madame Pushkina. Meanwhile, deeper in debt went Alexander Sergeievich. And even deeper into debt to the Emperor of all the Russias. The house resounded with violent quarrels, swearing, doors slamming, whimpering. Sometimes, Alexander Sergeievich felt like the meanest bastard in the world.

Of the three sisters only Alexandra had a deep respect and understanding of the importance of Alexander Pushkin, the writer. She fell in love with him and his poetry long before she had ever met him. Some nights she would stay at home while her sisters went to the balls. And she would tremble as she listened to the great man move around his study. She knew his every mood of restlessness. She knew his loneliness. She agonized. Her perceptive soul knew every pain his poor heart felt. Sometimes she would scold her sister for not treating this great man properly. Natalya accused Alexandra of being in love with her husband. The sister blushed but did not bother to deny it.

One day in the cold of winter, as he walked the frigid streets of Peter's city in his hareskin greatcoat and fur cap, Alexander Sergeievich saw a long line of people extending from a boulevard off Nevsky Prospekt. As he turned into Stable Street, he stopped and watched his countrymen and women trudging slowly toward the exhibit of a large canvas painting of *The Crucifixion*, by Bryullov. His chilled body heated up with outrage as he watched armed sentries in front of the Cathedral standing between the people and Bryullov's bleeding Savior, now and then shoving a feeble old muzhik with a gun for moving slowly. The spectacle infuriated Pushkin. That night, in a trembling rage he wrote his SECULAR.

When the supreme event had at long last transpired,
And God upon the cross in agony expired,
On either side the tree, two looked on one another:
One, Mary Magdalene, and one, the Virgin Mother—
In grief two women stood.
But now whom do we see beneath the holy rood,
As thought it were the porch of him who rules the city—
Not here the holy twain, borne down by pity,
But, shakos on their heads and bayonet in hand
Beside the crucifix two bristling sentries stand.
Are they set there to guard the cross as if 'twere state cargo?
Would you add dignity to the King of Kings?
What honor do you think your patronage thus brings,
You mighty of the earth,
What help by you is rendered
To him who's crowned with thorns, to him
who freely tendered
His body to the scourge, without complaint or fear,
The Christ who had to bear the cross, the nails, the spear?
Fear you the mob's affront to him who won remission,
But a broad oak above these dignified graves brooding
Bestirs its boughs in music . . .

He stared at what he had written in helpless anger. When would the people revolt? When would they say, "No more! No more! No goddamn more!"

One unusual winter evening Natalya stayed home from the Palace ball. She came into the study as he worked and sat in a corner on the other side of the room. And watched him. He could feel her presence in the room. He could smell her special-to-him fragrance when she came into the study. At first it irritated him, her interruption. But then, he thought, she's trying, isn't she? She wants to discuss your poetry with you, to try at least, you unreasonable bastard! She never professed to be an intellectual giant before you married her. You didn't marry her for that. He forced a smile on his face, as he turned from his desk toward Natalya.

"Why are you sitting over there so far away from me?" It was only then that he noticed she had a sheaf of writing paper in her lap.

She spoke just above a whisper. The fear in her dark eyes made him feel like the meanest son of a bitch in all of Russia. "I didn't mean to disturb you, but I wanted you to hear some of the poetry I have written."

He made himself say, "Very good," thinking to himself, what makes her think it is so easy to write a poem?

Natalya cleared her nervous throat. He could hear the pure-white kisses of the snow upon the window panes. She began to read, shakily at first, then clearly gaining confidence. And he thought to himself that her poetry was not bad at all. The ideas were definite and well written, the rhythm was true, as was the Russian idiom. All this time he had known her and he had underestimated her. So filled up with his own importance! His eyes widened as he listened to her further. There was something original about this work, a thing unusual for these times, something strangely strongly Russian rather than French.

His face filled up with pride for her. He heard himself say, "This is very good, Natasha!" He did not mean to patronize her.

She said, "Go ahead. Make fun of me! You can just go straight to hell for all I care."

"Make fun of you, my pet? I mean it, this is very good!"

He went to her and took her in his arms and found that she was trembling in her rage and indignation.

She pulled away from him. "Go ahead. Laugh at me!" She misunderstood the puzzled smile on his face, mistook the smile for veiled contempt.

He protested, "But I'm proud of you, my darling!"

She said, "Enjoy yourself at my expense. You know damn well it's only your own work, warmed over and served up again."

As soon as she spoke he knew she spoke the truth. He went toward her, as she stood, blinded now with angry tears. She dropped the papers on the floor. She was so beautiful in tears. He hated to see her cry but he loved her when she did. He tried to take her in his arms. "I really didn't know—I thought—"

"You thought!" She sneered. "You knew all along it was your own genius. But I don't care. You and your precious writing. What does it get you? It's me His Majesty adores, not you. They laugh at you behind your back. To the important people at the court, you're just a little boy, a Kammerjunker."

His open hand went up against her face, as if it had a will of its own.

"Go ahead," she shouted softly. "Slap me, beat me! I do everything I can to please you. All I am to you is something to sleep with and give babies to!"

"I'm sorry," he said. "I didn't mean to hit you! I'm just overwrought these days. Half of the time I don't know what I'm doing."

She turned from him and left him in his study.

He went back to his desk and began his work again. He wrote furiously, page after page. And tore the pages up again. It was no good. He could not get her off his mind. She had tried. She had cared enough to plagiarize him. At least it meant that she was reading his works. And he had rewarded her for her trouble by hitting her. He heard her coming down the hall again and entering the study. Her smell was strangely warmly different. His head bent over his desk encircled by his arms. He heard her placing something on the desk beside him. He smelled and felt the heat of steaming tea. And felt her hand gently stroking his wooly head. "Dear Alexander!" the woman sobbed.

He turned and put his arms around her waist. His hand caressed her tender buttocks. She trembled to his touch. She sobbed, "No! No! No, Alexander Sergeievich!" And he looked up into the soulful face of Natasha's sister, Alexandra. Her dark eyes were like two bright gems of smoky topaz. She ran quickly out of the room. He started to go after her, but turned and went back to his desk.

It was an impossible situation and it might have gone on like this endlessly, except that one day a handsome Frenchman by the name of George Charles d'Anthes came to Saint Petersburg under the sponsorship of Baron Heckeren, Ambassador to the Imperial Court from the Netherlands.

The world of Pushkin changed forever.

CHAPTER TWO

In Moscow the ladies of nobility would call him a handsome Don Juan dog or devil. He was so beautiful he was madly in love with his own reflection. He was Narcissus come back as a noble Frenchman to dwell among the living. In London he might have been Beau Brummel. In Scotland, Lochinvar. In Italy, Giovanni Casanova or Lothario. He was a coxcomb and a popinjay and a dandy of a Frenchman. He was George Charles d'Anthes, Alsatian-French and of a well connected family of the French nobility. A royalist by birth, persuasion and commitment. It was a time of revolutionary fervor when the spirit of "fraternité, liberté and egalité" was sweeping over France again. During his stay at the St. Cyr elitist military academy, his ennobled friends at court were overthrown, and he feared a repetition of the Reign of Terror, when his Royal Majesties fell victim to the wiles of Madame Guillotine.

Suddenly it became clear to this beautiful adventurer that he had to make other plans. The first thing to do, with his family's not inconsiderable influence, was to seek his fortune in the German military, but the most he could get was the rank of a noncommissioned officer. His Prussian sponsor was none other than the future German Emperor, Kaiser Wilhelm the One, who was linked to Russia by ties of a series of Imperial marriages. Wilhelm advised the handsome young blue-eyed mustachioed Frenchman to seek service in Saint Petersburg where the Emperor, who was Wilhelm's son-in-law, looked with favor upon Frenchmen with royalist sympathies.

D'Anthes fell ill with the bloody flux on the way to Saint Petersburg and stopped at a roadside inn just short of the Russian dominated Polish border to recuperate. Every morning, no matter how weak he felt, he would get out of his bed and stare in open admiration for hours at his reflection in the mirror over the washstand.

Several days later, a well appointed carriage pulled up in front of the very same roadside inn. The innkeeper, who had special nostrils for the smell of German marks, hastened out to the carriage to greet Baron Van Heckeren, Dutch Ambassador to the Imperial Court of Russia, on his way back to Saint Petersburg from vacation.

The little chubby innkeeper bowed deeply before this important personage.

"Your Excellency requires a room for the night?"

The portly Ambassador answered, "No, just see if you can prepare for me a proper supper. Then I'll be on my way."

"There is plenty of room here, Sire, and the accommodations are quite comfortable. There's only one other here. A young handsome ailing Frenchman."

"Oh, very well," the Ambassador said. "I suppose you could put me up for the night. But I shall have to have an early breakfast and get an early start tomorrow morning."

Later that evening Van Heckeren paid a visit to the ailing Frenchman. He went to the bed and felt the Frenchman's burning forehead. He went downstairs and inquired of the timid innkeeper as to the whereabouts of the best physician in the nearby village. He paid the man to go in his private berlin and fetch the doctor. "He must be the very best there is!" he shouted after the excited innkeeper as he ran out of the door. "Money is no object." He went back upstairs to attend to the beautiful young Frenchman.

The doctor came, examined the sickly Lochinvar, took his temperature, checked his pulse, bled him with leeches. He turned to the Ambassador. "He'll be all right in a few weeks. He just has dysentery and a pretty bad case of gonorrhea. It's not as bad as it might have been, since it's a new case."

"Don't fret yourself, dear boy. I shall nurse you back to health."

Baron Van Heckeren paid the doctor, rewarding him generously. He kept his word. He nursed the handsome d'Anthes back to health and brought him into Saint Petersburg under his paternal sponsorship. Through the efforts of the kindly Dutch Ambassador and the letter from the future Kaiser Wilhelm, d'Anthes secured a position as Lieutenant in the Czarist Guards.

D'Anthes was blonde of hair with a blonde mustache, devilishly pointed, sparkling light blue eyes filled with wickedness and mischief. A carefree kind of a fellow in a great hurry to make a success of himself. As a commissioned officer he was entitled to attend all of the balls at court, and he intended not to miss a single one, the Good Lord and the Emperor willing. He entered the royal circle with a tremendous splash, and he was an instant success. And one evening at an Imperial ball in the Winter Palace he met Natalya Goncharova Pushkina.

While Pushkin leaned on a long white column and sipped ices, this cavalier Frenchman danced almost every dance with Natalya, whispering into her tiny ears that she was the most beautiful woman the Lord in his eternal graciousness had ever created. The Imperial courtiers were delightfully titillated by the spectacle of these two beautiful people. At first Pushkin pretended not to notice. The dashing Lieutenant was cautiously circumspect. He was no fool. He'd heard of Alexander Pushkin. Although d'Anthes was no lover of great literature, he was aware of what the poet meant to the Russian people. Alexander Sergeievich Pushkin was a presence and a household word. But d'Anthes determined almost immediately that Natalya Nicholaevna Goncharova Pushkina would ultimately belong to him.

Months passed and as the winter season got underway, d'Anthes and Madame Pushkina became the principal attraction at the balls which went on every night in the week till late in the early morning. He carried on outrageously with her as if she were unmarried and totally available. And Natalya, on her part, did nothing to discourage this cavalier's attentiveness, as the Kammerjunker poet stood aside sipping Italian ices and pretending not to notice. The young Guardsman told Natalya that he loved her and could not live without her. He would kiss her quickly on the cheek or nose and nibble at her ears whenever they found themselves in a corner or an alcove of the ballroom. He was playing Russian roulette with his career and with his life, but he didn't seem to care. The courtiers were delighted and amused, at first. They were such a charming lovely couple. But after awhile, the proper people at the Court became alarmed at how the affair seemed headed along a course that could only end in scandal and disaster. Maybe even tragedy. For everyone knew that Alexander Sergeievich Pushkin was not a man to trifle with. His temper was of far and wide repute. And he was the deadliest duelist in all Saint Petersburg. Everyone noted that the once effervescent Pushkin had changed into a moody man with sallow complexion and demonic countenance. He seemed to live with thunderheads. On his face and in his deep dark eyes there was an almost perpetual look of evil and foreboding.

Natalya was deliriously happy about the whole thing and completely oblivious to the danger involved. She would come home and discuss her adventures with her husband-confidante. "He's so charming and so clever. He tells me the funniest, most risque stories! I haven't had so much fun in all my life!"

Pushkin would mutter darkly, "Be careful, you don't take this thing too far."

But Natalya could not hear Pushkin for the song she heard her own heart singing.

Alexandra warned her. Natalya retorted, "You're like all the other ladies at the court. You're jealous because d'Anthes pays you no attention."

Czar Nicholas and d'Anthes vied for Natalya's attention at the balls and parties. She thought this was how it was meant to be. Why else had the Good Lord made her so beautiful? Just as God had created her husband to write great literature, surely He had meant her to be adored by the handsomest of men. She lived in a heavenly paradise of Imperial unreality.

It could not go on like this continually. It was the unhappiest time in all of Alexander Pushkin's unhappy life. He was outside again, with his own wife and his very own family and household. Debts piled up. He would sit at his desk and imagine he could hear people laughing at him all over Saint Petersburg. His head throbbed. He placed his hands over both ears to shut out the sound of their laughter. One night at a ball at Anichkov Palace an infamous homosexual aristocrat by the name of Dolgorukov stood behind Pushkin and made the classic sign of the horns with fingers spread and a thumb in each ear indicating that Pushkin was being cuckolded by the dashing Lieutenant d'Anthes. Or Nicholas Romanov. Our poet's nerves were strained dangerously toward the breaking point. The flow of his genius had run dry. He wasn't writing. Could not concentrate, creatively. He thought constantly of death. And he remembered a poem he'd written in his moment of profound despair deep in exile in Southern Russia, GOD GRANT THAT I MAY NOT GO MAD!

Baroness Svetlina had ceased to visit him at breakfast time.

Some nights he would sit alone in his study fighting hard to bring his mind to focus on the work that lay before him. He told himself he didn't give a damn what those idiots at court said about him. He was above that. He had more important things to think about. Had his life to live, his work to finish. He would bite the tip of his pen and write furiously as if his life's blood were coming out of the nib of the goose quilled pen he wrote with. Time was running out for him, like the fluid of his pen. But it was no good when he forced it like that. He did care. It was his wife they laughed about. It was his own life they were disparaging.

Pray God that I may not go mad!

He sat there trying to get back to his work. His mind wandered. He was in Ekaterinaslav in the hovel he had shared with rats and roaches. He was in the camel-dung-heaped streets of Kishinev. Out in the Pale with large-eyed Nina. In Odessa with Eliza. Amelia was dead and lay rotting underneath Italian soil. And Olga Kalashnikova in that lonely graveyard in Boldino. "Rest in Peace." He was up on Holy Mountain with his nyanya. Grandma-ma and Grandpa-pa Hannibal. He sat there half awake and half with nightmare. Maybe after all there was a God. The peasants whom he loved believe it. Arina Rodionovna believed it. Perhaps he was already dead. Perhaps he had died and gone to hell where pagans like him were consigned to spend eternity. He closed his eyes. His head was screaming. He held it between his hands. He had to get himself together. There was work for him to do. He could not afford to lose his mind. What would happen to his children? What would happen to his work? What would happen to Natasha?

Pray God that I may not go mad!

He could hear his sister-in-law tiptoeing around the house outside his study. She walked softly in and put a cup of steaming tea on his desk. Her hands were trembling uncontrollably and she spilled tea on his manuscript.

"Goddammit, Alexandra, who in the hell asked you for tea?"

She stood there near him shaking like a slim birch in a wind out of the north. Tears were spilling from her warm dark eyes. "I'm sorry, Alexander Sergeievich. I didn't mean to upset you." A sob escaped her trembling lips.

He wanted to tell her that he understood, that he knew she loved him. He was sorry he had screamed at her, especially her. He looked up in her face and saw the great love there for him. He recognized the shameful want and the want in him reciprocating. Oh God, if only she were his Natalya. If only she had Natalya's face and her own spirit and intelligence. If only she were not Natalya's sister. The thought of making a mistress of his sister-in-law repelled him. She was too dear to him for that. Oh God, he mustn't do that to this one. Not to one like Alexandra! Yet he saw himself reaching out toward her.

She shouted, softly, "No, we mustn't!" She turned and ran out of the study sobbing down the hall to her bedroom. He got up and started down the hall after her, then he remembered that he mustn't. She was too dear to him. He mustn't.

He turned and went back to his desk.

After this emotional encounter with Pushkin, Alexandra began to accompany her two sisters to the balls and parties. And Pushkin would spend most of his nights alone, at home in his study, except for the children sleeping nearby and the servants downstairs in their quarters. He had to stop thinking of Alexandra in that way. She was his wife's sister and the sweetest woman ever in his life, and he must not debauch her.

He would stay out of her way. If she stayed at home, he would go out. If he could not resist temptation, then he'd avoid it. He mustn't give up on poor innocent Natalya so easily. He spent more time with the children now, told them stories, played with them.

He again tried to discuss his work with Natalya. He came home one evening from his research at the Imperial archives and found to his surprise that she was not going out that night. After supper, they sat together in his study. He tried to start a conversation with her on a project he was working on.

She stared at him blankly as if he spoke a language she was unfamiliar with. He thought, maybe she thinks I'm speaking a foreign language.

Try again. Don't lose your patience. Remember how she used to be in bed? You won that battle just by having patience. "The Russian people must have some written sense of their historic presence. The oral tradition is not enough." He sounded pompous even to himself.

She stared blank-faced at her tormentor who claimed to be in love with her. Her mind was elsewhere.

"I mean, Arina Rodionovna gave so much to me out of the oral tradition, and I must pass it on to the world in writing."

Natasha stared at Alexander.

"I know, the monks of Kiev and Novgorod wrote way back there in ancient times and Karamzin here in modern times. But I mean, someone has to dig deeper into us, into our nuances and idiom, into the meaning of the Russian peasantry. The Uzbeks, the Muzhiks, the Cossacks. Like Pugachev. And great heroes like Peter and—and Nevsky, and especially Ibrahim Petrovich Hannibal, my great-grandfather—"

She sat there thinking, why is he torturing me like this? I should have gone out tonight.

He asked her, "What are you thinking about, my pet?"

She said, "I have a headache. I must get something for it." And she left him in the study as she went to cure her headache. It seemed to be his mission in life to go around giving people whom he loved headaches. He'd always been a headache to his mother.

One winter night he worked late into the morning. Katerina and Natasha were at a ball at Anichkov Palace. He was working on his novel THE NEGRO OF PETER THE GREAT. Alexandrina had stayed behind to keep him company. There was nothing to worry about. Their love had conquered lust. Their common sense and character had overcome temptation. As she had done so many times before, she came into the room and sat quietly as she watched him work. Her presence in the room did not overly distract him. It was a tender thing that gave him solace. They were friends, nothing more or less. She was his wife's sister. This night, as he sometimes did, he turned to her and read a section of his work to her. He stopped reading and looked at her, as she sat there with tears spilling from her dear dark eyes.

His voice contained a terrible sadness mixed with pride.

"He was a great man, Alexandrina. A proud African in this Great White Russian world. And I know it wasn't easy for him. Right here in this same Saint Petersburg. They say my so-called savage temper and my sensuality come from him, but they refuse to give him credit for my genius. Somehow I know it comes from him." His voice choked off. "I've always felt the African in me very deeply."

Slyly and shyly she wiped the tears from her eyes. She looked up into his face and there was such a terrible sadness in the darkness of it. Like a dark and lonely winter night out there in the Russian steppes. She would do anything to erase the sorrow from those dear dark animated eyes, the anguish from that sensitive mouth. She wanted the beauty of his genius always to keep his countenance aglow. Her eyes began to fill again against her will. She could not forgive her younger sister's superficiality that prevented her from seeing the overwhelming beauty in his genius. That Natalya should find the empty-headed Lieutenant more attractive than Alexander Sergeievich was incomprehensible to Alexandra. Alexander Sergeievich saw the longing in her face, and he turned away from her. He thought he must be strong for both of them. He meant to tell her to please leave. He could not concentrate this night with her nearby. He turned again toward her and opened his mouth to speak. She had risen and had come near to him without his knowing, and now she stood within arm's reach. He said sadly, "Alexandrina—"

She misunderstood. She reached toward him and put her hand out and tenderly touched his woolen curls. And a sob slipped from her quaking lips.

"Oh my darling Alexander Sergeievich!" As he stood up and took her in his arms to keep this trembling one from falling. And it was all there in the dear dark wide eyes, the love and wanting, and the need and want and love in him reciprocating. His lonely heart knew a tender feeling it had never known before and a terrible need for love from her. And even as they both seriously agreed, "We simply mustn't," these two lovers did—almost. For they had reached the brimming brink from which there was no turning back. He held her tightly up against him and could not let himself release her, and he felt his manhood growing against the vortex of her maidenhood; it was as if he had entered by the warmest welcome the innermost chamber of her sensuality where no one else had ever ventured, and there had been a change of heart, an agonizing ambivalence; she wanted him to leave but desperately wanted him to remain forever; he felt the quivering response from the very depths of her womanhood to his self-asserting manliness; she felt that he was in her womb even as she had dreamed of it, shamefully, and at the same time dreaded it. So that even as she pleaded with him to spare her just this once, with the perspiration above her wet desiring lips, her mouth claimed his, she pushed further into his arms, his thighs. "Dear God, Alexander Sergeievich, we really mustn't!" And he held her with the strength of giants, for there was no such strength in this entire Russian earth enough for either of them, and if he turned her loose he knew he would undress her. And so he held her strongly as she wept there in his arms.

"Oh, my sweet, darling angel! My beautiful Alexander Sergeievich! I'm so ashamed! I love you! I love you! Let me go, my princely falcon! Please have pity on me!"

She went limp in his arms, her dear lips pale and parted, her cheeks now roseate, then losing color. He relaxed his hold on her and she almost went down to the floor. He took her in his arms again and took her to the couch and lay her there.

"Forgive me, Alexander Sergeievich! I feel so ashamed! I want to die! I want to kill myself!"

He told her, huskily, "There is nothing for you to be ashamed of. I'm so proud of you, dear angelic Alexandrina." He kissed the salty tears from her eyes.

He gathered her in his arms and he took her to her room and left her. She was Natasha's sister. He loved her much too deeply to debauch her.

After that evening, Alexandra seemed to think that all the rules of Christian conduct and morality no longer had any revelance to her. She was a changed woman. She went around the house with a serenity all her own. Her eyes always so dark and sorrowful were now aglow with the joy of living, breathing, her face suffused. She acted toward Alexander Sergeievich as if she were his wife instead of his sister-in-law. Sometimes she brought him coffee in the morning before he began his work. She anticipated what he would want for lunch and brought him that along with a glass of kvass. Between lunch and supper she brought his favorite wine. She inquired of him what he wanted for dinner and discussed it with the cook. She was the wife that Natasha might have been but never could be. But

Alexandra never went near him again in his study when he worked at night. It was as if she'd made up her mind after much agonizing that, if she could not be his wife, physically, romantically, she would be his wife in every other way.

One day she came down with a severe case of pneumonia. It frightened Pushkin. He almost went out of his mind with foreboding and apprehension. He was afraid she might pass away, as so many others who had loved him had done. The night after Alexandrina became ill he dreamed she had died, saw her lying with pale lips in a casket. His tears and weeping woke him and he could not go back to sleep. The next day he did not go to the archives but sat by her bedside as the doctor tended her, saw to it that she got her medication. She must not die. She loved him and he loved her and she must not die. This dearest of the dearest must not die. Alexandrina must not die! One day her temperature began to soar, and he, who wasn't sure there was a God, prayed silently to whatever God there might be. He gave her so much gentle care, Natasha became jealous, superficially, of her sister.

One day she mumbled to him, "You care for her more than you ever cared for me. You love her more."

If it were only true, Alexandrina thought. If it were only true! Her feverish dark eyes stared in envy at her younger sister, whom she knew Alexander Sergeievich worshiped.

"Alexandrina must get better!" was the poet's only answer.

When Natasha left the room Alexandrina asked him, "Do you really want me to get better?"

"I want it more than life itself. You are dearer to me than almost anyone on this earth!" He kissed her on her feverish lips.

She smiled. Her face lit up. The midnight left the deep deep darkness of her eyes. "I'll get better for you, Alexander Sergeievich."

"Get better for me, yes," he shouted softly, "but especially get better for your special, wonderful self!"

All night long that night Alexandrina tossed and turned restlessly as the perspiration drained from her. The next day her deep set eyes seemed to have sunken further, deeper into her forehead. Was she who loved him now about to leave him? Was his kiss actually the kiss of death?

"Alexandrina! You promised me!"

She smiled for him. He was standing near the bed. His eyes had filled with tears. She reached for his hand and placed it on her cheeks.

And he knew then the fever had left her and that she would indeed recover.

The announcement was made at one of the parties. The Dutch Ambassador had officially adopted d'Anthes. Printed cards were sent to close friends and acquaintances. Henceforth his name would be Lieutenant Georges Charles d'Anthes de Heckeren. Henceforth he would be known as the son of Baron Heckeren.

D'Anthes moved into his father's palace. The Baron pampered his new son. He indulged the blonde-haired Lieutenant with all kinds of expensive gifts like an old man coddling a new young lover. He showered so much obvious affection on the young Lieutenant rumors began to circulate that their relationship was an unnatural one.

The Baron was a very rich man totally devoid of scruples. Since coming to Russia he had used his considerable wealth and his influential friends, like Count Stroganov and Foreign Minister Count Nesselrode and Chief of Secret Police Benkendorf, to engage in illegal traffic in opium, expensive clothing from the Orient, expensive carpets from India and Persia, snuff, china, eunuchs, eastern spices, linens, arms and ammunition, scents, musk, jewels, girls, turquoise, topaz—all of it absolutely tax free. He committed crimes for which members of the Russian trade guilds would have been sentenced to a hundred lashes with the glue-dipped knout, hanged on the scaffold or banished to Siberia. If he had not received the powerful support and cover-up of men like Benkendorf and Nesselrode, the least he might have expected would be deportation back to Holland in disgrace. But the Baron became wealthier, more powerful and more arrogant.

Meanwhile, his beautiful young son ran the young ladies of the Imperial Court wild with his cavalier flirtations. But Natalya Nicholaevna Goncharova Pushkina was definitely the most favored one and the envy of all. Baron Van Heckeren did not begrudge his loving son his little flirtations with the young beauties of the opposite sex. As a matter of fact, he rather enjoyed it and encouraged it, as long as young d'Anthes always understood that his heart of hearts belonged to his adopted father.

Natasha came home one early before day morning apparently upset and told Pushkin that Baron Van Heckeren had approached her at the ball at which d'Anthes was absent due to illness, and implored her, "Give me back my son! For God's sakes, give him your undivided love! He is dying of a broken heart! If you do not give him your love, he will kill himself!"

Pushkin exploded. "Broken heart! He is sick in bed with syphilis! Stay away from those vultures. They're both of them despicable buggers!"

But Natasha did not heed her husband. The two young lovers took their innocent courtship from the ballroom out into the open. They went horseback riding with Natasha's sister, Katerina, as chaperone. Katerina had long ago fallen anguishly in love with d'Anthes. Pushkin's home became a place of endless arguments, intrigue and deceptions, of recriminations and weeping, of shouting and slamming doors. Muttered oaths. Threats. Dire warnings. Alexandra agonizing. Katerina was obviously envious of Natasha, who was loved ardently by d'Anthes. Natasha was romantically in love with d'Anthes but physically faithful to Pushkin and resentful of Pushkin's relationship with Alexandra. And Pushkin, ragingly annoyed by Natasha's flirtations with the young French Guardsman, thought often of the gypsy's warning to him in his young and gallivanting days, "Beware of a young white stranger. He spells danger to you."

Pushkin began to receive anonymous letters about Natasha and d'Anthes. Friends warned Natasha, but she laughed the warnings away.

She was only amusing herself she told them. There was no danger of serious involvement, she assured them, even as she sank deeper and deeper into a quagmire. And d'Anthes became *persona non grata* at several of the fashionable salons in Saint Petersburg. All this while Pushkin's mother lay dying and asking for her elder son.

Darkness had fallen by the time Alexander Sergeievich reached his dying mother. Gendarmes were already stationed outside the elder Pushkin's house in Moscow. Creditors and tradesmen were pacing back and forth outside like vultures smelling out their prey. When he walked into his mother's bedroom, she wept bitterly. "Forgive me, my son, my darling Sasha!"

Candles were burning, priests in long black cassocks were already reading the prayers for the dead, as she lay there in her brass four poster bed with the heavy damask canopy the delicate color of pinkish heather.

He fought desperately to control his feelings. "Forgive you for what, Ma-ma?" He remembered the years he had starved for the slightest show of affection from her, and from his father, but especially from her. He knew all this and yet he heard himself repeating, "Forgive you for what? For being a loving and devoted mother?" Her large dark eyes that had given her dear face so much beauty in her younger days had dimmed terribly with age. It was not until this very moment that he realized how much he really loved her—adored and worshiped her. Had always wanted her to love him and to demonstrate her love for him. He knew now he had always looked for her in the eyes of every beautiful woman he had ever loved. Her dark almost black eyes were not the same now, but he had looked for her in the dark eyes of Amelia and Svetlina and Eliza and perhaps even Natalya and Alexandrina.

Relatives and acquaintances were crowded around his mother's bed. Pushkin's father was weeping openly, sobbing now without control. Candles beneath icons glowed brightly all around the room.

She shook her head. "I'm on my death bed, son. I must put things right with my God and with the Holy Virgin. I ask their forgiveness, and I ask yours, for the way I treated you, the most excellent and virtuous of my children. Oh yes, I loved you, but I never understood you. God knows I tried. Heaven and the Blessed Virgin know I did my best. Can you find it in your generous heart to forgive your stupid mother? I always loved you, but I never knew how to show my love to you. Can you understand? Can you forgive me?"

It was in the dead of winter. All the windows were shut tight. There was a stifling smell of burning incense. She begged him. "Please! Pajalsta! Please, my angel, my brave bright falcon. Please forgive your stupid mother!"

He wept. He could not contain the tears. "There's nothing to forgive you for, Ma-ma, I love you! You know I have always loved you. I love you and I forgive you for whatever you think there is for me to forgive."

Her full lips that he had always loved were quivering now and seemed to him had somehow grown thinner. Her dear dark eyes lit up briefly now. She smiled, and held her hand out to him and he took it, and kissed her on her feverish lips, as quietly she gave up the ghost, with the head priest standing on the other side of the bed giving her extreme unction. Nadezda Osipovna Pushkina died with a beatific smile on her face, a great gift from her wayward son.

Again the thought of death haunted all his dreams that these days were usually nightmares. But he loved life in spite of everything. He remembered the poem he had written when he was in the deep and morbid doldrums of despondency in Boldino and thought continuously of death. He remembered.

O, nay, life has not grown stale for me.
I want to live, I do love life
Nor does my soul's flame fail entirely
Though no more stirred by youthful strife.
Still there exists a fascination
In curiosity's sharpened call,
In words dear to imagination
In feelings most of all.
The darkness of the grave—
Wherein is there a good of death?

Alexander Sergeievich ultimately reconciled himself to his mother's death, torturously, bitterly. Everyone had to die. Death was Fate's final grimmest joke on humans. But he himself had a long time to live, he told himself. He had too much work left still undone to waste time on thoughts of dying. Life is hard, life is endless struggle, life is sorrow; life can be vicious, but wherein is there the good of death?

After his return from his mother's burial on Holy Mountain near Mikhailovskoye, he applied for the fifth time to the Imperial Court for permission to publish his own magazine. To his great surprise the permission was granted. The magazine would be named SOVREMENNIK (The Contemporary). For this venture he gathered around him such writers as Turgenev, Zukovsky, Yazykov, Gogol and Vyazemsky. Especially did he encourage new young writers. They would meet at his apartment on the Moika Quay. The less than commodious study would be crowded with young writers who looked upon him as a kind of ancient sage. It embarrassed him, the admiration he saw in most of their faces.

When they had gathered one evening Alexandra had served them wine, and now she sat quietly in a corner.

Pushkin asked them why they wanted to be writers. "It is a crazy, lonely life, the hardest way in all this world to earn a livelihood."

A young Ukrainian writer by the name of Nikolai Gogol, large-eyed and intense, said, "What kind of a question is that? Asking me why I want to write is like asking me why I eat, why I breathe. I write because I cannot *not* write. Writing is as essential to me as sleeping. Sometimes I write against my will. It's a compulsion, an obsession. I write because I don't like the way things are on this crazy earth, especially in Holy Russia!"

Alexander Sergeievich exclaimed, "That's it! Of course! That's it! That is exactly why I write, to change the world. The world stinks to the Heavens, and I want it to smell a hell of a lot better."

"But," Nikolai Gogol objected, "I did not say I wrote to change the world. I don't believe that things can ever change."

Pushkin looked over into the large warm eyes of Alexandra. She was shocked at the temerity of anyone disputing Pushkin, especially another writer. He smiled to reassure her.

He turned again to Gogol. "The one thing I am as sure of as I am that it is snowing outside, is the inevitability of change. If I did not believe this I would not write another word. Each of us has changed since we gathered here this evening. Do you think the serfs are going to tolerate their situation forever? The serfs in Russia and the slaves in America will one day be liberated."

Gogol responded, "They have done little or nothing about their situation so far, and there seems to be very little possibility that they will do so in the future."

"What do you think the Decembrists were about?" Pushkin demanded.

Nikolai Gogol mumbled, "You're known as the bard of the Decembrists. Nevertheless the Czar is still with us. The serfs still remain in bondage."

Notwithstanding, Gogol was his favorite among the younger writers. Pushkin gave Nikolai two of his plots, inscribing them, "To Nikolai Gogol. I would have given them to no one else." Gogol later developed them into his DEAD SOULS and THE INSPECTOR GENERAL.

One evening Gogol visited alone with Pushkin. After dinner they retired to Pushkin's study. Natasha left for the ball at the Winter Palace along with her eldest sister. Alexandra brought them a bottle of vodka and two glasses and left. Nikolai began to read to Pushkin chapters from his novel, DEAD SOULS. They felt good about their friendship for each other. Gogol sat at the desk where the candelabrum gleamed brightly. Alexander Sergeievich sat on a couch across the room from him. They were relaxed in one another's company.

But as the story developed, Pushkin grew gloomier and gloomier. When Nikolai had finished reading, Alexander Sergeievich commented in a gruff voice all filled up with deep emotion, "My God! How sad our Russia is!"

"The saddest place in all this earth," Nikolai Gogol responded.

Pushkin's relationship with the younger writer grew and prospered. When Pushkin published THE CAPTAIN'S DAUGHTER, Gogol wrote in one of the Saint Petersburg journals:

In comparison with THE CAPTAIN'S DAUGHTER, all other novels and short stories are like watered porridge. In it, purity and restraint reach such heights that reality itself seems artificial, a caricature. For the first time, we have truly Russian characters: a simple officer commanding a fort, his wife, a sergeant, the fort itself with its lone cannon, the disorder of the period, the modest grandeur of ordinary people. Not only is it reality, it is better than reality.

Pushkin had immortalized the rebel, Pugachev, in Russian fiction. Gogol left Russia shortly afterwards. The country was too sad for him.

Alexander Sergeievich sorely missed the comradeship of Nikolai Gogol. He lived now in a state of deep depression. He began to think of death again. The meetings with the younger writers discontinued. His magazine SOVREMENNIK, was failing. He sunk deeper into debt. Alexandra stayed in her room at nights when her sisters left for a ball at the Stroganovs or the Nesselrodes or the Winter Palace. He sat alone in his study struggling vainly with his muse. The word was, in literary circles, especially at the court, that his career had run its course, the fountain of his talent had run dry. And sometimes he believed them. He spent all day at the archives, came home, had supper and sometimes played with his children.

Death became a phantom that haunted many of his waking hours. He felt a heavy premonition. It was during this time that he began to complete his EXEGI MONUMENTUM, the poem he started in Boldino.

One morning he awoke with a cold fear knifing at his heart that he had departed this particular version of his life for another dimension of existence, and a wave of sweet tranquility washed over him. Despite the vigilance of His Imperial Majesty's border guards, he had circumvented them, he had crossed over the Russian border at long last, into that other world where all was peace. He knew a subliminal feeling of his own soul soaring around with other souls in a heavenly existence. There were Grandpa-pa Ibrahim Petrovich and Grandma-ma Hannibal and Anna Rodionovna and Amelia Riznicha and Olga Kalashnikova and Anton Delvig. Even his dear and sorrowful mother. Ivan Pushchin was there also. He almost could not cope with so much serenity and blissfulness. It was a new experience for him. Then he heard the gentle breathing of the softness that lay next to him, he smelled the sharp sweet familiar fragrance of that softness, and he broke out in goose bumps of perspiration, and he was glad that he was still alive in this bedroom in this big brass bed with this loveliest of women next to him. Still death's premonition lingered. The cold taste in his mouth persisted. The house was chilled with the first days of November. He rose from his bed and stumbled down the hall to his study. It was one of the dying days of autumn. And he completed his EXEGI MONUMENTUM at one sitting.

Pushkin began to receive anonymous letters. "Dear Distinguished Friend: As an admirer who has adored your work ever since I can remember, I must painfully and hesitantly advise you that your wife is deceiving you with a certain gentleman who frequents the Imperial Court. Sincerely, Your devoted admirer. . . ." Then, "A certain young officer is regretfully deceiving you with your spouse." He began to get them two or three times a week. He thought at first they meant the Emperor, though he never believed, he told himself, that Natasha would actually deceive him. She was flirtatious, yes, but that was the fashion of the ladies at the court. She would just go so far and no further. She was his faithful wife, Natalya Nicholaevna Goncharova Pushkina.

The few times he would attend one of the balls, he usually stood there leaning on one of the long white columns in the vast ballroom looking bored and sipping ices, pretending not to watch the Emperor and the son of the Dutch Ambassador competing outrageously for the attention of Madame Natalya Goncharova Pushkina.

The number of letters increased. Now they became more specific. "The gay deceiver is a young handsome French Officer in the Emperor's Hussar Horse Guards." The image of the deceiver began to crystalize in Alexander Sergeievich's mind. Then one morning he received a letter that changed the course of Russian history. It was written in French. Pushkin's hands were shaking as he read it again and again.

> The Grand-cross Commanders and Chevaliers of the most serene order of cuckolds, convened in plenary assembly under the president of the venerable Grand Master of the Order, His Excellency D.I. Naryshkin, have unanimously elected M. Alexander Sergeievich Pushkin coadjutor of the Grand Master of the Order of Cucholds and historiographer of that Order.
>
> Permanent Secretary:
> Count I. Borch

He sat down at his desk and once more read the letter. His hand stopped trembling, as a calm spread over him.

PART EIGHT

TRAGEDY

CHAPTER ONE

He sat there beneath the piercing stare of his great-grandfather reading the letter again and again, but nothing changed. And he wondered why he kept reading, since he had understood every idiom, every nuance, every single innuendo, from the very first.

Naryshkin's wife had been the late and very pious Emperor Alexander's mistress. Common knowledge among the aristocracy. Count Borch's loving wife had played musical beds on many a conjugal couch at the Imperial Court. She had been a frequent participant in Emperor Alexander's monthly orgies.

The morning Alexander Sergeievich received his letter from "Count Borch," several of his friends and many of his enemies received identical communications.

As far as the harassed poet was concerned, war had been declared. He was quietly enraged. The first shot had been fired. Who fired the shot? What was it all about? Some thought it was a dangerous prank by someone with a macabre sense of humor, possibly meaning to point to the Emperor as the man cuckolding Pushkin to point the finger away from d'Anthes. There was a great debate among the ennobled people as to the meaning of the prank and the identity of the perpetrator. But Pushkin's mind was single pathed. He smelled a rat somewhere in the wainscoting, and the odor came from one quarter only. That quarter was Baron Van Heckeren and Georges Charles d'Anthes de Heckeren.

Having decided where the smell came from, there was no alternative but to act. Pushkin sat down that very morning and calmly sent a letter to d'Anthes challenging the guardsman to a duel. He felt good about it all day long.

Both men were expert marksmen. D'Anthes was the best shot in the Horse Guards. Alexander Sergeievich didn't remember how many duels he had fought. There'd been so many in his young eventful life. He'd won them all, those that had not been averted. This time it was different. This one would not be prevented. This time it was kill or be killed.

And he felt a kind of soft and sweet serenity settling over him. He went to his bedroom and stared at himself in the mirror above the washstand. He was pleased with what he saw. Nothing had changed except for a few wrinkles in the corners of his mouth, which was still thick and sensuous and African. He was still swarthy. And proud. Hell yes! *Da! Da!* Proud. There is so much to be proud about.

You gave the Russian people a literary tongue of their own. You gave them poetry, gave them prose, gave them tragedy. And most of all, you gave them the gift of loving themselves. And now the final gift—the finale. And you feel good about yourself.

He had not felt this way since the gendarme came for him in Mikhailovskoye to "face the abominable assassin." His heart knew a free and facile feeling, even as it palpitated in his animated chest.

It was not the happiest moment in our poet's life. He had been in a deep despondency and seemed doomed to remain in it forever. Life had not been very dear to this man who had always had a rage to live. Death could be a welcomed tranquilizer. If he killed d'Anthes he would have rid himself of a pestilence that plagued him day and night. If he himself were killed, he would win his peace and calm at last.

Either way he couldn't lose.

CHAPTER TWO

Unless Alexander Sergeievich's instincts and intelligence deceived him, the Dutch Ambassador had been playing with dangerous fireworks and they had exploded in his face. The rich baron with the rotten teeth was frightened. The script he and his ennobled cronies at Court had concocted had been mishandled by the actors. Alexander Sergeievich Pushkin was the kind of writer who wrote his own script and did not take kindly to any kind of editing or censorship. Pushkin felt that he could not lose no matter what Fate held in store for him. On the other hand, the Baron felt he could not win no matter who might fire the fatal shot. If his dear adopted son for whom he had planned so grandiosely should be killed, he himself would not want to live any longer. And in the event that his son, a foreigner, killed Alexander Sergeievich Pushkin, the African, the glory of the Russian people, the Emperor would have to censure his loving son and the Ambassador himself, no matter how the Great One himself might feel inwardly. History and the Russian people would demand it.

Fortunately, his d'Anthes was out of town doing extra guard duty as a penalty for some minor misconduct. Therefore the Ambassador received the letter and was the first to read it. He panicked momentarily. His old heart beat wildly in his chest, and he could hear it beating in the temples of his balding forehead. His whole face felt neuralgic. His gut erupted and he passed wind all morning long. Then he collected himself and moved to avert what could only be disaster for himself and his adopted son. The omnipresent Emperor was aware at all times of the developments, but at this stage he did nothing, one way or the other.

Meanwhile, the free and easy feeling Pushkin first knew after he had sent the challenge had gradually hardened into a cold outrage. He was a quietly seething volcano ready to erupt.

Also, meanwhile the royal tutor to the Czarevich, Zukovsky, had not been sitting idly by. The next morning after the challenge he was at Pushkin's apartment along the granite-embanked canal on Moika Street. They met in the poet's study amidst his cubicle of book-lined walls. Natalya would not leave. She sat there while they spoke heatedly to each other. "It's all my fault!" she sobbed suddenly. "I didn't mean to do it! I didn't understand."

Alexandra was also there, deathly frightened. Was it possible that her Alexander Sergeievich, her proud courageous falcon, Russia's greatest poet ever, might go to meet his death within several days?

Alexander Sergeievich himself was adamant. He wanted to kill. There was a quiet madness in his eyes that would not consider compromise. His honor and his dignity had been compromised too many times too many places. This would be the end of it. One way or the other. He laughed at his long time friend whom he loved and respected. "Why are you so interested in protecting the life of that worthless French bastard? Is he a friend of yours? What big loss would it be to the Russian people when I kill the son of a bitch?"

"You're letting your anger blind you," Zukovsky argued. "He's one of the best shots in the Emperor's Horse Guards. He's as good a shot as you are."

Alexander Sergeievich laughed at the Royal uchitol. The maniacal way he had of laughing when he was blind with anger. "So if he kills me all my troubles will be over. Everyone has to die some time. That's what Fate, God's Will and the Emperor have decreed for all of us."

Zukovsky lost his temper, a thing he seldom did. "Goddammit, Alexander Sergeievich, don't you know how important you are to Russia?"

Pushkin remembered what his wife had told him. "You're just a Kammerjunker—They all laugh at you."

"Don't you have the vaguest notion of what you mean to the Russian people?" Zukovsky continued. "You made the Russian language. You gave us a poetic tongue that is uniquely ours. You gave us the novel, gave us the tragedy. You molded the Russian psyche. You're a Russian of African descent."

"I know I'm African," Alexander Sergeievich answered with indignation and impatience. "I have always known it!"

"Don't you know what it means? You, Alexander Sergeievich Pushkin, a Russian of African descent, the greatest writer the Motherland has ever birthed. You are a national treasure. One of the greatest men who ever lived! And you're Russian and you're African! You have no right to recklessly risk your life like this. Don't you understand?"

"I understand how important it is for me to settle with this swinish bastard one way or the other," Pushkin replied heatedly.

Zukovsky got no satisfaction from the poet. His anger had been locked up in his heart too long. As Zukovsky was leaving, Natalya fell on her knees before her husband. "Forgive me, Alexander Sergeievich! Please forgive your stupid wife!"

He put his hand lightly on her lovely head. "There's nothing to forgive, my sweetheart. It's those sons of bitches at the Court. They've always hated me. There's never been any love lost between us." He remembered his mother's death bed, her dying request of him. Someone he loved was always asking his forgiveness.

Alexandra stared bleary-eyed at Alexander and Natalya, ashamed of the jealousy she felt of the great love she knew he still felt for her baby sister. She thought her undeserving of it. The feeling built up in her breasts. It overflowed. Against her will she blurted out, "It *is* all your fault! It *is* all your fault! You never appreciated him, never loved him!" She ran, sobbing, out of the study and down the hall to her own bedroom.

Zukovsky went directly to the Dutch Ambassador's palatial lodgings. All day they tried desperately for a compromise that would be acceptable to both Pushkin and d'Anthes.

The next morning Alexander Sergeievich was busy in his study when he heard announced, "Monsieur Le Baron Heckeren, Dutch Ambassador to the Court of Imperial Russia."

Pushkin, irritated, looked up at the smiling paunchy-faced Ambassador with the brown discolored teeth. His waxed and graying mustache made contact with the hair that sprouted from his nostrils like grasshoppper's antennae. Pushkin asked sarcastically, "To what do I owe this great honor, Your Highness?" He remained seated at his desk.

The nervous Ambassador mopped the brow of his wide receding forehead with a linen handkerchief. He began to pace the floor. Alexander Sergeievich watched him with a vague amusement. "I come on behalf of my son, Monsieur Pushkin." The bushy growth around his ears looked like earmuffs to the poet.

"Oh? So you have come as the lieutenant's second to make all the necessary arrangements? Good! Bravo! Please speak to Count Sollogub. He is my chosen second."

"There's been a terrible mistake, Monsieur. I—er—"

Alexander Sergeievich interrupted him. "Yes, and you and that scoundrel you call your son have made it. Speak to Sollogub."

"My son and I are blameless in this whole affair, Monsieur, I give you my sacred word."

"If that is all you have to say, Baron, I must ask you to leave. As you can see, I am rather busy at the moment."

"But, Monsieur, I do not understand. I beg of you—" The Baron pleaded.

"If you have not come to make the arrangements, please ask Nikita Koslov to show you out." Alexander Sergeievich turned his back on the Ambassador and to the business on his desk.

The Baron bowed stiffly, clicked his heels and left.

The next morning Baron Van Heckeren returned and asked for an extension of a week to make the necessary arrangements. D'Anthes was still away on guard duty. Alexander Sergeievich granted the extension.

That Friday night well appointed carriages, mink-lined barouches and berlins pulled up in front of the Stroganov palace all through the night. Winter weather had come early even for Northern Russia, and the snow had come down heavily and formed tremendous snowdrifts.

All day long a soft white icy snow had whirled wildly from the northern skies. Spitting, twisting, pirouetting. Roaring from across the Gulf of Finland like a crazy pack of howling Russian wolfhounds. Then suddenly at dusk it stopped, as if the trees, weary and heavy-laden, had altogether shouted, "Enough! Enough! Pajalsta!" And a great white hush fell softly on the land. The icicles on the frozen trees winked and blinked like rarest diamonds. A full moon cast a softened glow of beauty all around the palace. The Russian world was quiet, white and ominous. Apprehensive. Except that now and then a wind would come from out of nowhere and blow its cold white shrieking breath amongst the trees. The trees would creak and tremble, and here and there a frozen limb would fall to earth. The Stroganov palace was clothed in white, like a virgin bride. Lights from candled chandeliers glowed brightly from the giant windows.

The coachmen remained outside the palace in their tightly fitted red suits and hareskin coats throughout the evening and continually jumped up and down in the below-zero weather and flailed their bodies in order to keep from freezing to death. The horses snorted and pranced around for much the same reason. There was a great important ball at the Winter Palace, where all these ennobled personages belonged, but there was more important business to attend to at the Stroganovs'. This was the meeting of the powerful and ennobled enemies of Alexander Sergeievich Pushkin, important and aristocratic ones like Foreign Minister Nesselrode, Chief of Secret Police Benkendorf, Prince Gargarin, Bulgarin Poletika, Count and Countess Uvarov and Dolgorukov, the fabulous and flamboyantly homosexual prince.

"Your Highnesses," the Dutch Ambassador pleaded, "You must come to my assistance. That African savage will not listen to reason."

They were seated in the vast Stroganov drawing room. The fire burned brightly in the giant fireplace.

"It's true," Count Stroganov agreed. "The scribbling bastard is one of the deadliest shots in all of Russia."

Heavy silken drapes adorned the gargantuan windows. There were prodigious candelabra lit up like Christmas trees in two corners of the room, each with fifty lighted candles glowing.

Count Benkendorf inhaled long and deeply on his Turkish cigar and suggested, "Ask for another extension. Try again to negotiate a settlement. Meanwhile, get your son some guaranteed protection."

The Baron blinked his eyes and said, "I don't know what you mean."

"Gentlemen in duels have been known to wear breastplates beneath their jackets."

"That would be a violation of every ethical code of honor among noblemen. The very idea is revolting." The Dutch Ambassador looked around the room at all of those assembled.

Benkendorf scoffed. "You did not become one of the richest men in Russia by adhering strictly to some code of ethics."

The noblemen and ladies chuckled. Count Stroganov laughed heartily. The puffy-faced Dutch Ambassador turned scarlet, thinking to himself, what a peculiar sense of humor these barbaric Russians have. Codes of honor obviously meant nothing to them. He had always felt superior to them. He did not look upon them as Europeans. There were the French, Dutch, English and German, all were civilized Europeans. And then there were the Russians, a totally separate primitive breed. Barbaric Asiatics . . . Byzantines . . . Inscrutable! Orientals!

He stared from one face to the other. "Is everyone here accounted for? Can each of us be trusted?"

Nesselrode answered indignantly, "We are the Russian nobility, Sire. *La crème de la crème.*"

Heckeren spoke with a pomposity he did not feel at the moment. His years as a successful diplomat put him in good stead, most of the time. "My son and I are honorable men, Sires."

"Julius Caesar was an honorable man. It did not help to save him. The King and Queen of France were also honorable."

"We'll simply have to devise another plan," Heckeren continued. "The very thought of it is repulsive to a European gentleman."

"You are among European ladies and gentlemen at this very moment, Baron," the Chief of Secret Police retorted. "The fact of the matter is you want to save your son from being killed, and we want to help you, but if you are implying that we are not Europeans, you can go to hell with your code of ethics and your European arrogance."

Foreign Minister Count Nesselrode said, "Now-now, gentlemen. We have a common interest on two levels. One, we are all of the upper classes, the nobility. Not so?" They nodded their heads in agreement. "Two, we want to see this scribbling savage cut down to proper measurement."

Stroganov said, "We want to be rid of the arrogant African bastard!"

Chief of Secret Police Benkendorf cautioned, "But it has to be done properly and above board. At least, it must appear to be. The Emperor was very specific on this question. I have just left him before coming here. Do we understand each other? If we mishandle it, it could be a national disaster. This fellow Pushkin is an African nobody as far as we're concerned, but the intellectuals and the masses worship the hapless scribbler as if he were a god or something. That is why His

Majesty is so lenient with him. The Emperor must maintain his image as a benevolent autocrat."

Heckeren spoke again, more subdued this time. "I do not believe my son would consider one moment the use of a breastplate. I do, however, comprehend the gravity of the situation."

Meanwhile Zukovsky spent more time at Pushkin's than he did at his own apartment. He tried to persuade the poet to withdraw the challenge. "You can do it without any loss of honor, because you have no proof that the Heckerens are responsible for the letter."

Prince Paul Vyazemsky tried, as did Natalya's Aunt, Katerina Ivanovna. Alexander Sergeievich would not be moved from his position. Only Alexandra seemed to understand why he could not be dissuaded. Baron Van Heckeren came again and asked for another extension. He broke down into tears. "My son is very dear to me. He is oftentimes misguided in his actions, but I am sure you remember when you sowed your wild oats. It hasn't been that long ago. You're still a young man. I need an extension, because he is not here. He'll be on guard duty for another week."

Even though the poet knew men had the need for tears as much as anyone, he could not stand to see a man break down unrestrainedly into sobbing, especially an old man.

The Baron was weeping uncontrollably. "Please, Your Excellency! Show us a little mercy! I don't know what to do!"

Alexander Sergeievich gave the Baron a two week extension. The Baron thanked him profusely, took his hand and kissed it, and departed. After the Ambassador left, Pushkin stared in disgust at the back of his hand, poured water into a pewter bowl and washed it vigorously with soap before he went forward with his work.

Zukovsky went to see the Dutch Ambassador once more. By then the Baron had collected himself. After they had talked for hours getting nowhere, the Baron looked up into Zukovsky's face and said, "The irony of the whole thing is appalling."

"The irony?" Zukovsky questioned.

"Pushkin thinks my son is pursuing his wife, when all the time he has been infatuated by her sister, the beautiful Katerina. He worships her. He only associates with Natalya just so he can be near beautiful Katerina. The dear lad simply adores her."

Zukovsky's eyes lit up. Could it possibly be true? Could this be the solution? He hoped. Then he remembered the anger and the anguish that had been on Pushkin's face when he had left him. He shook his head.

"It will never work. He'll never believe such a story."

"But it's true! I tell you it's the gospel truth. I swear before the Virgin Mary."

359

Zukovsky smiled ironically. "I'm afraid my friend does not believe in the immaculateness of our Blessed Lady. You'll have to think of something much more convincing than that."

Heckeren said, "As a matter of fact he intends to ask her to marry him. He would have asked for her hand before now except he did not know how to approach Alexander Sergeievich Pushkin, since he is the head of the household in which she lives."

Zukovsky's heart leaped about jubilantly. Was this a solution to the problem? He asked the Baron, "And am I authorized to speak of this matter to Pushkin? I'm fairly sure he would withdraw his challenge."

Heckeren answered, "You must make it very clear that in his withdrawal of the challenge, there must be no mention of the engagement, lest it seem that my son is doing this out of cowardice. You do understand?"

A cloud enveloped Zukovsky's face. "I quite understand, dear Baron, and I just hope I can get my friend, Pushkin, to also understand."

Alexander Sergeievich laughed at Zukovsky. "Do I look like a damn fool? D'Anthes marry Katya?"

"He thinks she's beautiful. He adores her."

The angry poet laughed again. He rose and went toward the cabinet where the whiskey was kept.

He gave his friend a glass of vodka and he swallowed his with one protracted gulp. Zukovsky said, "He wants to announce their betrothal immediately."

Alexander Sergeievich said, "He might become betrothed to avoid the duel, but he still would not go through with it once the duel was called off."

"Have I ever given you bad advice?" Zukovsky's prominent Adams apple was nervously overactive. "Listen to me. Take them at their word that they're really going to get married."

Alexander Sergeievich laughed. "Certainly. Why not? He'll be the laughing stock of Saint Petersburg. Any infatuation Natasha might have had for the dashing Lieutenant will turn to contempt at his obvious cowardice. She'll be through with him forever."

Zukovsky felt he had to say to his long time friend and protégé, "I must tell you that your letter withdrawing the challenge must not mention the engagement. The engagement must not be interpreted as a ruse to avoid the field of honor. The Heckerens were very explicit on that point."

"The Heckerens can go to hell with their explicitness. What do they take me for? An idiot?" Pushkin replied angrily.

Zukovsky protested, "But Alexander Sergeievich. . . ."

"Not a chance. You tell your explicit Ambassador the challenge is still on. I will not withdraw! My final word!"

Negotiations went back and forward for over a week. When d'Anthes returned from extra guard duty and learned of what was taking place, he was infuriated. It was the first time in his association with his adopted father that they had fought except for innocent quarrels that were easily mended. But this time he railed at the old gentleman and swore at him with the vilest curses at his command. The pathetic old white-haired gentleman cried like a jilted and unrequited lover. "My darling boy, I did only what I thought was best for you. You don't understand your own predicament. I only did what any father would have done for his loving son."

"Father excrement! You decrepit old son of a bitch! If I allowed something like that to take place, I couldn't go back to the barracks. I'd be a disgrace to the Emperor's regiment. They'd probably run me out of the Hussars."

"Pushkin is a national hero. You forget we are foreigners in this barbaric country."

"The idea sickens me to think of it. I don't want to hear another word about it," d'Anthes replied.

"Calm down, dear boy," the Ambassador pleaded. "We have more than another week. Think it over. Perhaps you can come up with a better plan."

Zukovsky along with d'Archiac, a friend of d'Anthes authorized to speak on his behalf, came with yet another proposal. The letter of withdrawal must include a statement that absolves d'Anthes of any dishonorable motives to avoid the duel with Pushkin. Alexander Sergeievich refused at first. "That scoundrel hasn't the remotest intention of marrying poor Katya. It's a mere ruse, and I will not withdraw the challenge, unless I can expose the cowardly son of a bitch!"

Zukovsky and d'Archiac pleaded with him. They argued that in a duel of this kind there could be no winner. Only losers. "If d'Anthes kills you, he is certain to lose his position as officer of the Guards. If you kill d'Anthes, you will surely be interred in the Peter and Paul bastille or sent to the salt mines of Siberia."

Zukovsky emphasized, "It will be the excuse your enemies at the court seek, to put you away. For you, it will be a living death!"

D'Archiac pleaded, "I beg you to give this your serious consideration, Your Excellency. I guarantee for myself and Lieutenant d'Anthes de Heckeren that the marriage will take place."

Alexander Sergeievich finally wrote the following statement:

Monsieur d'Archiac has told me in confidence that Baron d'Anthes Heckeren has decided definitely to propose marriage to Katerina Goncharova. He hesitated from making the announcement for fear of being misunderstood. I, as head of the household of which my sister-in-law is a member, give my consent to this marriage. I withdraw my challenge to Lieutenant d'Anthes and I have no grounds for attributing his decision to marry my sister-in-law to motives unworthy of a man of honor.

Zukovsky, Sollogub, Natasha's aunt, Countess Katerina Ivanovna Zagryashskay, d'Archiac, all were overjoyed. Aunt Katerina, who had always been fond of her poet nephew-in-law, threw her arms around his neck and kissed him. "Thank you, Alexander Sergeievich! May the Holy Virgin bless you all of your days!" Zukovsky, Sollogub and d'Archiac and Turgenev shook his hand warmly and embraced him. Kissed him on his bearded cheeks.

D'Archiac told him elatedly, "Monsieur d'Anthes-Heckeren sends his best regards and told me to express his hope that the two of you will come shortly to look upon yourselves as brothers."

Alexander Sergeievich sneered. "Nyet! Never! Never shall I regard the swinish scoundrel as a brother. He has my permission to marry my sister-in-law, but that is the end of it and the extent of any personal relationship. He will never be welcomed in my house."

D'Archiac asked, nervously, "Is the Lieutenant to infer any disparagement on him as a gentleman of honor?"

Pushkin answered sarcastically, "It's merely that being a very busy man, as I am sure the Lieutenant is also, one must have priorities as to with whom one spends the little there is of one's leisure time."

D'Archiac bowed stiffly to the poet, clicked his heels and took his leave thinking to himself that he would forget to tell d'Anthes of the latter portion of this conversation.

Moments after they had left him alone in his study, Pushkin walked to the frosted window and stared out at the driving snowstorm. Early that morning a cold driving rain, changing to sleet then to snow, had come charging from the Baltic across the Finnish marshes. The wet snow softly kissed the windows with rough and wet and sloppy kisses. He heard the weird moaning of the northern wind and heard the sleighbells of the carriages as they departed. He thought, they were so happy when they left, confident that God was good and in his Heaven and all was right down on this frigid Russian earth. He smiled malevolently at their simplistic optimism. He had not settled yet with this Frenchman.

Alexander Sergeievich escorted the three sisters to the next party. In the midst of the festivities Baron Heckeren formally announced the engagement.

The party people applauded. The chandeliers gleamed and glittered. They drank to the health of the fiance and his bride-to-be. They gathered around the couple, as d'Anthes took it all in stride and Katerina glowed with a happiness she never dared to dream of. The guests chattered pleasantly, animatedly. They kissed the bride-to-be and shook the handsome bridegroom's hand. The Dutch Ambassador wept and kissed them both. Everyone present had expressed themselves to the couple excepting Alexander Sergeievich, who stood apart as if it were a thing that concerned him not in the least.

D'Anthes moved with his betrothed toward Pushkin for his blessings, so to speak. When he reached the poet and extended his hand in an obviously friendly gesture, Pushkin took Katya's hand and kissed it. Then he looked coldly past d'Anthes, turned his back and walked away.

The very proper party people gasped at such bad manners and such insolence. D'Anthes stood there pale as death. This was a pattern Alexander Sergeievich would follow from then on, much to everyone's outraged astonishment. He did not attend the wedding or the reception. Even Alexander Sergeievich's avowed comrades among the aristocracy, longtime friends like Prince and Princess Vyazemsky and Madame Karamzina, were offended by the poet's bad behavior and took sides with the debonair young Frenchman who conducted himself always as a gentleman of breeding. Pushkin was a bloody boor.

But Pushkin got the news from others that at the wedding reception d'Anthes reverted to form again and danced with Natalya Pushkina as if in fact she was the bride instead of homely hawk-faced Katerina. The courtly people understood that nothing had changed, essentially. D'Anthes had shrewdly avoided a duel and got himself into a situation where he could be even closer to Natalya. He was now a part of the family. Every party they attended he flirted with Natalya more than ever. Katerina was the unhappiest bride in all of Holy Russia. D'Anthes was safer than ever in these harmless flirtations, the way he understood and calculated it. He could go the limit without fear of challenge, since it was against the European code of ethics to challenge a member of one's family on the field of honor. It became so outrageous that Alexander Sergeievich forbade Natalya from dancing with her brother-in-law under any circumstances.

One day Natalya received a note from Princess Idalya Poletika, a long-time enemy of the poet ever since his days of sowing wild oats. Alexander Sergeievich had rejected a bedroom offer Princess Idalya had made to him years before, and she never forgave the arrogant African. He was busy in his study when the note arrived. Natalya didn't disturb him. She dressed warmly and went out into the freezing below-zero weather.

The Princess, a tall ungainly woman with large protruding teeth and freckled face, received Natalya in her reception room. After Natalya had taken off her outer garments the homely Princess asked to be excused for a moment. As Natalya waited wondering what the urgency of this meeting was about, d'Anthes suddenly stepped out of a side door and threw himself at her feet, professing his undying love for her.

Madame Pushkina was horrified, mortified.

"Get up off your knees," she ordered him in indignation. "You are my sister's husband, and I am a married woman."

"I only married your sister so I could be near you more often. You knew all the while I love you and only you."

Natalya said, "You are disgusting!"

"I love you! I worship you!" he professed. "Have pity on me!"

He took her in his arms and covered her face with kisses. She pulled away and slapped his face. "You are contemptible!"

She got her coat and hurried from the house.

The next day Alexander Sergeievich received a hand-delivered letter telling him of the meeting. He faced Natalya with the letter and she broke down and told him everything.

"I did nothing wrong, Alexander Sergeievich," she told him pleadingly. "I swear by the Holy Virgin I am innocent!"

"I know you're innocent, my pet," he told her. And he honestly believed it.

"Don't worry your head about it," he told Natalya calmly. "I'll take care of everything."

"What are you going to do?" she asked excitedly.

"Don't you worry," he repeated calmly.

But now it was clear to him that the masquerade was over. And he knew what he had to do. It didn't matter that the rascal was technically a part of the family, since even the marriage had been fraudulent. That very afternoon he wrote a letter to the Dutch Ambassador that was tantamount to a challenge.

Baron! Permit me to set down briefly everything that has transpired. The behavior of your son has been known to me for a long time past, and I could not remain indifferent. I contented myself with the role of observer, ready to intervene when I should consider it necessary. An incident, which at any other time would have been extremely unpleasant to me, presented an excellent opportunity: I received the anonymous letter. I knew the moment had come, and I put it to good advantage. The rest you already know. I obliged your son to play such an abject role that my wife, amazed at so much cowardice and truckling, could not refrain from laughing, and the emotions which she might have felt for this great and lofty passion, was extinguished in cold contempt and deserving repugnance.

I must confess, Baron, that your own conduct was not entirely seemly. You, the representative of your crown, acted as a parental pimp for your son; it appears that his conduct (rather inept, by the way) was guided entirely by you. It was you, probably, who suggested to him all the pitiful things he related and the idiotic things he wrote. Like an obscene old woman, you lay in wait for my wife in every corner, in order to tell her of the love of your bastard, as he is reputed to be, when, sick with the pox, he had to stay at home, you told her he was dying of love for her; you would murmur to her 'Give me back my son'.

You must agree, Baron, that after all this I cannot tolerate my family having any relation whatever with yours. It was on this condition that I agreed not to pursue the dirty business any further and not to dishonor you in the eyes of our court and yours—which I had the power to do and had intended to do. I do not care that my wife be imposed on by you with your paternal counsels. I cannot permit your son, after his disgusting behavior, to have the effrontery to speak to my wife and still less to tell her barrack room puns and to play the role of a devoted and unhappy lover, whereas he is actually a coward and a scoundrel. I am obliged to address myself to you and ask you to put an end to all these intrigues, if you wish to avoid a fresh scandal, to which I certainly will not hesitate to expose you. I have the honor to be, Baron, your humble and obedient servant,

A. S. Pushkin

Pushkin's letter had its intended effect. It had to evoke a challenge from the young Guardsman. He received the challenge two days later.

A beautiful tranquility settled quietly over the weary poet. This time there would be no turning back. No back and forth negotiations, no compromises. Everything would be settled on a field of honor. Live or die, he would, at last, have peace.

CHAPTER THREE

Even Alexander Sergeievich Pushkin would have agreed that events moved along at a turtle's pace in Holy Russia; then suddenly they happened like a bolt of lightning.

The challenge from the young French Guardsman was received, accepted and replied to. The busy Frenchman from the French Embassy showed up again as d'-Anthes' second. Alexander Sergeievich was working in his study at his desk. When asked to name his own second, the poet said, offhandedly, without looking up, "Tell your friend, since he made the challenge he can also select a second for me, his own servant for all I care. Let's just be done with it without delay or fanfare. The fewer people we involve the better."

A note came back hand-delivered telling Pushkin, since he wrote the insulting letter to d'Anthes' father, thereby precipitating the challenge, and having accepted the challenge, it was up to him to select his own second. Refusal to name a second would be considered in violation of the code of honor. Pushkin read the note and sighed. It was such a nuisance. Very well, he would select his own second. It was such a bother. And who would it be? Count Sollogub, thinking the matter settled, had left a few days before to spend several weeks in Moscow, so that if it had not been settled permanently, he would be too far away to be involved. What to do? Whom to choose? Then Pushkin remembered an old comrade of his Tsarskoye Selo school days, a carefree fun-loving hard-drinking predatory womanizer, now a Colonel in the Russian Army, Konstantin Danzas. It would be a lark for Danzas and he would also be discreet. Danzas lived in an apartment house on Nevsky Prospekt. He would go to see him in the morning, and before the day was over he would have his peace at last. He felt good, tranquil and uplifted.

January 27, 1837. Wake up shortly before eight A.M. It is still dark outside on the streets of Petersburg. Notwithstanding, the night street lights are slowly going out. Beautiful Natasha is still sleeping the innocent sleep of babes and angels. He stares down at her. Leans over and brushes his thick sensuous lips softly on her curving rosebud mouth. He feels her soft sweet breath upon his face, is titillated. He tiptoes around the chilly room, puts on a red-striped robe, does his toilet, thence to the study. Nikita brings him a cup of steaming tea. Bells resound outside for early mass. In his mind he pictures priests in black robes moving shadowly through the empty snowy streets. As usual, he sits down at his desk to do his mail, to answer correspondence before getting to the work for which he was created. He smiles confidently.

Nikita Koslov observes, "Master is feeling good today."

Pushkin answers jovially, "Why shouldn't I, Nikita, old friend? It's good to be alive!"

"It is for sure, Master."

He can hear the snow softly slapping the frost-bitten windows. It is a day like any other day of winter in the northern skies. It is snowing with a terrible vengeance in Sweden, Norway, Denmark, Finland. It comes howling across the Finnish marshes to Great Peter's city on the frozen Neva. The wind comes roaring off the Baltic. He thinks, the snow is snowing and day is breaking, and it will never break again for one of us, me or d'Anthes. And the world will go along its jocular way.

Mais, c'est la vie.

He wrote to Madame Ishimov, a translator of literature from English into Russia. He felt good! He complimented her on the crispness and the simplicity of her translation. "This is really the way to write!" He felt loose, relaxed, exhilarant. He sent her a book written by Barry Cornwall for her to translate portions of it for the next issue of his newly founded magazine, THE CONTEMPORARY. He felt free and easy. He expressed sincere regrets that he had to break an appointment with her for lunch that day to discuss a translation project. He read the latter pages of his unfinished novel, THE NEGRO OF PETER THE GREAT and promised himself he would finish this one day very very soon. He would set everything else aside to do so. He worked briefly on a little poem and he read it aloud.

"I have ripened for eternity,
And the torrent of my days
Has slowed. . . ."

He took his silver watch out of his vest pocket. It was already past eleven o'clock. He rose. It was time to locate Danzas. He dressed and went outside. The snow had ceased, but the howling wind slashed through the streets, cutting as sharply as a Cossack's saber. He went back inside for his bearskin greatcoat.

He came out again and hailed a cab. "To Nevsky Prospekt near the Tsepnoy Bridge!"

By now the streets had come alive with people on foot and troikas with their sleigh bells dashing to and fro, some on their way to manage the business of the Capital City, others on their way to bed from all night parties. His sleigh was heading across the Tsepnoy Bridge when he saw Danzas standing among a crowd on the pavement. He called upon the driver to stop.

"Danzas, you incorrigible reprobate! Where have you been hiding?"

Danzas was delighted to see his famous former schoolmate. "Reprobate! That's a compliment from one with your vaunted reputation."

"Are you busy at the moment?"

"I am always at your service, Alexander Sergeievich."

"Get in, my Colonel. I want you to go to the French Embassy with me and be witness to a conversation."

"What is it all about?"

"You'll find out when you get there."

On the way Alexander Sergeievich kept up a steady chatter about this and that and mostly about nothing of any consequence. Danzas was avid with curiosity, but too discreet to ask any further questions. Upon reaching the French Embassy they went directly to the office of Vicomte d'Archiac.

Colonel Danzas stood perspiration-drenched and wide-eyed as he listened to the conversation between the French attaché and Pushkin, after which Alexander Sergeievich turned to him and explained the situation rapidly in French, finally explaining that he desired Danzas to be his second, ending with "Consentez vous?"

Danzas collapsed in an office chair speechless and dumbfounded at first at the horrendous task history and Fate had chosen for him. When he found his voice he began to stammer.

"Well?" Pushkin asked the Colonel impatiently. Danzas jumped up nervously and bowed. "At your service, Alexander Sergeievich!" He still seemed in a state of shock. Why me? But there was simply nothing for it.

Pushkin thanked him and left him to work out the arrangements with d'-Archiac. "The bloodier the better," he admonished." We will meet at two o'clock at Wulf's Confectionery on Nevsky Prospekt."

He went home, and took a bath, combed his wooly locks, stared at himself in the mirror above the washstand, and donned his best suit and fur coat. Natasha had gone to some kind of tea party. He arrived at Wulf's ahead of Danzas. He was sipping a soda when Danzas arrived.

"Is everything set?" Pushkin asked.

Colonal Danzas looked around him before answering. "Everything is all arranged, and I have the pistols." He handed Alexander Sergeievich the rules of conduct. *Pistols at ten paces, the participants to stand five paces away from the barriers which would be ten paces apart; the two opponents at a signal from one of the seconds to advance toward the barrier and to fire from a distance of ten paces.*

Pushkin glanced cursorily at the conditions, as if it were a mere formality that had nothing to do with whether or not he would be living or dead by the morrow, while Danzas was trying to dissuade his former schoolmate from going through with the duel, pointing out that it was to the Dutch Ambassador to whom the insulting letter was sent. "It's he with whom the duel should be fought, Alexander Sergeievich!" He knew d'Anthes' reputation for being a crack duelist, an expert marksman. Pushkin ignored his friend's suggestion. He stared at Danzas blankly. His usually animated eyes were opaque, dead, unseeing, like the mad man in the Goncharov garret.

"Let's be on our way," Pushkin said.

Danzas was a tall and slimly constructed hard-drinking Colonel of a dragoon regiment in the Russian Army. He was thinly mustached and whitely handsome, very blond, with blue eyes and proud possessor of a Don Juan reputation with the ladies. Seriousness was not a part of his personality. But now, at this historic moment, he was as serious as he'd ever been in all his life.

Danzas began to wax nostalgic. He talked with Pushkin about the good old days at Tsarskoye Selo when they were young, carefree and innocent.

"By the Holy Virgin, Alexander Sergeievich, you were never innocent as far as the ladies were concerned." He laughed heartily, as he tried to involve his famous former schoolmate in his jolly reminiscences.

Alexander Sergeievich merely stared opaquely at the Colonel.

At which point the Colonel with the light blue eyes changed his strategy and tactics. "And to think you turned into such a domesticated homebody. It's unbelievable. How is your beautiful wife? And what are you planning for your wonderful children? A military career for the boys, eh? No, of course not, not you, the 'Bard of the Decembrists.' But what then? What else is there? I imagine every decision you make these days has to be predicated on how it will affect your wife and children. Perhaps that's why I never got married. I value my independence too zealously. I can commit the most outlandish, the most idiotic capers that come to mind. It's left entirely up to me. Nobody suffers the consequences of my idiocies excepting me. But you, I mean, you must always consider your wife and beautiful children—How—how—how many are there?"

Alexander Sergeievich stared blankly at his former schoolmate.

The consequences for his family. He had thought of nothing else these last few hours. There was nothing he could do about the emotional trauma they would suffer, inevitably. He could not spare them this. There was simply nothing for it. But he had written an official letter to the Imperial uchitol, Zukovsky, to be delivered in case of his most unlikely demise, bequeathing to him the power of attorney to settle his publishing affairs and his inconsiderable estate. He was sure that the Emperor would look out for Natalya and the children, he thought, bitterly. But there was simply nothing for it. It was Fate, God's Will and His Most Imperial Majesty. And that is how it had always been. He wiped a sole tear from his eye.

The duel was to take place at Black River, a suburb on the outskirts of the city not far from the place where the upper classes went sledding, and near the Commandant's mansion. Unknown to Pushkin, in desperation Colonel Danzas had notified Benkendorf, anonymously, of the location of the dueling grounds at Black River. At the last moment the Emperor had ordered that the duel be prevented at all costs. He feared trouble from the Russian people.

On the way to Black River the enormity of the historic role in which Fate had cast him overwhelmed Pushkin's fun-loving Tsarskoye Selo schoolmate. All the way to Black River Danzas tried to think of how he could avert the duel. He thought so hard his head began to throb. Surely something would happen at the last minute. Perhaps it was a nightmare that he would suddenly awake from.

Danza stared at the traffic of sleighs and troikas heading back to the city. Suddenly a smile spread over his face. His heart beat crazily. He was wild with jubilation. Fate had rescued him from history. Coming toward them he recognized the Pushkin carriage with Natalya Nicholaevna Goncharova Pushkina seated inside. She would see her husband and demand an explanation, and the whole thing would be called to a halt, temporarily at least. And while there was life and time, there was hope. In any event, he would get out of the role of the poet's second, even if it meant leaving the city. While the sledge approached, Pushkin was looking the other way, lost in his own thoughts.

For the briefest moment Danzas was certain that Natalya had seen them. She actually stared their way. But she was almost as near-sighted as her sister, Alexandra. He wanted to wave to her, but he had given his word to Alexander Sergeievich to be discreet. Those were the rules of this stupid game. The sledges passed each other, almost touching. Natalya was so close Danzas could almost have reached out and touched her. In fact, she recognized him and she smiled at him, and he was forced to speak to her, wishing her a pleasant evening, which she smilingly acknowledged. But the beautiful near-sighted woman did not recognize her husband whose face was still turned the other way. Had Alexander Sergeievich seen Natasha Goncharova Pushkina? In any event, the moment was lost forever.

Danzas decided to attract attention by taking out two pistols and holding them up under the pretext of examining them. Surely it would attract someone's attention, and they would see that policemen called a stop to this imminent Russian tragedy. He did not trust Chief Benkendorf.

A fun-loving fellow-nobleman from another sledge recognized Alexander Sergeievich and waved at him. "Hello Pushkin, why are you going to the hills so late? Everyone else is coming back."

Alexander Sergeievich laughed and waved back at them.

Danzas opened his mouth to scream at them, Somebody stop this madness, please! Pajalsta! But the code of honor kept him tongue-tied. He had promised to be discreet.

They reached the duel grounds seconds before the d'Anthes' party. The grounds were surrounded by a grove of trees shielding it from the view of people on the road. The drifting snow was deep. D'Archiac and Danzas began to jump up and down, stomping on the snow to pack it even and hard. D'Anthes pulled off his coat and joined in the stomping. Pushkin sat on the edge and watched absent-mindedly, as if the whole thing had nothing at all to do with him.

After awhile he called out to them, "Can we get this thing started? It will be dark shortly."

Moments passed. Danzas came over. "Does it look all right to you?"

"Fine! So long as we get the business done with."

They used their overcoats to construct the barrier ten feet apart. The sky was darkening every minute. The two seconds paced off the other five feet, each for the adversary that he seconded. The opponents took their positions, pistols to their sides.

What thoughts ran through the poet's mind those few seconds before Danzas gave the signal? Did the words of the gypsy woman cross his mind, the toothless old woman with the squeaky voice? "Beware of a white man in your life. He spells danger!" If he had remembered, he would have laughed it off. He didn't believe in fortune tellers. Did he remember Shakespeare's Othello, the proud and princely Blackamoor? And was d'Anthes the latter-day Iago? Was Natalya his Desdemona? Like the proud Othello he was in a struggle because his honor had been impinged upon. Honor—pride—dignity—What nobler causes on this earth were there to fight for to the death?

Perhaps he also thought of the passage in his own EUGENE ONEGIN? The duel in which Eugene the blasé roué had dueled with the fledgling poet Lansky and shot him dead. Did he wonder over the coincidence of the circumstances? The similarities. Had he been writing his own obituary? Was Fate actually that malevolent? Was it possible he had prophesied his own demise? Did he remember those immortal words written in his terrible solitude at Mikhailovskoye? The dueling grounds of his imagination had also been snow-covered.

"Ready—approach!"
And coldly glancing
With slow deliberate steps,
Not taking aim, the two advancing.
Four paces toward each other.
Four steps, four mortal steps.
But now, as he walks forward,
Unhurriedly, Eugene lifts his arm.
They walk. Five steps more.
Lansky takes aim too,
Squinting his left eye. Then Onegin fires.
And the fatal hour has struck.

The poet reels without a word:
The bells toll out his term, unheard. . . .

Just then a white hare scampered madly across the field of honor. Danzas gave the signal with his hat. The poet walked quickly toward the barrier. He reached the barrier ahead of his opponent. He began to raise his pistol to fire. D'Anthes had only walked four paces. He raised his pistol and fired. The pistol smoked in the freezing air. *The poet reels without a word.* Alexander Sergeievich Pushkin dropped, the pistol falling from his hand.

"I think he struck me in the thigh," he mumbled, as Danzas ran toward his famous comrade.

D'Anthes walked toward the barrier to get his cloak.

"Wait!" Alexander Sergievich shouted. "I think I'm strong enough to take my shot."

D'Anthes went back and took his position, turning sideways in profile, folding his arms to protect his heart.

The poet took another pistol (a dry one) from Danzas. He leaned up slightly and took careful aim, waiting a few minutes until his shaky hand was steadier. He pulled the trigger. Snowbirds took off from the icicled trees.

The bullet hit d'Anthes with so much force he fell, though it had only grazed his arm and hit a button on his military jacket in the area of his chest.

When Pushkin saw his opponent fall, he shouted, "Bravo!"

He inquired of Danzas, "Is he dead?"

Danzas answered, "I don't think so."

"Then we'll have to resume this again as soon as possible." He added confidentially, "You know I thought I'd be glad to kill him, but I don't feel that way at all. The whole damn affair is insane. Who needs to take another's life?" Meanwhile Danzas saw the poet's blood slowly spreading a red circle in the white snow like the strawberry ices Pushkin used to sip. It was then that Alexander Sergeievich lost consciousness. Danzas's heartbeat quickened as he saw his comrade was rapidly losing ground, as the blood continued to stain the snow in an ever-widening circle. Ambassador Heckeren had had a large troika nearby in case his son was badly wounded. D'Archiac and d'Anthes hastily improvised a bandage for the Guardsman's superficial wound, and they offered the use of the troika, a larger vehicle, to take the wounded Pushkin back to the city. Alexander Sergeievich never knew. D'Archiac and Danzas picked Alexander Sergeievich up carefully and laid him in the troika, and Danzas and his Lycée comrade began the painful journey back to Moika Street. Pushkin's consciousness would come and go as the troika bounced over the bumpy snowy road.

"Is it bad?" Alexander Sergeievich asked.

Danzas shook his head sadly. "I don't know. I don't think it is." But he was deathly frightened and wondered in anguish why Fate had chosen him to preside over the diabolic destruction of Russia's greatest living institution. He knew his famous friend had fallen victim to a hideous plot by people around the Imperial Court. Benkendorf had known about the duel and had chosen not to prevent it. Danzas learned only later that the Chief of Secret Gendarmes had mistakenly sent his policemen to another spot on the opposite side of the city. The information he had sent anonymously to Chief Benkendorf had been quite specific.

Danzas recalled now, smiling grimly, the days with Pushkin at Tsarskoye Selo. How many times he had boasted to others of knowing the famous poet, of the escapades and pranks they had executed together, the frolics and the capers, it seemed like centuries ago, and yet it seemed like yesteryear. After Lycée days he had watched his best friend evolve from a fun-loving hell-raising prankster to a world famous poet. The greatest writer in the Russian language. He'd always been proud of his friendship with the great Pushkin, the *petit génie*. And now an implacable Fate was exacting exhorbitant payment for that friendship.

The blood now was oozing through the poet's clothes and soaking into the floor of the expensively carpeted troika. Because of Pushkin's serious condition, the coach went slowly through the snowy darkening streets, as the long night of the northern skies began. And Danzas asked the coachman to hurry, but to drive carefully. It might be a matter of life and death. He looked into the poet's face, unrecognizable now, and distorted with pain. Alexander Sergeievich kept up a constant chatter as if pain were not cutting through his body like an angry scythe. Now the somber lights of the city appeared and the streets were filled with the sound of bells and shouts of idle talk and laughter. Already the elegant people were on their way to their parties as Alexander Pushkin lay mortally wounded in the coach with his friend Danzas beside him.

As the pain stabbed through his stomach like an actual dagger, Alexander Sergeievich thought, "Poor Natalya will be impatiently waiting supper for me. She has already dressed for the great party at Katerina Karamzina's. Poor dear, she may not be able to go tonight because of this. Such a bloody nuisance."

He had not known that he spoke aloud, till Danzas leaned toward him. "What did you say, Alexander Sergeievich?"

Pushkin answered feebly, "I want you to tell Dr. Arendt that if my wound is mortal, he should tell me straight away. I am not anxious to remain alive." Arendt was the official physician at the Imperial Court. He was also an ardent admirer of Alexander Pushkin.

Danzas' eyes immediately filled with tears. "Don't talk like that, Alexander Sergeievich!"

"It's true, Konstantine Ivanovich. I've lived an eventful life. I have no regrets. Though I've written many epigrams, most of life for me has been an elegy. Leaving this world is no terrible ordeal. I—" A stab of pain cut off his voice, as a look of wildness took possession of his face, and he bit his bottom lip till the blood began to trickle.

When they reached the house along the Moika embankment across from the bright lights of the Winter Palace, Pushkin told Danzas, "Go and prepare Natalya with the news. Send the servants for me."

The servants, along with Nikita Koslov, who had been with Alexander Sergeievich all of his remembered life, came and took him tenderly from the carriage to his study, weeping openly. He belonged to them. Their national pride and joy. They lay him in his study on a couch surrounded by his books that lined the walls.

CHAPTER FOUR

Meanwhile Danzas walked up to the second floor and into the dining room where the table was set awaiting the return of the man of the household. The chandelier above the oaken table glittered brightly as always. Danzas saw Natalya and her sister, Alexandra, seated at the other end of the room. A fire was burning brightly in the fireplace, casting softened shadows on the table and the Oriental carpet. It was a night no different for them than a hundred other nights. Before he could bring himself to speak his face told them enough. Natalya screamed and ran out towards the study. Alexandra sat motionless as Danzas related to her in quiet tones the occurrences of an hour ago. Before he could finish, Alexandra fell to the floor unconscious.

When Natalya reached the study she ran toward Pushkin as he lay on the couch. "Pushkin! My Pushkin! My darling Sasha! Forgive me! It's all my fault! I didn't understand!" She fell weeping upon the couch beside him.

He thought, painfully, Why was it so difficult for those whom he loved to understand him? Why was it so difficult to communicate with those whom he loved so desperately?

"Pajalsta," he begged her. "Please leave me till the doctor comes. I do not want you to see me like this. It is not your fault." Nikita took her from the room.

Colonel Danzas went in search of the most competent doctors in the Capital. Arendt, the Emperor's physician, Spassky, the Pushkins' family doctor, Solomon, the expert surgeon. None were to be found. It was the winter social season. Finally at a Foundling home, Danzas found a Dr. Shultz, who was a specialist in bringing babies into the world but had no expertise in matters of this nature or seriousness. Dr. Shultz would work with Pushkin until more expert help arrived. They undressed the poet. There was a black hole in his abdomen already turning purple and erupting like a miniature volcano, as it threw up the life blood of Alexander Sergeievich Pushkin, the people's poet. The bullet had struck his thigh, fractured his pelvis and entered his intestines. Dr. Shultz dressed the wound superficially, as the poet grimaced quietly, bravely, so as not to upset his Natasha who had come back into the study and sat distraught in a corner weeping silently and bitterly.

By the time Dr. Arendt arrived, Alexander Sergeievich's wife was sitting by his side holding his hand and mopping his perspiring forehead. Pushkin asked Natasha to leave the room again while the doctor removed the bandage and looked at the wound.

"It's very painful," Alexander Sergeievich told the doctor. "Tell me the truth. How serious is it?"

Dr. Arendt spoke gravely to the stricken poet. He was nattily attired in a black suit, white shirt and black necktie, dark-haired and thinly mustached, with a left eye that twitched noticeably. "I am duty bound to be candid with you, Alexander Sergeievich. The situation is very dangerous."

The news of the duel and Pushkin's condition swept over the city like a howling snowstorm. A crowd began to gather outside of his home in the freezing night. Pushkin's people, the "little people," the Third Estate, artists, writers, students, workers, women, youth. Nameless people in the faceless multitudes. For he had never seen himself as aiming the energies of his heart and brain at the elegant ones of the court. He wrote to the muzhiks, the serfs, to many who could neither read nor write. But they knew the name of Alexander Pushkin, his writings were read to them. *Lansky, Olga, Tatyana, Boris, Dmitri* and *Eugene Onegin* were a part of their cultural heritage, their own Russian psyche and identity. Alexander Pushkin belonged to them. To the solitary women and men far from Great Peter's City on the Neva, in the frozen stretches of Siberia, on the lonely steppes along the Don, in their pitiful isbas. Those now outside in the cold. Not to those across the way laughing gaily in the Winter Palace. Outside they moaned and shouted.

"Lord, have mercy on this crazy country!"

"Is he dead? Is he dying?"

"What about the foreign scoundrel?"

"Lord, save Pushkin for our country!"

"Poor Russia! The Blessed Virgin has forsaken us!"

All this for the man inside who had written GABRILIAD; poking fun at their Blessed Virgin. All over town candles were lighted for our poet, cynics, liberals, atheists, agnostics, unbelievers, true believers genuflected and crossed themselves before their icons.

"Save him for this godforsaken country!"

By midnight, thousands had gathered outside the poet's residence along the Moika embankment. Czarist guards were placed on duty at the doors leading to his apartment. Only very special friends were allowed to enter.

Inside Alexander Sergeievich fought a valiant fight with death like a Roman gladiator. All through the night and all day long the next day the battle raged unceasingly. Sometimes he welcomed death like a long sought friend, as he seemed to be drifting farther and farther out to sea on a ship without a compass toward some distant land where all was peace. Bravo! He thought, in his delirium, he was at long last leaving Russia! Neither Nicholas nor Benkendorf could do anything to stop him. Maybe that distant shore would be Africa, the land of mystery he had dreamed of all his life, the land of his great-grandfather Hannibal.

The doctors came and went. The pain increased, even as they stood around him mumbling to each other. Why didn't they let him go? He had never actually belonged, especially on this Holy Russian earth. He was of a different species with a highly superhuman sense of Russian consciousness. He was a Russian with the princely blood of Africa in his veins.

The doctors were all dressed in their black business suits, white shirts and black neckties, and as Pushkin looked up into their faces, they were, to him, like white-faced vultures dressed in black hovering malevolently above him. The pain slashing through his stomach seemed to tear him apart. Why was he not allowed to die in peace? He had sought peace all of his eventful life; it had eluded him like a willow-the-wisp. He could not even have a tranquil death.

Suddenly the doctors assumed different faces to him. He saw in their stead the satanic smirking faces of Benkendorf and Heckeren and Nicholas and Stroganov and—he had bitten his lips to suppress the screams struggling to erupt from the depths of him so many times he began to choke on his own blood, the pain stabbed him continuously.

Then suddenly he knew he wanted desperately to live. The songs he'd sung, the words he'd spoken to *his* Russia, *to the entire world!* The words rang through his feverish brain . . . EUGENE ONEGIN, THE BRONZE HORSEMAN, THE CAPTAIN'S DAUGHTER, ODE TO FREEDOM, THE VILLAGE, THE PRISONER OF THE CAUCASUS, THE DAGGER, THE COVETOUS KNIGHT, THE FOUNTAIN, GYPSIES, GABRILIAD, TALES OF BELKIN, THE QUEEN OF SPADES—He laughed aloud despite the pain. Was it possible that all of these words, perhaps millions of them, came from this consciousness that he kept losing and regaining, from his brain that soon would be no more? He had had a good productive life, but why must he leave it now? He was young and he had so much work to do. . . . He had not even finished THE NEGRO OF PETER THE GREAT. Why couldn't they have let him be to do the work that he was meant to do?

He would not have written his death script like this, dying of a stupid duel. If he had to go, he should have been shot down atop the barricades. He should have died to free the Motherland.

There was that optimistic moment when his soaring temperature dropped and his pulse went to a normal state. Natalya Nicholaevna screamed softly, "Sasha! Alexander Sergeievich! I knew in my heart you were going to live!"

He shook his head sadly. "Bring the children. I must see them." His great blue-black eyes began to fill. He would not live to see his children grow up, to share with them the joy and pain of childhood growth. He would never glow in pride at their achievements or suffer with them in their dismal failures.

Why? Why? It wasn't fair! He had so much unfinished work.

The children came in one by one, unable to comprehend the muffled tension and excitement, not understanding the import of this terrible moment in their lives. He kissed his son Alexander and held him tightly as if he would not let him go. "Stay strong, my son, and stand for truth and help your wonderful mother. Stand with the people. Always keep your head up high. Make a good life for yourself and your family." Alexander Alexandrovich stood there, his dear eyes full of sleepiness and wonder. The other children came near, and he kissed them. "Make a good life for yourselves, my sweethearts . . . Stay strong and beautiful, my darlings. Never desert the people! . . . Let my love go always with you my precious ones. . . ."

One day they would understand, he thought. One day they would read his books and each would say proudly, "That's my father!" After he smilingly blessed each one of them, he called Natalya to him.

She was weeping hysterically, as her sister, Alexandra, stood beside her, being strong for her private Pushkin. Alexander Sergeievich spoke softly to Natalya, "Don't be sad. I'm sorry that though you're entirely innocent, they will blame you. They will revile your good name. Leave this wretched city, dearest Natasha. Live in the country with the children for a time. Then come back and remarry."

"You're not going to die!" she pleaded with him. She held his hand tightly and kissed him repeatedly as her tears fell on his face.

He smiled painfully. "It's but the calm before the storm. Nature's playing its final joke on me."

Alexandra came to his bedside and kissed him fully on his blood-stained lips, then turned away from her beloved.

Zukovsky brought word from the Emperor that his wife and family would be taken care of with a governmental pension. His Imperial Majesty also requested that Alexander Sergeievich receive the last rites of the church before he left this world.

Pushkin smiled through his pain. An order from His Majesty on his death-bed. And the message from the Little Father was very clear. You want a pension for your widow and your children? Accept those last rites. Resignedly Pushkin asked them to send for a priest. The crowd in the street started weeping when the holy man arrived.

"Goodbye, Pushkin!"

"Farewell, fairest son!"

As the priest gave the poet extreme unction, a sculptor crouched quietly near the couch, sketching somberly, making ready the great man's death mask. It was the custom in Imperial Russia to make death masks for all the famous ones when they passed on into history.

"I want to say goodbye to all my friends. Where are they?" the poet asked in his delirium.

They came to his bedside and bade him farewell, Zukovsky, Turgenev, Vyazemsky, Danzas, Vera Vyazemsky, Pletnev.

When Madame Karamzina came to the bed, he remembered that she was one of his very first loves in Saint Petersburg, when he was seventeen and she was thirty eight. There was a terrible beauty now in his smiling face, as he took her hand and kissed it, and she kissed him softly on his forehead. She made the sign of the cross over him and turned away. When she looked back, he asked, "Make the sign of the cross over me again."

She came back and gazed upon his face, which, to her, was beautiful and beatific, as death hovered in the room. And she saw him now as he had been before, an innocent lad of seventeen, fresh from provincial Moscow, brimming over with all the juices of this life, so ragingly, madly in love with life.

It was only now at this very final moment that this elderly elegant widow woman realized that she had always loved him. She fell upon the couch beside him and could not keep herself from sobbing.

"You were too good for us. And even as we enjoyed you, we never understood you. You, who belonged to us, the greatest gift we ever knew. We blamed you, the blameless. How can you smile at us? When we are all guilty? We deserted you!"

He smiled through tears and motioned for her to leave his bedside. Her truth was too much for him. Too late to do him any good. He wanted to leave this world with forgiveness in his heart, especially for the ones he loved.

Another sharp pain knifed through his frail and slender body. He asked to be turned over on the right side. They turned him over, as he felt himself sinking now down down into a deep white irresistible void of nothingness.

He mumbled, "It's all over."

The doctor misunderstood. "Yes, we turned you over on your side."

It was 2:45 P.M. Outside the sun of Russian winter had already begun to set. He stared wordlessly at the doctor, with his great dark blue eyes glazed. And Dr. Arendt understood. The poet's great face now looked twice its size. Veins bulged blackly like whipcord on the poet's forehead, as if the vision he saw at this final moment was too much truth even for his noble forehead to contain. What was it, Pushkin? What great vision was it? It didn't matter anymore.

The father of Russian literature had reached the other shore. Where all was dignified tranquility.

He had left Russia at last!

Yebat! the Emperor and Benkendorf.

EXIGI MONUMENTUM

EXIGI MONUMENTUM

Pushkin was dead. The word went out all through the land all over Europe. "Pushkin is dead!" The Russian people wept without the Emperor's permission for the first time in the nation's history. Heretofore the Russian people neither laughed nor cried without a signal from the Little Father at the palace. But how could this be? An entire nation of people going, as if by prearrangement, immediately into mourning!

What was happening to Russia?

Full paged banners in the morning newspapers. "Pushkin is dead!" Bordered in black. Without the Emperor's permission.

In large headlines:

PUSHKIN IS DEAD!

Without the Emperor's permission.

THE SUN OF OUR POETRY IS SET. Pushkin is dead in the prime of his magnificent career. We have no strength to say more, and if so, to what purpose? Every Russian heart knows of this irreparable loss, every Russian heart is torn to bits by it. Pushkin! Our hope! Our joy! Our national genius! The glory of our people! Can it be? Is it really possible that we have no more Pushkin?

Newspaper publishers and editors were called upon the Imperial carpet. Chief of Secret Police Benkendorf demanded, "What is the meaning of these black borders around the obituaries of Alexander Pushkin? 'The sun of our poetry.' What magnificent career, pray tell? Was he a general? A minister? A statesman?" Benkendorf raged and ranted. He was red-faced and perspiring. "There must be no more of this nonsense. His Imperial Majesty has issued a *ukase* that there be no more mention of this trouble making scribbler. Not another word about him in your

382

publications, understand? Violation of this ukase will mean that your newspapers will be closed down, indefinitely! The Emperor does not want to see the name, Pushkin, anywhere in your publications!"

Meanwhile the Russian people moved inexorably toward the sudden void, the terrible quiet, the voice that would be heard no more.

They came toward the apartment on Moika Street, in troikas, in barouches, in dilapidated droschkys, in telegas, and horse-and-donkey carts, came by the thousands and on foot toward the awesome sudden silence on Moika Street.

"Hang the Frenchman!" some of them shouted.

They smashed the windows at the Dutch Embassy.

Thousands stood outside his apartment on Moika Street. The officials wrote *A. S. Pushkin* in chalk outside the door. The people jammed the little hall outside the study where he lay. Gendarmes were called in to control the ignorant and unruly mob. Old folks, young folks, middle aged people. A cordon of police was placed around Pushkin's house and in neighboring courtyards. The Third Estate came to pay tribute to a voice that had been silenced for all times. Muzhiks whom he dearly loved were there in the frigid weather.

"Farewell, Pushkin!"

"Goodbye, Oh noble son of Russia! Dosvidanya!"

"Safe journey to the other side!"

They came, especially did the old gray-bearded ones come and look down on his youthful wasted body, lying there so silently in black. Scrubby-faced old ones came, men and women, and sat awhile in the little room where the poet lay so peacefully, before moving along to make way for others. They came and sat with him for awhile, as if, weary from a long day's journey, they would gain some strength and wisdom from him for the long dark winter days and nights that lay ahead. They had had no chance to sit with him in real life.

They came to sit for a moment with Pushkin. Alexander Sergeievich. And years afterwards to tell their grandchildren, "My dears, I knew him. I sat with Alexander Pushkin in the same room. He was just like you and you—with eyes and mouth and ears and hands and feet. You know, of course he was a true genius. All the same he was a man. But oh, my children, what a man!"

There was a stifling smell in this little room where the faithful gathered; the smell of burning candles, melting wax, medicine and pungent incense. All mixed with the sickly fragrance of funereal flowers and the stench of human perspiration. This little room was the Mecca toward which the Pilgrims grimly marched.

Prince Vyazemsky, tall and stately, stared into some of their eloquent faces and thought to himself that they seemed more amazed than mournful. Astonished that their poet had proven not to be immortal.

CAN IT BE? IS IT REALLY POSSIBLE THAT WE HAVE NO MORE PUSHKIN?

These were Pushkin's people, the ones to whom he'd always written. This was the "Third Estate." There were no ambassadors here on Moika Street. No delicate ones here, no elegantly-stepping, lisping, proper talking French-accented ministers of state, no pretentious or affected counts or barons, no Frenchified Russians in this place. They were over at the Dutch Embassy, drinking to the poet's death and to the dashing Frenchman's health, albeit they drank uneasily. Imperial militia surrounded the Dutch Embassy to protect them from the angry and uncultured masses. But the little room on the Moika embankment had suddenly become the center of the universe for the Russian people, the working men and women, the peasants, students, the little businessmen, old women with their heads tied with babushkas, the artists and the intellectuals.

In his restless sleep the Emperor could hear those feet like an army on the march, moving toward Moika Street as if that little study were a beacon light to which they were irresistibly attracted.

The first night of Pushkin's death Czar Nicholas suffered indigestion, he had eaten very little that night. His appetite had disappeared. His stomach felt so bloated now, he thought it might really burst. He called Chief Benkendorf on the carpet. He paced back and forth agitatedly beneath a gleaming crystal chandelier. Bright lights shown all over the Winter Palace. The bulge above His Imperial midriff was more pronounced than ever. His heavy handsome face glowing now. He demanded of Benkendorf, "Why weren't my orders carried out? I specifically ordered you to prevent this duel from taking place."

Benkendorf bowed his head. "Your Majesty, we took all the necessary steps to prevent it, but we were given false information as to where it would take place. I assure you, though, there is absolutely nothing to be alarmed about. Everything is under—"

"Find out immediately where the false information came from and deal with the scoundrels summarily. It's obviously a damnable conspiracy!"

His Majesty's glazed desk already overflowed with communications, rumors of riots and revolution in the streets all over Russia, and here was his trusted Chief of Secret Police telling him he had nothing to worry about. He was surrounded by sycophants, imbeciles and nincompoops. He had just a few months ago received a hand-delivered letter from one of his very own and highly trusted staff urging that d'Anthes and Heckeren be arrested and dealt with summarily and severely "to demonstrate to the Russian masses that we are on their side. Even though we know that Russia is better off rid of this African scoundrel-of-a-scribbler. Nevertheless we must bow to the will of the people."

"Bow to the will of the people, must we?" Nicholas muttered to himself. "Who ever heard of a Czar of Russia bowing to the people's will?" He crushed the letter in his fist. Where did Anton Shishnikov get such dangerous revolutionary rubbish from? Subversion right here amongst his own Palace people. Well he knew how to deal with this now.

"Bring Anton Shishnikov here to me immediately!" he gruffly ordered Benkendorf.

All night long Pushkin's close friends sat in the study. Zukovsky, Prince Vyazemsky, Princess Vyazemskya, Madame Karamzina, Baroness Svetlina. They all sat and talked of Pushkin pranks and anecdotes. It almost seemed that Pushkin himself was a living presence in the room with them. Prince Vyazemsky stared at his weeping wife, Vera. He looked around the room, then toward the coffin, as if he hoped the poet would rise from his casket and speak to them, cheer them up, tell them it was all a joke, a typical Pushkin prank for which he was famous. Then, like old times, they would laugh, relieved, and all go home, and things would be just like they used to be. But Alexander Sergeievich *was* dead, his angel-tongued voice was silenced for all eternity. He could not save them from their sorrow.

They took solace from the memories he had left them. The carefree days at Tsarskoye Selo. Those first days after graduation in Saint Petersburg. The time he came as a naive brash boy to the Capital from the Lycée. They laughed together at the memory of his mischievous pranks. The day he caused a riot on the Nevsky Prospekt. They laughed till tears came to their eyes, because he could not join them in the laughter.

Meanwhile His Imperial Majesty declared war against a pesky ghost that would not lie quiescent. He banned the opening of Pushkin's play, THE COVETOUS KNIGHT, at the Alexandrinsky Theatre in Saint Petersburg, which had been scheduled for the night after his sudden and unscheduled demise. Thousands were turned away outside the theatre.

By Imperial Decree university professors and students were prohibited from leaving their classrooms to attend the funeral.

The police were instructed to destroy all copies of a new Pushkin portrait bordered in black with the caption:

THE FIRE HAS GONE OUT ON THE ALTAR.

The Smolensky Bookshop on the Nevsky Prospekt sold out EUGENE ONEGIN on the evening of Pushkin's death. All the next day thousands thronged the bookstore, while other thousands stood in line outside in the below-zero weather.

A young ensign by the name of Lermontov wrote *On The Death of Pushkin*.

The poet fell—a slave to honor—
He fell, maligned by slanderous talk;
Lead pierced the heart that craved for vengeance,
The poet's noble head had sunk!
And you, the insolent descendants
of men notorious for their foul deeds,
who trampled under foot, with slavish zeal, the remnants
of families upon whom fortune turned its back!
You stand around the throne, a greedy grasping crowd,
And kill or stifle freedom, genius, fame!
Behind the veil of law you found a shelter,
Before you—justice, truth must silent be!

385

By myrmidons of vice, there is a court of justice,
There is a sterner judge above;
He waits; no gold can ever tempt him
And all your thoughts and deeds he knows in advance.
Oh, then in vain will you resort to your habitual slander,
It will be of no avail.
All the black blood in your veins will not atone for
This righteous poet's sacred blood!

Pushkin's death inspired a plethora of poems all over Russia, some by men and women who had never dreamed a poem was in them. Another angry writer, Orgarev, wrote:

His assassin? Still running free!
Proud and handsome, full of health.
Lightly he struts about,
And the whole sinister clique
of Scandalmongers of fashion
Thrives too. There is no revenge—

Nikolai Gogol, wrote from Italy, "Russia without Pushkin! How strange, how strange, how utterly strange! It's impossible to believe! I can't imagine Russia without Alexander Pushkin! What will we do without him. What will we do? I weep deeply for my homeland."

Rumors from sources close to the Imperial Court spread all over Saint Pete like the howling snowstorm, that the Frenchman had worn an armored breastplate underneath his Hussar jacket; that the people's poet had fallen victim of a conspiracy plotted at the Winter Palace. Some said d'Anthes was a homosexual, the Baron's not so secret love. He felt no real desire for women. It was a trap, they said, to snare their poet. A dastardly conspiracy plotted carefully and many months in the unfolding. His Imperial Majesty was frightened and infuriated. His trust in Benkendorf was severely shakened.

The police raided the publishing house and destroyed the plates and printing presses of EUGENE ONEGIN. Nevertheless more than sixty thousand copies were sold in Saint Petersburg alone.

Organizations fought for the honor of carrying his remains. In the middle of that final night, as the friends of Pushkin sat with him for the very last time, a loud noise of *feldjagger* boots was heard as they stomped in the hall outside the study. The Emperor's feldjaggers, with bayonets and helmets, bullied their way into the study and took Pushkin's body away to the outrage of his comrades, by order of His Imperial Majesty. Natalya Goncharova Pushkina slept fitfully in a room nearby. Crying, weeping, tossing, turning. The world had become too much for her. Much too much.

Pushkin's long-time friend, Zukovsky, tutor to the heir apparent Czarevich Alexander II, made formal representations to the Emperor. "Extend to Pushkin the same recognition and largesse as was extended to the late Karamzin." Pushkin had succeeded Karamzin as the Imperial Historiographer. "Proclaim him as a national hero," Zukovsky requested. "Direct me to write an Imperial document proclaiming what Your Majesty intends to do on Pushkin's behalf."

The Emperor sat and wondered, had the world gone suddenly mad at this mad man's death? He was flatulent, his belly swollen. He answered the Imperial uchitol: "I will do something for Pushkin's widow and his children, but to issue a document similar to Karamzin's is simply out of the question. It was only through Imperial coercion that Pushkin died within the Grace of God. Whereas Karamzin died, as he lived, like a saint and an angel."

Nevertheless, he let it be widely known, though unofficially, that he, Nicholas Romanov, had done the following for the famous troublemaker:

1. Dissolved all of his debts.

2. Dissolved the mortgage on the Boldino estate.

3. Gave a handsome pension to the widow and children.

4. All of his works to be published, with the proceeds to go to his wife and children.

5. Immediate grant of 10,000 rubles to the Pushkin estate.

But no public proclamation of the African scribbler as a national hero. Friends of Alexander Pushkin wondered at the sudden generosity of Count Stroganov who volunteered to stand all of the expenses of the poet's funeral. Even in death Alexander Sergeievich could not escape Imperial intrigue. In making arrangements for the funeral the fat and pious Metropolitan of the Orthodox Church of Saint Petersburg refused Stroganov's request that he officiate. "I'll have nothing at all to do with that atheistic revolutionary scoundrel!" Father Lev Gregorovich Photius, the saintly monster, came forward and volunteered to perform the rites.

The funeral was announced to take place at St. Isaac Cathedral. Ten thousand turned out to attend the poet's funeral, only to find that the body was not there. The Imperial Gendarmerie had secreted his body to a church on Stable Street where they held a funeral service attended only by those to whom printed tickets had been extended. Pushkin dead and helpless lay there in his coffin amongst his enemies and family. His family was unable to locate and notify his brother, Leo, who was with an army regiment somewhere in Southern Russia. His sister, Olga was present at her brother's funeral. His father had come from Moscow the night before the funeral. He had sat at the Pushkin home that last night, numbed and mumbling to himself. He was not able to go to the funeral. They left him sitting in the poet's study staring into emptiness, and mumbling, "I love him—yes—I loved my son! The greatest man who ever lived. I love him! Everyone knows I loved him!"

The aristocrats were there enmasse, ambassadors, counts, barons, generals, ministers of state, men with countless decorations. While the little people were scurrying around the frozen city looking for their fallen poet. They stormed churches around the city, broke the doors of cathedrals. "Where is Alexander Pushkin?" "What have the bastards done with our noble bard?"

The church on Stable Street was pregnant with the smell of incense and funereal flowers and highly perfumed sophisticated bodies. And now it was that moment to bid a last Dosvidanya to the deceased. His enemies came up to the casket and kissed his hand and forehead, and breathed great sighs of deep relief. Souvenir hunters cut off locks of his hair, tore buttons from his frock. They bowed piously and made the sign of the cross on their bended knees. As the people searched the city for their poet's body.

Madame Karamzina was one of the few of his friends who received a ticket to his funeral. She stood above him now staring down into his peaceful face. All the memories of his young days swept over her. She realized that he was still a youth. Not yet thirty-eight years old. He who had such a stormy eagerness for life, a rage to live life to the ultimate, so much to give, so much to live for. She heard his sister, Olga Pushkina, and his sister-in-law, Alexandrina Goncharova, weeping bitterly behind her, and Madame Karamzina began to scream, "Pushkin! Pushkin! Alexander Sergeievich! Why did you leave us? Why?" She went into an hysteria of weeping and sobbing.

His sister, Olga kissed him on his frigid lips, as hot tears streamed down her cheeks.

Natalya Goncharova Pushkina kissed his noble brow. She kissed him on his thickened lips. She looked around her, lost, disoriented. At last she understood the enormity of her loss. The loss to the entire Russian people. Guilt, love, shame, sudden comprehension. It was too much—it was much too late—it was just too much for her mind and heart to emcompass and contain. She collapsed beside the casket.

At the very last moment Turgenev and Zukovsky threw their gloves into the casket. Chief Benkendorf caught his breath and raised his heavy beetled eyebrows. Was this some ritualistic revolutionary gesture? A republican signal for the masses to revolt? Russia would not be safe until this irreverent rascal was six feet underneath the earth.

Suddenly there was a tumultuous din outside the church. The people had finally found the funeral. Pushkin's people. A crowd outside the church did battle with the Emperor's Horse Guards. They smashed the lovely stained glass windows.

"Long live Alexander Pushkin!"

"Long live the Bard of Russia!"

The Horse Guards fought them off with knouts and bayonets. They locked and barricaded the doors of the church on Stable Street, and dispersed the angry mob.

Natalya was so completely devastated by her husband's death she could not possibly make the trip to the burial grounds at Mikhailovskoye. She formally asked the Emperor to allow Danzas to accompany the poet's body to Holy Mountain where he would be buried near his mother, grandmother and his great-grandfather. But the Emperor insisted that he had been liberal enough with Danzas, letting him stay out of prison till the funeral was over. Now he must be incarcerated. Czar Nicholas assigned Turgenev to represent the family and accompany the body. After much soul-searching Turgenev agreed to accompany his long-time protégé and comrade to his chamber of eternal sleep.

At midnight following the day of Alexander Sergeievich's funeral three troikas pulled up clandestinely in front of the padlocked church on Stable Street. The snow was falling steadily. A full brooding moon lit up the northern skies. Turgenev got shakily into the front troika. The casket tied up with stout rope and covered with canvas was placed into the middle sledge. Nikita Koslov climbed laboriously into the second sledge and crouched behind his dead master to accompany him on this final journey. He had been so many places with this man who lay so quietly in front of him. This man with whom he had shared so much: exile, loneliness, hardships, laughter, tears, tribulations, triumphs, alienation. His old eyes were dazed with wondering. How was it that the soul and spirit of his master had slipped so quietly and violently from this virile body? Two Imperial feldjaggers of the Secret Police hoisted themselves into the third troika. Within fifteen or twenty minutes they set out single file heading southward through the snowy night to accompany Alexander Sergeievich Pushkin to his final resting place.

Official orders had been sent ahead to the Governor of the Pskov province that no demonstrations or ceremonies were to be engaged in upon their arrival at the burial grounds. "A.S. Pushkin's funeral has already been held here in Saint Petersburg. No further rites are necessary, or desirable." Get the revolutionary rascal into the ground as quickly and as quietly as possible.

Three surreptitious troikas hurried through the frozen night. Benkendorf had choreographed the entire procedure, leaving nothing to coincidence or happenstance. From posting station to posting station, from posted gendarmes to posted gendarmes, nine Imperial horses galloped, at appointed points along the way changing horses and policemen. It stopped snowing as the day was breaking. All day long the next day the three troikas dashed across the great white Russian vastness.

Turgenev grew weary and exhausted from the ordeal. His eyes teared, his nostrils ran, his teeth chattered. He thought his entire body must be frostbitten. He could not keep his mind off the silence that lay in the coffin in the sledge behind him. The last few days had seemed totally unreal to him. Was it really possible that there was no more Alexander Pushkin!

389

Nikita Koslov remained in a half crouched position throughout the entire journey, straightening up only at the posting stations. How had it happened that the Frenchman killed his master? Was it possible that there really was no more Pushkin? No more Sasha?

The two feldjaggers in the sledge behind, rigid from the cold and their military conformity, took turns catching short dozes, one of them forever keeping a sharp eye on the coffin up ahead of him, as if each thought Pushkin's phantom, out of some perverse and revolutionary nature, would steal his body and thereby frustrate his grave and the Emperor.

Just as darkness began to blanket the cold white frozen earth of Russia, the Svyatogorsk Monastery atop the hill on Holy Mountain came into view. Pushkin would be buried there on the morrow. They reached Trigorskoye and the Wulf-Osipov home around nine o'clock that evening. Turgenev sat up most of the night with the Wulf-Osipovs in a kind of soirée of Pushkin reminiscences. Exchanging Pushkin anecdotes. The younger girls who had been mere babes in Pushkin's time had grown into young ladies. Zizi and Annettie with tear-filled eyes kept looking toward the front room window as if they expected Pushkin to gallop up on his great red stallion and leap nimbly through the window. Madame Wulf-Osipovna sat most of the time silently reflective. Every now and then she would remember some specific Pushkinism and become hysterical with laughter.

Zizi began to laugh and laugh until her laughter turned to tears. "I can't believe it! I can't believe it! "How could they let it happen to him?"

Turgenev put his arms around Zizi's shoulders. He attempted to console her. "Pushkin *is* dead." He had not allowed himself to utter the fatal words before. "It's true, he's dead. But we must remember how much life he gave us while he lived. We must be thinking: 'Joy to the World! Pushkin lived! His noble spirit still lives. The grave cannot defeat a spirit such as Alexander Sergeievich. We must gain pride and strength and sustenance from this greatest of great sons of Russia." He tried to keep Zizi from crying even as his own eyes filled with tears.

Early the next morning they took Alexander Sergeievich Pushkin to the hill on Holy Mountain. It was still black dark outside. A feeble light gleamed and glittered in the grill-worked windows of the monastery. Muzhiks from the Mikhailovskoye estate had awakened earlier and had almost finished digging Pushkin's grave. Turgenev tried to warm himself by a miserable fire near the peasants while they completed the terrible chore. It had begun to snow again.

The sun, a great ball of burning ice, came up blood-filled through the falling snow, just as distraught Nikita Koslov and some weeping peasants lowered the coffin into the grave. Nikita wept for the years he had shared with his beloved friend and master. Turgenev was crying openly now as he threw a handful of dirt upon the casket. The gendarmes stood nearby flailing their bodies to keep from freezing to death.

What did Turgenev think of as he stood there at the graveside? Did he remember Pushkin's EXEGI MONUMENTUM? Did the poet's voice speak to his beloved comrade from the grave? For he had completed his monumental statement just a short time before this fateful moment:

> Unto myself I reared a monument not built
> By hands, a track thereto the people's feet will tread;
> Not Emperor Alexander's shaft is as lofty as my pillar
> That proudly lifts its unsubmissive head.
>
> Not wholly shall I die—but in my lyre my spirit
> Shall incorruptible and bodiless, survive—
> And I shall know renown as long as under heaven
> One poet yet remains alive.
>
> The rumor of my fame will sweep through vasty Russia,
> And all its people speak this name, whose light shall reign
> Alike for haughty Slav, and Finn, and savage Tungus
> And Kalmuk riders of the Plain.
>
> I shall be loved, and long the people will remember
> The kindly thoughts I stirred—my music's brightest crown,
> How in this cruel age I celebrated freedom,
> And fought for truth toward those cast down.
>
> Oh, Muse, as ever, now, obey your God's commandments,
> of insults, unafraid, to praise and slander cool,
> Demanding no reward, sing on, but in your wisdom,
> Be silent when you meet a fool.
>
> But in your wisdom,
> Be silent when you meet a fool.

The book was designed by Joanne E. Kinney. The typeface for the text is Garamond. The display type is MGB Patrician from Letraset. The book is printed on 50# Glatfelter and is bound in Holliston Mills Black Linen cloth.

Manufactured in the United States of America.